David Collins

An account of the English colony in New South Wales

David Collins

An account of the English colony in New South Wales

ISBN/EAN: 9783741194337

Manufactured in Europe, USA, Canada, Australia, Japa

Cover: Foto ©Andreas Hilbeck / pixelio.de

Manufactured and distributed by brebook publishing software
(www.brebook.com)

David Collins

An account of the English colony in New South Wales

AN
ACCOUNT
OF THE
ENGLISH COLONY
IN
NEW SOUTH WALES.

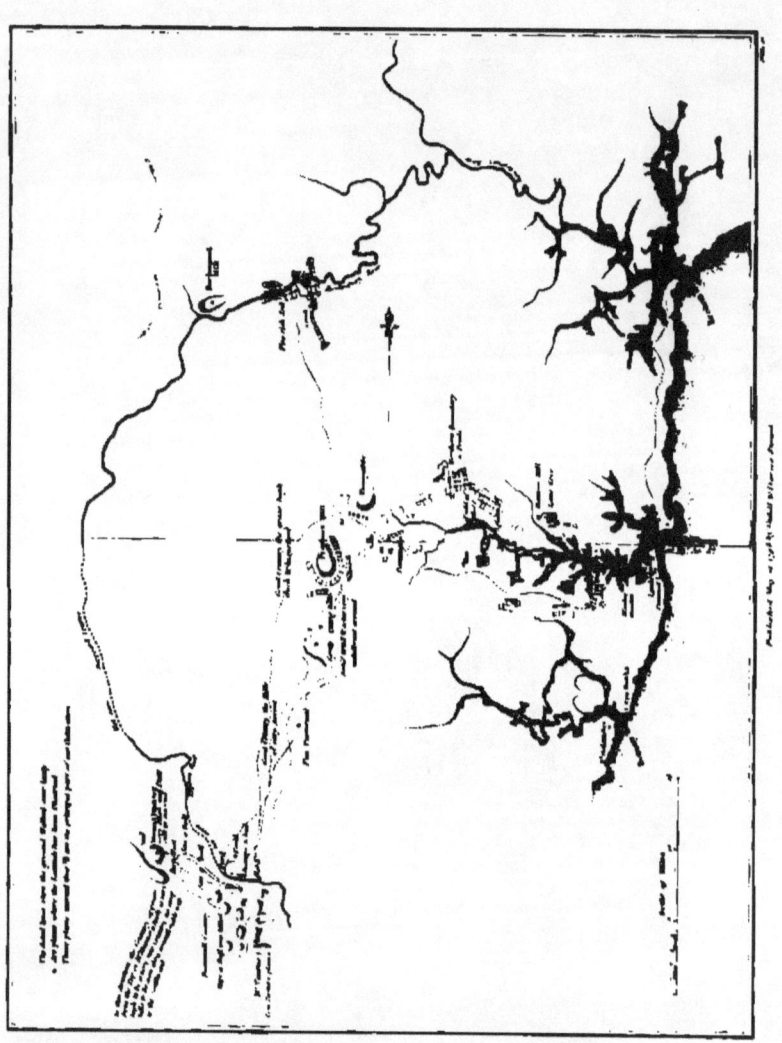

AN

ACCOUNT

OF THE

ENGLISH COLONY

IN

NEW SOUTH WALES:

WITH

REMARKS ON THE DISPOSITIONS, CUSTOMS, MANNERS, &c. OF
THE NATIVE INHABITANTS OF THAT COUNTRY.

TO WHICH ARE ADDED,

SOME PARTICULARS OF NEW ZEALAND;

COMPILED, BY PERMISSION,

FROM THE MSS. OF LIEUTENANT-GOVERNOR KING.

By DAVID COLLINS, Esquire,

LATE JUDGE ADVOCATE AND SECRETARY OF THE COLONY.

ILLUSTRATED BY ENGRAVINGS.

" Many might be saved who now suffer an ignominious and an early death; and many
" might be so much purified in the furnace of punishment and adversity, as to
" become the ornaments of that society of which they had formerly been the bane. The
" vices of mankind must frequently require the severity of justice; but a wise State will
" direct that severity to the greatest moral and political good." ANON.

LONDON:

PRINTED FOR T. CADELL JUN. AND W. DAVIES, IN THE STRAND.
1798.

THOMAS Lord Viſcount SYDNEY,

ONE OF HIS MAJESTY'S MOST HONOURABLE PRIVY COUNCIL,
CHIEF JUSTICE IN EYRE SOUTH OF TRENT,
A GOVERNOR OF THE CHARTER-HOUSE,
AND A VICE-PRESIDENT OF THE ASYLUM.

MY LORD,

THE Honour that YOUR LORDSHIP has done me, in permitting this Volume to go forth into the World under the Sanction of YOUR NAME, demands my warmeſt Acknowledgments. I can only wiſh that the Work had been more worthy of its PATRON.

The ORIGINATOR of the PLAN of COLONIZATION for NEW SOUTH WALES was too conſpicuous a Character to be overlooked by the Narrator of its Riſe and Progreſs. The benevolent Mind of YOUR LORDSHIP led you to conceive this Method of redeeming many Lives that might

A   be

be forfeit to the offended Laws; but which, being preserved, under salutary Regulations, might afterward become useful to Society: and to your Patriotism the Plan
presented a Prospect of commercial and political Advantage. The following Pages will, it is hoped, serve to
evince, with how much Wisdom the Measure was suggested and conducted; with what beneficial Effects its
Progress has been attended; and what future Benefits the
Parent Country may with Confidence anticipate.

That YOUR LORDSHIP may long live to enjoy those
grateful Reflections which a Sense of having advanced the
public Welfare must be presumed to excite; and that
OUR MOST GRACIOUS SOVEREIGN, THE FATHER OF HIS
PEOPLE, may long, very long reign over these Kingdoms,
and continue to be served by Statesmen of tried Talents
and Integrity, is the earnest Prayer of,

MY LORD,

Your Lordship's much obliged,

and most devoted Servant,

DAVID COLLINS.

POLAND-STREET,
May 25, 1798.

PREFACE.

To the Public the following Work is with refpectful deference fubmitted by its Author, who trufts that it will be found to comprife much information interefting in its nature, and that has not been anticipated by any former productions on the fame fubject. If he fhould be thought to have been fometimes too minute in his detail, he hopes it will be confidered, that the tranfactions here recorded were penned as they occurred, with the feelings that at the moment they naturally excited in the mind; and that circumftances which, to an indifferent reader, may appear trivial, to a fpectator and participant feem often of importance. To the defign of this Work, (which was, to furnifh a complete record of the tranfactions of the Colony from its foundation,) accuracy and a degree of minutenefs in detail feemed effential; and on reviewing his manufcript, the Author faw little that, confiftently with his plan, he could perfuade himfelf to fupprefs.

For his labours he claims no credit beyond what may be due to the ftricteft fidelity in his narrative. It was not a romance that he had to give to the world; nor has he gone out of the track that actual circumftances prepared for him, to furnifh food for fickly minds, by fictitious relations of adventures that never happened, but which are by a certain defcription of readers perufed with avidity, and not unfrequently confidered as the only paffages deferving of notice.

Though to a work of this nature a ftyle ornamental and luxuriant would have been evidently inapplicable, yet the Author has not been wholly inattentive to this particular, but has endeavoured to temper the dry and formal manner of the mere journalift, with fomething of the hiftorian's eafe. Long fequeftered, however, from literary fociety, and from convenient accefs to books, he had no other models than thofe which memory could fupply; and therefore does not prefume to

A 2   think

think his Volume proof against the rigid cenſor: but to liberal criticiſm he ſubmits, with the confidence of a man conſcious of having neither negligence nor preſumption to impute to himſelf. He wrote to beguile the tedium of many a heavy hour; and when he wrote looked not beyond the ſatisfaction which at ſome future period might be afforded to a few friends, as well as to his own mind, by a review of thoſe hardſhips which in common with his colleagues he had endured and overcome; hardſhips which in ſome degree he ſuppoſes to be inſeparable from the firſt eſtabliſhment of any colony; but to which, from the peculiar circumſtances and deſcription of the ſettlers in this inſtance, were attached additional difficulties.

In the progreſs of his not unpleaſing taſk, the Author began to think that his labours might prove intereſting beyond the ſmall circle of his private friends; that ſome account of the gradual reformation of ſuch flagitious characters as had by many (and thoſe not illiberal) perſons in this country been confidered as paſt the probability of amendment, might be not unacceptable to the benevolent part of mankind; but might even tend to cheriſh the ſeeds of virtue, and to open new ſtreams from the pure fountain of mercy *.

Nor was he without hope, that through the humble medium of this Hiſtory, the untutored ſavage, emerging from darkneſs and barbariſm, might find additional friends among the better-informed members of civilized ſociety.

With theſe impreſſions, therefore, he felt it a ſort of duty to offer his Book to the world; and ſhould the objects alluded to be in any degree promoted by it, he ſhall confider its publication as the moſt fortunate circumſtance of his life.

---

* "It often happens," ſays Dr. Johnſon, " that in the looſe and thoughtleſs and diſſi-
" pated, there is a ſecret radical worth, which may ſhoot out by proper cultivation;
" that the ſpark of heaven, though dimmed and obſtructed, is yet not extinguiſhed, but
" may, by the breath of counfel and exhortation, be kindled into flame.

* * * * * * * * * * * * * * * *

" Let none too haſtily conclude that all goodneſs is loſt, though it may for a time be
" clouded and overwhelmed; for moſt minds are the ſlaves of external circumſtances,
" and conform to any hand that undertakes to mould them; roll down any torrent of
" cuſtom in which they happen to be caught; or bend to any importunity that bears hard
" againſt them." RAMBLER, No. 70.

Occurrences

Occurrences such as he has had to relate are not often presented to the Public; they do not, indeed, often happen. It is not, perhaps, once in a century that colonies are established in the most remote parts of the habitable globe; and it is seldom that men are found existing perfectly in a state of nature. When such circumstances do occur, curiosity, and still more laudable sentiments, must be excited. The gratification even of curiosity alone might have formed a sufficient apology for the Author; but he has seen too much of virtue even among the vicious to be indifferent to the sufferings, or backward in promoting the felicities of human nature.

A few words, he hopes, may be allowed him respecting the Colony itself, for which he acknowledges what, he trusts, will be considered as at least an excusable partiality. He bore his share of the distresses and calamities which it suffered; and at his departure, in the ninth year of its growth, with pleasure saw it wear an aspect of ease and comfort that seemed to bid defiance to future difficulties. The hardships which it sustained were certainly attributable to mischance, not to misconduct. The Crown was fortunate in the selection of its Governors, not less with respect to the gentlemen who were sent out expressly in that capacity, than in those on whom the temporary administration occasionally devolved.

Under GOVERNOR HUNTER, who at present presides there, the resources of the Country and the energies of the Colonists will assuredly be called forth. The intelligence, discretion, and perseverance of that officer will be zealously applied to discover and fix every local advantage. His well-known humanity will not fail to secure the savage islander from injury or mortification; reconcile him to the restraints, and induce him to participate in the enjoyments, of civilized society; and instruct him to appreciate justly the blessings of rational freedom, whose salutary restrictions are not less conducive to individual benefit than to the general weal.

With respect to the resources of the Settlement, there can be little doubt, that at this moment it is able to support itself in the article of grain; and the wild stock of cattle to the westward of the Nepean will soon render it independent on this country in the article of animal food. As to its utility, beside the circumstance of its freeing the mother

country

country from the depraved branches of her offspring, in some instances reforming their dispositions, and in all cases rendering their labour and talents conducive to the public good, it may prove a valuable nursery to our East India possessions for soldiers and seamen.

If, beside all this, a Whale Fishery should be established, another great benefit may accrue to the parent country from the coast of New South Wales.

The Island, moreover, abounds with fine timber in every respect adapted to the purposes of ship-building: iron too it possesses in abundance. Coal has been found there, and some veins of copper; and however inconsiderable the quantity of these articles that has been hitherto found, yet the proof of their existence will naturally lead to farther research, and most probably terminate in complete success.

The flax plant grows spontaneously, and may, with the assistance of proper implements and other necessaries, be turned to very profitable account.

The climate is for the most part temperate and healthy; cattle are prolific; and fruits and culinary vegetables thrive with almost a tropical luxuriance.

To be brief: Such is the ENGLISH COLONY IN NEW SOUTH WALES, for which the Author is anxiously solicitous to obtain the candid consideration of his countrymen; among whom it has been painful to him to remark a disposition too prevalent for regarding it with odium and disgust.

LONDON,
May 25, 1798.

CONTENTS.

INTRODUCTION.

An Account of the English Colony in New South Wales.

CONTENTS.

a

CONTENTS.

CONTENTS.

CONCLU-

CONCLUSION:

Comprising Particulars of the BRITANNIA's VOYAGE to ENGLAND; with Remarks on the STATE of NORFOLK ISLAND, and some Account of NEW ZEALAND.

APPENDIX.

A P P E N D I X.

AN

INTRODUCTION.

A Voyage to New South Wales.

SECTION I.

THE Commissioners of his Majesty's Navy, near the end of the year 1786, advertised for a certain number of vessels to be taken up for the purpose of conveying between seven and eight hundred male and female felons to Botany Bay in New South Wales, on the eastern coast of New Holland; whither it had been determined by Government to transport them, after having sought in vain upon the African coast for a situation possessing the requisites for the establishment of a colony.

The following vessels were at length contracted for, and assembled in the River to fit, and take in stores and provisions, viz. the Alexander, Scarborough, Charlotte, Lady Penrhyn, and Friendship, as transports; and the Fishbourn, Golden Grove, and Borrowdale, as store-ships. The Prince of Wales was afterwards added to the number of transports, on a representation being made to the Treasury Board that such an addition was necessary. The transports were immediately prepared for the reception of the convicts, and the store-ships took on board provisions for two years, with tools, implements of agriculture, and such other articles as were considered necessary to a colonial establishment.

Oᴀ

On the 24th of October, Captain Arthur Phillip hoisted a pendant on board his Majesty's ship the Sirius of 20 guns, then lying at Deptford. This ship was originally called the Berwick, and intended for the East India Company; but having, while on the stocks, met with some accident by fire, was purchased by Government for a store-ship, and as such had performed one voyage to America. Her burden was about 520 tons; and being, from her construction, well-calculated for this expedition, she was taken into the service as a man of war, and with her capacity changed also her name.

As the government of the intended colony, as well as the command of the Sirius, was given to Captain Phillip, it was thought necessary to appoint another captain to her, who might command her on any service in which she might be employed for the colony, while Captain Phillip should be engaged in his government. For this purpose an order was signed by his Majesty in Council, directing the Lords Commissioners of the Admiralty to appoint John Hunter esquire (then a master and commander) second captain of the Sirius, with the rank of post. Although this ship mounted only 20 guns, and those but six-pounders, yet on this particular service her establishment was not confined to what is usual in a ship of that class; but, with a first and second captain, she had also three lieutenants, a master, purser, surgeon and two mates, a boatswain, a gunner, and a subaltern's detachment of marines.

The Supply brig was also put into commission, and the command given to Lieutenant Henry Lidgbird Ball. This vessel was to accompany the Sirius as an armed tender; and both ships, having completed their equipment at Deptford-yard, dropped down on the 10th of December to Long Reach, where they took in their guns, powder, and other stores.

They were here joined by some of the transports, and continued waiting for orders until the 30th of January 1787, when they sailed for Spithead; which port, however, they were prevented from reaching, by heavy and contrary gales of wind, which they continued to experience both in the Downs and on their passage, until the latter end of the following month.

One or two of the transports had in the mean time arrived at Portsmouth, and the Charlotte and Alexander proceeded to Plymouth, where they were to receive the male and female convicts that were ready for them.

On the 5th of March, the order for their embarkation, together with that of the detachment of marines provided as an escort, was sent from the Secretary of State's office, with directions for their immediately joining the other ships of the expedition at the Mother-bank. This was done accordingly; and, every necessary arrangement having taken place, the troops intended for the garrison embarked, and the convicts, male and female, were distributed in the different transports.

On

On Monday the 7th of May Captain Phillip arrived at Portsmouth, and took the command of his little fleet, then lying at the Mother-bank. Anxious to depart, and apprehensive that the wind, which had for a considerable time been blowing from the quarter favourable to his passage down the Channel, might defert him at the moment when he moft wifhed for its continuance, he on the Thursday following made the fignal to prepare for failing. But here a demur arofe among the failors on board the transports, who refufed to proceed to fea unlefs they fhould be paid their wages up to the time of their departure, alleging as a ground for this refufal, that they were in want of many articles neceffary for fo long a voyage, which this money, if paid, would enable them to purchafe. The cuftom of their employ, however, being againft a demand which yet appeared reafonable, Captain Phillip directed the different mafters to put fuch of their people as refufed to proceed with them to fea, on board of the Hyæna frigate, and to receive an equal number of her feamen, who fhould afterwards be re-exchanged at fea, her captain being directed to accompany the fleet to a certain diftance.

This difficulty being removed, and the fhip's companies of the Sirius and the Supply having received the ufual advance of two months' wages, on Saturday the 12th the men of war and fome of the transports got under fail, with a view of dropping down to St. Helen's, and thence proceeding to fea; but the wind falling fhort, and proving unfavourable, they brought up at Spithead for the night, and at day-break next morning the whole fleet weighed with a fresh breeze, and, having a leading wind, paffed without any accident through the Needles.

The transports were of the following tonnage, and had on board the undermentioned number of convicts, and other perfons, civil and military, viz.

The Alexander, of 453 tons, had on board 192 male convicts; 2 lieutenants, 2 ferjeants, 2 corporals, 1 drummer, and 29 privates, with 1 affiftant furgeon to the colony.

The Scarborough, of 418 tons, had on board 205 male convicts; 1 captain, 2 lieutenants, 2 ferjeants, 2 corporals, 1 drummer, and 26 privates, with 1 affiftant furgeon to the colony.

The Charlotte, of 346 tons, had on board 89 male and 20 female convicts; 1 captain, 2 lieutenants, 3 ferjeants, 3 corporals, 1 drummer, and 35 privates, with the principal furgeon of the colony.

The Lady Penrhyn, of 338 tons, had on board 101 female convicts; 1 captain, 2 lieutenants, and 3 privates, with a perfon acting as a furgeon's mate.

The Prince of Wales, of 334 tons, had on board 2 male and 50 female convicts; 2 lieutenants, 3 ferjeants, 2 corporals, 1 drummer, and 24 privates, with the furveyor-general of the colony.

The Friendship, (fnow,) of 228 tons, had on board 76 male and 21 female convicts; 1 captain, 2 lieutenants, 2 ferjeants, 3 corporals, 1 drummer, and 36 privates, with 1 affiftant furgeon to the colony.

There were on board, befide thefe, 28 women, 8 male and 6 female children, belonging to the foldiers of the detachment, together with 6 male and 7 female children belonging to the convicts.

The Fifhbourn ftore-fhip was of 378 tons; the Borrowdale of 272 tons; and the Golden Grove of 331 tons. On board this laft fhip was embarked the chaplain of the colony, with his wife and a fervant.

Not only thefe as ftore-fhips, but the men of war and tranfports, were ftored in every part with provifions, implements of agriculture, camp equipage, clothing for the convicts, baggage, &c.

On board of the Sirius were taken, as fupernumeraries, the major command-ant of the corps of marines embarked in the tranfports *, the adjutant and quar-ter-mafter, the judge-advocate of the fettlement, and the commiffary; with 1 fer-jeant, 3 drummers, 7 privates, 4 women, and a few artificers.

Proper day and night fignals were eftablifhed by Captain Phillip for the regu-lation of his convoy, and every neceffary inftruction was given to the mafters to guard againft feparation. On board the tranfports a certain number of prifoners were allowed to be upon deck at a time during the day, the whole being pro-perly fecured at night: and as the mafter of each fhip carrying convicts had in-dented for their fecurity in a penalty of forty pounds for every one that might efcape, they were inftructed conftantly to confult with the commanding marine officer on board the tranfports, both as to the number of convicts that were to be fuffered to come on deck during the paffage, and the times when fuch in-dulgence fhould be granted. To the military was left the care of thofe effential fervices, the prefervation of their health, the infpection of their provifions, and the diftribution of the centinels who were to guard them. Their allowance of provifions during the voyage (two-thirds of the ufual allowance to a feaman in the navy) was contracted for in London †; and Mr. Zachariah Clark was fent out in one of the tranfports as the agent refponfible for the due performance of the contract. This allowance was to be fufpended on their arrival at any fo-reign port, the commiffary of the fettlement being then to furnifh them with frefh provifions.

At our outfet we had the mortification to find that two of our convoy were very heavy failers, and likely to be the occafion of much delay in fo long a voy-age as that in which we had embarked. The Charlotte was on the firft and

* This officer was alfo lieutenant-governor of the colony.

† By William Richards jun. efquire, of Walworth in the county of Surry.

second day taken in tow by the Hyæna, and the Lady Penrhyn fell confiderably aftern. As the feparation of any of the fleet was a circumftance to be moft fedulously guarded againft and prevented, the Sirius occafionally fhortened fail to afford the fternmoft fhips time to come up with her; at the clofe of evening fhe was put under an eafy fail for the night, during which time fhe carried, for the guidance of the whole, a confpicuous light in the main-top.

On the 15th the fignal was made for the tranfports to pafs in fucceffion within hail under the ftern of the Sirius, when, on inquiry, it appeared, that the pro-voft-marfhal of the fettlement (who was to have taken his paffage on board the Prince of Wales) was left behind, together with the third mate of the Charlotte tranfport, and five men from the Fifhbourn ftore-fhip: the lofs of thefe five per-fons was fupplied by as many feamen from on board the Hyæna.

Light or unfavourable winds prevented our getting clear of the Channel until the 16th, at which time we had the fatisfaction of finding that we had accom-plifhed it without returning, or putting in at any of the ports which offered themfelves in our way down.

Sunday the 20th was marked by the difcovery of a defign formed among the convicts on board the Scarborough tranfport to mutiny and take poffeffion of the fhip. The information was given by one of the convicts to the command-ing marine officer on board, who, on the lying-to of the convoy at noon to dif-patch Captain De Courcy to England, waited on the major-commandant on board the Sirius, and communicated the particulars to him and Captain Phillip, who, after fome deliberation, directed that the ringleaders (two in number) fhould be brought on board the Sirius, there punifhed, and afterwards fecured in the Prince of Wales tranfport. This was accordingly put in execution, and two dozen lafhes were inflicted by the boatfwain's mate of the Sirius on each of the offenders, who ftedfaftly denied the exiftence of any fuch defign as was im-puted to them.

A boat from each of the tranfports coming on board the Sirius with letters for England, fome additional fignals were given to the mafters, with directions to thofe who had convicts on board to releafe from their irons fuch as might by their behaviour have merited that indulgence; but with orders to confine them again with additional fecurity on the leaft appearance among them of irre-gularity.

Thefe neceffary regulations being adjufted, and the Hyæna fent off with the commanding officer's letters, the fleet made fail again in the evening. But it fhould have been obferved, that when the Hyæna's boat came on board fhe brought fome neceffaries for the five men belonging to her, who had been lent to the Fifhbourn ftore-fhip, and who, animated with a fpirit of enterprife, chofe rather to remain in her than return in the frigate to England.

The

The wind was more favourable to the Hyæna's return to Plymouth (which port she was directed to make) than to our progress southward, for the two following days; but it then coming round to the N. W., by the 24th we had reached the latitude of Cape Ortegal.

On the 25th, the signal was made for Lieutenant Shortland, the agent on board the Alexander, who, at his coming on board, was directed to visit the several transports, and collect from each a list of the different trades and occupations of the respective convicts, agreeably to a form given him for that purpose by Captain Phillip. From this time to the 29th the wind continued favourable, but blowing exceedingly fresh, and attended with a heavy rolling sea. The Supply was now directed to make sail and keep six miles a-head during the day, and two during the night; and to look out for the land, as it was expected that the fleet would on the morrow be in the neighbourhood of the Madeira Isles. Accordingly, soon after day-break the following morning, she made the signal for seeing land, and at noon we were a-breast of the Deserters—certain high barren rocks so named, to the S. S. E. of the Island of Madeira, and distant about three leagues.

In the afternoon of the 31st, the Supply a-head again made the signal for seeing land; and shortly after we were a-breast of the ridge of rocks situated between the Madeira and Canary Isles, called the Salvages.

Our strong trade-wind appeared to have here spent its force, and we were baffled (as frequently happens in the vicinity of islands) by light airs or calms. With these and contrary winds our patience was exercised until the evening of the 2d of June, when a favourable breeze sprang up, which continued during that night. At six the next morning the island of Teneriffe was seen right a-head; and about seven in the evening the whole fleet came to an anchor in the road of Santa Cruz. The ships were immediately moored, taking the precaution of buoying their cables with empty casks, to prevent their being injured by rocks or foul ground, an inconvenience which had frequently been experienced by navigators in this road. We found riding here a Spanish packet, an English brig bound to London, and some smaller vessels.

Captain Phillip designed to have sent an officer forward in the Supply, to announce his arrival to the governor, and to settle as well the hour of his waiting upon him, as some necessary arrangements respecting fresh provisions, water, &c.; but as it was growing dark before the fleet anchored, and night coming on, when business of that nature could not well be transacted, his visit was postponed until the morning. Before we came to an anchor the port-officer, or harbour-master, came on board to make the customary inquiries, accompanied by some Spanish officers and gentlemen of the town. The ceremony of a salute was on their side declined, having, as was alleged, but two or three guns

mounted

mounted for use; and on our part this omission was readily acquiesced in, as expediting the service which brought us thither, that of watering the ships, and taking on board wine and such other refreshments as could be procured; an object of more consequence than the scrupulous observance of compliment and etiquette, particularly in the then necessarily crowded state of the Sirius. And as it was afterwards understood, that it was not usual at this place to return an equal number of guns upon those occasions, (a circumstance always insisted on by his Majesty's ships when they salute,) all unpleasant discussion of this point was thereby avoided.

Early in the morning the officer was dispatched on shore by Captain Phillip to learn at what time he might pay his respects to the governor. The hour of noon was appointed for that ceremony; and accordingly at that time Captain Phillip, accompanied by the civil, military, and naval officers under his orders, waited on his excellency the Marquis De Branceforte, and were received by him with the utmost politeness.

The same reasons which induced Captain Phillip to acquiesce in omitting to salute on his arrival at this port, operated against his taking public notice of his Majesty's birth-day, which he would otherwise have made a point of celebrating with every mark of respect.

In the afternoon of this day the marquis sent an officer on board the Sirius, politely offering Captain Phillip whatever assistance he might stand in need of, and that was in his power to furnish. In the forenoon of Wednesday the 6th, he came in person on board, attended by several of his officers, to return Captain Phillip's visit; and afterwards entertained him, the lieutenant-governor, and other officers of the settlement, navy, and marines, to the number of ten, at dinner.

The next being the day of Corpus Christi, a day of great religious observance and ceremony in Roman Catholic countries, no boats were sent from the transports to the shore. The business of watering, getting off wine, &c. was suspended by Captain Phillip's directions until the morrow, to prevent the least interruption being given by any of the people under his command to the ceremonies and processions which were to take place. Those officers, whose curiosity led them to observe the religious proceedings of the day, very prudently attended uncovered, and knelt, wherever kneeling was required, in the streets, and in their churches; for, when it was considered that the same great Creator of the universe was worshipped alike by Protestant and Catholic, what difficulty could the mind have in divesting their pageant of its tinsel, its trappings, and its censers, and joining with sincerity in offering the purest incense, that of a grateful heart?

The

The Marquis De Branceforte, whom we found in the government of the Canary Isles, was, we were informed, a major-general in the Spanish service, and having been three years in the government, only waited, it was said, for his promotion to the rank of lieutenant-general to return to Spain.   The salary annexed to this government, as we understood, was not quite equal to fifteen hundred pounds a-year.   His Excellency's house was situated at the upper end of the High Street, or Square, as it was called, and was by no means the best in the town, Mr. Carter (the treasurer) and some private merchants appearing to reside in larger and much better habitations.   The houses in most of the streets were built with quadrangles, a gallery running round the interior sides of the first floor, on which indeed the families chiefly resided, appropriating the ground floor to offices for domestic purposes.   The dwelling-rooms were not ceiled, but were open to the roof of the building, which rarely exceeded two stories in height.   The upper part of the windows was glazed with very bad glass; the lower part consisted of close lattice-work, through the small apertures of which, as we traversed the streets, we had now and then opportunities of noticing the features of the women, whom the custom of the country had confined within doors to the lattice, and in the street to the *reba zilia*, or veil.   There were but few objects in the town sufficiently striking to draw the attention of a stranger.

The landing-place was commodious, being formed by a stone pier, alongside of which two boats at a time might lie with great ease and take in their fresh water.   It appeared by an inscription in Spanish, that the pier, having fallen nearly into a state of entire ruin, was indebted for its present convenience to the liberality of the governor, assisted indeed by some merchants, who superintended and contributed largely to its repair, which was completed in the year 1786.

At the lower end of the High Street was observed a light and well-finished monument of white marble, commemorating the marvellous appearance of the image or bust of Our Lady at Candelaria, to the Guanches, the aborigines of the country, who were thereby converted to Christianity 104 years before the preaching of the gospel.   The four sides of the monument bore long inscriptions to this effect, and further intimated, that it was erected, as an act of piety and cordial devotion, at the expence of Don Bartholoni di Montagnes, perpetual captain of the Royal Marine Castle at Candelaria.

In the centre of this street were a stone basin and fountain, from which the inhabitants were supplied with a stream of very good water, conveyed from the neighbouring hills by wooden troughs supported on slight posts, and reaching quite to the town.   At the head of the street, near the government-house, stood a large stone cross, and at a small distance the church of St. Francis, annexed to which was a monaftery of Francifcans. The name of Santa Cruz, the Holy Crofs, feemed not inapplicable to this town, for one or more crucifixes of wood or ftone were to be found in moft of the ftreets, and in others the form of the Crofs was painted upon the walls of the houfes. Over the entrances of fome houfes we obferved, inclofed in fmall glafs-cafes, the images and pictures of favourite faints, with lamps before them, which were lighted in the evenings and on certain public occafions.

There were not any fortifications upon the commanding ground above the town; but at each end of the bay ftood a fort, between which were erected three or four circular redoubts, connected with each other by a low parapet wall, wearing the appearance of a line of communication between the forts; but very few cannon were to be feen in the works.

On the fkirts of the town to the fouthward we vifited a workhoufe, which had been originally defigned for the reception of the mendicants with which the town had been very much infefted. About forty families had fubfcribed a certain fum to erect this building, and to furnifh it in a manner every way convenient and confiftent with fuch a defign. But we were informed that the governor had filled it with the daughters of the labouring poor, who were here inftructed in weaving and fpinning, and were brought up in induftry and cleanlinefs, remaining in the houfe untill of a marriageable age, when a portion equal to ten pounds fterling was given with each on the day of her nuptials. This and the other expences of the houfe were furnifhed by a fund produced from the labour of the young people, who appeared all in the fame drefs, plain indeed, but cleanly and neat.

We heard with furprife, and not without regret, that this inftitution was likely to fall to the ground whenever the governor's departure fhould take place, the fubfcribers being diffatisfied with the plan that was then purfued, alleging that their money had been given to get rid of their beggars, whofe numbers were not diminifhed; and that the children were only taught what they could learn from their mothers at home. To us however, judging without prejudice or partiality, the defign of the inftitution appeared to have been more effectually anfwered by ftriking at the root of beggary, than if the charity had been merely confined to objects who would have been found daily to multiply, from the comfortable provifion held out to them by that charity.

A whole-length picture of the governor was hung up in the working-room of the houfe. He was reprefented, agreeably to the end that was at firft propofed by the inftitution, conducting a miferable object to the gate of the workhoufe; a front view of which was alfo given.

Thefe iflands, known to the Romans by the appellation of the Fortunate iflands, appeared even at this day to deferve that epithet; for the inhabitants

c　　　　　　　　were

were so fortunate, and the soil so happy, that no venomous creature had been found to live there; several toads, adders, and other poisonous reptiles, which had been brought thither for proof, having died almost immediately after their arrival. The air of this place is very salubrious; an instance of which was remarked in a gentleman who was said to be 113 years of age, and who had been happy enough to preserve his faculties through such a series of time, nearly entire, his memory alone appearing to be impaired. He came from Waterford in Ireland, and had been vice-consul at this port ever since the year 1709.

We were informed that a slight shock of an earthquake had been felt here in the month of February preceding, but was unattended with any eruption from the Peak, which had not alarmed the island since the year 1703, when it destroyed the port of Guarrachica.

When the weather was very hot at Santa Cruz, the better sort of the inhabitants chose cooler residences higher up in the mountains, and these they could establish in whatever degree of temperature they chose; for in proportion as they ascended the air became cooler, the famous Peak being (though a volcano) clad in perpetual snow at its summit. We understood that the rain fell very heavy at certain seasons; and, on the sides of the hills which surrounded the town, ridges or low walls of stone were constructed at short distances, with intervals in them, to break the force of the water, which otherwise, descending in torrents, would sweep away every thing before it. Around Santa Cruz, indeed, there appeared but little vegetation for which to be apprehensive, nor did the prospect brighten till we came within view of the town named Laguna, an inland settlement, and once the capital of the island.

For this place a party of us set forward on the 8th, mounted, according to the custom of the country, upon mules or asses. Our route lay over hills and mountains of rock continually ascending, until within a short distance of the town, at which we arrived in between two and three hours from our leaving Santa Cruz. The road over which we passed was wide, but for the greatest part of it we travelled over loose stones that bore all the appearance of cinders; in some places resembling a regular pavement, and in others our beasts were compelled to scramble as well as they could over the hard solid rock. We found that Laguna, which was somewhat better than three English miles distant from Santa Cruz, had formerly been a populous city; the streets were spacious, and laid out at right angles with each other.

Here were two monasteries and as many convents. The monastery of St. Augustine we visited; and the good fathers of it with great civility conducted us to their chapel, though it was preparing for the celebration of some religious ceremony. We found the altar-piece, on which was commonly displayed all their finery and taste, neat, light, and elegant. Few paintings were to be seen;

3   the

the best were half-lengths of some of the saints disposed round the pulpit. The form of this building was a quadrangle, the centre of which was laid out in garden-ground, elegantly divided into walks, bordered with roses, myrtle, and a variety of other shrubs and flowers. Hence we proceeded to the retreat of religious females, but had not chosen the proper time for paying our respects, which ceremony we therefore deferred until our return in the evening from an excursion into the adjacent country.

The town of Laguna (a name which signifies Lake or Swamp) is situated upon a plain surrounded by high hills, and watered by the same means as Santa Cruz, from a great distance up the country. We noticed, indeed, two stone-basins, and fountains playing in different streets of the place. The buildings here had a manifest superiority over those of Santa Cruz, the streets were far more spacious, and the houses larger. In some of the former we perceived a regular line of shops filled chiefly with articles from England. The insalubrity of the air of this place, however, had driven, and was continuing to drive, such numbers almost daily from its influence, that it had more the appearance of a deserted than of an inhabited town, weeds and grass literally growing in the streets. As this town decreased in its population, Santa Cruz, with some others on the island, received the benefit; and it must be acknowledged, that although in quitting Laguna they removed from fertile fields and a romantic pleasant country, to uncouth and almost barren rocks at Santa Cruz, they changed a noxious for a very healthy situation.

After viewing the town we remounted our beasts, and proceeded by the side of the aqueduct into a most delightful country, where we found the people cheerfully employed in gathering their harvest, and singing their rural roundelays. The soil produced oats, barley, wheat, and Indian corn; but, though it bore always two, and sometimes three crops, it was nevertheless unequal in the whole of its produce to the consumption of the island, the deficiency being supplied from the Grand Canary.

The sides of the hills were clothed with woods, into one of which we rode, and arriving at a place named Il Plano de los Viejos, or the Plain of the Old People, we rested for some little time, and afterward, crossing through a cultivated valley, ascended the hill on the opposite side, where we visited the source of the streams that supplied the aqueduct. Returning thence, we refreshed under the walls of a small chapel, where a friar occasionally performed mass for the neighbouring country people. About five o'clock we again entered Laguna, with the intention of paying our compliments to the sisterhood of the convent which we had visited in the morning; but whether our party was too numerous, or from what other cause it proceeded we could not learn, we were only favoured with the company of four or five of the elder ladies of the house, who talked very loud and very fast. After purchasing some few bunches of artificial fruit, we took our leave, and proceeded to Santa Cruz, cautiously indeed, down the hills and rocks which we had ascended in the morning, and arrived about sun-set.

An outward-bound Dutch East-Indiaman had anchored in the road since the morning.

In the evening of this day John Powers, a convict, made his escape from the Alexander transport, in a small boat which by some accident was suffered to lie unattended to alongside the ship, with a pair of oars in it ; he was however retaken at day-break the next morning, by the activity of the master and a party of marines belonging to the transport, and brought on board the Sirius, whence he was removed to his own ship, with directions for his being heavily ironed.

It appeared that he had at first conceived hopes of being received on board the Dutch East-India ship that arrived in the morning; but, meeting with a disappointment there, rowed to the southern part of the island, and concealed himself among the rocks, having first set his boat and oars adrift, which fortunately led to a discovery of the place he had chosen for his retreat. The Marquis de Brancesorte, on hearing of his escape, expressed the greatest readiness to assist in his recovery ; and Captain Phillip offered a considerable reward for the same purpose.

Having completed the provisioning and watering of the fleet, and being again ready to proceed on our voyage, in the afternoon of Saturday the 9th the signal was made from the Sirius for all boats to repair on board; shortly after which she unmoored, and that night lay at single anchor.

At day-break the following morning the whole fleet got under way.

SECTION II.

Proceed on the Voyage.—Altitude of the Peak of Teneriffe.—Pass the Isles of Sal, Bonavista, May, and St. Iago.—Cross the Equator.—Progress.—Arrive at the Brazils.—Transactions at Rio de Janeiro—Some Particulars of that Town—Sail thence.—Passage to the Cape of Good Hope—Transactions there.—Some Particulars respecting the Cape.—Depart for New South Wales.

LIGHT airs had, by the noon of Monday the 11th, carried the fleet midway between the islands of Teneriffe and the Grand Canary, which latter was now very distinctly seen. This island wore the same mountainous appearance as its opposite neighbour Teneriffe, from which it seemed to be divided by a space of about eleven leagues. Being the capital of the Canary Islands, the chief bishop had his residence there, and evinced in his diocese the true spirit of a primitive Christianity, by devoting to pious and charitable purposes the principal part of a revenue of ten thousand pounds *per annum*. The chief officers of justice also reside in this island, before whom all civil causes are removed from Teneriffe and the other Canary Islands, to be finally decided.

While detained in this spot, we had a very fine view of the Peak of Teneriffe, lifting its venerable and majestic head above the neighbouring hills, many of which were also of considerable height, and perhaps rather diminished the grandeur of the Peak itself, the altitude of which we understood was 15,396 feet, only 148 yards short of three miles.

On the 14th, the wind began to blow steady from the north-east; and on the 15th, about eleven in the forenoon, we crossed the tropic of Cancer. Our weather now became hot and close, and we rolled along through a very heavy sea, the convoy, however, keeping well together.

At six o'clock in the morning of the 18th, the Supply, then a-head of the fleet, made the signal for seeing land. The weather being very hazy, we had but an indistinct view of the Isle of Sal, one of the Cape de Verd islands, bearing N. W. by W. ½ W. distant eight leagues; and at one the same day, we came in sight of the Island of Bonavista, bearing S. W. distant two leagues.

Captain Phillip designing to anchor for a few hours at the Island of St. Iago, to procure water and other refreshments, if he could get in without any risk or difficulty, in the evening shortened sail, and made the convoy's signal to close, the run from thence to that island being too great to admit of our reaching it before dark. The Supply was directed at the same time to keep a-head with a

light.

light during the night; and at twelve o'clock the night-signal was made for the fleet to bring-to.

At six the next morning we made sail again, and soon after passed the Isle of May, distant about four leagues, bearing N. W. by W. of us. Between nine and ten o'clock we made the south end of the Island of St. Iago, and at the distance of about two leagues. The wind freshening soon after we saw the island, at noon we were ranging along the south side of it, with the signal flying for the convoy to prepare to anchor; but at the moment of our opening Praya-bay, and preparing to haul round the southern extremity of it, the fleet was suddenly taken aback, and immediately after baffled by light airs. We could however perceive, as well by the colours at the fort, as by those of a Portuguese snow riding in the bay, that the wind blew directly in upon the shore, which would have rendered our riding there extremely hazardous; and as it was probable that our coming to an anchor might not have been effected without some accident happening to the convoy, Captain Phillip determined to wave, for the superior consideration of the safety of the fleet under his care, the advantages he might otherwise have derived from the supply of fresh provisions and vegetables to be procured there: the breeze therefore coming off the land, and with sufficient effect to carry us clear of the island and its variable weather, the anchoring signal was taken in, and we made sail about two o'clock, the fleet standing away due south. Our sudden departure from the island, we imagined, must have proved some disappointment to the inhabitants, as we noticed that a gun was fired at the fort, shortly after our opening the bay; a signal, it was supposed, to the country people to bring down their articles for trade and barter.

On the 14th of July the fleet crossed the equator in the 26th degree of east longitude. Such persons as had never before crossed the Line were compelled to undergo the ridiculous ceremonies which those who were privileged were allowed to perform on them.

From this time our weather was pleasant, and we had every appearance of soon reaching our next port, the Rio de Janeiro, on the Brazil coast.

The track which we had to follow was too beaten to afford us any thing new or interesting. Captain Phillip proposed making the Island of Trinidada; but the easterly winds and southerly currents which we had met with to the northward of the Line having set us so far to the westward when we crossed it, he gave up all expectation of seeing it, and on the 28th altered his course, steering S. W. Trinidada is laid down in 20° 25' south latitude, and 28° 35' west longitude, while we at noon on the 29th were in 19° 36' south latitude, and 33° 18' west longitude.

The longitude, when calculated by either altitudes of the sun, for the time-piece, (of Kendal's construction, which was sent out by the Board of Longitude,)

of

or by the means of several sets of lunar observations, which were taken by Captain Hunter, Lieutenant Bradley, and Lieutenant Dawes, was constantly shewn to the convoy, for which purpose the signal was made for the whole to pass under the stern of the Sirius, when a board was set up in some conspicuous part of the ship with the longitude marked on it to that day at noon.

A good look-out (to make use of the sea-phrase usual on these occasions) was kept for an island, not very well known or described, which was laid down in some charts, nearly in the track which we were to cross, but it was not seen by any of the ships of the fleet; nor was implicit credit given to its existence, although named, (the Island of Ascension,) and a latitude and longitude assigned to it. It was conjectured, that the islands of Martin Vas and Trinidada, lying within about five leagues of each other, had given rise to the idea of a new island, and that Ascension was in reality one or other of those islands.

Only two accidents happened during the passage to the Brazils. A seaman belonging to the Alexander was so unfortunate as to fall overboard, and could not be recovered—and a female convict on board the Prince of Wales was so much bruised by the falling of a boat from off the booms, (which, owing to the violent motion of the ship, had got loose,) that she died the following day, notwithstanding the professional skill and humane attention of the principal surgeon; for as the boat in launching forward fell upon the neck and crushed the vertebræ and spine, all the aid he could render her was of no avail.

On Thursday the 2d of August we had the coast of South America in sight; and the head-land, named Cape Frio, was distinctly seen before the evening closed in. Our time-piece had given us notice when to look out for it, and the land was made precisely to the hour in which it had taught us to expect it. It was not, however, until the evening of the 4th that we anchored within the islands at the entrance of the harbour of Rio de Janeiro.

At day-break the next morning an officer was dispatched from the Sirius to inform the viceroy of the arrival of the fleet; and he most readily and politely promised us every assistance in his power. A ship bound to Lisbon passing us about noon, that opportunity was taken of sending an account to England of the fortunate progress which we had so far made in the long voyage before us; soon after which the port-officer, or harbour-master, came on board, and, the sea-breeze beginning to blow, the fleet got under sail. About five in the afternoon we crossed the bar, and soon after passing the fort of Santa Cruz, saluted it with thirteen guns, which were returned by an equal number of guns from the fort. While saluting, it fell calm; but by the assistance of a light breeze which afterwards sprung up, and the tide of flood, the Sirius was enabled to reach far enough in by seven o'clock to come to an anchor in the harbour of Rio de Janeiro;

Janeiro; the convoy also anchored as they came up, at the distance of about a mile and a half from the landing-place, which was found very commodious.

Our paſſage from Teneriffe, although rather a long one, had fortunately been unattended with any diſeaſe, and the ſurgeon reported that we had brought in only ninety-five perſons ſick, comprehending every deſcription of people in the fleet. Many, however, of this number were bending only under the preſſure of age and its attendant infirmities, having no other complaints among them.

On the morning after our arrival the intendant of the port, with the uſual officers, repaired on board the Sirius, requiring the cuſtomary certificates to be given, as to what nation ſhe belonged to, whither bound, the name of her commander, and his reaſon for coming into that port; to all which ſatisfactory anſwers were given; and at eleven o'clock the day following Captain Phillip, accompanied by the officers of the ſettlement, civil and military, waited upon Don Louis Vaſconcellos, the viceroy of the Brazils, at his excellency's palace, who received them with much politeneſs, readily aſſenting to a tent being pitched on ſhore for the purpoſe of an obſervatory; as well as to the drawing of the Seine in different parts of the bay for fiſh; only pointing out the reſtrictions that would be neceſſary to prevent the ſailors from ſtraggling into the country. On their taking leave, it was moſt politely intimated, that no reſtraint would be impoſed upon the officers, whenever they came on ſhore to the town, in which they were free to paſs wherever they deſired. A conduct ſo oppoſite to that in general obſerved to foreigners in this port could by us be attributed only to the great eſteem in which Captain Phillip was held here by all ranks of people during the time of his commanding a ſhip in the Portugueſe ſervice; for on being informed of the employment he now held, the viceroy's guard was directed to pay him the ſame honours during his ſtay here, that were paid to himſelf as the repreſentative of the crown of Portugal.

The palace of the viceroy ſtood in the Royal Square, of which, together with the public priſon, the mint, and the opera-houſe, it formed the right wing. Of theſe buildings the opera-houſe alone was ſhut up; and we were informed, that the gloom which was thrown over the court and kingdom of Portugal by the death of the late king, had extended in full force to the colonies alſo; all private and public amuſements being ſince that time diſcouraged as much as poſſible, the viceroy himſelf ſetting the example. Once a-week, indeed, his excellency had a muſic-meeting at the palace for the entertainment of himſelf and a few ſelect friends; but nothing more.

The town of St. Sebaſtian (or, as it is more commonly named, the town of Rio de Janeiro, which was in fact the name of the river forming the bay, on the weſtern ſide of which was built the town) is large, and was originally deſigned to

have

have had an elevated and airy situation, but was, unfortunately for the inhabit-ants, erected on low ground along the shore, and in a recess almost wholly out of the reach of the refreshing sea-breeze, which was observed to be pretty regular in its visitations. The inhabitants, nevertheless, deemed the air salubrious; and we were informed that epidemic distempers were rare among them. In their streets, however, were frequently seen objects of wretchedness and misery crawl-ing about with most painful and disgusting swellings in their legs and privities. The hospital, which had formerly been a Jesuit's convent, stood near the summit of the hill, in an open situation, at the back of the town. From the great esti-mation in which English surgeons were held here, it would seem that the town is not too well provided in that respect. Senor Ildefonse, the principal in the place, had studied in England, where he went under the course of surgical educa-tion called walking the hospitals, and might by his practice in this place, which was considerable, and quite as much as he could attend to, have soon realised a handsome fortune; but we understood, that to the poor or necessitous sick he always administered gratis.

The township of the Rio de Janeiro was said to contain on the whole not less than 40,000 people, exclusive of the native Indians and negroes. These last ap-pear to be very numerous, of a strong robust appearance, and are brought from the coast of Guinea, forming an extensive article of commerce. With these people of both sexes the streets were constantly filled, scarcely any other description of people being seen in them. Ladies or gentlemen were never seen on foot in the streets during the day; those whose business or inclination led them out being carried in close chairs, the pole of which came from the head of the vehicle, and rested on the shoulders of the chairmen, having, notwithstanding the gaudiness of the chair itself, a very awkward appearance.

The language spoken here by the white people was that of the mother coun-try—Portuguese. The ecclesiastics in general could converse in Latin; and the negro slaves spoke a corrupt mixture of their own tongue with that of the people of the town. The native Indians retained their own language, and could be distinctly discerned from the natives of Guinea, as well by the colour of the skin, as by the hair and the features of the face. Some few of the military con-versed in French; but this language was in general little used.

The town appeared to be well supplied with water, which was conveyed into it from a great distance by means of an aqueduct, (or carioca,) which in one place having to cross a road or public way was raised upon a double row of strong lofty arches, forming an object that from the bay, and at the entrance of the harbour, added considerably to the beauty of the imagery. From this aque-

duct

duct the water was received into stone fountains, constructed with capacious ba-
sins, whither the inhabitants sent their linen, to have the dirt rather beaten than
washed out of it, by slaves. One of these fountains of a modern construction
was finished with great taste and neatness of execution.

We also observed several large and rich convents in the town. The chief of
these were, the Benedictine and the Carmelite; one dedicated to St. Anthony,
another to Our Lady of Assistance, and another to Sᵗ Theresa. The two last
were for the reception of nuns; and of the two, that of Sᵗ Theresa was reported the severest in its religious duties, and the strictest in its restraints and regulations. The convent D. Ajuda, or of Assistance, received as pensioners, or
boarders, the widows of officers, and young ladies having lost their parents, who
were allowed to remain, conforming to the rules of the convent, until married,
or otherwise provided for by their friends. There were many inferior convents
and churches, and the whole were under the spiritual direction of a bishop,
whose palace was in the town, a short distance from one of the principal
convents.

Near the carioca, or aqueduct, stood the seminary of St. Joseph, where the
servants of the church received their education, adopting on their entrance the
clerical habit and tonsure. The chapel to the seminary was neat, and we were
conducted by a sensible well-informed father of the Benedictine Order to a small
library belonging to it.

To a stranger nothing could appear more remarkable than the innumerable
religious processions which were to be seen at all hours in this town. At the
close of every day an image of the Virgin was borne in procession through the
principal streets, the attendants arrayed in white surplices, and bearing in their
hands lighted tapers; chanting at the same time praises to her in Latin. To this,
as well as to all other religious processions, the guards turned out, grounded
their arms, kneeled, and shewed the most submissive marks of respect; and the
bells of each church or convent in the vicinity of their progress sounded a peal
while they were passing.

Every church, chapel, or convent, being under the auspices of some tutelary
saint, particular days were set apart as the festival of each, which were opened
with public prayers, and concluded with processions, music, and fireworks. The
church and altars of the particular saint whose protection was to be solicited
were decorated with all the splendor of superstition *, and illuminated both
within and without. During several hours after dark, on these solemn festivals,
the inhabitants might be seen walking to and from the church, dressed in their

---

* We were informed that they never permitted any base metals near their altars, all their vessels,
&c. being of the purest gold or silver.

best

beſt habiliments, accompanied by their children, and attended by their ſlaves and their carriages.

An inſtance was related to us, of the delay that was thrown in the way of labour by this extravagant parade of public worſhip, and the ſtrict obſervance of ſaints' days, which, though calculated, no doubt, by the glare which ſurrounds the ſhrine, and decorates the veſture of its prieſts, to impreſs and keep in awe the minds of the lower ſort of people, Indians and ſlaves, had neverthelefs been found to be not without its evil effects:

A ſhip from Liſbon, laden chiefly with bale goods, was burnt to the water's edge, with her whole cargo, and much private property, the fourth day after her anchoring in the harbour, owing to the intervention of a ſabbath and two ſaints' days which unfortunately enſued that of her arrival. All that could be done was, to tow the veſſel on ſhore near the Iſland of Cobres, clear of the ſhipping in the bay, where grounding, ſhe was totally conſumed. One of the paſſengers, whoſe whole property was deſtroyed with her, came out to fill an high judicial employment, and had with all his family removed from Liſbon for that purpoſe, bringing with him whatever he had valuable in Europe.

At a corner of almoſt every ſtreet in the town we obſerved a ſmall altar, dedicated generally to the Virgin, and decorated with curtains and lamps. Before theſe altars, at the cloſe of every evening, the negroes aſſembled to chant their veſpers, kneeling together in long rows in the ſtreet. The policy of thus keeping the minds of ſo large a body, as that of the black people in this town, not only in conſtant employment, but in awe and ſubjection, by the almoſt perpetual exerciſe of religious worſhip, was too obvious to need a comment. In a colony where the ſervants were more numerous than the maſters, a military, however excellent, ought not to be the only control; to keep the mind in ſubjection muſt be as neceſſary as to provide a check on the perſonal conduct.

The trades-people of the town have adopted a regulation, which muſt prove of infinite convenience to ſtrangers, as well as to the inhabitants. We found the people of one profeſſion or trade dwelling together in one, two, or as many ſtreets as were neceſſary for their numbers to occupy. Thus, for inſtance, the apothecaries reſided in the principal ſtreet, or Rua Direita, as it was named; one or more ſtreets were aſſigned to the jewellers; and a whole diſtrict appeared to be occupied by the mercers. By this regulation the labour of traverſing from one ſtreet to another, in ſearch of any article which the purchaſer might wiſh to have a choice of, was avoided *. Moſt of the articles were from Europe, and were ſold at a high price.

* The ſame uſeful regulation is obſerved at Aleppo.

d 2   Houſes

Houses here were built, after the fashion of the mother-country, with a small wooden balcony over the entrance; but to the eye of one accustomed to the cheerful appearance of glass windows, a certain sombre cast seemed to pervade even their best and widest streets, the light being conveyed through window-frames of close lattice-work. Some of these, indeed, being decorated on the outside with paint and some gilding, rather improved the look of the houses to which they belonged.

The winter, we were informed, was the only season in which the inhabitants could make excursions into the country; for when the sun came to the southward of the Line, the rain, as they most energetically assured us, descended for between two and three months rather in seas than in torrents. At this season they confined themselves to their houses in the town, only venturing out by the unscorching light of the moon, or at those intervals when the rains were moderated into showers. But, though the summer season is so extremely hot, the use of the cold bath, we found, was wholly unknown to the inhabitants.

The women of the town of Rio de Janeiro, being born within the tropics, could not be expected to possess the best complexions; but their features were in general expressive—the eye dark and lively, with a striking eye-brow. The hair was dark, and nature had favoured them with that ornament in uncommon profusion: this they mostly wore with powder, strained to a high point before, and tied in several folds behind. By their parents they were early bred up to much useful knowledge, and were generally mistresses of the polite accomplishments of music, singing, and dancing. Their conversation appeared to be lively, at times breaking out in sallies of mirth and wit, and at others displaying judgment and good *sense*. In their dress for making or receiving visits, they chiefly affected silks and gay colours; but in the mornings, when employed in the necessary duties of the house, a thin but elegant robe or mantle thrown over the shoulders was the only upper garment worn. Both males and females were early taught to dress as men and women; and we had many opportunities of seeing a hoop on a little Donna of three years of age, and a bag and a sword on a Senor of six. This appearance was as difficult to reconcile as that of the saints and virgins in their churches being decorated with powdered perruques, swords, laced clothes, and full-dressed suits.

Attentions to the women were perhaps carried farther in this place than is customary in Europe. To a lady, in the presence of a gentleman, a servant never was suffered to hand even a glass of water, the gentleman (with a respect approaching to adoration) performing that office; and these gallantries appeared to be received as the homage due to their superior rank in the creation. It was said, indeed, that they were not disinclined to intrigues, but in public the strictest

decorum

decorum and propriety of behaviour was always obferved in the women, fingle as well as married. At houfes where feveral people of both fexes were met together, the eye, on entering the room, was inflantly hurt, at perceiving the female part of the company ranged and feated by themfelves on one fide, and the gentlemen on the other, an arrangement certainly unfavourable to private or particular converfation. Thefe daughters of the Sun fhould, however, neither be cenfured nor wondered at, if found indulging in pleafures againft which even the conflitutions of colder regions are not proof. If frozen Chaflity be not always found among the children of ice and fnow, can fhe be looked for among the inhabitants of climates where froft was never felt? Yet heartily fhould fhe be welcomed wherever fhe may be found, and doubly prized if met with unexpectedly.

The mines, the great fource of revenue to the crown of Portugal, and in the government of this place the great caufe of jealoufy both of ftrangers and of the inhabitants, were fituated fomewhat more than a week's journey hence, except fome which had been lately difcovered in the mountains near the town. Sufficient employment was found for the Mint, at which was ftruck all the coin that was current here, befides what was fent to Europe. The diamond-trade had been for fome time taken into the hands and under the infpection of Government; but the jewellers' fhops abounded with topazes, chryfolites, and other curious and precious ftones.

Befide the forts at the entrance of the harbour, there were two others of confiderable force, one at either extremity of the place, conftructed on iflands in the bay. On an eminence behind the town, and commanding the bay, ftood the Citadel. The troops in thefe works were relieved regularly on the laft day of every month, previous to which all the military in the garrifon paffed in review before the viceroy in the quadrangle of the palace. About 250 men with officers in proportion were on duty every day in the town, diftributed into different guards, from which centinels were ftationed in various parts of the place, who, to keep themfelves alert, challenge and reply to each other every quarter of an hour. In addition to thefe centinels, every regiment and every guard fent parties through the ftreets, patroling the whole night for the prefervation of peace and good order.

An officer from each regiment attended every evening at the palace to take orders for the following day, which were delivered by the adjutant of orders, who himfelf received them directly from the viceroy. At the palace every tranfaction in the town was known, and thence, through the adjutant of orders, the inhabitants received the viceroy's commands and directions whenever he thought it neceffary to guide or regulate their conduct.

The regiments that came here from Lifbon had been twenty years in the country, although, on leaving Europe, they were promifed to return at the

expiration

expiration of the third. They were recruited in the Brazils; and such officers as might wish to visit Portugal obtained leave of absence on application to the court, through the viceroy. To each regiment is attached an officer, who is styled an Auditeur, and whose office is to inquire into all crimes committed by the soldiers of his regiment. If he sees it necessary, he has power to inflict corporal punishment, or otherwise, as the offender may in his judgment merit; but his authority does not extend either to life or limb. For exercising this employment he is allowed the pay of a captain of infantry.

The barracks for the troops appeared to be commodious, and to be kept in good order. A small number of cavalry were always on duty, employed in the antichamber of the palace, or in attending the viceroy either on days of parade, or in his excursions into the country. A captain's guard of infantry with a standard mounted every day at the palace.

During our stay in this port all the transports struck their yards and top-masts, and overhauled their rigging preparatory to our passage to the Cape of Good Hope. An observatory was erected on the Island of Enchados, where Lieutenant Dawes, with two young gentlemen from the Sirius as assistants, went on shore, taking with them the instruments requisite for ascertaining the exact rate of going of the time-piece; and for making other necessary observations. Sailmakers were also sent to the island; and some of the camp-equipage of the settlement was landed to be inspected and thoroughly aired, with proper guards for its security.

Some propensities to the practice of their old vices manifesting themselves among the convicts* soon after their arrival in this port had given them an opportunity, the governor, with the lieutenant-governor, visited the transports, and informed the prisoners, both male and female, that in future any misbehaviour on their part should be attended with severe punishment, while on the other hand propriety of conduct should be particularly distinguished and rewarded with proportionate indulgence.

On the 21st, being the birth-day of the prince of Brazil, the Sirius, in compliment to the court of Portugal, displayed a Portuguese flag at her fore-top-mast-head, and, on the saluting of the fort on the Island of Cobras, saluted also with twenty-one guns. At ten o'clock the same morning, Captain Phillip, with the principal officers of the settlement and garrison, went on shore to pay their compliments to the viceroy in honour of the day, who on this and similar occasions had a court, at which all the civil and military officers and principal inhabitants of the town attended to pay their respects to his excellency as the representative

---

* Counterfeit coin was offered by some of them to a boat which came alongside one of the transports.

of

of the sovereign, who received them standing under a canopy in the presence-chamber of the palace.

Preparations were now making for putting to sea; and on Saturday the 1st of September, having appointed to sail on the Monday following, the governor, lieutenant-governor, and other officers, waited upon and took leave of the viceroy, who expressed himself in the handsomest terms at their departure.

During their stay in this port of refreshment, the convicts were each served daily with a pound of rice and a pound and an half of fresh meat (beef), together with a suitable proportion of vegetables. Great numbers of oranges were at different times distributed among them, and every possible care was taken to refresh and put them into a state of health and condition to resist the attacks of the scurvy, should it make its appearance in the long passage over the ocean which was yet between them and New South Wales. The Reverend Mr. Johnson gave also his full share of attention to their welfare, performing divine service on board two of the transports every Sunday of their stay in port.

We were unluckily not in season for any other of the fruits of this country than oranges and bananas; but these were truly delicious, and amply compensated, both in quantity and quality, for the want of others. Some few guavas, and a pine-apple or two, were purchased; but we were informed that their flavour then, and when in perfection, was not to be compared. Vegetables (which were brought from the opposite shore) were in great plenty. The beef was small and lean, and sold at about two-pence halfpenny *per* pound: mutton was in proportion still smaller, and poultry dear, but not ill-tasted. The market-place was contiguous to the palace.

On the evening of Sunday the 2d of September, a Portuguese boat, just at the close of the day, after once or twice rowing round the Sirius, dropped a soldier of the island on board, who, it appeared from his own account, had been for five or six days absent from his duty, and dreading perhaps to return, or perhaps wishing to change his situation, requested that he might be received on board, and permitted to sail to New Holland with Captain Phillip; who, however, not chusing to comply with his request, caused him to be immediately conveyed on shore in one of the ship's boats; but with great humanity permitted him to be landed wherever he thought he might chance to escape unobserved, and have an opportunity of returning to his duty.

An officer was this day sent to signify Captain Phillip's intention of saluting the forts when he took his departure, which would be the following morning, and presuming that an equal number of guns would be fired in return. The viceroy answered, that no mark of attention or respect should on his part be omitted that might testify his esteem for Captain Phillip, and the high sense he entertained

entertained of the decorum observed by those under his command during their stay in that port.

The land-wind not blowing on Monday morning, all idea of sailing was given up for that day. In the afternoon the signal was made for unmooring, and for all boats to cease communication with the shore.

At day-break the following morning the harbour-master came on board the Sirius, and, a light land breeze favouring her departure, took charge of that ship over the bar; the Supply and convoy getting under sail, and following her out of the bay. When the Sirius arrived nearly a-breast of the fort of Santa Cruz, it was saluted with one-and-twenty guns; a marked compliment paid by the viceroy to Captain Phillip, who immediately returned it with the like number of guns. Shortly after this the harbour-master left the ship, taking with him Mr. Morton, the master of the Sirius, who from ill health was obliged to return to England in the Diana, a whaler, which was lying here on our arrival. By this gentleman were sent the public and private letters of the fleet.

The land-breeze carrying us clear of the islands in the offing, the Supply was sent to speak a ship that was perceived at some little distance a-head, and which proved to be a ship from Oporto. By her we learned that the viceroy was superseded in his government, and it was imagined that his successor was standing into the harbour in a royal yacht which we then saw under the land. Toward evening it fell calm, and the islands and high land were still in sight. The calm continued during the greatest part of the following day; but toward evening a light and favourable breeze sprung up, which enabled us to cross the tropic of Capricorn, and bend our course toward the Cape of Good Hope.

On the night of Friday the 7th we had heavy squalls of rain, thunder, and lightning. From that time until the 11th the wind was rather unfavourable; but shifting to the northward on that day, it blew during the two following in strong gales, with squalls of heavy rain, attended with much sea.

These strong gales having, on Friday the 14th, terminated in a calm, Lieutenant Shortland, the day following, reported to the commanding officer, that there were eleven soldiers sick on board the Alexander, and five or six convicts on board the Charlotte. The calm continued until the 16th, when a favourable breeze sprung up; but those ships of the fleet which could sail were prevented from making the most of the fair wind, by the Lady Penrhyn transport and others, which were inattentive, and did not make sail in proper time.

On the 19th the wind was fresh, and frequently blew in squalls, attended with rain. In one of these squalls the Charlotte suddenly hove-to, a convict having fallen overboard; the man, however, was drowned. Our weather was at this time extremely cold; and the wind, which had for some days been unfavourable, shifting

shifting on the 22d, we again looked towards the Cape. At one o'clock the next morning it came on to blow very hard, accompanied with a great sea; we had nevertheless the satisfaction to observe, that the convoy appeared to get on very well, though some of them rolled prodigiously. This gale continued with very little variation until the morning of the 28th, when it moderated for a few hours, and shifted round to the S. E. It now again blew in fresh gales, attended with much rain and sea. But a calm succeeding all this violence shortly after, on Sunday morning the 30th the weather was sufficiently clear to admit of some altitudes being taken for the time-keeper, when our longitude was found to be 3° 04'. Thence to the 4th of October both wind and weather were very uncertain, the wind sometimes blowing in light airs, very little differing from a calm, with clear skies; at others, in fresh breezes, with rain. On the 4th, Captain Phillip was informed that thirty of the convicts on board of the Charlotte were ill; some of them, as it was feared, dangerously. To render this information still more unpleasant, the wind was foul during the two succeeding days.

In the forenoon of Saturday the 6th, four seamen of the Alexander transport were sent on board the Sirius, under a charge of having entered into a conspiracy to release some of the prisoners while the ship should be at the Cape of Good Hope, and of having provided those people with instruments for breaking into the fore-hold of the ship (which had been done, and some provisions stolen thereout). The four seamen were ordered to remain in the Sirius, a like number of her people being sent in lieu of them on board the transport.

On Thursday the 11th, by an altitude of the sun taken that morning, the fleet was found to be in the longitude of 15° 35' E. at which time there was an unfavourable change of the wind, and the sick on board the Charlotte were not decreasing in number.

On the next day, as it was judged from the information given by the time-keeper that we were drawing nigh the land, the Supply was sent forward to make it; but it was not seen until the following morning.

At noon on the 13th the Supply was sent to instruct the sternmost ships of the convoy in what direction they should keep to enter the bay; and about four in the afternoon, the harbour-master getting on board the Sirius, that ship was brought safely to an anchor in Table Bay, the convoy doing the same before dark; having crossed over from one Continent to the other, a distance of upwards of eleven hundred leagues, in the short space of five weeks and four days, fortunately without separation, or any accident having happened to the fleet.

e   Imme-

Immediately on our anchoring, an officer from the Sirius was sent on shore to the governor, who politely promised us every assistance in his power; and at sun-rise the next morning the Sirius saluted the garrison with thirteen guns, which were returned by an equal number from the fort.

From the great uncertainty of always getting readily on shore from the bay, and the refreshments found at the Cape of Good Hope being so necessary after, and so well adapted to the fatigues and disorders consequent on a long voyage, we found it a custom with most strangers on their arrival to take up their abode in the town, with some one or other of the inhabitants, who would for two rix-dollars, (eight shillings of English money,) or a ducatoon, (six shillings English,) per week, provide very good lodgings, and a table amply furnished with the best meats, vegetables, and fruits which could be procured at the Cape. This custom was, as far as the nature of our service would admit, complied with by several officers from the ships; and, on the second day after our arrival, Captain Phillip, with the principal officers of the navy and settlement, proceeded to the government-house in the Company's garden, where they were introduced to Mr. Van de Graaf, (the governor, for the Dutch East-India Company, of this place and its dependencies,) and by him politely received.

With a requisition made by Captain Phillip of a certain quantity of flour and corn, the governor expressed his apprehensions of being unable to comply, as the Cape had been very lately visited by that worst of scourges—a famine, which had been most severely felt by every family in the town, his own not excepted. This was a calamity which the settlement had never before experienced, and was to be ascribed rather to bad management of, than any failure in, the late crops. Measures were however taking to guard, as much as human precaution could guard, against such a misfortune in future; and magazines were erecting for the reception of grain on the public account, which had never been found necessary until fatal experience had suggested them. Captain Phillip's request was to be laid before the Council, without whose concurrence in such a business the governor could not act, and an answer was promised with all convenient dispatch. This answer, however, did not arrive until the 23d, when Captain Phillip was informed that every article which he had demanded was ordered to be furnished.

In the mean time the ships of the fleet had struck their yards and topmasts, (a precaution always necessary here to guard against the violence of the south-east wind, which had been often known to drive ships out of the bay,) and began filling their water. On board of the Sirius and some of the transports, the carpenters were employed in fitting up stalls for the reception of the cattle that was to be taken hence as stock for the intended colony at New South Wales. These were not ready until the 8th of the next month, November, on which day, 1 bull, 1 bull-calf, 7 cows, 1 stallion, 3 mares, and 3 colts, together with as great a number of rams, ewes, goats, boars, and breeding sows, as room could be provided for, were embarked in the different ships, the bulls and cows on board the Sirius, the horses on board the Lady Penrhyn; the remainder were put into the Fishbourn store-ship and Friendship transport.

Shortly after our arrival in the bay, a soldier belonging to the Swiss regiment of Muron, quartered here, swam off from his post and came on board one of the transports, requesting to be permitted to proceed in her to New South Wales; but, as an agreement had been mutually entered into between the Dutch and English commanders, that deserters in the service of, or subjects of either nation, should be given up, Captain Phillip sent him on shore, previously obtaining a promise of his pardon from the regiment.

On the 9th the watering of the fleet being completed, corn and hay for the stock, and flour, wine, and spirits for the settlement, being all on board, preparations were made for putting to sea, and on the 10th the signal was made to unmoor.

The convicts while in this port had been served, men and women, with one pound and an half of soft bread each *per diem;* a pound of fresh beef, or mutton, and three quarters of a pound for each child, together with a liberal allowance of vegetables.

While in this harbour, as at Rio de Janeiro, Mr. Johnson, the chaplain, preached on board two of the transports every Sunday; and we had the satisfaction to see the prisoners all wear the appearance of perfect health on their being about to quit this port, the last whereat any refreshment was to be expected before their arrival in New South Wales.

As it was earnestly wished to introduce the fruits of the Cape into the new settlement, Captain Phillip was ably assisted in his endeavours to procure the rarest and the best of every species, both in plant and seed, by Mr. Mason, the king's botanist, whom we were so fortunate as to meet with here, as well as by Colonel Gordon, the commander in chief of the troops at this place; a gentleman whose thirst for natural knowledge amply qualified him to be of service to us, not only in procuring a great variety of the best seeds and plants, but in pointing out the culture, the soil, and the proper time of introducing them into the ground.

The following plants and seeds were procured here and at Rio de Janeiro:

At Rio de Janeiro.	At the Cape of Good Hope.
Coffee—both seed and plant.	The Fig-tree.
Cocoa—in the nut.	Bamboo.
Cotton—seed.	Spanish Reed.
Banana—plant.	Sugar Cane.
Oranges—various sorts, seed and plant.	Vines of various sorts.
Lemon—seed and plant.	Quince.
Guava—seed.	Apple.
Tamarind.	Pear.
Prickly pear—plant, with the cochineal on it.	Strawberry.
	Oak.
Eugenia, or Pomme Rose—a plant bearing a fruit in shape like an apple, and having the flavour and odour of a rose.	Myrtle.
Ipecacuana—three sorts.	To these must be added all sorts of grain, as Rice, Wheat, Barley, Indian corn, &c. for seed, which were purchased to supply whatever might be found damaged of these articles that were taken on board in England.
Jalap.	

During our stay here, the Ranger packet, Captain Buchanan, arrived after a passage of twelve weeks from Falmouth, bound to Bengal. She sailed again immediately. One officer alone of our fleet was fortunate enough to receive letters by her from his connexions in England.

At the time of our arrival the inhabitants of this agreeable town had scarcely recovered from the consternation into which they had been thrown by one of the black people called Malays, with whom the place abounded; and who, taking offence at the governor for not returning him to Batavia, (where, it seemed, he was of consequence among his own countrymen, and whence he had been sent to the Cape as a punishment for some offence,) worked himself up to phrenzy by the effect of opium, and, arming himself with variety of weapons, rushed forth in the dusk of the evening, killing or maiming indiscriminately all who were so unfortunate as to be in his route, women alone excepted. He stabbed the centinel at the gate of the Company's gardens, and placed himself at his post, waiting some time in expectation of the governor's appearance, who narrowly escaped the fate intended for him, by its falling on another person accidentally passing that way. On being pursued, he fled with incredible swiftness to the Table Mountain at the back of the town, whence this single miscreant, still animated by the effect of the opium, for two days resisted and defied every force that was sent against him. The alarm and terror into which the town was thrown were inconceivable; for two days none ventured from within their houses, either masters or slaves; for an order was issued, (as the most likely means of destroying him, should he appear in the town,) that whatever Malay was seen in the streets should be instantly killed by the soldiery. On the evening of the second day, however, he was taken alive on the Table Mountain, having done much injury to those who took him, and was immediately consigned to the death he merited, being broken on the wheel, and his head and members severed after the execution, and distributed in different parts of the country.

Of this man, who had killed fourteen of the inhabitants, and desperately wounded nearly double that number, it was remarked, that in his progress his fury fell only on men, women passing him unhurt; and it was as extraordinary as it was unfortunate, that among those whom his rage destroyed, were some of the most deserving and promising young men in the town. This, at Batavia, was called running a muck, or amocke, and frequently happened there, but was the first instance of the kind known at the Cape. Since that time, every Malay or other slave, having business in the street after a certain hour in the evening, is obliged to carry a lighted lantern, on pain of being stopped by the centinel and kept in custody until morning. Murder and villany are strongly depicted on the features of the slaves of that nation; and such of them as dared to speak of this dreadful catastrophe clearly appeared to approve the behaviour of their countryman.

The government of the Cape we understood to be vested in a governor and council, together with a court of justice. The council is composed of the governor, the second or lieutenant-governor, the fiscal, the commanding officer of the troops for the time being, and four counsellors. With these all regulations for the management of the colony originate; and from them all orders and decrees are issued. The court of justice is composed of the fiscal, the second governor, a secretary, and twelve members, six of whom are from among the burghers, and six from among the Bourgeoisie. The fiscal, who was the first magistrate, had hitherto been styled independent, that is to say, his decisions were not subject to the interference of the governor and council; but we were informed, that since the death of the late fiscal, M. Serrurier, it had been determined by the States, that the decrees of the fiscal should be subject to the revision of the council. Before this officer were tried all causes both civil and criminal. He had a set of people belonging to him who constantly patroled the streets armed, to apprehend all vagrant and disorderly persons. Every fourteen days offences were tried. The prison was adjacent to and had communication with the court-house. The place where all sentences were executed stood to the left of the landing-place, a short distance above the fort or castle. The ground on which it stood was raised by several steps above the road. Within the walls were to be seen (and seen with horror) six crosses for breaking criminals, a large gibbet, a spiked pole for impalements, wheels, &c. &c. together with a flight wooden building, erected for the reception of the ministers of justice upon

execution-

execution-days. Over the entrance was a figure of Justice, with the usual emblems of a sword and balance, and the following apposite inscription:

" Felix quem faciunt aliena pericula cautum."

The bodies of those broken on the wheel were exposed in different parts of the town, several instances of which, and some very recent ones, were still to be seen.

It had been always imagined, that the police of the Cape-town was so well regulated as to render it next to impossible for any man to escape, after whom the fiscal's people were in pursuit. This, however, did not appear to be the case; for very shortly after our arrival four seamen belonging to a ship of our fleet deserted from her; and although rewards were offered for apprehending them, and every effort made that was likely to insure success, two only were retaken before our departure.

Since the attempt meditated upon the Cape by the late Commodore Johnstone, the attention of the government appeared to have been directed to its internal defence. To this end additional works had been constructed on each side of the town, toward the hill called the Lion's Rump, and beyond the castle or garrison. But the defence in which they chiefly prided themselves, and of which we were fortunate enough to arrive in time to be spectators, consisted of two corps of cavalry and one of infantry, formed from the gentlemen and inhabitants of the town. We understood that these corps were called out annually to be exercised during seven days, and were reviewed on the last day of their exercise by the governor attended by his whole council. They appeared to be stout and able-bodied men, particularly those who composed the two corps of cavalry, and who were reputed to be excellent marksmen. Their horses, arms, and appointments were purchased at their own expence, and they were expected to hold themselves in readiness to assemble whenever their services might be required by the governor. For uniform, they wore a blue coat with white buttons, and buff waistcoat and breeches. Their parade was the Square or Market-place, where they were attended by music, and visited by all the beauty of the place, who animated them by their smiles from the balcony of the town-hall, and if the weather was favourable accompanied them to the exercising ground, where tents were pitched for their reception, and whence they beheld these patriotic Africans (for few of them knew Holland but by name) enuring themselves to the toils of war, " pro aris et " focis." We were however told, that at the least idea of an enemy coming on the coast, the women were immediately sent to a distance in the country.

The militia throughout the whole district of the Cape were assembled at this time of the year, exercised for a week, and reviewed by the governor or his deputy, commencing with the militia of the Cape-town.

The

The present governor of the Cape, Mr. Van de Graaf, though a colonel of engineers in the service of the States, yet holds his commission as governor under the authority of the Dutch East India Company, to which body the settlement wholly belongs. Every ship or vessel wearing a pendant of the States, be her rate what it may, is on entering the harbour saluted by the fort, which salute she returns with an inferior number of guns. The governor, at the landing-place, with his officers and carriages, attends the coming on shore of her captain or senior officer, to receive his commands, and escort him to his lodgings in the town, treating him with every mark of respect in his power. Such an humiliation of the Company's principal servant and officers in a commercial community bore, it must be confessed, rather an extraordinary appearance; but such, as we were informed, was the distinction between the two services; and Mr. Van de Graaf was obliged to obtain his prince's permission before he could accept of the government of the Cape from the East India Company.

Residence at the Cape would be highly agreeable, were it not for the south-east wind. This during the summer season blows with such violence, and drives every where such clouds of sand before it, that the inhabitants at certain times dare not stir out of their houses. Torrents of dust and sand, we were told, had been frequently known to fall on board of ships in the road. This circumstance accounted for every thing we got here being gritty to the taste; sand mixing with their flour, their rice, their sugar, and with whatever was capable of receiving it, finding its way in at doors, windows, and wherever there was an entrance for it. From the great height of the Table Mountain*, whatever clouds are within its influence are attracted when the south-east wind prevails; and as it increases in violence, these clouds hang over the side of the mountain, and descend into the valley, sometimes rolling down very near the town. From the curling of the vapour over the mountain, the inhabitants predict the arrival of the south-easter, and say, " The Table-cloth is spread;" but with all its violence, and the inconvenience of the dust and sand, it has a good effect, for the climate and air of the Cape Town (though wonderfully beneficial and refreshing to strangers after a long voyage) is not reckoned salubrious by the inhabitants, who, we understood, were at times visited by pains in the chest, sore throats, and putrid fevers; and the place would certainly be still more unhealthy were it not for this south-east wind, which burns as it blows, and while it sweeps disorder before it purifies the air.

The Cape is celebrated for producing in the highest perfection all the tropical and other fruits; but of the few that were in season during our stay we could not pronounce so favourably. The oranges and bananas in particular were not

* 3555 Rhineland feet—a Rhineland foot left; twelve inches and ₇/₁₀ths English.

equal

equal to those of Rio de Janeiro. The grape we could only taste from the bottle; that of Constantia, so much famed, has a very fine, rich, and pleasant flavour, and is an excellent cordial; but much of the wine that is sold under that name was never made of the grape of Constantia; for the vineyard is but small, and has credit for a much greater produce than it could possibly yield: this reminds us of those eminent masters in the art of painting, to whom more originals are ascribed than the labour of the longest life of man could produce.

Wines of their own growth formed a considerable article of traffic here; and the neatness, regularity, and extent of their wine-vaults, were extremely pleasing to the eye; but a stranger should not visit more than one of them in a day; for almost every cask has some peculiarity to recommend it, and its contents must be tasted.

We found the paper currency here very inconvenient, from its lightness; as more than one instance occurred among ourselves during our stay, of its being torn from our hands by the violence of the south-east wind, when we were about to make a payment in the street, or even at the door of a shop.

The meat of the Cape was excellent; the black cattle were large, very strong, and remarkable for the great space between their horns. It was not uncommon to see twelve, fourteen, or sixteen oxen yoked in pairs to a waggon, and galloping through the streets of the town, preceded by a Hottentot boy, who accompanied them on foot, conducting the foremost couple by a leathern thong, which caution they are compelled to observe by an order of government, some accidents having formerly happened from some of these large teams having been imprudently driven through the streets without any one to lead them; the lash of the charioteer (for the driver of such a team deserves a more honourable appellation than that of waggoner) had been sometimes heard, we were told, on board of ships in the bay.

The sheep are fat, well-flavoured, and remarkable for the weight and size of their tails. Wonders have been related of them by travellers; but travellers from this part of the world are privileged to exaggerate in their narrations, if they choose so to do; the truth however is, that their tails weigh from eight to sixteen pounds; some few perhaps may be heavier by a pound or two; but though the sheep itself will very well endure the voyage to Europe, yet its tail considerably decreases in size and weight during the passage.

Strangers coming into the bay are served with beef, mutton, &c. by the Company's butcher, who contracts to supply the Company, its officers and ships, with meat at a certain price, which is fixed at about three halfpence *per* pound, although he may have to purchase the cattle at three or four times that sum; but in return for this exaction, he has the sole permission of selling to strangers, and at a much higher price, though even in that instance his demand is not allowed to exceed a certain quota. Four-pence *per* pound was the price given for all the meat served to our ships after we came in.

During our stay here we made frequent visits to the Company's garden, pleasantly situated in the midst of the town. The ground on each side of the principal walk, which was from eight to nine hundred paces in length, was laid out in fruit and kitchen gardens, and at the upper end was a paddock where we saw three large oftriches, and a few antelopes. Behind this paddock was a menagerie, which contained nothing very curious :—a vicious zebra, an eagle, a caffowary, a falcon, a crowned falcon, two of the birds called fecretaries, a crane, a tiger, an hyæna, two wolves, a jackall, and a very large baboon, compofed the entire catalogue of its inhabitants.

In the town are two churches, one for the Calvinifts, and another for the followers of Luther. In the first of thefe was a handfome organ ; four large plain columns fupported the roof, and the walls were ornamented with efcutcheons and armorial quarterings. The body of the church was filled with chairs for the women, the men fitting in pews round the fides. By the pulpit ftood an hourglafs, which, we were told, regulated the duration of the minifter's admonition to his congregation. In the church-yards the grave-ftones, inftead of bearing the names of the deceafed, were all numbered, and the names were regiftered in a book kept for the purpofe.

Weddings were always folemnized on a Sunday at one or other of thefe churches, and the parties were habited in fables, a drefs furely more congenial with the fenfations felt on the laft than on the firft day of fuch an union.

To the care of an officer belonging to a regiment in India, who was returning to Europe in a Danifh veffel, Captain Phillip committed his difpatches ; and by this fhip every officer gladly embraced the laft opportunity of communicating with their friends and connections, until they fhould be enabled to renew their correfpondence from the new world to which they were now bound.

Nothing remaining to be done that need detain the convoy longer in this port, every article having been procured that could tend to the prefent refrefhment of the colonifts, or to the future advantage of the colony, the Sirius was unmoored in the evening of Sunday the 11th, Captain Phillip purpofing to put to fea the following morning ; but the wind at that time not being favourable, the boats from the Sirius were once more fent on fhore for a load of water, in order that no veffel which could be filled with an article fo effential to the prefervation of the ftock might be taken to fea empty.

The fouth-eaft wind now beginning to blow, the fignal was made for weighing, and at ten minutes before two in the afternoon of Monday the 12th of November the whole fleet was under fail ftanding out with a frefh of wind to the northward of Robin Ifland.

E

It was natural to indulge at this moment a melancholy reflection which obtruded itself upon the mind. The land behind us was the abode of a civilized people; that before us was the residence of savages. When, if ever, we might again enjoy the commerce of the world, was doubtful and uncertain. The refreshments and the pleasures of which we had so liberally partaken at the Cape, were to be exchanged for coarse fare and hard labour at New South-Wales. All communication with families and friends now cut off, we were leaving the world behind us, to enter on a state unknown; and, as if it had been necessary to imprint this idea more strongly on our minds, and to render the sensation still more poignant, at the close of the evening we spoke a ship from London *. The metropolis of our native country, its pleasures, its wealth, and its consequence, thus accidentally presented to the mind, failed not to afford a most striking contrast with the object now principally in our view.

Before we quitted the Cape Captain Hunter determined the longitude of the Cape-town in Table-bay to be, by the mean of several sets of lunar observations taken on board the Sirius, 18° 23' 55" east from Greenwich.

* The Kent—southern whaler.

SECTION III.

Proceed on the Voyage.—Captain Phillip sails onward in the Supply, taking with him three of the Transports.—Pass the Island of St. Paul.—Weather, January 1788.—The South Cape of New Holland made.—The Sirius and her Convoy anchor in the Harbour of Botany Bay.

EVERY precaution being absolutely necessary to guard against a failure of water on board the different ships, the whole were put upon an allowance of three pints *per* man *per diem* soon after our departure from the Cape. This regulation was highly proper, as from the probable continuance of the easterly wind which then blew, the fleet might be detained a considerable time at sea.

For several days after we had sailed, the wind was unfavourable, and blowing fresh, with much sea, some time elapsed before we had reached to the eastward of the Cape of Good Hope. On the 16th, Captain Phillip signified his intention of proceeding forward in the Supply, with the view of arriving in New South Wales so long before the principal part of the fleet, as to be able to fix on a clear and proper place for the settlement. Lieutenant Shortland was at the same time informed, that he was to quit the fleet with the Alexander, taking on with him the Scarborough and Friendship transports. These three ships had on board the greater part of the male convicts, whom Captain Phillip had sanguine hopes of employing to much advantage, before the Sirius, with that part of the fleet which was to remain under Captain Hunter's direction, should arrive upon the coast. This separation, the first that had occurred, did not take place until the 25th, on which day Captain Phillip went on board the Supply, taking with him, from the Sirius, Lieutenants King and Dawes, with the time-keeper. On the same day Major Ross, with the adjutant and quarter-master of the detachment, went into the Scarborough, in order to co-operate with Captain Phillip in his intention of preparing, as far as time might allow, for the reception of the rest of the convoy.

The Supply and the three transports having taken their departure, Captain Hunter drew his little convoy into the order of sailing prescribed for them; and the boats, which had been employed passing and repassing between the Sirius and the transports, being hoisted in, about noon the fleet made sail to the south-east, having a fresh breeze at west-north-west.

On Sunday the 16th of December, by computation, we were a-breast of the Island of St. Paul, passing it at the distance of about sixty leagues.

f 2　　　　　　　　　The

The following day, on the return of a boat from the Fishbourn store-ship, which had been sent to inquire into the state of the stock, we heard that several of the sheep were dead, as well as eight of the hogs belonging to the public stock.

Christmas-day found us in the latitude of 42° 10′ south, and steering, as we had done for a considerable time, an east-south-east course. We complied, as far as was in our power, with the good old English custom, and partook of a better dinner this day than usual; but the weather was too rough to admit of much social enjoyment.

With the wind at south-west, west-south-west, and south and by west, the weather was clear and cold, while to the northward of east or west it generally blew in strong gales.

We now often noticed pieces of sea-weed floating by the ships; and on the 28th the sun just appeared in time to shew us we were in the latitude of 42° 58′ south.

On the 29th, being in latitude 43° 35′ south, the course was altered to east and by south half south, in order to run down our easting without going any further to the southward. The run at noon on this day was found to be the greatest we had made in any twenty-four hours since our departure from England, having 182 miles on the log-board since twelve o'clock the preceding day.

By lunar observations taken on the 30th the longitude was found to be 118° 19′ east.

1788.] The new year opened with a gale of wind from the northward, which continued with much violence all the day, moderating towards evening.

The evening of the third proved fine and moderate, and the sun setting clear gave a good observation for the amplitude, when the variation was found to be 1° 00′ east. At noon the fleet was in the latitude of 44° 00′ south, and longitude by lunar observation 135° 32′ east, of which the convoy was informed.

At noon on the 4th preparations were made on board the Sirius for falling in with the land; her cables were bent, signal-guns prepared, and every possible precaution taken to ensure the safety of the fleet.

About ten at night on the 5th, a very beautiful aurora australis was observed bearing about south-west of the fleet; and for some nights a luminous phenomenon had been seen resembling lights floating on the surface of the water.

By a lunar observation taken at ten o'clock of the forenoon of Monday the 7th, the fleet was then distant seventeen leagues from the South Cape of New Holland; and at five minutes past two in the afternoon the signal was made for seeing the land. The rocks named the Mewstone and Swilly were soon visible, and the fleet stood along shore with fair moderate weather and smooth water, the land of New Holland distant from three to five miles.

Nothing

Nothing could more strongly prove the excellence and utility of lunar observations, than the accuracy with which we made the land in this long voyage from the Cape of Good Hope, there not being a league difference between our expectation of seeing it, and the real appearance of it.

A thick haze hanging over the land, few observations could be made of it. What we first saw was the South-west Cape of New Holland, between which and the South Cape the land appeared high and rocky, rising gradually from the shore, and wearing in many places a very barren aspect. In small cavities, on the summit of some of the high land, was the appearance of snow. Over the South Cape the land seemed covered with wood; the trees stood thick, and the bark of them appeared in general to have a whitish cast. The coast seemed very irregular, projecting into low points forming creeks and bays, some of which seemed to be deep; very little verdure was any where discernible; in many spots the ground looked arid and steril. At night we perceived several fires lighted on the coast, at many of which, no doubt, were some of the native inhabitants, to whom it was probable our novel appearance must have afforded matter of curiosity and wonder.

In all the preceding passage we had been scarcely a day without seeing birds of different kinds; and we also met with many whales. The weather was in general very rough, and the sea high, but the wind favourable, blowing mostly from north-west to south-west.

The convoy behaved well, paying more attention and obedience to signals than ships in the merchant service are commonly known to do. The ships, however, began to grow foul, not one of them being coppered, and we now anxiously wished for a termination of the voyage, particularly as the hay provided for the horses was on the point of being wholly expended.

The fair wind which had accompanied us to New Holland suddenly left us, shifting round to north-east and by east; we were obliged to lay our heads off shore, in order to weather Swilly and the Eddystone, (a perpendicular rock about a league to the eastward of Swilly,) and the next day we had the mortification of a foul wind, a thing to which we had been long unaccustomed.

In the night of the 9th the Golden Grove shipped a sea, which stove in all her cabin-windows: it was nearly calm at the time, with a confused heavy swell*.

At two o'clock in the afternoon of the following day a very heavy and sudden squall took the Sirius and laid her considerably down on her starboard side: it blew very fresh, and was felt more or less by all the transports, some of which suffered in their sails.

* This circumstance has since occurred to other ships nearly in the same situation.

2   Our

Our progress along the coast to the northward was very slow, and it was not until the 19th that we fell in with the land, when we were nearly a-breast of the Point named by Captain Cook Red Point. Before evening, however, we were gratified with the sight of the entrance into Botany Bay, but too late to attempt standing into it with the transports that night. The convoy therefore was informed by Captain Hunter how the entrance of the bay bore, and directed to be very attentive in the morning when the Sirius made sail or bore up.

When the morning came we found the fleet had been carried by a current to the southward as far as a clump of trees which had the preceding day obtained, from some resemblance in the appearance, the name of Post-down Clump; but with the assistance of a fine breeze we soon regained what we had lost in the night; and at ten minutes before eight in the morning the Sirius came to an anchor in Botany Bay. The transports were all safe in by nine o'clock.

AN

ACCOUNT

OF THE

ENGLISH COLONY

IN

NEW SOUTH WALES.

AN ACCOUNT

OF THE

ENGLISH COLONY

IN

NEW SOUTH WALES.

CHAP. I.

ARRIVAL OF THE FLEET AT BOTANY BAY.—THE GOVERNOR PROCEEDS TO PORT JACKSON, WHERE IT IS DETERMINED TO FIX THE SETTLEMENT.—TWO FRENCH SHIPS UNDER M. DE LA PEROUSE ARRIVE AT BOTANY BAY.—THE SIRIUS AND CONVOY ARRIVE AT PORT JACKSON.—TRANSACTIONS.—DISEMBARKATION.—COMMISSION AND LETTERS-PATENT READ.—EXTENT OF THE TERRITORY OF NEW SOUTH WALES.—BEHAVIOUR OF THE CONVICTS.—THE CRIMINAL COURT TWICE ASSEMBLED.—ACCOUNT OF THE DIFFERENT COURTS.—THE SUPPLY SENT WITH SOME SETTLERS TO NORFOLK ISLAND.—TRANSACTIONS.—NATIVES.—WEATHER.

WHEN the Sirius anchored in the bay, Captain Hunter was informed that the Supply had preceded him in his arrival only two days; and that the agent Lieutenant Shortland, with his detachment from the fleet, had arrived but the day before the Sirius and her convoy.

Thus, under the blessing of God, was happily completed, in eight months and one week, a voyage which, before it was undertaken, the mind hardly dared venture to contemplate, and on which it was impossible to reflect without some apprehensions as to its termination. This fortunate completion of it, however, afforded even to ourselves as much matter of surprise as of general satisfaction; for in the above space of

B   time

time we had failed five thousand and twenty-one leagues; had touched
at the American and African Continents; and had at last rested within
a few days sail of the antipodes of our native country, without meeting
any accident in a fleet of eleven sail, nine of which were merchantmen
that had never before sailed in that distant and imperfectly explored
ocean: and when it is considered, that there was on board a large body
of convicts, many of whom were embarked in a very sickly state, we
might be deemed peculiarly fortunate, that of the whole number of all
descriptions of persons coming to form the new settlement, only thirty-
two had died since their leaving England, among whom were to be included one or two deaths by accidents; although previous to our departure it was generally conjectured, that before we should have been a
month at sea one of the transports would have been converted into an
hospital ship. But it fortunately happened otherwise; the high health
which was apparent in every countenance was to be attributed not only
to the refreshments we met with at Rio de Janeiro and the Cape of
Good Hope, but to the excellent quality of the provisions with which
we were supplied by Mr. Richards junior, the contractor; and the
spirits visible in every eye were to be ascribed to the general joy and fatisfaction which immediately took place on finding ourselves arrived at
that port which had been so much and so long the subject of our most
serious reflections, the constant theme of our conversations.

The governor, we found, had employed the time he had been here
in examining the bay, for the purpose of determining where he should
establish the settlement; but as yet he had not seen any spot to which
some strong objection did not apply. Indeed, very few places offered
themselves to his choice, and not one sufficiently extensive for a thousand people to sit down on. The southern shore about Point Sutherland seemed to possess the soil best adapted for cultivation, but it was
deficient in that grand essential fresh water, and was besides too confined for our numbers. There was indeed a small run of water there;
but it appeared to be only a drain from a marsh, and by no means promised that ample or certain supply which was requisite for such a settlement as ours. The governor, therefore, speedily determined on examining the adjacent harbours of Port Jackson and Broken Bay, in one of
which he thought it possible that a better situation for his young colony
                                          might

might be found. But as his search might possibly prove fruitless, and that the few days which it should occupy might not be altogether thrown away, he left the lieutenant-governor at Botany Bay, with instructions to clear the ground about Point Sutherland, and make preparations for disembarking the detachment of marines and the convicts on his return, should that place at last be deemed the most eligible spot. At the same time Lieutenant King, of the Sirius, was directed to examine such parts of the bay as, from want of time, the governor had not himself been able to visit.

The governor set off on Monday the 21st, accompanied by Captain Hunter, Captain Collins (the judge advocate), a lieutenant, and the master of the Sirius, with a small party of marines for their protection, the whole being embarked in three open boats. The day was mild and serene, and there being but a gentle swell without the mouth of the harbour, the excursion promised to be a pleasant one. Their little fleet attracted the attention of several parties of the natives, as they proceeded along the coast, who all greeted them in the same words, and in the same tone of vociferation, shouting every where " Warra, warra, warra,"—words which, by the gestures that accompanied them, could not be interpreted into invitations to land, or expressions of welcome. It must however be observed, that at Botany Bay the natives had hitherto conducted themselves sociably and peaceably toward all the parties of our officers and people with whom they had hitherto met, and by no means seemed to regard them as enemies or invaders of their country and tranquillity [*].

The coast, as the boats drew near Port Jackson, wore so unfavourable an appearance, that Captain Phillip's utmost expectation reached no farther than to find what Captain Cook, as he passed by, thought might be found, shelter for a boat. In this conjecture, however, he was most agreeably disappointed, by finding not only shelter for a boat, but a harbour capable of affording security to a much larger fleet than would probably ever seek for shelter or security in it. In

[*] How grateful to every feeling of humanity would it be could we conclude this narrative without being compelled to say, that these unoffending people had found reason to change both their opinions and their conduct!

one of the coves of this noble and capacious harbour, equal if not superior to any yet known in the world, it was determined to fix the settlement; and on the 23d, having examined it as fully as the time would allow, the governor and his party left Port Jackson and its friendly and peaceful inhabitants, (for such he every where found them,) and returned to Botany Day.

In the report of the survey made by Lieutenant King, during the governor's absence, the latter found nothing to induce him to alter his resolution of fixing in Port Jackson: directions were therefore given, that the necessary supply of water and grass for the stock should be immediately sent off to the ships, and the next morning was appointed for their departure from Botany Bay.

Several trees had been cut down at Point Sutherland, a saw-pit had been dug, and other preparations made for disembarking, in case the governor had not succeeded as, to the great satisfaction of every one, it was found he had; for had he been compelled to remain in Botany Bay, the swampy ground every where around it threatened us with unhealthy situations; neither could the shipping have ridden in perfect security when the wind blew from the S. E. to which the bay lay much exposed, the sea at that time rolling in with a prodigious swell. A removal therefore to Port Jackson was highly applauded, and would have taken place the next morning, but at day-light we were surprised by the appearance of two strange sail in the offing. Of what nation they could be, engaged the general wonder for some time, which at last gave way to a conjecture that they might be the French ships under M. de la Perouse, then on a voyage round the world. This was soon strengthened by the view of a white pendant, similar in shape to that of a commodore in our service, and we had no longer a doubt remaining that they were the ships above mentioned. They were, however, prevented by a strong southerly current from getting into the bay until the 26th, when it was known that they were the Boussole and Astrolabe, French ships, which sailed, under the command of M. de la Perouse, from France in the year 1785, on a voyage of discovery. As Captain Hunter, with whom the governor had left the charge of bringing the Sirius and transports round to Port Jackson, (whither he had preceded them in the Supply the day before,)

was

was working out when M. de la Perouse entered Botany Bay, the two commanders had barely time to exchange civilities; and it must naturally have created some surprise in M. de la Perouse to find our fleet abandoning the harbour at the very time he was preparing to anchor in it: indeed he afterwards said, that " until he had looked " round him in Botany Bay, he could not divine the cause of our " quitting it, which he was so far from expecting, that having heard " at Kamschatka of the intended settlement, he imagined he should " have found a town built and a market established; but from what " he had seen of the country since his arrival, he was convinced of " the propriety and absolute necessity of the measure." M. de la Perouse sailed into the harbour by Captain Cook's chart of Botany Bay, which lay before him on the binnacle; and we had the pleasure of bearing him more than once pay a tribute to our great circumnavigator's memory, by acknowledging the accuracy of his nautical observations.

The governor, with a party of marines, and some artificers selected from among the seamen of the Sirius and the convicts, arrived in Port Jackson, and anchored off the mouth of the cove intended for the settlement on the evening of the 25th; and in the course of the following day sufficient ground was cleared for encamping the officer's guard and the convicts who had been landed in the morning. The spot chosen for this purpose was at the head of the cove, near the run of fresh water, which stole silently along through a very thick wood, the stillness of which had then, for the first time since the creation, been interrupted by the rude sound of the labourer's axe, and the downfal of its ancient inhabitants;—a stillness and tranquillity which from that day were to give place to the voice of labour, the confusion of camps and towns, and " the busy hum of its new possessors." That these did not bring with them

" Minds not to be changed by time or place,"

was fervently to have been wished; and if it were possible, that on taking possession of Nature, as we had thus done, in her simplest, purest garb, we might not sully that purity by the introduction of vice, profaneness, and immorality. But this, though much to be
wished,

wifhed, was little to be expected;—the habits of youth are not eafily laid afide, and the utmoft we could hope in our prefent fituation was to oppofe the foft harmouifing arts of peace and civilifation to the baneful influence of vice and immorality.

In the evening of this day the whole of the party that came round in the Supply were affembled at the point where they had firft landed in the morning, and on which a flag-ftaff had been purpofely erected and an union jack difplayed, when the marines fired feveral vollies; between which the governor and the officers who accompanied him drank the healths of his Majefty and the Royal Family, and fuccefs to the new colony. The day, which had been uncommonly fine, concluded with the fafe arrival of the Sirius and the convoy from Botany Bay,—thus terminating the voyage with the fame good fortune that had from its commencement been fo confpicuoufly their friend and companion.

The difembarkation of the troops and convicts took place from the following day until the whole were landed. The confufion that enfued will not be wondered at, when it is confidered that every man ftepped from the boat literally into a wood. Parties of people were every where heard and feen varioufly employed;—fome in clearing ground for the different encampments; others in pitching tents, or bringing up fuch ftores as were more immediately wanted; and the fpot which had fo lately been the abode of filence and tranquillity was now changed to that of noife, clamour, and confufion: but after a time order gradually prevailed every where. As the woods were opened and the ground cleared, the various encampments were extended, and all wore the appearance of regularity.

A portable canvas houfe, brought over for the governor, was erected on the Eaft fide of the cove, (which was named Sydney, in compliment to the principal fecretary of ftate for the home department,) where alfo a fmall body of convicts was put under tents. The detachment of marines was encamped at the head of the cove near the ftream, and on the Weft fide was placed the main body of the convicts. The women did not difembark until the 6th of February; when, every perfon belonging to the fettlement being landed, the numbers amounted to 1030

11   perfons

persons. The tents for the sick were placed on the West side, and it was observed with concern that their numbers were fast increasing. The scurvy, that had not appeared during the passage, now broke out, which, aided by a dysentery, began to fill the hospital, and several died. In addition to the medicines that were administered, every species of esculent plants that could be found in the country were procured for them ; wild celery, spinach, and parsley, fortunately grew in abundance about the settlement ; those who were in health, as well as the sick, were very glad to introduce them into their messes, and found them a pleasant as well as wholesome addition to the ration of salt provisions.

The public stock, consisting of one bull, four cows, one bull-calf, one stallion, three mares, and three colts, (one of which was a stone-colt,) were landed on the East point of the cove, where they remained until they had cropped the little pasturage it afforded ; and were then removed to a spot at the head of the adjoining cove, that was cleared for a small farm, intended to be placed under the direction of a person brought out by the governor.

Some ground having been prepared near his excellency's house on the East side, the plants from Rio-de-Janeiro and the Cape of Good Hope were safely brought on shore in a few days ; and we soon had the satisfaction of seeing the grape, the fig, the orange, the pear, and the apple, the delicious fruits of the Old, taking root and establishing themselves in our New World.

As soon as the hurry and tumult necessarily attending the disembarkation had a little subsided, the governor caused his Majesty's commission, appointing him to be his captain-general and governor in chief in and over the territory of New South Wales and its dependencies, to be publicly read, together with the letters patent for establishing the courts of civil and criminal judicature in the territory, the extent of which, until this publication of it, was but little known even among ourselves. It was now found to extend from Cape York, (the extremity of the coast to the northward,) in the latitude of 10° 37' South, to the South Cape, (the southern extremity of the coast,) in the latitude of 43° 39' South ; and inland to the westward as far as 135° of East longitude, comprehending all the islands adjacent

in

in the Pacific Ocean, within the latitudes of the above-mentioned capes.

By this definition of our boundaries it will be seen that we were confined along the coast of this continent to such parts of it solely as were navigated by Captain Cook, without infringing on what might be claimed by other nations from the right of discovery. Of that right, however, no other nation has chosen to avail itself. Whether the western coast is unpromising in its appearance, or whether the want of a return proportioned to the expence which the mother-country must sustain in supporting a settlement formed nearly at the farthest part of the globe, may have deterred them, is not known; but Great Britain alone has followed up the discoveries she had made in this country, by at once establishing in it a regular colony and civil government.

The ceremony of reading these public Instruments having been performed by the judge advocate, the governor, addressing himself to the convicts, assured them, among other things, that " he should " ever be ready to shew approbation and encouragement to those " who proved themselves worthy of them by good conduct and at- " tention to orders; while on the other hand, such as were determined " to act in opposition to propriety, and observe a contrary conduct, " would inevitably meet with the punishment which they deserved." He remarked how much it was their interest to forget the habits of vice and indolence in which too many of them had hitherto lived; and exhorted them to be honest among themselves, obedient to their overseers, and attentive to the several works in which they were about to be employed. At the conclusion of this address three vollies were fired by the troops, who thereupon returned to their parade, where the governor, attended by Captain Hunter and the principal officers of the settlement, passed along the front of the detachment, and received the honours due to a captain-general; after which he entertained all the officers and gentlemen of the settlement at dinner, under a large tent pitched for the purpose at the head of the marine encampment.

The convicts had been mustered early in the morning, when nine were reported to be absent. From the situation which we had unavoidably

avoidably adopted, it was impossible to prevent these people from
straggling. Fearless of the danger which must attend them, many
had visited the French ships in Botany Bay, soliciting to be taken on
board, and giving a great deal of trouble. It was soon found that
they secreted at least one-third of their working tools, and that any
sort of labour was with difficulty procured from them.

The want of proper overseers principally contributed to this. Those
who were placed over them as such were people selected from among
themselves, being recommended by their conduct during the voyage;
few of these, however, chose to exert the authority that was requisite
to keep the gangs at their labour, although assured of meeting with
every necessary support. Petty thefts among themselves began soon
to be complained of; the sailors from the transports, although repeatedly forbidden, and frequently punished, still persisted in bringing spirits on shore by night, and drunkenness was often the consequence.

To check these enormities, the court of criminal judicature was
assembled on the 11th of February, when three prisoners were tried;
one for an assault, of which being found guilty, he was sentenced to
receive one hundred and fifty lashes; a second, for taking some biscuit
from another convict, was sentenced to a week's confinement on bread
and water, on a small rocky island near the entrance of the cove;
and a third, for stealing a plank, was sentenced to receive fifty lashes,
but, being recommended to the governor, was forgiven.

The mildness of these punishments seemed rather to have encouraged than deterred others from the commission of greater offences;
for before the month was ended the criminal court was again assembled
for the trial of four offenders, who had conceived and executed a plan
for robbing the public store during the time of issuing the provisions.
This crime, in its tendency big with evil to our little community,
was rendered still more atrocious by being perpetrated at the very time
when the difference of provisions, which had till then existed, was
taken off, and the convict saw the same proportion of provision issued
to himself that was served to the soldier and the officer, the article of
spirits only excepted. Each male convict was that day put upon the
following weekly ration of provisions, two-thirds of which was served

to the female convicts; viz.—7 pounds of biscuit; 1 pound of flour; 7 pounds of beef, or 4 pounds of pork; 3 pints of pease; and 6 ounces of butter.

It was fair to suppose that so liberal a ration would in itself have proved the security of the store, and have defended it from depredation; but we saw with concern, that there were among us some minds so habitually vicious that no consideration was of any weight with them, nor could they be induced to do right by any prospect of future benefit, or fear of certain and immediate punishment. The charge being fully proved, one man, James Barrett, suffered death: his confederates were pardoned, on condition of their being banished from the settlement. Another culprit was sentenced to receive three hundred lashes; but, not appearing so guilty as his companions, was pardoned by the governor, the power of pardoning being vested in him by his Majesty's commission.

His excellency, having caused one example to be made, extended lenity to some others who were tried the following day; and one convict, James Freeman, was pardoned on condition of his becoming the public executioner.

It appeared by the letters patent under the great seal of Great Britain, which were read after the governor's commission, that " the appoint- " ment of the place to which offenders should be transported having " been vested in the crown by an act of parliament, his Majesty, by " two several orders in council, bearing date the 6th of December " 1786, had declared, that certain offenders named in two lists an- " nexed to the orders in council should be transported to the eastern " coast of New Holland, named New South Wales, or some one or " other of the islands adjacent:" and it being deemed necessary that a colony and civil government should be established in the place to which such felons should be transported, and that a court of criminal jurisdiction should also be established therein, with authority to proceed in a more summary way than is used within the realms of Great Britain, according to the known and established laws thereof, his Majesty, by the 27th Geo. 3. cap. 56. was enabled to authorise, by his commission under the great seal, " the governor, or in his absence " the lieutenant-governor of such place, to convene from time to " time,

" time, as occasion may require, a court of criminal jurisdiction,
" which court is to be a court of record, and is to consist of the judge-
" advocate and such six officers of the sea and land service as the go-
" vernor shall, by precept issued under his hand and seal, require to
" assemble for that purpose." This court has power to inquire of,
hear, determine, and punish all treasons, misprisions of treasons, murders, felonies, forgeries, perjuries, trespasses, and other crimes whatsoever that may be committed in the colony; the punishment for such
offences to be inflicted according to the laws of England as nearly as
may be, considering and allowing for the circumstances and situation
of the settlement and its inhabitants. The charge against any offender
is to be reduced into writing, and exhibited by the judge-advocate :
witnesses are to be examined upon oath, as well for as against the
prisoner; and the court is to adjudge whether he is guilty or not
guilty by the opinion of the major part of the court. If guilty, and
the offence is capital, they are to pronounce judgment of death, in
like manner as if the prisoner had been convicted by the verdict of
a jury in England, or of such corporal punishment as the court, or
the major part of it, shall deem meet. And in cases not capital, they
are to adjudge such corporal punishment as the majority of the court
shall determine. But no offender is to suffer death, unless five members of the court shall concur in adjudging him to be guilty, until the
proceedings shall have been transmitted to England, and the king's pleasure signified thereupon. The provost-marshal is to cause the judgment
of the court to be executed according to the governor's warrant under
his hand and seal.

The resemblance of this to the military courts may be easily traced
in some particulars. The criminal court is assembled, not at stated
times, but whenever occasion may require. It is composed of military officers, (the judge advocate excepted, whose situation is of a
civil nature,) who assemble as such in their military habits, with the
insignia of duty, the sash and the sword. Their judgments are to be
determined by the majority; and the examination of the witnesses is
carried on by the members of the court, as well as by the judge-
advocate. But in other respects it differs from the military courts.
The judge advocate is the judge or president of the court; he frames

and

and exhibits the charge against the prisoner, has a vote in the court, and is sworn, like the members of it, well and truly to try and to make true deliverance between the king and the prisoner, and give a verdict according to the evidence.

When the state of the colony and the nature of its inhabitants are considered, it must be agreed, that the administration of public justice could not have been placed with so much propriety in any other hands. The outward form of the court, as well as the more essential part of it, are admirably calculated to meet the characters and dispo-sition of the people who form the major part of the settlement. As long confinement would be attended with a loss of labour, and other evils, the court is assembled within a day or two after the apprehension of any prisoner whose crime is of such magnitude as to call for a criminal proceeding against him. He is brought before a court com-posed of a judge and six men of honour, who hear the evidence both for and against him, and determine whether the crime exhibited be or be not made out; and his punishment, if found guilty, is ad-judged according to the laws of England, considering and allowing for the situation and circumstances of the settlement and its inhabitants; which punishment, however, after all, cannot be inflicted without the ratification of the governor under his hand and seal.

Beside this court for the trial of criminal offenders, there is a civil court, consisting of the judge-advocate and two inhabitants of the set-tlement, who are to be appointed by the governor; which court has full power to hear and determine in a summary way all pleas of lands, houses, debts, contracts, and all personal pleas whatsoever, with autho-rity to summon the parties upon complaint being made, to examine the matter of such complaint by the oaths of witnesses, and to issue warrants of execution under the hand and seal of the judge-advocate. From this court, on either party, plaintiff or defendant, finding himself or themselves aggrieved by the judgment or decree, an appeal lies to the governor, and from him, where the debt or thing in demand shall exceed the value of three hundred pounds, to the king in council: but these appeals must be put in, if from the civil court, within eight days, and if from the governor or superior court, within fourteen days after pronouncing the said judgments.

To

To this court is likewise given authority to grant probates of wills and administration of the personal estates of intestates dying within the settlement. But as property must be acquired in the country before its rights can come into question, few occasions of assembling this court can occur for many years.

In addition to these courts for the trial of crimes, and the cognisance of civil suits, the governor, the lieutenant-governor, and the judge-advocate for the time being, are by his Majesty's letters patent constituted justices for the preservation of the peace of the settlement, with the same power that justices of the peace have in England within their respective jurisdictions. And the governor, being enabled by his Majesty's commission, soon after our arrival, caused Augustus Alt esq. (the surveyor-general of the territory) to be sworn a justice of the peace, for the purpose of sitting once a week, or oftener as occasion might require, with the judge-advocate, to examine all offences committed by the convicts, and determine on and punish such as were not of sufficient importance for trial by the criminal court.

There is also a vice-admiralty court for the trial of offences committed upon the high seas, of which the lieutenant-governor is constituted the judge, Mr. Andrew Miller the registrar, and Mr. Henry Brewer the marshal. The governor has, beside that of captain-general, a commission constituting him vice-admiral of the territory; and another vesting him with authority to hold * general courts-martial, and to confirm or set aside the sentence. The major-commandant of the detachment had the usual power of assembling regimental or battalion courts-martial for the trial of offences committed by the soldiers under his command.

By this account of the different modes of administering and obtaining justice, which the legislature provided for this settlement, it is evident that great care had been taken on our setting out, to furnish us with a stable foundation whereon to erect our little colony, a foundation which was established in the punishment of vice, the

* Captain Collins, the judge advocate of the settlement, had also a warrant from the Admiralty appointing him judge advocate to the marine detachment.

security

security of property, and the preservation of peace and good order in our community.

The governor having also received instructions to establish a settlement at Norfolk Island, the Supply sailed for that place about the middle of the month of February, having on board Lieutenant King of the Sirius, named by Capt. Phillip superintendant and commandant of the settlement to be formed there. Lieutenant King took with him one surgeon, (Mr. Jamieson, surgeon's mate of the Sirius,) one petty officer, (Mr. Cunningham, also of the Sirius,) two private soldiers, two persons who pretended to some knowledge in flax-dressing, and nine male and six female convicts, mostly volunteers. This little party was to be landed with tents, clothing for the convicts, implements of husbandry, tools for dressing flax, &c. and provisions for six months; before the expiration of which time it was designed to send them a fresh supply.

Norfolk Island is situated in the latitude of 29° south, and in longitude 168° 10′ east of Greenwich, and was settled with a view to the cultivation of the flax plant, which at the time when the island was discovered by Captain Cook was found growing most luxuriantly where he landed; and from the specimens taken to England of the New Zealand flax, (of which sort is that growing at Norfolk Island,) it was hoped some advantages to the mother country might be derived from cultivating and manufacturing it.

Mr. King, previous to his departure for his little government, was sworn in as a justice of the peace, taking the oaths necessary on the occasion, by which he was enabled to punish such petty offences as might be committed among his people, capital crimes being reserved for the cognisance of the criminal court of judicature established here.

Our own preservation depending in a great measure upon the preservation of our stores and provisions, houses for their reception were immediately begun when sufficient ground was found to be cleared; and the persons who had the direction of these and other works carrying on, found it most to the advantage of the public service to employ the convicts in task work, allotting a certain

quantity

quantity of ground to be cleared by a certain number of perſons in a given time, and allowing them to employ what time they might gain, till called on again for public ſervice, in bringing in materials and erecting huts for themſelves. But for the moſt part they preferred paſſing in idleneſs the hours that might have been ſo profitably ſpent, ſtraggling into the woods for vegetables, or viſiting the French ſhips in Botany Bay. Of this latter circumſtance we were informed by M. de Clonard, the captain of the Aſtrolabe, in an excurſion he made from the ſhips, to bring round ſome diſpatches from M. de la Perouſe, which that officer requeſted might·be forwarded to the French ambaſſador at the court of London by the firſt of our tranſports that might ſail from hence for Europe. He informed us, that they were daily viſited by the convicts, many of whom ſolicited to be received on board before their departure, promiſing (as an inducement) to be accompanied by a number of females. M. de Clonard at the ſame time aſſured us, that the general (as he was termed by his officers and people) had given their ſolicitations no kind of. countenance, but had threatened to drive them away by force.

Among the buildings that were undertaken ſhortly after our arrival, muſt be mentioned an obſervatory, which was marked out on the weſtern point of the cove, to receive the aſtronomical inſtruments which had been ſent out by the Board of Longitude, for the purpoſe of obſerving the comet which was expected to be ſeen about the end of this year. The conſtruction of this building was placed under the direction of Lieut. Dawes of the marines, who, having made this branch of ſcience his particular ſtudy, was appointed by the Board of Longitude to make aſtronomical obſervations in this country.

The latitude of the obſervatory was - - - 33° 52′ 30″ S.

The longitude, from Greenwich, - - - - 151° 19′ 30″ E.

Governor Phillip, having been very much preſſed for time when he firſt viſited this harbour, had not thoroughly examined it. The completion of that neceſſary buſineſs was left to Captain Hunter, who, with the firſt lieutenant of the Sirius, early in the month of February, made an accurate ſurvey of it. It was then found to be far more extenſive to the weſtward than was at firſt imagined, and

Captain

Captain Hunter described the country as wearing a much more favourable countenance toward the head or upper part, than it did immediately about the settlement. He saw several parties of the natives, and, treating them constantly with good humour, they always left him with friendly impressions.

It was natural to suppose that the curiosity of these people would be attracted by observing, that, instead of quitting, we were occupied in works that indicated an intention of remaining in their country; but during the first six weeks we received only one visit, two men strolling into the camp one evening, and remaining in it for about half an hour. They appeared to admire whatever they saw, and after receiving each a hatchet (of the use of which the eldest instantly and curiously shewed his knowledge, by turning up his foot, and sharpening a piece of wood on the sole with the hatchet) took their leave, apparently well pleased with their reception. The fishing-boats also frequently reported their having been visited by many of these people when hauling the seine, at which labour they often assisted with cheerfulness, and in return were generally rewarded with part of the fish taken.

Every precaution was used to guard against a breach of this friendly and desirable intercourse, by strictly prohibiting every person from depriving them of their spears, fizgigs, gum, or other articles, which we soon perceived they were accustomed to leave under the rocks, or loose and scattered about upon the beaches. We had however great reason to believe that these precautions were first rendered fruitless by the ill conduct of a boat's crew belonging to one of the transports, who, we were told afterwards, attempted to land in one of the coves at the lower part of the harbour, but were prevented, and driven off with stones by the natives. A party of them, consisting of sixteen or eighteen persons, some time after landed on the island * where the people of the Sirius were preparing a garden, and with much artifice, watching their opportunity, carried off a shovel, a spade, and a pick-axe. On their being fired at and hit

* Since known by the name of Garden Island.

on

on the legs by one of the people with fmall fhot, the pick-axe was dropped, but they carried off the other tools.

To fuch circumftances as thefe muft be attributed the termination of that good underftanding which had hitherto fubfifted between us and them, and which Governor Phillip laboured to improve whenever he had an opportunity. But it might have been forefeen that this would unavoidably happen: the convicts were every where ftraggling about, collecting animals and gum to fell to the people of the tranfports, who at the fame time were procuring fpears, fhields, fwords, fifhing-lines, and other articles from the natives, to carry to Europe; the lofs of which muft have been attended with many inconveniences to the owners, as it was foon evident that they were the only means whereby they obtained or could procure their daily fubfiftence; and although fome of thefe people had been punifhed for purchafing articles of the convicts, the practice was carried on fecretly, and attended with all the bad effects which were to be expected from it. We alfo had the mortification to learn, that M. De la Peroufe had been compelled to fire upon the natives at Botany Bay, where they frequently annoyed his people who were employed on fhore. This circumftance materially affected us, as thofe who had rendered this violence neceffary could not difcriminate between us and them. We were however perfectly convinced that nothing fhort of the greateft neceffity could have induced M. De la Peroufe to take fuch a ftep, as we heard him declare, that it was among the particular inftructions that he received from his fovereign, to endeavour by every poffible means to acquire and cultivate the friendfhip of the natives of fuch places as he might difcover or vifit; and to avoid exercifing any act of hoftility upon them. In obedience to this humane command, there was no doubt but he forbore ufing force until forbearance would have been dangerous, and he had been taught a leffon at Maouna, one of the Ifles des Navigateurs, that the tempers of favages were not to be trufted too far; for we were informed, that on the very day and hour of their departure from that ifland, the boats of the two fhips, which were fent for a laft load of water, were attacked by the natives with ftones and clubs,

D   and

and M. De l'Angle, the captain of the Aftrolabe, with eleven officers and men, were put to death; thofe who were fo fortunate as to get off in the fmall boats that attended on the watering launches, (which were deftroyed,) efcaped with many wounds and contufions, fome of which were not healed at the time of their relating to us this unfortunate circumftance. It was conjectured, that fome one of the feamen, unknown to the officers, muft have occafioned this outrage, for which there was no other probable reafon to affign, as the natives during the time the fhips were at the ifland had lived with the officers and people on terms of the greateft harmony. And this was not the firft misfortune that thofe fhips had met with during their voyage; for on the north-weft coaft of America, they loft two boats with their crews, and feveral young men of family, in a furf.

Notwithftanding the preffure of the important bufinefs we had upon our hands after our landing, the difcharge of our religious duties was never omitted, divine fervice being performed every Sunday that the weather would permit: at which time the detachment of marines paraded with their arms, the whole body of convicts attended, and were obferved to conduct themfelves in general with the refpect and attention due to the occafion on which they were affembled.

It was foon obferved with fatisfaction, that feveral couples were announced 'for marriage; but on ftrictly fcrutinizing into the motive, it was found in feveral inftances to originate in an idea, that the married people would meet with various little comforts and privileges that were denied to thofe in a fingle ftate; and fome, on not finding thofe expectations realifed, repented, wifhed and actually applied to be reftored to their former fituations; fo ignorant and thoughtlefs were they in general. It was however to be wifhed, that matrimonial connexions fhould be promoted among them; and none who applied were ever rejected, except when it was clearly underftood that either of the parties had a wife or hufband living at the time of their leaving England.

The weather during the latter end of January and the month of February was very clofe, with rain, at times very heavy, and attended with much thunder and lightning. In the night of the 6th

of

of February, six sheep, two lambs, and one pig, belonging chiefly to the lieutenant-governor, having been placed at the foot of a large tree, were destroyed by the lightning. But accidents of this kind were rather to be expected than wondered at, until the woods around us could be opened and cleared.

CHAP. II.

BROKEN BAY VISITED.—M. DE LA PEROUSE SAILS.—TRANSACTIONS.—THE SUPPLY RETURNS.—LORD HOWE ISLAND DISCOVERED.—THE SHIPS FOR CHINA SAIL.—SOME CONVICTS WOUNDED BY THE NATIVES.—SCURVY.—NEW STORE-HOUSE.—NECESSARY ORDERS AND APPOINTMENTS.—EXCUR-SIONS INTO THE COUNTRY.—NEW BRANCH OF THE HARBOUR INTO PORT JACKSON.—SHEEP.

March.] EARLY in March the governor, accompanied by some officers from the settlement and the Sirius, went round by water to the next adjoining harbour to the northward of this port, which is laid down in the charts by the name of Broken Bay, from the broken appearance of the land by which it is formed. The intention of this visit was, not only to survey the harbour, if any were found to exist, but to examine whether there were within it any spots of ground capable of cultivation, and of maintaining a few families; but in eight days that he was absent, though he found an harbour equal in magnitude to Port Jackson, the governor saw no situation that could at all vie with that which he had chosen for the settlement at Sydney Cove, the land at Broken Bay being in general very high and in most parts rocky and barren. The weather proved very un-favourable to an excursion in a country where the residence for each night was to be provided by the travellers themselves; and some of the party returned with dysenteric complaints. The weather at Port Jackson had been equally adverse to labour, the governor finding at

D 2   his

his return upwards of two hundred patients under the surgeon's care, in consequence of the heavy rains that had fallen. A building for the reception of the sick was now absolutely neceffary, and one, eighty-four feet by twenty-three, was put in hand, to be divided into a dispensary, (all the hospital-stores being at that time under tents,) a ward for the troops, and another for the convicts. It was to be built of wood, and the roof to be covered in with shingles, made from a species of fir that is found here. The heavy rains also pointed out the neceffity of sheltering the detachment, and until barracks could be built, most of them covered their tents with thatch, or erected for themselves temporary clay huts. The barracks were begun early in March; but much difficulty was found in providing proper materials, the timber being in general shakey and rotten. They were to consist of four buildings, each building to be sixty-seven feet by twenty-two, and to contain one company. They were placed at a convenient distance asunder for the purpose of air and cleanliness, and with a space in the centre for a parade.

On or about Monday the 10th of March, the French ships failed from Botany Bay, bound, as they said, to the northward, and carrying with them the most unfavourable ideas of this country and its native inhabitants; the officers having been heard to declare, that in their whole voyage they no where found so poor a country, nor such wretched miserable people. During their stay in Botany Bay, they set up the frames of two large boats which they brought out from Europe, to replace those they lost at Maouna, and on the north-west coast of America. We had, during their stay in this country, a very friendly and pleasant intercourse with their officers, among whom we observed men of abilities, whose observations, and exertions in the search after knowledge, will most amply illustrate the history of their voyage: And it reflected much credit on the minister when he arranged the plan of it, that people of the first talents for navigation, astronomy, natural history, and every other science that could render it conspicuously useful, should have been selected for the purpose.

We found after their departure the grave of the Abbé L. Receveus, who died but a short time before they failed: he was buried not very

far

far from the spot where their tents were erected, at the foot of a
tree, on which were nailed two pieces of board with the following
inscription:

Hic jacet
L. Receveur
Ex F. F. Minoribus
Galliæ Sacerdos
Physicus in Circumnavigatione Mundi
Duce D. de la Perouse
Obiit Die 17 Febr. Anno
1788.

Governor Phillip, on hearing that these boards had fallen down from
the tree, caused the inscription to be engraven on a plate of copper,
which was put up in place of the boards; but rain, and the oozing of
gum from the tree, soon rendered even that illegible.

We continued to be still busily employed; a wharf for the convenience of landing stores was begun under the direction of the surveyor-general: the ordnance, consisting of two brass six-pounders on
travelling carriages, four iron twelve-pounders, and two iron six-
pounders, were landed; the transports, which were chartered for China,
were clearing; the long-boats of the ships in the cove were employed
in bringing up cabbage-tree from the lower part of the harbour,
where it grew in great abundance, and was found, when cut into
proper lengths, very fit for the purpose of erecting temporary huts,
the posts and plates of which being made of the pine of this country,
and the sides and ends filled with lengths of the cabbage-tree, plastered
over with clay, formed a very good hovel. The roofs were generally
thatched with the grass of the gum-rush; some were covered with
clay, but several of these failed, the weight of the clay and heavy
rain soon destroying them.

A gang of convicts was employed, under the direction of a person
who understood the business, in making bricks at a spot about a mile
from the settlement, at the head of Long Cove; at which place also
two acres of ground were marked out for such officers as were willing
to cultivate them and raise a little grain for their stock; it not being
the

the intention of government to give any grants of land until the neceffary accounts of the country, and of what expectations were likely
to be formed from it, fhould be received.

Great inconvenience was found from the neceffity that fubfifted of
fuffering the ftock of individuals to run loofe amongft the tents and
huts; much damage in particular was fuftained by hogs, who frequently forced their way into them while the owners were at labour,
and deftroyed and damaged whatever they met with. At firft thefe
loffes were ufually made good from the ftore, as it was unreafonable
to expect labour where the labourer did not receive the proper fuftenance; but this being foon found to open a door to much impofition,
and to give rife to many fabricated tales of injuries that never exifted,
an order was given, that any hog caught trefpaffing was to be killed
by the perfon who actually received any damage from it.

The principal ftreet of the intended town was marked out at the
head of the cove, and its dimenfions were extenfive. The government-
houfe was to be conftructed on the fummit of a hill commanding a
capital view of Long Cove, and other parts of the harbour; but this
was to be a work of after-confideration; for the prefent, as the ground
was not cleared, it was fufficient to point out the fituation and define
the limits of the future buildings.

On the 19th the Supply returned from Norfolk Ifland, having been
abfent four weeks and fix days. We learned that fhe made the ifland
on the 29th of laft month, but for the five fucceeding days was not
able to effect a landing, being prevented by a furf which they found
breaking with violence on a reef of rocks that lay acrofs the principal
bay. Lieutenant King had nearly given up all hopes of being able
to land, when a fmall opening was difcovered in the reef wide enough
to admit a boat, through which he was fo fortunate as to get fafely
with all his people and ftores. When landed, he could nowhere find
a fpace clear enough for pitching a tent; and he had to cut through
an almoft impenetrable wildernefs before he could encamp himfelf and
his people. Of the ftock he carried with him, he loft the only fhe-
goat he had, and one ewe. He had named the bay wherein he
landed and fixed the fettlement Sydney Bay, and had given the names
                                                                    of

of Phillip and Nepean to two small islands which are situated at a small distance from it.

Lieutenant King, the commandant, wrote in good spirits, and spoke of meeting all his difficulties like a man determined to overcome them. The soil of the island appeared to be very rich, but the landing dangerous, Sydney Bay being exposed to the southerly winds, with which the surf constantly breaks on the reef. The Supply lost one of her people, who was washed off the reef and drowned. There is a small bay on the other side of the island, but at a distance from the settlement, and no anchoring ground in either. The flax plant (the principal object in view) he had not discovered when the Supply sailed. Lieutenant Ball, soon after he left this harbour, fell in with an uninhabited island in lat. 31° 56′ S. and in long. 159° 4′ East, which he named Lord Howe Island. It is inferior in size to Norfolk Island, but abounded at that time with turtle, (sixteen of which he brought away with him,) as well as with a new species of fowl, and a small brown bird, the flesh of which was very fine eating. These birds were in great abundance, and so unused to such visitors, that they suffered themselves to be knocked down with sticks, as they ran along the beach.

Pines, but no small trees, grow on this island, in which there is a good bay, but no anchoring ground. Of the pines at Norfolk Island, one measured nine feet in diameter, and another, that was found lying on the ground, measured 182 feet in length.

As the scurvy was at this time making rapid strides in the colony, the hope of being able to procure a check to its effects from the new island, rendered it in every one's opinion a fortunate discovery.

The Scarborough, Charlotte, and Lady Penrhyn transports being cleared, were discharged from government service in the latter end of the month, and the masters left at liberty to proceed on their respective voyages pursuant to the directions of their owners.

In the course of this month several convicts came in from the woods; one in particular dangerously wounded with a spear, the others very much beaten and bruised by the natives. The wounded man had been employed cutting rushes for thatching, and one of the others was a convalescent from the hospital, who went out to collect a

J J   few

few vegetables. All these people denied giving any provocation to the natives: it was, however, difficult to believe them; they well knew the consequences that would attend any acts of violence on their part, as it had been declared in public orders early in the month, that in forming the intended settlement, any act of cruelty to the natives being contrary to his Majesty's most gracious intentions, the offenders would be subject to a criminal prosecution; and they well knew that the natives themselves, however injured, could not contradict their assertions. There was, however, too much reason to believe that our people had been the aggressors, as the governor on his return from his excursion to Broken Bay, on landing at Camp Cove, found the natives there who had before frequently come up to him with confidence, unusually shy, and seemingly afraid of him and his party; and one, who after much invitation did venture to approach, pointed to some marks upon his shoulders, making signs they were caused by blows given with a stick. This, and their running away, whereas they had always before remained on the beach until the people landed from the boats, were strong indications that the man had been beaten by some of our stragglers. Eleven canoes full of people passed very near the Sirius, which was moored without the two points of the cove, but paddled away very fast upon the approach of some boats toward them.

The curiosity of the camp was excited and gratified for a day or two by the sight of an emu, which was shot by the governor's game-killer. It was remarkable by every stem having two feathers proceeding from it. Its height was 7 feet 2 inches, and the flesh was very well flavoured.

The run of water that supplied the settlement was observed to be only a drain from a swamp at the head of it; to protect it, therefore, as much as possible from the sun, an order was given out, forbidding the cutting down of any trees within fifty feet of the run, than which there had not yet been a finer found in any one of the coves of the harbour.

April.] As the winter of this hemisphere was approaching, it became absolutely necessary to expedite the buildings intended for the detachment; every carpenter that could be procured amongst the
convicts

convicts was sent to assist, and as many as could be hired from the transports were employed at the hospital and storehouses. The long-boats of the ships still continued to bring up the cabbage-tree from the lower part of the harbour, and a range of huts was begun on the west side for some of the female convicts.

Our little camp now began to wear the aspect of distress, from the great number of scorbutic patients that were daily seen creeping to and from the hospital tents; and the principal surgeon suggested the expediency of another supply of turtle from Lord Howe Island: but it was generally thought that the season was too far advanced, and the utmost that could have been procured would have made but a very trifling and temporary change in the diet of those afflicted with the disorder.

On the 6th, divine service was performed in the new storehouse, which was covered in, but not sufficiently completed to admit provisions. One hundred feet by twenty-five were the dimensions of this building, which was constructed with great strength; yet the mind was always pained when viewing its reedy combustible covering, remembering the livid flames that had been seen to shoot over every part of this cove: but no other materials could be found to answer the purpose of thatch, and every necessary precaution was taken to guard against accidental fire.

An elderly woman, a convict, having been accused of stealing a flat iron, and the iron being found in her possession, the first moment she was left alone she hung herself to the ridge-pole of her tent, but was fortunately discovered and cut down before it was too late.

Although several thefts were committed by the convicts, yet it was in general remarked, that they conducted themselves with more propriety than could have been expected from people of their description; to prevent, however, if possible, the commission of offences so prejudicial to the welfare of the colony, his excellency signified to the convicts his resolution that the condemnation of any one for robbing the huts or stores should be immediately followed by their execution. Much of their irregularity was perhaps to be ascribed to the intercourse that subsisted, in spite of punishment, between them and the seamen from the ships of war and the transports, who at least one day in the week found means to get on shore with spirits.

E   Notwithstanding

Notwithstanding it was the anxious care of every one who could prevent it, that the venereal disease might not be introduced into the settlement, it was not only found to exist amongst the convicts, but the very sufferers themselves were known to conceal their having it. To stop this evil, it was ordered by the governor, that any man or woman having and concealing this disorder should receive corporal punishment, and be put upon a short allowance of provisions for six months.

Lieutenant Dawes of the marines was directed in public orders to act as officer of artillery and engineers; in consequence of which the ordnance of the settlement, and the constructing of a small redoubt on the east side, were put under his direction.

Mr. Zachariah Clark, who came out of England as agent to Mr. Richards the contractor, was at the same time appointed an assistant to the commissary; and the issuing of the provisions, which was in future to be once a week, was put under his charge.

In the course of this month a stone building was begun on the west side for the residence of the lieutenant-governor, one face of which was to be in the principal street of the intended town.

The governor, desirous of acquiring a knowledge of the country about the seat of his government, and profiting by the coolness of the weather, made during the month several excursions into the country; in one of which having observed a range of mountains to the westward, and hoping that a river might be found to take its course in their neighbourhood, he set off with a small party, intending if possible to reach them, taking with him six days provisions; but returned without attaining either object of his journey,—the mountains, or a river.

He penetrated about thirty miles inland, through a country most amply clothed with timber, but in general free from underwood. On the fifth day of his excursion he had, from a rising ground which he named Belle Vue, the only view of the mountains which he obtained during the journey; and as they then appeared at too great a distance to be reached on one day's allowance of provisions, which was all they had left, he determined to return to Sydney Cove.

In

In Port Jackson another branch extending to the northward had been difcovered; but as the country furrounding it was high, rocky, and barren, though it might add to the extent and beauty of the harbour, it did not promife to be of any benefit to the fettlement.

The governor had the mortification to learn on his return from his weftern expedition, that five ewes and a lamb had been deftroyed at the farm in the adjoining cove, fuppofed to have been killed by dogs belonging to the natives.

The number of fheep which were landed in this country were confiderably diminifhed; they were of neceffity placed on ground, and compelled to feed on grafs, that had never before been expofed to air or fun, and confequently did not agree with them; a circumftance much to be lamented, as without ftock the fettlement muft for years remain dependent on the mother-country for the means of fubfiftence.

CHAP. III.

TRANSACTIONS.—TRANSPORTS SAIL FOR CHINA.—THE SUPPLY SAILS FOR LORD HOWE ISLAND.—RETURN OF STOCK IN THE COLONY IN MAY.—THE SUPPLY RETURNS.—TRANSACTIONS.—A CONVICT WOUNDED.—RUSH-CUTTERS KILLED BY THE NATIVES.—GOVERNOR'S EXCURSION.—HIS MAJESTY'S BIRTH-DAY.—BEHAVIOUR OF THE CONVICTS.—CATTLE LOST.—NATIVES. — PROCLAMATION. — EARTHQUAKE. — TRANSPORTS SAIL FOR ENGLAND.—SUPPLY SAILS FOR NORFOLK ISLAND.—TRANSACTIONS.—NATIVES—CONVICTS WOUNDED.

THE month of May opened with the trial, conviction, and execution of James Bennett, a youth of feventeen years of age, for breaking open a tent belonging to the Charlotte tranfport, and ftealing thereout property above the value of five fhillings. He confeffed that he had often merited death before he committed the crime for which he was then about to fuffer, and that a love of idlenefs and bad connexions had been his ruin. He was executed immediately on re-

R 2				ceiving

ceiving his sentence, in the hope of making a greater impression on the convicts than if it had been delayed for a day or two.

There being no other shelter for the guard than tents, great inconvenience was found in placing under its charge more than one or two prisoners together. The convicts, therefore, who were confined at the guard until they could be conveyed to the southward, were sent to the Hare Island at the entrance of this cove, where they were to be supplied weekly with provisions from the store, and water from the Sirius, until an opportunity offered of sending them away.

The three transports sailed on the 5th, 6th, and 7th of this month for China. The Supply also sailed on the 6th for Lord Howe Island, to procure turtle and birds for the settlement, the scurvy continuing to resist every effort that could be made to check its progress by medicine; from the lateness of the season, however, little hope was entertained of her success.

The governor having directed every person in the settlement to make a return of what live-stock was in his possession, the following appeared to be the total amount of stock in the colony :

1 Stallion,	25 Pigs,
3 Mares,	5 Rabbits,
3 Colts,	18 Turkies,
2 Bulls,	29 Geese,
5 Cows,	35 Ducks,
29 Sheep,	122 Fowls,
19 Goats,	87 Chickens.
49 Hogs,	

There having been found among the convicts a person qualified to conduct the business of a bricklayer, a gang of labourers was put under his direction, and most of the huts which grew up in different parts of the cleared ground were erected by them. Another gang of labourers was put under the direction of a stone-mason, and on the 15th the first stone of a building, intended for the residence of the governor until the government-house could be erected, was laid on the east side of the cove.

The

The following inscription, engraven on a piece of copper, was placed in the foundation:

> His Excellency
> ARTHUR PHILLIP Esq.
> Governor In Chief and Captain General
> in and over the Territory of New South Wales,
> landed in this Cove,
> with the first Settlers of this Country,
> the 24th Day of January 1788;
> and on the 15th Day of May
> in the same Year,
> being the 28th of the Reign of His present Majesty
> GEORGE the THIRD,
> The First of these Stones was laid.

The large store-house being completed, and a road made to it from the wharf on the west side, the provisions were directed to be landed from the victuallers, and proper gangs of convicts placed to roll them to the store.

Carpenters were now employed in covering in that necessary building the hospital, the shingles for the purpose being all prepared; these were fastened to the roof (which was very strong) by pegs made by the female convicts.

The timber that had been cut down proved in general very unfit for the purpose of building, the trees being for the most part decayed, and when cut down were immediately warped and split by the heat of the sun. A species of pine appeared to be the best, and was chiefly used in the frame-work of houses, and in covering the roofs, the wood splitting easily into shingles.

The Supply returned in the afternoon of the 25th from Lord Howe Island, without having procured any turtle, the weather being much too cold and the season too late to find them so far to the southward.

To the southward and eastward of Lord Howe Island there is a rock, which may be seen at the distance of eighteen leagues, and which from its shape Lieutenant Ball has named Ball Pyramid.

On

On the 26th a foldier and a failor were tried by the criminal court of judicature for affaulting and dangeroufly wounding James M'Neal, a feaman. Thefe people belonged to the Sirius, and were employed on the ifland where the fhip's company had. their garden, the feamen in cultivating the ground, and the foldier in protecting them; for which purpofe he had his firelock with him. They all lived together in a hut that was built for them, and on the evening preceding the affault had received their week's allowance of fpirits, with which they intoxicated themfelves, and quarrelled. They were found guilty of the affault, and, as pecuniary damages were out of the queftion, were each fentenced to receive five hundred lafhes.

Farther and ftill more unpleafant confequences of the ill-treatment which the natives received from our people were felt during this month. On the evening of the 21ft a convict belonging to the farm on the eaft fide was brought into the hofpital, very dangeroufly wounded with a barbed fpear, which entered about the depth of three inches into his back, between the fhoulders. The account he gave of the tranfaction was, that having ftrayed to a cove beyond the farm with another man, (who did not return with him,) he was fuddenly wounded with a fpear, not having feen any natives until he received the wound. His companion ran away when the natives came up, who ftripped him of all his clothes but his trowfers, which they did not take, and then left him to crawl into the camp. A day or two afterwards the clothes of the man that was miffing were brought in, torn, bloody, and pierced with fpears; fo that there was every reafon to fuppofe that the poor wretch had fallen a facrifice to his own folly and the barbarity of the natives.

On the 30th an officer, who had been collecting rufhes in a cove up the harbour, found and brought to the hofpital the bodies of two convicts who had been employed for fome time in cutting rufhes there, pierced through in many places with fpears, and the head of one beaten to a jelly. As it was improbable that thefe murders fhould be committed without provocation, inquiry was made, and it appeared that thefe unfortunate men had, a few days previous to their being found, taken away and detained a canoe belonging to the

11   natives,

natives, for which act of violence and injuſtice they paid with their lives.

Notwithſtanding theſe circumſtances, a party of natives in their canoes went alongſide the Sirius, and ſome ſubmitted to the operation of ſhaving: after which they landed on the weſtern point of the cove, where they examined every thing they ſaw with the greateſt attention, and went away peaceably, and apparently were not under any apprehenſion of reſentment on our parts for the murders above-mentioned.

/June, 1788.] The governor, however, on hearing that the two ruſh-cutters had been killed, thought it abſolutely neceſſary to en-deavour to find out, and, if poſſible, ſecure the people who killed them; for which purpoſe he ſet off with a ſtrong party well armed, and landed in the cove where their bodies had been found; whence he ſtruck acroſs the country to Botany Bay, where on the beach he ſaw about fifty canoes, but none of their owners. In a cove on the ſea-ſide, between Botany Bay and Port Jackſon, he ſud-denly fell in with an armed party of natives, in number between two and three hundred, men, women, and children. With theſe a friendly intercourſe directly took place, and ſome ſpears, &c. were exchanged for hatchets; but the murderers of the ruſh-cutters, if they were amongſt them, could not be diſcovered in the crowd. The governor hoped to have found the people ſtill at the place where the men had been killed, in which caſe he would have endeavoured to ſecure ſome of them; but, not having any fixed reſidence, they had, perhaps, left the ſpot immediately after glutting their ſanguinary reſentment.

His Majeſty's birth-day was kept with every attention that it was poſſible to diſtinguiſh it by in this country; the morning was uſhered in by the diſcharge of twenty-one guns from the Sirius and Supply; on ſhore the colours were hoiſted at the flag-ſtaff, and at noon the detachment of marines fired three vollies; after which the officers of the civil and military eſtabliſhment waited upon the governor, and paid their reſpects to his excellency in honor of the day. At one o'clock the ſhips of war again fired twenty-one guns each; and

and the transports in the cove made up the fame number between them, according to their irregular method on thofe occafions. The officers of the navy and fettlement were entertained by the governor at dinner, and, among other toafts, named and fixed the boundaries of the firft *county* in his Majefty's territory of New South Wales. This was called Cumberland County, in honor of his Majefty's fecond brother; and the limits of it to the northward were fixed by the northernmoft point of Broken Bay, to the fouthward by the fouthernmoft point of Botany Bay, and to the weftward by Lanfdown and Carmarthen hills (the name given to the range of mountains feen by the governor in an excurfion to the northward). At fun-fet the fhips of war paid their laft compliment to his Majefty by a third time firing twenty-one guns each. At night feveral bonfires were lighted; and, by an allowance of fpirits given on this particular occafion, every perfon in the colony was enabled to drink his Majefty's health.

Some of the worft among the convicts availed themfelves of the opportunity that was given them in the evening, by the abfence of feveral of the officers and people from their tents and huts, to commit depredations. One officer on going to his tent found a man in it, whom with fome difficulty he fecured, after wounding him with his fword. The tent of another was broken into, and feveral articles of wearing apparel ftolen out of it; and many fmaller thefts of provifions and clothing were committed among the convicts. Several people were taken into cuftody, and two were afterwards tried and executed. One of thefe had abfconded, and lived in the woods for nineteen days, exifting by what he was able to procure by nocturnal depredations among the huts and ftock of individuals. His vifits for this purpofe were fo frequent and daring, that it became abfolutely neceffary to proclaim him an outlaw, as well as to declare that no perfon muft harbour him after fuch proclamation.

Exemplary punifhments feemed about this period to be growing daily more neceffary. Stock was often killed, huts and tents broke open, and provifions conftantly ftolen about the latter end of the week; for among the convicts there were many who knew not how

to

to hufband their provifions through the feven days they were intended to ferve them, but were known to have confumed the whole at the end of the third or fourth day. One of this defcription made his week's allowance of flour (eight pounds) into eighteen cakes, which he devoured at one meal; he was foon after taken fpeechlefs and fenfelefs, and died the following day at the hofpital, a loathfome putrid object.

The obvious confequence of this want of œconomy was, that he who had three days to live, and nothing to live on, before the ftore would be again open to fupply his wants, muft fteal from thofe who had been more provident. Had a few perfons been fent out who were not of the defcription of convicts, to have acted as overfeers, or fuperintendants, regulations for their internal œconomy, as well in the articles of cloathing as provifions, might have been formed which would have prevented thefe evils: it would then too have been more practicable to detect them in felling or exchanging the flops which they received, and their provifions would have been fubject to a daily infpection. But overfeers drawn from among themfelves were found not to have that influence which was fo abfolutely neceffary to carry any regulation into effect. And although the convicts, previous to the birth-day, were affembled, and their duty pointed out to them, as well as the certain confequence of a breach or neglect thereof, both by his excellency the governor and the lieutenant-governor, yet it foon appeared that there were fome among them fo inured to the habits of vice, and fo callous to remonftrance, that they were only reftrained until a favourable opportunity prefented itfelf.

The convicts who had been fent to the rock, in the hope that lenity to them might operate alfo upon others, were, on the occafion of his Majefty's birth-day, liberated from their chains and confinement, and his excellency forgave the offences of which they had been refpectively guilty, and which had occafioned their being fent thither.

By fome ftrange and unpardonable neglect in the convict who had been entrufted with the care of the cattle, the two bulls and four cows were loft in the beginning of this month. The man had been accuftomed to drive them out daily to feek the frefheft grafs and heft

F

pafturage,

pasturage, and was ordered never on any pretence to leave them. To this order, as it afterwards appeared, he very seldom attended, frequently coming in from the woods about noon to get his dinner, leaving them grazing at some little distance from the farm where they were kept; and in this manner they were lost. They had strayed from the spot he expected to find them on, or perhaps had been driven from it by the natives, and he spent two days in searching for them before the governor was made acquainted with the accident.

Several parties were successively sent out to endeavour the recovery of stock so essential to the colony; but constantly returned without success.

On the 27th a party of the natives, supposed to be in number from twenty to thirty, landed at the point on the east side of the cove, between the hours of eleven and twelve at night, and proceeded along close by the centinels, stopping for some time at the spot where the governor's house was building, and in the rear of the tents inhabited by some of the women. It was said that they appeared alarmed on hearing the centinels call out " All is well," and, after standing there for some time, went off toward the run of water. The centinels were very positive that they saw them, and were minute in their relation of the above circumstances; notwithstanding which, it was conjectured by many to be only the effect of imagination. It is true, the natives might have chosen that hour, of the night to gratify a curiosity that would naturally be excited on finding that we still resided among them; and perhaps for the purpose of observing whether we all passed the night in sleep.

The cold weather which we had at this time of the year was observed to affect our fishing, and the natives themselves appeared to be in great want. An old man belonging to them was found on the beach of one of the coves, almost starved to death.

It having been reported, that one of the natives who had stolen a jacket from a convict had afterwards been killed or wounded by him in an attempt to recover it, the governor issued a proclamation, promising a free pardon, with remission of the sentence of transportation, to such male or female convict as should give information of any such offender or offenders, so that he or they might be brought to trial,

and

and profecuted to conviction; but no difcovery was made in confequence of this offer.

In the afternoon of the 22d a flight fhock of an earthquake was obferved, which lafted two or three feconds, and was accompanied with
a diftant noife like the report of cannon, coming from the fouthward;
the fhock was local, and fo flight that many people did not feel it.

July.] The Alexander, Prince of Wales, and Friendfhip tranfports, with the Borrowdale ftorefhip, having completed their preparations for fea, failed together on the 14th of the month for
England. Two officers from the detachment of marines, Lieutenant
Maxwell and Lieutenant Collins, were embarked as paffengers; thefe
gentlemen having obtained permiffion to return to Europe for the recovery of their healths, which had been in a bad ftate from the time
of their arrival in the country.

The following report was made by the principal furgeon, of the
ftate of the fick in the fettlement, at the time of the departure of the
fhips:

The number of marines under medical treatment were 36
The number of convicts ditto ditto 66
Convicts unfit for labour from old age and infirmities 52

And if idlenefs might have been taken into the account, as well it
might, fince many were thereby rendered of very little fervice to the
colony, the number would have been greatly augmented.

It was now neceffary to think of Norfolk Ifland; and on the 20th
the Supply failed with ftores and provifions for that fettlement.

Only two transports remained of the fleet that came out from
England; thefe were the Golden Grove and Fifhburn, and preparations were making for clearing and difcharging them from government fervice. The people were employed in conftructing a cellar on
the weft fide for receiving the fpirits which were on board the Fifhburn, and in landing provifions from the Golden Grove, which were
ftowed in the large ftorehoufe by fome feamen belonging to the Sirius,
under the infpection of the mafter of that fhip.

From the nature of the materials with which moft of the huts occupied by the convicts were covered in, many accidents happened by
fire, whereby the labour of feveral people was loft, who had again to

feek

seek shelter for themselves, and in general had to complain of the destruction of provisions and clothing. To prevent this, an order was given, prohibiting the building of chimnies in future in such huts as were thatched.

Several thefts were committed by and among the convicts. Wine was stolen from the hospital, and some of those who had the care of it were taken up on suspicion and tried, but for want of sufficient evidence were acquitted. There was such a tenderness in these people to each other's guilt, such an acquaintance with vice and the different degrees of it, that unless they were detected in the fact, it was generally next to impossible to bring an offence home to them. As there was, however, little doubt, though no positive proof of their guilt, they were removed from the hospital, and placed under the direction of the officer who was then employed in constructing a small redoubt on the east side.

The natives, who had been accustomed to assist our people in hauling the seine, and were content to wait for such reward as the person who had the direction of the boat thought proper to give them, either driven by hunger, or moved by some other cause, came down to the cove where they were fishing, and, perceiving that they had been more successful than usual, took by force about half of what had been brought on shore. They were all armed with spears and other weapons, and made their attack with some shew of method, having a party stationed in the rear with their spears poized, in readiness to throw, if any resistance had been made. To prevent this in future, it was ordered that a petty officer should go in the boats whenever they were sent down the harbour.

No precautions, however, that could be taken, or orders that were given, to prevent accidents happening by misconduct on our part, had any weight with the convicts. On the evening of the 27th one of them was brought in wounded by the natives. He had left the encampment with another convict, to gather vegetables, and, contrary to the orders which had been repeatedly given, went nearly as far as Botany Bay, where they fell in with a party of the natives, who made signs to them to go back, which they did, but unfortunately ran different ways. This being observed by the natives, they threw their

spears

spears at them. One of them was fortunate enough to escape unhurt, but the other received two spears in him, one entering a little above his left ear, the other in his breast. He took to an arm of the bay, which, notwithstanding his wounds, he swam across, and reported that the natives stood on the bank laughing at him.

Much credit, indeed, was not to be given to any of their accounts; but it must be remarked, that every accident that had happened was occasioned by a breach of positive orders repeatedly given.

Still, notwithstanding this appearance of hostility in some of the natives, others were more friendly. In one of the adjoining coves resided a family of them, who were visited by large parties of the convicts of both sexes on those days in which they were not wanted for labour, where they danced and sung with apparent good humour, and received such presents as they could afford to make them; but none of them would venture back with their visitors.

CHAP. IV.

HEAVY RAINS.—PUBLIC WORKS.—SHEEP STOLEN.—PRINCE OF WALES'S BIRTH-DAY.—FISH.— IMPOSITION OF A CONVICT.—NATIVES.—APPREHENSIVE OF A FAILURE OF PROVISIONS.—NATIVES.—JUDICIAL ADMINISTRATION.—A CONVICT MURDERED.

August.] ALL public labour was suspended for many days in the beginning of the month of August by heavy rain; and the work of much time was also rendered fruitless by its effects; the brick-kiln fell in more than once, and bricks to a large amount were destroyed; the roads about the settlement were rendered impassable; and some of the huts were so far injured, as to require nearly as much labour to repair them as to build them anew. It was not until the 14th of the month, when the weather cleared up, that the people were again able to work. The public works then in hand were, the barracks for the marine detachment; an observatory on the west point of the cove; the

houses

houses erecting for the governor and the lieutenant-governor ; and the shingling of the hospital.

Thefts among the convicts during the bad weather were frequent; and a sheep was stolen from the farm on the east side a few nights prior to the birth-day of his royal highnefs the Prince of Wales, for celebrating of which it had been for some time kept separate from the others and fattened; and although a proclamation was issued by the governor offering a pardon, and the highest reward his excellency could offer, emancipation, to any male or female convict who should discover the person or persons concerned in the felony, except the person who actually stole or killed the sheep, no information was given that could lead to a discovery of the perpetrators of this offence.

The anniversary of the Prince of Wales's birth was observed by a cessation from all kinds of labour. At noon the troops fired three vollies at the flag-staff on the east side, after which the governor received the compliments usual on this occasion. The Sirius fired a royal salute at one o'clock, and a public dinner was given by the governor. Bonfires were lighted on each side of the cove at night, with which the ceremonies of the day concluded.

It had been imagined in England, that some, if not considerable savings of provisions might be made, by the quantities of fish that it was supposed would be taken; but nothing like an equivalent for the ration that was issued to the colony for a single day had ever been brought up.

We were informed, that the French ships, while in Botany Bay, had met with one very successful haul of large fish, that more than amply supplied both ships companies; but our people were not so fortunate. Fish enough was sometimes taken to supply about two hundred persons; but the quantity very rarely exceeded this. Three sting-rays were taken this month, two of which weighed each about three hundred weight, and were distributed amongst the people.

His royal highness Prince William Henry's birth-day was distinguished by displaying the colours at the flag-staff; and this compliment was paid to other branches of the royal family whose birth-days were not directed to be observed with more ceremony.

On

On the 26th the Supply returned from Norfolk Island, having been absent five weeks and two days. From the commandant the most favourable accounts were received of the richness and depth of the soil and salubrity of the climate, having been visited with very little rain, or thunder and lightning. His search after the flax-plant had been successful; where he had cleared the ground he found it growing spontaneously and luxuriant: a small species of plantain also had been discovered. His gardens promised an ample supply of vegetables; but his seed-wheat, having been heated in the long passage to this country, turned out to be damaged, and did not vegetate. The landing was found to be very dangerous, and he had the misfortune to lose Mr. Cunningham, the midshipman, with three people, and the boat they were in, by the surf on the reef, a few days before the Supply sailed. Short, however, as the time was, the carpenter of that vessel replaced the boat by building him a coble of the timber of the island, constructed purposely for going without the reef, and for the hazardous employ she must often be engaged in.

The settlement at Sydney Cove was for some time amused with an account of the existence and discovery of a gold mine; and the impostor had ingenuity enough to impose a fabricated tale on several of the officers for truth. He pretended to have found it at some distance down the harbour; and, offering to conduct an officer to the spot, a boat was provided; but immediately on landing, having previously prevailed on the officer to send away the boat, to prevent his discovery being made public to more than one person, he made a pretence to leave him, and, reaching the settlement some hours before the officer, reported that he had been sent up by him for a guard. The fellow knew too well the consequences that would follow on the officer's arrival to wait for that, and therefore set off directly into the woods, whence he returned the day following, when he was punished with fifty lashes for his imposition. Still, however, persisting that he had discovered a metal, a specimen of which he produced, the governor, who was absent from the settlement at the opening of the business, but had now returned, ordered him to be taken again down the harbour, with directions to his adjutant to land him on the place the man should point out, and keep him in his sight; but on being assured by

that

that officer, that if he attempted to deceive him he would put him to death, the man saved him the trouble of going far with him, and confessed that his story of having discovered a gold mine was a falsehood which he had propagated in the hope of imposing on the people belonging to the Fishburn and Golden Grove, from whom, being about to prepare for Europe, he expected to procure cloathing and other articles in return for his promised gold-dust; and that he had fabricated the specimens of the metal which he had exhibited, from a guinea and a brass buckle; the remains of which he then produced.

For this imposture he was afterwards ordered by the magistrates before whom he was examined to receive a hundred lashes, and to wear a canvas frock, with the letter R cut and sewn upon it, to distinguish him more particularly from others as a rogue.

Among the people of his own description, there were many who believed, notwithstanding his confession and punishment, that he had actually made the discovery he pretended, and was induced to say it was a fabrication merely to secure it to himself, to make use of at a future opportunity. So easy is it to impose on the minds of the lower class of people!

The natives continued to molest our people whenever they chanced to meet any of them straggling and unarmed; yet, although forcibly warned by the evil and danger that attended their straggling, 'the latter still continued to give the natives opportunity of injuring them. About the middle of the month a convict, who had wandered beyond the limits of security which had been pointed out for them, fell in with a party of natives, about fourteen in number, who stripped and beat him shockingly, and would have murdered him had they not heard the report of a musquet, which alarming them, they ran away, leaving him his clothes. On the 21st a party of natives landed from five canoes, near the point where the observatory was building, where, some of them engaging the attention of the officers and people at the observatory, the others attempted forcibly to take off a goat from the people at the hospital; in which attempt finding themselves resisted by a seaman who happened to be present, they menaced him with their spears, and, on his retiring, killed the animal and took it off in a canoe, making off toward Long Cove with

with much expedition. They were followed immediately by the governor, who got up with some of the party, but could neither recover the goat, nor meet with the people who had killed it.

It was much to be regretted, that none of them would place a confidence in and reside among us; as in such case, by an exchange of languages, they would have found that we had the most friendly intention toward them, and that we would ourselves punish any injury they might sustain from our people.

. September.] The seed-wheat that was sown here did not turn out any better than , that at Norfolk Island; in some places the ground was twice cropped, and there was reason to apprehend a failure of seed for the next year. The governor, therefore, early in this month, signified his intention of sending the Sirius to the Cape of Good Hope, to procure a sufficient quantity of grain for that purpose; together with as much flour for the settlement as she could stow, after laying in a twelvemonth's provisions for her ship's company. Her destination was intended to have been to the northward; but on making a calculation, and comparing the accounts of those navigators who had procured refreshments among the islands, it was found, that although she might provide very well for herself, yet, after an absence of three or four months, which would be the least time she would be gone, she could not bring more than would support the colony for a fortnight. At the same time his excellency made known his intention of establishing a settlement on some ground which he had seen at the head of this harbour when he made his excursion to the westward in April last, and which, from its form, he had named the Crescent. This measure appeared the more expedient, as the soil in and about the settlement seemed to be very indifferent and unproductive, and by no means so favourable for the growth of grain as that at the Crescent.

The Sirius was therefore ordered to prepare for her voyage with all expedition; and as she would be enabled to stow a greater quantity of flour by not taking all her guns, eight of them were landed on the west point of the cove, and a small breast-work thrown up in front of them.

The

The master of the Golden Grove storeship also was ordered to prepare for sea, the governor intending to employ that ship in taking provisions and stores, with a party of convicts, to Norfolk Island.

The stores of the detachment having been kept on board the Sirius until a building could be erected for their reception, and a storehouse for that purpose being now ready, they were removed on shore.

Two boats, one of eight and another of sixteen oars, having been sent out in frame for the use of the settlement, the carpenter of the Supply was employed in putting them together during that vessel's stay in port, and one of them, the eight-oared boat, was got into the water this month; but the want of a schooner or two, of from thirty to forty tons burden, to be employed in surveying this coast, was much felt and lamented.

We had now given up all hope of recovering the cattle which were so unfortunately lost in May last; and the only cow that remained not being at that time with calf, and having since become wild and dangerous, the lieutenant-governor, whose property she was, directed her to be killed; she was accordingly shut at his farm, it being found impracticable to secure and slaughter her in the common way.

About the middle of September several canoes passed the Sirius, and above 30 natives landed from them at the observatory or western point of the cove. They were armed, and, it was imagined, intended to take off some sheep from thence; but, if this was their intention, they were prevented by the appearance of two gentlemen who happened to be there unarmed; and, after throwing some stones, they took to their canoes and paddled off.

On the 25th the people in the fishing-boat reported that several spears were thrown at them by some of the natives; for no other reason, than that, after giving them freely what small fish they had taken, they refused them a large one which attracted their attention.

On the 30th one midshipman and two seamen from the Sirius, one serjeant, one corporal, and five private marines, and twenty-one male and eleven female convicts, embarked on board the Golden Grove for Norfolk Island, and the day following she dropped down, with his Majesty's ship Sirius, to Camp Cove, whence both ships sailed on the 2d of October.

October.]

October.] Captain Hunter, having been sworn as a magistrate soon
after the arrival of the fleet, continued to act in that capacity until his
departure for the Cape of Good Hope, sitting generally once a week,
with the judge-advocate and the surveyor-general, to inquire into petty
offences. Saturday was commonly set apart for these examinations;
that day being given to the convicts for the purpose of collecting vegetables and attending to their huts and gardens.

The detachment also finding it convenient to collect vegetables, and
being obliged to go for them as far as Botany Bay, the convicts were
ordered to avail themselves of the protection they might find by going
in company with an armed party; and never, upon any account, to
straggle from the soldiers, or go to Botany Bay without them, on pain
of severe punishment. Notwithstanding this order and precaution,
however, a convict, who had been looked upon as a good man, (no
complaint having been made of him since his landing, either for dis-
honesty or idleness,) having gone out with an armed party to procure
vegetables at Botany Bay, straggled from them, though repeatedly
cautioned against it, and was killed by the natives. On the return of
the soldiers from the bay, he was found lying dead in the path, his
head beat to a jelly, a spear driven through it, another through his
body, and one arm broken. Some people were immediately sent out
to bury him; and in the course of the month the parties who went by
the spot for vegetables three times reported that his body was above
ground, having been, it was supposed, torn up by the natives' dogs.
This poor wretch furnished another instance of the consequences that
attended a disobedience of orders which had been purposely given to
prevent these accidents; and as nothing of the kind was known to
happen, but where a neglect and contempt of all order was first shewn,
every misfortune of the kind might be attributed, not to the manners
and disposition of the natives, but to the obstinacy and ignorance of
our people.

On the departure of the Sirius, one pound of flour was deducted
from the weekly ration of those who received the full proportion, and
two-thirds of a pound from such as were at two-thirds allowance. The
settlement was to continue at this ration until the return of the Sirius,
which was expected not to exceed six months. But public labour was

not affected by this reduction. The cellar being completed and ready for the reception of the spirits that were on board the Fishburn, they were landed from that ship; and she, being cleared and discharged from government employ, hove down, and prepared for her return to England.

A gang of convicts were employed in rolling timber together, to form a bridge over the stream at the head of the cove; and such other public works as were in hand went on as usual; those employed on them in general barely exerting themselves beyond what was necessary to avoid immediate punishment for idleness.

A warrant having about this time been granted by the governor, for the purpose of assembling a general court-martial, a defect was discovered in the marine mutiny act; and it was determined by the officers, that, as marine officers, they could not sit under any other than a warrant from the Lords Commissioners of the Admiralty. The marines are so far distinct from his Majesty's land forces, that while on shore in any part of his Majesty's dominions, they are regulated by an act of parliament passed expressly for their guidance; and when it was found necessary to employ a corps of marines during the late war in America, they were included in the mutiny act passed for his Majesty's forces employed in that country. This provision having been neglected on the departure of the expedition for this country, and not being discovered until the very instant when it was wanted, all that could be done was to state their situation to the governor, which they did on the 13th, and at the same time requested, " That they might " be understood to be acting only in conformity with an act of the " British legislature, passed expressly for their regulation while on " shore in any part of his Majesty's dominions; and that they had not " in any shape been wanting in the respect that belonged to the high " authority of his Majesty's commission, or to the officer invested with " it in this country."

On the 24th a party of natives, meeting a convict who had straggled from the settlement to a fence that some people were making for the purpose of inclosing stock, threw several spears at him; but, fortunately, without doing him any injury. The governor, on being made acquainted with the circumstance, immediately went to the spot
with

with an armed party, where some of them being heard among the bushes, they were fired at; it having now become absolutely necessary to compel them to keep at a greater distance from the settlement.

CHAP. V.

SETTLEMENT OF ROSE HILL.—THE GOLDEN GROVE RETURNS FROM NOR-FOLK ISLAND.—THE STORESHIPS SAIL FOR ENGLAND.—TRANSACTIONS.—JAMES DALEY TRIED AND EXECUTED FOR HOUSEBREAKING.—BOTANY BAY EXAMINED BY THE GOVERNOR.—A CONVICT FOUND DEAD IN THE WOODS.—CHRISTMAS DAY.—A NATIVE TAKEN AND BROUGHT UP TO THE SETTLEMENT.—WEATHER.—CLIMATE.—REPORT OF DEATHS FROM THE DEPARTURE OF THE FLEET FROM ENGLAND TO THE 31ST OF DECEMBER, 1788.

November.] THE month of November commenced with the esta-blishment of a settlement at the head of the harbour. On the 2d, his excellency the governor went up to the Crescent, with the surveyor-general, two officers, and a small party of marines, to choose the spot, and to mark out the ground for a redoubt and other necessary build-ings; and two days after a party of ten convicts, being chiefly people who understood the business of cultivation, were sent up to him, and a spot upon a rising ground, which his excellency named Rose Hill, in compliment to G. Rose esq. one of the secretaries of the treasury, was ordered to be cleared for the first habitations. The soil at this spot was of a stiff clayey nature, free from that rock which every where covered the surface at Sydney Cove, well clothed with timber, and unobstructed by underwood.

The party of convicts having, during the course of the month, been gradually increased, the subaltern's command was augmented by a captain with an additional number of private men; and it being found necessary that the commanding officer should be vested with civil power and authority sufficient to inflict corporal punishment on the

the convicts for idleness and other petty offences, the governor constituted him a justice of the peace for the county of Cumberland for that purpose.

10th. While this little settlement was establishing itself, the Golden Grove returned from Norfolk Island, having been absent five weeks and four days. It brought letters from Lieutenant King, the commandant, who wrote in very favourable terms of his young colony. His people continued healthy, having fish and vegetables in abundance; by the former of which he was enabled to save some of his salted provisions. He had also the promise of a good crop from the grain which had been last sown, and his gardens wore the most flourishing appearance.

A cocoa-nut perfectly fresh, and a piece of wood said to resemble the handle of a fly-flap as made at the Friendly Islands, together with the remains of two canoes, had been found among the rocks, perhaps blown from some island which might lie at no great distance.

The Golden Grove, on her return to this port, saw a very dangerous reef, the south end of which, according to the observation of Mr. Blackburn, (the master of the Supply,) who commanded her for the voyage, lay in the latitude of 29° 25′ South, and longitude 159° 29′ East. It appeared to extend, when she was about four leagues from it, from the N. E. by N. to N.

The Golden Grove brought from Norfolk Island a lower yard and a top-gallant-mast for herself, and the like for the Fishburn.

A soldier belonging to the detachment, who was employed with some others in preparing shingles at a little distance from the settlement, was reported by his comrades, toward the latter end of last month, to be missing from the hut or tent, and parties were sent out in search of him; but returning constantly without success, he was at length given up; and a convict who was employed in assisting the party, and who had been the last person seen with him, was taken into custody; but on his examination nothing appeared that could at all affect him.

Another soldier of the detachment died at the hospital of the bruises he received in fighting with one of his comrades, who was, with three others, taken into custody, and afterward tried upon a charge of murder,

der, but found guilty of manslaughter. Instead of burning in the hand, (which would not have been in this country an adequate punishment,) each was sentenced to receive two hundred lashes.

The two storeships sailed for England on the 19th. By these ships the governor sent home dispatches, and he strongly recommended to the masters to make their passage round by the south cape of this country; but it was conjectured that they intended to go round Cape Horn, and touch at Rio de Janeiro.

The small redoubt that was begun in July last being finished, a flag-staff was erected, and two pieces of iron ordnance placed in it.

In order to prevent, if possible, the practice of thieving, which at times was very frequent, an order was given, directing that no convict, who should in future be found guilty of theft, should be supplied with any other clothing than a canvas frock and trowsers. It was at the same time ordered, that such convicts as should in future fail to perform a day's labour, should receive only two thirds of the ration that was issued to those who could and did work.

Unimportant as these circumstances may appear when detailed at a distance from the time when they were necessary, they yet serve to show the nature of the people by whom this colony (whatever may be its fate) was first founded; as well as the attention that was paid by those in authority, and the steps taken by them, for establishing good order and propriety among them, and for eradicating villany and idleness.

December.]   James Daley, the convict who in August pretended to have discovered an inexhaustible source of wealth, and was punished for his imposition, was observed from that time to neglect his labour, and to loiter about from hut to hut, while others were at work. He was at last taken up and tried for breaking into a house, and stealing all the property he could find in it; of this offence he was convicted, and suffered death; the governor not thinking him an object of mercy. Before he was turned off, he confessed that he had committed several thefts, to which he had been induced by bad connections, and pointed out two women who had received part of the property for the acquisition of which he was then about to pay so dear a price. These women were immediately apprehended, and one of them made

a public

I I

a public example of, to deter others from offending in the like manner. The convicts being all assembled for muster, she was directed to stand forward, and, her head having been previously deprived of its natural covering, she was clothed with a canvas frock, on which was painted, in large characters, R. S. G. (receiver of stolen goods,) and threatened with punishment if ever she was seen without it. This was done in the hope that shame might operate, at least with the female part of the prisoners, to the prevention of crimes; but a great number of both sexes had too long been acquainted with each other in scenes of disgrace, for this kind of punishment to work much reformation among them. This, however, must be understood to be spoken only of the lowest class of these people, among whom the commission of offences was chiefly found to exist; for there were convicts of both sexes who were never known to associate with the common herd, and whose conduct was marked by attention to their labour, and obedience to the orders they received.

On the 11th, the governor set off with a small party in boats, to examine the different branches of Botany Bay, and, after an excursion of five days, returned well satisfied that no part of that extensive bay was adapted to the purpose of a settlement; thus fully confirming the reports he had received from others, and the opinions he had himself formed.

A convict having been found dead in the woods near the settlement, an enquiry into the cause of his death was made by the provost-marshal; when it appeared from the evidence of Mr. Balmain, one of the assistant-surgeons who attended to open him, and of the people who lived with the deceased, that he died through want of nourishment, and through weakness occasioned by the heat of the sun. It appeared that he had not for more than a week past eaten his allowance of provisions, the whole being found in his box. It was proved by those who knew him, that he was accustomed to deny himself even what was absolutely necessary to his existence, abstaining from his provisions, and selling them for money, which he was reserving, and had somewhere concealed, in order to purchase his passage to England when his time should expire.

Mr.

Mr. Reid, the carpenter of the Supply, now undertook the conftruction of a boat-houfe on the eaft fide, for the purpofe of building, with the timber of this country, a launch or hoy, capable of being employed in conveying provifions to Rofe Hill, and for other ufeful and neceffary purpofes. The working convicts were employed on Saturdays, until ten o'clock in the forenoon, in forming a landing-place on the eaft fide of the cove. At the point on the weft fide, a magazine was marked out, to be conftructed of ftone, and large enough to contain fifty or fixty barrels of powder.

Chriftmas-day was obferved with proper ceremony. Mr. Johnfon preached a fermon adapted to the occafion, and the major part of the officers of the fettlement were afterward entertained at dinner by the governor.

It being remarked with concern, that the natives were becoming every day more troublefome and hoftile, feveral people having been wounded, and others, who were neceffarily employed in the woods, driven in and much alarmed by them, the governor determined on endeavouring to feize and bring into the fettlement, one or two of thofe people, whofe language it was become abfolutely neceffary to acquire, that they might learn to diftinguifh friends from enemies.

Accordingly, on the 30th a young man was feized and brought up by Lieutenant Ball of the Supply, and Lieutenant George Johnfton of the marines. A fecond was taken; but, after dragging into the water beyond his depth the man who feized him, he got clear off. The native who was fecured was immediately on his landing led up to the governor's, where he was cloathed, a flight iron or manacle put upon his wrift, and a trufty convict appointed to take care of him. A fmall hut had been previoufly built for his reception clofe to the guardhoufe, wherein he and his keeper were locked up at night; and the following morning the convict reported, that he flept very well during the night, not offering to make any attempt to get away.

The weather, during the month of December, was for the firft part hot and clofe; the middle was fine; the latter variable, but moftly fine:—upon the whole the month was very hot. The climate was allowed by every one, medical as well as others, to be fine and falu-briou.

H

brious. The rains were heavy, and appeared to fall chiefly on or about the full and change of the moon. Thunder and lightning at times had been severe, but not attended with any bad effects since the month of February last.

The following report of the casualties which had happened from the day of our leaving England to the 31st of December 1788, was given in at this time; viz.—

Casualties from May 13, 1787, to December 31, 1788.	Garrison.			Convicts.			Total
	Men.	Women	Children	Men.	Women	Children	
Died on the passage, from May 13, 1787, to January 26, 1788, — — —	1	1	1	20	4	9	36
Died between January 26, 1788, and January 1, 1789, — — —	5		1	28	13	9	56
Killed by the natives in the above time, —				4			4
Executed in the above time, — —				5			5
Missing in the above time, — — —	1			12	1		14
Total	7	1	2	69	18	18	115

CHAP. VI.

NEW YEAR'S DAY.—CONVICTS, HOW EMPLOYED.—THEIR DISPOSITION TO
IDLENESS AND VICE.—HER MAJESTY'S BIRTH-DAY KEPT.—NATIVES.—
CAPTAIN SHEA DIES.—REGULATIONS RESPECTING THE CONVICTS.—IN-
STANCES OF THEIR MISCONDUCT.—TRANSACTIONS.—THE SUPPLY SAILS
FOR NORFOLK ISLAND.—PUBLIC WORKS.—NATIVES.—CONVICTS KILLED.
—STORES ROBBED.—THE SUPPLY RETURNS.—INSURRECTION PROJECTED
AT NORFOLK ISLAND.—HURRICANE THERE.—TRANSACTIONS AT ROSE
HILL.

January, 1789.] THE first day of the new year was marked as a
holiday by a suspension of all kinds of labour, and by hoisting the colours at the fort. The ration of provisions, though still less by a
pound of flour than the proper allowance, was yet so sufficient as not
to be complained of; nor was labour diminished by it. Upon a calculation of the different people employed for the public in cultivation,
it appeared, that of all the numbers in the colony there were only two
hundred and fifty so employed:—a very small number indeed to
procure the means of rendering the colony independent of the mother-
country for the necessaries of life. The rest were occupied in carrying on various public works, such as stores, houses, wharfs, &c.
A large number were incapable, through age or infirmities, of being
called out to labour in the public grounds; and the civil establishment,
the military, females, and children, filled up the catalogue of those
unassisting in cultivation.

The soil immediately about the settlement was found to be of too
sandy a nature to give much promise of yielding a sufficient produce
even for the small quantity of stock it possessed. At Rose Hill the prospect was better; indeed whatever expectations could be formed of successful cultivation in this country rested as yet in that quarter. But the
convicts by no means exerted themselves to the utmost; they foolishly
conceived, that they had no interest in the success of their labour;

H 2　　　　　　　　　　and,

and, if left to themselves, would at any time rather have lived in idleness, and depended upon the public stores for their daily support so long as they had any thing in them, than have contributed, by the labour of their hands, to secure themselves whereon to exist when those stores should be exhausted.

Idleness, however, was not the only vice to be complained of in these people. These were frequent among them; and one fellow, who, after committing a robbery ran into the woods, and from thence coming at night into the settlement committed several depredations upon individuals, and one upon the public stores, was at length taken and executed, in the hope of holding out an example to others. His thefts had been so frequent and daring, that it became necessary to offer a reward of one pound of flour to be given weekly, in addition to the ration then issued, for his apprehension. Another convict, named Ruglass, was tried for stabbing Ann Fowles, a woman with whom he cohabited, and sentenced to receive seven hundred lashes, half of which were inflicted on him while the other unhappy wretch was suffering the execution of his sentence.

The 19th was observed as the birth-day of her Majesty.—The colours were displayed at sun-rise; at noon the detachment of marines fired three rounds; after which the governor received the compliments of the day; and at one o'clock the Supply, the only vessel in the country, fired twenty-one guns. The governor entertained the officers at dinner, and the day concluded with a bonfire, for which the country afforded abundant materials.

A day or two after this the place was agitated by a report that a great gun had been fired at sea; but on sending a boat down without the harbour's mouth, nothing was seen there that could confirm a report which every one anxiously wished might be true.

A boat having been sent down the harbour with some people to cut rushes, a party of natives came to the beach while they were so employed, and took three of their jackets out of the boat. On discovering this theft, the cockswain pursued a canoe with two men in it as far as a small island that lay just by, where the natives landed, leaving the canoe at the rocks. This the cockswain took away, (contrary to an order, which had been made very public, on no account to

touch

touch a canoe, or any thing belonging to a native,) and towed it to the bay where they had been cutting rushes. The natives returned to the same place unobserved, and, while the cockswain and his people were collecting what rushes they had cut, threw a spear at the cockswain, which wounded him in the arm, notwithstanding they must have known that at that time we had one of their people in our possession, on whom the injury might be retaliated. He, poor fellow, did not seem to expect any such treatment from us, and began to seem reconciled to his situation. He was taken down the harbour once or twice, to let his friends see that he was alive, and had some intercourse with them which appeared to give him much satisfaction.

For fifteen days of this month the thermometer rose in the shade above eighty degrees. Once, (on the 8th,) at one in the afternoon, it stood at 105° in the shade.

February 2d.] Captain John Shea, of the marines, who had been for a considerable time in a declining state of health, died, and was interred with military honours the day following; the governor and every officer of the settlement attending his funeral. The major-commandant of the detachment shortly after filled up the vacancy which this officer's death had occasioned by appointing Captain Lieutenant Meredith to the company; and First Lieutenant George Johnston succeeded to the captain-lieutenancy. Second Lieutenant Ralph Clarke was appointed a First, and volunteer John Ross a Second Lieutenant; but their commissions were still to receive the confirmation of the lords commissioners of the Admiralty.

The convicts being found to continue the practice of selling their clothing, an order was issued, directing, that if in future a convict should give information to the provost-marshal against any person to whom he had sold his clothes, the seller should receive them again, be permitted to keep whatever was paid him for them, and receive no punishment himself for the sale. It was also found necessary to direct, that all stragglers at night who, on being challenged by the patrole, should run from them, should be fired at; but orders, in general, were observed to have very little effect, and to be attended to only while the impression made by hearing them published remained upon the mind; for the convicts had not been accustomed to
live

live in fituations where their conduct was to be regulated by written
orders.   There was here no other mode of communicating to them
fuch directions as it was found neceffary to iffue for their obfervance ;
and it was very common to have them plead in excufe for a breach
of any regulation of the fettlement, that they had never before heard
of it ; nor had they any idea of the permanency of an order, many
of them feeming to think it iffued merely for the purpofe of the
moment.

It was much to be regretted, that there exifted a neceffity for
placing a confidence in thefe people, as in too many inftances the truft
was found to be abufed: but unfortunately, to fill many of thofe
offices to which free people alone fhould have been appointed in this
colony, there were none but convicts. From thefe it will be readily
fuppofed the beft characters were felected, thofe who had merited by
the propriety of their conduct the good report of the officers on board
the fhips in which they were embarked, and who had brought with
them into thofe fhips a better name than their fellows from the prifons
in which they had been confined.   Thofe alfo who were qualified
to inftruct and direct others in the exercife of profeffions in which
they had fuperior knowledge and experience, were appointed to act
as overfeers, with gangs under their direction ; and many had given
evident proofs or ftrong indications of returning difpofitions to honeft
induftry.

There were others, however, who had no claim to this praife.
Among thefe muft be particularifed William Bryant, to whom, from
his having been bred from his youth to the bufinefs of a fifherman
in the weftern part of England, was given the direction and management of fuch boats as were employed in fifhing ; every encouragement
was held out to this man to keep him above temptation; an hut was
built for him and his family ; he was always prefented with a certain
part of the fifh which he caught ; and he wanted for nothing that was
neceffary, or that was fuitable to a perfon of his defcription and
fituation. But he was detected in fecreting and felling large quantities
of fifh ; and when the neceffary enquiry was made, this practice appeared to have been of fome ftanding with him. For this offence
he was feverely punifhed, and removed from the hut in which he
                                                                    had

had been placed; yet as, notwithstanding his villainy, he was too useful a person to part with and send to a brick cart, he was still retained to fish for the settlement; but a very vigilant eye was kept over him, and such steps taken as appeared likely to prevent him from repeating his offence, if the sense of shame and fear of punishment were not of themselves sufficient to deter him.

A person of the name of Smith having procured a passage from England in the Lady Penrhyn, with a design to proceed to India in the event of his not finding any employment in this country, on his offering his services, and professing to have some agricultural knowledge, was received into the colony, and, being judged a discreet prudent man, was placed about the provision store under the assistant to the commissary at Rose Hill, and was moreover sworn in as a peace-officer, to act as such immediately under the provost-marshal; a line wherein, from the circumstance of his being a free man, it was supposed he might render essential aid to the civil department of the colony. It was farther intended, at a future period, to place some people under his direction, to give him an opportunity of exercising the abilities he was said to possess as a practical farmer.

14th.] The magazine at the Point being now completed, the powder belonging to the settlement was lodged safely within its walls.

It being of importance to the colony to ascertain the precise situation and extent of the reefs seen by Mr. Blackburn, in the Golden Grove storeship, in November last, Lieutenant Ball (who was proceeding to Norfolk Island with provisions and convicts) was directed to perform that duty on his return. He sailed with the vessel under his command on the 17th, having on board twenty-one male and six female convicts, and three children; of the latter two were to be placed under Mr. King's care as children of the public. They were of different sexes; the boy, Edward Parkinson, who was about three years of age, had lost his mother on the passage to this country; the girl, who was a year older, had a mother in the colony; but as she was a woman of abandoned character*, the child was taken from

* The same who was wounded by Ruglass, p. 51.

her

her to fave it from the ruin which would otherwife have been its inevitable lot. Thefe children were to be inftructed in reading and writing, and in hufbandry. The commandant of the ifland was directed to caufe five acres of ground to be allotted and cultivated for their benefit, by fuch perfon as he fhould think fit to entruft with the charge of bringing them up according to the fpirit of this intention, in promoting the fuccefs of which every friend of humanity feemed to feel an intereft.

The cove was now, for the firft time, left without a fhip; a circum- ftance not only ftriking by its novelty, but which forcibly drew our attention to the peculiarity of our fituation. The Sirius was gone upon a long voyage to a diftant country for fupplies, the arrival of which were affuredly precarious. The Supply had left us, to look after a dangerous reef; which fervice, in an unknown fea, might draw upon herfelf the calamity which fhe was feeking to inftruct others to avoid. Should it have been decreed, that the arm of misfortune was to fall with fuch weight upon us, as to render at any time the falvation of this little veffel neceffary to the falvation of the colony, how deeply was every one concerned in her welfare! Reflection on the bare poffibility of its mifcarriage made every mind anxious during her abfence from the fettlement.

From the evident neceffity that exifted of maintaining a ftrict dif- cipline among the military employed in this country, it became re- quifite to punifh with fome feverity any flagrant breach of military fubordination that might occur. Jofeph Hunt, a foldier in the de- tachment, having been found abfent from his poft when ftationed as a centinel, was tried by a court-martial, and fentenced to receive feven hundred lafhes; which fentence was put in execution upon him at two periods, with an interval of three weeks.

Toward the end of this month the detachment took poffeffion of their barracks; two of which, having been nearly twelve months in hand, were now completed, and ready for their reception. A brick houfe, forty feet by thirteen, was begun on the eaft fide for the commiffary; and materials were preparing for a guard-houfe.

At Rofe Hill the people were principally employed in clearing and cultivating land; but the labour of removing the timber off the ground

14   when

when cut down very much retarded the beft efforts of the people fo
employed. The military and convicts ftill lived under tents ; and, as
a proof of the fmall fpace which they occupied, two Emus or Caffo-
waries, who muft have been feeding in the neighbourhood, ran
through the little camp, and were fo intermingled with the people,
who ran out of their tents at fo ftrange an appearance, that it became
dangerous to fire at them ; and they got clear off, though literally fur-
rounded by a multitude of people, and under the very muzzles of
fome of their mufquets.

Very little moleftation was at this time given by the natives ; and
had they never been ill treated by our people, inftead of hoftility, it
is more than probable that an intercourfe of friendfhip would have
fubfifted.

March.] The impracticability of keeping the convicts within the
limits preferibed for them became every day more evident. Almoft
every month fince our arrival had produced one or more accidents,
occafioned principally by a non-compliance with the orders which had
been given folely with a view to their fecurity; and which, with
thinking beings, would have been of fufficient force as examples to
deter others from running into the fame danger. But neither orders
nor dangers feemed to be at all regarded where their own temporary
convenience prompted them to difobey the one, or run the rifque of
incurring the other. A convict belonging to the brick-maker's gang
had ftrayed into the woods for the purpofe of collecting fweet tea ;
an herb fo called by the convicts, and which was in great eftimation
among them. The leaves of it being boiled, they obtained a beverage
not unlike liquorice in tafte, and which was recommended by fome
of the medical gentlemen here, as a powerful tonic. It was difcovered
foon after our arrival, and was then found clofe to the fettlement ;
but the great confumption had now rendered it fcarce. It was fuppofed, that the convict in his fearch after this article had fallen in with
a party of natives, who had killed him. A few days after this accident, a party of the convicts, fixteen in number, chiefly belonging to
the brick-maker's gang, quitted the place of their employment, and,
providing themfelves with ftakes, fet off toward Botany Bay, with a
determination to revenge, upon whatever natives they fhould meet,

I   the

the treatment which one of their brethren had received at the close of
the last month. Near Botany Bay they fell in with the natives, but
in a larger body than they expected or defired. According to their
report, they were fifty in number; but much dependance was not
placed on what they faid in this refpect, nor in their narrative of the
affair; it was certain, however, that they were driven in by the
natives, who killed one man and wounded fix others. Immediately
on this being known in the fettlement, an armed party was fent out
with an officer, who found the body of the man that had been killed,
ftripped, and lying in the path to Botany Bay. They alfo found a
boy, who had likewife been ftripped and left for dead by the natives.
He was very much wounded, and his left ear nearly cut off. The
party, after burying the body of the man, returned with the wounded
boy, but without feeing any of the perpetrators of this mifchief; the
other wounded people had reached the fettlement, and were taken to
the hofpital. The day following, the governor, judging it highly
neceffary to make examples of thefe mifguided people, who had fo
daringly and flagrantly broken through every order which had been
given to prevent their interfering with the natives as to form a party
exprefsly to meet with and attack them, directed that thofe who were
not wounded fhould receive each one hundred and fifty lafhes, and
wear a fetter for a twelvemonth; the like punifhment was directed to
be inflicted upon thofe who were in the hofpital, as foon as they fhould
recover from their wounds; in purfuance of which order, feven of
them were tied up in front of the provifion ftore, and punifhed (for
example's fake) in the prefence of all the convicts.

The fame day two armed parties were fent, one toward Botany Bay,
and the other in a different direction, that the natives might fee that
their late act of violence would neither intimidate nor prevent us from
moving beyond the fettlement whenever occafion required.

Such were our enemies abroad: at home, within ourfelves, we had
enemies to encounter of a different nature, but in their effects more
difficult to guard againft. The gardens and houfes of individuals, and
the provifion ftore, were overrun with rats. The fafety of the provifions was an object of general confequence, and the commiffary
was for fome time employed in examining into the ftate of the ftore.
                                                                One

One morning, on going early to the store, he found the wards of a key which had been broken in the padlock that secured the principal door, and which it was the duty of the patroles to visit and inspect every night. Entering the storehouse, he perceived that an harness-cask had been opened and some provisions taken out. It being supposed that the wards of the key might lead to a discovery of the perpetrator of this atrocious act, they were sent to a convict blacksmith, an ingenious workman through whose hands most of the work passed that was done in his line, who immediately knew them to belong to a soldier of the name of Hunt, the same who in the course of the preceding month received seven hundred lashes, and who had some time back brought the key to this blacksmith to be altered. On this information, Hunt was taken up; but offering to give some material information, he was admitted an evidence on the part of the crown, and made an ample confession before the lieutenant-governor and the judge-advocate, in which he accused six other soldiers of having been concerned with him in the diabolical practice of robbing the store for a considerable time past of liquor and provisions in large quantities. This crime, great enough of itself, was still aggravated by the manner in which it was committed. Having formed their party, seven in number, and sworn each other to secrecy and fidelity, they procured and altered keys to fit the different locks on the three doors of the provision store; and it was agreed, that whenever any one of the seven should be posted there as centinel during the night, two or more of the gang, as they found it convenient, were to come during the hours in which they knew their associate would have the store under his charge, when, by means of their keys, and sheltered in the security which he afforded them, (by betraying in so flagrant a manner the trust and confidence reposed in him as a centinel,) they should open a passage into the store, where they should remain shut up until they had procured as much liquor or provisions as they could take off. If the patroles visited the store while they chanced to be within its walls, the door was found locked and secure, the centinel alert and vigilant on his post, and the store apparently safe.

Fortunately for the settlement, on the night preceding the discovery one of the party intended to have availed himself of his situation as

I 2 centinel,

centinel, and to enter the store alone, purposing to plunder without the participation of his associates. But while he was standing with the key in the lock, he heard the patrole advancing. The key had done its office, but as he knew that the lock would be examined by the corporal, in his fright and haste to turn it back again, he mistook the way, and, finding that he could not get the key out of the lock, he broke it, and was compelled to leave the wards in it; the other part of the key he threw away.

On this information, the six soldiers whom he accused were taken up and tried; when, the evidence of the accomplice being confirmed by several strong corroborating circumstances, among which it appeared that the store had been broken into and robbed by them at various times for upwards of eight months, they were unanimously found guilty, and sentenced to suffer that death which they owned they justly merited. Their defence wholly consisted in accusing the accomplice of having been the first to propose and carry the plan into execution, and afterwards the first to accuse and ruin the people he had influenced to associate with him. A crime of such magnitude called for a severe example; and the sentence was carried into execution a few days after their trial.

Some of these unhappy men were held in high estimation by their officers; but the others, together with the accomplice Hunt, had been long verging toward this melancholy end. Four of them had been tried for the death of their comrade Bulmore, which happened in a contest with one of them in November last; and their manner of conducting themselves at various times appeared to have been very reprehensible. The liquor which they procured from the store was the cause of drunkenness, which brought on affrays and disorders, for which, as soldiers, they were more than once punished. To these circumstances must be added (what perhaps must be considered as the root of these evils) a connexion which subsisted between them and some of the worst of the female convicts, at whose huts, notwithstanding the internal regulations of their quarters, they found means to enjoy their ill-acquired plunder.

On the morning of their execution, one of them declared to the clergyman who attended him, that the like practices had been carried

on

on at the store at Rose Hill by similar means and with similar success.
He named two soldiers and a convict as the persons concerned; these
were afterwards apprehended, and underwent an examination of several
hours by the lieutenant-governor and the judge-advocate, during which
nothing being drawn from either that could affect the others, they
were all discharged. It was, however, generally believed, that the
soldier would not in his dying moments have falsely accused three men
of a crime which they had never committed; and that nothing but
their constancy to each other had prevented a discovery of their guilt.

While these transactions were passing at Sydney, the little colony at
Norfolk Island had been threatened with an insurrection. The Supply
returned from thence the 24th, after an absence of five weeks, and
brought from Lieutenant King, the commandant, information of the
following chimerical scheme :—The capture of the island, and the
subsequent escape of the captors, was to commence by the seizure of.
Mr. King's person, which was intended to be effected on the first
Saturday after the arrival of any ship in the bay, except the Sirius.
They had chosen that particular day in the week, as it had been for
some time Mr. King's custom on Saturdays to go to a farm which he
had established at some little distance from the settlement, and the
military generally chose that day to bring in the cabbage palm from
the woods. Mr. King was to be secured in his way to his farm.
A message, in the commandant's name, was then to be sent to Mr.
Jamison, the surgeon, who was to be seized as soon as he got into
the woods; and the serjeant and the party were to be treated in the
same manner. These being all properly taken care of, a signal was
to be made to the ship in the bay to send her boat on shore, the
crew of which were to be made prisoners on their landing; and two
or three of the insurgents were to go off in a boat belonging to the
island, and inform the commanding officer that the ship's boat had
been stove on the beach, and that the commandant requested another
might be sent a-shore; this also was to be captured: and then, as
the last act of this absurd scheme, the ship was to be taken, with which
they were to proceed to Otaheite, and there establish a settlement.
They charitably intended to leave some provisions for the commandant
and his officers, and for such of the people as did not accompany them
in their escape.—This was their scheme. Not one difficulty in the
execution

execution of it ever occurred to their imagination: all was to happen with as much facility as it was planned; and, had it not been fortunately revealed to a seaman belonging to the Sirius, who lived with Mr. King as a gardener, by a female convict who cohabited with him, there was no doubt but that all these improbabilities would have been attempted.

On being made acquainted with these circumstances, the commandant took such measures as appeared to him necessary to defeat them; and several who were concerned in the scheme confessed the share which they were to have had in the execution of it. Mr. King had hitherto, from the peculiarity of his situation,—secluded from society, and confined to a small speck in the vast ocean, with but a handful of people,—drawn them round him, and treated them with the kind attentions which a good family meets with at the hands of a humane master; but he now saw them in their true colours, and one of his first steps, when peace was restored, was to clear the ground as far as possible round the settlement, that future villainy might not find a shelter in the woods for its transactions. To this truly providential circumstance, perhaps, many of the colonists afterwards were indebted for their lives. .

On Thursday the 26th of February the island was visited by a hurricane, which came on early in the morning in very heavy gales of wind and rain. By four o'clock several pines of 180 and 200 feet in length, and from 20 to 30 feet in circumference, were blown down. From that hour until noon the gale increased to a dreadful hurricane, with torrents of heavy rain. Every instant pines and live oaks, of the largest dimensions, were borne down by the fury of the blast, which, tearing up roots and rocks with them, left chasms of eight or ten feet depth in the earth. Those pines that were able to resist the wind bent their tops nearly to the ground; and nothing but horror and desolation everywhere presented itself. A very large live oak-tree was blown on the granary, which it dashed to pieces, and stove a number of casks of flour; but happily, by the activity of the officers and free people, the flour, Indian corn, and stores, were in a short time collected, and removed to the commandant's house, with the loss only of about half a cask of flour, and some small stores. At noon the gale blew with the utmost violence, tearing up whole forests

by

by the roots. At one o'clock there were as many trees torn up by the roots as would have required the labour of fifty men for a fortnight to have felled. Early in the forenoon the swamp and vale were overflowed, and had every appearance of a large navigable river. The gardens, public and private, were wholly destroyed; cabbages, turnips, and other plants, were blown out of the ground; and those which withstood the hurricane seemed as if they had been scorched. An acre of Indian corn which grew in the vale, and which would have been ripe in about three weeks, was totally destroyed*.

His people continued to be healthy, and the climate had not forfeited the good opinion he had formed of it. He acquainted the governor, that for his internal defence he had formed all the free people on the island into a militia, and that a military guard was mounted every night as a piquet. There were at this time victualled on the island sixteen free people, fifty-one male convicts, twenty-three female convicts, and four children.

The arrival of the Supply with an account of these occurrences created a temporary variety in the conversation of the day; and a general satisfaction appeared when the little vessel that brought them dropped her anchor again in the cove. Lieutenant Ball, having lost an anchor at Norfolk Island, did not think it prudent to attempt to fall in with the shoal seen by the Golden Grove storeship; his orders on that head being discretionary.

We now return to the transactions of the principal settlement. The person who was noticed in the occurrences of the last month as being employed at Rose Hill under the commissary, had been also intrusted with the direction of the convicts who were employed in clearing and cultivating ground at that place; but, being advanced in years, he was found inadequate to the task of managing and controlling the people who were under his care, the most of whom were always inventing plausible excuses for absence from labour, or for their neglect of it while under his eye. He was therefore removed, and succeeded

* The direction of the hurricane was across the island from the South-east; and as its surf had blown down more trees than were found lying on the ground when Mr. King looked on it, he conjectured that it was not an annual visitant of the island. This conjecture seems now to be justified, as nothing of the kind has since occurred there.

by

by a perfon who came out from England as a fervant to the governor. This man joined to much agricultural knowledge a perfect idea of the labour to be required from, and that might be performed by the convicts ; and his figure was calculated to make the idle and the worthlefs fhrink if he came near them. He had hitherto been employed at the fpot of ground which was cleared foon after our arrival at the adjoining cove, fince diftinguifhed by the name of Farm Cove, and which, from the natural poverty of the foil, was not capable of making an adequate return for the labour which had been expended on it. It was, however, ftill attended to, and the fences kept in repair ; but there was not any intention of clearing more ground in that fpot.

Toward the latter end of the month two of the birds diftinguifhed in the colony by the name of Emus were brought in by fome of the people employed to fhoot for the officers. The weight of each was feventy pounds.

CHAP. VII.

NEUTRAL BAY.—SMALL-POX AMONG THE NATIVES.—CAPTAIN HUNTER IN THE SIRIUS RETURNS WITH SUPPLIES FROM THE CAPE OF GOOD HOPE.—MIDDLETON ISLAND DISCOVERED.—DANGER OF WANDERING IN THE FORESTS OF AN UNKNOWN COUNTRY.—CONVICTS.—THE KING'S BIRTH-DAY KEPT.—CONVICTS PERFORM A PLAY.—A REINFORCEMENT UNDER LIEUTENANT CRESSWELL SENT TO NORFOLK ISLAND.—GOVERNOR PHILLIP MAKES AN EXCURSION OF DISCOVERY.—TRANSACTIONS.—HAWKESBURY RIVER DISCOVERED.—PROGRESS AT ROSE HILL.—IMPORTANT PAPERS LEFT BEHIND IN ENGLAND.

April.] THE governor thinking it probable that foreign fhips might again vifit this coaft, and perhaps run into this harbour for the purpofe of procuring refrefhments, directed Mr. Blackburn to furvey a large bay on the north fhore, contiguous to this cove; and a fufficient depth of water being found, his excellency inferted in the port orders,
that

that all foreign ships coming into this harbour should anchor in this
bay, which he named Nentral Bay, bringing Rock Island to bear
S. S. E. and the hospital on the west side of Sydney Cove to bear
S. W. by W.

Early in the month, and throughout its continuance, the people
whose business called them down the harbour daily reported, that they
found, either in excavations of the rock, or lying upon the beaches
and points of the different coves which they had been in, the bodies of
many of the wretched natives of this country. The cause of this
mortality remained unknown until a family was brought up, and the
disorder pronounced to have been the small-pox. It was not a desirable circumstance to introduce a disorder into the colony which was
raging with such fatal violence among the natives of the country ; but
the saving the lives of any of these people was an object of no small
importance, as the knowledge of our humanity, and the benefits
which we might render them, would, it was hoped, do away the evil
impressions they had received of us. Two elderly men, a boy, and a
girl were brought up, and placed in a separate hut at the hospital.
The men were too far overcome by the disease to get the better of it ;
but the children did well from the moment of their coming among us.
From the native who resided with us we understood that many families had been swept off by this scourge, and that others, to avoid it,
had fled into the interior parts of the country. Whether it had ever
appeared among them before could not be discovered, either from
him or from the children ; but it was certain that they gave it a
name (gal-gal-la) ; a circumstance which seemed to indicate a pre-
acquaintance with it.

The convicts, among other public works, were now employed in
forming a convenient road on the west side from the hospital and
landing-place to the storehouses ; and in constructing a stable at Farm
Cove, with some convenient out-houses for stock.

May.] Of the native boy and girl who had been brought up in the
last month, on their recovery from the small-pox, the latter was taken
to live with the clergyman's wife, and the boy with Mr. White, the
surgeon, to whom, for his attention during the cure, he seemed to be
much attached.

K   While

While the eruptions of this diforder continued upon the children, a feaman belonging to the Supply, a native of North America, having been to fee them, was feized with it, and foon after died; but its baneful effects were not experienced by any white perfon of the fettlement, although there were feveral very young children in it at the time.

From the firft hour of the introduction of the boy and girl into the fettlement, it was feared that the native who had been fo inftrumental in bringing them in, and whofe attention to them during their illnefs excited the admiration of every one that witneffed it, would be attacked by the fame diforder; as on his perfon were found none of thofe traces of its ravages which are frequently left behind. . It happened as the fears of every one predicted; he fell a victim to the difeafe in eight days after he was feized with it, to the great regret of every one who had witneffed how little of the favage was found in his manner, and how quickly he was fubftituting in its place a docile, affable, and truly amiable deportment.

6th.] After an abfence of feven 'months and fix days, to the great fatisfaction of every one, about five in the evening his Majefty's fhip Sirius anchored in the cove from the Cape of Good Hope. Captain Hunter failed from this port on the 2d of October 1788, and, during the fpace which had elapfed between his departure and his return, had circumnavigated the globe. He made his paffage by Cape Horn, arriving on the 2d of laft January at the Cape of Good Hope, from which place he failed on the 20th of the following month. Off the fouthern extremity of this country the Sirius met with a gale of wind, when fo clofe in with the land that it was for fome time doubtful whether fhe would clear it. In this gale fhe received confiderable damage; the head of the fhip, the figure of the Duke of Berwick, was torn from the cutwater, and fhe was afterwards found to have been very much weakened.

The Sirius brought 127,000 weight of flour for the fettlement, and a twelvemonth's provifions for her fhip's company; but this fupply was not very flattering, as the fhort fpace of four months, at a full ration, would exhauft it. It was, however, very welcome, and her return feemed to have gladdened every heart. Eager were our in-

14   quiries

quiries after intelligence from that country from which we had been
now two years divided, and to whose transactions we were entire
strangers. With joy, mingled with concern that we were not personal
sharers in the triumph, did we hear of our country's successful efforts
in the cause of the Stadtholder, and of the noble armaments which our
ministers had fitted out to support it. We trusted, however, that while
differently employed, our views were still directed to the same object;
for, though labouring at a distance, and in an humbler scene, yet the
good, the glory, and the aggrandizement of our country were prime
considerations with us. And why should the colonists of New South
Wales be denied the merit of endeavouring to promote them, by establishing civilization in the savage world; by animating the children of
idleness and vice to habits of laborious and honest industry; and by
shewing the world that to Englishmen no difficulties are insuperable?

We heard with concern that Lieutenant Shortland was near five
months in reaching Batavia in the Alexander, in which ship he sailed
from this port on the 14th of last July, in company with the Friendship, Borrowdale, and Prince of Wales. From this ship and the Borrowdale he parted company very shortly after leaving our harbour;
they proceeded round Cape Horn, to Rio de Janeiro, where in last
December they were left lying ready for sea. The Alexander and
Friendship proceeding to the northward kept company together as far
as the island of Borneo, where, the crews of both ships being so much
reduced by the scurvy, (the Alexander had buried seventeen of her
seamen,) that it was impossible to navigate both vessels against the
strong currents which they met with, and the western monsoon which
had then set in, both ships were brought to an anchor, and most of
the Friendship's stores, with all her people, being taken out and received on board the Alexander, she was scuttled and sunk. When the
Alexander arrived at Batavia, she had, of both ship's crews, but one
man who was able to go aloft.

Lieutenant Shortland, in his letter, noticed some discoveries which
he had made; particularly one of an extensive and dangerous shoal,
which obtained the name of Middleton Shoal, and was reckoned to be
in the latitude of 29° 20′ South, and in the longitude of 158° 40′ East.
He had also discovered an island, which he placed in the latitude of

K 2   28°

28° 10' South, and in the longitude of 159° 50' East, and named Sir Charles Middleton Island: his other discoveries, not being so immediately in the vicinity of this territory, were not likely to be of any advantage to the settlement; but it was of some importance to it to learn that an extensive reef was so near, and to find its situation ascertained to be in the track of ships bound from hence to the northward; for if Sir Charles Middleton Island should hereafter be found to possess a safe and convenient harbour, it might prove an interesting discovery for this colony.

A Dutch ship, bound for Europe, sailing from the Cape of Good Hope on the 9th of last January, Captain Hunter took that opportunity of forwarding the dispatches with which he had been charged by Governor Phillip. He was informed by the master of the Harpy Whaler, who had put into Table Bay, that in England there had been a general anxiety to hear of our safety and arrival in this country, and that ships to be taken up had been advertised for, but had not been engaged, as the government waited for accounts from Governor Phillip.

Of these accounts it was hoped that ministers had been some time in possession, and that in consequence supplies were at this hour on their passage to New South Wales.

Our attention was now directed to receiving from the Sirius the provisions she had brought us; and as the flour had been packed in bags at the Cape of Good Hope, the coopers were immediately employed in setting up and preparing casks for its reception on shore. These being soon completed, the flour was landed and deposited in the store. This, with the building and covering-in of a new hut for the smith's work, formed the principal labour of the convicts at Sydney during this month.

The boats in the colony not being found sufficient for the purpose of transporting provisions from the store at Sydney to the settlement at Rose Hill, a launch or hoy was put upon the stocks, under the direction of Mr. Reid, the carpenter of the Supply, to be employed for that and other necessary purposes. She was to be built of the timber of the country, and to carry ten tons.

From

From that settlement, early in the month, two soldiers of the detachment doing duty there were reported to be missing; and, though parties had been sent out daily in different directions to seek for them, yet all was unavailing. It was supposed that they must have lost their way in some of the thick and almost impenetrable brushes which were in the vicinity of Rose Hill, and had there perished miserably. They had gone in search of the sweet tea plant already mentioned; and perhaps when they resigned themselves to the fate which they did not see how to avoid, oppressed with hunger, and unable to wander any farther, they may have been but a short distance from the relief they must so earnestly have desired. A dog that was known to have left the settlement with them reached Rose Hill, almost famished, nine days after they had left it. The extreme danger attendant on a man's going beyond the bounds of his own knowledge in the forests of an unsettled country could no where be more demonstrable than in this. To the westward was an immense open track before him, in which, if unbefriended by either sun or moon, he might wander until life were at an end. Most of the arms which extended into the country from Port Jackson and the harbour on each side of Port Jackson, were of great length, and to round them without a certain and daily supply of provisions was impossible *.

To guard as much as possible against these accidents every measure which could be suggested was adopted. A short time after the settlement was established at Rose Hill, the governor went out with some people in a direction due South, and caused a visible path to be made; that if any person who had strayed beyond his own marks for returning, and knew not where he was, should cross upon this path, he might by following it have a chance of reaching the settlement; and orders were repeatedly given to prohibit straggling beyond the limits which were marked and known.

* In many of these arms, when sitting with my companions at my ease in a boat, I have been struck with horror at the bare idea of being lost in them; as, from the great similarity of one cove to another, the recollection would be bewildered in attempting to determine any relative situation. It is certain, that if destroyed by no other means, infinity would accelerate the miserable end that must ensue.

Toward

Toward the end of the month, fome convicts having reported that they had found the body of a white man lying in a cove at a fhort diftance from the fettlement, a general mufter of the convicts at Sydney was directed; but no perfon was unaccounted for except Cæfar, an incorrigibly ftubborn black, who had abfconded a few days before from the fervice of one of the officers, and taken to the woods with fome provifions, an iron pot, and a foldier's mufket, which he had found means to fteal.

Garden robberies, after Cæfar's flight, were frequent, and fome feeds belonging to a feine being ftolen, a reward of a pardon was held out to any of the accomplices on difcovering the perfon who ftole them; and the like reward was alfo offered if, in five days, he fhould difcover the perfon who had purchafed them; but all was without effect. It was conjectured that they had been ftolen for the purpofe of being converted into fhot by fome perfon not employed or authorized to kill the game of this country.

The weather during the latter part of this month was cold; notwithftanding which a turtle was feen in the harbour.

June 4.] The anniverfary of his Majefty's birth-day, the fecond time of commemorating it in this country, was obferved with every diftinction in our power; for the firft time, the ordnance belonging to the colony were difcharged; the detachment of marines fired three vollies, which were followed by twenty-one guns from each of the fhips of war in the cove; the governor received the compliments due to the day in his new houfe, of which he had lately taken poffeffion as the government-houfe of the colony, where his excellency afterwards entertained the officers at dinner, and in the evening fome of the convicts were permitted to perform Farquhar's comedy of the Recruiting Officer, in a hut fitted up for the occafion. They profeffed no higher aim than " humbly to excite a fmile," and their efforts to pleafe were not unattended with applaufe.

In addition to the fteps taken by the commandant of Norfolk Ifland for his internal fecurity, the governor thought an increafe of his military force abfolutely neceffary. Accordingly, the day after his Majefty's birth-day, Lieutenant Crefwell, with fourteen privates from the detachment of marines, embarked on board the Supply for Norfolk Ifland;

Island; and at the same time she received a written order from his excellency to take upon himself the direction and execution of the authority vested in Mr. King, in the event of any accident happening to that officer, until a successor should be formally appointed and sent from hence.

The Supply, on her return from Norfolk Island, was to visit the island seen by Lieutenant Shortland, and laid down by him, in the latitude of 28° 10′ South. She was also to cruise for the shoal seen by that officer, and stated to be in the latitude of 29° 20′ South, and for the shoal seen by Mr. Blackburn, the south end of which lay in the latitude of 29° 25′ South; all of which, if the observations of both officers were equally correct, would, it was supposed, be found contiguous to each other. Lieutenant Ball was directed to land upon the island, if landing should be found practicable; and to determine, if he could, the extent and situation of the shoals.

On these services the Supply sailed the 6th of this month; on which day the governor set off with a party on a second excursion to Broken Bay, in the hope of being able, from the head of that harbour, to reach the mountains inland. His excellency returned to the settlement on the evening of the 16th, having discovered a capacious freshwater river, emptying itself into Broken Bay, and extending to the westward. He was compelled to return without tracing it to its source, not having a sufficient quantity of provisions with him; but immediately made the necessary preparations for returning to finish his examination of it; and set off on that design with an increased party, and provisions for twenty-one days, on Monday the 29th.

Cæsar, being closely attended to, was at length apprehended and secured. This man was always reputed the hardest working convict in the country; his frame was muscular and well calculated for hard labour; but in his intellects he did not very widely differ from a brute; his appetite was ravenous, for he could in any one day devour the full ration for two days. To gratify this appetite he was compelled to steal from others, and all his thefts were directed to that purpose. He was such a wretch, and so indifferent about meeting death, that he declared while in confinement, that if he should be hanged, he would create a laugh before he was turned off, by playing
                                                                    off

off some trick upon the executioner. Holding up such a mere animal
as an example was not expected to have the proper or intended effect;
the governor therefore, with the humanity that was always conspicuous in his exercise of the authority vested in him, directed that he
should be sent to Garden Island, there to work in fetters; and in
addition to his ration of provisions he was to be supplied with vegetables from the garden.

The Sirius had, in the gale of wind which she met with off Tasman's
Head, sustained much more damage, and was, upon inspection, found
to have been weakened much more than was at first conjectured.
This was the more unfortunate, as, from the nature of our situation,
many important services were yet to be rendered by her to the colony.
It became, therefore, a matter of public concern to have her damages
repaired and the ship strengthened as expeditiously and as efficaciously
as our abilities would admit. A convenient retired cove on the north
shore being fixed on for the purpose of a careening cove, she dropped
down and took possession of it toward the latter end of the month.
She could have been refitted with much ease at Sydney; but there was
no doubt that the work necessary to be done to her would meet with
fewer interruptions, if the people who were engaged in it were removed from the connections which seamen generally form where
there are women of a certain character and description.

The gang under the direction of the overseer employed at the brick
fields had hitherto only made ten thousand bricks in a month. A kiln
was now constructed in which thirty thousand might be burnt off in
the same time, which number the overseer engaged to deliver.

The carpenter of the Supply, who had undertaken the construction
of the hoy, being obliged to proceed with that vessel on her going to
sea, the direction of the few people employed upon her was left with
the carpenter of the Sirius during his absence.

July 14.] The governor returned from his second visit to the river,
which he named the Hawkesbury, in honor of the noble lord at the
head of the committee of council of trade and plantations. He
traced the river to a considerable distance to the westward, and was
impeded in his further progress by a shallow which he met with a short
distance above the hill formerly seen, and then named by him Richmond

mond Hill, to the foot of which the course of the Hawkesbury conducted him and his party. They were deterred from remaining
any time in the narrow part of the river, as they perceived evident
traces of the freshes having risen to the height of from twenty to forty
feet above the level of the water. They represented the windings of
the river as beautiful and picturesque; and toward Richmond Hill
the face of the country appeared more level and open than in any
other part. The vast inundations which had left such tokens behind
them of the height to which they swell the river seemed rather unfavourable for the purpose of settling near the banks, which otherwise
would have been convenient and desirable, the advantages attending
the occupation of an allotment of land on the margin of a fresh-water
river being superior to those of any other situation. The soil on the
banks of the river was judged to be light; what it was further inland
could not be determined with any certainty, as the travellers did not
penetrate to any distance, except at Richmond Hill, where the soil
appeared to be less mixed with sand than that on the branches.

During the governor's absence the sail-maker of the Sirius had
strayed into the woods about the cove where she was repairing, and,
not knowing the country, wandered so far that he could not find his
way back to the ship. Fortunately for him, the governor, on his return from Broken Bay, met with him in the north arm of this harbour,
but so weakened by hunger and fatigue, as to have all the appearance
of intoxication when first discovered and spoken to, and in a situation
so remote from a probability of assistance, that perhaps a few days
more would have fixed the period of his existence.

On visiting the settlement at Rose Hill, the convicts were all found
residing in very good huts, apparently under proper regulations, and
encouraged to work in the gardens, which they had permission to cultivate during those hours which were not dedicated to public labour.
A barrack for the soldiers was erected in the small redoubt which had
been constructed, and in which also stood the provision store. Some
ground had been opened on the other side of the stream of water which
ran into the creek, where a small house had been built for the superintendant Dodd, under whose charge were to be placed a barn and
granaries, in which the produce of the ground he was then filling with

L   wheat

wheat and barley was to be depofited. The people of all defcriptions continued very healthy; and the falubrity of the climate rendered medicine of little ufe.

Notwithftanding little more than two years had elapfed fince our departure from England, feveral convicts about this time fignified that the refpective terms for which they had been tranfported had expired, and. claimed to be reftored to the privileges of free men. Unfortunately, by fome unaccountable overfight, the papers neceffary to afcertain thefe particulars had been left by the mafters of the tranfports with their owners in England, inftead of being brought out and depofited in the colony; and as, thus fituated, it was equally impoffible to admit or to deny the truth of their affertions, they were told to wait until accounts could be received from England; and in the mean time, by continuing to labour for the public, they would be entitled to fhare the public provifions in the ftore. This was by no means fatisfactory, as it appeared that they expected an affurance from the governor of receiving fome gratuity for employing their future time and labour for the benefit of the fettlement. One of thefe people having, in the prefence of his excellency, expreffed himfelf difrefpectfully of the lieutenant-governor, he was brought before a criminal court and tried for the fame, of which offence being found guilty, he was fentenced to receive fix hundred lafhes, and to wear irons for the fpace of fix months.

It muft be acknowledged, that thefe people were moft peculiarly and unpleafantly fituated. Confcious in their own minds that the fentence of the law had been fulfilled upon them, it muft have been truly diftreffing to their feelings to find that they could not be confidered in any other light, or received into any other fituation, than that in which alone they had been hitherto known in the fettlement. In the infancy of the colony, however, but little was to be gained by their being reftored to the rights and privileges of free people, as no one was in poffeffion of fuch abundance as to afford to fupport another independent of the public ftore. Every man, therefore, muft have wrought for his provifions; and if they had been gratified in their expectation of being paid for their labour, the price of provifions in this country would certainly have been found equal, if not fuperior,

to

to any value they could have set upon their time and labour for the public. As these considerations must have offered themselves to the notice of many good understandings which were among them, it was rather conjectured, that the dissatisfaction which evidently prevailed on this subject was set on foot and fomented by some evil-designing spirits and associates in former iniquities. The governor, however, terminated this business for the present, by directing the judge-advocate to take the affidavits of such persons as would make oath that they had served the term prescribed by the law, and by recommending them to work for the public until some information was received from government on that head.

The observatory which was erected on our first landing being found small and inconvenient, as well for the purpose of observing as for the residence of Lieutenant Dawes and the reception of the astronomical instruments, the stone-cutters began preparing stone to construct another, the materials for which were found in abundance upon the spot, the west point of the cove.

CHAP. VIII.

BARRACKS. — STOCK. — INTELLIGENCE FROM NORFOLK ISLAND. — POLICE ESTABLISHED AT THE PRINCIPAL SETTLEMENT. — A SUCCESSFUL HAUL OF FISH. — A SOLDIER TRIED FOR A RAPE. — PROVISIONS BEGIN TO FAIL. — NATIVES. — A LAUNCH COMPLETED. — RATE. — RATION REDUCED TO TWO-THIRDS. — SIRIUS RETURNS TO THE COVE. — ONE OF HER MATES LOST IN THE WOODS. — SUPPLY SAILS FOR NORFOLK ISLAND. — UTILITY OF THE NIGHT WATCH. — A FEMALE CONVICT EXECUTED FOR HOUSE-BREAKING. — TWO NATIVES TAKEN. — SERIOUS CHARGE AGAINST THE ASSISTANT COMMISSARY SATISFACTORILY CLEARED UP. — LIEUTENANT DAWES'S EXCURSION. — THE SUPPLY RETURNS. — TRANSACTIONS.

August.] OF the four barracks which were begun in March 1788, and at that time intended to be finished as such, two had been for some time occupied by the detachment, two companies residing in each; a

L 2   third

third was at the beginning of this month converted into a storehouse; and the wood-work of the fourth was taken down and applied to some other purpose; the labour and time required to finish it being deemed greater than the utility that would be derived from it as a barrack, the two that were already occupied conveniently and comfortably accommodating the detachment.

As every circumstance became of importance that might in its tendency forward or retard the day whereon the colony was to be pronounced independent of the mother-country for provisions, it was soon observed with concern, that hitherto by far a greater proportion of males than females had been produced by the animals we had brought for the purpose of breeding. This, in any other situation, might not have been so nicely remarked; but here, where a country was to be stocked, a litter of twelve pigs whereof three only were females became a subject of conversation and inquiry. Out of seven kids which had been produced in the last month, one only was a female; and many similar instances had before occurred, but no particular notice was attracted until their frequency rendered them remarkable. This circumstance excited an anxious care in every one for the preservation of such females as might be produced; and at the moment now spoken of no person entertained an idea of slaughtering one of that sort; indeed males were so abundant that fortunately there was no occasion.

On the 7th Lieutenant Ball returned from Norfolk Island, and from an unsuccessful cruise of nearly six weeks in search of the island and shoals for which he was directed to look. He sailed over the identical spot on which Mr. Shortland had fixed the latitudes and longitudes of his island and his shoal, without seeing either, and therefore concluded, that they had not been placed far enough to the northward. The error might have lain in copying the account from his log-book into his letter.

From Norfolk Island Lieutenant King wrote, that he had cleared seventeen acres of ground upon the public account, all of which were either sown or ready for sowing; that caterpillars had done much damage to some wheat which had just come up; and that he was erecting a storehouse capable of containing a large quantity of stores

and

and provisions, and had made a visible road from Sydney Bay to Cascade Bay. The pine trees, of the utility of which such sanguine hopes had been entertained, were found to be unfit for large masts or yards, being shakey or rotten at thirty or forty feet from the butt; the wood was so brittle that it would not make a good oar, and so porous that the water soaked through the planks of a boat which had been built of it. Mr. King also lamented their ignorance of the proper mode of preparing the flax plant, which rendered it useless to them. A single pod of cotton had been found on the island, and a tree had been discovered, the bark of which was strong, and of a texture like cotton. A species of bird also had been met with which burrowed in the ground, and had been seen in such numbers about the summit of Mount Pitt, the highest hill on the island, that they were contemplated as a resource in any future season of distress, should they be found to visit the island at stated periods, and to deposit their eggs on it. Mr. King spoke well of the general behaviour of the subjects of his little government since the detection of their late scheme to overturn it.

From the frequent commission of offences in this settlement and at Rose Hill, where scarcely a night passed but complaint was made on the following morning of a garden being robbed, or a house broken into, so favourable a report could not be given of the general conduct of the people. The frequency of these enormities had become so striking, that it appeared absolutely necessary to devise some plan which might put a stop to an evil that was every day increasing. The convicts who were employed in making bricks, living in huts by themselves on the spot where their work was performed, were suspected of being the perpetrators of most of the offences committed at Sydney; and orders had been given, forbidding, under pain of punishment, their being seen in town after sunset. These depredations continuing, however, a convict of the name of Harris presented to the judge-advocate a proposal for establishing a night-watch, to be selected from among the convicts, with authority to secure all persons of that description who should be found straggling from the huts at improper hours. This proposal being submitted to the governor, and the plan thoroughly digested and matured, the first attempt toward a police in this settle-

ment

14

ment commenced on Saturday the 8th of August. The following are
the heads of the plan :

The settlement was divided into four districts, over each of which
was placed a watch consisting of three persons, one principal and two
subordinate watchmen. These, being selected from among those convicts whose conduct and character had been unexceptionable since their
landing, were vested with authority to patrole at all hours in the night,
to visit such places as might be deemed requisite for the discovery of
any felony, trespass, or misdemeanor, and to secure for examination
all persons that might appear to be concerned therein ; for which
purpose they were directed to enter any suspected hut or dwelling
or to use any other means that might appear expedient. They
were required to detain and give information to the nearest guard-
house of any soldier or seaman who should be found straggling after
the taptoo had been beat. They were to use their utmost endeavours to trace out offenders on receiving accounts of any depredation ;
and in addition to their night duty, they were directed to take cognizance of such convicts as gamed, or sold or bartered their slops or provisions, and report them for punishment. A return of all occurrences
during the night was to be made to the judge-advocate ; and the military were required to furnish the watch with any assistance they might
be in need of, beyond what the civil power could give them. They
were provided each with a short staff, to distinguish them during the
night, and to denote their office in the colony ; and were instructed
not to receive any stipulated encouragement or reward from any individual for the conviction of offenders, but to expect that negligence
or misconduct in the execution of their trust would be punished with
the utmost rigour. It was to have been wished, that a watch established for the preservation of public and private property had been
formed of free people, and that necessity had not compelled us, in
selecting the first members of our little police, to appoint them from a
body of men in whose eyes, it could not be denied, the property of
individuals had never before been sacred. But there was not any choice.
The military had their line of duty marked out for them, and between
them and the convict there was no description of people from whom
overseers or watchmen could be provided. It might, however, be
                                                    supposed,

supposed, that among the convicts there must be many who would feel
a pride in being distinguished from their fellows, and a pride that
might give birth to a returning principle of honesty. It was hoped
that the convicts whom we had chosen were of this description; some
effort had become necessary to detect the various offenders who were
prowling about with security under cover of the night; and the convicts who had any property were themselves interested in defeating
such practices. They promised fidelity and diligence, from which the
scorn of their fellow-prisoners should not induce them to swerve, and
began with a confidence of success the duty which they had themselves offered to undertake.

The Sirius, on being closely inspected and surveyed by her own
carpenter and the carpenter of the Supply, was found to be so much
weakened, that the repairs which were requisite to put her in a state
fit to encounter the storms of this coast would require the labour of
four men for six months and twenty-four days, not including Sundays
in the calculation. This was unfortunate; the resources of a king's
yard were not to be found in the careening cove in Port Jackson;
people who looked forward beyond the event of the morrow began to
think that her services might be wanted before she could be in a condition to render them; and it was considered a matter of the utmost
moment, to bestow the labour that she required in as little time
and with as much skill as the circumstances of our situation would
admit.

12th.] Such attentions as were within our power were shewn to
the anniversary of his royal highness the Prince of Wales's birth-day;
and although the table of our festivity was not crowned with luxuries
or delicacies, yet the glass that was consecrated on that occasion to
his royal highness's name was in no part of the British dominions
accompanied with more sincere wishes for his happiness.

On the 20th, Daniel Gordon, a convict, was brought to trial for
stealing a quantity of provisions and clothes, the property of persons
employed by the lieutenant-governor at some ground which he had in
cultivation near the settlement. The prisoner appearing wild and in-
coherent on being brought before the court, the principal surgeon of
the settlement was directed to examine him, and giving it as his
                                                            opinion,

opinion, upon oath, that the man's pulse very strongly indicated either a delirium or intoxication, his trial was put off until the following morning, when, the same appearances of wildness continuing on him, witnesses were examined as to the tenor of his conduct during his being in confinement for the offence; and the court were of opinion from their testimony, " That the prisoner was not in a state of mind to " be put upon his trial." He was therefore placed under the care of the surgeon at the hospital, and the court broke up.

It was generally supposed, that a firm belief that his offence would be fixed upon him occasioned the derangement of intellect which appeared. He was a notorious offender, and had been once pardoned in this country under the gallows. Many of his fellow-prisoners gave him credit for the ability with which he had acted his part, and perhaps he deserved their applause; but disordered as he appeared before the court, their humanity would not suffer them to proceed against a wretch who either had not, or affected not to have, a sufficient sense of his situation.

Slops were served to the convicts during this month, and the detachment received the remainder of the shoes which they brought from England.

September.] In England some dependence had been placed on fish as a resource for the settlement, but sufficient for a general distribution had not hitherto been caught at any one time. On the 4th of this month the people belonging to the Supply had a very large haul; their seine was so full, that had they hauled it ashore it must have burst; the ropes of it were therefore made fast on shore, and the seine was suffered to lie until left dry by the tide. The fish were brought up to the settlement, and distributed among the military and convicts. A night or two after this, a fishing-boat caught about one hundred dozen of small fish; but this was precarious, and, happening after the provisions were served, no other advantage could be derived from the circumstance, than that of every man's having a fish meal.

On the 10th a criminal court of judicature was assembled for the trial of Henry Wright, a private soldier in the detachment, for a rape on a child of eight years of age; of which heinous offence being found guilty, he received sentence to die; but being recommended by the

court

court to the governor, his excellency was pleased to pardon him, on condition of his residing, during the term of his natural life, at Norfolk Island. This was an offence that did not seem to require an immediate example; the chastity of the female part of the settlement had never been so rigid, as to drive men to so desperate an act; and it was believed, that beside the wretch in question there was not in the colony a man of any description who would have attempted it.

On the 12th, the butter, which had hitherto been served at six ounces per week to each man in the settlement, being expended, the like quantity of sugar was directed to be issued in its stead. This was the first of the provisions brought from England which had wholly failed; and, fortunately, the failure was in an article which could be the best spared. It never had been very good, and was not, strictly speaking, a necessary of life.

A small boat belonging to a gentleman of the settlement, having been too deeply laden with cabbage-trees which had been collected in a bay down the harbour for the purpose of building, was overset on her return to the cove, by touching on a rock which lay off one of the points. There were three people in her, two of whom swam on shore; the third remained five hours on her keel, and was accidentally met with and picked up by the people of a fishing boat.

Captain Hunter, unwilling to lose any opportunity of rendering a service to the colony, while the repairs of his ship were going on, surveyed the two adjoining harbours of Broken Bay and Botany Bay; and correct charts were thus obtained of these two harbours, so admirably situated with relation to Port Jackson.

The natives, who had for some time past given very little interruption, toward the end of the month attacked Henry Hacking, one of the quarter-masters of the Sirius, who, being reckoned a good shot, was allowed to shoot for the officers and ship's company. His account was, that, being in the woods, a stone was thrown at him from one of two natives whom he perceived behind him, and that on looking about he found dispersed among the trees a number that could not be less than forty. Wishing to intimidate them, he several times only presented his piece toward them; but, finding that they followed him, he at last gave them the contents, which happened to be small shot for birds.

M

birds. Thefe he replaced with buckfhot, and got rid of his troublefome and defigning followers by difcharging his piece a fecond time.
They all made off; but fome of them ftumbling as they ran, he apprehended they had been wounded. This account met with more credit
than could ufually be allowed to fuch tales, as the perfon who gave it
was held in great eftimation by the officers of his fhip both as a man
and as a feaman.

Mr. Palmer, the purfer of the Sirius, having occafion to cut timber
in a cove down the harbour, was vifited by fome natives, who took an
opportunity of concealing two of his axes in the bufhes. On his
miffing the implements, the natives went off in fome confternation,
leaving two children behind them, whom Mr. Palmer detained, and
would have brought up to the fettlement, had not their friends ran-
fomed them with the property that had been ftolen.

At Rofe Hill, where the corn promifed well, an Emu had been
killed, which ftood feven feet high, was a female, and when opened
was found to contain exactly fifty eggs.

October.] The launch that was begun in May laft by the carpenter
of the Supply, being completed, was put into the water the 5th of
October. From the quantity of wood ufed in her conftruction fhe appeared to be a mere bed of timber, and, when launched, was named
by the convicts, with an happinefs that is fometimes vifible in the allu-
fions of the lower order of people, The Rofe Hill Packet *. She was
very foon employed in tranfporting provifions to Rofe Hill, and going
up with the tide of flood, at the top of high water, paffed very well
over the flats at the upper part of the harbour.

Our enemies the rats, who worked unfeen, and attacked us where
we were moft vulnerable, being again obferved in numbers about the
provifion ftore, the commiffary caufed the provifions to be moved out
of one ftore into another; for, alas! at this period they could be all
contained in one. Thefe pernicious vermin were found to be very
numerous, and the damage they had done much greater than the ftate
of our ftores would admit. Eight cafks of flour were at one time

---

* She was afterwards generally known by the name of The Lamp, a word more
briefly applying to her fize and conftruction.

found

found wholly deftroyed. From the ftore, fuch as efcaped the hunger of the different dogs that were turned loofe upon them flew to the gardens of individuals, where they rioted upon the Indian corn which was growing, and did confiderable mifchief.

The prefence of a captain being no longer deemed neceffary at Rofe Hill, the military guard there for the protection of the ftores was reduced to a fubaltern officer, and a proportionate number of privates. Mr. Dodd, who had for fome time been authorized by the governor to inflict corporal punifhment on the convicts for idlenefs, rioting, or other mifdemeanors, had obtained fuch an influence over them, that military coercion was not fo neceffary as when the fettlement was firft eftablifhed. Of this perfon, the officers who had been on duty at Rofe Hill from time to time gave the moft favourable reports, fpeaking of him as one in every refpect qualified to execute the truft which had been repofed in him by the governor.

During this month a gang of convicts were employed at Sydney in forming a convenient road from the hofpital to the magazine and obfervatory on the point; and a fmall hut, for the reception of a corporal's guard at the hofpital, was erected.

Of the few people who died in October, (one foldier, three women, and one child,) one was an unhappy woman who had been fent on board in a ftate of infanity, and who had remained in that condition until the day of her death; fhe and another of the three women died in child-bed; and the foldier was carried off by a diforder which he brought with him into the country. Thefe circumftances tended to eftablifh the good opinion which was at firft formed of the falubrity of the climate of New South Wales.

November.] This month opened with a ferious, but prudent and neceffary alteration in our provifions. The ration which had hitherto been iffued was, on the firft of the month, reduced to two thirds of every fpecies, fpirits excepted, which continued as ufual. This meafure was calculated to guard againft accidents; and the neceffity of it was obvious to every one, from the great uncertainty as to the time when a fupply might arrive from England, and from the loffes which had been and ftill were occafioned by rats in the provifion ftore. Two years provifions were landed with us in the colony: we had

M 2   been

been within two months of that time disembarked, and the public store had been aided only by a small surplus of the provisions which remained of what had been furnished by the contractor for the passage, and the supply of four months flour which had been received by the Sirius from the Cape of Good Hope. All this did not produce such an abundance as would justify any longer continuance of the full ration; and although it was reasonable to suppose, as we had not hitherto received any supplies, that ships would arrive before our present stock was exhausted; yet, if the period of distress should ever arrive, the consciousness that we had early foreseen and strove to guard against its arrival would certainly soften the bitterness of our reflections; and, guarding thus against the worst, that worst providentially might never happen. The governor, whose humanity was at all times conspicuous, directed that no alteration should be made in the ration to be issued to the women. They were already upon two thirds of the man's allowance; and many of them either had children who could very well have eaten their own and part of the mother's ration, or they had children at the breast; and although they did not labour, yet their appetites were never so delicate as to have found the full ration too much, had it been issued to them. The like reduction was enforced afloat as well as on shore, the ships' companies of the Sirius and Supply being put to two thirds of the allowance usually issued to the king's ships. This, as a deduction of the eighths allowed by custom to the purser was made from their ration, was somewhat less than what was to be issued in the settlement.

Thus opened the month of November in this settlement; where, though we had not the accompanying gloom and vapour of our own climate to render it terrific to our minds, yet we had that before us, in the midst of all our sunshine, which gave it the complexion of the true November so inimical to our countrymen.

It was soon observed, that of the provisions issued at this ration on the Saturday the major part of the convicts had none left on the Tuesday night; it was therefore ordered, that the provisions should be served in future on the Saturdays and Wednesdays. By these means, the days which would otherwise pass in hunger, or in thieving from the few who were more provident, would be divided, and the

14

people

people themfelves be more able to perform the labour which was required from them. Overfeers and married men were not included in this order.

On the 7th Captain Hunter brought the Sirius into the cove completely repaired. She had been ftrengthened with riders placed within board, her copper had been carefully examined, and fhe was now in every refpect fit for fea. Previous to her quitting the careening cove, Mr. Hill, one of the mafter's mates, having had fome bufinefs at Sydney, was landed on his return early in the morning on the north fhore, oppofite Sydney Cove, from whence the walk to the fhip was fhort; but he was never afterwards heard of. Parties were fent day after day in queft of him for feveral days. Guns were fired from the Sirius every four hours, night and day, but all to no effect. He had met with fome fatal accident, which deprived a wife of the pleafurable profpect of ever feeing him return to her and to his friends. He had once before miffed his way; and it was reported, when his lofs was confirmed, that he declared on the fatal morning, when ftepping out of the boat, that he expected to lofe himfelf again for a day or two. His conjecture was more than confirmed; he loft himfelf for ever, and thus added one to the number of thofe unfortunate perfons who had perifhed in the woods of this country.

On the 11th the Supply failed for Norfolk Ifland, having on board provifions and fix male and eight female convicts for that colony. She was to ftop at Lord Howe Ifland, to endeavour to procure turtle for this fettlement; a fupply of which, in its prefent fituation, would have been welcomed, not as a luxury, but as a neceffary of life.

The night-watch was found of infinite utility. The commiffion of crimes, fince their inftitution, had been evidently lefs frequent, and they were inftrumental in bringing forward for punifhment feveral offenders who would otherwise have efcaped. The fear and deteftation in which they were held by their fellow-prifoners was one proof of their affiduity in fearching for offences and in bringing them to light; and it poffibly might have been afferted with truth, that many ftreets in the metropolis of London were not fo well guarded and watched as the fmall, but rifing town of Sydney, in New South Wales.

By

By their activity, a woman (a female convict of the name of Ann Davis alias Judith Jones) was apprehended for breaking into the house of Robert Sidaway (a convict) in the day-time, and stealing several articles of wearing apparel thereout. The criminal court being assembled, she was tried and found guilty. On receiving sentence to die, she pleaded being quick with child; but twelve of the discreetest women among the convicts, all of whom had been mothers of children, being impanelled as a jury of matrons, they pronounced that she was not pregnant; on which she was executed the Monday following, acknowledging at that fatal moment which generally gives birth and utterance to truth, that she was about to suffer justly, and that an attempt which she made, when put on her defence, to criminate another person, (a woman whose character was so notorious that she hoped to establish her own credit and innocence upon her infamy,) as well as her plea of pregnancy, were advanced merely for the purpose of saving her life. She died generally reviled and unpitied by the people of her own description.

The summer was observed to be the chief season of fish. A fishing-boat belonging to the colony had so many fish in the seine, that had it not burst at the moment of landing, it was imagined that a sufficiency would have been taken to have served the settlement for a day; as it was, a very considerable quantity was brought in; and not long after a boat belonging to the Sirius caught seven-and-forty of the large fish which obtained among us the appellation of Light Horse Men, from the peculiar conformation of the bone of the head, which gave the fish the appearance of having on a light-horse-man's helmet.

The governor, after the death of the native who was carried off by the small-pox in May last, never had lost sight of a determination to procure another the first favourable opportunity. A boat had several times gone down the harbour for that purpose; but without succeeding, until the 25th of this month, when the first lieutenant of the Sirius, accompanied by the master, fortunately secured two natives, both men, and brought them up to the settlement without any accident. Being well known to the children, through their means every assurance was given them of their perfect safety in our possession.

They

They were taken up to the governor's, the place intended for their future refidence, where fuch reftraint was laid upon their perfons as was judged requifite for their fecurity.

The affurances of fafety which were given them, and the fteps which were taken to keep them in a ftate of fecurity, were not perfectly fatisfactory to the elder of the two; and he fecretly determined to take the firft opportunity which offered of giving his attendants no further trouble upon his account. The negligence of his keeper very foon gave him the opportunity he defired; and he made his efcape, taking with him into the woods the fetter which had been rivetted to his ancle, and which every one, who knew the circumftance, imagined he would never be able to remove. His companion would have joined him in his flight, but fear detained him a few minutes too late, and he was feized while tremblingly alive to the joyful profpect of efcaping.

During the month of November a brick houfe was begun on the eaft fide of the cove for the judge-advocate. The huts which were got up on our firft landing were flight and temporary; every fhower of rain wafhed a portion of the clay from between the interftices of the cabbage-tree of which they were conftructed; their covering was never tight; their fize was neceffarily fmall and inconvenient; and although we had not hitherto been fo fortunate as to difcover lime-ftone any where near the fettlement, yet to occupy a brick houfe put together with mortar formed of the clay of the country, and covered with tiles, became, in point of comparative comfort and convenience, an object of fome importance.

December.] Among the various bufinefs which came before the magiftrates at their weekly meetings, was one which occupied much of their time and attention. The convicts who were employed about the provifion ftore informed the commiffary, by letter, that from certain circumftances, they had reafon to accufe Mr. Zachariah Clark, his affiftant, of embezzling the public provifions. A complaint of fuch a nature, as well on account of its importance to the fettlement, as of its confequence to the perfon accufed, called for an immediate enquiry; and the judge-advocate and Captain Hunter loft no time in bringing forward the neceffary inveftigation. The convicts charged Mr. Clark with having made at different times, and applied to his own ufe, a
                                                                        confiderable

considerable over-draught of every species of provisions, and of the liquor which was in store. A dread of these circumstances being one day discovered by others, when the blame of concealment might involve them in a suspicion of participation, induced them to step forward with the charge. The suspicious appearances, however, were accounted for by Mr. Clark much to the satisfaction of the magistrates under whose consideration they came. He stated, that expecting to be employed in this country, he had brought out with him large quantities of provisions, wine, rum, draught and bottled porter, all of which he generally kept at the store; that when parties have applied to him for provisions or spirits at an hour when the store was shut, he had frequently supplied them from his own case, or stock which he had for present use in his tent or in his house, and afterwards repaid himself from the store; and that being ill with the scurvy for several months after his arrival, he did not use any salt provisions, which gave him a considerable credit for such articles at the store: from all which circumstances the convicts who accused him might, as they were unknown to them, be induced to imagine that he was taking up more than his ration from time to time.

With Mr. Clark's ample and public acquittal from this accusation, a commendation equally public was given to the convicts, who, noticing the apparent over-draught of spirits and provisions, and ignorant at the same time of the causes which occasioned it, had taken measures to have it explained.

From the peculiarity of our situation, there was a sort of sacredness about our store; and its preservation pure and undefiled was deemed as necessary as the chastity of Cæsar's wife. With us, it would not bear even suspicion.

In the course of this month the harvest was got in; the ground in cultivation at Rose Hill produced upwards of two hundred bushels of wheat, about thirty-five bushels of barley, and a small quantity of oats and Indian corn; all of which was intended to be reserved for seed. At Sydney, the spot of ground called the Governor's Farm had been sown only with barley, and produced about twenty-five bushels.

A knowledge of the interior parts of this extensive country was anxiously desired by every one; but the difficulty of attaining it, and
the

the various employments in which we had all been neceffarily engaged, had hitherto prevented any material refearches being made. The governor had penetrated to the weftward as far as Richmond Hill, perhaps between fifty and fixty miles inland ; but beyond that diftance all was a blank. Early in this month Lieutenant Dawes with a fmall party, taking with them juft as much provifions as they could conveniently carry, fet off on an attempt to reach the weftern mountains by and from the banks of the frefh water river, firft feen, fome time fince, by Captain Tench, and fuppofed to be a branch of the Hawkefbury. From this excurfion he returned on the ninth day, without accomplifhing his defign, meeting with nothing, after quitting the river, but ravines that were nearly inacceffible. He had, notwithftanding the danger and difficulty of getting on through fuch a country, reached within eleven miles of the mountains, by computation. During his toilfome march he met with nothing very remarkable, except the impreffions of the cloven feet of an animal differing from other cloven feet by the great width of the divifion in each. He was not fortunate enough to fee the animal that had made them.

In this journey Lieutenant Dawes's line of march, unfortunately and unpleafantly for him, happened to lie, nearly from his fetting out, acrofs a line of high and fteep rocky precipices, which required much caution in defcending, as well as labour in afcending. Perhaps an open country, which might have led him readily and conveniently to the point he propofed to attain, was lying at no great diftance from him either to his right or left. To feek for that, however, might have required more time than his ftock of provifions would have admitted ; and he was compelled to return through the fame unprofitable country which he had paffed.

On the 21ft, between ten and eleven o'clock at night, the Supply returned from Norfolk Ifland, having been abfent fix weeks within a day. From thence Lieutenant King wrote that he expected his harveft would produce from four to fix months flour for all his inhabitants, exclufive of a referve of double feed for twenty acres of ground. Befide this promifing appearance, he had ten acres in cultivation with Indian corn, which looked very well. His gardens had fuffered much by the grub-worm and from a want of rain, of which they had had

N   fcarcely

scarcely any since the 23d of September last. The ground which was cleared for the crown amounted to about twenty-eight acres, and he was busied in preparations for building a redoubt on an eminence named by him Mount George.

The Supply, in her visit at Lord Howe Island, turned eighteen turtle; several of which unluckily dying before she reached Norfolk Island, she could leave only four there, and but three survived the short voyage thence to this place.

Several thefts having been lately committed by the convicts, and the offenders discovered by the vigilance of the members of our new police, several of them were tried before the criminal court of judicature. Cæsar the black, whose situation on Garden Island had been some time back rendered more eligible, by being permitted to work without irons, found means to make his escape, with a mind insensible alike to kindness and to punishment, taking with him a canoe which lay there for the convenience of the other people employed on the island, together with a week's provisions belonging to them; and in a visit which he made them a few nights after in his canoe, he took off an iron pot, a musket, and some ammunition.

The working convicts at Sydney had lately been principally employed in constructing two convenient kitchens and ovens for the use of the detachment, adjoining to the quarters; building a house for the judge-advocate; forming roads either in or leading to the town; and removing the provisions from the old thatched storehouse to that in the marine quarters, which, by being covered in with tiles, was not so liable to an accident by fire, nor likely to prove so great an harbour for rats, to guard against whom it had become necessary to take as many precautions as against any other enemy. They, however, in defiance of every care which was taken to shut them out, when the provisions were removed, found means, by working under ground, to get in; and as it was now a matter of much moment to preserve every ounce of provisions that belonged to us, they were all taken out, and re-stowed with an attention suitable to their important value.

At Rose Hill, where as yet there was not any night-watch established, petty thefts and depredations were frequently committed, particularly on the wheat as it ripened. The bakehouse also was robbed

of

of a quantity of flour by a perſon unknown. Theſe offences were generally attributed to the reduction which had taken place in the ration of proviſions; and every one dreaded how much the commiſſion of them might be increaſed, if accident or delay ſhould render a ſtill greater reduction neceſſary.

Mr. Dodd, the ſuperintendant at that ſettlement, a few days before Chriſtmas, cut and ſent down a cabbage which weighed ſix-and-twenty pounds. The other vegetable productions of his garden, which was by no means a rich mould, were plentiful and luxuriant.

Some people who had been out with a gun from Roſe Hill brought in with them, on their return, a tinder-box, to which chance conducted them in a thick bruſh diſtinguiſhed by the name of the New Bruſh, about ſix miles from the ſettlement. This article was known to have belonged to the two unfortunate ſoldiers who had been unaccounted for ſince laſt April, and who, in great probability, found there a miſerable period to their exiſtence. They alſo picked up in the ſame bruſh a piece of linen, ſaid to have formed part of a petticoat which belonged to Anne Smith, a female convict who abſconded a few days after our landing in the country. This might have been carried thither and dropped by ſome natives in their way through the bruſh; but it gave a ſtrong colour to the ſuppoſition of her having likewiſe periſhed, by ſome means or other, in the woods.

CHAP. IX.

A CONVICT MADE A FREE SETTLER.—A PLEASING DELUSION.—EXTRAOR-
DINARY SUPPLY OF FISH.—CÆZAR'S NARRATIVE.—ANOTHER CONVICT
WOUNDED BY THE NATIVES.—THE SUPPLY ARRIVES FROM NORFOLK
ISLAND.—A LARGE NUMBER OF SETTLERS SENT THITHER ON BOARD THE
SIRIUS AND SUPPLY.—HEAVY RAINS.—SCARCITY OF PROVISIONS INCREAS-
ING IN AN ALARMING DEGREE.—LIEUTENANT MAXWELL'S INSANITY.—
NEWS BROUGHT OF THE LOSS OF THE SIRIUS.—ALLOWANCE OF PROVISIONS
STILL FURTHER REDUCED.—THE SUPPLY SENT TO BATAVIA FOR RELIEF.
ROBBERIES FREQUENT AND DARING.—AN OLD MAN DIES OF HUNGER.—
ROSE HILL.—SALT AND FISHING-LINES MADE.—THE NATIVE ESCAPES.—
TRANSACTIONS.

January, 1790.] EARLY in the new year the Supply sailed again
for Norfolk Island with twenty-two male and two female convicts, and
one child; Lieutenant King having in his last letters intimated, that
he could very well find employment for a greater number of people
than he then had under his orders. With those convicts and some
stores she sailed on the 7th, and on her return was to touch at Lord
Howe Island to procure turtle.

Of the convicts the period of whose sentences of transportation had
expired, and of whom mention was made in the transactions of July
last, one, who signified a wish of becoming a settler, had been sent up
to Rose Hill by the governor; where his excellency, having only waited
to learn with certainty that he had become a free man before he gave
him a grant of land, caused two acres of ground to be cleared of the
timber which stood on them, and a small hut to be built for him.
This man had been bred to the business of a farmer, and during his
residence in this country had shewn a strong inclination to be industrious, and to return to honest habits and pursuits. Rewarding him,
therefore, was but holding out encouragement to such good dispositions. The governor had, however, another object in view, beside a
wish to hold him up as a deserving character: he was desirous of
trying,

trying, by his means, in what time an induſtrious active man, with
certain aſſiſtance, would be enabled to ſupport himſelf in this country
as a ſettler; and for that purpoſe, in addition to what he cauſed to be
done for him at firſt, he furniſhed him with the tools and implements
of huſbandry neceſſary for cultivating his ground, with a proportion of
grain to ſow it, and a ſmall quantity of live ſtock to begin with. He
took poſſeſſion of his ground the 21ſt of November 1789, and under
ſome diſadvantages. An opinion had prevailed, and had been pretty
generally diſſeminated, that a man could not live in this country; and
in addition to this diſcouragement, although he ſtill received a ration
from the public ſtore, yet it was not a ration that bore any proportion
to the labour which his ſituation required from him. The man himſelf, however, reſolved to be induſtrious, and to ſurmount as well as
he was able whatever difficulties might lie in his way.

The flour which had been brought from England did not ſerve
much beyond the beginning of this month, and that imported from
the Cape now ſupplied its place. Every one began to look forward
with much anxiety to the arrival of ſupplies from England; and as it
was reaſonable to conclude that every day might bring them on the
coaſt, Captain Hunter, accompanied by Mr. Worgan, the ſurgeon of
the Sirius, and Mr. White, with ſix or eight ſeamen, having choſen
a ſpot proper for their purpoſe, erected a flagſtaff on the ſouth head of
this harbour, whence, on the appearance of a ſhip in the offing, a
ſignal might be made, as well to convey the wiſhed-for information
to the ſettlement, as to ſerve as a mark for the ſtranger. An hut
was built for their accommodation, and this little eſtabliſhment was
of ſuch importance, that our walks were daily directed to a ſpot
whence it could be ſeen; thus fondly indulging the deluſion, that
the very circumſtance of looking out for a ſail would bring one into
view.

A ſufficient quantity of fiſh having been taken one night in this
mouth, to admit the ſerving of two pounds to each man, woman,
and child belonging to the detachment, the governor directed, that a
boat ſhould in future be employed three times in the week to fiſh for
the public; and that the whole quantity caught ſhould be iſſued at the
above rate to every perſon in turn. This allowance was in addition

to

to the ration of provisions; and was received with much satisfaction several times during the month.

Cæsar, after his escape from and subsequent visit at Garden Island, found his way up to Rose Hill, whence he was brought on the 30th, very much wounded by some natives whom he had met with in the woods. Being fearful of severe punishment for some of his late offences, he reported, on being brought in, that he had fallen in with our cattle which had been so long lost; that they were increased by two calves; that they seemed to be under the care of eight or ten natives, who attended them closely while they grazed; and that, on his attempting to drive the cattle before him, he was wounded by another party of the natives. The circumstance of his being wounded was the only part of his story that met with any credit, and that could not well be contradicted, as he had several spear wounds about him in different parts of his body; but every thing else was looked upon as a fabrication (and that not well contrived) to avert the lash which he knew hung over him. He was well known to have as small a share of veracity as of honesty. His wounds however requiring care and rest, he was secured, and placed under the surgeon's care at the hospital.

Information was also received at this time from Rose Hill, that a convict who had been employed to strike the sting ray, with another, on the flats, having gone on shore, engaged in some quarrel with the natives, who took all his clothes from him, severely wounded, and would inevitably have killed him, but for the humane, friendly, and disinterested interference of one of their own women, who happened to be present. This accident, and many others of the same nature, could not have happened, had the orders which he had received, not to land upon any account, been attended to.

The bricklayers, having finished the judge-advocate's house, were employed in building a dispensary on the west side contiguous to the hospital, the medicines and chirurgical instruments being much exposed to damps in the place where they had hitherto been necessarily kept.

Garden robberies were frequent, notwithstanding the utmost care and vigilance were exerted to prevent them. A rainy tempestuous
night

night always afforded a cloak for the thief, and was generally followed in the morning by some one complaining of his or her garden having been stripped of all its produce.

February.]   The first signal from the flagstaff at the south head was displayed on the 10th of February; and though every imagination first turned toward the expected stranger, yet happening about the time at which the Supply was expected from Norfolk Island, conjecture soon fixed on the right object; and the temporary suspence was put an end to, by word being brought up to the settlement, that the Supply, unable to get into Port Jackson, had borne up for Botany Bay, in which harbour she anchored in the dusk of the evening. The next morning the letters which she had brought were received. Lieutenant King wrote, that his people continued healthy, and his settlement went on well. His wheat had returned twenty fold, notwithstanding he had had much dry weather. He had relinquished his intention of throwing up a redoubt on Mount George; but, instead of that work, had employed his people in constructing a stoccade of piles round his house, inclosing an oblong square of one hundred feet by one hundred and forty, within which he purposed erecting storehouses, and a barrack for the military. He stated, that the convicts under his orders had in general very good gardens, and that many of them would have a very large produce of Indian corn.

The Supply having in her way to Norfolk Island touched at Lord Howe Island, Lieutenant Ball left the gunner and a small party to turn turtle, but they met with no success; so that no dependance was to be placed on that island for any material relief. The gunner examined the island, and found fresh water in cavities, but not in any current.

The Supply could not get round from Botany Bay until the 12th, when she came to anchor in the cove, whence she had been absent just five weeks.

Lieutenant King having constantly written in high terms of the richness of the soil of Norfolk Island, the governor, on comparing the situation of the convicts there and in this settlement, where their gardens had not that fertility to boast of, and where the ration from the store was with too many hastily devoured, and with most derived but

an

an uncertain and fcanty aid from any other fource, determined, and about the middle of the month announced his determination, to detach thither a large body of convicts, male and female, together with two companies of the marines. Some immediate advantages were expected to be derived from this meafure; the garden ground that would be left by thofe who embarked would be poffeffed by thofe who remained, while the former would inftantly on their arrival at Norfolk Ifland participate in the produce of luxuriant gardens, in a more conftant fupply of fifh, and in the affiftance that was occafionally obtained from the birds which fettled on Mount Pitt.

At the fame time that this intention was made public, the day of their departure was fixed. The whole were to embark on board the Sirius and the Supply in the beginning of the following month, and were, if no fhip arrived from England to prevent them, to fail on the 5th. Should, unfortunately, the neceffity of adopting the meafure then exift, the Sirius was to proceed to China directly from Norfolk Ifland to procure a fupply of provifions for the colony. China was chofen, under an idea that falt provifions were to be obtained there, and that it was preferable to fending to any of the iflands in thofe feas, or to the Cape of Good Hope at this feafon of the year, when the Sirius and her crew would have had to encounter the cold and boifte-rous weather of a winter's paffage thither.

As the numbers on Norfolk Ifland would be confiderably increafed by the arrival of this detachment from hence, the governor judged the prefence of Major Rofs neceffary there, as lieutenant-governor of the territory. Lieutenant King was to be recalled and return to this fet-tlement.

Preparations were immediately fet on foot for the embarkation of the marines and other perfons who were to quit this colony. It had been a part of the firft determinations on this bufinefs, that the Sirius fhould, as I have mentioned, proceed directly from Norfolk Ifland on her voyage to China; but Captain Hunter having reprefented the abfo-lute neceffity he fhould be under of touching fomewhere to wood and water, owing to the numbers he fhould have on board, that idea was given up, and Captain Hunter was directed to return with the Sirius

to

to this port for the above purposes of wooding and watering. An additional reason offered itself to influence this determination; it was hoped, that before she could return, the arrival of the expected supplies would have rendered the voyage altogether unnecessary; and it was but reasonable to suppose that this would happen. The governor had, in all his dispatches, uniformly declared the strong necessity there was of having at least two years provisions in store for some time to come; and as this information, together with an exact account of the situation of the colony, had been transmitted by seven different conveyances, if only one had arrived safe, it could not reasonably be doubted that supplies would be immediately dispatched. From the length of time too which had elapsed since the departure of the last ships * that sailed from hence direct for England, (full fifteen months,) it was as reasonable to suppose that they might arrive within the time that the Sirius would be absent.

The month passed in the arrangements and preparations requisite on this occasion, to which the weather was extremely unfavourable, heavy rains, with gales of wind, prevailing nearly the whole time. The rain came down in torrents, filling up every trench and cavity which had been dug about the settlement, and causing much damage to the miserable mud tenements which were occupied by the convicts. By these rains, a pit which had been dug for the purpose of procuring clay to plaister the walls of a hut, was filled with water; and a boy upwards of two years of age, belonging to one of the female convicts, falling into it, was drowned. The surgeons tried, but without success, to save his life, using the methods practised by the Humane Society. Yet bad as the weather was, several gardens were robbed, and, as at this time they abounded with melons and pumpkins, they became the objects of depredation in common with other productions of the garden.

A brick building, fifty-nine feet in front, designed for a guard-house, of which the foundation had been laid a few days before the heavy rains commenced, suffered much by their continuance. The situation

---

* The Golden Grove and the Fishburn sailed from this port the 19th of November 1788, intending to make their passage round by Cape Horn, to which the season was most favourable.

of

of this building was on the east side of the cove, at the upper part, contiguous to the bridge over the run of water, and convenient for detaching affistance to any part of the place where it might be requifite.

On the 1st of March a reduction in the allowance of fpirits took place; the half pint *per diem*, which had hitherto been iffued to each man who was entitled to receive it, was to be difcontinued, and only the half of that allowance ferved. Thus was the gradual decreafe in our ftores followed by a diminution of our daily comforts and neceffaries.

One immediate confequence, and that an evil one, was the effect of the intended embarkation for Norfolk Ifland. It being found that great quantities of ftock were killed, an order was immediately given to prevent the further deftruction of an article fo effential in our prefent fituation, until fome neceffary regulations could be publifhed; but the officers and people who were about to embark were not included in this prohibition. The mention of future regulations in this order inftantly begat an opinion among the convicts, that on the departure of the fhips all the live ftock in the colony would be called in, or that the owners would be deprived of the benefits which might refult from the poffeffion of it. Under colour, therefore, of its belonging to thofe who were exempted in the late order, nearly all the ftock in the fettlement was in the courfe of a few nights deftroyed; a wound being thereby given to the independence of the colony that could not eafily be falved, and whofe injurious effects time and much attention alone could remove.

The expected fupplies not having arrived, on the 3d, the two companies of marines with their officers and the colours of the corps embarked on board the Sirius and the Supply. With them alfo embarked the lieutenant-governor, and Mr. Confiden the fenior affiftant furgeon of the fettlement. On the day following, one hundred and fixteen male and fixty-eight female convicts, with twenty-feven children, were put on board; among the male convicts the governor had fent the troublefome and incorrigible Cæfar, on whom he had beftowed a pardon. With thefe alfo was fent, though of a very different defcription, a perfon whofe exemplary conduct had raifed him from the fituation

14   of

of a convict to the privileges of a free man.   John Irving had since our landing in the country been employed as an assistant at the hospital. He was bred a surgeon, and in no instance whatever, since the commission of the offence for which he was transported, had he given cause of complaint.   He was now sent to Norfolk Island, to act as an assistant to the medical gentlemen there.

On the 5th the Sirius and the Supply left the cove, but did not get to sea until the following day, when at the close of the evening they were scarcely to be discerned from the south head.   At the little post at this place Captain Hunter left the gunner, a midshipman, and six of the Sirius's people.   Mr. Maxwell, one of her lieutenants, having been for a considerable time past in a melancholy and declining way, and his disorder pronounced by the surgeons to be insanity, he was discharged from the ship, and had taken up his residence on shore under the care of the surgeon, with proper people who were left from the ship to attend him.   This was the second officer whose situation in the Sirius it became necessary to have filled.   Lieutenant King, the commandant of Norfolk Island, had for some time been discharged from the ship's books; and Mr. Newton Fowell, a young gentleman of the Sirius's quarter-deck, being deemed well qualified, was appointed by the governor (as the naval commanding officer) to succeed him.   To fill the vacancy occasioned by Mr. Maxwell's unfortunate state of health, Mr. Henry Waterhouse, a young gentleman of promising abilities, was taken from the quarter-deck.   Both these appointments were to wait the confirmation of the lords commissioners of the admiralty.

Immediately after the departure of these ships, the governor directed his attention to the regulation of the people who were left at Sydney, and to the preservation of the stock in the colony.   For these purposes, he himself visited the different huts and gardens whose tenants had just quitted them, distributing them to such convicts as were either in miserable hovels, or without any shelter at all.   It was true, that by this arrangement the idle found themselves provided for by the labour of many who had been industrious; but they were at the same time assured, that unless they kept in good cultivation the gardens which they were allowed to possess, they would be turned out from the

O 2   comforts

comforts of a good hut, to live under a rock or a tree. That they might have time for this purpose, the afternoon of Wednesday and the whole of Saturday in each week were given to them. Much room was made every where by the numbers who had embarked (in all two hundred and eighty-one persons); the military quarters had a deserted aspect; and the whole settlement appeared as if famine had already thinned it of half its numbers. The little society that was in the place was broken up, and every man seemed left to brood in solitary silence over the dreary prospect before him.

With respect to the stock, his excellency directed, that no hogs under three months old should be killed, nor were any to be butchered without information being first given at head-quarters.

Those who bred poultry were left at liberty to dispose of it in such manner as they thought proper; and the commissary was directed to purchase for the use of the hospital such live stock as the owners were desirous of selling, complying with the above regulations, and receiving one shilling a pound as the price.

Some provisions which yet remained in the old large thatched store were removed for greater security into the store in the marine quarters. It was strongly suspected, that an attempt had been made to obtain some part of these provisions in the night; and some convicts were examined before the judge-advocate on suspicion of having taken some flour from the store; but nothing appeared that could materially affect them. The provisions, when all collected together under one roof and into one view, afforded but a melancholy reflection,—it was well that we had even them.

On the 27th of the month, the long-expected signal not having been displayed, it became necessary to put the colony upon a still shorter ration of provisions. It was a painful but a necessary duty. The governor directed that the provisions should in future be served daily; for which purpose the store was to be opened from one to three in the afternoon. The ration for the week was to consist of

> Four pounds of flour,
> Two pounds and a half of pork, and
> One pound and a half of rice;

and

and these were to be issued to every person in the settlement without distinction; but as the public labour must naturally be affected by this reduction, the working hours were in future to be from sun-rise, with a small interval for breakfast, until one o'clock: the afternoons were to be allowed the people to receive their provisions and work in their gardens. These alterations in the ration and in the hours of labour, however, were not to commence until the 1st of the following month.

At Rose Hill similar regulations were made by the governor. The garden ground was enlarged; those who were in bad huts were placed in better; and every thing was said that could stimulate them to be industrious. This, with a few exceptions, appeared to be the principal labour both there and at Sydney; and the night-watch were called upon by the common interest to be more than ever active and sedulous in their efforts to protect public and private property; for robberies of gardens and houses were daily and nightly committed. Damage was also received from the little stock which remained alive; the owners, not having wherewith to feed them, were obliged to turn them loose to browse among the grass and shrubs, or turn up the ground for the fern-root; and as they wandered without any one to prevent their doing mischief, they but too often found an easy passage over fences and through barriers which were now grown weak and perishing. It was however ordered, that the stock should be kept up during the night, and every damage that could be proved to have been received during that time was to be made good by the owners of the stock that might be caught trespassing; or the animals themselves were to be forfeited.

The carpenters were employed in preparing a roof for a new store-house, those which were first erected being now decaying, and having been always insecure. It was never expected to get up a building of one hundred feet in front, which this was designed to be, upon so reduced a ration as the present; but while the people did labour, it was proper to turn that little labour to the public account.

The working gangs being now so much reduced by the late embarkation, the hoy was employed in bringing the timber necessary for this building from the coves where it was cut down and deposited for that purpose. This vessel, when unemployed for public services, was given to the officers, and by them sent down the harbour to procure cabbage-tree for their stock, in the preservation and maintenance of which every one felt an immediate and anxious concern.

The weather had been very wet during this month; torrents of rain again laid every place under water; many little habitations, which had withstood the inundations of the last month, now suffered considerably; several chimnies fell in; but this was owing, perhaps, as much to their being built by job or task-work, (which the workmen hurried over in general to get a day or two to themselves,) as to the heavy rains.

April.] The reduced ration and the change in the working hours commenced, as was directed, on the 1st of this month; much time was not consumed at the store, and the people went away to dress the scanty allowance which they had received.

Attention to our religious duties was never omitted. Divine service was performed in one of our emptied storehouses on the morning of the next day, being Good-Friday; and the convicts were recommended to employ the remainder of it in their gardens. But, notwithstanding the evident necessity that existed for every man's endeavouring to assist himself, very few were observed to be so profitably occupied.

As every saving that could be made in the article of provisions was of consequence in the present situation of the stores, it was directed on the 3d, that such fish as should in future be taken by the public boats should be issued at the store, in the proportion of ten pounds of fish to two pounds and a half of pork; and one hundred and fifty pounds of fish, which had been brought up before the issuing of provisions commenced on that day, were served out agreeable to that order.

Mr. Maxwell, whose disorder at times admitted of his going out alone, was fortunately brought up from the lower part of the harbour, where he had passed nearly two days, without sustenance, in rowing from one side to the other, in a small boat by himself. He was noticed by a serjeant who had been fishing, and who observed him rowing under the dangerous rocks of the middle-head, where he must soon have been dashed to pieces, but for his fortunate interposition. After this escape he was more narrowly watched.

                                                                While

While occupied in liftening to the tale of his diftreffes, the Supply returned from Norfolk Ifland, with an account that was of itfelf almoft fufficient to have deranged the ftrongeft intellect among us. A load of accumulated evils feemed burfting at once upon our heads. The fhips that were expected with fupplies were ftill to be anxioufly looked for; and the Sirius, which was to have gone in queft of relief to our diftreffes, was loft upon the reef at Norfolk Ifland, on the 19th of laft month. This was a blow which, as it was unexpected, fell with increafed weight, and on every one the whole weight feemed to have fallen.

This untoward accident happened in the following manner: " Captain Hunter was extremely fortunate in having a fhort paffage hence " to Norfolk Ifland, arriving there in feven days after he failed. The " foldiers, and a confiderable part of the convicts, were immediately " landed in Cafcade Bay, which happened at the time to be the leeward " fide of the ifland. Bad weather immediately enfued, and continuing " for feveral days, the provifions could not be landed, fo high was the " furf occafioned by it. This delay, together with a knowledge that " the provifions on the ifland were not adequate to the additional " numbers that were now to be victualled, caufed him to be particu- " larly anxious to get the provifions on fhore. The bad weather had " feparated the Sirius from the Supply; but meeting with a favourable " flant of wind on the 19th, Captain Hunter gained the ifland from " which he had been driven, and flood for Sydney Bay, at the fouth " end of it, where he found the Supply; and it being fignified by " fignal from the fhore, (where they could form the beft judgment,) " that the landing might be effected with any boat, he brought to in " the windward part of the bay, with the fhip's head off the fhore, " got out the boats, and loaded them with provifions. When the " boats had put off from the fhip, it being perceived that fhe fettled " very much to leeward, the tacks were got on board, and every fail " fet that was poffible to get her free from the fhore. Notwithftand- " ing which, fhe could not weather the reef off the fouth-weft end of " the bay, the wind having at that time very unfavourably fhifted two " points. The fhip was then thrown in flays, which fhe miffed, " being with great difficulty wore clear of the breakers, and brought
" to

" to the wind on the other tack, when every fail was again set.
" Finding that she still drifted faft upon the shore, another attempt
" was made to flay her; but being out of trim, it did not succeed.
" All the sheets and hallyards were then ordered to be let fly, and
" an anchor to be cut away; but before it reached the ground, she
" struck with violence on the reef, very soon bulged, and was irreco-
" verably loft. Her officers and people were all faved, having been
" dragged on shore, through the furf, on a grating."

This day, which untoward circumstances had rendered fo gloomy to
us, was 'remarkably fine, and at the unfortunate moment of this calamity there was very little wind. On the next or fecond day after, per-
million was given to two convicts (one of whom, James Brannegan,
was an overfeer) to get off to the ship, and endeavour to bring on
shore what live hogs they might be able to fave; but with all that
lamentable want of refolution and confideration which is characteriftic
of the lower order of people when temptations are placed before them,
they both got intoxicated with the liquor which had efcaped the plunder of the feamen, and fet the ship on fire in two places. A light on
board the ship being obferved from the shore, feveral shot were fired at
it, but the wretches would neither put it out, nor come on shore;
when a young man of the name of Afcott, a convict, with great in-
trepidity went off through the furf, extinguished the fire, and forced
them out of the ship.

The lieutenant-governor, immediately after the lofs of the Sirius,
called a council of all the naval and marine officers in the fettlement,
when it was unanimoufly determined that martial law should be pro-
claimed; that all private flock, poultry excepted, should be confidered
as the property of the flate; that juftice should be adminiftered by a
court-martial to be compofed of feven officers, five of whom were to
concur in a fentence of death; and that there should be two locks upon
the door of the public flore, whereof one key was to be in the keeping
of a perfon to be appointed by Captain Hunter in behalf of the feamen; the other to be kept by a perfon to be appointed in behalf of the
military. The day following, the troops, feamen, and convicts, being
affembled, thefe refolutions were publicly read, and the whole confirmed

firmed their engagement of abiding by them by passing under the king's colour, which was displayed on the occasion.

In the Supply arrived the late commandant of Norfolk Island, two lieutenants, four petty officers, twenty-four seamen, and two marines, lately belonging to the Sirius. These officers spoke in high terms of the activity and conduct of Mr. Keltie the master, Mr. Brooks the boatswain, and Mr. Donovan a midshipman of the Sirius, who ventured off to the ship in one of the island boats through a very dangerous surf, and brought on shore the end of the hawser, to which was slung the grating that saved the lives of the officers and people. They likewise somewhat blunted the edge of this calamity, by assurances that it was highly probable, from the favourable appearance of the weather when the Supply left Norfolk Island, that all or at least the greatest part of the provisions would be landed from the Sirius.

The general melancholy which prevailed in this settlement when the above unwelcome intelligence was made public need not be described; and when the Supply came to an anchor in the cove every one looked up to her as to their only remaining hope.

In this exigency the governor thought it necessary to assemble all the officers of the settlement, civil and military, to determine on what measures were necessary to be adopted. At this meeting, when the situation of the colony was thoroughly weighed and placed in every point of view, it was determined to reduce still lower what was already too low; the ration was to be no more than two pounds and a half of flour—two pounds of pork—one pint of pease, and one pound of rice, for each person for seven days. This allowance was to be issued to all descriptions of people in the colony, children under eighteen months excepted, who were to have only one pound of salt meat. Every exertion was to be made here, and at Botany Bay, in fishing for the general benefit. All private boats were to be surrendered to the public use; every effort was to be put in practice to prevent the robbing of gardens; and, as one step toward this, all suspicious characters were to be secured and locked up during the night. People were to be employed to kill, for the public, the animals that the country afforded; and every step was to be taken that could save a pound of the salt provisions in store. It was proposed to take all the hogs in the settlement as public property; but as it was absolutely necessary to keep some breeding sows, and the flock being small and very poor, that idea was abandoned.

In pursuance of these resolutions, the few convicts who had been employed to shoot for individuals were given up for the public benefit; and a fishery was established at Botany Bay, under the inspection of one of the midshipmen of the Sirius. But this plan, not being found to answer, was soon relinquished. The quantity of fish that was from time to time taken was very inconsiderable, and the labour of transporting it by land from thence was greater than the advantage which was expected to be derived from it. The boats were therefore recalled, and employed with rather more success at Sydney.

It was well known, that the integrity of the people employed in fishing could not be depended upon; the officers of the settlement therefore voluntarily took upon themselves the unpleasant task of superintending them; and it became a general duty, which every one chearfully performed. The fishing-boat never went out without an officer, either by night or by day.

On the 7th, about four hundred weight of fish being brought up, it was issued agreeable to the order; and could the like quantity have been brought in daily, some saving might have been made at the store, which would have repaid the labour that was employed to obtain it. But the quantity taken during this month, after the 7th, was not often much more than equal to supplying the people employed in the boats with one pound of fish per man, which was allowed them in addition to their ration. The small boats, the property of individuals, were therefore returned to their owners, and the people who had been employed in them, together with the seamen of the Sirius now here, were placed in the large boats belonging to the settlement.

Neither was much advantage obtained by employing people to shoot for the public. At the end of the month only three small kangooroos had been brought in. The convicts who were employed on this service, three in number, were considered as good marksmen, and were allowed a ration of flour instead of their salt provisions, the better to enable them to sustain the labour and fatigue of traversing the woods of this country.

The

The neceffity of procuring relief became every day more preffing. The voyage of the Sirius to China was at an end; and nothing had yet arrived from England, though hourly expected. It was the natural and general opinion, that our prefent fituation was to be attributed to accident rather than to procraftination. It was more probable, that the veffels which had been difpatched by the Britifh government had met with fome diftrefs, that had either compelled them to return or had wholly prevented them from any further profecution of the voyage, than that any delay fhould have taken place in their departure. The governor, therefore, determined on fending the Supply armed tender to Batavia; and, as her commander was moft zealoufly active in his preparations for the voyage, fhe was foon ready for fea. Her tonnage, however, was trifling when compared with our neceffities. Lieutenant Ball was, therefore, directed to procure a fupply of eight months provifions for himfelf, and to hire a veffel and purchafe 200,000 pounds of flour, 80,000 pounds of beef, 60,000 pounds of pork, and 70,000 pounds of rice; together with fome neceffaries for the hofpital, fuch as fugar, fago, hogs lard, vinegar, and dongaree. The expectation of this relief was indeed diftant, but yet it was more to be depended upon than that which might be coming from England. A given time was fixed for the return of the Supply; but it was impoffible to fay when a veffel might arrive from Europe. Whatever might be our diftrefs for provifions, it would be fome alleviation to look on to a certain fixed period when it might be expected to be removed. Lieutenant Ball's paffage lay through the regions of fine weather, and the hope of every one was fixed upon the little veffel that was to convey him; yet it was painful to contemplate our very exiftence as depending upon her fafety; to confider that a rough fea, a hidden rock, or the violence of elemental ftrife, might in one fatal moment precipitate us, with the little bark that had all our hopes on board, to the loweft abyfs of mifery. In the well-known ability and undoubted exertions of her commander however, under God, all placed their dependance; and from that principle, when fhe failed, inftead of predicting mifchance, we all, with one wifh for her fafe return, fixed and anticipated the period at which it might reafonably be expected.

F 2　　　　　　　　　　　　　　　　　　She

She failed on Saturday the 17th of April, having on board Lieutenant King, the late commandant of Norfolk Island, who was charged with the governor's dispatches for the secretary of state, and Mr. Andrew Miller, the late commissary, whose ill state of health obliging him to resign that employment, the governor permitted him to return to England, and had appointed Mr. John Palmer, the purser of the Sirius, to supply his place.

Lieutenant Newton Fowell, of the Sirius, was, together with the gunner of that ship, also embarked. The Supply was to touch at Norfolk Island, if practicable, and take on board Lieutenant Bradley of the Sirius, who, from his knowledge of the coast, was chosen by the governor to proceed to Batavia, and was to return to this port in whatever vessel might be freighted by Lieutenant Ball; Mr. Fowell and the gunner were to be left at the island.

Mr. Palmer received his appointment from his excellency on the 12th of this month, on which day the following was the state of the provisions in the public store; viz.

Pork	-	23,851	} pounds,	{ Which was		
Beef	-	1,280		to serve	26th Aug.—4 months 14 days.	
Rice	-	24,455 pounds,	}	at the		
Pease	-	17 bushels,	}	ration	13th Sept.—5 months 1 day.	
Flour	-	56,884	} pounds,	then issued		
Biscuit	-	1,934		until	19th Dec.—8 months 7 days.	

The duration of the Supply's voyage was generally expected to be six months; a period at which, if no relief arrived in the mean time from England, we should be found without salt provisions, rice, and pease.

In the above statement three hundred bushels of wheat, which had been produced at Rose Hill, were not included, being reserved for seed.

The governor, from a motive that did him immortal honor, in this season of general distress, gave up three hundred weight of flour which was his excellency's private property, declaring that he wished not to see any thing more at his table than the ration which was received in common from the public store, without any distinction of persons;

4

and

and to this resolution he rigidly adhered, wishing that if a convict complained, he might see that want was not unfelt even at Government house.

On the 20th of the month, the following was the ration issued from the public store to each man for seven days, or to seven people for one day,

Flour,	- - -	2½ pounds.
Rice,	- - -	2 pounds.
Pork,	- - -	2 pounds.

The pease were all expended. Was this a ration for a labouring man? The two pounds of pork, when boiled, from the length of time it had been in store, shrunk away to nothing; and when divided among seven people for their day's sustenance, barely afforded three or four morsels to each.

The inevitable consequences of this scarcity of provisions ensued; labour stood nearly suspended for want of energy to proceed; and the countenances of the people plainly bespoke the hardships they underwent. The convicts, however, were employed for the public in the forenoons; and such labour was obtained from them as their situation would allow. The guard-house on the east side was finished and taken possession of during the month.

There being many among the convicts who availed themselves of this peculiar situation to commit thefts, it became necessary to punish with severity all who were fully convicted before the court of criminal jurisdiction. One convict was executed for breaking into a house, and several others were sentenced to severe corporal punishments. Garden robberies were the principal offences committed. These people had been assembled by the governor, and informed that very severe punishment would follow the conviction of persons guilty of robbing gardens, as a necessary step toward preventing the continuance of such an evil; and he strongly inculcated the absolute necessity that existed for every man to cultivate his own garden, instead of robbing that of another. To the few who, from never having been industrious, had not any ground sown or planted with vegetables, he allotted a small but sufficient spot for their use, and encouraged them in their labour by his presence and directions; but they preferred any thing to honest industry.

industry. These people, though the major part of them were, during the night, locked up in the building lately occupied as a guard-house, were ever on the watch to commit depredations on the unwary during the hours in which they were at large, and never suffered an opportunity to escape them. A female convict, who came down from Rose Hill, was robbed of her week's provisions; and as it was impossible to replace them from the public store, she was left to subsist on what she could obtain from the bounty (never more truly laudable than at this distressing juncture) of others who commiserated her situation.

One male convict was executed; one female convict and one child died. The female convict occasioned her own death, by overloading her stomach with flour and greens, of which she made a mess during the day, and ate heartily; but, not being satisfied, she rose in the night and finished it. This was one of the evil effects of the reduced ration.

May.] The expedient of shooting for the public not being found to answer the expectations which had been formed of it, sixty pounds of pork only having been saved, the game-killers were called in, and the general exertion was directed to the business of fishing. The seine and the hooks and lines were employed, and with various success; the best of which afforded but a very trifling relief.

As the Sirius was fated not to return to perform her intended voyage to India, the biscuit which had been baked for that purpose was issued, in lieu of flour, that article being served again when the biscuit was expended; and it lasted only through seven days.

It was naturally expected, that the miserable allowance which was issued would affect the healths of the labouring convicts. A circumstance occurred on the 12th of this month, which seemed to favor this idea: an elderly man dropped down at the store, whither he had repaired with others to receive his day's subsistence. Fainting with hunger, and unable through age to hold up any longer, he was carried to the hospital, where he died the next morning. On being opened, his stomach was found quite empty. It appeared, that not having any utensil of his own wherein to cook his provisions, nor share in any, he was frequently compelled, short as his allowance for the day was, to give a part of it to any one who would supply him with a vessel to dress his

his victuals; and at those times when he did not choose to afford this deduction, he was accustomed to eat his rice and other provisions undressed, which brought on indigestion, and at length killed him.

It might have been supposed, that the severity of the punishments which had been ordered by the criminal court on offenders convicted of robbing gardens would have deterred others from committing that offence; but while there was a vegetable to steal, there were those who would steal it, wholly regardless as to the injustice done to the person they robbed, and of the consequences that might ensue to themselves. For this sort of robbery the criminal court was twice assembled in the present month. The clergyman had taken a convict in his garden in the act of stealing potatoes. Example was necessary, and the court that tried him, finding that the severity of former courts did not prevent the commission of the same offence, instead of the great weight of corporal punishment which had marked their former sentences, directed this prisoner to receive three hundred lashes, his ration of flour to be stopped for six months, and himself to be chained for that time to two public delinquents who had been detected in the fact of robbing the governor's garden, and who had been ordered by the justices to work for a certain time in irons.

This sentence was carried into execution; but the governor remitted, after some days trial, that part of it which respected the prisoner's ration of flour, without which he could not long have existed.

The governor's garden had been the object of frequent depredation; scarcely a night passed that it was not robbed, notwithstanding that many received vegetables from it by his excellency's order. Two convicts had been taken up, who confessed that within the space of a month they had robbed it seven or eight times, and that they had killed a hog belonging to an officer. These were the people who were ordered by the justices to work in irons. A soldier, a man of infamous character, had been detected robbing the garden while centinel in the neighbourhood of it, and, being tried by a court-martial for quitting his post, was sentenced and received five hundred lashes. Yet all this was not sufficient; on the evening of the 26th, a seaman belonging to the Sirius got into the governor's garden, and was fired

at

at by a watchman who had been stationed there for some nights past, and wounded, as it afterwards appeared, but so slightly as not to prevent his effecting his escape; leaving, however, a bag behind him, filled with vegetables. On close examination it was fixed upon him, and, being brought before a criminal court, he was sentenced to receive five hundred lashes; but at the same time was recommended to the governor's clemency, on account of a good character which had been given him in court. The governor, as it was his garden that was robbed, attended to the recommendation, remitting four out of the five hundred lashes which had been ordered him *. Being, after this, villain enough to accuse some of his shipmates of crimes which he acknowledged existed only in his own malicious mind, he received, by order of the justices, a further punishment of fifty lashes.

So great was either the villany of the people, or the necessities of the times, that a prisoner lying at the hospital under sentence of corporal punishment, (having received a part of it, five hundred lashes,) contrived to get his irons off from one leg, and in that situation was caught robbing a farm. On being brought in, he received another portion of his punishment.

Among other thefts committed in this season of general distress, was one by a convict employed in the fishing-boat, who found means to secrete several pounds of fish in a bag, which he meant to secure in addition to the allowance which was to be made him for having been out on that duty. To deter others from committing the like offence, which might, by repetition, amount to a serious evil, he was ordered to receive one hundred lashes.

At Rose Hill the convicts conducted themselves with much greater propriety; not a theft nor any act of ill behaviour having been for some time past heard of among them †.

At that settlement a kangooroo had been killed of one hundred and eighty pounds weight; and the people reported that they were much

* Sixty pounds of flour, which had been offered as a reward for bringing to justice a garden-thief, were paid to the watchman who fired at him.

† They had vegetables in great abundance.

molested

molested by the native dogs, which had been seen together in great numbers, and, coming by night about the settlement, had killed some hogs which were not housed.

The colony had hitherto been supplied with salt from the public stores, a quantity being always shaken off from the salt provisions, and reserved for use by the store-keepers; but the daily consumption of salt provisions was now become so inconsiderable, and they had been so long in store, that little or none of that article was to be procured. Two large iron boilers were therefore erected at the east point of the cove; some people were employed to boil the salt water, and the salt which was produced by this very simple process was issued to the convicts.

Our fishing tackle began now, with our other necessaries, to decrease. To remedy this inconvenience, we were driven by necessity to avail ourselves of some knowledge which we had gained from the natives; and one of the convicts (a rope-maker) was employed to spin lines from the bark of a tree which they used for the same purpose.

The native who had been taken in November last convinced us how far before every other consideration he deemed the possession of his liberty, by very artfully effecting his escape from the governor's house, where he had been treated with every indulgence and had enjoyed every comfort which it was in his excellency's power to give him. He managed his escape so ingeniously, that it was not suspected until he had completed it, and all search was rendered fruitless. The boy and the girl appeared to remain perfectly contented among us, and declared that they knew their countryman would never return.

During this month the bricklayer's gang and some carpenters were sent down to the Look-out, to erect two huts for the midshipmen and seamen of the Sirius who were stationed there, where the stone-mason's gang were employed quarrying stone for two chimnies.

The greatest quantity of fish caught at any one time in this month was two hundred pounds. Once the seine was full; but through either the wilfulness or the ignorance of the people employed to land it, the greatest part of its contents escaped. Upwards of two thousand pounds were taken in the course of the month, which produced a

Q   saving

saving of five hundred pounds of pork at the store, the allowance of thirty-one men for four weeks.

Very little labour could be enforced from people who had nothing to eat. Nevertheless, as it was necessary to think of some preparations for the next season, the convicts were employed in getting the ground ready both at Sydney and at Rose Hill for the reception of wheat and barley. The quantity of either article, however, to be now sown, fell far short of what our necessities required.

CHAP. X.

THE LADY JULIANA TRANSPORT ARRIVES FROM ENGLAND.—THE GUARDIAN.
—HIS MAJESTY'S BIRTH-DAY.—THANKSGIVING FOR HIS MAJESTY'S RECO-
VERY.—THE JUSTINIAN STORESHIP ARRIVES.—FULL RATION ORDERED.—
THREE TRANSPORTS ARRIVE.—HORRID STATE OF THE CONVICTS ON
BOARD.—SICK LANDED.—INSTANCE OF SAGACITY IN A DOG.—A CONVICT
DROWNED.—MORTALITY AND NUMBER OF SICK ON THE 13TH.—CONVICTS
SENT TO ROSE HILL.—A TOWN MARKED OUT THERE.—WORKS IN HAND
AT SYDNEY.—INSTRUCTIONS RESPECTING GRANTS OF LAND.—MR. FER-
GUSSON DROWNED.—CONVICTS' CLAIMS ON THE MASTER OF THE NEPTUNE.
—TRANSACTIONS.—CRIMINAL COURT.—WHALE.

June.] THE first and second days of this month were exceedingly unfavourable to our situation; heavy rain and blowing weather obstructed labour and prevented fishing. But it was decreed that on the 3d we should experience sensations to which we had been strangers ever since our departure from England. About half past three in the afternoon of this day, to the inexpressible satisfaction of every heart in the settlement, the long-looked-for signal for a ship was made at the South Head. Every countenance was instantly cheered, and wore the lively expressions of eagerness, joy, and anxiety; the whole settlement was in motion and confusion. Notwithstanding it blew very strong at the time, the governor's secretary, accompanied by Captain Tench and Mr.

Mr. White, immediately went off, and at some risk (for a heavy sea was running in the harbour's mouth) reached the ship for which the signal had been made just in time to give directions which placed her in safety in Spring Cove. She proved to be the Lady Juliana transport from London, last from Plymouth; from which latter place we learned, with no small degree of wonder and mortification, that she sailed on the 29th day of last July (full ten months ago) with two hundred and twenty-two female convicts on board.

We had long conjectured, that the non-arrival of supplies must be owing either to accident or delays in the voyage, and not to any backwardness on the part of government in sending them out. We now found that our disappointment was to be ascribed to both misfortune and delay. The Lady Juliana, we have seen, sailed in July last, and in the month of September following his majesty's ship Guardian, of forty-four guns, commanded by Lieutenant Edward Riou, sailed from England, having on board, with what was in the Lady Juliana, two years provisions, viz. 295,344 pounds of flour, 149,856 pounds of beef, and 303,632 pounds of pork, for the settlement; a supply of clothing for the marines serving on shore, and for those belonging to the Sirius and Supply; together with a large quantity of sails and cordage for those ships and for the uses of the colony; sixteen chests of medicines; fifteen casks of wine; a quantity of blankets and bedding for the hospital; and a large supply of unmade clothing for the convicts; with an ample assortment of tools and implements of agriculture.

At the Cape of Good Hope Lieutenant Riou took on board a quantity of stock for the settlement, and completed a garden which had been prepared under the immediate direction of Sir Joseph Banks, and in which there were near one hundred and fifty of the finest fruit trees, several of them bearing fruit.

There was scarcely an officer in the colony that had not his share of private property embarked on board of this richly freighted ship; their respective friends having procured permission from government for that purpose.

But it was as painful then to learn, as it will ever be to recollect, that on the 23d day of December preceding, the Guardian struck

Q 2   against

against an island of ice in latitude 45° 54′ South, and longitude 41° 30′ East, whereby she received so much injury, that Lieutenant Riou was compelled, in order to save her from instantly sinking, to throw overboard the greatest part of her valuable cargo both on the public and private account. The stock was all killed, (seven horses, sixteen cows, two bulls, a number of sheep, goats, and two deer,) the garden destroyed, and the ship herself saved only by the interposition of Providence, and the admirable conduct of the commander.

The Guardian was a fast-sailing ship, and would probably have arrived in the latter end of January or the beginning of February last. At that period the large quantity of live stock in the colony was daily increasing; the people required for labour were, comparatively with their present state, strong and healthy; the necessity of dividing the convicts, and sending the Sirius to Norfolk Island, would not have existed; the ration of provisions, instead of the diminutions which had been necessarily directed, would have been increased to the full allowance; and the tillage of the ground consequently proceeded in with that spirit which must be exerted to the utmost before the settlement could render itself independent of the mother country for subsistence.

But to what a distance was that period now thrown by this unfortunate accident, and by the delay which took place in the voyage of the Lady Juliana! Government had placed a naval officer in this transport, Lieutenant Thomas Edgar *, for the purpose of seeing justice done to the convicts as to their provisions, cleanliness, &c. and to guard against any unnecessary delays on the voyage. Being directed to follow the route of the Sirius and her convoy, he called at Teneriffe and St. Iago, stayed seven weeks at Rio de Janeiro, and one month at the Cape of Good Hope; completing his circuitous voyage of ten months duration by arriving here on the 3d day of June 1790.

On Lieutenant Edgar's arrival at the Cape he found the Guardian lying there, Lieutenant Riou having just safely regained that port, from which he had sailed but a short time, with every fair prospect of speedily and happily executing the orders with which he was entrusted, and of conveying to this colony the assistance of which it stood so much

* He had sailed with the late Captain Cook.

in

in need. Unhappily for us, she was now lying a wreck, with difficulty and at an immenfe expence preferved from finking at her anchors.

Befide the common fhare which we all bore in this calamity, we had to lament that the efforts of our feveral friends, in amply fupplying the wants that they concluded muft have been occafioned by an abfence of three years, were all rendered ineffectual, the private articles having been among the firft things that were thrown overboard to lighten the fhip*.

Government had fent out in the Guardian twenty-five male convicts, who were either farmers or artificers, together with feven perfons engaged to ferve as fuperintendants of convicts, for three years from their landing, at falaries of forty pounds per annum each. Of thefe, two, who were profeffed gardeners, were fuppofed to be drowned, having left the fhip foon after fhe ftruck, with feveral other perfons in boats, and not been heard of when the Lady Juliana left the Cape. The fuperintendants who remained came on in the tranfport; but the convicts, of whofe conduct Lieutenant Riou fpoke in the higheft terms, were detained at the Cape.

A clergyman alfo was on board the Guardian, the Rev. Mr. Crowther, who had been appointed, at a falary of eight fhillings per diem, to divide the religious duties of the fettlement with Mr. Johnfon. This gentleman left the fhip with the mafter and purfer in the long-boat, taking provifions and water with them; and of five boats which were launched on the fame perilous enterprife, this was the only one that conducted her paffengers into any fafety. They were fortunately, after many days failing, picked up by a French fhip, which took them into the Cape, and thence to Europe.

One-third of the ftores and provifions intended for the colony were put on board the tranfport, the remaining two-thirds were on board the Guardian; none of which it was fuppofed would ever reach the fettlement, the fmall quantity excepted (feventy-five barrels of flour) which was put on board the tranfport at the Cape. The Dutch at that place were profiting by our misfortune, their warehoufes being let out

* The private property of the officers was all ftowed, as the beft and fafeft place in the fhip, in the gun-room. Some officers were great lofers.

at

at an immense expence to receive such of the provisions and stores as remained on board the Guardian when she got in.

In addition to the above distressing circumstances, we learned that one thousand convicts of both sexes were to sail at the latter end of the last year, and that a corps of foot was raising for the service of this country under the command of a major-commandant, Francis Grose esq. from the 29th foot, of which regiment he was major. The transports which sailed hence in May, July, and November 1788 (the Friendship excepted) arrived in England within a very short time of each other; and their arrival relieved the public from anxiety upon our account.

The joy that was diffused by the arrival of the transports was considerably checked by the variety of unpleasant and unwelcome intelligence which she brought. We learned that our beloved Sovereign had been attacked and for some months afflicted with a dangerous and alarming illness, though now happily recovered. Our distance from his person had not lessened our attachment, and the day following the receipt of this information being the anniversary of his Majesty's birth, it was kept with every mark of distinction that was in our power. The governor pardoned all offenders who were under confinement, or under sentence of corporal punishment; the ration was increased for that day, that every one might rejoice; at the governor's table, where all the officers of the settlement and garrison were met, many prosperous and happy years were fervently wished to be added to his Majesty's life; and Wednesday the 9th was appointed for a public thanksgiving on occasion of his recovery.

The Lady Juliana was, by strong westerly winds and bad weather, prevented from reaching the cove until the 6th, when, the weather moderating, she was towed up to the settlement. The convicts on board her appeared to have been well treated during their long passage, and preparations for landing them were immediately made; but, in the distressed situation of the colony, it was not a little mortifying to find on board the first ship that arrived, a cargo so unnecessary and unprofitable as two hundred and twenty-two females, instead of a cargo of provisions; the supply of provisions on board her was so inconsiderable as to permit only an addition of one pound and a half of flour

being

being made to the weekly ration. Had the Guardian arrived, perhaps
we should never again have been in want.

On the 9th, being the day appointed for returning thanks to Al-
mighty God for his Majesty's happy restoration to health, the attendance on divine service was very full. A sermon on the occasion was
preached by the Rev. Mr. Johnson, who took his text from the book
of Proverbs, " By me kings reign." The officers were afterwards
entertained at the governor's, when an address on the occasion of the
meeting was resolved to be sent to his Majesty.

When the women were landed on the 11th, many of them appeared to be loaded with the infirmities incident to old age, and to be
very improper subjects for any of the purposes of an infant colony.
Instead of being capable of labour, they seemed to require attendance
themselves, and were never likely to be any other than a burden to
the settlement, which must sensibly feel the hardship of having to support by the labour of those who could toil, and who at the best were
but few, a description of people utterly incapable of using any exertion
toward their own maintenance.

When the women were disembarked, and the provisions and stores
landed, it was found that twenty casks of flour (from the unfitness of
the ship to perform such a voyage, being old and far from tight) were
totally destroyed. This was a serious loss to us, when only four
pounds of flour constituted the allowance of that article for one man
for seven days.

From this situation of distress, however, we were in a short time
afterwards effectually relieved, and the colony might be pronounced
to be restored, by the arrival (on the 20th) of the Justinian storeship,
Mr. Benjamin Maitland master, from England, after a short passage
of only five months. Mr. Maitland, on the 2d of this month, the
day preceding the arrival of the Lady Juliana, was off the entrance of
this harbour, and would certainly have been found by that ship at
anchor within the heads, had he not, by a sudden change of the wind,
aided by a current, been driven as far to the northward as Black Head,
in latitude 32° S. where he was very nearly lost in an heavy gale of
wind; but which he providentially rode out, having been obliged to
come to an anchor, though close in with some dangerous rocks. The
wind

wind was dead on the shore, and the rocks so close when he anchored, that the rebound of the wave prevented him from riding any considerable strain on his cable. Had that failed him, we should never have seen the Justinian or her valuable cargo, which was found to consist of stores and provisions, trusted, it was true, to one ship; but as she had happily arrived in safety, and was full, we all rejoiced that we had not to wait for the arrival of a second before the colony could be restored to its former plenty.

We now learned that three transports might be hourly expected, having on board the thousand convicts of whose destination we had received some information by the Lady Juliana, together with detachments of the corps raised for the service of this country. The remainder of this corps (which was intended to consist of three hundred men) were to come out in the Gorgon man of war, of forty-four guns. This ship was also to bring out Major Grose, who had been appointed lieutenant-governor of the territory in the room of Major Ross, which officer, together with the marines under his command, were intended to return to England in that ship.

Of the change which had been effected in the system of government in France we now first received information, and we heard with pleasure that it was not likely to interrupt the tranquillity of our own happy nation—happy in a constitution which might well excite the admiration and become the model of other states not so free.

The Justinian had sailed on the 17th of last January from Falmouth, and touched only at St. Iago, avoiding, as she had not any convicts on board, the circuitous passage by the Rio de Janeiro and the Cape of Good Hope.

On the day following her arrival, every thing seemed getting into its former train; the full ration was ordered to be issued; instead of daily, it was to be served weekly as formerly; and the drum for labour was to beat as usual in the afternoons at one o'clock. How general was the wish, that no future necessity might ever occasion another deduction in the ration, or an alteration in the labour of the people!

That Norfolk Island, whose situation at this time every one was fearful might call loudly for relief, should as quickly as possible reap

her

her share of the benefit introduced among us by their arrivals, it was
intended to send the Lady Juliana thither; and as she required some
repairs, without which she could not proceed to sea, some carpenters
from the shore were sent on board her, and employed to sheath her
bends, which were extremely defective.

A shop was opened on shore by the master of this ship, at the hut
lately occupied as a bakehouse for the Supply, for the sale of some
articles of grocery, glass, millinery, perfumery, and stationary; but
the risk of bringing them out having been most injudiciously estimated too highly, as was evident from the increase on the first cost,
which could not be disguised, they did not go off so quickly as the
owners supposed they would.

A report having been circulated soon after the establishing of this
settlement, that a considerable sum of money had been subscribed in
England, to be expended in articles for the benefit of the convicts who
embarked for this country, which articles had been entrusted to the
Rev. Mr. Johnson, to be disposed of according to the intention of the
subscribers after our arrival, Mr. Johnson wrote to his friends in
England to confute this report; and by accounts lately received, it
appeared that no such public collection had ever been made; at
Mr. Johnson's request, therefore, the governor published a contradiction of the above report in the general orders of the settlement.
The convicts had hitherto imagined that they had a right to the articles which had from time to time been distributed among them; but
Mr. Johnson now thought it necessary that they should know it was to
his bounty they were indebted for them, and that consequently the
partakers of it were to be of his own selection.

The female convicts who had lately arrived attending at divine
service on the first Sunday after their landing, Mr. Johnson, with much
propriety, in his discourse, touched upon their situation, and described
it so forcibly as to draw tears from many who were the least hardened
among them.

Early in the morning of the 23d, one of the men at the Look-out
discerned a sail to the northward, but, the weather coming on thick,
soon lost sight of it. The bad weather continuing, it was not seen again
until the 25th, when word was brought up to the settlement, that a

R   large

large ship, apparently under jury-masts, was seen in the offing; and on the following day the Surprise transport, Nicholas Anstis master, (late chief mate of the Lady Penrhyn,) anchored in the cove from England, having on board one captain, one lieutenant, one surgeon's mate, one serjeant, one corporal, one drummer, and twenty-three privates of the New South Wales corps; together with two hundred and eighteen male convicts. She sailed on the 19th of January from Portsmouth in company with two other transports, with whom she parted between the Cape of Good Hope and this place.

We had the mortification to learn, that the prisoners in this ship were very unhealthy, upwards of one hundred being now in the sick list on board. They had been very sickly also during the passage, and had buried forty-two of these unfortunate people. A portable hospital had fortunately been received by the Justinian, and there now appeared but too great a probability that we should soon have patients enough to fill it; for the signal was flying at the south head for the other transports, and we were led to expect them in as unhealthy a state as that which had just arrived.

On the evening of Monday the 28th, the Neptune and Scarborough transports anchored off Garden Island, and were warped into the cove the following morning.

We were not mistaken in our expectations of the state in which they might arrive. By noon the following day, two hundred sick had been landed from the different transports. The west side afforded a scene truly distressing and miserable; upwards of thirty tents were pitched in front of the hospital, the portable one not being yet put up; all of which, as well as the hospital and the adjacent huts, were filled with people, many of whom were labouring under the complicated diseases of scurvy and the dysentery, and others in the last stage of either of those terrible disorders, or yielding to the attacks of an infectious fever.

The appearance of those who did not require medical assistance was lean and emaciated. Several of these miserable people died in the boats as they were rowing on shore, or on the wharf as they were lifting out of the boats; both the living and the dead exhibiting more horrid spectacles than had ever been witnessed in this country. All this was to be attributed to confinement, and that of the worst species, confine-

ment

ment in a small space and in irons, not put on singly, but many of them chained together. On board the Scarborough a plan had been formed to take the ship, which would certainly have been attempted, but for a discovery which was fortunately made by one of the convicts (Samuel Burt) who had too much principle left to enter into it. This necessarily, *on board that ship*, occasioned much future circumspection; but Captain Marshall's humanity considerably lessened the severity which the insurgents might naturally have expected. On board the other ships, the masters, who had the entire direction of the prisoners, never suffered them to be at large on deck, and but few at a time were permitted there. This consequently gave birth to many diseases. It was said, that on board the Neptune several had died in irons; and what added to the horror of such a circumstance was, that their deaths were concealed, for the purpose of sharing their allowance of provisions, until chance, and the offensiveness of a corpse, directed the surgeon, or some one who had authority in the ship, to the spot where it lay.

A contract had been entered into by government with Messrs. Calvert, Camden, and King, merchants of London, for the transporting of one thousand convicts, and government engaged to pay 17l. 7s. 6d. per head for every convict they embarked. This sum being as well for their provisions as for their transportation, no interest for their preservation was created in the owners, and the dead were more profitable (if profit alone was consulted by them, and the credit of their house was not at stake) than the living.

The following accounts of the numbers who died on board each ship were given in by the masters:

	Men.	Women.	Children.
On board the Lady Juliana	0	5	2
the Surprise	42	0	0
the Scarborough	68	0	0
the Neptune	151	11	2
Total	261	16	4

All possible expedition was used to get the sick on shore; for even while they remained on board many died. The bodies were taken over to the north shore, and there interred.

R 2   Parties

Parties were immediately sent into the woods to collect the acid berry of the country, which for its extreme acetosity was deemed by the surgeons a most powerful antiscorbutic. Among other regulations, orders were given for baking a certain quantity of flour into pound loaves, to be distributed daily among the sick, as it was not in their power to prepare it themselves. Wine and other necessaries being given judiciously among those whose situations required such comforts, many of the wretches had recourse to stratagem to obtain more than their share by presenting themselves, under different names and appearances, to those who had the delivery of them, or by exciting the compassion of those who could order them.

Blankets were immediately sent to the hospital in sufficient numbers to make every patient comfortable; notwithstanding which, they watched the moment when any one died to strip him of his covering, (although dying themselves,) and could only be prevented by the utmost vigilance from exercising such inhumanity in every instance.

The detachment from the New South Wales corps, consisting of one captain, three subalterns, and a proportionate number of non-commissioned officers and privates, was immediately disembarked, and room being made in the marine barracks, they took possession of the quarters allotted for them.

Lieutenant Shapcote, the naval agent on board of the Neptune, died between the Cape of Good Hope and this place. A son of this gentleman arrived in the Justinian, to which ship he belonged, and received the first account of his father's death, on going aboard the Neptune to congratulate him on his arrival.

An instance of sagacity in a dog occurred on the arrival of the Scarborough, too remarkable to pass unnoticed; Mr. Marshall, the master of the ship, on quitting Port Jackson in May 1788, left a Newfoundland dog with Mr. Clark, (the agent on the part of the contractor, who remained in the colony,) which he had brought from England. On the return of his old master, Hector swam off to the ship, and getting on board, recognised him, and manifested, in every manner suitable to his nature, his joy at seeing him; nor could the animal be persuaded to quit him again, accompanying him always when he went on shore, and returning with him on board.

At

A View of the Governor's House at St. Mary's the Antigua. Bloomsbury

At a mufter of the convicts which was directed during this month, one man only was unaccounted for, James Haydon. Soon after the mufter was over, word was brought to the commiffary, that his body had been found drowned in Long-Cove, at the back of the fettlement. Upon inquiry into the caufe of his death, it appeared that he had a few days before ftolen fome tobacco out of an officer's garden in which he had been employed, and, being threatened with punifhment, had ab-fconded. He was confidered as a well-behaved man; and if he pre-ferred death to fhame and punifhment, which he had been heard to declare he did, and which his death feemed to confirm, he was de-ferving a better fate.

The total number of fick on the laft day of the month was three hundred and forty-nine.

July.] The melancholy fcenes which clofed the laft month appeared unchanged at the beginning of this. The morning generally opened with the attendants of the fick paffing frequently backwards and for-wards from the hofpital to the burying-ground with the miferable victims of the night. Every exertion was made to get up the portable hofpital; but, although we were informed that it had been put up in London in a very few hours, we did not complete it until the 7th, when it was inftantly filled with patients. On the 13th, there were four hundred and eighty-eight perfons under medical treatment at and about the hofpital,—a dreadful fick lift!

Such of the convicts from the fhips as were in a tolerable ftate of health, both male and female, were fent up to Rofe Hill, to be em-ployed in agriculture and other labours. A fubaltern's detachment from the New South Wales corps was at the fame time fent up for the military duty of that fettlement in conjunction with the marine corps.

There alfo the governor in the courfe of the month laid down the lines of a regular town. The principal ftreet was marked out to extend one mile, commencing near the landing-place, and running in a direc-tion weft, to the foot of the rifing ground named Rofe Hill, and in which his excellency purpofed to erect a fmall houfe for his own refidence whenever he fhould vifit that fettlement. On each fide of this ftreet, whofe width was to be two hundred and five feet, huts
were

were to be erected capable of containing ten perfons each, and at the
diftance of fixty feet one from the other; and garden ground for each
hut was allotted in the rear. As the huts were to be built of fuch
combuftible materials as wattles and plafter, and to be covered with
thatch, the width of the ftreet, and the diftance they were placed from
each other, operated as an ufeful precaution againft fire; and by beginning on fo wide a fcale the inhabitants of the town at fome future
day would poffefs their own accommodations and comforts more readily, each upon his own allotment, than if crowded into a fmall fpace.

While thefe works were going on at Rofe Hill, the labouring convicts at Sydney were employed in conftructing a new brick ftorehoufe,
difcharging the tranfports, and forming a road from the town to the
brick-kilns, for the greater eafe and expedition in bringing in bricks to
the different buildings.

Our ftores now wore a more refpectable appearance than they had
done for fome time. In addition to the provifions put on board the
tranfports in England, Lieutenant Riou had forwarded by thofe fhips
four hundred tierces of beef and two hundred tierces of pork, which
he had faved from the wreck of the Guardian, and which we had the
fatisfaction to find were nothing the worfe for the accident which befel
her. Thefe, with the feventy-five cafks of flour which were brought
on by the Lady Juliana, formed the amount of what we were now to
receive of the large cargo of that unfortunate fhip.

Lieutenant Riou alfo fent by thefe fhips the twenty male convicts
which had been felected as artificers and put on board the Guardian in
England; and with them he fent the moft pointed recommendations in
their favour, defcribing their conduct, both before and after the accident which happened to the fhip under his command, in the ftrongeft
terms of approbation.

The Lady Juliana being found on infpection to require fuch extenfive repairs as would too long delay the difpatching the neceffary
fupplies to Norfolk Ifland, the governor directed the Surprife tranfport
and Juftinian ftorefhip to proceed thither.

By the 19th, the Juftinian was cleared of her cargo, excepting about
five hundred cafks of provifions, which were not to be taken out until
the

She arrived at Norfolk Island; and both that ship and the Surprise were preparing with all expedition for sailing. The Justinian, however, from the circumstance of retaining some part of her large cargo on board, was ready first, and sailed on the 28th. The master, Mr. Benjamin Maitland, was directed to follow his former orders after landing his stores and provisions at Norfolk Island, and proceed to Canton to freight home with teas upon account of government. She was hired by the month at fifteen shillings and sixpence per ton, and was to be in government employ until her return to Deptford. By this ship the governor sent dispatches to the secretary of state.

The Lady Juliana, having received some repairs by the carpenters of the colony at the time when it was designed she should go to Norfolk Island, and some others by the assistance of her own carpenters, sailed a day or two after the Justinian for Canton From the extravagant price set on his goods by the master, his shop had turned out badly; and it was said that he took many articles to sea, which he must of necessity throw overboard before he reached Canton.

The governor received by these ships dispatches from the secretary of state, containing, among other articles of information, instructions respecting the granting of lands and the allotting of ground in townships. Soon after their arrival it was declared in public orders:

That, in consequence of the assurances that were given to the non-commissioned officers and men belonging to the detachment of marines, on their embarking for the service of this country, that such of them as should behave well should be allowed to quit the service on their return to England, or be discharged abroad upon the relief, and permitted to settle in the country; his Majesty had been graciously pleased to direct the following terms to be held out as an encouragement to such non-commissioned officers and private men of the marines as might be desirous of becoming settlers in this country, or in any of the islands comprised within the government of the continent * of New South Wales, on the arrival of the corps raised and intended for the service of this country, and for their relief; viz.

To every non-commissioned officer, an allotment of one hundred and thirty acres of land if single, and one hundred and fifty if married.

* Now so called officially for the first time.

To

To every private man, eighty acres of land if single, one hundred if married; and ten acres of land for each child at the time of granting the allotment; free of all fees, taxes, quit-rents, and other acknowledgments, for the term of five years; at the expiration of which term to be liable to an annual quit-rent of one shilling for every fifty acres.

As a further encouragement, a bounty was offered of three pounds per man to every non-commissioned officer and private man who would enlist in the new corps, (to form a company to be officered from the marines,) and an allotment of double the above proportion of land if they behaved well for five years, to be granted them at the expiration of that time; the said allotments not to be subject to any fee or tax for ten years, and then to be liable to an annual quit-rent of one shilling for every fifty acres.

And upon their discharge at either of the above periods they were to be supplied with clothing and one year's provisions, with seed grain, tools, and implements of agriculture. The service of a certain number of convicts was to be assigned to them for their labour when they could make it appear that they could maintain, feed, and clothe them. In these instructions no mention was made of granting lands to officers; and to other persons who might emigrate and be desirous of settling in this country, no greater proportion of land was to be allotted than what was to be granted to a non-commissioned officer of the marines.

Government, between every allotment, reserved to itself a space equal to the largest grant, on either side, which, as crown land, was not to be granted, but leased only to individuals for the term of fourteen years.

Provision was made for the church, by allotting in each township which should be marked out four hundred acres for the maintenance of a minister; and half of that number was to be allotted for the maintenance of a school master.

If the allotments should happen to be made on the banks of any navigable river or creek, care was to be taken that the breadth of each track did not extend along the banks thereof more than one-third of the length of such track, in order that no settler should engross more than his proportion of the benefit which would accrue from such a situation. And it was also directed, that the good and the bad land should be as equally divided as circumstances would allow.

No

No new regulations were directed to take place in respect of granting lands to convicts emancipated or discharged; the original instructions, under which each male convict if single was to have thirty, if married fifty, and ten acres for every child he might have at the time of settling, remained in force.

The particular conditions required by the crown from a settler were, the residing upon the ground, proceeding to the improvement and cultivation of his allotment, and reserving such of the timber thereof as might be fit for naval purposes for the use of his Majesty.

The period fixed by government for victualling a settler from the public stores, twelve months, was in general looked upon as too short, and it was thought not practicable for any one at the end of that period to maintain himself, unless during that time he should have very great assistance given him, and be fortunate in his crops.

About the latter end of this month a spermaceti whale was seen in the harbour, and some boats from the transports went after it with harpoons; but, from the ignorance of the people in the use of them, the fish escaped unhurt. In a few days afterwards word was received that a punt belonging to Lieutenant Poulden had been pursued by a whale and overset, by which accident young Mr. Ferguson (a midshipman of the Sirius) and two soldiers were unfortunately drowned. The soldiers, with another of their companions, who saved his life by swimming, had been down the harbour fishing, and, calling at the Look-out, took in Mr. Ferguson, who had sat up all the preceding night to write to his father, (Captain James Ferguson, lieutenant-governor of Greenwich hospital,) and was now bringing his letters to Sydney for the purpose of sending them by the Justinian.

Mr. Ferguson was a steady well-disposed young man, and the service, in all probability, by this extraordinary accident, lost a good officer.

The Scarborough was cleared this month, and, being discharged from government employ, the master was left at liberty to proceed to Canton, where he was to load home with teas.

Much irregularity was committed by the seamen of the transports, who found means to get on shore at night, notwithstanding the port orders; and one, a sailor from the Neptune, was punished with twenty-five lashes for being found on shore without any permission at eleven o'clock at night.

s   The

The sick list, now consisting of only three hundred and thirty-two persons, was found to be daily decreasing, and the mortality was infinitely less at the end, than at the beginning of the month.

August.] The Surprise transport sailed on the first of August for Norfolk Island, having on board thirty-five male and one hundred and fifty female convicts, two of the superintendants lately arrived, and one deputy commissary, Mr. Thomas Freeman, appointed such by the governor's warrant. There came out in the Neptune a person of the name of Wentworth, who, being desirous of some employment in this country, was now sent to Norfolk Island to act as an assistant to the surgeon there, being reputed to have the necessary requisites for such a situation.

On the 8th, the Scarborough sailed for Canton, and the Neptune was preparing to follow her as soon as she could be cleared of the cargo she had on board upon account of government. While this was delivering, some of the convicts who came out in that ship put in before the judge-advocate their claims upon the master, Mr. Donald Trail, not only for clothing and other articles, but for money, which they stated to have been taken from them at the time of their embarkation, and had never since been returned to them. Many of these claims were disputed by Mr. Trail, and others were settled to the satisfaction of the claimants; but of their clothing, knives, buckles, &c. he could give no other account, than that he was directed by the naval agent, Lieutenant Shapcote, to destroy them at their embarkation for obvious reasons, tending to the safety of the ship and for the preservation of their health.

On the 19th the Neptune was cleared and discharged the service, having landed the cargo she brought out on government account in good condition. Preparatory to her sailing for China, she quitted the cove on the 22d; soon after which, information being received that several convicts purposed to attempt making their escape in her from the colony, a small armed party of soldiers was sent on board her, under the direction of Lieutenant Long * of the marines, to search the ship, when one man and one woman were found on board. The man

---

* Appointed by Governor Philip, after the arrival of the New South Wales corps, to do the duty of town-adjutant.

was one who had juft arrived in the colony, and, being foon tired of
his fituation, had prevailed on fome of the people to fecrete him among
the fire-wood which they had taken on board. In the night another
perfon fwam off to the fhip, and was received by the guard. He
pleaded being a free man, but as he had taken a very improper mode
of quitting the colony, he was, by order of the governor, punifhed the
day following, together with the convict who had been found concealed
among the fire-wood. The Neptune failed on the 24th, leaving behind
her one mate Mr. Forfar, and two feamen ; and the cove was once
more without a fhip.

An excurfion into the country had been undertaken this month by
Captain Tench and fome other officers. They were abfent fix days,
and on their return we learned, that they had proceeded in a direction
S. S. W. of Rofe Hill ; that they met with frefh water running to the
northward ; found the traces of natives wherever they went, and paffed
through a very bad country interfected every where with deep ravines.
They had reafon to think, that in rainy weather the run of water
which they met with rofe above its ordinary level between thirty and
forty feet. They faw a flock of emu's twelve in number.

It having been found that the arms and ammunition which were
entrufted to the convicts refiding at the diftant farms for their protection againft the natives, were made a very different ufe of, an order
was given recalling them, and prohibiting any convicts from going out
with arms, except M'Intire, Burn, and Randall, who were licenfed
game-killers.

The clergyman complaining of non-attendance at divine fervice,
which it muft be obferved was generally performed in the open air,
alike unfheltered from wind and rain, as from the fervor of the fummer's fun, it was ordered that three pounds of flour fhould be deducted
from the ration of each overfeer, and two pounds from that of each
labouring convict, who fhould not attend prayers once on each Sunday, unlefs fome reafonable excufe for their abfence fhould be affigned.

Toward the latter end of the month a criminal court was held for
the trial of Hugh Low, a convict, who had been in the Guardian, and
who was in cuftody for ftealing a fheep, the property of Mr. Palmer
the commiffary. Being moft clearly convicted of the offence by the

s 2   evidence

evidence of an accomplice and others, he received sentence of death, and, the governor not deeming it advisable to pardon an offence of that nature, suffered the next day, acknowledging the commission of the fact for which he died.

The preservation of our stock was an object of so much consequence to the colony, that it became indispensably necessary to protect it by every means in our power. Had any lenity been extended to this offender on account of his good conduct in a particular situation, it might have been the cause of many depredations being made upon the stock, which it was hoped his punishment would prevent.

On the 28th a pair of shoes was served to each convict. The female convicts were employed in making the slops for the men, which had been now sent out unmade. Each woman who could work at her needle had materials for two shirts given her at a time, and while so employed was not to be taken for any other labour.

The storehouse which was begun in July was finished this month, and was got up and covered in without any rain. Its dimensions were one hundred feet by twenty-two.

At Rose Hill the convicts were employed in constructing the new town which had been marked out, building the huts, and forming the principal street. The governor, who personally directed all these works, caused a spot of ground for a capacious garden to be allotted for the use of the New South Wales corps, contiguous to the spot whereon his excellency meant to erect the barracks for that corps.

In addition to the flag-staff which had been erected on the south head of the harbour, the governor determined to construct a column, of a height sufficient to be seen from some distance at sea, and the stone-masons were sent down to quarry stone upon the spot for the building.

The body of one of the unfortunate people who were drowned at the latter end of July last with Mr. Ferguson was found about the close of this month, washed on shore in Rose Bay, and very much disfigured. The whale which occasioned this accident, we were informed, had never found its way out of the harbour, but, getting on shore in Manly Bay, was killed by the natives, and was the cause of numbers of them being at this time assembled to partake of the repasts which it afforded them.

CHAP. XI.

GOVERNOR PHILLIP WOUNDED BY A NATIVE.—INTERCOURSE OPENED WITH
THE NATIVES.—GREAT HAUL OF FISH.—CONVICTS ABSCOND WITH A
BOAT.—WORKS.—WANT OF RAIN.—NATIVES.—SUPPLY RETURNS FROM
BATAVIA.—TRANSACTIONS THERE.—CRIMINAL COURTS.—JAMES BLOOD-
WORTH EMANCIPATED.—OARS FOUND IN THE WOODS.—A CONVICT
BROUGHT BACK IN THE SUPPLY.—A BOAT WITH FIVE PEOPLE LOST.—
PUBLIC WORKS.—A CONVICT WOUNDED BY A NATIVE.—ARMED PARTIES
SENT OUT TO AVENGE HIM.—A DUTCH VESSEL ARRIVES WITH SUPPLIES
FROM BATAVIA.—DECREASE BY SICKNESS AND CASUALTIES IN 1790.

September.] SINCE the escape of Bennillong the native in May
last, nothing had been heard of him, nor had any thing worthy of
notice occurred among the other natives. In the beginning of this
month, however, they were brought forward again by a circumstance
which seemed at first to threaten the colony with a loss that must have
been for some time severely felt; but which was succeeded by an opening of that amicable intercourse with these people which the governor
had always laboured to establish, and which was at last purchased by a
most unpleasant accident to himself, and at the risk of his life.

The governor, who had uniformly directed every undertaking in
person since the formation of the colony, went down in the morning
of the 7th to the south head, accompanied by Captain Collins and
Lieutenant Waterhouse, to give some instructions to the people employed in erecting a column at that place. As he was returning to
the settlement, he received information, by a boat which had landed
Mr. White and some other gentlemen in the lower part of the harbour,
(they were going on an excursion towards Broken Bay,) that Bennillong had been seen there by Mr. White, and had sent the governor
as a present a piece of the whale which was then lying in the wash of
the surf on the beach. Anxious to see him again, the governor, after
taking some arms from the party at the Look-out, which he thought
the more requisite in this visit as he heard the cove was full of natives,
went

went down and landed at the place where the whale was lying.   Here
he not only saw Bennillong, but Cole-be also, who had made his escape
from the governor's house a few days after his capture.   At first his excellency trusted himself alone with these people; but the few months
Bennillong had been away had so altered his person, that the governor,
until joined by Mr. Collins and Mr. Waterhouse, did not perfectly
recollect his old acquaintance.   Bennillong had been always much
attached to Mr. Collins, and testified with much warmth his satisfaction at seeing him again.   Several articles of wearing apparel were
now given to him and his companions (taken for that purpose from
the people in the boat, who, all but one man, remained on their oars
to be ready in case of any accident), and a promise was exacted from
the governor by Bennillong to return in two days with more, and also
with some hatchets or tomahawks.   The cove was full of natives
allured by the attractions of a whale feast; and it being remarked
during the conference that the twenty or thirty which appeared were
drawing themselves into a circle round the governor and his small
unarmed party, (for that was literally and most inexcusably their
situation,) the governor proposed retiring to the boat by degrees;
but Bennillong, who had presented to him several natives by name,
pointed out one, whom the governor, thinking to take particular
notice of, stepped forward to meet, holding out both his hands
toward him.   The savage not understanding this civility, and perhaps
thinking that he was going to seize him as a prisoner, lifted a spear
from the grass with his foot, and fixing it on his throwing-stick, in
an instant darted it at the governor.   The spear entered a little above
the collar bone, and had been discharged with such force, that the
barb of it came through on the other side.   Several other spears were
thrown, but happily no further mischief was effected.   The spear was
with difficulty broken by Lieutenant Waterhouse, and while the governor was leading down to the boat the people landed with the arms,
but of four musquets which they brought on shore one only could be
fired.

    The boat had five miles to row before it reached the settlement;
but the people in her exerting themselves to the utmost, the governor

was

was landed and in his house in something less than two hours. The spear was extracted with much skill by Mr. Balmain, one of the assistant-surgeons of the hospital, who immediately pronounced the wound not mortal. An armed party was dispatched that evening toward Broken Bay for Mr. White, the principal surgeon, who returned the following day, and reported that in the cove where the whale lay they saw several natives; but being armed nothing had happened.

No other motive could be assigned for this conduct in the savage, than the supposed apprehension that he was about to be seized by the governor, which the circumstance of his advancing toward him with his hands held out might create. But it certainly would not have happened had the precaution of taking even a single musket on shore been attended to. The governor had always placed too great a confidence in these people, under an idea that the sight of fire arms would deter them from approaching; he had now, however, been taught a lesson which it might be presumed he would never forget.

This accident gave cause to the opening of a communication between the natives of this country and the settlement, which, although attended with such an unpromising beginning, it was hoped would be followed with good consequences.

A few days after the accident, Bennillong, who certainly had not any culpable share in the transaction, came with his wife and some of his companions to a cove on the north shore not far from the settlement, where, by means of Boo-roong, the female who lived in the clergyman's house, an interview was effected between the natives and some officers, Mr. White, Mr. Palmer, and others, who at some personal risk went over with her.

At this time the name of the man who had wounded the governor was first known, Wil-le-me-ring; and Bennillong made many attempts to fix a belief that he had beaten him severely for the aggression. Bennillong declared that he should wait in that situation for some days, and hoped that the governor would be able, before the expiration of them, to visit him. On the tenth day after he had received the wound, his excellency was so far recovered as to go to the place, accom-

accompanied by several officers all armed, where he saw Bennillong and his companions. Bennillong then repeated his assurances of his having, in conjunction with his friend Cole-be, severely beaten Wil-le-me-ring; and added that his throwing the spear at the governor was entirely the effect of his fears, and done from the impulse of self-preservation.

The day preceding the governor's visit, the fishing boats had the greatest success which had yet been met with; near four thousand of a fish, named by us, from its shape only, the salmon, being taken at two hauls of the seine. Each fish weighed on an average about five pounds; they were issued to this settlement, and to that at Rose Hill; and thirty or forty were sent as a conciliating present to Bennillong and his party on the north shore.

These circumstances, and the visit to the natives, in which it was endeavoured to convince them that no animosity was retained on account of the late accident, nor resentment harboured against any but the actual perpetrator of the fact, created a variety in the conversation of the day; and those who were desirous of acquiring the language were glad of the opportunity which the recently-opened intercourse seemed to promise them.

In the night of the 26th a desertion of an extraordinary nature took place. Five male convicts conveyed themselves, in a small flat boat called a punt, from Rose Hill undiscovered. They there exchanged the punt, which would have been unfit for their purpose, for a boat, though very small and weak, with a mast and sail, with which they got out of the harbour. On sending to Rose Hill, people were found who could give an account of their intentions and proceedings, and who knew that they purposed steering for Otaheite. They had each taken provisions for one week; their cloaths and bedding; three iron pots, and some other utensils of that nature. They all came out in the last fleet, and took this method of speedily accomplishing their sentences of transportation, which were for the term of their natural lives. Their names were, John Tarwood, a daring, desperate character, and the principal in the scheme; Joseph Sutton, who was found secreted on board the Neptune and punished; George Lee;
George

George Connoway, and John Watson. A boat with an officer was
sent to search for them in the north-west branch of this harbour, but
returned, after several hours search, without discovering the least trace
of them. They no doubt pushed directly out upon that ocean which,
from the wretched state of the boat wherein they trusted themselves,
must have proved their grave.

The governor purposing to erect a capacious storehouse and a range
of barracks at Rose Hill, a convict who understood the business of
brick-making was sent up for the purpose of manufacturing a quantity
sufficient for those buildings, a vein of clay having been found which it
was supposed would burn into good bricks. A very convenient wharf
and landing place were made at that settlement, and twenty-seven huts
were in great forwardness at the end of the month.

Very small hopes were entertained of the wheat of this season;
extreme dry weather was daily burning it up. Toward the latter end
of the month some rain fell, the first which deserved the name of
a heavy rain since last June.

October.] The little rain which fell about the close of the preceding
month soon ceased, and the gardens and the corn grounds were again
parching for want of moisture. The grass in the woods was so dried,
that a single spark would have set the surrounding country in flames;
an instance of this happened early in the month, with the wind blowing strong at N. W. It was however happily checked.

Bennillong, after appointing several days to visit the governor, came
at last on the 8th, attended by three of his companions. The welcome reception they met with from every one who saw them inspired
the strangers with such a confidence in us, that the visit was soon
repeated; and at length Bennillong solicited the governor to build him
a hut at the extremity of the eastern point of the cove. This the
governor, who was very desirous of preserving the friendly intercourse
which seemed to have taken place, readily promised, and gave the
necessary directions for its being built.

19th.] While we were thus amusing ourselves with these children
of ignorance, the signal for a sail was made at the South Head, and
shortly after the Supply anchored in the cove from Batavia, having
been absent from the settlement six months and two days. Lieutenant

T   Ball

Ball arrived at Batavia on the 6th of July last, where he hired a vessel, a Dutch snow, which was to sail shortly after him with the provisions that he had purchased for the colony. While the Supply lay at Batavia the season was more unhealthy than had ever been known before; every hospital was full, and several hundreds of the inhabitants had died. Lieutenant Ball, at this grave of Europeans, buried Lieutenant Newton Fowell, Mr. Ross the gunner, and several of his seamen. He tried for some days to touch at Norfolk Island, but ineffectually, being prevented by easterly winds. Mr. King and Mr. Miller (the late commissary) had sailed on the 4th of last August in a Dutch packet for Europe.

By the return of this vessel several comforts were introduced into the settlement; her commander, with that attention to the wants of the different officers which always characterised him, having procured and taken on board their respective investments.

In his passage to Batavia, Lieutenant Ball saw some islands, to which, conjecturing, from not finding them in any charts which he had on board, that he might claim being the discoverer of them, he gave names accordingly. Although anxious to make an expeditious passage, he had the mortification to be baffled by contrary winds both to and from Batavia; and at that settlement, instead of finding the governor-general (to whom in his orders he was directed to apply for permission to purchase provisions, and for a ship to bring them) ready to forward the service he came on, which he represented as requiring the utmost expedition, he was referred to the Sabandhaar, Mr. N. Engelhard, who, after much delay and pretence of difficulty in procuring a vessel, produced one, a snow, which they estimated at three hundred and fifty tons burthen, and demanded to be paid for at the rate of eighty rix dollars for every ton freight, amounting together to twenty-eight thousand rix dollars, each rix dollar being computed at forty-eight Dutch pennies; and the freight was to be paid although the vessel should be lost on the passage.

As it was impossible to hire any vessel there upon cheaper terms, Lieutenant Ball was compelled to engage for the Waaksamheyd (that being her name, which, englished, signified " Good look out ") upon the terms they proposed. Of the provisions which he was instructed

10

to procure, the whole quantity of flour, two hundred thousand pounds, was not to be had, he being able only to purchase twenty thousand and twenty-one pounds, for which they charged ten stivers per pound, and an addition of about one-third of a penny per pound was charged for grinding it *. Instead of the flour Lieutenant Ball purchased two hundred thousand pounds of rice, at one rix dollar and forty-four stivers per hundred weight, over and above the seventy thousand pounds he was directed to procure. The salt provisions were paid for at the rate of seven stivers per pound, and the amount of the whole cargo, including the casks for the flour, wood for dunnage, hire of cooleys, and of craft for shipping the provisions, was thirty thousand four hundred and forty-one rix dollars and thirty-three stivers; which added to the freight (twenty-eight thousand rix dollars) made a total of fifty-eight thousand four hundred and forty-one rix dollars and thirty-three stivers, or 11,688 l. 6 s. 9 d. sterling.

Mr. Ormsby, a midshipman from the Sirius, was left to come on with the snow, which it was hoped would sail in a few weeks after the Supply.

The criminal court was twice assembled during this month. At the first a soldier was tried for a felony, but acquitted. At the second William Harris and Edward Wildblood were tried for entering a hut at Parramatta, in which was only one man, and that a sick person, whom they knocked down, and then robbed the hut. They were clearly convicted of the offence, and, being most daring and flagrant offenders, were executed at Rose Hill, near the hut which they had robbed. These people had given a great deal of trouble before they committed the offence for which they suffered. At the latter end of the last month they took to the woods, having more than once or twice robbed their companions at Rose Hill. As they were well known, the watch soon brought them in to the settlement at Sydney. They confessed, that the night before they were apprehended they killed a goat belonging to Mr. White. The governor directed them immediately to

* The flour, without the freight, including one hundred and ten rix dollars which were charged for twenty-two half leagers in which it was contained, amounted as nearly as possible to tre-pence three farthings per pound.

T 2	be

be linked together by the leg, and fent them back to Rofe Hill, there to labour upon bread and water. It was in this fituation that, taking advantage of their overfeer's abfence for a few minutes, they went to the hut, of the fituation of which they had previous knowledge, and robbed it of every thing they could carry away.

While thefe people were fuffering the punifhment they deferved, James Bloodworth, mentioned before in this narrative, received the moft diftinguifhing mark of approbation which the governor had in his power to give him, being declared free, and at liberty to return to England whenever he fhould choofe to quit the colony. Bloodworth had approved himfelf a moft ufeful member of the fettlement, in which there was not a houfe or building that did not owe fomething to him; and as his lofs would be feverely felt fhould he quit it while in its infancy, he bound himfelf by an agreement with the governor to work for two years longer in the colony, ftipulating only to be fed and clothed during that time.

Encouraged by the facility with which Tarwood and his companions made their efcape from the colony, fome others were forming plans for a fimilar enterprife. A convict gave information that a fcheme nearly ripe for execution was framed, and that the parties had provided themfelves with oars, mafts, fails, &c. for the purpofe, which were concealed in the woods; and as a proof of the veracity of his account, he fo clearly defcribed the place of depofit, that on fending to the fpot, four or five rude unfinifhed ftakes were found, which he faid were to be fafhioned into oars. The perfon who gave the information dreaded fo much being known as the author, that no further notice was taken of it than deftroying the oars, and keeping a very vigilant eye on the conduct of the people who had been named by him as the parties in the bufinefs.

Attempts of this fort were always likely to be made, at leaft as long as any difficulty occurred in their quitting the colony after the term had expired for which by law they were fentenced to remain abroad. There muft be many among them who would be anxious to return to their wives or children, or other relations, and who, perhaps, might not refort again to the companions of their idle hours. If thefe people found any

obftacles

obstacles in their way, they would naturally be driven to attempt the attainment of their wishes in some other mode; and it would then become an object of bad policy, as well as cruelty, to detain them.

The weather about this period was evidently becoming warmer every day; and although the trees never wholly lost their foliage, yet they gave manifest signs of the return of spring.

November.]   James Williams, who was missing on the sailing of the Supply for Batavia, was found by Lieutenant Ball to have secreted himself on board that vessel, and on her return he delivered him up as a prisoner to the provost-marshal. Williams owned that his flight was to avoid a punishment which he knew awaited him; and Lieutenant Ball spoke so favourably of his conduct while he was under his observation, that the governor would have forgiven him, had he not feared that others might, from such an example, think to meet the same indulgence: he therefore directed him to receive two hundred and fifty lashes, (half of the punishment which by the court that tried him he was sentenced to receive,) and remitted the remainder.

A small boat belonging to Mr. White, which had been sent out with a seine, was lost this month somewhere about Middle Head. She had five convicts in her; and, from the reports of the natives who were witnesses of the accident, it was supposed they had crossed the harbour's mouth, and, having hauled the seine in Hunter's Bay, were returning loaded, when, getting in too close with the rocks and the surf under Middle Head, she filled and went down. The first information that any accident had happened was given by the natives, who had secured the rudder, mast, an oar, and other parts of the boat, which they had fixed in such situations as were likely to render them conspicuous to any boat passing that way. Mr. White and some other gentlemen, going down directly, found their information too true. One of the bodies was lying dead on the beach; with the assistance of Cole-be and the other natives he recovered the seine which was entangled in the rocks, and brought away the parts of his boat which they had secured.

This appeared to be a striking instance of the good effect of the intercourse which had been opened with these people; and there seemed only to be a good understanding between us and them wanting to establish

blish

blish an harmony which would have been productive of the best confequences, and might have been the means of preventing many of the
unfortunate accidents that had happened. The governor, however,
thought it neceffary to direct, that offenfive weapons should not be
given to thefe people in exchange for any of their articles; being apprehenfive that they might ufe them among themselves, and not wishing by any means to arm them againft each other.

At Rofe Hill a ftorehoufe was begun and finished during the month,
without any rain ; its dimenfions were one hundred feet by twenty-
four feet. The bricks there, either from forne error in the procefs, or
defect in the clay, were not fo good in quality as thofe made at Sydney.
—In their colour they were of a deep red when burned, but did not
appear to be durable.

At Sydney, a good landing-place on the eaft fide was completed; and
two fmall brick huts, one for a cutler's shop, and another for the purpofe of boiling oil or melting tallow, were built on the fame fide. A
wharf was alfo marked out on the weft fide, which was to be carried
far enough out into deep water to admit of the loaded hoy coming
along-fide at any time of tide. The hut, a brick one twelve feet fquare
and covered with tiles, was finished for Bennillong, and taken poffeffion of by him about the middle of the month.

Notwithftanding the accidents which had happened to many who
had ftrayed imprudently beyond the known limits of the different fettlements, two foldiers of the New South Wales corps, who had had
every neceffary caution given them on the arrival of their detachment
at Rofe Hill, ftrayed into the woods, and were miffing for four or
five days, in which time they had fuffered feverely from anxiety and
hunger.

December.] The temporary barrack which had been erected within
the redoubt at Rofe Hill, formed only of pofts and shingles nailed or
faftened with pegs on battens, going faft to decay, and being found inadequate to guard againft either the rain or wind of the winter months
and the heat of thofe of the fummer, the foundation of a range of brick
buildings for the officers and foldiers ftationed there was laid early in the
month. The governor fixed the fituation contiguous to the ftorehoufe
lately erected there, to which they might ferve as a protection. They
were

were defigned for quarters for one company, with the proper number
of officers, a guard-room, and two fmall ftore-rooms.

On the 10th, John M'Intire, a convict who was employed by the
governor to fhoot for him, was dangeroufly wounded by a native
named Pe-mul-wy *, while in queft of game in the woods at fome
confiderable diftance from the fettlement. When brought in he declared, and at a time when he thought himfelf dying, that he did not
give any offence to the man who wounded him; that he had even
quitted his arms, to induce him to look upon him as a friend, when
the favage threw his fpear at about the diftance of ten yards with a
fkill that was fatally unerring. When the fpear was extracted, which
was not until fuppuration took place, it was found to have entered his
body under the left arm, to the depth of feven inches and a half. It
was armed for five or fix inches from the point with ragged pieces of
fhells faftened in gum. His recovery was immediately pronounced
by Mr. White to be very doubtful.

As the attack on this man was wanton, and entirely unprovoked on
the part of M'Intire, not only from his relation of the circumftance,
but from the account of thofe who were with him, and who bore tefti-
mony to his being unarmed, the governor determined to punifh the
offender, who it was underftood reforted with his tribe above the head
of Botany Bay. He therefore directed that an armed party from the
garrifon fhould march thither, and either deftroy or make prifoners of
fix perfons (if practicable) of that tribe to which the aggreffor belonged,
carefully avoiding to offer any injury to either women or children.
To this meafure the governor reforted with reluctance. He had always wifhed that none of their blood might ever be fhed; and in his
own cafe, when wounded by Wille-me-ring, as he could not punifh him
on the fpot, he gave up all thoughts of doing it in future. As, however, they feemed to take every advantage of unarmed men, fome
check appeared abfolutely neceffary. Accordingly, on Tuefday the
14th a party, confifting of two captains, (Tench, of the marines, and
Hill of the New South Wales corps) with two fubalterns, three fer-

* His name was readily obtained from the natives who lived among us, and who foon
became acquainted with the circumftances.

jeants,

---

jeants, two corporals, one drummer, and forty privates, attended by two surgeons, set off with three days' provisions for the purpose above-mentioned.

There was little probability that such a party would be able so unexpectedly to fall in with the people they were sent to punish, as to surprise them, without which chance, they might hunt them in the woods for ever; and as the different tribes (for we had thought fit to class them into tribes) were not to be distinguished from each other, but by being found inhabiting particular residences, there would be some difficulty in determining, if any natives should fall in their way, whether they were the objects of their expedition, or some unoffending family wholly unconnected with them. The very circumstance, however, of a party being armed and detached purposely to punish the man and his companions who wounded M'Intire, was likely to have a good effect, as it was well known to several natives, who were at this time in the town of Sydney, that this was the intention with which they were sent out.

On the third day after their departure they returned, without having wounded or hurt a native, or made a prisoner. They saw some at the head of Botany Bay, and fired at them, but without doing them any injury. Whenever the party was seen by the natives, they fled with incredible swiftness; nor had a second attempt, which the governor directed, any better success.

The governor now determining to avail himself as much as possible of the health and strength of the working convicts, while by the enjoyment of a full ration they were capable of exertion, resolved to proceed with such public buildings as he judged to be necessary for the convenience of the different settlements. Accordingly, during this month, the foundation of another storehouse was laid, equal in dimensions and in a line with that already erected on the east side of the cove at Sydney.

On the 17th the Dutch snow the Waakfamheyd anchored in the cove from Batavia, from which place she failed on the 20th day of last September, meeting on her passage with contrary winds. She was manned principally with Malays, sixteen of whom she buried during the passage. Mr. Ormsby the midshipman arrived a living picture of the ravages made in a good constitution by a Batavian fever. He was

2   in

in such a debilitated state, that it was with great difficulty he supported himself from the wharf on which he landed to the governor's house.

The master produced a packet from the sabandhaar (his owner) at Batavia, inclosing two letters to the governor, one written in very good English, containing such particulars respecting the vessel as he judged it for his interest to communicate; the other, designed to convey such information as he was possessed of respecting European politics, being written in Dutch, unfortunately proved unintelligible; and we could only gather from Mr. Ormsby and the master, (who spoke bad English,) that a misunderstanding subsisted between Great Britain and Spain; but on what account could not be distinctly collected.

On the first working day after her arrival the people were employed in delivering the cargo from the snow. The quantity of rice brought in her was found to be short of that purchased and paid for by Lieutenant Ball 42,900 weight, and the governor consented to receive in lieu a certain proportion of butter *, the master having a quantity of that article on board very good. This deficiency was ascertained by weighing all the provisions which were landed; a proceeding which the master acquiesced in with much reluctance and some impertinence.

The numbers who died by sickness in the year 1790, were two seamen, one soldier, one hundred and twenty-three male convicts, seven females, and ten children; in all, one hundred and forty-three persons.

In the above time four male convicts were executed; one midshipman, two soldiers, and six male convicts were drowned; one male convict perished in the woods, and two absconded from the colony, supposed to be secreted on board a transport; making a total of decrease one hundred and fifty-nine persons.

* One pound of butter to eighteen pounds of rice.

CHAP. XII.

NEW YEAR'S DAY.—A CONVICT DROWNED.—A NATIVE KILLED.—SIGNAL COLOURS STOLEN.—SUPPLY SAILS FOR NORFOLK ISLAND.—H. E. DODD, SUPERINTENDANT AT ROSE HILL, DIES.—PUBLIC WORKS.—TERMS OFFERED FOR THE HIRE OF THE DUTCH SNOW TO ENGLAND.—THE SUPPLY RETURNS.—STATE OF NORFOLK ISLAND.—FISHING-BOAT OVERSET.—EXCESSIVE HEATS.—OFFICERS AND SEAMEN OF THE SIRIUS EMBARK IN THE SNOW.—SUPPLY SAILS FOR NORFOLK ISLAND, AND THE WAAKSAMHEYD FOR ENGLAND.—WILLIAM BRYANT AND OTHER CONVICTS ESCAPE FROM NEW SOUTH WALES.—RUSE, A SETTLER, DECLARES HE CAN MAINTAIN HIMSELF WITHOUT ASSISTANCE FROM THE PUBLIC STORES.—RATION REDUCED.—ORDERS RESPECTING MARRIAGE.—PORT REGULATIONS.—SETTLERS.—PUBLIC WORKS.

January 1791.] ON the first day of the new year the convicts were excused from all kind of labour. At Rose Hill, however, this holiday proved fatal to a young man, a convict, who, going to a pond to wash his shirt, slipped from the side, and was unfortunately drowned.

The Indian corn beginning to ripen at that settlement, the convicts commenced their depredations, and several of them, being taken with corn in their possession, were punished; but nothing seemed to deter them, and they now committed thefts as if they stole from principle; for at this time they received the full ration, in which no difference was made between them and the governor, or any other free person in the colony. When all the provisions brought by the Dutch snow were received into the public stores, the governor altered the ration, and caused five pounds of rice to be issued in lieu of four pounds of flour, which were taken off.

Information having been received toward the close of the last month, that some natives had thrown a spear or fiz-gig at a convict in a garden on the west side, where they had met together to steal potatoes, the governor sent an armed party to disperse them, when a club being thrown by one of the natives at the party, the latter fired, and one man was wounded. This circumstance was at first only surmised, from tracing a quantity of blood from the spot to the water; but in a few
days

days afterward the natives in the town told us the name of the wounded
man, and added, that he was then dead, and to be found in a cove
which they mentioned. On going to the place, a man well known in
the town fince the intercourfe between us and his countrymen had been
opened was found dead, and difpofed of for burning. He had been
fhot under the arm, the ball dividing the fubclavian artery, and Mr.
White was of opinion that he bled to death.

It was much to be regretted that any neceffity exifted for adopting
thefe fanguinary punifhments, and that we had not yet been able to
reconcile the natives to the deprivation of thofe parts of this harbour
which we occupied. While they entertained the Idea of our having
difpoffeffed them of their refidences, they muft always confider us as
enemies; and upon this principle they made a point of attacking the
white people whenever opportunity and fafety concurred. It was alfo
unfortunately found, that our knowledge of their language confifted
at this time of only a few terms for fuch things as, being vifible,
could not well be miftaken; but no one had yet attained words enough
to convey an idea in connected terms. It was alfo conceived by fome
among us, that thofe natives who came occafionally into the town did
not defire that any of the other tribes fhould participate in the enjoyment of the few trifles they procured from us. If this were true, it
would for a long time retard the general underftanding of our friendly
intentions toward them; and it was not improbable but that they
might for the fame reafon reprefent us in every unfavourable light they
could imagine.

About the middle of the month a theft of an extraordinary nature
was committed by fome of the natives. It had been the cuftom to
leave the fignal colours during the day at the flag-ftaff on the fouth head,
at which place they were feen by fome of thefe people, who, watching
their opportunity, ran away with them, and they were afterwards feen
divided among them in their canoes, and ufed as coverings.

On the 18th the Supply quitted the cove, preparatory to her failing
for Norfolk Ifland, which fhe did on the 22d, having fome provifions
on board for that fettlement. She was to bring back Captain Hunter,
with the officers and crew of his Majefty's late fhip Sirius. Her com-

U 2   mander,

mander, Lieutenant Ball, labouring under a very severe and alarming indisposition, Mr. David Blackburn, the master, was directed by the governor to take charge of her until Mr. Ball should be able to resume the command.

The wound which M'Intire had received proved fatal to him on the 22d of this month. He had appeared to be recovering, but in the afternoon of that day died somewhat suddenly. On opening the body, the spear appeared to have wounded the left lobe of the lungs, which was found adhering to the side. In the cavity were discovered some of the pieces of stone and shells with which the weapon had been armed. This man had been suspected of having wantonly killed or wounded several of the natives in the course of his excursions after game; but he steadily denied, from the time he was brought in to his last moment of life, having ever fired at them but once, and then only in defence of his own life, which he thought in danger.

26th. Our colours were hoisted in the redoubt, in commemoration of the day on which formal possession was taken of this cove three years before.

On the night of the 28th Henry Edward Dodd, the superintendant of convicts employed in cultivation at Rose Hill, died of a decline. He had been ill for some time, but his death was accelerated by exposing himself in his shirt for three or four hours during the night, in search after some thieves who were plundering his garden. His body was interred in a corner of a large spot of ground which had been inclosed for the preservation of stock, whither he was attended by all the free people and convicts at Rose Hill. The services rendered to the public by this person were visible in the cultivation and improvements which appeared at the settlement where he had the direction. He had acquired an ascendancy over the convicts, which he preserved without being hated by them; he knew how to proportion their labour to their ability, and, by an attentive and quiet demeanor, had gained the approbation and countenance of the different officers who had been on duty at Rose Hill.

Mr. Thomas Clark, a superintendant who arrived here in the last year, was directed by the governor to carry on the duties with which Mr. Dodd
had

had been charged, in which, it must be remarked, the care of the public grain was included.

At Rose Hill great progress was made in the building of the new barracks.

At Sydney, the public works in hand were, building the new storehouse, and two brick houses, one for the Rev. Mr. Johnson, and the other for Mr. Alt, the surveyor-general. These two buildings were erected on the east side of the cove, and in a line with those in the occupation of the commissary and judge-advocate.

February.]   The master of the Dutch snow having received instructions from his owner, the sabandhaar at Batavia, to offer the vessel to the governor, either for sale or for hire, after she should be cleared of her cargo, mentioned the circumstance to his excellency, and proposed to him to sell the vessel with all her furniture and provisions for the sum of thirty-three thousand rix dollars, about 6,600l. or to let her to hire at fifteen rix dollars per ton per month ; in either of which cases a passage was to be provided for his people to the Cape of Good Hope. The governor was desirous of sending this vessel to England with the officers and people of the Sirius; but it was impossible to close with either of these offers, and he rejected them as unreasonable. Her master therefore dropped the vessel down to the lower part of the harbour, meaning to sail immediately for Batavia. Choosing, however, to try the success of other proposals, he wrote from Camp Cove to the secretary, offering to let the vessel for the voyage to England for twenty-thousand rix dollars, stipulating that thirty thousand rix dollars should be paid for her in the event of her being lost; the crew to be landed at the Cape, and himself to be furnished with a passage to England.   On receiving this his second offer, the governor informed him, that instead of his proposal one pound sterling per ton per month should be given for the hire of the snow, to be paid when the voyage for which she was to be taken up should be completed.   With this offer of the governor's, the master, notwithstanding his having quitted the cove on his first terms being rejected, declared himself satisfied, and directly returned to the cove, saluting with five guns on coming to an anchor.

In

In adjusting the contract or charter-party, the master displayed the greatest ignorance and the most tiresome perverseness, throwing obstacles in the way of every clause that was inserted. It was however at length finally settled and signed by the governor on the part of the crown, and by Detmer Smith, the master, on the part of his owners, he consenting to be paid for only three hundred tons instead of three hundred and fifty, for which she had been imposed upon Lieutenant Ball at Batavia. The carpenter of the Supply measured her in this cove.

Directions were now given for fitting her up as a transport to receive the Sirius's late ship's company and officers; and Lieutenant Edgar, who came out in the Lady Juliana transport, was ordered to superintend the fitting her, as an agent; in which situation he was to embark on board her and return to England.

26th. The Supply, after an absence of just five weeks, returned from Norfolk Island, having on board Captain Hunter, with the officers and people of the Sirius; and Lieutenant John Johnson of the marines, whose ill state of health would not permit him to remain there any longer.

We now found that our apprehensions of the distressed situation of that settlement until it was relieved were well founded. The supply of provisions which was dispatched in the Justinian and Surprise reached them at a critical point of time, there being in store on the 7th of August, when they appeared off the island, provisions but for a few days at the ration then issued, which was three pounds of flour and one pint of rice; or, in lieu of flour, three pounds of Indian meal or of wheat, ground, and not separated from the husks or the bran. Their salt provisions were so nearly expended, that while a bird or a fish could be procured no salt meat was issued. The weekly ration of this article was only one pound and an half of beef, or seventeen ounces of pork. What their situation might have been but for the providential supply of birds which they met with, it was impossible to say; to themselves it was too distressing to be contemplated. On Mount Pitt they were fortunate enough to obtain, in an abundance almost incredible, a species of aquatic birds, answering the description

of

of that known by the name of the Puffin. These birds came in from
the sea every evening, in clouds literally darkening the air, and,
descending on Mount Pitt, deposited their eggs in deep holes made by
themselves in the ground, generally quitting them in the morning,
and returning to seek their subsistence in the sea. From two to three
thousand of these birds were often taken in a night. Their seeking
their food in the ocean left no doubt of their own flesh partaking of
the quality of that upon which they fed; but to people circumstanced
as were the inhabitants on Norfolk Island, this lessened not their importance; and while any Mount Pitt birds (such being the name given
them) were to be had, they were eagerly sought. The knots of the
pine tree, split and made into small bundles, afforded the miserable
occupiers of a small speck in the ocean sufficient light to guide them
through the woods, in search of what was to serve them for their
next day's meal. They were also fortunate enough to lose but a few
casks of the provisions brought to the island in the Sirius, by far the
greater part being got safely on shore; but so hazardous was at all
times the landing in Sydney Bay, that in discharging the two ships,
the large cutter belonging to the Sirius was lost upon the reef, as she
was coming in with a load of casks, and some women; by which
accident, two seamen of the Sirius, (of whom James Coventry, tried
at Sydney in 1788, for assaulting M'Neal on Garden Island, was one,)
three women, one child, (an infant at the breast whose mother got safe
on shore,) and one male convict who swam off to their assistance,
were unfortunately drowned. The weather, notwithstanding this accident, was so favourable at other times, that in one day two hundred
and ninety casks of provisions were landed from the ships.

The experience of three years had now shewn, that the summer was
the only proper season for sending stores and provisions to Norfolk
Island, as during that period the passage through the reef had been
found as good, and the landing as practicable as in any cove in Port
Jackson. But this was by no means certain or constant; for the surf
had been observed to rise when the sea beyond it was perfectly calm,
and without the smallest indication of any change in the weather.
A gale of wind at a distance from the island would suddenly occasion
such a swell, that landing would be either dangerous or impracticable.

It

It was matter of great satisfaction to learn, that the Sirius's people, under the direction of Captain Hunter, had been most usefully and successfully employed in removing several rocks which obstructed the passage through the reef; and that a correct survey of the island had been made by Lieutenant Bradley, by which several dangers had been discovered, which until then had been unknown.

The lieutenant-governor had, since taking upon him the command of the settlement, caused one hundred and fourteen acres of land to be cleared; and the late crops of maize and wheat, it was supposed, would have proved very productive had they not been sown somewhat too late, and not only retarded by too dry a season but infested by myriads of grubs and caterpillars, which destroyed every thing before them, notwithstanding the general exertions which were made for their extirpation. These vermin were observed to visit the island during the summer, but at no fixed period of that season.

Two pieces of very coarse canvas manufactured at Norfolk Island were sent to the governor; but, unless better could be produced from the looms than these specimens, little expectation was to be formed of this article ever answering even the common culinary purposes to which canvas can be applied.

Those officers who had passed some time in both settlements remarked, that the air of Norfolk Island was somewhat cooler than that of ours, here at Sydney; every breeze that blew being, from its insular situation, felt there.

Martial law continued in force until the supplies arrived; and of the general demeanor of the convicts during that time report spoke favourably.

The Lady Juliana, passing the island in her way to China, was the first ship that was seen; but, to the inexpressible disappointment and distress of those who saw her, as well as to the surprise of all who heard the circumstance, the master did not send a boat on shore. Nor were they relieved from their anxiety until two days had passed, when the other ships arrived.

This was the substance of the information received from Norfolk Island. From an exact survey which had been made, it was computed, that not more than between three and four hundred families

could

could be maintained from the produce of the island; and that even from that number in the course of twenty years many would be obliged to emigrate.

On the Supply's coming to an anchor, the Sirius's late ship's company, whose appearance bore testimony to the miserable fare they had met with in Norfolk Island for several months, were landed, and lodged in the military or portable hospital, until the Waaksamheyd Dutch snow could be got ready to receive them.

William Bryant, who had been continued in the direction of the fishing-boat after the discovery of his mal-practices, was, at the latter end of the month, overheard consulting in his hut after dark, with five other convicts, on the practicability of carrying off the boat in which he was employed. This circumstance being reported to the governor, it was determined that all his proceedings should be narrowly watched, and any scheme of that nature counteracted. The day following this conference, however, as he was returning from fishing with a boat-load of fish, the hook of the fore tack giving way in a squall of wind, the boat got stern-way, and filled, by which the execution of his project was for the present prevented. In the boat with Bryant was Dennillong's sister and three children, who all got safe on shore, the woman swimming to the nearest point with the youngest child upon her shoulders. Several of the natives, on perceiving the accident, paddled off in their canoes, and were of great service in saving the oars, mast, &c. and in towing the boat up to the cove.

In addition to other works in hand this month, the surveyor was employed in clearing and deepening the run of water which supplied the settlement at Sydney, and which, through the long drought, was at this time very low, although still sufficient for the consumption of the place. Fresh water was indeed every where very scarce, most of the streams or runs of water about the cove being dried up.

At Rose Hill the heat on the 10th and 11th of the month, on which days at Sydney the thermometer stood in the shade at 105°, was so excessive, (being much increased by the fire in the adjoining woods,) that immense numbers of the large fox bat were seen hanging at the

X

boughs

boughs of the trees, and dropping into the water, which, by their
stench, was rendered unwholesome. They had been observed for
some days before regularly taking their flight in the morning from
the northward to the southward, and returning in the evening.
During the excessive heat many dropped dead while on the wing; and
it was remarkable, that those which were picked up were chiefly males.
In several parts of the harbour the ground was covered with different
sorts of small birds, some dead, and others gasping for water.

The relief of the detachment at Rose Hill unfortunately took place
on one of these sultry days, and the officer having occasion to land
in search of water was compelled to walk several miles before any could
be found, the runs which were known being all dry; in his way
to and from the boat he found several birds dropping dead at his feet.
The wind was about north-west, and did much injury to the gardens,
burning up every thing before it. Those persons whose business compelled them to go into the heated air declared, that it was impossible
to turn the face for five minutes to the quarter from whence the
wind blew.

	9 a.m.	3 p.m.	10 p.m.
The greatest height of the thermometer during this month was,	90	105	84
The least height of - ditto - - - - - - was,	62	64½	61

March.] On the 2d of March Lieutenant Thomas Edgar hoisted a
pendant on board the snow, in quality of naval agent, on which occasion she fired five guns. The preparations which were making on
board that vessel were not completed until toward the latter end of the
month, at which time the officers and seamen who were to go home
in her were embarked.

Of the Sirius's late ship's company, ten seamen and two marines
chose rather to settle here than return to their friends. Two of the
seamen made choice of their lands in this country, the others in Norfolk Island. The majority of them had formed connections with
women, for whose sake they consented to embrace a mode of life
for which the natural restlessness of a sailor's disposition was but ill calculated. This motive, it is true, they disavowed; but one of the
stipulations which they were desirous of making for themselves being
the

the indulgence of having the women who had lived with them permitted still to do so, and it appearing not the least important article in their confideration, feemed to confirm the foregoing opinion.

The number of officers who were to embark was leffened by Mr. Jamifon, the furgeon's mate of the Sirius, receiving the governor's warrant appointing him an affiftant furgeon to the colony, in which capacity he was to be employed at Norfolk Ifland. For that fettlement the Supply was now ready to fail; and on the 21ft, one captain, two fubalterns, one ferjeant, one corporal, one drummer, and eighteen privates of the New South Wales corps, embarked on board that veffel, to relieve a part of the marine detachment doing duty there. Mr. Jamifon and the ten fettlers from the Sirius were alfo put on board, together with fome ftores that had been applied for. Allotments of fixty acres each were to be marked out for the fettlers, which they were to poffefs under the fame conditions as were impofed on fettlers in this country.

The Supply failed the following morning, carrying an inftrument under the hand and feal of the governor, reftoring to the rights and privileges of a free man John Afcott, a convict at Norfolk Ifland, who had rendered himfelf very confpicuous by his exertions in preventing the Sirius from being burnt foon after fhe was wrecked.

On Monday the 28th the Waakfamheyd tranfport failed for England, having on board Captain Hunter, with the officers and crew of his majefty's late fhip Sirius. By Captain Hunter's departure, which was regretted by every one who fhared the pleafure of his fociety, the adminiftration of the country would now devolve upon the lieutenant-governor, in cafe of the death or abfence of the governor; a dormant commiffion having been figned by his majefty invefting Captain Hunter with the chief fituation in the colony in the event of either of the above circumftances taking place.

In the courfe of the night of the 28th, Bryant, whofe term of tranfportation, according to his own account, expired fome day in this month, eluded the watch that was kept upon him, and made his efcape, together with his wife and two children, (one an infant at the breaft,) and feven other convicts, in the fifhing-boat, which, fince the accident at the latter end of the laft month, he had taken care to

X 2   keep

keep in excellent order. Their flight was not discovered until they had been some hours without the Heads.

They were traced from Bryant's hut to the Point, and in the path were found a hand-saw, a scale, and four or five pounds of rice, scattered about in different places, which, it was evident, they had dropped in their haste. At the Point, where some of the party must have been taken in, a seine belonging to government was found, which, being too large for Bryant's purpose, he had exchanged for a smaller that he had made for an officer, and which he had from time to time excused himself from completing and sending home.

The names of these desperate adventurers were,

Came in the first fleet,	William Bryant,	His sentence was expired.
	Mary Braud his wife, and two children,	She had two years to serve.
	James Martin,	He had one year to serve.
	James Cox,	He was transported for life.
	Samuel Bird,	He had one year and four months to serve.
Came in the second fleet,	William Allen,	He was transported for life.
	Samuel Broom,	He had four years and four months to serve.
	Nathaniel Lilly,	He was transported for life.
	William Morton,	He had five years and one month to serve.

So soon as it was known in the settlement that Bryant had got out of reach, we learned that Detmer Smith, the master of the Waaksamheyd, had sold him a compass and a quadrant, and had furnished him with a chart, together with such information as would assist him in his passage to the northward. On searching Bryant's hut, cavities under the boards were found, where he had secured the compass and such other articles as required concealment: and he had contrived his escape with such address, that although he was well known to be about making an attempt, yet how far he was prepared, as well as the time when he meant to go, remained a secret. Most of his companions were connected with women; but if these knew any thing, they were too faithful to those they lived with to reveal it. Had the women been bound to them by any ties of affection, fear for their safety, or the dislike to part, might have induced some of them to have defeated the enterprise; but not having any interest either in their flight, or in their

remaining

remaining here, they were silent on the subject. For one young woman, Sarah Young, a letter was found the next morning, written by James Cox, and left at a place where he was accustomed to work in his leisure hours as a cabinet-maker, conjuring her to give over the pursuit of the vices which, he told her, prevailed in the settlement, leaving to her what little property he did not take with him, and assigning as a reason for his flight the severity of his situation, being transported for life, without the prospect of any mitigation, or hope of ever quitting the country, but by the means he was about to adopt. It was conjectured that they would steer for Timor, or Batavia, as their assistance and information were derived from the Dutch snow.

The situation of these people was very different from that of Tarwood and his associates, who were but ill provided for an undertaking so perilous; but Bryant had long availed himself of the opportunities given him by selling fish to collect provisions together, and his boat was a very good one, and in excellent order; so that there was little reason to doubt their reaching Timor, if no dissension prevailed among them, and they had but prudence enough to guard against the natives wherever they might land. William Morton was said to know something of navigation; James Cox had endeavoured to acquire such information on the subject as might serve him whenever a fit occasion should present itself; and Bryant and Bird knew perfectly well how to manage a boat. What story they could invent on their arrival at any port, sufficiently plausible to prevent suspicion of their real characters, it was not easy to imagine.

The depredations committed on the Indian corn at Rose Hill were now so frequent and so extensive, that it became absolutely necessary to punish such offenders as were detected with a severity that might deter others; to this end, iron collars of seven pounds weight were ordered as a punishment for flagrant offenders, who were also linked together by a chain, without which precaution they would still have continued to plunder the public grounds. The baker at that settlement absconded with a quantity of flour with which he had been entrusted, belonging to the military on duty there, and other persons. He was taken some days afterward in the woods near Sydney. It must be remarked, however,

however, that all thefe thefts were for the procuring of provifions, and that offences of any other tendency were very feldom heard of.

Some time in this month, James Rufe, the firft fettler in this country, who had been upon his ground about fifteen months, having got in his crop of corn, declared himfelf defirous of relinquifhing his claim to any further provifions from the ftore, and faid that he was able to fupport himfelf by the produce of his farm. He had fhewn himfelf an induftrious man; and the governor, being fatisfied that he could do without any further aid from the ftores, confented to his propofal, and informed him that he fhould be forthwith put in poffeffion of an allotment of thirty acres of ground in the fituation he then occupied.

To fecure our frefh water, which, though very low, might ftill be denominated *a run*, the governor caufed a ditch to be dug on each fide of it at fome diftance from the ftream, and employed fome people to erect a paling upon the bank, to keep out ftock, and protect the fhrubs within from being deftroyed.

April.] The fupplies of provifions which had been received in the laft year not warranting the continuing any longer at the ration now iffued, the governor thought it expedient to make a reduction of flour, rice, and falt provifions. Accordingly, on the firft Saturday in this month each man, woman, and child above ten years of age, was to receive,

3 pounds of flour,   1 pound being taken off;
3 pounds of rice,   ditto;
3 pounds of pork,   ditto;
or when beef fhould be ferved,
4½ pounds of beef,   2½ pounds being taken off.

A fmall proportion was to be given to children under ten years of age; and this ration the commiffary was directed to iffue until further orders. Of this allowance the flour was the beft article; the rice was found to be full of weevils; the pork was ill-flavoured, rufty, and fmoked; and the beef was lean, and, by being cured with fpices, truly unpalatable. Much of both thefe articles when they came to be dreffed could not be ufed, and, being the beft that could be procured at
Batavia,

Batavia, no inclination was excited by these specimens to try that market again.

It having been reported to the governor, that Bryant had been frequently heard to express, what was indeed the general sentiment on the subject among the people of his description, that he did not consider his marriage in this country as binding; his excellency caused the convicts to be informed, that none would be permitted to quit the colony who had wives or children incapable of maintaining themselves and likely to become burdensome to the settlement, until they had found sufficient security for the maintenance of such wives or children as long as they might remain after them. This order was designed as a check upon the erroneous opinion which was formed of the efficacy of Mr. Johnson's nuptial benediction; and if Bryant had thought as little of it as he was reported to do, his taking his wife with him could only be accounted for by a dread of her defeating his plan by discovery if she was not made personally interested in his escape.

This order was shortly after followed by another, limiting the length of such boats as should be built by individuals to fourteen feet from stem to stern, that the size of such boats might deter the convicts from attempts to take them off.

About this time some information being received, that it was in agitation to take away the sixteen-oared boat belonging to the colony, or some one or two of the smaller boats, a centinel was placed at night on each wharf; and the officer of the guard was to be spoken to before any boat could leave the cove. In addition to this regulation, it was directed, that the names of all such people as it might be necessary to employ in boats after sun-set should be given in writing to the officer of the guard, to prevent any convicts not belonging to officers or to the public boats from taking them from the wharfs under pretence of fishing or other services.

Mr. Schaffer, who came out from England as a superintendant of convicts, finding himself, from not speaking the language, (being a German,) inadequate to the just discharge of that duty, gave up his appointment as a superintendant, and accepted of a grant of land; and an allotment of one hundred and forty acres were marked out for him on the south side of the creek leading to Rose Hill. On the same side

14   of

of the creek, but nearer to Rose Hill, two allotments of sixty acres each were marked out for two settlers from the Sirius. On the opposite side the governor had placed a convict, Charles Williams, who had recommended himself to his notice by extraordinary propriety of conduct as an overseer, giving him thirty acres; and James Ruse received a grant of the same quantity of land at Rose Hill. These were all the settlers at this time established in New South Wales; but the governor was looking out for some situations in the vicinity of Rose Hill for other settlers, from among the people whose sentences of transportation had expired.

During this month the governor made an excursion to the westward, but he reached no farther than the banks of the Hawkesbury, and returned to Rose Hill on the 6th, without making any discovery of the least importance. At that settlement, the Indian corn was nearly all gathered off the ground; but it could not be said to have been all gathered in, for much of it had been stolen by the convicts. So great a desire for tobacco prevailed among these people, that a man was known to have given the greatest part of his week's provisions for a small quantity of that article; and it was sold, the produce of the place, for ten and even fifteen shillings per pound. The governor, on being made acquainted with this circumstance, intimated an intention of prohibiting the growth of tobacco, judging it to be more for the true interest of the people to cultivate the necessaries than the luxuries of life.

The public works at Rose Hill consisted in building the officers barracks; a small guardhouse near the governor's hut; a small house for the judge-advocate (whose occasional presence there as a magistrate was considered necessary by the governor), and for the clergyman; and in getting in the Indian corn.

At Sydney, the house for the surveyor-general was covered in; and the carpenters were employed in finishing that for the clergyman. Bricks were also brought in for a house for the principal surgeon, to be built near the hospital on the west side.

Many thefts, and some of money, were committed during the month at both settlements. A hut belonging to James Davis, employed as a coxswain to the public boats, was broken into; but nothing was stolen,

Davis

Davis having taken his money with him, and nothing elfe appearing to have been the object of their fearch. His hut was fituated out of the view of any centinel, and a night was chofen for the attempt when it was known that he was on duty at Rofe Hill.

_____

CHAP. XIII.

A MUSQUET FOUND BY A NATIVE.—REPORTS OF PLANS TO SEIZE BOATS.—
SUPPLY ARRIVES FROM NORFOLK ISLAND.—THE KING'S BIRTH DAY.—
A CANOE DESTROYED.—ITS EVIL EFFECTS.—CORN SOWN.—BATTERY BE-
GUN.—ONE HUNDRED AND FORTY ACRES INCLOSED FOR CATTLE.—THE
MARY ANN ARRIVES.—TWO CRIMINAL COURTS HELD.—RATION IM-
PROVED.—THE MATILDA ARRIVES.—THE MARY ANN SAILS FOR NORFOLK
ISLAND.—SETTLERS.—THE ATLANTIC AND SALAMANDER ARRIVE.—FULL
RATION ISSUED.—THE WILLIAM AND ANN ARRIVES.—NATIVES.—PUBLIC
WORKS.

May.] COLE-BE, the native who fince our communication with thefe people had attached himfelf to Mr. White, the principal furgeon, made his appearance one morning in the beginning of the month with a mufquet, which, on diving into the fea for fomething elfe, he had brought up with him. It was fuppofed to have been loft from Mr. White's boat in November laft at the lower part of the harbour.

The fcheme for feizing one of the boats was refumed in this month, and appeared to be in great forwardnefs. The boat however was changed, the long-boat being chofen inftead of that which was at firft thought of. She was to be feized the firft time fhe fhould be employed in towing the hoy with provifions to Rofe Hill; out of which they were to take what quantity they required for their purpofe, land the crew, and run her afhore. On receiving this information, the governor, inftead of fending the hoy up with different fpecies of provifions, caufed her to be loaded with rice, and a fmall quantity of flour, in fome meafure to defeat their fcheme, at leaft for that time, as the information did not ftate that they had collected any falt provifions. She

Y   was

was accordingly difpatched with flour and rice, and returned fafely, no attempt having been made to ftop her. It was then faid, that they were at a lofs for a perfon to navigate her; and that a depofit of powder and ball was made at a farm near the brick-fields; where however, on fearching, nothing of the kind was found. Various other reports were whifpered during the month, which, whether founded in truth or not, had this good effect, that every neceffary precaution was taken to prevent their fucceeding in any attempt of that kind which they might be defperate enough to make.

Much anxiety was excited on account of the long and unufual abfence of the Supply, which failed for Norfolk Ifland on the 22d day of March, and did not return to this harbour until the 30th of this month, which completed ten weeks within a day fince fhe failed. Contrary winds and heavy gales had prevented her arrival at the time fhe might have been reafonably expected. She was three weeks in her paffage hither, and was blown off the ifland for eleven days.

Captain Johnfton, Lieutenants Crefwell and Kellow, one ferjeant, one corporal, one drummer, and twenty privates of the marine detachment, arrived in the Supply; with two prifoners, one a foldier for fome irregularity of conduct when centinel, the other a convict.

The weather had been as dry at Norfolk Ifland as it had been here; which, with the blighting winds, had confiderably injured all the gardens, and particularly fome crops of potatoes. Of the great fertility of the foil every account brought the ftrongeft confirmation; and by attending to the proper feafon for fowing, it was the general opinion that two crops of corn might be got off in a year.

Their provifions, like ours, were again at fo low an ebb, that the lieutenant-governor had reduced the ration. The whole number victualled when the Supply failed amounted to fix hundred and twenty-nine perfons; and for that number there were in ftore at the *full* ration, flour and Indian corn for twenty weeks, beef for eighteen weeks, and pork for twenty-nine weeks; and thefe, at the ration then iffued, would be prolonged, the grain to twenty-feven, the beef to forty-two, and the pork to twenty-nine weeks.

It muft however be remarked, that the ration at Norfolk Ifland was often uncertain, being regulated by the plenty or fcarcity of the Mount

Pitt

Pitt birds. Great numbers of these birds had been killed for some time before the Supply failed thence; but they were observed about that time to be quitting the island.

On board the Supply were some planks, and such part of the stores belonging to the Sirius as the lieutenant-governor could get on board. That ship had not then gone to pieces; the side of her which was on the reef was broken in and much injured, but the side next the sea (the larboard side) appeared fresh and perfect.

At Sydney, by an account taken at the latter end of the month of the provisions then remaining in store, there appeared to be at the ration then issued of

> Flour and rice 40 weeks, a supply till 31st March 1792;
> Beef   - 12 weeks, ditto, - 31st August 1791;
> Pork   - 27 weeks, ditto, - 21st December 1791.

In this account the rice and flour were taken together as one article, but the rice bore by far the greatest proportion.

It was remarked by many in the settlement, that both at Sydney and at Rose Hill the countenances of the labouring convicts indicated the shortness of the ration they received; this might be occasioned by their having suffered so much before from the same cause, from the effects of which they had scarcely been restored when they were again called upon to experience the hardship of a reduced ration of provisions. The convicts who arrived in June had not recovered from the severity of their passage to this country.

It having been said that James Ruse, who in March last had declared his ability to support himself independent of the store, was starving, the governor told him, that in consideration of his having been upon a short allowance of provisions during nearly the whole of the time he had been cultivating ground upon his own account, the storekeeper should be directed to supply him with twenty pounds of salt provisions. The man assured his excellency that he did not stand in need of his bounty, having by him at the time a small stock of provisions; a quantity of Indian corn, (which he found no difficulty in exchanging for salt meat,) and a bag of flour; all which enabled him to do so well, that he absolutely begged permission to *decline* the offer. So very contradictory was his own account of his situation to that which had been reported.

The

The barracks at Rose Hill, being so far completed as to admit of being occupied, were taken possession of this month by the New South Wales corps.

Several thefts of provisions were committed; two, that were of some consequence, appeared as if the provisions had been collected for some particular purpose; and, if so, perhaps only passed from the possession of one thief to that of another. While a stalk of Indian corn remained upon the ground, the convicts resolved to plunder it, and several were severely punished; but it did not appear that they were amended by the correction, nor that others were deterred by the example of their punishment. So truly incorrigible were many of these people!

Finishing the clergyman's and surveyor's houses; bringing in bricks for other buildings; posts and paling for a fence round the run of water; and making cloathing for the people, occupied the convicts at Sydney.

June.] The bad weather met with by the Supply during her late voyage to Norfolk Island had done her so much injury, that, on a careful examination of her defects, it appeared that she could not be got ready for sea in less than three months. In addition to other repairs which were indispensable, her main mast was found so defective, that after cutting off eighteen feet from the head of it, and finding the heel nearly as bad, the carpenter was of opinion that she must be furnished with an entire new mast. This, when the difficulty of finding timber for her foremast (which, it must be remarked, bore the heavy gales of wind she met with, as well as could be desired even of wood the fittest for masts) was recollected, was an unlucky and an ill-timed want; for, should it happen that supplies were not received from England by the middle or end of the month of July, the services of this vessel would be again required; and, to save the colony, she must at that time have been dispatched to some settlement in India for provisions. She was therefore forthwith hauled along-side the rocks, and people were employed to look for sound timber fit for a mast.

On his majesty's birth-day an extra allowance of provisions was issued to the garrison and settlements; each man receiving one pound of salt meat, and the like quantity of rice; each woman half a pound of

Ny water-house Greenwater, with a distant view of the western mountains taken from the Third mill

of meat and one pound of rice; and each child a quarter of a pound of meat and half a pound of rice. And to make it a chearful day to every one, all offenders who had for stealing Indian corn been ordered to wear iron collars were pardoned.

The town which had been marked out at Rose Hill, and which now wore something of a regular appearance, on this occasion received its name. The governor called it Par-ra-mat-ta, being the name by which the natives distinguished the part of the country on which the town stood.

Notwithstanding the lenity and indulgence which had been shewn on his majesty's birth-day, in pardoning the plunderers of gardens and the public grounds, and by issuing an extra allowance of provisions to every one, the governor's garden at Parramatta was that very night entered and robbed by six men, who assaulted the watchman (Thomas Ocraft) and would have escaped all together, had he not, with much resolution, secured three of them for punishment.

Indulgences of this nature were certainly thrown away upon many who partook of them; but as it was impossible to discriminate so nicely between the good and the bad as wholly to exclude the undeserving, no distinction could be made.

The people who had assaulted the watchman were severely punished, as his authority could never have been supported without such an example; but either his vigilance, or the countenance which was shewn to him on account of his strict performance of his duty, created him many enemies; and it became necessary to give him arms, as well for his own defence, as for the more effectual protection of the district he watched over. Some nights after, in a turnip ground at Parramatta, he was obliged to fire at a convict, whom he wounded, but not dangerously, and secured. He was sent down to the hospital at Sydney.

Since the establishment of that familiar intercourse which now subsisted between us and the natives, several of them had found it their interest to sell or exchange fish among the people at Parramatta; they being contented to receive a small quantity of either bread or salt meat in barter for mullet, bream, and other fish. To the officers who resided there this proved a great convenience, and they encouraged the natives to visit them as often as they could bring them fish. There

were,

were, however, among the convicts some who were so unthinking, or so depraved, as wantonly to destroy a canoe belonging to a fine young man, a native, who had left it at some little distance from the settlement, and as he hoped out of the way of observation, while he went with some fish to the huts. His rage at finding his canoe destroyed was inconceivable; and he threatened to take his own revenge, and in his own way, upon all white people. Three of the six people who had done him the injury, however, were so well described by some one who had seen them, that, being closely followed, they were taken and punished, as were the remainder in a few days after.

The instant effect of all this was, that the natives discontinued to bring up fish; and Bal-loo-der-ry, whose canoe had been destroyed, although he had been taught to believe that one of the six convicts had been hanged for the offence, meeting a few days afterwards with a poor wretch who had strayed from Parramatta as far as the Flats, he wounded him in two places with a spear. This act of Ballooderry's was followed by the governor's strictly forbidding him to appear again at any of the settlements; the other natives, his friends, being alarmed, Parramatta was seldom visited by any of them, and all commerce with them was destroyed. How much greater claim to the appellation of · savages had the wretches who were the cause of this, than the native who was the sufferer?

During this month some rain had fallen, which had encouraged the sowing of the public grounds, and one hundred and sixteen bushels of wheat were sown at Parramatta. Until these rains fell, the ground was so dry, hard, and literally burnt up, that it was almost impossible to break it with a hoe, and until this time there had been no hope or probability of the grain vegetating.

In the beginning of the month, the stone-mason, with the people under his direction, had begun working at the west point of the cove, where the governor purposed constructing out of the rock a spot whereon to place the guns belonging to the settlement, which was to wear the appearance of a *work.* The flag-staff was to be placed in the same situation. The house for the principal surgeon was got up and covered in during this month.

Among

Among the convicts who died about this time, was —— Frazer, a man who came out in the first fleet, and who, since his landing, had been employed as a blacksmith. He was an excellent workman, and was supposed to have brought on an untimely end by hard drinking, as he seldom chose to accept of any article but spirits in payment for work done in his extra hours.

July.] To guard against a recurrence of the accident which happened to our cattle soon after we had arrived, the governor had for some time past employed a certain number of convicts at Parramatta in forming inclosures; and at the commencement of this month not less than one hundred and forty acres were thinned of the timber, surrounded by a ditch, and guarded by a proper fence.

In addition to the quantity of ground sown with wheat, a large proportion was cleared to be sown this season with Indian corn; and the country about Parramatta, as well as the town itself, where eight huts were now built, wore a very promising appearance.

At Sydney, the little ground that was in cultivation belonged to individuals; the whole labour of the convicts employed in clearing ground being exerted at Parramatta, where the soil, though not the best for the purposes of agriculture, (according to the opinion of every man who professed any knowledge of farming,) was still better than the sand about Sydney, where, to raise even a cabbage after the first crop, manure was absolutely requisite.

On the morning of the ninth, the signal for a sail was made at the South-head; and before night it was made known that the Mary Ann transport was arrived from England, with one hundred and forty-one female convicts on board, six children, and one free woman, some clothing, and the following small quantity of provisions: one hundred and thirty-two barrels of flour; sixty-one tierces of pork; and thirty-two tierces of beef.

This ship sailed alone; but we were informed that she was to be followed by nine sail of transports, on board of which were embarked, (including one hundred and fifty women, the number put into the Mary Ann,) two thousand and fifty male and female convicts; the whole of which were to be expected in the course of six weeks or two months, together with his Majesty's ship Gorgon.

We

We also learned that Lieutenant King, who sailed hence the 17th April 1790, arrived in London the 20th day of December following, having suffered much distress after leaving Batavia, whence he was obliged to go to the Mauritius, having lost nearly all the crew of the packet he was in by sickness. Mr. Millar, the late commissary, died on the 28th of August.

With great satisfaction we heard, that from our government having adopted a system of sending out convicts at two embarkations in every year, at which time provisions were also to be sent, it was not probable that we should again experience the misery and want with which we had been but too well acquainted, from not having had any regular mode of supply. Intimation was likewise given, that a cargo of grain might be expected to arrive from Bengal, some merchants at that settlement having proposed to Lord Cornwallis, on hearing of the loss of the Guardian, to freight a ship with such a cargo as would be adapted to the wants of the colony, and to supply the different articles at a cheaper rate than they could be sent hither from England. We were also to expect a transport with live stock from the north-west coast of America.

The master, Mark Monroe, had not any private letters on board; but (what added to the disappointment every one experienced) he had not brought a single newspaper; and, having been but a few weeks from Greenland before he sailed for this country, he was destitute of any kind of information.

The Mary Ann had a quick passage, having been only four months and sixteen days from England. She touched nowhere, except at the island of St. Iago, where she remained ten days. The master landed a boat in a bay on this coast about fifteen miles to the southward of Botany Bay; but made no other observation of any consequence to the colony, than that there was a bay in which a boat might land.

The women, who were all very healthy, and who spoke highly of the treatment which they had experienced from Mr. Monroe, were landed immediately after the arrival of the transport in the cove, and were distributed among the huts at Sydney, while the governor went up to Parramatta to make such preparation as the time would admit for the numbers he expected to receive.

The

The convicts whose terms of transportation had expired were now collected, and by the authority of the governor informed, that such of them as wished to become settlers in this country should receive every encouragement; that those who did not, were to labour for their provisions, stipulating to work for twelve or eighteen months certain; and that in the way of such as preferred returning to England no obstacles would be thrown, provided they could procure passages from the masters of such ships as might arrive; but that they were not to expect any assistance on the part of Government to that end. The wish to return to their friends appeared to be the prevailing idea, a few only giving in their names as settlers, and none engaging to work for a certain time.

We had twice in this month found occasion to assemble the court of criminal judicature. In the night of Saturday the 16th, a soldier of the marine detachment was detected by the patroles in the spirit cellar adjoining to the deputy-commissary's house, the lock of which he had forced. On being taken up, he offered, if he could be admitted an evidence, to convict two others; which being allowed, the court was assembled on the 19th, when two of his brother soldiers were tried; but for want of evidence sufficiently strong to corroborate the testimony of the accomplice, they were of necessity acquitted. Godfrey the accomplice was afterwards tried by a military court for neglect of duty and disobedience of orders in quitting his post when centinel; which offence being proved against him, he was sentenced to receive eight hundred lashes, and to be drummed out of the corps. In the evening of the day on which he was tried (the 21st) he received three hundred lashes, and was drummed out with every mark of disgrace that could be shewn him. In a short time afterwards the two soldiers who had been acquitted were sent to do duty at the South Head. There was little room to doubt, but that in concert with Godfrey they had availed themselves of their situations as centinels, and frequently entered the cellar; and it was judged necessary to place them where they would *. be disabled from concerting any future scheme with him.

A convict was tried for a burglary by the same court, but was acquitted. On the 27th another court was assembled for the trial of James Chapman, for a burglary committed in the preceding month

z   in

in the house of John Petree, a convict, in which he stole several articles of wearing apparel. Charles Crofs and Joseph Hatton, two
convicts, were also tried for receiving them knowing them to be stolen.
Chapman the principal, refusing to plead any thing but guilty, received sentence of death. Against the receivers it appeared in evidence,
that after the burglary was committed the property was concealed in
the woods between Sydney and Parramatta, at which place all the
parties resided, that having suffered it to remain some weeks, Chapman
and Crofs went from Parramatta to bring it away; and while they
were so employed, Hatton found that the watchmen were going in
pursuit of Chapman; on which he directly set off to meet and adver-
tise them of it, and receive the property, which; by a clear chain of
evidence, he was proved to have taken and concealed again in the
woods. Hatton was found guilty, and sentenced to receive eight
hundred lashes. Crofs was acquitted. Chapman was executed the
following day at noon. Half an hour before he died, he informed
the judge-advocate and the clergyman who attended him, that a plan
was formed of breaking into the government-house, and robbing it of
a large sum of money which it was imagined the governor kept in it;
and that it was to be executed by himself and three other convicts, all
of whom were, however, very far from being of suspicious characters.
But as there was no reason to suppose that a person in such an awful
situation would invent an accusation by which he could not himself
be benefited, and which might injure three innocent people, the governor took all the precautions that he thought necessary to guard
against the meditated villany.

A practice having been discovered, of purchasing the soldiers regimental neceffaries for the purpose of disposing of them among the
shipping, and this requiring a punishment that should effectually check
it, Bond, a convict who baked for the hospital and others, was brought
before two magistrates, and, being convicted of having bought several
articles of wearing apparel which had been served to a soldier, was
sentenced to pay the penalty prescribed by act of parliament, five
pounds; or, on failure within a certain time, to go to prison. Having
made some considerable profits in the exercise of his trade as a baker,
he preferred paying the penalty.

It

It being always defirable to go as near the eftablifhed ration as the ftate of the ftores would allow, and the governor never wifhing to keep the labouring man one moment longer than was abfolutely neceffary upon a reduced allowance of provifions, he directed two pounds of rice to be added to the weekly proportion of that article; but, although by this addition eight pounds of grain were iffued, (viz. three pounds of flour and five pounds of rice,) the ration was far from being brought up to the ftandard eftablifhed by the Treafury for the colony; five pounds of bad worm-eaten rice making a moft inadequate fubftitute for the fame quantity of good flour. In the article of meat the labouring man fuffered ftill more; for in a given quantity of fixty pounds, which were iffued on one ferving day to two meffes, there were no lefs than forty pounds of bone, and the remainder, which was intended to be eaten, was almoft too far advanced in putrefaction for even hunger to get down. It muft be obferved that it came in the fnow from Batavia.

Patrick Burn, a perfon employed to fhoot for the commanding officer of the marine detachment, died this month; and the hut that he had lived in was burnt down in the night a few hours after his deceafe, by the carelefnefs of the people, who were Irifh and were fitting up with the corpfe, which was with much difficulty faved from the flames, and not until it was much fcorched.

Auguft.] On Monday, the 1ft of Auguft, the Matilda, the firft of the expected fleet of tranfports, arrived, after an extraordinary paffage of four months and five days, from Portfmouth; having failed from thence on the 27th day of March laft, with four fail of tranfports for this place, with whom fhe parted company that night off Dunnoze. Another divifion of tranfports had failed a week before from Plymouth Sound. On board the Matilda were two hundred and five male convicts, one enfign, one ferjeant, one corporal, one drummer, and nineteen privates, of the New South Wales corps; and fome ftores and provifions calculated as a fupply for the above number for nine months after their arrival.

The mafter of this fhip anchored for two days in a bay of one of Schoeten's Iflands, diftant from the main land about twelve miles, in the latitude of 42° 15′ S.; where, according to his report, five or fix

Z 2   fhips

ships might find shelter. Those who were on shore saw the footsteps of different kinds of animals, and traces of natives, such as huts, fires, broken spears, and the instrument which they use for throwing the spear. They spoke of the soil as sandy, and observed that the ground was covered with shrubs such as were to be found here.

The convicts in this ship, on their landing, appeared to be aged and infirm, the state in which they were said to have been embarked. It was not therefore to be wondered at, that they had buried twenty-five on the passage. One soldier also died. Twenty were brought in sick, and were immediately landed at the hospital.

It was intended by the governor that this ship should have proceeded immediately to Norfolk Island with the greater part of the convicts she had on board, together with all the stores and provisions; but the master, Mr. Matthew Weatherhead, requesting that as the ship was very leaky the Mary Ann might be permitted to perform the service required, instead of the Matilda, (both ships belonging to the same owners,) and the Mary Ann being perfectly ready for sea, the governor consented to this proposal; and that ship was hauled alongside the Matilda to receive her cargo. Fifty-five of the convicts brought in this ship, selected from the others as farmers or artificers, were sent up to Parramatta; of the remainder, those whose health would permit them to go were put on board the Mary Ann, together with thirty-two convicts of bad character from among those who came out in the preceding year, and eleven privates of the New South Wales corps. On the Monday following (the 8th) the Mary Ann sailed for Norfolk Island.

At Parramatta the only accommodation which the shortness of the notice admitted of being provided for the people who were on their passage was got up; two tent huts, one hundred feet long, thatched with grass, were erected; and, independent of the risk which the occupiers might run from fire, they would afford good and comfortable shelter from the weather.

The governor had now chosen situations for his settlers, and fixed them on their different allotments. Twelve convicts, whose terms of transportation had expired, he placed in a range of farms at the foot of a hill named Prospect Hill, about four miles west from Parramatta;

fifteen

fifteen others were placed on allotments in a diftrict named the Ponds, from a range of fresh-water ponds being in their vicinity; these were situated two miles in a direction north-east of Parramatta. Between every allotment, a space had been reserved equal to the largest grant on either side, pursuant to the instructions which the governor had received; but it was soon found that this distribution might be attended with much disadvantage to the settler; a thick wood of at least thirty acres must lie between every allotment; and a circumstance happened which shewed the inconvenience consequent thereon, and determined the governor to deviate from the instructions, whenever, by adhering to them, the settlers were likely to be material sufferers.

In the beginning of the month information was received, that a much larger party of the natives than had yet been seen assembled at any one time had destroyed a hut belonging to a settler at Prospect Hill, who would have been murdered by them, but for the timely and accidental appearance of another settler with a musquet. There was no doubt of the hut having been destroyed, and by natives, though perhaps their numbers were much exaggerated; the governor, therefore, determined to place other settlers upon the allotments which had been reserved for the crown; by which means assistance in similar or other accidents would be more ready.

After the arrival of the Matilda, the governor, judging that his stores would admit of increasing the weekly allowance of flour, directed that (instead of three) five pounds of that article should be issued to each man; and to each woman an addition of half a pound to the three which they before received. The other articles of the ration remained as before.

The platform which had been constructing on the West Point since June last being ready for the reception of the cannon, they were moved thither about the middle of the month; in doing which, a triangle which was made use of, not being properly secured, slipped and fell upon a convict, (an overseer,) by which accident his thigh was dislocated, and his body much bruised. He was taken to the hospital, where, fortunately, Mr. White immediately reduced the luxation.

About noon on Saturday the 20th, the Atlantic transport anchored in the cove from Plymouth, whence she sailed with two other trans-

ports,

ports, and parted with them about five weeks since in bad weather between Rio de Janeiro and this port, the passage from which had not been more than ten weeks. She had on board a serjeant's party of the new corps as a guard to two hundred and twenty male convicts, eighteen of whom died on the passage. The remainder came in very healthy, there being only nine sick on board. The evening before her arrival she stood into a capacious bay, situated between Long Nose and Cape St. George, where they found good anchorage and deep water. Lieutenant Richard Bowen, the naval agent on board, who landed, described the soil to be sandy, and the country thickly covered with timber. He did not see any natives, but found a canoe upon the beach, whose owners perhaps were not far off. This canoe, by Lieutenant Bowen's account, appeared to be on a somewhat stronger construction than the canoes of Port Jackson.

The signal for another sail was made the next morning at the Look-out, and about one o'clock the Salamander transport arrived. She sailed from England under Lieutenant Bowen's orders, with a serjeant's party of the new corps and one hundred and sixty male convicts on board, one hundred and fifty-five of whom she brought in all healthy, except one man who was in the sick list. The party arrived without the serjeant, he having deserted on their leaving England.

Both these transports having brought a supply of provisions calculated to serve nine months for the convicts that were embarked, the governor directed the commissary to issue the full ration of provisions, serving rice in lieu of pease; the reduced ration having continued from Saturday the 2d day of last April to Saturday the 27th of August; twenty-one weeks.

A party of one hundred convicts were sent from the Atlantic to Parramatta, the remainder were landed and disposed of at Sydney. The Salamander was ordered to proceed to Norfolk Island with the people and the cargo she had on board.

There were at this time not less than seventy persons from the Matilda and Atlantic under medical treatment, being weak, emaciated, and unfit for any kind of labour; and the list was increasing. It might have been supposed that on changing from the unwholesome air of a ship's between-decks to the purer air of this country, the weak would have

gathered

gathered ftrength; but it had been obferved, that in general foon after landing, the convicts were affected with dyfenteric complaints, perhaps caufed by the change of water, many dying, and others who had ftrength to overcome the difeafe recovering from it but flowly.

On the 28th the William and Ann tranfport arrived (the laft of Lieutenant Bowen's divifion). She had on board one ferjeant and twelve privates of the new corps, one hundred and eighty-one male convicts, with her proportion of ftores and provifions. She failed with one hundred and eighty-eight convicts from England, but loft feven on the paffage; the remainder came in very healthy, five only being fo ill as to require removal. The firft mate of this fhip, Mr. Simms, formerly belonged to the Golden Grove tranfport.

The town beginning to fill with ftrangers, (officers and feamen from the tranfports,) and fpirituous liquors finding their way among the convicts, it was ordered that none fhould be landed until a permit had been granted by the judge-advocate; and the provoft-marfhal, his affiftant, and two principals of the watch, were deputed to feize all fpirituous liquors which might be landed without.

Ballooderry, the profcribed native, having ventured into the town with fome of his friends, one or two armed parties were fent to feize him, and a fpear having been thrown, (it was faid by him,) two mufquets were fired, by which one of his companions was wounded in the leg; but Ballooderry was not taken. On the following day it was given out in orders, that he was to be taken whenever an opportunity offered; and that any native attempting to throw a fpear in his defence, as it was well known among them why vengeance was denounced againft him, was, if poffible, to be prevented from efcaping with impunity.

Thofe who knew Ballooderry regretted that it had been neceffary to treat him with this harfhnefs, as among his countrymen we had no where feen a finer young man. The perfon who had been wounded by him in the month of June laft was not yet recovered.

Difcharging the tranfports formed the principal labour of the month; the fhingles on the roof of the old hofpital being found to decay faft, and many falling off, the whole were removed, and the building was covered with tiles.

The

The convicts at Parramatta were employed in opening some ground about a mile and a half above that settlement, along the south side of the creek ; and it was expected from the exertions which they were making, that between forty and fifty acres would be soon ready for sowing with Indian corn for this season. Their labour was directed by Thomas Daveney, a free person who came out with the governor.

CHAP. XIV.

THE SALAMANDER SAILS FOR, AND THE MARY ANN ARRIVES FROM NOR-
FOLK ISLAND.—BONDEL, A NATIVE, RETURNS.—A SEAMAN, FOR SINK-
ING A CANOE, PUNISHED.—THE GORGON ARRIVES.—COMMISSION OF
EMANCIPATION, AND PUBLIC SEAL.—THE ACTIVE AND QUEEN ARRIVE.—
COMPLAINTS AGAINST THE MASTER OF THE QUEEN.—SUPPLY ORDERED
HOME.—ALBEMARLE ARRIVES.—MUTINY ON BOARD.—BRITANNIA AND
ADMIRAL BARRINGTON ARRIVE.—FUTURE DESTINATION OF THE TRANS-
PORTS.—THE ATLANTIC AND QUEEN HIRED.—ATLANTIC SAILS FOR BEN-
GAL.—SALAMANDER RETURNS FROM NORFOLK ISLAND.—TRANSACTIONS.
—PUBLIC WORKS.—SUICIDE.

September.] IT became necessary to land the cargo brought out in the Salamander, for the purpose of re-stowing it in a manner convenient for getting it out at Norfolk Island while the ship was under sail. The great inconvenience attending landing a cargo in such a situation had been pointed out in letters which could not yet have been attended to. It was at the same time suggested, that ships should be freighted pur-posely for Norfolk Island, with casks and bales adapted to the size of the island boats, which would in a great measure lessen the inconveni-ence above mentioned.

On the 3d, near two hundred male convicts, with a serjeant's party of the New South Wales corps, some stores and provisions, having been put on board the Salamander, she sailed for Norfolk Island the follow-ing morning : and the Mary Ann returned from that settlement on the 8th, having been absent only four weeks and two days. The convicts,

troops,

troops, ftores, and provifions were all landed fafely; but an unexpected furf rifing at the back of the reef, filling the only boat (a Greenland whale-boat) which the mafter took with him, fhe was dafhed upon the reef, and ftove; the people, who all belonged to the whaler, fortunately faved themfelves by fwimming.

From Norfolk Ifland we learned, that the crops of wheat then in the ground promifed well, having been fown a month earlier than thofe of the laft feafon. Of the public ground ninety acres were in wheat, and one hundred in Indian corn: of the ground cleared by the convicts, and cultivated by themfelves for their own maintenance, there were not lefs, at the departure of the tranfport, than two hundred and fifty acres.

Bondel, a native boy, who went thither with Captain Hill, to whom he was attached, in the month of March laft, came back by this conveyance to his friends and relations at Port Jackfon. During his refidence on the Ifland, which Mr. Monroe faid he quitted reluctantly, he feemed to have gained fome fmattering of our language, certain words of which he occafionally blended with his own.

Some prifoners having been fent from Norfolk Ifland, the criminal court was affembled on the 15th for the trial of one of them for a capital offence committed there; but for want of fufficient evidence he was acquitted. Great inconvenience was experienced from having to fend prifoners from that ifland with all the neceffary witneffes. In the cafe juft mentioned the profecutor was a fettler, who being obliged to leave his farm for the time, the bufinefs of which was neceffarily fufpended until he could return, was ruined: and one of the witneffes was in nearly the fame fituation. But as the courts in New South Wales would always be the fuperior courts, it was not eafy to difcover a remedy for thefe inconveniences.

A feaman of one of the tranfports having been clearly proved to have wantonly funk a canoe belonging to a native, who had been paddling round the fhip, and at laft ventured on board, he was ordered to be punifhed, and to give the native a complete fuit of wearing apparel, as a fatisfaction for the injury he had done him, as well as to induce him to abandon any defign of revenge which he might have formed. The corporal punifhment was however afterwards remitted, and the fea-

A A   man

man ordered to remain on board his ship while she should continue in this port.

Some of the soldiers who came out in the William and Ann transport having exhibited complaints against the master, whom they accused of assaulting and severely beating them during the passage, the affair was investigated before three magistrates, and a fine laid upon the master, which he paid.

On Wednesday the 21st his Majesty's ship Gorgon of forty-four guns, commanded by Captain John Parker, anchored within the heads of the harbour, reaching the settlement the following morning, and anchoring where his Majesty's late ship Sirius used to moor.

The Gorgon sailed from England on the 15th of March last, touching on her passage at the islands of Teneriffe and St. Iago, and at the Cape of Good Hope, where she remained six weeks, taking in three bulls, twenty-three cows, sixty-eight sheep, eleven hogs, two hundred fruit trees, a quantity of garden seed, and other articles for the colony. Unfortunately, the bulls and seven of the cows died; but a bull-calf, which had been produced on board, arrived in good condition.

Six months provisions for about nine hundred people, with stores for his Majesty's armed tender the Supply, and for the marine detachment, were sent out in the Gorgon; wherein also was embarked Mr. King, the late commandant of Norfolk Island, now appointed by his Majesty lieutenant-governor of that settlement, and a commander in the navy; together with Mr. Charles Grimes, commissioned as a deputy surveyor-general to be employed at Norfolk Island; the chaplain and quarter-master of the New South Wales corps, and Mr. David Burton, a superintendant of convicts.

By this ship we received a public seal to be affixed to all instruments drawn in his Majesty's name, and a commission under the great seal empowering the governor for the time being to remit, either absolutely or conditionally, the whole or any part of the term for which felons, or other offenders, should have been or might hereafter be transported to this country. Duplicates of each pardon were to be sent to England, for the purpose of inserting the names of the persons so emancipated in the first general pardon which should afterwards issue under the great seal of the kingdom.

To

To deserving characters, of which description there were many convicts in the colony, a prospect of having the period of their banishment shortened, and of being restored to the privilege which by misconduct they had forfeited, had something in it very cheering, and was more likely to preserve well intentioned men in honest and fair pursuits, than the fear of punishment, which would seldom operate with good effect on a mind that entertained no hope of reward for propriety of conduct. The people with whom we had to deal were not in general actuated by that nice sense of feeling which draws its truest satisfaction from self approbation; they looked for something more substantial, something more obvious to the external senses.

In determining the device for the seal of the colony, attention had been paid to its local and peculiar circumstances. On the obverse were the king's arms, with the royal titles in the margin; on the reverse, a representation of convicts landing at Botany Bay, received by Industry, who, surrounded by her attributes, a bale of merchandise, a beehive, a pickaxe, and a shovel, is releasing them from their fetters, and pointing to oxen ploughing and a town rising on the summit of a hill, with a fort for its protection. The masts of a ship are seen in the bay. In the margin are the words *Sigillum. Nov. Camb. Aust.*; and for a motto " *Sic fortis Etruria crevit.*" The seal was of silver; its weight forty-six ounces, and the devices were very well executed.

The cattle were immediately landed, and turned into the inclosures which had been prepared for them. One cow died in the boat going up.

The remaining transports of the fleet were now dropping in. On the 26th the Active from England, and the Queen from Ireland, with convicts of that country, arrived and anchored in the cove. On board of the Active, beside the serjeant's guard, were one hundred and fifty-four male convicts. An officer's party was on board the Queen, with one hundred and twenty-six male and twenty-three female convicts, and three children.

These ships had been unhealthy, and had buried several convicts in their passage. The sick which they brought in were landed immediately; and many of those who remained, and were not so ill as to

A A 2   require

require medical affiſtance, were brought on ſhore in an emaciated and feeble condition, particularly the convicts from the Active. They in general complained of not having received the allowance intended for them; but their emaciated appearance was to be aſcribed as much to confinement as to any other cauſe. The convicts from the Queen, however, accuſing the maſter of having withheld their proviſions, an inquiry took place before the magiſtrates, and it appeared beyond a doubt, that great abuſes had been practiſed in the iſſuing of the proviſions; but as to the quantity withheld, it was not poſſible to aſcertain it ſo clearly, as to admit of directing the deficiency to be made good, or of puniſhing the parties with that retributive juſtice for which the heinouſneſs of their offence ſo loudly called; the proceedings of the magiſtrates were therefore ſubmitted to the governor, who determined to tranſmit them to the ſecretary of ſtate.

Nothing could have excited more general indignation than the treatment which theſe people appeared to have met with; for, what crime could be more offenſive to every ſentiment of humanity, than the endeavour, by curtailing a ration already not too ample, to derive a temporary advantage from the miſeries of our fellow-creatures!

By the arrival of theſe ſhips ſeveral articles of comfort were introduced among us, there being ſcarcely a veſſel that had not brought out ſomething for ſale. It could not, however, be ſaid that they were procurable on eaſier terms than what had been ſold here in the laſt year. The Spaniſh dollar was the current coin of the colony, which ſome of the maſters taking at five ſhillings and others at four ſhillings and ſix-pence, the governor, in conſideration of the officers having been obliged to receive the dollars at five ſhillings ſterling when given for bills drawn in the ſettlement, iſſued a proclamation fixing the currency of the Spaniſh dollar at that ſum.

The Supply was now carefully ſurveyed, when it appeared, that her defects were ſuch as to render it by no means difficult to put her into a ſtate that would enable her to reach England; but that if ſhe remained ſix months longer in this country, ſhe would become wholly unſerviceable. It was therefore determined to diſpatch her immediately to England. Timber had with infinite labour been procured

for

for her main-mast, and her other repairs were put in train for her sailing hence in the course of the next month.

October.] The remainder of the transports expected did not arrive until the middle of October. The Albemarle was off the coast some days, being prevented by a southerly current from getting in. She arrived on Thursday the 13th, with two hundred and fifty male and six female convicts, her proportion of stores and provisions, and one serjeant, one corporal, one drummer, and twenty privates of the new corps.

The convicts of this ship had made an attempt, in conjunction with some of the seamen, to seize her on the 9th of April, soon after she had sailed from England; and they would in all probability have succeeded,·but for the activity and resolution shewn by the master Mr. George Bowen, who, hearing the alarm, had just time to arm himself with a loaded blunderbuss, which he discharged at one of the mutineers, William Syney, (then in the act of aiming a blow with a cutlass at the man at the wheel,) and lodged its contents in his shoulder. His companions, seeing what had befallen him, instantly ran down below; but the master, his officers, and some of the seamen of the ship, following them, soon secured the ringleaders, Owen Lyons and William Syney. A consultation was held with the naval agent, Lieutenant Robert Parry Young, the ship's company, and the military persons on board, the result of which was, the immediate execution of those two at the fore-yard arm. They had at this time parted company with the other transports, and no other means seemed so likely to deter the convicts from any future attempt of the like nature. It afterwards appearing that two of the seamen had supplied them with instruments for sawing off their irons, these were left at the island of Madeira, where the Albemarle touched, to be sent prisoners to England.

On the day following the Britannia arrived, with one hundred and twenty-nine male convicts, stores, and provisions on board; and on the 16th the Admiral Barrington, the last of the ten sail of transports, anchored in the cove. This ship had been blown off the coast, and fears were entertained of her safety, as she left the cape with a crippled main-mast and other material defects. She had on board a captain

14   and

and a party of the New South Wales corps, with two hundred and sixty-four male convicts, four free women, and one child. She had been unhealthy too, having lost thirty-six convicts in the passage, and brought in eighty-four persons sick, who were immediately landed. Her stores and proportion of provisions were the same as on board of the other ships.

The whole number of convicts now received into the colony, including thirty on board the Gorgon, were, male convicts one thousand six hundred and ninety-five; female convicts one hundred and sixty-eight; and children nine. There were also eight free women (wives of convicts) and one child; making a total number of one thousand eight hundred and eighty-one persons, exclusive of the military. Upwards of two hundred convicts, male and female, did not reach the country.

Of the ten sail of transports lately arrived, five, after delivering their cargoes, were to proceed on the southern whale fishery, viz. the Mary Ann, Matilda, William and Ann, Salamander, and Britannia. Melville, the master of the Britannia, conceiving great hopes of success on this coast from the numbers of spermaceti whales which he saw between the south cape and this port, requested to be cleared directly on his coming in, that he might give it a trial; and, the governor consenting, his ship was ready by the 22d (a week after her arrival), and sailed on the 24th with the other whalers.

The Queen, Atlantic, Active, Albemarle, and Admiral Barrington, after being discharged from government employ, were to proceed to Bombay, by consent of the East India Company, and load home with cotton upon private account under the inspection of the company's servants at that settlement, provided the cotton should be afterwards sold at the company's sales, subject to the usual expences (their duty only excepted), and provided the ships did not interfere with any other part of the company's exclusive commerce *.

---

* Notwithstanding this proviso, which was expressed more at large in the licence given by the company, and which extended to the prohibition of every article except the stores and provisions put on board by government, there was on board of these ships a very large quantity of iron, steel, and copper, intended for sale as a foreign settlement in India, with the produce of which they were to purchase the homeward-bound investment of cotton.

The

The quantity of provisions received by these ships being calculated for the numbers on board of each for nine months only after their arrival, and as, so large a body of convicts having been sent out, it was not probable that we should soon receive another supply, the governor judged it expedient to send one of the transports to Bengal, to procure provisions for the colony; for which purpose he hired the Atlantic at fifteen shillings and sixpence per ton per month. In the way thither she was to touch at Norfolk Island, where Lieutenant Governor King, with some settlers, was to be landed; and the Queen transport was hired for the purpose of bringing back Lieutenant Governor Ross, and the marine detachment serving there, relieved by a company of the New South Wales corps.

On the 25th, the anniversary of his Majesty's accession to the throne, a salute of one and twenty guns was fired by the Gorgon, and the public dinner given on the occasion at the government house was served to upwards of fifty officers, a greater number than the colony had ever before seen assembled together.

The following morning the Atlantic sailed for Norfolk Island and Calcutta. For the first of these places, she had on board Lieutenant Governor King and his family; Captain Paterson of the New South Wales corps (lately arrived in the Admiral Barrington); Mr. Balmain, the assistant surgeon, sent to relieve Mr. Considen; the Rev. Mr. Johnson, who voluntarily visited Norfolk Island for the purpose of performing those duties of his office which had hitherto been omitted through the want of a minister to perform them; twenty-nine settlers discharged from the marines; several male and female convicts, and some few settlers from that class of people.

At Calcutta, Lieutenant Bowen, who was continued in his employment of naval agent, was to procure a cargo of flour and pease, in the proportion of two tons of flour to one ton of pease; and was for that purpose furnished with letters to the merchants who had made proposals to Lord Cornwallis to supply the colony, the governor meaning for that reason to give their house the preference.

The Salamander had returned from Norfolk Island, where every person and article she had on board were safely landed. By letters received thence, we learned that it was supposed there had formerly

merly been inhabitants upon the island, several stone hatchets, or rather stones in the shapes of adzes, and others in the shapes of chissels, having been found in turning up some ground in the interior parts of the island. Lieutenant-Governor King had formerly entertained the same supposition from discovering the banana tree growing in regular rows.

It was not to be doubted but that the tranquillity and regularity of our little town would in some degree be interrupted by the great influx of disorderly seamen who were at times let loose from the transports. Much less cause of complaint on this score, however, arose than was expected. The port orders, which were calculated to preserve the peace of the place, were from time to time enforced; and on one occasion ten seamen belonging to the transports were punished for being found in the settlement after nine o'clock at night.

At Parramatta, whither the greatest part of the convicts lately arrived had been sent, petty offences were frequently committed, and the constant presence of a magistrate became daily more requisite. The convicts at that place were chiefly employed in opening some new ground at a short distance from the settlement.

The foundation of a new storehouse was begun this month at Sydney, on the spot where the redoubt had hitherto stood; which, since the construction of the platform near the magazine on the east point of the cove, had been pulled down, and the mould removed into the garden appropriated to government-house. This, and clearing the transports, formed the principal labour at Sydney.

On the last day of this month, James Downey was found hanging in his hut. The cause of this rash action was said to have been the dread of being taken up for a theft which, according to some intimation he had received, was about to be alleged against him. He came out in the first fleet, had served his term of transportation, had constantly worked as a labourer in the bricklayers gang, and was in general considered as a harmless fellow.

From Parramatta two convicts were missing, and were said to be killed by the natives.

CHAP. XV.

A PARTY OF IRISH CONVICTS ABSCOND.—THE QUEEN SAILS FOR NORFOLK
ISLAND.—WHALE-FISHERY.—RATION ALTERED.—THE SUPPLY SAILS FOR
ENGLAND.—LIVE STOCK (PUBLIC) IN THE COLONY.—GROUND IN CULTI-
VATION.—SICK.—RUN OF WATER DECREASING.—TWO TRANSPORTS SAIL
—WHALE-FISHERY GIVEN UP.—THE QUEEN ARRIVES FROM NORFOLK
ISLAND.—THE MARINES EMBARK IN THE GORGON FOR ENGLAND.—RA-
TION FURTHER REDUCED.—TRANSACTIONS—CONVICTS WHO WERE IN
THE GUARDIAN EMANCIPATED.—STORE FINISHED.—DEATHS IN 1791.

November.] ON the first day of this month, information was received from Parramatta, that a body of twenty male convicts and one
female, of those lately arrived in the Queen transport from Ireland,
each taking a week's provisions, and armed with tomahawks and knives,
had absconded from that settlement, with the chimerical idea of walking to China, or of finding in this country a settlement wherein they
would be received and entertained without labour. It was generally
supposed, however, that this improbable tale was only a cover to the
real design, which might be to procure boats, and get on board the
transports after they had left the cove. An officer with a party was
immediately sent out from Parramatta in pursuit of them, who traced
them as far down the harbour as Lane Cove, whence he reached the
settlement at Sydney, without seeing or hearing any thing more of
them. A few days afterward the people in a boat belonging to the
Albemarle transport, which had been down the harbour to procure
wood on the north shore, met with the wretched female who had accompanied the men. She had been separated from them for three
days, and wandered by herself, entirely ignorant of her situation, until
she came to the water side, where, fortunately, she soon after met the
boat. Boats were sent down the next day, and the woman's husband
was found and brought up to the settlement. They both gave the
same absurd account of their design as before related, and appeared to
have

have suffered very confiderably by fatigue, hunger, and the heat of the weather. The man had loft his companions eight-and-forty hours before he was himself difcovered; and no tidings of them were received for feveral days, although boats were conftantly fent in to the north-weft arm, and the lower part of the harbour.

Three of thefe miferable people were fome time after met by fome officers who were on an excurfion to the lagoon between this harbour and Broken Bay; but, notwithftanding their fituation, they did not readily give themfelves up, and, when queftioned, faid they wanted nothing more than to live free from labour. Thefe people were fent up to Parramatta, whence, regardlefs of what they had experienced, and might again fuffer, they a fecond time abfconded in a few days after they had been returned. Parties were immediately difpatched from that fettlement, and thirteen of thofe who firft abfconded were brought in, in a ftate of deplorable wretchednefs, naked, and nearly worn out with hunger. Some of them had fubfifted chiefly by fucking the flowering fhrubs and wild berries of the woods; and the whole exhibited a picture of mifery, that feemed fufficient to deter others from the like extravagant folly. The practice of flying from labour into the woods ftill, however, prevailing, the governor caufed all the convicts who arrived this year to be affembled, and informed them of his determination to put a ftop to their abfconding from the place where he had appointed them to labour, by fending out parties with orders to fire upon them whenever they fhould be met with; and he declared that if any were brought in alive, he would either land them on a part of the harbour whence they could not depart, or chain them together with only bread and water for their fubfiftence, during the remainder of their terms of tranfportation. He likewife told them, that he had heard they were intending to arm themfelves and feize upon the ftores (fuch a defign had for fome days been reported); but that if they made any attempt of that kind, every man who might be taken fhould be inftantly put to death. Having thus endeavoured to imprefs them with ideas of certain punifhment if they offended in future, he forgave fome offences which had been reported by the magiftrate, exhorted them to go cheerfully to their labour, and changed their hours of work, agreeably to a requeft which they had made.

Four

Four hundred and two of thefe miferable, people had received medicines from the hofpital in the morning of the day when the governor had thus addreffed them. The prevailing difeafe was a dyfentery, which was accompanied by a general debility.

The Queen failed early in the month with an officer and a detachment of the New South Wales corps, fome convicts, ftores and provifions, for Norfolk Ifland. The Salamander failed at the fame time on her fifhing voyage.

From her intended trial of the whale-fifhery on the coaft the Britannia arrived on the 10th, and was followed the next day by the Mary Ann. Mr. Melvill killed, in company with the William and Ann, the day after he went out, feven fpermaceti whales, two only of which they were able to fecure from the bad weather which immediately fucceeded. From the whale which fell to the Britannia's fhare, although but a fmall one, thirteen barrels of oil were procured; and in the opinion of Mr. Melvill, the oil, from its containing a greater proportion of that valuable part of the fifh called by the whalers the head-matter, was worth ten pounds more per ton than that of the fifh of any other part of the world he had been in. He thought that a moft advantageous voyage might be made upon this coaft, as he was confident upwards of fifteen thoufand whales were feen in the firft ten days that he was abfent, the greater number of which were obferved off this harbour; and he was prevented from filling his fhip by bad weather alone, having met with only one day fince he failed in which he could lower down a boat.

The fuccefs and report of the mafter of the Mary Ann were very different; he had been as far to the fouthward as the latitude of 45° without feeing a whale; and in a gale of wind fhipped a fea that ftove two of his boats, and wafhed down the veffels for boiling the oil, which were fixed in brick-work, and to repair which he came into this harbour.

The Matilda came in a few days afterwards from Jervis Bay, (in latitude 35° 6′ S. and longitude 152° 0′ E.) where fhe had anchored for fome days, being leaky. The mafter of this fhip, Mr. Matthew Weatherhead, faw many whales, but was prevented from killing any by the badnefs of the weather.

B B 2   The

The William and Ann. came in soon after, confirming the report of the great numbers of fish which were to be seen upon the coast, and the difficulty of getting at them. She had killed only one fish, and came in to repair and shorten her main-mast.

A difference of opinion prevailed among the masters of the ships which had been out respecting the establishing a whale-fishery upon this coast. In one particular, however, they all agreed, which was, that the coast abounded with fish; but the major part of them thought that the currents and bad weather prevailing at this season of the year, and which appeared to be also the season of the fish, would prevent any ships from meeting with that success, of which on their setting out they themselves had had such sanguine hopes. One of them thought that the others, in giving this opinion, were premature, and that they were not sufficiently acquainted with the weather on the coast to form any judgment of the advantage to be derived from future attempts. They were determined, nevertheless, to give it another trial, on the failure of which they meant to prosecute their voyage to the coast of Peru. Having set up their rigging, they went out again toward the latter end of the month.

About the middle of the month an alteration took place in the ration; two pounds of flour were taken off, and one pint of pease and one pint of oatmeal were issued in their stead; the full ration, which was first served on the 27th of August last, having been continued not quite three months.

The Supply armed tender, having completed her repairs, sailed for England on the 26th, her commander, Lieutenant Ball, purposing to make his passage round Cape Horn, for which the season of the year was favourable. Lieutenant John Cresswell of the marines went in her, charged with the governor's dispatches.

The services of this little vessel had endeared her, and her officers and people, to this colony. The regret which we felt at parting with them was, however, lessened by a knowledge that they were flying from a country of want to one of abundance, where we all hoped that the services they had performed would be rewarded by that attention and promotion to which they naturally looked up, and had an indisputable claim.

At

At this time the public live stock in the settlement consisted of one stallion aged, one mare, two young stallions, two colts, sixteen cows, two calves, one ram, fifty ewes, six lambs, one boar, fourteen sows (old and young), and twenty-two pigs.

The ground in cultivation at and about Parramatta amounted to three hundred and fifty-one acres in maize, forty-four in wheat, six in barley, one in oats, two in potatoes, four in vines, eighty-six in garden ground, and seventeen in cultivation by the New South Wales corps. In addition to these there were one hundred and fifty acres cleared to be sown with turnips, ninety-one acres were in cultivation by settlers, twenty-eight by officers civil and military at and about Sydney; and at Parramatta one hundred and forty acres were inclosed and the timber thinned for cattle; making a total of nine hundred and twenty acres of land thinned, cleared, and cultivated.

The platform at the west point of the cove was completed during this month. The flag-staff had been for some time erected, and the cannon placed on the platform. A corporal's guard was also mounted daily in the building which had been used as an observatory by Lieutenant Dawes.

The mortality during this month had been great, fifty male and four female convicts dying within the thirty days. Five hundred sick persons received medicines at the end of the month. That list however was decreasing. The extreme heat of the weather during the month had not only increased the sick list, but had added one to the number of deaths. On the 4th, a convict attending upon Mr. White, in passing from his house to his kitchen, without any covering upon his head, received a stroke from a ray of the sun, which at the time deprived him of speech and motion, and, in less than four-and-twenty hours, of his life. The thermometer on that day stood at twelve o'clock at 94° ½ and the wind was at N. W.

By the dry weather which prevailed our water had been so much affected, beside being lessened by the watering of some of the transports, that a prohibition was laid by the governor on the watering of the remainder at Sydney, and their boats were directed to go to a convenient place upon the north shore. To remedy this evil the governor had employed the stone-mason's gang to cut tanks out of the rock, which

14   would

would be refervoirs for the water large enough to fupply the fettlement for fome time.

December.] On the 3d of this month the fhips Albemarle and Active failed for India. After their departure feveral people were miffing from the fettlement; fome whofe fentences of tranfportation had expired, and others who were yet convicts. Previous to their failing (it having been reported that the feamen intended to conceal fuch as had made intereft among them to get off) the governor in-ftructed the mafter to deliver any perfons whom he might difcover to be on board without permiffion to quit the colony, as prifoners to the commanding officer of the firft Britifh fettlement they fhould touch at in India. About this time a boat belonging to Mr. White was taken from its mooring; and it was for a time fuppofed that fhe had been taken off by fome runaways to get on board one of the fhips then about to fail, and afterwards fet adrift; but fhe was found by fome gentle-men of the Gorgon the day after their departure, between this harbour and Broken Bay, with two men in her, who on the appearance of the party which found her ran into the woods. The gentlemen left her with a plank knocked out, an oar and the rudder broken, and other-wife rendered ufelefs to the people who ran away with her. They alfo fell in with a convict, an Irifhman, who had been abfent five weeks from Parramatta, and who had fet off with fome others to pro-ceed along the coaft in fearch of another fettlement. The boat was brought up a few days afterwards.

Two of the whalers, the Matilda and Mary Ann, came in from fea the day on which the other fhips failed. The former landed a boat in a bay on the coaft about fix miles to the fouthward of Port Stephens, where the feine was hauled and a large quantity of fifh taken; but of the fifh which they went to procure (whales) they faw none.

The Mary Ann was rather more fortunate. By going to the fouth-ward, fhe killed nine fifh; of five of them fhe fecured enough to pro-cure about thirty barrels of oil; but was prevented by bad weather from getting more. Thefe fhips failed again immediately, and both ran down the coaft as far to the fouthward as 36° 30', and returned on the 16th without killing a fifh. The mafters attributed their bad fuccefs to currents; and, giving up all hopes of a fifhery here, they deter-

mined,

mined, after refitting, to quit the coaſt. The Salamander and Britannia whalers came in at the ſame time, and with like ill fortune. Melvill the maſter of the Britannia, who had been formerly ſo ſanguine in his hopes of a fiſhery, ſeemed now to have adopted a different opinion, and hinted to ſome in the colony, that he did not think he ſhould try the coaſt any longer. It muſt be remarked however, that the whalers were not out of port at any one time long enough to enable them to ſpeak with any great degree of preciſion either for or againſt the probability of ſucceſs. They ſeemed more deſirous of obtaining a knowledge of the harbours on the coaſt: the William and Ann had been ſeen in Broken Bay; others had viſited Botany Bay and Jervis Bay; the Salamander had remained long enough in Port Stephens (an harbour to the northward, until then not viſited by any one) to take an eye-ſketch of the harbour and of ſome of its branches or arms; and Port Jackſon was found to have its conveniences. After a well-manned and well-found whaler ſhould have kept the ſea for an entire ſeaſon, the ſucceſs might be determined.

The Queen tranſport having returned from Norfolk Iſland, with the lieutenant-governor and the officers and ſoldiers of the marine corps, who were to take their paſſage to England in the Gorgon, the greateſt part of the marine detachment embarked on board of that ſhip on the 13th. Thoſe who did not embark were left for the duty of the place until the remainder of the New South Wales corps ſhould arrive.

By the Queen ſeveral convicts whoſe ſentences of tranſportation had expired were allowed to return to this ſettlement, purſuant to a promiſe made them on their going thither; and we were informed, that the Atlantic ſailed from Norfolk Iſland for Calcutta on the 13th of the laſt month. Both ſhips landed ſafely every article they had on board for the colony, being favoured by very fine weather while ſo employed. Lieutenant-governor King, on taking upon him the government of the iſland, pardoned all offenders whom he found in cuſtody.

Governor Phillip having no further occaſion for the ſervices of the Gorgon, that ſhip ſailed for England on Sunday the 18th. Two convicts had the folly to attempt making their eſcape from the colony in this ſhip, but they were detected and brought back. A woman was alſo ſuppoſed to have effected her eſcape; but ſhe was found diſguiſed

In

in men's apparel at the native's hut on the east point of the cove.

On board of the Gorgon were embarked the marines who came from England in the first ships; as valuable a corps as any in his Majesty's service. They had struggled here with greatly more than the common hardships of service, and were now quitting a country in which they had opened and smoothed the way for their successors, and from which, whatever benefit might hereafter be derived, must be derived by those who had the easy task of treading in paths previously and painfully formed by them.

The cove and the settlement were now resuming that dull uniformity of uninteresting circumstances which had generally prevailed. The Supply and the Gorgon had departed, and with them a valuable portion of our friends and associates. The transports which remained were all preparing to leave us, and in a few days after the Gorgon, the Matilda and Mary Ann sailed for the coast of Peru. These ships had some convicts on board, who were permitted to ship themselves with the masters.

A further reduction of the ration was directed to take place at the end of the month, one pound being taken from the allowance of flour served to the men. From the state of the provision stores, the governor, on Christmas-day, could only give one pound of flour to each woman in the settlement. On that day divine service was performed here and at Parramatta, Mr. Bayne, the chaplain of the new corps, assisting Mr. Johnson in the religious duties of the morning. There were some among us, however, by whom even the sanctity of this day was not regarded; for at night the marine store was robbed of two-and-twenty gallons of spirits.

At Parramatta various offences were still committed, notwithstanding the lenity which had been shewn to several offenders at the close of the last month. Many of the convicts there not having any part of their ration left when Tuesday or Wednesday night came, the governor directed, as he had before done from the same reason, that the provisions of the labouring convicts should be issued to them daily. This measure being disapproved of by them, they assembled in rather a tumultuous manner before the governor's house at Parramatta on the

last

laft day of the month, to requeft that their provifions might be ferved as ufual on the Saturdays. The governor, however, difperfed them without granting their requeft; and as they were heard to murmur, and talk of obtaining by different means what was refufed to entreaty, (words fpoken among the crowd, and the perfon who was fo daring not being diftinguifhable from the reft,) he affured them that as he knew the major part of them were led by eight or ten defigning men to whom they looked up, and to whofe names he was not a ftranger, on any open appearance of difcontent, he fhould make immediate examples of them. Before they were difmiffed they promifed greater propriety of conduct and implicit obedience to the orders of their fuperiors, and declared their readinefs to receive their provifions as had been directed.

This was the firft inftance of any tumultuous affembly among thefe people, and was now to be afcribed to the fpirit of refiftance and villany lately imported by the new comers from England and Ireland.

Among the public works of the month the moft material was the completing and occupying the new ftore on the eaft fide, which was begun in October laft; its dimenfions were eighty by twenty-four feet; and as it was built for the purpofe of containing dry ftores, the height was increafed beyond that commonly adopted here, and a fpacious loft was formed capable of containing a large quantity of bale goods. This was by far the beft ftore in the country.

In the courfe of the month a warrant of emancipation paffed the feal of the territory to John Lowe, Henry Cone, Richard Chearn, Thomas Fifk, Daniel Cubitt, Charles Pafs, George Bolton, William Carelefs, William Curtis, John Chapman Morris, Thomas Merrick, William Skinner, and James Weavers, convicts who left England in the Guardian, on condition of their refiding within the limits of this government, and not returning to England within the period of their refpective fentences. Inftructions to this effect had been received from home, Lieutenant Riou having interefted himfelf much in their behalf. They were to be at liberty to work at any trade they might be acquainted with; but during their continuance in the country they were to be difpofed of wherever the governor fhould think proper. They were alfo at liberty to fettle land upon their own account.

c c   The

The numbers who died by sickness in the year 1791 were, one of the civil establishment (H. E. Dodd); two soldiers; one hundred and fifty-five male and eight female convicts; and five children: in all one hundred and seventy-one persons (twenty-eight more than had died during the preceding year).

In the above time one male convict was executed; one drowned; four lost in the woods (exclusive of the Irish convicts who had absconded, of whom no certain account was procured); one destroyed himself; and eight men, one woman, and two children, had run from the settlement; making a loss of one hundred and eighty-nine persons.

————————

CHAP. XVI.

THE QUEEN SAILS FOR NORFOLK ISLAND.—WHALERS ON THEIR FISHING VOYAGES.—CONVICTS MISSING.—VARIOUS DEPREDATIONS.—DISPENSARY AND BAKE-HOUSE ROBBED.—PROCLAMATION.—A CRIMINAL COURT HELD.—CONVICT EXECUTED.—TRANSACTIONS.—THE PITT WITH LIEUTENANT-GOVERNOR GROSE ARRIVES.—MILITARY DUTY FIXED FOR PARRAMATTA.—GOODS SELLING AT SYDNEY FROM THE PITT.—THE PITT ORDERED TO BE DISPATCHED TO NORFOLK ISLAND.—COMMISSIONS READ.—SICKNESS.—THE PITT SAILS.—MR. BURTON KILLED.—STORMY WEATHER.—PUBLIC WORKS.—REGULATIONS RESPECTING PERSONS WHO HAD SERVED THEIR TERMS OF TRANSPORTATION.—NATIVES.

January 1792.] EARLY in this month sixty-two people, settlers and convicts, with Mr. Bayne, the chaplain of the New South Wales corps, (who offered his services, as there never had been a clergyman there,) embarked on board the Queen transport for Norfolk Island, the master of that ship having engaged to carry them and a certain quantity of provisions thither for the sum of 150l. Of the settlers twenty-two were lately discharged from the marine service, and the remainder were convicts; some of the latter, whose terms of transportation

ation had expired, had chosen Norfolk Island to settle in, and others
were sent to be employed for the public.

This ship, with the Admiral Barrington for India, sailed on the
6th; and the Salamander and Britannia whalers on the 7th, the masters
of the two latter ships signifying an intention of cruising for three
months upon this coast; at the end of which time, according to their
success, they would either return to this port, or pursue their voyage
to the northward.

Several convicts attempted to escape from the settlement on board
of these ships, some of whom were discovered before they sailed, and,
being brought on shore, were punished; but there was great reason
to suppose that others were secreted by the connivance of the seamen,
and eluded the repeated searches which were made for them.

In addition to this exportation, the colony lost some useful people
whom it could ill spare; but who, their terms of transportation
having expired, would not be induced to remain in the settlement,
and could not be prevented from quitting it.

By the commissary's report of the muster it appeared, that forty-
four men and nine women were absent and unaccounted for; among
which number were included those who were wandering in the woods,
seeking for a new settlement, or endeavouring to get into the path to
China! Of these people many, after lingering a long time, and existing merely on roots and wild berries, perished miserably. Others
found their way in, after being absent several weeks, and reported the
fate of their wretched companions, being themselves reduced to nearly
the same condition, worn down and exhausted with fatigue and want
of proper sustenance. Yet, although the appearance of these people
confirmed their account of what they had undergone, others were still
found ignorant and weak enough to run into the woods impressed
with the idea of either reaching China by land, or finding a new settlement, where labour would not be imposed on them, and where the
inhabitants were civil and peaceable. Two of these wretches at the
time of their absconding met a convict in their way not far from the
new grounds, whom they robbed of his provisions, and beat in so cruel
a manner that, after languishing for some time, he died in the hospital
at Parramatta. He described their persons, and mentioned their

names,

names, with the precife circumftances attending their treatment of him, and it was hoped that they would have lived to return, and receive the reward of their crime; but one of their companions who furvived them brought in an account of their having ended a wicked and miferable exiftence in the woods.

Depredations being nightly committed at the fkirts of the town, and at the officers' farms, by fome of thefe vagrants, who were fuppofed to lurk between this place and Parramatta, it was thought neceffary to fend armed parties out at night for a certain diftance round the fettlement, with orders to feize, or fire on, all perfons found ftraggling; and feveral were detected by them in the act of robbing the gardens at the different farms. Indeed neither the property nor the perfons of individuals were fafe for fome time. Two villains came to a hut which was occupied by one Williams a fawyer, and which he had erected at a fpot at fome diftance from the town where he could have a little garden ground, and attempted to rob him; but the owner furprifed them, and, in endeavouring to fecure them, was wounded fo feverely in the arm with a tomahawk, that the tendon was divided; and it was fuppofed that he never would recover the perfect ufe of the limb. They even carried their audacity fo far, as to be fecretly meditating an attempt upon the barrack and ftorehoufe at Parramatta; at leaft, information of fuch a plan was given by fome of the convicts; and as there had been feen among them people filly enough to undertake to walk to the other fide of this extenfive continent, expecting that China would be found there, it was not at all improbable that fome might be mad enough to perfuade others that it would be an eafy matter to attempt and carry the barracks and ftores there. But no other ufe was made of the report than the exertion of double vigilance in the guards, which was done without making public the true motive. To the credit of the convicts who came out in the firft fleet it muft be remarked, that none of them were concerned in thefe offences; and of them it was faid the new comers ftood fo much in dread, that they never were admitted to any fhare in their confidence.

As the Indian corn began to ripen the convicts recommenced their depredations, and many were punifhed with a feverity feemingly calculated to deter others, but actually without effect. They appeared

to

to be a people wholly regardless of the future, and not dreading any thing that was not immediately present to their own feelings. It was well known that punishment would follow the detection of a crime; but their constant reliance was on a hope of escaping that detection; and they were very rarely known to stand forward in bringing offenders to punishment, although such rewards were held out as one would imagine were sufficient to induce them. It being necessary to secure four dangerous people, who, after committing offences, had withdrawn into the woods, a reward of fifty pounds of flour was offered for the apprehension of either of them, but only one was taken.

The easy communication between Sydney and Parramatta had been found to be a very great evil from the time the path was first made; but since the numbers had been so much augmented at Parramatta, it became absolutely necessary to put a stop to the intercourse. The distance was about sixteen miles; and, unless information was previously given, a person would visit Sydney and return without being missed: and as stolen property was transferred from one place to another by means of this quick conveyance, orders were given calculated to cut off all unlicensed intercourse.

A report having been falsely propagated at Parramatta, that it was intended by the governor to take the corn of individuals on the public account, the settlers and convicts who had raised maize or other grain, and who were not provided with proper places to secure it in, were informed, that they might send it to the public store, and draw it from thence as their occasions required; and farther, that they were at liberty to dispose of such live stock, corn, grain, or vegetables, which they might raise, as they found convenient to themselves, the property of every individual being equally secured to him, and by the same law, whether belonging to a free man or a convict. Such of the above articles as they could not otherwise dispose of, they were told, would be purchased by the commissary on the public account at a fair market-price.

Toward the latter end of the month some villains broke into the dispensary at the hospital, and stole two cases of portable soup, one case of camomile flowers, and one case containing sudorific powder. These articles had been placed in the dispensary on the very evening
it

it was broken into, to be sent to Parramatta the following morning. The cafes with the camomile and sudorific powder (which perhaps they had taken for sugar or flour) were found at the back of the hill behind the hospital; and, in order to discover the persons concerned in this theft, (as well as those who maimed the sawyer, as before related,) a proclamation was published, offering to any person or persons giving such information as should convict the principal offenders, a free pardon for every offence which he, she, or they might have committed since their arrival in this country; and that a full ration of provisions should be issued to such person or persons during the remainder of their respective terms of transportation.

Several people died at Parramatta, some of whom were at labour, apparently in health, and dead in four-and-twenty hours. An extraordinary circumstance attended, though it was not the cause of the death of one poor creature: while dragging with others at a brick cart he was seized with a fainting fit, and when he recovered was laid down under a cart which stood in the road, that he might be in the shade. Being weak and ill, he fell asleep. On waking, and feeling something tight about his neck, he put up his hand, when, to his amazement and horror, he grasped the folds of a large snake which had twined itself round his neck. In endeavouring to disengage it, the animal bit him by the lip, which became instantly tumid. Two men, passing by, took off the snake and threw it on the ground, when it erected itself and flew at one of them; but they soon killed it. The man who had fainted at the cart died the next morning, not, however, from any effect of the bite of the snake, but from a general debility.

At Parramatta the public bakehouse was broken into, and robbed of a large quantity of flour and biscuit. The robber had made his way down the chimney of the house, and, though a man and woman slept in the place, carried off his booty undiscovered.

The convicts having assembled there at the latter end of the last month in an improper and tumultuous manner, the governor now thought proper to issue a proclamation, directing that " in case of any " riot or disturbance among the convicts, every one who was seen out " of his hut would (if such riot or disturbance should happen in the " night, or during the hours of rest from labour, or if he were ab-
" sent

" sent from his labour during the hours of work) be deemed to be
" aiding and assisting the rioters, and be punished accordingly."

The convicts were strictly forbidden ever to assemble in numbers
under any pretence of stating a complaint, or for any other cause
whatever, all complaints being to be made through the medium of the
superintendants or overseers.

A disobedience to this proclamation was to be punished with the
utmost severity; and any person who, knowing of any intended riot
or tumultuous and unlawful assembly among the convicts, did not take
the first opportunity of informing either the commanding officer of the
military or one of the superintendants thereof, would be deemed and
punished as a principal in such riot.

An instance of the profligacy of the convicts which occurred at this
time is deserving of notice: a woman who had been entrusted to
carry the allowance of flour belonging to two other women to the
bakehouse, where she had run in debt for bread which she had taken
up on their account, mixed with it a quantity of pounded stone, in
the proportion of two-thirds of grit, to one of flour. Fortunately,
she was detected before it had been mixed with other flour at the
bakehouse, and was ordered to wear an iron collar for six months as a
punishment.

February.] A criminal court was held at Parramatta on the 7th of
this month for the trial of James Collington, who, as before mentioned,
had broken into the public bakehouse at that place by getting down
the chimney in the night. It appeared that he had taken off about
fifty pounds of flour, which he tied up in an apron that he found in
the room, and the leg of a pair of trowsers. He deposited the property under a rock, and occasionally visited it; but it was soon seized
by some other nocturnal adventurer, and Collington then broke into
another hut, wherein eight people were sleeping, and took thereout a
box containing wearing apparel and provisions, without disturbing
them, so soundly did fatigue make them sleep; but he was detected in
a garden with the property, and secured. Being found guilty, he received sentence of death, and was executed early the following morning. At the tree he addressed the convicts, warning them to avoid
the paths he had pursued; but said, that he was induced by hunger to

14   commit

commit the crime for which he suffered. He appeared defirous of death, declaring that he knew he could not live without ftealing.

Information having been received, that a great body of convicts at the new grounds intended to feize fome arms which had been given to the fettlers for their protection againft the natives, and (after robbing their huts) to proceed to the fea-coaft, where, deftroying every perfon who fhould oppofe them, they were to build a veffel, a convict who was faid to be a ringleader was taken up, and, upon the information which he gave, five others were apprehended and chained together; in which fituation they continued for fome time, when their fcheme having been defeated, and other fteps taken to prevent their putting it in execution, they were liberated, and returned to their ufual labour.

Information would have been at all times more readily procured from thefe people, had they not been conftantly apprehenfive of receiving ill-treatment not only from the parties concerned, but from others who were not; and although every affurance of protection was given by thofe who were authorifed to hold it out, yet it was not found fufficient to do away the dread they were faid to labour under. Accident, or a quarrel among themfelves, fometimes furnifhed information that was not otherwife to be procured; and in general to one or other of thefe caufes was to be attributed every information that was received of any mal-practices among them.

A perfon who had been employed under one of the fuperintendants at Parramatta, and in whom, from an uniformity of good conduct during his refidence in this country, fome truft was at times placed, was detected in giving corn to a fettler from the public granary, to which he had occafional accefs. The offence being fully proved, he was fentenced to receive three hundred lafhes, and the perfon to whom he had given the corn two hundred lafhes. It was feen with great concern, that there were but few among them who were honeft enough to refift any temptation that was placed in their way.

A convict who had abfconded five weeks fince was apprehended by fome of the military at the head of one of the coves leading from Parramatta. He had built himfelf a hut in the woods, and faid when brought in, that he had preferved his exiftence by eating fuch fifh as he was fortunate enough to catch, rock oyfters, and wild berries; and

that

that the natives had more than once purfued him when employed in thefe refearches. But very little credit was given to any account he gave, and it was generally fuppofed that he had lived by occafionally vifiting and robbing the huts at Sydney and Parramatta. He had taken to the woods to avoid a punifhment which hung over him, and which he now received.

Early in the month eight fettlers from the marines received their grants of land fituated on the north fide of the harbour near the Flats, and named by the governor the Field of Mars.

The convicts employed in cultivating and clearing public ground beyond Parramatta, having been landed in a weak and fickly ftate, wore in general a moft miferable and emaciated appearance, and numbers of them died daily. The reduced ration by no means contributed to their amendment; the wheat that was raifed laft year, (four hundred and fixty-one bufhels,) after referving a fufficiency for feed, was iffued to them at a pound per man per week, and a pound of rice per week was iffued to each male convict at Sydney.

On Tuefday the 14th the fignal was made for a fail, and fhortly after the Pitt, Captain Edward Manning, anchored in the cove from England. She failed the 17th of laft July from Yarmouth Roads, and had rather a long paffage, touching at St. Iago, Rio de Janeiro, and the Cape of Good Hope. She had on board Francis Grofe, Efq. the lieutenant-governor of the fettlements, and major-commandant of the New South Wales corps, one company of which, together with the adjutant and furgeon's mate, came out with him.

She brought out three hundred and nineteen male and forty-nine female convicts, five children, and feven free women; with falt provifions calculated to ferve that number of people ten months, but which would only furnifh the colony with provifions for forty days. The fupply of provifions was confined to falt meat, under an idea that the colony was not in immediate want of flour, and that a fupply had been fent from Calcutta, which, together with what had been procured from Batavia, that which had been fent before from England, and the grain that might have been raifed in the fettlements, would be adequate to our confumption for the prefent. The difpatches, however, which had been forwarded from this place by the Juftinian in July 1790 having

D D   been

been received by the secretary of state, what appeared from those communications to be necessary for the colony were to be sent in one or more ships to be dispatched in the autumn of last year, with an additional number of convicts, and the remaining company of the New South Wales corps. A sloop in frame, of the burden of forty-one tons, was sent out in the Pitt; to make room for which, several bales of cloathing, and many very useful articles, were obliged to be shut out.

By this conveyance information was received, that the Dædalus hired storeship, which was sent out to carry provisions to the Sandwich Islands for two ships employed in those parts on discovery, was directed to repair to this settlement after performing that service, to be employed as there should be occasion, and that she might be expected in the beginning of the year 1793.

The Pitt brought in many of her convicts sick; and several of her seamen and fifteen soldiers of the New South Wales corps had died shortly after her leaving St. Iago, owing to her having touched there during an unhealthy season.

The whole of the New South Wales corps, except one company, being now arrived, the numbers requisite for the different duties were settled; and one company, consisting of a captain, two lieutenants, one ensign, three serjeants, three corporals, two drummers, and seventy privates, was fixed for the duty of Parramatta; a like number for Norfolk Island, and the remainder were to do duty at Sydney, the head quarters of the corps.

Permission having been obtained, a shop was opened at a hut on shore for the sale of various articles brought out in the Pitt; and notwithstanding a fleet of transports had but lately sailed hence, notwithstanding the different orders which had been sent to Bengal, and the high price at which every thing was sold, the avidity with which all descriptions of people grasped at what was to be purchased was extraordinary, and could only be accounted for by the distance of our situation from the mother country, the uncertainty of receiving supplies thence, and the length of time which we had heretofore the mortification to find elapse without our receiving any.

March.] It being necessary to send to Norfolk Island a proportion of what provisions were in store, the Pitt was engaged for that purpose;
and

and for performing this service her owners were to receive 651l. a sum
equal to six weeks demurrage for that ship. From Norfolk Island she
was to proceed, upon her owners account, to Bengal; and her commander was charged with duplicates of the letters and instructions given
to Lieutenant Bowen. In the event of any accident having prevented
the arrival of that officer at Calcutta, Captain Manning was to cause the
service with which he was entrusted to be executed, by applying to the
governor-general, and the house of Messrs. Lambert, Ross, and company, for the supply of provisions, which the Atlantic was to have
brought, to be forwarded to this country either by the Pitt, or by vessels
to be hired by that house at Calcutta.

This precaution was taken rather to guard against the worst that
might happen, than from any probability that the Atlantic would not
have reached Calcutta, that ship being well fitted for such a voyage,
strong, well manned, and under the direction of an able and an active
officer. To her arrival, however, we looked forward at this period
with some anxiety, as the flour and salt provisions in the settlement already occupied but a small portion of the stores which contained them,
there being only fifty-two days flour, and twenty-one weeks salt meat
in store at the ration now issued.

On the morning of Saturday the 17th the marines and **New South
Wales** corps formed under arms on the parade in front of the quarters,
when his Majesty's commission appointing Francis Grose, Esquire, to be
lieutenant-governor of this territory, and the letters patent under the
great seal for establishing the civil and criminal courts of judicature,
were publicly read by the judge-advocate. The governor and the
principal officers of the settlement attended, and his excellency received
from the corps under arms the honours due to his rank in the colony.
At the conclusion of the ceremony, the Pitt, by a well-concerted signal,
saluted with fifteen guns, as a compliment to the lieutenant-governor.

A person who came out to this country in the capacity of a carpenter's mate on board the Sirius, and who had been discharged from that
ship's books into the Supply, having been left behind when that vessel
sailed for England, offered his services to put together the vessel that
arrived in frame in the Pitt; and being deemed sufficiently qualified as
a shipwright, he was engaged at two shillings *per diem* and his provi-

DD 2

sions to set her up. Her keel was accordingly laid down on blocks placed for the purpose near the landing-place on the east side. As this person was the only shipwright in the colony, the vessel would much sooner have rendered the services which were required of her, had she been put together, coppered, and sent out manned and officered from England; by these means too the colony would have received many articles which were of necessity shut out of the Pitt to make room for her stowage.

About this time a malady of an alarming nature was perceived in the colony. Four or five of the convicts were seized with insanity; and, as the major part of those who were visited by this calamity were females, who on account of their sex were not harassed with hard labour, and who in general shared largely of such little comforts as were to be procured in the settlement, it was difficult to assign a cause for this disorder.

April.] With a dreadful sick list, and with death making rapid strides among us, the month of April commenced: a lamentable circumstance to those who had to provide by their labour for the support of a colony, in which, from its great distance, not only from the parent country, but from every port where supplies could be procured, it became an object of the first magnitude and importance to endeavour speedily, and by every possible exertion, to place its inhabitants in a situation that accident or delay might not affect. His Majesty's ship Guardian afforded a melancholy recollection how much this colony had already felt from misadventure, and the delay which occurred in the voyage of the Lady Juliana transport had proved equally calamitous. The recent circumstance of a ship arriving without a supply of flour, and other contingencies, spoke with a warning voice, and loudly demanded that every arm which could be raised should be exerted to make provision against the hour of want. Few, however, in comparison with the measure of our necessities, were the numbers daily brought into the field for the purpose of cultivation; and of those who could handle the hoe or the spade by far the greater part carried hunger in their countenances; but it was earnestly hoped and anxiously expected, that by the speedy arrival of supplies from England the full ration of every species of provisions would be again issued, when labour

bour would be renewed with additional vigour and effect; health
and strength be seen residing among us; and the approaches of independence on Great Britain be something more than a sanguine hope
or visionary speculation.

The convicts, and such stores and provisions as the governor thought
it necessary to send to Norfolk Island, being embarked, the Pitt sailed
on the 7th. Previous to her departure, a female convict was found
secreted on board, who declaring in her justification that the fourth
mate of the ship had assisted her in her escape, he was tried by the
civil court of judicature for taking a convict from the settlement, but,
for want of sufficient proof, was acquitted.

The practicability of being secreted on board of ships would always
operate as an inducement to wretches who saw a long term of servitude before them to attempt their escape; but it certainly behoved
every master of a merchantman bound from this port to be very vigilant and sedulous to prevent their succeeding, as the safety of the
ship might be very much endangered by having numbers of such
people on board mixing with their ship's company.

On Friday the 13th died Mr. David Burton, of a gun-shot wound
which he received on the preceding Saturday. This young man, on
account of the talents he possessed as a botanist, and the services which
he was capable of rendering in the surveying line, could be but ill
spared in this settlement. His loss was occasioned by one of those
accidents which too frequently happen to persons who are inexpe-
rienced in the use of fire-arms. Mr. Burton had been out with Ensign
Beckwith, and some soldiers of the New South Wales corps, intending
to kill ducks on the Nepean. With that sensation of the mind which
is called presentiment he is said to have set out, having more than once
observed, that he feared some accident would happen before his return;
and he did not cease to be tormented with this unpleasant idea, until
his gun, which he carried rather aukwardly, went off, and lodged its
contents in the ground within a few inches of the feet of the person
who immediately preceded him in the walk through the woods.
Considering this as the accident which his mind foreboded, he went
on afterwards perfectly freed from any apprehension. But he was
deceived. Reaching the banks of the river, they found on its surface
                                                          innumerable

innumerable flocks of those fowl of which they were in search. Mr. Burton, in order to have a better view of them, got upon the stump of a tree, and, resting his hand upon the muzzle of his piece, raised himself by its assistance as high as he was able. The butt of the piece rested on the ground, which was thickly covered with long grass, shrubs, and weeds. No one saw the danger of such a situation in time to prevent what followed. By some motion of this unfortunate young man the piece went off, and the contents, entering at his wrist, forced their way up between the two bones of his right arm, which were much shattered, to the elbow. Mr. Beckwith, by a very happy presence of mind, applying bandages torn from a shirt, succeeded in stopping the vast effusion of blood which ensued, or his patient must soon have bled to death. This accident happened at five in the afternoon, and it was not, till ten o'clock at night of the following day that Mr. Burton was brought into Parramatta. The consequence was, such a violent fever and inflammation had taken place that any attempt to save life by amputation would only have hastened his end. In the night of the 12th the mortification came on, and he died the following morning, leaving behind him, what he universally enjoyed while living, the esteem and respect of all who knew him.

A person of a far different character and description met with an accidental death the following day. He had been employed to take some provisions to a settler who occupied a farm on the creek leading to Parramatta, and was killed by a blow from the limb of a tree, which fell on his head and fractured his skull, without having allowed him that time for repentance of which a sinful life stood so much in need. His companions and fellow prisoners (for he was a convict) declared him to have been so great a reprobate, that he was scarcely ever known to speak without an oath, or without calling on his Maker as a witness to the truth of the lie he was about to utter.

The weather had been for some days extremely bad, heavy storms of wind and rain having generally prevailed from Monday the 9th till Friday the 13th, when fair weather succeeded. At Parramatta the gale had done much damage; several huts which were built in low grounds were rendered almost inaccessible, and the greater part of the wattled huts suffered considerably. A large portion of the cleared
ground

ground was laid under water, and such corn as had not been reaped was beaten down. At Sydney the effects of the storm, though it had been equally violent, were not so severe. Most of the houses were rendered damp, and had leaks in different parts; seeds which had been recently sown were washed out of the ground, and the bridge over the stream was somewhat injured. In the woods it had raged with much violence; the people employed to kill game reported that it was dangerous to walk in the forests; and the ground, covered with huge limbs or whole trunks of trees, confirmed the truth of their report.

The bricklayers were immediately sent up to Parramatta, to repair the damages effected by the storm; and the bridge at Sydney was not only repaired, but considerably widened.

On Saturday the 13th an alteration took place in the ration. Three pounds of flour, and two pounds of maize, with four pounds of pork, were served to each man, and three pounds of flour, and one pound of maize, with four pounds of pork, were served to each woman in the settlement. The children received the usual proportion. To such alterations the settlement had now for some years been habituated; and although it was well known that they never were imposed but when the state of the stores rendered them absolutely necessary, it was impossible to meet the deduction without reflecting, that the established ration would have been adequate to every want; the plea of hunger could not have been advanced as the motive and excuse for thefts; and disease would not have met so powerful an ally in its ravages among the debilitated and emaciated objects which the gaols had crowded into transports, and the transports had landed in these settlements.

The works in hand were, building brick huts at Sydney for convicts, consisting of two apartments, each hut being twenty-six feet in front, and fourteen feet in width, and intended to contain ten people, with a suitable allotment of garden ground; completing tanks for water; widening the bridge, &c. One day in each week was dedicated to issuing provisions, and the labour of the other five (with interruptions from bad weather, and the plea of the reduced ration) did not amount in all to three good working days.

At

At Parramatta the principal labour was the getting in and houfing the maize, and preparing ground for the next year's grain. The foundations of two material buildings were laid, a town-hall and an hofpital. The town-hall was intended to include a market-place for the fale of grain, fifh, poultry, live flock, wearing apparel, and every other article that convicts might purchafe or fell. An order eftablifhing this regulation had been given out at Parramatta, and a clerk of the market appointed to regifter every commodity that was brought for fale or barter; directing, in the cafe of non-compliance, the forfeiture both of the purchafe-money and of the article, to be given, one moiety to the informer, and the other to the hofpital for the benefit of the fick.

This order was meant to prevent the felling or interchanging of ftolen goods among the convicts; a meafure that appeared to be daily becoming more neceffary. The depredations which were committed, hourly it might be faid, upon the maize, were very ferious, and called for the interpofition of fome meafure that might prevent them, as punifhments, however fevere, were not found effectually to anfwer the end. A convict who lived as a fervant with an officer was tried by the criminal court for robbing his mafter, and being found guilty was fentenced to receive three hundred lafhes.

The colony had now been fo long eftablifhed, that many convicts who had come out in the firft fleet, and might be termed the firft fettlers in the country, had ferved the feveral terms of tranfportation to which they had been fentenced. Of the people of this defcription, fome had become fettlers; fome had left the country; others, to ufe their own expreffions, had taken themfelves off the ftores, that is to fay, had declined receiving any farther provifions from the public ftores or doing any public labour, but derived their fupport from fuch fettlers or other perfons as could employ and maintain them; while others, with fomewhat more difcretion, continued to labour for government, and to receive their provifions as ufual from the commiffary. Of the latter defcription, fourteen who were indulged with the choice of the place where they were to labour, preferred the fettlement at Sydney, and there had one hut affigned to them for their refidence. To prevent any impofition on the part of thofe who profeffed to be fupported by fettlers, they were directed to render an

14   account

account at the end of each week of their respective employments; for people who had not any visible means of living would soon have become nuisances in the settlement.

It required something more than common application to adapt remedies to the various irregularities which from time to time grew up in the settlement, and something more than common ingenuity to counteract the artifices of those whose meditations were hourly directed to schemes of evasion or depredation.

The natives had not lately given us any interruption by acts of hostility. Several of their young people continued to reside among us, and the different houses in the town were frequently visited by their relations. Very little information that could be depended upon respecting their manners and customs was obtained through this intercourse; and it was observed, that they conversed with us in a mutilated and incorrect language formed entirely on our imperfect knowledge and improper application of their words.

CHAP. XVII.

MORTALITY IN APRIL.—APPEARANCE AND STATE OF THE CONVICTS.—
RATION AGAIN REDUCED.—QUANTITY OF FLOUR IN STORE.—SETTLERS.—
STATE OF TRANSACTIONS WITH THE NATIVES.—INDIAN CORN STOLEN.—
PUBLIC WORKS.—AVERAGE PRICES OF GRAIN, &c. AT SYDNEY, AND AT
PARRAMATTA.—MORTALITY DECREASES.—KING'S BIRTH-DAY.—THE AT-
LANTIC RETURNS FROM BENGAL.—ACCOUNT RECEIVED OF BRYANT AND
HIS COMPANIONS.—RATION FARTHER REDUCED.—ATLANTIC CLEARED.—
SHEEP-PENS AT PARRAMATTA ATTEMPTED.—QUALITY OF PROVISIONS
RECEIVED FROM CALCUTTA.—THE BRITANNIA ARRIVES FROM ENG-
LAND.—RATION INCREASED.—A CONVICT EMANCIPATED.—PUBLIC
WORKS.

May.]   THE mortality in the last month had been extremely great. Distressing as it was, however, to see the poor wretches daily dropping into the grave, it was far more afflicting to observe the countenances and emaciated persons of many that remained soon to follow their

E R   miserable

miferable companions. Every ftep was taken that could be devifed to fave them; a fithery was eftablithed at the South-head, exclufively for the ufe of the fick, under the direction of one Barton, who had been formerly a pilot, and who, in addition to this duty, was to board all fhips coming into the harbour and pilot them to the fettlement. The different people who were employed by individuals to kill game were given up for the ufe of the hofpital; and to ftimulate them to exertion, two pounds of flour in addition to the ration were ordered for every kangooroo that they fhould bring, befide the head, one fore-quarter, and the pluck of the animal.

The weakeft of the convicts were excufed from any kind of hard labour; but it was not hard labour that deftroyed them; it was an entire want of ftrength in the conftitution to receive nourifhment, to throw off the debility that pervaded their whole fyftem, or to perform any fort of labour whatever.

This dreadful mortality was chiefly confined to the convicts who had arrived in the laft year; of one hundred and twenty-two male convicts who came out in the Queen tranfport from Ireland, fifty only were living at the beginning of this month. The different robberies which were committed were alfo confined to this clafs of the convicts, and the wretches who were concerned in the commiffion of them were in general too weak to receive a punifhment adequate to their crimes. Their univerfal plea was hunger; but it was a plea that in the then fituation of the colony could not be fo much attended to as it certainly would have been in a country of greater plenty.

The quantity of Indian corn ftolen and deftroyed this feafon was not afcertained, but was fuppofed to have been at leaft one fixth of what was raifed. The people employed in bringing it in daily reported that they found immenfe piles of the hufks and ftalks concealed in the midft of what was ftanding, having been there fhelled and taken off at different times. This was a very ferious lofs, and became an object of immediate confideration in fuch a fcarcity as the colony then experienced; moft anxioufly it expected fupplies from England, which did not arrive, though the time had elapfed in which they fhould have appeared had their departure taken place at the period mentioned by the fecretary of ftate (the autumn of laft year). His excellency therefore
14   thought

thought it prudent still farther to abridge the ration of flour which was then issued; and on the 9th of the month directed the commissary to serve weekly, until further orders, one pound and an half of flour with four pounds of maize to each man; and one pound and an half of flour with three pounds of maize to each woman, and to every child ten years of age; but made no alteration in the ration of salt provisions.

This ration was to take place on Saturday the 12th; and as maize or Indian corn was now necessarily become the principal part of each person's subsistence, hand-mills and querns were set to work to grind it coarse for every person both at Sydney and at Parramatta; and at this latter place, wooden mortars, with a lever and a pestle, were also used to break the corn, and these pounded it much finer than it could be ground by the hand-mills; but it was effected with great labour.

On comparing this ration with that issued in the month of April 1790, it will appear that the allowance then received from the public store was in most respects better than that now ordered. We then received, in addition to two pounds and a half of flour, two pounds of rice, which taken together yielded more nutritive substance than the four pounds of maize and one pound and a half of flour; for the maize when perfectly ground, sifted, and divested of the unwholesome and unprofitable part, the husk, would not give more than three pounds of good meal; and the rice was used by the convicts in a much greater variety of modes than it was possible to prepare the maize in.

As at this period the flour in store was reduced to a very inconsiderable quantity, twenty-four days at the new ration, (one pound and a half per week,) and the salt provisions at the present ration not affording a supply for a longer time than three months, it became a melancholy, although natural reflection, that had not such numbers died, both in the passage and since the landing of those who survived the voyage, we should not at this moment have had any thing to receive from the public stores; thus strangely did we derive a benefit from the miseries of our fellow-creatures!

Several of the settlers who had farms at or near Parramatta, notwithstanding the extreme drought of the season preceding the saving of their corn, had such crops that they found themselves enabled to take

off

off from the public store, some one, and others two convicts, to assist in preparing their grounds for the next season. The salt provisions with which they supplied them they procured by bartering their corn for that article, reserving a sufficiency for the support of themselves and families, and for seed. Mr. Schaffer from a small patch of ground got in about two hundred bushels of Indian corn; and with the assistance of four convicts expected to have thirty acres in cultivation the next season. But others of the settlers, inattentive to their own interests, and more desirous of acquiring for the present what they deemed comforts, than studious to provide for the future, not only neglected the cultivation of their lands, but sold the breeding stock with which they had been supplied by order of the governor. Two settlers of the former description having clearly forfeited their grants, and it being understood that they did not intend to proceed to cultivation any further than to save appearances till they could get away, their grants were taken from them, and other settlers placed on the grounds. But exclusive of the idle people, of which there were but few, the settlers were found in general to be doing very well, their farms promising to place them shortly in a state of independence on the public stores in the articles of provisions and grain; and it must not be omitted in this account, that they had to combat with the bad effects of a short and reduced ration nearly the whole of the time that they had been employed in cultivating ground on their own account.

Many complaints having been made by the settlers, of depredations committed on their Indian corn by some of the convicts, it was ordered, that every convict residing at Parramatta, who should be fully convicted before a magistrate of stealing Indian corn, should, in addition to such corporal punishment as he might think it necessary to adjudge, be sent from Parramatta to the New Grounds, there to be employed in cultivation. Mr. Richard Atkins, who came out in the Pitt, and who had been sworn a justice of the peace, went up to Parramatta to reside there, the constant presence of a magistrate being deemed by the governor indispensable at that settlement.

It was soon perceived, that the punishment of being sent from Parramatta was more dreaded by the convicts than any corporal correction, however severe, that could have been inflicted on them. The being

deprived

deprived of a comfortable hut and garden, and quitting a place whence the communication with Sydney was frequent, particularly when shipping were in the cove, operated so powerfully with one offender, who was ordered out to the New Grounds, that he chose rather to make an attempt to destroy himself than be sent thither; and had very nearly effected his purpose, having made an incision in his neck of such depth as to lay bare the carotid artery.

In addition to the depredations of our own people, the natives had for some time been suspected of stealing the corn at the settlements beyond Parramatta. On the 18th a party of the tribe inhabiting the woods, to the number of fifteen or sixteen, was observed coming out of a hut at the middle settlement, dressed in such clothing as they found there, and taking with them a quantity of corn in nets. The person who saw them imagined at first from their appearance that they were convicts; but perceiving one of them preparing to throw a spear at him, he levelled his piece, which was loaded with small shot, and fired at him. The native instantly dropped his spear, and the whole party ran away, leaving behind them the nets with the corn, some blankets, and one or two spears. It was supposed that the native was wounded; for in a few days information was received from Parramatta, that a convict who was employed in well-digging at Prospect Hill, having come in from thence to receive some slops which were issued, was on his return met midway and murdered, or rather butchered by some of the natives. When the body was found, it was not quite cold, and had at least thirty spear wounds in it. The head was cut in several places, and most of the teeth were knocked out. They had taken his clothing and provisions, and the provisions of another man which he was carrying out to him. The natives with whom we had intercourse said, that this murder was committed by some of the people who inhabited the woods, and was done probably in revenge for the shot that was fired at the natives who some time before were stripping the hut.

Toward the end of the month the corn was all got in and housed at Parramatta. As the grounds were cleared of the stalks, the depredations which had been committed became visible; and several of the convicts were detected by the night-watch in bringing in large quantities of shelled corn which had been stolen, buried or concealed in the woods,

and

and shelled as they could find opportunity. Seven bushels were recovered in one night by the vigilance of the watch; and as different quantities were found from time to time in the huts, the people who resided in them were all ordered to the New Grounds.

The works during this month, both at Sydney and at Parramatta, went on but slowly. At Sydney a tank that would contain about seven thousand nine hundred and ninety-six gallons of water, with a well in the centre fifteen feet deep, was finished, and the water let into it. Brick huts were in hand for the convicts in room of the miserable hovels occupied by many, which had been put up at their first landing, and in room of others which, from having been erected on such ground as was then cleared, were now found to interfere with the direction of the streets which the governor was laying out. People were also employed in cutting paling for fencing in their gardens. At Parramatta and the New Grounds, during the greatest part of the month, the people were employed in getting in the maize and sowing wheat. A foundation for an hospital was laid, a house built for the master carpenter, and roofs prepared for the different huts either building, or to be built in future.

The following were the prices of grain and other articles, as they were sold during this month at Sydney, and at the market-place at Parramatta.

At Sydney.

Flour from 6d. to 1s. per lb.
Maize per bushel from 12s. 6d. to 15s.
Laying hens from 7s. to 10s. each.
Cocks for killing from 4s. to 7s. each.
Half grown chickens from 2s. 6d. to 3s. 6d. each.
Chickens six weeks old 1s. each.
Eggs 3s. per dozen, or 3d. a-piece.
Fresh pork 1s. per lb.
Potatoes 3d. per lb.
Good white beart cabbages 1d. each.
Greens per dozen 6d.
Turnips 6d. per dozen.
Sows in pig from 4l. 10s. to 6l. 6s.
Sows just taken the boar from 3l. to 4l. 4s.

At Parramatta.

Flour, 1s. per lb.
Maize per bushel from 11s. to 13s.
Laying hens from 7s. 6d. to 10s. each.
Cocks for killing from 4s. 6d. to 5s. each.
Chickens two months old 3s. each.
Eggs per dozen 3s.
Fresh pork per lb from 1s. 1d. to 1s. 3d.
Salt pork per lb. from 10d. to 1s.
Potatoes per lb. from 3d. to 4d.
A lot of cabbages, per hundred 10s.
Tea per lb. from 16s. to 1l. 1s.
Coffee per lb. from 2s. to 3s.
Moist sugar from 2s. to 2s. 6d. per lb.
Tobacco grown in the country from 1s. 6d. to 2s. per lb.

Growing

At Sydney.	At Parramatta.
Growing pigs from 1 L. to 2 L. 10 s. each.	Virginia or Brazil from 4 s. to 6 s.
Sucking pigs 10 s. each.	Soap from 1 s. 6 d. to 2 s. 6 d. per lb.
Moist sugar from 1 s. 6 d. to 2 s. 6 d. per lb.	Cheese from 1 s. 6 d. to 2 s. per lb.
Coffee 2 s. to 2 s. 6 d. per lb.	
Salt pork per lb. from 8 d. to 9 d.	
Tobacco, Brazil, per lb. from 3 s. to 5 s.	

June.] With infinite satisfaction it was observed at the beginning of the month, that the mortality and sickness among the people had very much decreased. This was attributed by the medical gentlemen to the quantities of fresh meat which had been obtained at Parramatta by the people who were employed to shoot for the hospital; a sufficiency having been brought in at one time to supply the sick with fresh meat for a week; and for the remainder of the month in the proportion of twice or three times a week. Great quantities of vegetables had also been given to those who were in health, as well as to the sick, both from the public ground at the farther settlement, (which had been sown, and produced some most excellent turnips,) and from the governor's garden.

4th.] The anniversary of his Majesty's birth-day was observed with as much distinction as was in our power. The governor always wished to celebrate that day in the year in a manner that should render it welcome to all descriptions of people in the different settlements. Heretofore on the same occasion he had increased the ration of provisions; but the situation of the public stores not admitting of such increase at the present, the commissary was directed to issue on that day half a pint of rum to each person of the civil and military department, and a quarter of a pint of rum to each female in the settlement. At noon the New South Wales corps fired three vollies, and the governor received the compliments of the day; after which the officers of each department were entertained by his Excellency at dinner at government-house. Bonfires were made at night, and the day concluded joyfully, without any interruption to the peace of the settlement.

The small allowance of spirits which was given for the day to the convalescents, and to such sick in the hospital as the surgeon judged proper, being found of infinite service to them, the governor directed
that

that the surgeon should receive a certain quantity, and at his discretion issue it from time to time to such sick under his care as he thought would derive benefit from it; the remainder was ordered to be reserved for the use of the sloop when it might be necessary to send her to sea. The spirits at this time in the colony were the surplus of what had been sent out for his majesty's ship Sirius, and the Supply armed tender.

As it had been customary too, on this day, to grant a pardon to such offenders as might be in custody or under sentence of corporal punishment, his Excellency was pleased a few days after to release such convicts as were sentenced to work in irons for a limited time at Parramatta and the New Grounds, and who were not very notorious offenders. This lenity was the rather shewn at this time, as the convicts were in general giving proofs of a greater disposition to honesty than had for some time been visible among them. The convicts at the New Grounds being assembled for this purpose, the governor acquainted them, " that the state of the colony requiring a still farther " reduction in the ration, it would very shortly take place; but that " he hoped soon to have it in his power to augment it. The deficien- " cies in the established ration, he informed them, should at a future " period be made up; but in the meantime he expected that every " man would continue to exert himself and get the corn into the " ground to insure support for the next year." Indeed these exertions became every day more necessary. On the 6th of this month there was only a sufficiency of flour in store to serve till the 2d of July, and salt provisions till the 6th of August following, at the ration then issued ; and neither the Atlantic storeship from Calcutta, nor the expected supplies from England, had arrived.

Notwithstanding the mortality and sickness which had prevailed among the convicts who came out in the last ships, much labour had been performed at the New Grounds by those who were capable of handling the hoe and the spade. At this time the quantity of ground in wheat, and cleared and broken up for maize, there and at Parramatta, was such as (if not visited again by a dry season) would at least, computing the produce even at what it was the last year, yield a sufficiency of grain for all our numbers for a twelvemonth. But every
one

one doubted the possibility of getting all the corn into the ground within the proper time, unless the colony should be very speedily relieved from its distresses, as the reduction in the ration would inevitably be followed by a diminution of the daily labour.

On the 20th however, to the inexpressible joy of all ranks of people in the settlements, the Atlantic storeship anchored safely in the cove, with a cargo of rice, soujee, and dholl, from Calcutta, having been much longer performing her voyage than was expected, owing to some delays at Calcutta, in settling and arranging the contract for the supply of provisions which had been required. The merchants who, in the year 1790, had made a tender to supply this colony with certain articles at a stipulated price, were, from several concurring circumstances, unable to furnish what was required by Lieutenant Bowen, agreeable to the prices then stipulated; it was therefore determined by the members of the council at Calcutta, to whom Lieutenant Bowen delivered his letters and instructions, (Earl Cornwallis, who had, several months previous to his arrival, been desired by the secretary of state to direct any supplies which might be required for this settlement, being absent with the army,) to invite offers for supplying the different articles which were required by contract. Lieutenant Bowen arrived at Calcutta on the 4th of February, and it was not till the 27th of the following month that the business was finally arranged, and a contract entered into by the house of Lambert, Ross, and Co. satisfactory to the council and to Lieutenant Bowen.

It appearing that the flour of Bengal, unless it was dressed for the purpose, which would have taken a great deal of time, was not of a quality to keep even for the voyage from Calcutta to this country, a large proportion of rice, of that sort which was said to be the fittest for preservation, was purchased. A small quantity of flour too was put on board, but merely for the purpose of experiment. It was called soujee by the natives, but was much inferior in quality to the flour prepared in Europe, and more difficult to make into bread.

The Atlantic left Calcutta the 28th of March, and on her passage met with much bad weather, and some heavy gales of wind. She brought two bulls and a cow of the Bengal breed, together with twenty sheep and twenty goats; but these were of so diminutive a species,

P P   that,

that, unless the breed could be confiderably improved by that already in the country, very little benefit was for a length of time to be expected from their importation. Various feeds and plants alfo were received from the company's botanical garden; and much commendation was due to Colonel Kydd, the gentleman who fuperintended the felection and arrangement of them for the voyage; as well as to Lieutenant Bowen, for his care, and for the accommodation which he gave up, both to them and to the cattle, in the cabin of the fhip.

Information was received by the Calcutta papers of the loſs of his Majefty's fhip Pandora, Captain Edwards, who had been among the Friendly Iflands in fearch of Chriftian and his piratical crew, fourteen of whom he had fecured, and was returning with the purpofe of furveying Endeavour Straits purfuant to his inftructions, when he unfortunately ftruck upon a reef in latitude 23° S. eleven degrees only to the northward of this port. By his boats he providentially reached Timor with ninety-nine of his officers and people, being the whole of his fhip's company which were faved. At Timor, on his arrival, he found Bryant and his companions, who made their efcape from this place in the fifhing cutter in the night of the 28th of March 1791. Thefe people had framed and told a plaufible tale of diftrefs, of their having been caft away at fea; and this for a time was believed; but they foon, by their language to each other, and by practifing the tricks of their former profeffion, gave room for fufpicion; and being taken up, their true characters and the circumftances of their efcape were divulged. The Dutch governor of Timor delivered them to Captain Edwards, who took them on with him to Batavia, whence he was to proceed to England. The circumftance of thefe people having reached Timor confirmed what was fuggefted immediately after their departure, that the mafter of the fnow Waakfambeyd had furnifhed Bryant with inftructions how to proceed, and with every thing he ftood in need of for his voyage; and it muft be remembered, that though this man, during his ftay in this port, had conftantly faid that every fort of refrefhment was to be procured at Timor, yet when Captain Hunter, while at fea, propofed to fteer for that ifland, he declared that nothing was to be got there, and fo prevented that officer from going thither. There cannot be a doubt that, expecting to find

his

his friends at Timor, he did not choose either to endanger them, or risk a discovery of the part he had acted in aiding their escape.

Had it not been for the fortunate discovery and subsequent delivery of these people to a captain of a British man of war, the evident practicability of reaching Timor in an open boat might have operated with others to make the attempt, and to carry off boats from the settlements; which, during the absence of the king's ships belonging to the station, was never difficult; and it was now hoped, that the certainty of every boat which should reach that or any other Dutch settlement under similar circumstances being suspected and received accordingly, would have its due effect here.

The supply of provisions received by the Atlantic being confined to grain, it became necessary to reduce the ration of salt meat. It was therefore ordered on the 21st, that after the Friday following only two pounds of pork should be issued in lieu of four. The allowance of one pound and a half of flour and four pounds of maize was continued, but one pound of rice and one quart of pease were added.

The general order given out on this occasion stated,

" That the arrival of ships with further supplies of provisions might
" be daily looked for; but as it was possible that some unforeseen ac-
" cident might have happened to the ships which were expected to
" have sailed from England shortly after the departure of the Pitt, it
" became necessary to reduce the ration of provisions then issued, in
" order that the quantity in store might hold out till the arrival of
" those ships, which might be supposed to have sailed for this country
" about the months of January or February last; it having been the
" intention of government that ships should sail from England for this
" colony twice in every year. And as all deficiencies in the ration
" were to be made good hereafter, the following extract from the in-
" structions which fixed the ration for the colony was inserted, viz.

" Ration for each marine and male convict for seven days
successively:

7 pounds of bread, or in lieu thereof 7 pounds of flour;
7 pounds of beef, or in lieu thereof 4 pounds of pork;
3 pints of pease;
6 ounces of butter;
1 pound of flour,   or in lieu thereof 1 a pound of rice:

" Being

" Being the fame as are allowed his Majefty's troops ferving in the
" Weft-India Iflands, excepting only the allowance of fpirits.

" And two thirds of the above ration were directed to be iffued to
" each woman in the fettlement." So far the general order.

As, however, a fufficient quantity of rice could not be landed in
time to iffue on the Saturday, one pound of maize was iffued in lieu of
the fame quantity of rice.

At this ration the rice and flour or foujee were calculated to laft five
months; and the peafe or dholl for nearly a twelvemonth. But if the
Atlantic had not arrived, the profpect in the colony would have been
truly dreary and diftreffing; as it was intended to have iffued only
one pound and a half of flour, three pounds of maize, and two pounds
of pork per week, on Saturday the 23d; a ration that would have derived very little affiftance from vegetables, as at that feafon of the year
the gardens had fcarcely any thing in them. Gloomy and unpro-
mifing, however, as was the fituation of the fettlements before her
arrival, that event, which happened the very day on which, two
years before, the colony had been relieved by the arrival of the
Juftinian ftorefhip, caft a gleam of funfhine which penetrated every
one capable of reflection, and, by effecting a fudden change in the
ideas, operated fo powerfully on the mind, that we all felt alike, and
found it impoffible to fit for one minute ferioufly down to any
bufinefs or accuftomed purfuit.

A black, the fame who had fecreted himfelf on board the Supply
when fhe went to Batavia, having found means to conceal himfelf on
board the Atlantic on her departure for Calcutta, and to remain concealed until fhe had left Norfolk Ifland, was brought back again to the
fettlement, notwithftanding he endeavoured to efcape from the fhip in
the Ganges. As it appeared that he had ferved the term for which
he was fentenced to be transported even before he got off on board the
Atlantic, (of which Lieutenant Bowen had only his affertion,) no punifhment was inflicted upon him, and he was left at liberty to get
away in any fhip that would receive him on board.

The little live ftock that was received by the Atlantic was landed at
Parramatta directly after her arrival, and placed in an inclofure feparated from the others.

About

About two hundred and fifty gallons of Bengal rum having been received, the governor directed, that in consequence of the ration being reduced, that quantity, together with what was in store, and had been intended for the use of the sloop at a future time, should be issued to the civil and military, reserving a proportion for those at Norfolk Island.

The flag-staff which had been erected at the South Head under the direction of Captain Hunter, in the month of January 1790, being found too short to shew the signal at any great distance, a new one was taken down the harbour, and erected the day the Atlantic arrived, within a few feet of the other; its height above ground was sixty feet.

It was not found that the return of the Atlantic had caused any diminution in the price of grain or stock, either at Parramatta or at Sydney. At this latter place a market had been established for the sale of grain, fish, or poultry, similar to that at Parramatta; a clerk being appointed to superintend it, and take account of the different articles brought for sale, to prevent the barter of goods stolen by the convicts.

On the last day of the month, some natives residing at the south shore of Botany Bay, whether from a hope of reward, or from actually having seen some ships at a distance, informed the governor that a few days before they had perceived four or five sail, one of which they described to be larger than the others, standing off the land, with a westerly wind. Little credit was however given to their report.

July.] As the merchants who supplied the provisions received by the Atlantic were only to be paid for such part of the cargo as was actually landed, and found to be in a merchantable condition, it became necessary to weigh and survey the whole of the cargo; for which purpose two surveyors were appointed by the governor. This of course proved a very tedious business, from the weakness of the 'gangs at Sydney. Seldom more than four hundred bags, each bag containing one hundred and sixty-four pounds, were at first landed in a day; latterly, this number was by great exertions got up to somewhat more than five hundred in a day. It was not, however, till the 21st of the month that she was cleared.

Having discharged her cargo, she began the serious labour of ballasting, and it being wished to expedite her preparations for Norfolk Island,

her

her ship's company were assisted with twelve convicts from the settlement, and the occasional use of such boats as could be spared to convey the ballast to the ship. The governor was anxious to learn the state of that dependency, not having heard from it since the return of the Queen transport early in the last December.

The maize being all got in, it was hoped that the convicts would not find any new object for their depredations, and that order and tranquillity would for a time at least be restored among them. But the houses of individuals soon became their prey, and three or four daring burglaries were committed this month : I say daring burglaries, as the houses which were broken into were either within the view of a centinel, or within the round of a watchman. This, however, must not be otherwise understood than as a proof of the perseverance and cunning of these people, who could find means to elude any vigilance that was opposed to their designs. An attempt to steal some of the sheep at Parramatta was also made by two notorious offenders, who, from being deemed incorrigible, were not included in the pardon which the governor granted to the wretches in irons after his Majesty's birth-day, but were ordered to be chained together for some longer time. Being fortunately overheard by the person who lived in the inclosure, and had the care of the stock, he snapped a piece at them, and, finding it miss fire, gave an alarm to the watch, by whose activity they were apprehended two miles from the place. They were provided with every thing necessary for their design, such as a tomahawk, an iron kettle, knives, spoons, platters, and a quantity of vegetables. It was found, that with the assistance of the tomahawk they had divided the chain that linked them together, and had secured round the leg the iron that remained with each, so as not to be heard when they moved.

The different species of provisions which had been received from Calcutta were not much esteemed by the people. The flour or soujee, from our not knowing the proper mode of preparing it for bread, soon became sour, particularly if not assisted with some other grain ; the dholl, or pease, were complained of as boiling hard, and not breaking, though kept on the fire for a greater length of time than the impatience of those who were to use it would in general admit of; and the rice,

though

though termed the beſt of the cargo, was found to be full of huſks, and ill dreſſed. Some pork alſo, of which eight caſks had been ſent as an experiment, was, on being iſſued, found to be for the moſt part putrid, and, in the language of ſurveyors of proviſions, not ſit for men to eat. Theſe circumſtances, together with the extreme minute-neſs of the Bengal breed of cattle, excited a general hope, that theſe ſettlements would not have to depend upon that country for ſupplies. To the parent country every one anxiouſly looked for a ſpeedy and ſubſtantial aſſiſtance; and day after day uſed to paſs in a fruitleſs hope that the morrow would come accompanied with the long wiſhed-for arrival of ſhips.

The natives who lived among us aſſured us from time to time, that the report formerly propagated of ſhips having been ſeen on the coaſt had a foundation in reality; and as every one remembered that the Juſtinian, after making the heads of Port Jackſon, had been kept at ſea for three weeks, a fond hope was cheriſhed that the ſun had ſhone upon the whitened ſails of ſome approaching veſſel, which had been diſcovered by the penetrating eyes of our ſavage neighbours at Botany Bay. In this anxiety and expectation we remained till the 26th, when the long-wiſhed-for ſignal was made, and in a few hours after the Britannia ſtore-ſhip, Mr. William Raven maſter, anchored in the cove, after a paſſage of twenty-three weeks from Falmouth, having ſailed from thence on the 15th of laſt February, the day after the arrival of the Pitt in this country.

The Britannia was the firſt of three ſhips that were to be diſpatched hither, having on board twelve months clothing for the convicts, four months flour, and eight months beef and pork for every deſcription of perſons in the ſettlements, at full allowance, calculating their numbers at four thouſand ſix hundred and thirty-nine, which it was at home ſuppoſed they might amount to after the arrival of the Pitt. It was ſtill a matter of uncertainty in England, even at the departure of the Britannia, whether the merchants of Calcutta had ſupplied this country with proviſions; and under the idea that ſome circumſtance might have prevented them, this ſupply was ordered to be forwarded. The Kitty tranſport, one of the three ſhips which were to contain theſe ſupplies, had ſailed from Dept-ford, at the time the Britannia paſſed through the Downs; her arrival therefore might be daily expected—and in her, or on board of the other ſhip,

ship, it was imagined that fifteen families of Quakers, who had made proposals to government to be received in this country as settlers, were to take their passage.

It was with great pleasure heard in the colony, that some steps had been taken toward prosecuting Donald Trail, the master of the Neptune transport, for his treatment of the convicts with which he sailed from England for this settlement in the year 1790. The sickness and mortality which prevailed among them excited a suspicion that they had been improperly treated; and information upon oath was soon procured of many acts of neglect, ill usage, and cruelty toward them.

In consequence of the arrival of the Britannia, the commissary was on the following day directed to issue, *until further orders*, the following weekly ration; viz.

    To each man 4 pounds of maize,
           3 pounds of soujee,
           7 pounds of beef, or in lieu thereof 4 lbs. of pork,
           3 pints of pease or dholl, and
           ½ a pound of rice.

Two thirds of the man's ration was directed to be issued to each woman and to every child above ten years of age; one half of the man's ration to each child above two, and under ten years of age; and one fourth of the man's ration to each child under two years of age.

Thus happily was the colony once more put upon something like a full ration of provisions; a change in our situation that gave universal satisfaction, as at the hour of the arrival of the Britannia there were in the public store only twenty-four days salt provisions for the settlement at the ration then issued. A delay of a month in her voyage would have placed the colony in a state that must have excited the commiseration of its greatest enemies; a vast body of hard-working people depending for their support upon one pound and a half of soujee, or bad Bengal flour, four pounds of maize, one pound of rice, and one quart of pease for one man per week, without one ounce of meat! But with this new ration all entertained new hopes, and trusted that their future labours would be crowned with success, and that the necessity of sending out supplies from the mother country until the colony could support itself without assistance would have become so evident from the

        1   frequency

frequency of our diftreffes and the reduction of the ration, that the
journalift would no longer have occafion to fill his page with compari-
fons between what we might have been and what we were; to lament
the non-arrival of fupplies; nor to paint the miferies and wretchednefs
which enfued; but might adopt a language to which he might truly
be faid to have been hitherto a ftranger, and paint the glowing pro-
fpects of a golden harveft, the triumph of a well-filled ftore, and the
increafing and confequent profperity of the fettlements.

His excellency this month thought fit to exercife the power vefted
in him by act of parliament, and by his Majefty's commiffion under
the great feal, of remitting either wholly, or in part, the term for
which felons might be tranfported, by granting an abfolute remiffion
of the term for which Elizabeth Perry had been fentenced. This
woman came out in the Neptune in 1790, and had married James Rufe
a fettler. The good conduct of the wife, and the induftry of the hufband, who had for fome time fupported himfelf, his wife, a child, and
two convicts, independent of the public ftore, were the reafons affigned
in the inftrument which reftored her to her rights and privileges as a
free woman, for extending to her the hand of forgivenefs.

This power, fo pleafing to the feelings of its poffeffor, had hitherto
been very fparingly exercifed; and thofe perfons who had felt its influence were not found to have been undeferving. I fpeak only of fuch
convicts as had been deemed proper objects of this favour by the governor himfelf; the convicts, however, who came out in the Guardian
were emancipated by the King's command, and of thefe by far the
greater part conducted themfelves with propriety.

Preparing roofs for new barracks, bringing in bricks to the fpot appointed for their conftruction, and difcharging the Atlantic and the
Britannia, were the principal works in hand at Sydney during the
month.—At the fettlements beyond Parramatta (which had lately obtained and were in future to be diftinguifhed by the name of Toon-
gab-be) the convicts were employed in preparing the ground for the
reception of next year's crop of maize. At and near Parramatta, the
chief bufinefs was erecting two houfes on allotments of land which
belonged to Mr. Arndell the affiftant furgeon, and to John Irving, (one
of thofe perfons whofe exemplary conduct and meritorious behaviour

o o   both

both in this country and on the paffage to it had been rewarded with
unconditional freedom by the governor,) each of whom had been put
in poffeffion, the former of fixty and the latter of thirty acres of land
on the creek leading to Parramatta ; erecting chimnies for the different
fettlers at the ponds, preparing roofs for various buildings, fawing timber, cutting pofts and railing for inclofures, and hoeing and preparing
ground for maize.

CHAP. XVIII.

THE BRITANNIA CLEARED.—SURVEY OF PROVISIONS.—TOTAL OF CARGO
RECEIVED FROM BENGAL.—ATLANTIC SAILS WITH PROVISIONS FOR NOR-
FOLK ISLAND.—TRANSACTIONS.—GENERAL BEHAVIOUR OF CONVICTS.—
CRIMINAL COURTS.—PRISONER PARDONED CONDITIONALLY.—ANOTHER
ACQUITTED.—NEW BARRACKS BEGUN.—THEFTS.—THE ATLANTIC RE-
TURNS FROM NORFOLK ISLAND.—INFORMATION.—SETTLERS THERE DIS-
CONTENTED.—PRINCIPAL WORKS.—THE BRITANNIA TAKEN UP BY THE
OFFICERS OF THE NEW SOUTH WALES CORPS TO PROCURE STOCK.—THE
ROYAL ADMIRAL EAST INDIAMAN ARRIVES FROM ENGLAND.—REGULA-
TIONS AT THE STORE.—A BURGLARY COMMITTED.—CRIMINAL COURT.—
THE BRITANNIA SAILS.—SHOPS OPENED.—BAD CONDUCT OF SOME SET-
TLERS.—OIL ISSUED.—SLOPS SERVED.—GOVERNOR PHILIPS SIGNIFIES HIS
INTENTION OF RETURNING TO ENGLAND.

Auguft.] THE Britannia was cleared, and difcharged from government employ, on the 17th of this month. A deficiency appearing in
the weight of the falt provifions delivered from that fhip, a furvey
was immediately ordered ; and it appeared from the report of the perfons employed to conduct it, (and who from their fituations were well
qualified to judge, Mr. Bowen, a lieutenant in the navy, and Mr.
Raven, the commander of the Britannia and a mafter of a man of war,)
that the cafks of beef were deficient, on an average, thirty-fix pounds
and one-third, and the tierces twenty-one pounds and one-third.   It
alfo appeared that the meat was lean, coarfe, and boney, and worfe
                                        than

than they had ever feen iffued in his Majefty's fervice. A deception of this nature would be more feverely felt in this country, as its inhabitants had but lately experienced a change from a very fhort ration of falt provifions ; and every ounce loft here was of importance, as the fupply had been calculated on a fuppofition of each cafk containing its full weight.

It having been covenanted, as already mentioned, by Meffrs. Lambert, Rofs, and Company, that only fuch part of the cargo as on its arrival here fhould be found to be in a merchantable ftate fhould be paid for, the following quantity, having been deemed merchantable by the perfons appointed to take the furvey, was received into the ftore ; viz.

	Tons.	Cwt.	Qrs.	Ibs.
Rice - - -	190	3	2	3
Dholl - - -	152	18	2	13
Peafe - - -	15	9	2	23
Soujee - -	57	3	0	4
Wheat - -	1	15	1	24
Total of Grain	417	10	1	11

Eight cafks of pork, (as an experiment,) from Lambert and Company ; and two cafks of rum containing one hundred and twenty-fix gallons, fupplied at 3s. per gallon. Four cafks of flour, and four cafks of foujee from Mr. Cockraine, (fent likewife as an experiment,) were alfo received into the ftore.

The unmerchantable articles, confifting of foujee, dholl, and rice, were fold at public auction ; and though wholly unfit for men to eat, yet being not too bad for flock, were quickly purchafed, and in general went off at a great price. Several lots, confifting of five bags of the foujee, each bag containing about one hundred and fourteen pounds, fold for 4 l. 14 s. The whole quantity of damaged grain which was thus difpofed of amounted to nine hundred and ninety-one bags, and fold for 373 l. 9 s. making a moft defirable and acceptable provifion for the private flock in the colony. For this fum of 373 l. 9 s. credit was given to the merchants at the final fettling of the account ; at which time it appeared, that the whole of the Atlantic's cargo of rice,

o o 2

dholl,

dholl, peafe, foujee, wheat, and rum, which was to be paid for by government, amounted to the fum of 7538l. 14s. 4d.

This cargo might be termed an experiment, to which it was true we were driven by neceffity; and it had become the univerfal and earneft wifh that no caufe might ever again induce us to try it.

The maize being expended, except a certain proportion which was referved for feed, feven pounds of foujee were iffued per week to each man; but as the quantity of this article which had been received from India was but fmall (fifty-feven tons) compared with the rice and dholl, toward the latter end of the month it became neceffary to make up a new ration compounded of the various grain which had been introduced from Calcutta, and the different articles of food which had been received from England.

One third of the provifions received from Bengal by the Atlantic, and the like proportion of the ftores and provifions which had been landed from the Britannia, having been put on board the former of thofe fhips, fhe failed on the 19th for Norfolk Ifland, having alfo on board two fettlers from the marine detachment, twenty-two male convicts, an incorrigible lad who had been drummed out of the New South Wales corps, three natives, and a free woman, wife to one of the convicts. Among the latter defcription of perfons were fome of very bad character; others who were fuppofed to have formed a defign of efcaping from the colony; fome who profeffed to be flax dreffers, and a few artificers who might be ufeful at that ifland.

At the head of a party of convicts who were faid to have formed a defign of feizing a boat and effecting their efcape, was J. C. Morris, one of thofe convicts who left England in the Guardian, and who, from their meritorious behaviour before and after the difafter that befel that fhip, received conditional emancipation by his Majefty's command. Morris was at Norfolk Ifland when the intimation of the royal bounty reached this country. Being permitted to return to this fettlement, he obtained a grant of thirty acres of land at the Eaftern Farms, in an advantageous fituation on the north-fide of the creek leading to Parramatta. Here it foon became evident that he had not the induftry neceffary for a bona fide fettler, and that, inftead of cultivating his own ground, he lent himfelf to his neighbours, who were

to

to repay his labour by working for him at a future day. The governor deemed this a clear forfeiture of his grant, in which it was unequivocally expressed, that he held the thirty acres on condition of his residing within the same, and proceeding to the improvement and cultivation thereof. Being no longer a settler, he declared himself able to procure his daily support without the assistance of the public stores, from which, it must be remarked, he had been maintained all the time he held his grant. Soon after this, it was said, he formed the plan of going off with a boat; yet not so cautiously, but that information was given of it to the governor, who resolved to send him back to Norfolk Island, whence an escape was by no means so practicable as from this place; and he was, very much against his inclination, put on board the Atlantic for that purpose. He found means, however, to get on shore in the night preceding her departure; and she sailed without him. A reward being offered for apprehending him, he was soon taken, and sent up to Parramatta, there to be confined on a reduced ration, until an opportunity offered of sending him to Norfolk Island.

During the month the governor thought it necessary to issue some regulations to be observed by those convicts whose sentences of transportation had expired. The number of people of this description in the colony had been so much increased of late, that it had become requisite to determine with precision the line in which they were to move. Having emerged from the condition of convicts, and got rid of the restraint which was necessarily imposed on them while under that subjection, many of them seemed to have forgotten that they were still amenable to the regulations of the colony, and appeared to have shaken off, with the yoke of bondage, all restraint and dependence whatsoever. They were, therefore, called upon to declare their intentions respecting their future mode of living. Those who wished to be allowed to provide for themselves were informed, that on application to the judge advocate, they would receive a certificate of their having served their several periods of transportation, which certificate they would deposit with the commissary as his voucher for striking them off the provision and clothing lists; and once a week they were to report in what manner and for whom they had been employed.

Such

Such as should be desirous of returning to England were informed, that no obstacle would be thrown in their way, they being at liberty to ship themselves on board of such vessels as would give them a passage. And those who preferred labouring for the public, and receiving in return such ration as should be issued from the public stores, were to give in their names to the commissary, who would victual and clothe them as long as their services might be required.

Of those, here and at Parramatta, who had fulfilled the sentence of the law, by far the greater part signified their intention of returning to England by the first opportunity; but the getting away from the colony was now a matter of some difficulty, as it was understood that a clause was to be inserted in all future contracts for shipping for this country, subjecting the masters to certain penalties, on certificates being received of their having brought away any convicts or other persons from this settlement without the governor's permission; and as it was not probable that many of them would, on their return, refrain from the vices or avoid the society of those companions who had been the causes of their transportation to this country, not many could hope to obtain the sanction of the governor for their return.

With very few exceptions, however, the uniform good behaviour of the convicts was still to be noted and commended.

September.] The month of September was ushered in with rain, and storms of wind, thunder, and lightning. At Parramatta and Toongabbe too, as well as at Sydney, much rain fell for several days. On the return of fine weather, it was seen with general satisfaction, that the wheat sown at the latter settlement looked and promised well, and had not suffered from the rain.

Early in the month the criminal court was assembled for the trial of Benjamin Ingram, a man who had served the term for which he was ordered to be transported. He had broken into a house belonging to a female convict, in which he was detected packing up her property for removal. Being found guilty, he received sentence of death; but, on the recommendation of the court, the governor was induced to grant him a pardon, upon condition of his residing for life on Norfolk Island. With this extension of mercy the culprit was not made ac-

quainted

quainted till that moment had arrived which he thought was to separate him from this world for ever. Upon the ladder, and expecting to be turned off, the condition on which his life was spared was communicated to him; and with gratitude both to God and the governor, he received the welcome tidings. He afterwards confessed, that he had for some time past been in the habit of committing burglaries and other depredations; for, having taken himself off the stores to avoid working for the public, he was frequently distressed for food, and was thus compelled to support himself at the expence perhaps of the honest and industrious. He readily found a rascal to receive what property he could procure for sale, and for a long time escaped detection. This depraved man had two brothers in the colony; one who came out with him in the first fleet, and who had been for some time a sober, hard-working, industrious settler, having also served the term of his transportation; the other brother came out in the last year, and bore the character of a well-behaved man. There was also a fourth brother; but he was executed in England. It was said, that these unfortunate men had honest and industrious people for their parents; they could not, however, have paid much attention to the morals of their family; or, out of four, some might surely have laid claim to the character of the parents.

The criminal court was again assembled on the 20th of this month, for the trial of William Godfrey, who was taken up on a suspicion of having seized the opportunity of some festivity on board of the Britannia, then nearly ready for sea, and taken half a barrel of powder out of the gun-room, about nine o'clock at night. Proof however was not brought home to him; although many circumstances induced every one to suppose he was the guilty person.

This month was fixed for beginning the new barracks. For the private soldiers there were to be five buildings, each one hundred feet by twenty-four in front, and connected by a slight brick wall. At each end were to be two apartments for officers, seventy-five feet by eighteen; each apartment containing four rooms for their accommodation, with a passage of sixteen feet. Of these barracks, one at each end was to be constructed at right angles with the front, forming a wing to the centre building. Kitchens were to be built, with other

convenient

convenient offices, in the rear, and garden ground was to be laid out at the back. Their fituation promifed to be healthy, and it was certainly pleafant, being nearly on the fummit of the high ground at the head of the cove, overlooking the town of Sydney, and the fhipping in the cove, and commanding a view down the harbour, as well of the fine piece of water formiug Long Cove, as that branching off to the weftward at the back of the lieutenant governor's farm.

The foundation of one of the buildings defigned for an officer's barrack having been dug, and all the neceffary materials brought together on the fpot, the walls of it were got up, and the whole building roofed and covered in, in eleven days.

Their fituation being directly in the neighbourhood of the ground appropriated to the burial of the dead, it became neceffary to choofe another fpot for the latter purpofe; and the governor, in company with the Rev. Mr. Johnfon, fet apart the ground formerly cultivated by the late Captain Shea of the marines.

Several thefts were committed at Sydney and at Parramatta, from which latter place three male convicts abfconded, taking with them the provifions of their huts, intending, it was fuppofed, to get on board the Britannia. Rewards being offered, fome of them were taken in the woods. It had been found, that the mafters of fhips would give paffages to fuch people as could afford to pay them from ten to twenty pounds for the fame, and the perpetrators of fome of the thefts which were committed appeared to have had that circumftance in view, as one or two huts, whofe proprietors were well known to have amaffed large fums of money for people in their fituations, were broken into; and in one inftance they fucceeded. On the night of the 22d the hut of Mary Burne, widow of a man who had been employed as a game-killer, was robbed of dollars to the amount of eleven pounds; with which the pillagers got off undifcovered.

On the 30th the Britannia left the cove, dropping down below Bradley's Point, preparatory to failing on her intended voyage to Dufky Bay in New Zealand; and while every one was remarking, that the cove (being left without a fhip) again looked folitary and uncomfortable, the fignal was made at the South Head, and at ten o'clock at night the Atlantic anchored in the cove from Norfolk Ifland, where,

we

A Modern View of Sydney Cove.

we had the satisfaction to learn, the large cargo which she had on board was landed in safety, although at one time the ship was in great danger of running ashore at Cascade Bay. We now learned that the expectations which had been formed of the crops at Norfolk Island had been too sanguine; but their salt provisions lasted very well. Governor King, however, wrote that the crops then in the ground promised favourably, although he would not venture to speak decidedly, as they were very much annoyed by the grub. This was an enemy produced by the extreme richness of the soil; and it was remarked, that as the land was opened and cleared, it was found to be exposed to the blighting winds which infest the island.

The great havoc and destruction which the reduced ration had occasioned among the birds frequenting Mount Pitt had so thinned their numbers, that they were no longer to be depended upon as a resource. The convicts, senseless and improvident, not only destroyed the bird, its young, and its egg, but the hole in which it burrowed; a circumstance that ought most cautiously to have been guarded against; as nothing appeared more likely to make them forsake the island.

The stock in the settlement was plentiful, but, from being fed chiefly on sow thistle during the general deficiency of hard food, the animals looked ill, and were as badly tasted. The Pitt, however, took from the island a great quantity of stock; barrow pigs and fowls, pumkins and other vegetables; for which Captain Manning and his officers paid the owners with many articles of comfort to which they had long been strangers.

The convicts in general wore a very unhealthy cadaverous appearance, owing, it was supposed, not only to spare diet, but to the fatigue consequent on their traversing the woods to Mount Pitt, by night, for the purpose of procuring some slender addition to their ration, instead of reposing after the labours of the day. They had committed many depredations on the settlers, and one was shot by a person of that description in the act of robbing his farm.

Governor King, having discovered that the island abounded with that valuable article lime-stone, was building a convenient house for his own residence, and turning his attention to the construction of

permanent

permanent ftorehoufes, barracks for the military, and other neceffary buildings.

The weather had been for fome time paft very bad, much rain having fallen accompanied with ftorms of wind, thunder, and lightning. In fome of thefe ftorms the wreck of his Majefty's ship Sirius went to pieces and difappeared, no part of that unfortunate ship being left together, except what was confined by the iron ballaft in her bottom.

On board of the Atlantic came fixty-two perfons from Norfolk Island, among whom were feveral whofe terms of tranfportation had expired; thirteen offenders; and nine of the marine fettlers, who had given up the hoe and the fpade, returned to this place to embrace once more a life to which they certainly were, from long habit, better adapted than to that of independent fettlers. They gave up their eftates, and came here to enter as foldiers in the New South Wales corps.

Mr. Charles Grimes, the deputy-furveyor, arrived in the Atlantic, being fent by Mr. King to ftate to the governor the fituation of the fettlers late belonging to the Sirius, whofe grounds had, on a careful furvey by Mr. Grimes, been found to interfect each other. They had been originally laid down without the affiftance of proper inftruments, and being fituated on the fide of the Cafcade Stream, which takes feveral windings in its courfe, the different allotments, being clofe together, naturally interfered with each other when they came to be carried back. The fettlers themfelves faw how difadvantageoufly they were fituated, and how utterly impoffible it was for every one to poffefs a diftinct allotment of fixty acres, unlefs they came to fome agreement which had their mutual accommodation in view; but this, with an obftinacy proportioned to their ignorance, they all declined: as their grounds were marked out fo would they keep them, not giving an inch in one place, though certain of poffeffing it with advantage in another. Thefe people proved but indifferent fettlers; failors and foldiers, feldom bred in the habits of induftry, but ill brooked the perfonal labour which they found was required from them day after day, and month after month. Men who from their infancy had been accuftomed to have their daily fubfiftence found them were but ill
calculated

calculated to procure it by the sweat of their brows, and must very unwillingly find that without great bodily exertions they could not provide it at all. A few months experience convinced them of the truth of these observations, and they grew discontented; as a proof of which they wrote a letter to the judge-advocate, to be submitted to the governor, stating, as a subject of complaint among other grievances, that the officers of the settlement bred stock for their own use, and requesting that they might be directed to discontinue that practice, and purchase stock of them.

Very few of the convicts at Norfolk Island whose terms of transportation had expired were found desirous of becoming permanent settlers; the sole object with the major part appearing to be, that of taking ground for the purpose of raising by the sale of the produce a sum sufficient to enable them to pay for their passages to England. The settler to benefit this colony, the *bona fide* settler, who should be a man of some property, must come from England. He is not to be looked for among discharged soldiers, shipwrecked seamen, or quondam convicts.

Governor King finding, after trying every process that came within his knowledge for preparing and dressing the flax-plant, that unless some other means were devised, it never would be brought to the perfection necessary to make the canvas produced from it an object of importance, either as an article of clothing for the convicts or for maritime purposes, proposed to Mr. Ebor Bunker, the master of the William and Ann, who had some thoughts of touching at Dusky-Bay in New Zealand, to procure him two natives of that country, if they could be prevailed on to embark with him, and promised him one hundred pounds if he succeeded, hoping from their perfect knowledge of the flax-plant, and the process necessary to manufacture it into cloth, that he might one day render it a valuable and beneficial article to his colony; but Captain Bunker had never returned.

Norfolk Island had been visited by all the whalers which sailed from this port on that fishery. The Admiral Barrington and Pitt left with Mr. King eleven men and two female convicts, who had secreted themselves at this port on board of those ships.

October.]

October.] The Britannia, which had quitted the cove on the last day of September, preparatory to her departure on a fishing voyage, (a licence for which had been granted by the East-India Company for the space of three years,) returned to the cove on the third of this month for the purpose of fitting for the Cape of Good Hope, the officers of the New South Wales corps having engaged the master to proceed thither and return on their account with a freight of cattle, and such articles as would tend to the comfort of themselves and the soldiers of the corps, and which were not to be found in the public stores. Mr. Raven, the master, let his ship for the sum of 2000 l.; and eleven shares of 200 l. each were subscribed to purchase the stock and other articles. The ship was well calculated for bringing cattle, having a very good between-decks; and artificers from the corps were immediately employed to fit her with stalls proper for the reception and accommodation of cows, horses, &c. A quantity of hay was put on board sufficient to lessen considerably the expence of that article at the Cape; and she was ready for sea by the middle of the month. Previous to her departure, on the 7th, the Royal Admiral East-Indiaman, commanded by Captain Essex Henry Bond, anchored in the cove from England, whence she had sailed on the 30th of May last. Her passage from the Cape of Good Hope was the most rapid that had ever been made, being only five weeks and three days from port to port.

On board of the Royal Admiral came stores and provisions for the colony; one serjeant, one corporal, and nineteen privates, belonging to the New South Wales corps; a person to be employed in the cultivation of the country; another as a master miller; and a third as a master carpenter; together with two hundred and eighty-nine male and forty-seven female convicts. She brought in with her a fever, which had been much abated by the extreme attention paid by Captain Bond and his officers to cleanliness, that great preservative of health on board of ships, and to providing those who were ill with comforts and necessaries beyond what were allowed for their use during the passage. Of three hundred male convicts which she received on board, ten only died, and one made his escape from the hospital at False Bay; in return for whom, however, Captain Bond brought on with him

Thomas

Thomas Watling, a male convict, who found means to get on shore from the Pitt when at that port in December last, and who had been confined by the Dutch at the Cape town from her departure until this opportunity offered of sending him hither.

We had the satisfaction of hearing that the Supply armed tender made good her passage to England in somewhat less than five months, arriving at Plymouth on the 21st of April last. It was, however, matter of much concern to all who were acquainted with him, to learn at the same time, that Captain Hunter, who sailed from this port in March 1791, in the Dutch snow Waaksambeyd, and who had anxiously desired to make a speedy passage, had been thirteen months in that vessel striving to reach England, where he at last let go his anchor a day after the termination of Lieutenant Ball's more successful voyage in the Supply, arriving at Spithead on the evening of the 22d of April last. His Majesty's ship Gorgon had been at the Cape of Good Hope, but had not arrived in England when the Royal Admiral left that country.

We were also informed, that the Kitty transport had sailed with provisions and a few convicts from England some weeks before the Royal Admiral; and Captain Bond left at False Bay an American brig, freighted on speculation with provisions for this colony, and whose master intended putting to sea immediately after him.

The sick, to the number of eighty, were all immediately disembarked from the Indiaman; the remainder of her convicts were sent up to be employed at Parramatta and the adjoining settlement. At these places was to be performed the great labour of clearing and cultivating the country; and thither the governor judged it necessary at once to send such convicts as should arrive in future, without permitting them to disembark at Sydney, which town (from the circumstance of its being the only place where shipping anchored) possessed all the evils and allurements of a sea port of some standing, and from which, if once they got into huts, they would be with difficulty removed when wanted; they pleaded the acquirement of comforts, of which, in fact, it would be painful though absolutely necessary to deprive them. At once to do away therefore the possibility of any attachment to this part of the colony, the governor gave directions for their being immediately

6

sent

sent from the ship to the place of their future residence and employment; and, having no other thoughts, they went with cheerfulness.

There arrived in the Royal Admiral as a superintendant charged with the care of the convicts, Mr. Richard Alley, who formerly belonged to the Lady Juliana transport, in quality of surgeon, in the memorable voyage of that ship to this colony; a voyage that could never be thought on by any inhabitant of it without exciting a most painful sensation. This gentleman went to England in the snow with Captain Hunter, whither the comforts of long voyages seemed to accompany him. Immediately on his arrival there, he was appointed by the commissioners of the navy to come out in the Royal Admiral as surgeon and superintendant of the convicts embarked in that ship, with an allowance of twelve shillings and sixpence *per diem* until his arrival in England, exclusive of his half pay as surgeon of the navy.

It had always been an object of the first consequence, that the people employed about the stores, if not free, should at least have been so situated as to have found it their interest to resist temptation. This had never hitherto been accomplished; capital and other exemplary punishments did not effect it; the stores were constantly robbed, although carefully watched, and as well secured as bolts, locks, and iron fastenings could make them. The governor therefore now adopted a plan which was suggested to him; and, discharging all the convicts employed at the provision-store, replaced them by others, to whom he promised absolute emancipation at the end of a certain number of years, to be computed from the dates of their respective arrivals in this country.

If any thing could produce the integrity so much to be desired, this measure seemed the best calculated for the purpose; an interest was created superior to any reward that could have been held out, a certain salary, an increase of ration, a greater proportion of cloathing, or even emancipation itself, if given at the time. To those who had no other prospect but that of passing their lives in this country, how cheering, how grateful must have been the hope of returning to their families at no very distant period, if not prevented by their own misconduct! There were two in this situation among those placed at the stores, Samuel Burt and William Sutton, both of whom had conducted

ducted themselves with the greatest propriety since their conviction, and who beheld with joy the probability that appeared of their being again considered and ranked in the class of honest men and good members of society; estimations that depended wholly upon themselves.

As a store-keeper was a person on whom much dependence must necessarily be placed, (it being his duty to be constantly present whenever the stores were opened, and with a vigilant eye to observe the conduct of the inferior servants,) at the strong recommendation of the officers under whom he had served, Serjeant Thomas Smyth was discharged from the marine detachment, and placed upon the list of superintendants of convicts as a store-keeper. This appointment gave general satisfaction; and the commissary now felt himself, under all these arrangements, more at ease respecting the safety of the stores and provisions under his charge.

On the night of the 10th a daring burglary was committed. Mr. Raven, the master of the Britannia, occupied a hut on shore, which was broken open and entered about midnight, and from the room in which he was lying asleep, and close to his bedside, his watch and a pair of knee-buckles were stolen; a box was forced open, in which was a valuable time-piece and some money belonging to Mr. Raven, who, fortunately waking in the very moment that the thief was taking it out at the door, prevented his carrying it off. Assistance from the guard came immediately, but too late—the man had got off unseen. In a day or two afterwards, however, Charles Williams, a settler, gave information that a convict named Richard Sutton, the morning after the burglary, had told him that he had stolen and secured the property, which he estimated at sixty pounds, and which he offered to put into his possession for the purpose of sale, first binding him by a horrid ceremony * and oath not to betray him. Williams, on receiving the watch, which proved a metal one, worth only about ten pounds, (and the disproportion of which to the value he had expected, probably had induced him to make the discovery,) immediately caused him to be taken into custody, and delivered the pro-

* They cut each other on the cheek with their knives.

perty

perty to a magistrate, giving at the same time an account how he came
by them. All these circumstances were produced in evidence before a
criminal court; but the prisoner, proving an *alibi* that was satisfactory
to the court, was acquitted. With the evidence that he produced
in his defence it was impossible to convict him; but the court and the
auditors were in their consciences persuaded that the prisoner had committed the burglary and theft, and that he intended to have employed
Williams to dispose of the property; which the latter had undertaken,
and would have performed, had the watch proved to have been a time-
piece which the prisoner imagined he had been lucky enough to secure. Williams, had he been put to prove where he was at the very
time the house was entered, had people ready to depose that he was on
his way by water to his farm near Parramatta. This man had formerly been remarkable for propriety of conduct; but, after he became
a settler, gave himself up to idleness and dissipation, and went away
from the court in which he had been giving his testimony, much de-
graded in the opinion of every man who heard him.

The Britannia sailed on the 24th for the Cape of Good Hope, Mr.
Raven taking with him Governor Philip's dispatches for England, (in
which was contained a specific demand for twelve months provisions
for the colony,) and the wishes as well of those whom he considered
as his employers, as of those who were not, for the safe and speedy
execution of his commission; as his return to the colony would introduce many articles of comfort which were not to be found in the public stores among the articles issued by government.

At Sydney and at Parramatta shops were opened for the sale of the
articles of private trade brought out in the Royal Admiral. A licence
was given for the sale of porter; but, under the cover of this, spirits
found their way among the people, and much intoxication was the
consequence. Several of the settlers, breaking out from the restraint
to which they had been subject, conducted themselves with the greatest
impropriety, beating their wives, destroying their stock, trampling on
and injuring their crops in the ground, and destroying each other's
property. One woman, having claimed the protection of the magistrates, the party complained of, a settler, was bound over to the good
behaviour for two years, himself in twenty pounds, and to find two

sureties

sureties in ten pounds each. Another settler was at the same time set an hour in the stocks for drunkenness. The indulgence which was intended by the governor for their benefit was most shamefully abused; and what he suffered them to purchase with a view to their future comfort, was retailed among themselves at a scandalous profit; several of the settlers houses being at this time literally nothing else but porter-houses, where rioting and drunkenness prevailed as long as the means remained. It was much to be regretted that these people were so blind to their own advantage, most of them sacrificing to the dissipation of the moment what would have afforded them much comfort and convenience, if reserved for refreshment after the fatigue of the day.

The only addition made to the weekly ration in consequence of the arrival of the Royal Admiral was an allowance of six ounces of oil to each person; a large quantity, nine thousand two hundred and seventy-eight gallons, having been put on board that ship and the Kitty transport, to be issued in lieu of butter; as an equivalent for which it certainly would have answered well, had it arrived in the state in which it was reported to have been put on board; but it grew rancid on the passage, and was in general made more use of to burn as a substitute for candles, than for any other purposes to which oil might have been applied.

Toward the latter end of the month, the convicts received a general serving of clothing, and other necessary articles. To each male were issued two frocks made of coarse and unsubstantial osnaburgs, in which there were seldom found more than three weeks wear; two pairs of trowsers made of the same slight materials as the frocks, and open to the same observation as to wear; one pair of yarn stockings; one hat; one pair of shoes; one pound of soap; three needles; a quarter of a pound of thread, and one comb.

The females received each one cloth petticoat; one coarse shift; one pair of shoes; one pair of yarn stockings; one pound of soap; a quarter of a pound of thread; two ounces of pins; six needles; one thimble, and one pair of scissars.

These articles were supplied by commission; and Mr. Davison, the person employed by government, was limited in the price of each article, which was fixed too low to admit of his furnishing them of the

quality

quality abfolutely neceffary for people who were to labour in this country. The ofnaburgs in particular had always been complained of; for it was a fact, that the frocks and trowfers made of them were oftener known to have been worn out within a fortnight, than to have lafted three weeks.

The month clofed with a circumftance that excited no fmall degree of concern in the fettlement: Governor Philip fignified a determination of quitting his government, and returning to England in the Atlantic. To this he was induced by perceiving that his health hourly grew worfe, and hoping that a change of air might contribute to his recovery. His Excellency had the fatisfaction, at the moment that he came to this refolution, of feeing the public grounds wear every appearance of a productive harveft. At Toongabbe, forty-two acres of wheat, fown about the middle of laft March, looked as promifing as could be wifhed; the remainder of the wheat, from being fown fix weeks later; did not look fo fine and abundant, but ftill held out hopes of an ample return. The Indian corn was all got into the ground, and fuch of it as was up looked remarkably well.

CHAP. XIX.

A VESSEL FROM AMERICA ARRIVES.—PART OF HER CARGO PURCHASED.—GEORGE BARRINGTON AND OTHERS EMANCIPATED CONDITIONALLY.—THE ROYAL ADMIRAL SAILS.—ARRIVAL OF THE KITTY TRANSPORT.—1001 L RECEIVED BY HER.—HOSPITAL BUILT AT PARRAMATTA.—HARVEST BEGUN AT TOONGABBE.—RATION INCREASED.—THE PHILADELPHIA SAILS FOR NORFOLK ISLAND.—STATE OF THE CULTIVATION PREVIOUS TO THE GOVERNOR'S DEPARTURE.—SETTLERS.—GOVERNOR PHILIP SAILS FOR ENGLAND.—REGULATIONS MADE BY THE LIEUTENANT-GOVERNOR.—THE HOPE, AN AMERICAN SHIP, ARRIVES.—HER CARGO PURCHASED FOR THE COLONY.—THE CHESTERFIELD WHALER ARRIVES.—GRANT OF LAND TO AN OFFICER.—EXTREME HEAT AND CONFLAGRATION.—DEATHS IN 1792.—PRICES OF STOCK, &c.

November.] ON the 1ft of November, about eleven o'clock at night, the Philadelphia brigantine, Mr. Thomas Patrickfon mafter, anchored in

in the cove from Philadelphia. Lieutenant-governor King, on his
paſſage to this country in the Gorgon in the month of July 1791, had
ſeen Mr. Patrickſon at the Cape of Good Hope, and learning at that
time from the Lady Juliana and Neptune tranſports, which had juſt
arrived there from China, that the colony was in great diſtreſs for
proviſions, ſuggeſted to him the advantage that might attend his
bringing a cargo to this country on ſpeculation. On this hint Captain Patrickſon went to England, and thence to Philadelphia, from
which place he ſailed the beginning of laſt April with a cargo conſiſting chiefly of American beef, wine, rum, gin, ſome tobacco, pitch,
and tar. He ſailed from Philadelphia with thirteen hands; but, in
ſome very bad weather which he met with after leaving the African
ſhore, his ſecond mate was waſhed overboard and loſt, it blowing too
hard to attempt ſaving him.

The governor directed the commiſſary to purchaſe ſuch part of the
Philadelphia's cargo as he thought was immediately wanting in the colony; and five hundred and ſixty-nine barrels of American cured beef,
each barrel containing one hundred and ninety-three pounds, and
twenty-ſeven barrels of pitch and tar, were taken into ſtore; the expence of which amounted to 2829 l. 11 s.

, Notwithſtanding the great length of time Captain Patrickſon had been
on his voyage, (from the beginning of April to November,) his ſpeculation did not prove very diſadvantageous to him. A great part of his
cargo, that was not taken by government, was diſpoſed of among the
officers and others of the ſettlement; and the governor hired his veſſel
to take proviſions to Norfolk Iſland, giving him 150 l. for the run.
Captain Patrickſon had formed ſome expectation of diſpoſing of his
veſſel in this country; but the governor, having received intimation
that the Kitty might be detained in the ſervice as long as he found it
neceſſary after her arrival, did not judge it expedient to purchaſe the
veſſel.

On the 3d of the month three warrants of emancipation paſſed the
ſeal of the territory: one to John Trace, a convict who came out in the
firſt fleet; having but three months of his term of tranſportation remaining, that portion of it was given up to him, that he might become
a ſettler. The ſecond was granted to Thomas Reſtil, (alias Crowder,)

on the recommendation of the lieutenant-governor of Norfolk Island, on condition that he should not return to England during the term of his natural life, his sentence of transportation being *durante vitæ*. The third warrant was made out in favour of one who, whatever might have been his conduct when at large in society, had here not only demeaned himself with the strictest propriety, but had rendered essential services to the colony—George Barrington. He came out in the Active; on his arrival the governor employed him at Toongabbe, and in a situation which was likely to attract the envy and hatred of the convicts, in proportion as he might be vigilant and inflexible. He was first placed as a subordinate, and shortly after as a principal watchman; in which situation he was diligent, sober, and impartial; and had rendered himself so eminently serviceable, that the governor resolved to draw him from the line of convicts; and, with the instrument of his emancipation, he received a grant of thirty acres of land in an eligible situation near Parramatta *. Here was not only a reward for past good conduct, but an incitement to a continuance of it; and Barrington found himself, through the governor's liberality, though not so absolutely free as to return to England at his own pleasure, yet enjoying the immunities of a free man, a settler, and a civil officer, in whose integrity much confidence was placed.

On the 13th the Royal Admiral sailed for Canton. Of the private speculation brought out in this ship, they sold at this place and at Parramatta to the amount of 3600l. and left articles to be sold on commission to the amount of 750l. more.

Captain Bond was obliged to leave behind him one of his quartermasters and six sailors, who ran away from the ship. The quartermaster had served in the same capacity on board of the Sirius, and immediately after his arrival in England (in the snow) engaged himself with Captain Bond for the whole of the voyage; but a few days before the departure of the ship from this port, he found means to leave her, and, assisted by some of the settlers, concealed himself in the woods until concealment was no longer necessary. On giving himself up, he entered on board the Atlantic; but on his declaring that he did not

* He was afterwards sworn in as a peace officer.

intend

intend returning to England, the governor ordered him into confinement. The sailors were put into one of the longboats, to be employed between this place and Parramatta, until they could be put on board a ship that might convey them hence.

It was never desirable that seamen should receive encouragement to run from their ships; they became public nuisances here; the masters of such ships would find themselves obliged to procure convicts at any rate to supply their places; indeed, so many might be shipped or secreted on board, as might render the safety of the vessel very precarious; and as the governor determined to represent the conduct of any master who carried away convicts without his approbation, so he resolved never to deprive them of their seamen. Under this idea, a hut, in which a seaman from the Royal Admiral was found concealed, was pulled down, and two convicts who had been secreted on board that ship were sent up to Toongabbe, as a punishment, as well as to be out of the way of another attempt.

On the 18th the Kitty transport anchored in the cove from England, after a circuitous passage of thirty-three weeks, round by the Rio de Janeiro and the Cape of Good Hope. She twice sailed from England. On her first departure, which was in March last, she had on board thirty female and ten male convicts; but being obliged to put back to Spithead, to stop a leak which she sprung in her raft port, eight of her ten male convicts found means to make their escape. This was an unfortunate accident; for they had been particularly selected as men who might be useful in the colony. Of the two who did remain, the one was a brick-maker and the other a joiner.

When her cargo was landing, it was found to have suffered considerably by the bad weather she had experienced; the flour in particular, an article which could at no time bear any diminution in this country, was much damaged. The convicts had for a long time been nearly as much distressed for utensils to dress their provisions, as they had been for provisions; and we had now the mortification to find, that of the small supply of iron pots which had been put on board, a great part were either broken or cracked, having been literally stowed among the provision casks in the hold.

7   There

There arrived in this ship two chests, containing three thousand eight hundred and seventy ounces of silver, in dollars, amounting to 1001 L. This remittance was sent out for the purpose of paying such sums as were due to the different artificers who had been employed in this country. It was also applied to the payment of the wages due to the superintendants, who had experienced much inconvenience from not receiving their salaries here; and indeed the want of public money had been very much felt by every one in the colony. When the marines, who became settlers before and at the relief of the detachment, were discharged for that purpose, they would have suffered great difficulties from the want of public money to pay what was due to them, had not the commissary taken their respective powers of attorney, and given them notes on himself, payable either in cash, or in articles which might be the means of rendering them comfortable, and of which he had procured a large supply from Calcutta. These notes passed through various hands in traffic among the people of the description they were intended to serve, and became a species of currency which was found very convenient to them.

The female convicts who arrived in the Kitty, twenty-seven in number, were immediately sent up to Parramatta.

Government had put on board the Kitty a naval agent, Lieutenant Daniel Woodriff, for the purpose of seeing that no unnecessary delays were made in the voyage, and that the convicts on board were not oppressed by the master or his people. This officer, on his arrival, stated to the governor his opinion that the master had not made the best of his way, and that he had remained longer in the port of Rio de Janeiro than there could possibly be occasion for. He likewise stated several disagreements which had occurred between him and the master, and in which the latter seemed to think very lightly of the authority of a naval agent on board his ship. There was also on board this ship, on the part of the crown, a medical gentleman who was appointed for the express purpose of attending to such convicts as might be ill during the voyage; so extremely solicitous were the members of Administration to guard against the evils which had befallen the convicts in former passages to this country.

A4

At Parramatta a brick hospital, confisting of two wards, was finished this month; and the sick were immediately removed into it. The spot chosen for this building was at some distance from the principal street of the town, and convenient to the water; and, to prevent any improper communication with the other convicts, a space was to be inclosed and paled in round the hospital, in which the sick would have every neceffary benefit from air and exercise.

At the other settlement they had begun to reap the wheat which was sown in April last; and for want of a granary at that place it was put into stacks. From not being immediately thrashed out, there was no knowing with certainty what the produce of it was; but it had every appearance of turning out well. The ear was long and full, and the straw remarkably good.

December.] On the 3d of this month, the governor, as one of his last acts in the settlement, ordered one pound of flour to be added to the weekly ration, which, by means of this addition, stood on his departure at

> 3 pounds of flour;
> 5 pounds of rice;
> 4 pounds of pork, or 7 pounds of beef;
> 3 pounds of dholl; and
> 6 ounces of oil.

On the 7th the Philadelphia failed for Norfolk Island, having on board for that settlement Mr. Grimes, the deputy surveyor; Mr. Jamieson, who was to superintend the convicts employed there in cultivation; Mr. Peat, the master-carpenter (there being a person* in that situation here of much ability); a convict who came out in the Royal Admiral, to be employed as a master-taylor; two convicts sawyers, and one convict carpenter, the same who came out with his family in the Kitty; together with some provisions and stores. His excellency had always attended to this little colony with a parental care; often declaring, that from the peculiarity of its situation he would rather that want should be felt in his own government than in

---

* Mr. Thomas Livingstone, at a salary of 50 l. per annum.

that

that dependency; and as they would be generally eight or ten weeks later than this colony in receiving their supplies, by reason of the time which the ships necessarily required to refit after coming in from sea, he purposed furnishing them with a proportion of provisions for three months longer than the provisions in store at this place would last: and his excellency took leave of that settlement, by completing, as fully as he was able, this design.

He was now about taking leave of his own government. The accommodations for his excellency and the officers who were going home in the Atlantic being completed, the detachment of marines under the command of Lieutenant Poulden embarked on the 5th, and at six o'clock in the evening of Monday the 10th Governor Phillip quitted the charge with which he had been entrusted by his Sovereign, and in the execution of which he had manifested a zeal and perseverance that alone could have enabled him to surmount the natural and artificial obstacles which the country and its inhabitants had thrown in his way.

The colony had now been established within a few weeks of five years; and a review of what had been done in cultivation under his excellency's direction in that time cannot more properly be introduced than at the close of his government. .

Previous to the sailing of the Britannia on the 24th of last October, an accurate survey of the whole ground in cultivation, both on account of the crown, and in the possession of individuals, was taken by the surveyor-general, and transmitted to England by that ship; and from the return which he then made, the following particulars were extracted:

Ground

Ground in cultivation, the 16th October 1792.

	Acres in wheat.	Acres in barley.	Acres in maize.	Garden ground.	Ground clear'd of timber.	Total number of acres.
At Parramatta, - - -	1	7½	308	—	—	316½
At and leading to Toongabbe -	171½	14	511	—	—	696½
Total public ground,	172½	21½	819	—	—	1012½
Belonging to Settlers and others.						
At Parramatta, - - -				{ 1		
The governor's garden, - -	—	½	2	{ 3 vines.	—	6½
Garden ground belonging to different people, including convicts' gardens,	—	—	—	104	—	104
At Parramatta, 1 settler, - -	3	—	18	1	7	29
At Prospect Hill, four miles to the westward of Parramatta, 18 settlers,	11¼	—	84	—	—	95¼
At the Ponds, two miles to the north-east of Parramatta, 16 settlers,	10¼	2½	63	3½	16½	95¾
At the Northern boundary farms, two miles from Parramatta, 5 settlers,	3	—	35	2¾	11	51¾
At the Field of Mars, on the north shore, near the entrance of the creek leading to Parramatta, 8 settlers, (marines,) - - - -	4	—	44½	2	31	81½
At the Eastern farms, 12 settlers,	—	—	40½	—	12½	53
On the creek leading to Parramatta, 7 settlers, - - - -	4½	—	80½	4	22	111½
In cultivation by the civil and military at Sydney, - - - -	—	—	—	—	62½	62½
Total,	208½	24½	1186½	121½	162½	1703

Of the sixty-seven settlers above enumerated, one, James Ruse, who had a grant of thirty acres at Parramatta, went upon his farm the latter end of November 1789; but none of the others began to cultivate ground upon their own accounts earlier than the middle of July 1791; but many of them at a much later date. The eight marine settlers at the Field of Mars took possession of their allotments at the beginning of February 1792. The conditions held out to settlers were, to be victualled and clothed from the public store for eighteen months from the term of their becoming settlers; to be furnished with tools and implements of husbandry; grain to sow their grounds, and such

 stock

flock as could be spared from the public. They were likewise to have
assigned them the services of such a number of convicts as the governor
should think proper, on their making it appear that they could employ,
feed, and clothe them. Every man had a hut erected on his farm at
the public expence. At the time of the governor's departure, many of
them, by their own industry, and the assistance he had afforded them,
were enabled to have one or two convicts off the store, and employed
by them at their farms; and such as were not married were allowed
a convict hutkeeper. In general they were not idle, and the major
part were comfortably situated.

At this time the quantity of land which had passed to settlers * in
this territory under the seal of the colony amounted to three thousand
four hundred and seventy acres; of which quantity four hundred and
seventeen acres and a half were in cultivation, and the timber cleared
from one hundred more, ready for sowing; which, compared with
the total of the *public ground* in cultivation, (one thousand and twelve
acres and three quarters,) will be found to be by eleven acres more
than equal to one half of it. A striking proof of what some settlers
had themselves declared, on its being hinted to them that they had not
always been so diligent when labouring for the whole—" We are now
" working for ourselves." One material good was, however, to be
expected from a tract of land of that extent being cultivated by individuals, if at any time an accident should happen to the crop on the
public ground, they might be a resource, though an inconsiderable
one. Fortunately, no misfortune of that nature had ever fallen upon
the colony; but it had been, at the beginning of this month, very
near experiencing a calamity that would have blasted all the prospects
of the next season, and in one moment have rendered ineffectual the
labour of many hands and of many months. Two days after the
wheat had been reaped, and got off the ground at Toongabbe, the
whole of the stubble was burnt. The day on which this happened
had been unusually hot, and the country was every where on fire.
Had it befallen us while the wheat was upon the ground, nothing
could have saved the whole from being destroyed. From this circum-

* Some few had been added since the surveyor's return of the 16th October.

stance,

ftance, however, one good refulted; precautions againft a fimilar accident were immediately taken, by clearing the timber for a certain
diftance round the cultivated land.

The flock belonging to the public was kept at Parramatta. It
confifted of three bulls *, two bull calves, fifteen cows, three calves,
five ftallions, fix mares, one hundred and five fheep, and forty-three
hogs.

Of the fheep, the governor gave to each of the married fettlers from
the convicts, and to each fettler from the marines, and from the Sirius,
one ewe for the purpofe of breeding; and to others he gave fuch
female goats as could be fpared. This flock had been procured at much
expence; and his excellency hoped that the people among whom he
left it would fee the advantage it might prove to them, and cherifh it
accordingly.

His excellency, at embarking on board the Atlantic, was received
near the wharf on the eaft-fide, (where his boat was lying,) by Major
Grofe, at the head of the New South Wales corps, who paid him, as
he paffed, the honors due to his rank and fituation in the colony. He
was attended by the officers of the civil department, and the three
marine officers who were to accompany him to England.

At daylight on the morning of the 11th, the Atlantic was got under
way, and by eight o'clock was clear of the Heads, ftanding to the
E. S. E. with a frefh breeze at fouth. By twelve o'clock fhe had
gained a confiderable offing.

With the governor there embarked, voluntarily and cheerfully, two
natives of this country, Bennillong and Yem-mer-ra-wan-nie, two men
who were much attached to his perfon; and who withftood at the
moment of their departure the united diftrefs of their wives, and the
difmal lamentations of their friends, to accompany him to England, a
place that they well knew was at a great diftance from them.

One or two convicts alfo who had conducted themfelves to his fatisfaction, and whofe periods of tranfportation were expired, were permitted by the governor to return to England in the fame fhip with
himfelf.

* Two from Calcutta, and one which was calved on board the Gorgon.

K K 2   The

The Atlantic had likewise on board various specimens of the natural productions of the country, timber, plants, animals, and birds. Among the animals were four fine kangooroos, and several native dogs.

The Atlantic had been put into excellent condition for the voyage which she had to perform; she was well found and well manned, and there appeared no reason to doubt her reaching England in six months from her departure. A safe and speedy passage to her was the general wish, not only on account of the governor, whose health and constitution (already much impaired) might suffer greatly by the fatigues of a protracted voyage; but that the information of which his excellency was in possession respecting these settlements, from their establishments to the moment of his quitting them, might as quickly as possible be laid before administration.

The government of the colony now devolved, by his Majesty's letters patent under the great seal of Great Britain, upon the lieutenant-governor. This office was filled by the major-commandant of the New South Wales corps, Francis Grose, Esq. who arrived in February last in the Pitt transport. At his taking upon himself the government, on which occasion the usual oaths were administered by the judge-advocate, he gave out the following order, regulating the mode of carrying on the duty at Parramatta:

" All orders given by the captain who commands at Parramatta,
" respecting the convicts stationed there, are to be obeyed; and all
" complaints or reports that would be made to the lieutenant-governor
" when present, are in his absence to be communicated to captain Fo-
" veaux, or such other captain as may be doing duty with the detach-
" ment."

The alteration which this order produced, consisted in substituting the military for the civil officer. Before this period, all complaints had been inquired into by the civil magistrate, who, in the governor's absence from Parramatta, punished such slight offences as required immediate cognizance, reporting to the governor from time to time whatever he did; and all orders and directions which regarded the convicts, and all reports which were made respecting them, went through him.

The military power had hitherto been considered as requisite only for the protection of the stores, and the discharge of such duties as
belonged

belonged to their profeffion, without having any fhare in the civil direction of the colony * ; but as it was provided by his Majefty's commiffion already fpoken of, that, in cafe of the death or abfence both of
the governor and lieutenant-governor of the territory, the officer next
in rank on fervice in the colony fhould take upon himfelf and exercife the functions of the governor, until fuch time as inftructions
fhould be received from England ; under this idea, the lieutenant-
governor iffued the above order, placing the captain commanding the
detachment of the New South Wales corps at Parramatta, in the
direction of the civil duties of that fettlement.

Similar regulations took place at Sydney, where " the captain of
" the day was directed to report to the commanding officer all con-
" vict prifoners, ftating by whom and on what account they might be
" confined ;" and this order was in a few days after enforced by
another, which directed " that all inquiries by the civil magiftrate
" were in future to be difpenfed with, until the lieutenant-governor
" had given directions on the fubject ; and the convicts were not on
" any account to be puuifhed but by his particular order."

At Sydney, it had been ufual for the magiftrates to take examinations, and make enquiry into offences, either weekly, or as occafion
required, and to order fuch punifhment as they thought necellary,
always reporting their proceedings to the chief authority.

It muft be noticed, that at this time the civil magiftrates in the
colony confifted of the lieutenant-governor and the judge-advocate,
who were juftices of the peace by virtue of their refpective commiffions ; the Rev. Mr. Johnfon ; Auguftus Alt and Richard Atkins †, Efquires, who had been fworn in as magiftrates by authority
of the governor.

As no inconvenience had ever been experienced in the mode which
was practifed of conducting the bufinefs of the fettlement, the neceffity or caufe of thefe alterations was not directly obvious, and could
not be accounted for from any other motive than that preference which

* The commanding officer of the corps or regiment ferving in the territory excepted,
who held likewife the *civil* appointment of lieutenant-governor.

† This gentleman had been appointed regiftrar of the court of vice-admiralty by Governor Phillip.

a military

a military man might be supposed to give to carrying on the service by means of his own officers, rather than by any other.

On Saturday the 15th the convicts received their provisions according to the ration that was issued before the governor's departure; but on the Monday following, the usual day of serving provisions to the civil and military, a distinction was made, for the first time, in the ration they received; the commissary being directed to issue to the officers of the civil and military departments, the soldiers, superintendants, watchmen, overseers, and settlers from the marines, six pounds of flour, and but two pounds of rice per man, per week, instead of three pounds of flour, and five pounds of rice, which was the allowance of the convicts. This distinction was intended to be discontinued whenever the full ration could be served.

The stock which had been distributed among the married settlers and others by Governor Phillip for the purpose of breeding from, (as has been already observed,) appeared to have been thrown away upon them when viewed as a breeding stock for settlers. No sooner had the Atlantic sailed, than the major part of them were offered for sale; and there was little doubt, (many of their owners making no scruple to publish their intentions,) that had they not been bought by the officers, in a very few weeks many of them would have been destroyed. By this conduct, as far as their individual benefit was concerned, they had put it out of their own power to reap any advantage from the governor's bounty to them; but the stock by this means was saved, and had fallen into hands that certainly would not wantonly destroy it. There were a few among the settlers who exchanged their sheep for goats, deeming them a more profitable stock; but, in general, spirits were the price required by the more ignorant and imprudent part of them; and several of their farms, which had been, and ought to have always been, the peaceful retreats of industry, were for a time the seats of inebriety and consequent disorder.

About this time there anchored in the cove an American ship, the Hope, commanded by a Mr. Benjamin Page, from Rhode Island, with a small cargo of provisions and spirits for sale. The cause of his putting into this harbour, the master declared, was for the purpose of procuring wood and water, of which he stated his ship to be much in

want;

want; thus making the sale of his cargo appear to be but a secondary object with him.

As the colony had not yet seen the day when it could have independently said, " We are not in want of provisions; procure your " wood and your water, and go your way," the lieutenant-governor directed the commissary to purchase such part of his cargo as the colony stood in need of; and two hundred barrels of American cured beef, at four pounds per barrel; eighty barrels of pork, at four pounds ten shillings per barrel; forty-four barrels of flour, at two pounds per barrel; and seven thousand five hundred and ninety-seven gallons of (new American) spirits at four shillings and sixpence per gallon, were purchased; amounting in all to the sum of 2957l. 6s. 6d.

This ship had touched at the Falkland Islands for the purpose of collecting skins from the different vessels employed in the seal trade from the United States of America, with which she was to proceed to the China market. From the Cape of Good Hope her passage had been performed in two months and one day. The master said, he found the prevailing winds were from the N. W. and described the. weather as the most boisterous he had ever known for such a length of time. By one sea, his caboose was washed over the side, and one of his people going with it was drowned. He observed, when about the South-cape of this country, that the weather was clear; but after passing the latitude of the Maria Islands, he found it close, hazy, and heated, and had every appearance of thick smoke. About that time we had the same sort of weather here; and the excessive heats which at other times have been experienced in the settlements have been also noticed at sea when at some distance from the land.

By this ship we were not fortunate enough to receive any European news. The master saw only one English ship at the Cape, the Chesterfield whaler, commanded by a Mr. Alt, who had formerly been a midshipman in his Majesty's ship Sirius, and who went home on board of the Neptune transport.

In a few days after the arrival of the Hope, the signal was again made at the South-head, and in a few hours the Chesterfield, the ship just mentioned to us by the American, anchored in the cove. She sailed from the Cape of Good Hope shortly after Mr. Page; and the

                                                                    master

master said he touched at Kerguelan's Land, where, some other ship having very recently preceded him, (which he judged from finding several sea elephants dead on the beach, and a club which is used in killing them,) he remained but a short time, having very bad weather. He supposed the ship which preceded him to have been the first which had visited those desolate islands since Captain Cook had been there, as he found the fragments of the bottle in which that officer had deposited a memorial of his having examined them. This was conjecture and might be erroneous, as the mere pieces of the bottle afforded no proof that it had been recently broken.

Mr. Alt spoke of meeting with very bad weather, and of his ship having thereby suffered such injury, that he was compelled on the representation of his people to put in here for the purpose of getting repairs. Indeed her appearance very amply justified their representations; and it was a wonder how she had swam so far, for her complaints must have been of very long standing.

To expedite the building of the new barracks, which formed the most material labour at Sydney, two overseers and forty men were sent down from Parramatta. One barrack being now completed, towards the latter end of the month it was occupied by Captain George Johnston, a party-wall having been thrown down adapting the building to the accommodation of one instead of two officers.

On the last day of the month, two warrants of emancipation passed the seal of the territory, together with a grant of twenty-five acres of land to Ensign Cummings of the New South Wales corps. In the instructions for granting lands in this country, no mention of officers had yet been made; it was however fairly presumed that the officers could not be intended to be precluded from the participation of any advantages which the crown might have to bestow in the settlements; particularly as the greatest in its gift, the free possession of land, was held out to people who had forfeited their lives before they came into the country.

Among the regulations which took place at Sydney, must be noticed the dispensing with the officer's guard which had always mounted there; and the changing the hours of labour. The convicts now had more time given to them, for the purpose not only of avoiding the heat

of

of the day, but of making themselves comfortable at home. They were directed to work from five in the morning until nine; rest until four in the afternoon, and then labour until sun-set.

The Kitty, having delivered her cargo, began to prepare for taking some stores and provisions and a detachment of the New South Wales corps to Norfolk Island.

The weather during this month was very hot. The 5th was a day most excessively sultry. The wind blew strong from the northward of west; the country, to add to the intense heat of the atmosphere, was every where on fire. At Sydney, the grass at the back of the hill on the west side of the cove, having either caught or been set on fire by the natives, the flames, aided by the wind which at that time blew violently, spread and raged with incredible fury. One house was burnt down, several gardens with their fences were destroyed; and the whole face of the hill was on fire, threatening every thatched hut with destruction. The conflagration was with much difficulty (notwithstanding the exertions of the military) got under, after some time, and prevented from doing any further mischief. At different times during this uncomfortable day distant thunder was heard, the air darkened, and some few large drops of rain fell. The apparent danger from the fires drew all persons out of their houses; and on going into the parching air, it was scarcely possible to breathe; the heat was insupportable; vegetation seemed to suffer much, the leaves of many culinary plants being reduced to a powder. The thermometer in the shade rose above one hundred degrees. Some rain falling toward evening, the excessive heat abated.

At Parramatta and Toongabbe also the heat was extreme; the country there too was every where in flames. Mr. Arndell was a great sufferer by it. The fire had spread to his farm; but by the efforts of his own people and the neighbouring settlers it was got under, and its progress supposed to be effectually checked, when an unlucky spark from a tree, which had been on fire to the topmost branch, flying upon the thatch of the hut where his people lived, it blazed out; the hut with all the out-buildings, and thirty bushels of wheat just got into a stack, were in a few minutes destroyed. The erecting of the hut and out-houses had cost 15l. a short time before.

The

The day preceding that of the excessive heat, James Castles, an industrious and thriving settler at Prospect Hill, had his hut accidentally burnt down, with all his comforts, and three bushels of wheat which he had just reaped. The governor ordered his hut to be rebuilt, and every assistance given which the stores afforded to repair his loss.

There died between the 1st of January and 31st of December 1792, two of the civil department, six soldiers, four hundred and eighteen male convicts, eighteen female convicts, and twenty-nine children ; one male convict was executed ; and three male convicts were lost in the woods ; making a decrease by death of four hundred and eighty-two persons.

The following were the prices of stock, grain, and other articles, as they were sold at Sydney, and at Parramatta, at the close of the year :

At Sydney.	At Parramatta.
Maize per lb. 3d.	Maize per lb. 3d.
Rice per lb. 3d.	Rice per lb. 3d.
Pease or dholl from 1½d. to 2d. per lb.	Pease or dholl 2d. per lb.
Flour 9d. per lb.	Flour, 6d. per lb.
Potatoes 3d. per lb.	Potatoes 2d. per lb.
Sheep 10l. 10s. each.	Sheep 10l. 10s. each.
Milch goats from 8l. 8s. to 10l. 10s.	Milch goats from 5l. 5s. to 10l.
Kids from 2l. 10s. to 4l.	
Breeding sows from 6l. 6s. to 7l. 7s. and 10l. 10s.	Breeding sows from 6l. 6s. to 10l. 10s.
Young ditto from 3l. to 4l.	Pigs of a month old 12s.
Laying hens 10s.	Laying hens from 7s. to 10s.
Full grown fowls from 5s. to 7s. 6d.	Full grown fowls from 7s. to 10s.
Chickens 1s. 6d.	Chickens 1s. 6d.
Fresh pork per lb. 1s.	Fresh pork per lb. 1s.
Prime salt pork from 6d. to 8d.	Prime salt pork 6d.
Salt beef 4d.	Salt beef 4d.
Eggs per dozen from 2s. to 3s.	Eggs per dozen 2s.
Moist sugar per lb. 1s. 6d.	Moist sugar per lb. 1s. 6d.
Tea from 8s. to 16s.	Tea from 6s. to 16s.
Soap 1s.	Soap 1s.
Butter from 1s. 6d. to 2s.	Coffee 2s.
Cheese from 1s. 6d. to 2s.	Tobacco, American Brazil, 4s.
Hams from 1s. 6d. to 2s.	Tobacco of the colony 2s.
Bacon from 1s. 6d. to 2s.	

The

The price of fish and vegetables varied from day to day; spirits in exchange were estimated at from twelve to twenty shillings per gallon; porter was sold from nine to ten pounds per hogshead, or from one shilling to one shilling and three pence per quart.

It did not appear that the settlers had brought any new wheat or other grain to market.

CHAP. XX.

ORDER RESPECTING SPIRITS.—SEAMEN PUNISHED.—CONVICTS ENLISTED IN-TO THE NEW CORPS.—REGULATIONS RESPECTING DIVINE SERVICE.—THE HOPE SAILS.—THE BELLONA ARRIVES.—CARGO DAMAGED.—INFORMA-TION.—TWO WOMEN AND A CHILD DROWNED.—THE KITTY SAILS FOR NORFOLK ISLAND.—RATION.—AN OFFICER SENT UP TO INSPECT THE CULTIVATION AT PARRAMATTA.—A THEFT COMMITTED.—WORKS.—KANGOOROO GROUND OPENED.—SETTLERS.—LIBERTY PLAINS.—CONDI-TIONS.—BELLONA SAILS.—TRANSACTIONS.—THE SHAH HORMUZEAR FROM CALCUTTA ARRIVES.—INFORMATION RECEIVED BY HER.—THE DHOLL EXPENDED.—SICKNESS AND DEATH OCCASIONED BY THE AMERICAN SPIRITS.—THE CHESTERFIELD SENT TO NORFOLK ISLAND.—CONVICTS SELL THEIR CLOTHING.—TWO SPANISH SHIPS ARRIVE.—INFORMATION.—EPITAPH.—A CRIMINAL COURT.—THE KITTY RETURNS FROM NORFOLK ISLAND.—FRAUD AT THE STORE AT PARRAMATTA.

January 1793.] THE lieutenant governor having directed the commissary to dispose of the spirits purchased from the American to the military and civil officers of the colony, in which were included the superintendants, and some others in that line, it was found that it had been purchased by many individuals of the latter description with the particular view of retailing it among the convicts. He therefore found it necessary to declare in public orders, "That it was his intention to make " frequent inquiries on the subject; and it might be relied upon, that if " it ever appeared that a convict was possessed of any of the liquor so " supplied by the commissary, the conduct of those who had thought

L L 2   " proper

" proper to abuse what was designed as an accommodation to the offi-
" cers of the garrison, would not be passed over unnoticed."

Some such order had indeed become very necessary; for the American spirit had by some means or other found its way among the
convicts; and, a discreet use of it being wholly out of the question with
those people, intoxication was become common among them. The
free use of spirits had been hitherto most rigidly prohibited in the colony; that is to say, it was absolutely forbidden to the convicts. It
might therefore have been expected, that when that restraint was in
ever so small a degree removed, they would break out into acts of disorder and contempt of former prohibitions. It was therefore indispensable to the preservation of peace and good order in the settlement, to
prevent, if possible, the existence of so great an evil as drunkenness;
which, if suffered, would have been the parent of every irregularity.
The fondness expressed by these people for even this pernicious American spirit was incredible; they hesitated not to go any lengths to procure it, and preferred receiving liquor for labour, to every other article
of provisions or clothing that could be offered them.

The master of the Kitty having represented to the lieutenant governor that the conduct of his ship's company was at times so irregular
and mutinous (some of them refusing to do their duty, going on shore
and taking boats from the ship without permission) that he found it
impossible to carry on the business of the ship, unless he could receive
some assistance from the civil authority, the lieutenant-governor directed
one, of whom the master particularly complained, Benjamin Williams,
to receive one hundred lashes, and another, —— Adams, to receive
twenty-five lashes. This in some measure checked the spirit of disobedience in the ship, and the duty was carried on better than before.
Her preparations for Norfolk Island however went on but slowly, four
or five of her hands having left her. These, together with some other
seamen who had been left behind from the Royal Admiral, were either
employed in the public boats belonging to the colony, or had entered
into the New South Wales corps; into which corps also several convicts of good character had been lately received, to complete the company that had been formed from the marines under the command of

Captain

Captain Johnflon. This company was a valuable addition, being compofed of many excellent foldiers from the marines; who entered into it voluntarily, and whofe conduct had met the entire approbation of their officers.

On the departure of the governor, the houfe that he had lived in was taken poffeffion of by the oldeft captain of the corps, his apartments in the officers quarters being confined, and tumbling to pieces.

Divine fervice was now performed at fix o'clock in the morning. For want of a building dedicated to that purpofe, many inconveniences were fuffered, as well by the clergyman as by thofe who attended him. The lieutenant-governor therefore did not require the ceremony to be performed more than once a day; and that the health of the convicts might not be injured from the heat of the fun, which at this feafon of the year was exceffive, he directed the church call to be beat at a quarter before fix in the morning. The overfeers were enjoined to be particularly careful to collect as many of their gangs to attend Mr. Johnfon as could conveniently be brought together; for, although it was not wifhed that the huts fhould be left without proper perfons to look after them, it was neverthelefs expected, that no idle excufes fhould keep the convicts from attending divine fervice.

On the 10th the Hope failed for Canton, the mafter having been allowed to fhip three convicts, whofe fentences of tranfportation had expired; viz. Murphy, a fail-maker; Sheppard, a joiner; and Bateman, a lad who had been employed as an attendant on an officer.

At fix o'clock in the evening of Tuefday the 15th, the fignal which always gave fatisfaction in the colony was made at the South head; feveral boats went down, but when night clofed it was only known that a fhip was off. A large fire for the information of the ftranger was made at the South head; and at about ten o'clock the following morning, the Bellona tranfport, Mr. Mathew Boyd commander, anchored in the cove from England; from which place fhe failed on the 8th day of Auguft laft, having on board a cargo of ftores and provifions for the colony; feventeen female convicts; five fettlers, and their families; —— Thorpe, a perfon engaged as a mafter mill-wright at a falary of 100l. per annum; and Walter Broady, who returned to New South Wales to be employed in his former capacity of mafter blackfmith.

blackfmith. The quaker families which had been expected for some time past had engaged to take their passage in the Bellona; but it was said, that they had been diverted from their purpose by some misrepresentations which had been made to them respecting this country.

Among other articles now received were five pipes of port wine and a quantity of rum, which were configned to the governor for the purpose of being fold to the officers of the civil and military establishments at prime cost; and three thousand pounds of tobacco for the use of the foldiers of the garrison and others.

The shameful impositions which had been practised by many who had brought out articles for sale in the colony, and the advantage which had been taken in too many instances of our necessities, had been properly stated at home, and this measure had been adopted by Government for our accommodation. The wine was immediately distributed; coming to the officer, after every expence of wharfage, &c. at 19 l. 10 s. per hogshead, and the rum at five shillings per gallon. The tobacco was likely to remain for some time undisposed of, as a quantity had been lately brought into the fettlement, and was felling at a lower price than could be taken for that imported by this ship; and tobacco formed a material article of the different investments in the Britannia.

With great pleasure we also found that Government, in consequence of the representations of Governor Phillip, had directed a strong substantial Russia duck to be substituted for the flight unserviceable Ofnaburghs with which the convicts had been hitherto supplied.

We learned by the Bellona, that his Majesty's ship Gorgon arrived at Spithead on the 19th of June last. In her passage, which she made by Cape Horn, on the 18th of February last, being in the latitude of 51° 30' S. and longitude 34° 07' W. variation 13° 37' E. she fell in with twenty-nine islands of ice. When the ship reached within three or four miles of the first of these islands, they observed one compact body, without the smallest appearance of any opening, bearing from N. N. E. to W. N. W. and which with some difficulty, being embayed *, they were enabled to clear, by hauling the ship from N. to

* When near this great body of ice, the thermometer was as low as thirty-six degrees; and it rose from that point, as she drew off, to forty degrees.

W. S. W.

W. S. W. This was done at ten in the forenoon; they did not reach the extreme weſtern point of the ice until five in the evening; and from the rate at which the ſhip failed, from her coming up with the firſt iſland of ice, until ſhe cleared the north-weſt point of the field abovementioned, it was computed that ſhe had run full twenty leagues.

It muſt be remarked, that the Sirius, in the month of December 1788, ſaw ſeveral iſlands of ice in nearly the ſame latitude and longitude.

At the Cape of Good Hope Captain Parker had met with Captain Edwards of the Pandora, who delivered to him Mary Braud, the widow of Bryant, (who eſcaped to Timor in the fiſhing cutter,) with one of the children, and only four of the male convicts who accompanied Bryant in his flight. Bryant died at Batavia, with the other child, and two of his companions; one of them, James Cox, was ſaid to be drowned in the Straits of Sunda. On their arrival in England the ſtory of their ſufferings in the boat excited much compaſſion; and, before the Bellona failed, they had been brought up to the bar of the Old Bailey, and ordered by the court to remain in Newgate until the period of their original ſentence of tranſportation ſhould expire, there to finiſh their unſucceſsful attempts to regain their liberty.

While the cargo of the Bellona was landing much of it was found to be damaged; the ſhip had been overloaded, and had met with very boiſterous weather on her paſſage. This practice of crowding too much into one ſhip had in many inſtances been very prejudicial to the colony; in the preſent inſtance, of the Ruſſia duck, which was excellent in its kind, and which had coſt the ſum of 6636 L. 0 s. 9 d.; ſixty-eight bales, containing thirteen thouſand one hundred and forty-eight yards, were damaged; ſixty-nine caſks of flour alſo were found to be much injured. Of ſeventy-ſix hogſheads of molaſſes, eleven hundred and ſeventy-two gallons were found to have leaked out; one caſk of pork was ſtinking and rotten; ſeventy-nine gallons of rum, and one hundred and ninety-eight gallons of wine, were deficient, owing to improper ſtowage; three hundred and thirty-five hammocks, thirteen rugs, five hundred and twenty-ſeven yards of brown cloths, and one caſe of ſtationary, were rendered totally unfit for uſe. Of the articles

articles thus found to be unserviceable to the colony, there was not one which in its proper state would not have been valuable ; and when the expence attending their conveyance, the risk of the passage, the inconvenience that must be felt from the want of every damaged article, and the impossibility of getting them replaced for a great length of time, were considered, it was difficult to ascertain their precise value.

Among the occurrences of this month one appears to deserve particular notice. On Friday the 18th, Eleanor M'Cave, the wife of Charles Williams, the settler, was drowned, together with an Infant child, and a woman of the name of Green. These unfortunate people had been drinking and revelling with Williams the husband and others at Sydney, and were proceeding to Parramatta in a small boat, in which was a bag of rice belonging to Green. The boat heeling considerably, and some water getting at the bag, by a movement of Green's to save her rice the boat overset near Breakfast Point, and the two women and the child were drowned. If assistance could have been obtained upon the spot, the child might have been saved ; for it was forced from the wretched mother's grasp just before she finally sunk, and brought on shore by the father; but for want of medical aid it expired. The parents of this child were noted in the colony for the general immorality of their conduct ; they had been rioting and fighting with each other the moment before they got into the boat; and it was said, that the woman had imprecated every evil to befal her and the infant she carried about her, (for she was six months gone with child,) if she accompanied her husband to Parramatta. The bodies of these two unfortunate women were found a few days afterwards, when the wretched and rascally Williams buried his wife and child within a very few feet of his own door. The profligacy of this man indeed manifested itself in a strange manner: a short time after he had thus buried his wife, he was seen sitting at his door, with a bottle of rum in his hand, and actually drinking one glass and pouring another on her grave until it was emptied, prefacing every libation by declaring how well she had loved it during her life. He appeared to be in a state not far from insanity, as this anecdote certainly testifies; but the melancholy event had not had any other effect upon his mind.

4   The

The Kitty transport being ready for sea, on Sunday the 20th two subalterns, three serjeants, three corporals, one drummer, and sixty privates, of the New South Wales corps, were embarked, for the purpose of relieving the detachment from that corps now on duty at Norfolk Island under the command of a captain, who received orders to return to this settlement.

On board of this ship were also embarked, Mr. Clarke, the deputy-commissary for Norfolk Island; Mr. Peate, the master carpenter, who came out in the Royal Admiral; two coopers; two taylors; two officers' servants; John Chapman Morris, Benjamin Ingram (pursuant to the conditional pardon which he received from Governor Phillip), and a few women: and on the 25th she sailed.

On Saturday the 26th, the rice being expended, the convicts received three pounds of flour, and the civil and military one pound of flour in addition to the former allowance.

In the course of this month the lieutenant-governor judged it necessary to send an officer to Parramatta, whom he could entrust with the direction of the convicts employed there and at Toongabbe in cultivation, as well as to take charge of the public grain. This business had always been executed by one of the superintendants, under the immediate inspection and orders of the governor, who latterly had dedicated the greatest part of his time and attention to these settlements. But it was attended with infinite fatigue to his excellency; and the business had now grown so extensive, that it became absolutely necessary that the person who might have the regulation of it should reside upon the spot, that he might personally enforce the execution of his orders, and be at all times ready to attend to the various applications which were constantly making from settlers.

The lieutenant-governor, therefore, (his presence being required at Sydney, the head-quarters of his regiment, and the seat of the government of the country,) deputed this trust to Lieutenant John M'Arthur, of the New South Wales corps; the superintendants, storekeepers, overseers, and convicts at the two settlements, being placed under his immediate inspection.

Charles Gray, a man who had rendered himself notorious in the registers of this colony by repeated acts of villany, exhibited himself

M M   again

again to public view at the close of this month, and at a time when every one thought him a reclaimed man. He had been sent to Norfolk Island as a place where he would have fewer opportunities of exercising his predatory abilities than at Sydney; but the law having spent its force against him, he returned to this settlement as a free man in September last. On his declaring that he was able to provide for himself, he was allowed to work for his own support, and for some time past he had cut wood and drawn water for a drummer in the New South Wales corps, a man who, by much self-denial and economy, had got together and laid up thirty-three guineas, for the prudent and laudable purpose of hereafter apprenticing his children; but having unfortunately and most indiscreetly suffered this man to know, not only that he had such a sum, but where he kept it, Gray availed himself of a convenient opportunity, and carried off the whole sum, together with a shirt which lay in his way. On being taken up, (for suspicion was directly fixed on him,) he readily acknowledged the theft, and either was, or pretended to be, very much in liquor. On being urged to restore the property, he sent the watchmen to search for it in different places, but without directing them to the spot where he had concealed it. At last he was taken out himself, when accidentally meeting the lieutenant-governor he threw himself on the ground, pretending to be in a fit; on which he was directly ordered to be tied up and punished with one hundred lashes. After this he would not make any discovery, and was sent to the hospital. The drummer who had suffered so materially by this wretch, although the object of pity, yet, knowing as he must have done the character of the man, was certainly entitled to no small degree of blame for trusting with a secret of such importance to his family a man who he must have known could not have withstood so great a temptation.

The lieutenant-governor proposing to open and cultivate the ground commonly known by the name of the Kangooroo Ground, situate to the westward of the town of Sydney between that settlement and Parramatta, a gang of convicts was sent from the latter place for that purpose. The soil here was much better for agriculture than that immediately adjoining to the town of Sydney, and the ground lay well for cultivation; but it had hitherto been neglected, from its being deficient

deficient in the very effential requifite of water; on which account Parramatta had been preferred to it. The eligibility of cultivating it was however now going to be tried; and, permiffion having been received by the Bellona to grant lands to thofe officers who might defire it, provided the fituations of the allotments were fuch as might be advantageous to *bonâ fide* fettlers hereafter, if they ever fhould fall into fuch hands, feveral officers chofe this as the fpot which they would cultivate, and allotments of one hundred acres each were marked out for the clergyman, (who, to obtain a grant here, relinquifhed his right to cultivate the land allotted for the maintenance of a minifter,) for the principal furgeon, and for two officers of the corps.

February.] The fettlers who came out in the Bellona having fixed on a fituation at the upper part of the harbour above the Flats, and on the fouth fide, their different allotments were furveyed and marked out; and early in this month they took poffeffion of their grounds. Being all free people, one convict excepted, who was allowed to fettle with them, they gave the appellation of " *Liberty Plains*" to the diftrict in which their farms were fituated. The moft refpectable of thefe people, and apparently the beft calculated for a *bonâ fide* fettler, was Thomas Rofe, a farmer from Dorfetfhire, who came out with his family, confifting of his wife and four children. An allotment of one hundred and twenty acres was marked out for him. With him came alfo Frederic Meredith, who formerly belonged to the Sirius, Thomas Webb, who alfo belonged to the Sirius, with his nephew, and Edward Powell, who had formerly been here in the Lady Juliana tranfport. Powell having fince his arrival married a free woman, who came out with the farmer's family, and Webb having brought a wife with him, had allotments of eighty acres marked out for each; the others had fixty each. The conditions under which they engaged to fettle were, " To " have their paffages provided by government*; an affortment of tools " and implements to be furnifhed them out of the public ftores; to be " fupplied with two years' provifions; their lands to be granted free of " expence; the fervice of convicts alfo to be affigned them free of ex-

* Government paid for each perfon above ten years of age the fum of eight pounds eight fhillings; and allowed one fhilling *per diem* for victualling them; and fixpence *per diem* for every one under that age.

" pence; and those convicts whose services might be assigned them to
" be supplied with two years' rations and one year's clothing." The
convict who settled with them (Walter Rouse, an industrious quiet man)
came out in the first fleet, and being a bricklayer by trade they thought
he might be of some service to them in constructing their huts. He
had an allotment of thirty acres marked out for him.

Many more officers availed themselves of the assent given by government to their occupying land, and fixed, some at Parramatta and
others in different parts of the harbour, where they thought the ground
most likely to turn out to their convenience and advantage. They
began their settlements in high spirits; the necessary tools and implements of husbandry were furnished to them from the stores; and they
were allowed each the use of ten convicts. From their exertions the
lieutenant-governor was sanguine in his hopes of being enabled to increase considerably the cultivation of the country; they appeared indeed to enter vigorously into these views, and not being restrained
from paying for labour with spirits, they got a great deal of work
done at their several farms (on those days when the convicts did not
work for the public) by hiring the different gangs; the great labour of
burning the timber after it was cut down requiring some such extra aid.

On the 5th of the month the Bellona was discharged from government employ. Twenty-one days were allowed for the delivery of her
cargo; but, by taking off the people from the brick carts, and from
some other works, she was cleared within the time. This ship was of
four hundred and fifty-four tons burthen, and was paid by government at the rate of four pounds four shillings per ton per month. A
clause was inserted in the charter-party, forbidding the master to
receive any person from the colony, without the express consent and
order of the governor. The governor was also empowered to take
her up for the purposes of the colony should he want her; but as the
Dædalus was expected, and the Kitty was already here, both in the
service of government, it was not necessary to detain her, and she
sailed on the 19th for Canton.

The master having been permitted to receive on board two convicts
(the number he requested) whose terms of transportation had expired,
consented to his ship being smoked, when four people were found
                                                        secreted

secreted on board, two of whom had not yet served the full periods of
their sentences.

To prevent this ship's coming on demurrage while her cargo was
delivering, the convicts worked in their own hours, as well as those
allotted to the public, under a promise of having the extra time allowed them at a future day. While this labour was in hand, the
building of the barracks stood still for want of materials; it therefore
became necessary, when the brick carts could again be manned, to lose
no time in bringing in a sufficient number of bricks to employ the
bricklayers. This having performed, they claimed their extra time,
which now amounted to sixteen days. As it would have proved very
inconvenient to have allowed them to remain unemployed for that
number of days, the lieutenant-governor directed the commissary to
issue to each person so employed half a pint of spirits *per diem* for sixteen days. Liquor given to them in this way operated as a benefit
and a comfort to them : it was the intemperate use of spirits, procured
at the expence of their clothing or their provisions, which was to be
guarded against, and which operated as a serious evil.

For want of sufficient store room, it was found necessary to stow a
great part of the wet provisions and flour arrived by the Bellona in
tiers before the provision-store. Care was taken to shelter them from
the sun and from the weather; and when the pile was completed, it
was, until the eye was accustomed to the sight, an object of novelty
and wonder; it never having occurred to us since we first built a store,
to have more provisions than our stores could contain.

Gray, who had recovered from his last punishment, being now
again urged to discover what he had done with the drummer's money,
trifled until he was again punished, and then declared he had buried it
in the man's garden ; but being taken to the spot he could not find it,
and in fact did not seem to know were to look for it. It was supposed, that, being in liquor when he committed the robbery, he was
ignorant how he had disposed of the property, or that it had fallen
into the hands of some person too dishonest to give it to the right
owner. He was afterwards sent to the hospital, whence he made his
escape into the woods.

On

On the evening of Sunday the 24th the signal was made at the South-head, a short time before dark, but too late to be observed at the settlement; at nine o'clock, however, information was received by the boat belonging to the South-head, that a ship from Calcutta was at anchor in the lower part of the harbour. In the morning she worked up, and anchored just without the cove. She proved to be the Shah Hormuzear, of about four hundred tons burthen, commanded by Mr. Matthew Wright Bampton, from Calcutta, who had embarked some property on a private speculation for this country. Mr. Bampton, in September last, had sailed from Bombay, with a cargo of provisions and stock for this settlement; but when near the Line, his ship springing a leak, he was obliged to return, and got to Bengal, where, with the sanction of Lord Cornwallis, he took on board a fresh cargo for the colony. At Bengal he had met with Captain Manning, who sailed from hence in the Pitt in April last, and who mentioned to him such articles as he thought were most wanted in these settlements.

Mr. Bampton had on board when he sailed, one bull, twenty-four cows, two hundred and twenty sheep, one hundred and thirty goats, five horses, and six asses; together with a quantity of beef, flour, rice, wheat, gram, paddy, and sugar; a few pipes of wine, some flat iron, and copper sufficient for the sloop's bottom which had been received in frame by the Pitt, and which Captain Manning remembered to have been sent out without that necessary article; a large quantity of spirits, and some canvas. In the article of stock, however, Mr. Bampton had been very unfortunate. His cattle died; of the sheep more than half perished; one horse and three asses died; and very few of the goats survived the voyage, a voyage by no means a long one, having been performed in eight weeks wanting three days, and in good weather. This mortality evidently did not proceed from any want of proper care, but was to be ascribed to their having been embarked immediately on being taken from the fields, and consequently wanting that stamina which a sea-voyage required.

The cattle that survived was purchased by the different officers of the colony, while the other part of the cargo, the spirits and canvas excepted, were taken by government. The amount of the whole purchased chafed by government was 960 3l. 5 s. 6 d; for although a fupply of provifions had been lately received from England, it was but a fmall one, and we were not yet in poffeffion of that plenty which would have warranted our rejecting a cargo of provifions, particularly when brought on fpeculation. The hour of diftrefs might again arrive, and occafions might occur that would excite a wifh, perhaps in vain, for a cargo of provifions from Bengal. In addition to thefe reafons, it muft be remarked, that the different articles which were purchafed were of the beft quality, and offered on reafonable terms.

By this fhip we received information, that the Queen tranfport had arrived fafe at Bombay; but it was much feared that the Admiral Barrington, which failed in company with the Queen from this place on the 6th of January 1792, was loft, as no accounts had been received of her at any port in India, a confiderable time after her arrival at Bombay from Batavia might reafonably have been expected. There arrived in the Chefterfield a perfon who had been a convict in this country, but who had been allowed to take his paffage on board the Admiral Barrington. This man quitted the Admiral Barrington at Batavia, and got to the Cape in a Dutch fhip, where meeting with Mr. Alt, he embarked with him, and by the accident which brought the Chefterfield hither returned to this colony. On his arrival here, he circulated a report, that feveral of the convicts who had got on board of thefe two fhips had been landed by order of the mafters at an ifland which they met with in their paffage to Batavia, inhabited indeed, but by favages; and that thofe who remained experienced fuch inhuman treatment, that they were glad to run away from them at the firft port where any civilifed people were to be found. He was himfelf among this number, and now declared that he was ready to make oath to the truth of his relation if it fhould be required. If there was any truth in his account, and the mafters of thefe fhips did actually turn any people on fhore in the manner already defcribed, it was more than probable that an act of fuch apparent cruelty had been occafioned by fome attempt of the convicts to take the fhips from them; and the numbers which were fuppofed to have been on board (feventeen) rather juftified the fuppofition. Captain Manning, of the Pitt, who had taken from this fettlement twenty men and nine wo-

men,

men, found them fo ufelefs and troublefome, that he was very glad to leave the greatteft part of them at Batavia *, and now declared that he regretted ever having received them on board. When thefe circum-ftances fhould be made public, it was thought that the mafters of fhips would not be fo defirous of recruiting their fhips' 'companies from among the inhabitants of this colony.

The grain called dholl, which had been iffued as part of the ration at the rate of three pints per man per week fince the arrival of the Atlantic, was difcontinued on the 25th, the whole of that article having been ferved out. It had been found ufeful for ftock.

At Toongabbe the workmen were now employed in conftructing a barn and granary upon a very extenfive fcale.

Among the females who died this month was one, a ftout healthy young woman, of the name of Martha Todd, who came out in the Mary Ann, and fell a victim to a dyfenteric complaint, which feized her after drinking too freely of the pernicious fpirits which had been lately introduced into the colony. The fame fate attended James Hatfield, a man who had been looked upon as a fober good character. He was on the point of obtaining a grant of land, and came from Parramatta to Sydney for the purpofe of fpeaking about his allotment, when, unfortunately, he met with fome of his friends, and partaking intemperately of the American rum, he was feized with a dyfentery, which carried him off in a few days. In this way many others were affected after drinking, through want of a fufficient ftamina to overcome the effect of the fpirit.

March.] The repairs of the Chefterfield having been completed, fhe was on the point of proceeding to fea, when the lieutenant-governor propofed to the mafter for the fum of 120l. to take on board a freight of provifions for Norfolk Ifland; which he confenting to, fhe was hauled alongfide the fhip from Bengal, and a certain proportion of grain was put into her; after which, fuch falt provifions and ftores as were intended to be conveyed by her were fent from the colony, and on the 10th fhe failed for Norfolk Ifland.

In lieu of the three pints of dholl, which were now difcontinued, an additional pound of flour was ferved; the civil and military receiv-

At that grave of Europeans the Pitt loft eighteen of her people.

1 4   ing

ing eight pounds, and the convicts seven pounds of flour per week, from the 9th; and in order to make a little room in the store, and that the officers might be accommodated with a better kind of flour, they were permitted to receive from the commissary two casks of American flour each, which were to be deducted from their ration.

The ship from Bengal, which was manned with Lascars, had no sooner hauled into the cove, and opened a communication with the shore, than a practice commenced among the convicts of disposing of the slops and blankets which they had lately received to the Lascars, who, trembling with the cold even of this climate, very readily availed themselves of their propensity to part with them; which was so great, that it became necessary to punish with severity such offenders as were detected.

On Tuesday the 12th the signal was made at the South Head, and by the noon of the following day two Spanish ships anchored in the lower part of the harbour. An officer from one of them arriving at the settlement, we learned that they were the two ships of whose expected arrival information had been received from government in the year 1790; and to whom it was recommended that every attention should be paid. They were named the Descuvierta and Atrevida (the Discovery and the Intrepid); the former commanded by Don Alexandro Malaspina, with a broad pendant as the commander of the expedition, and the latter by Don José de Bustamante y Guerra. They had been three years and a half from Europe on a voyage of discovery and information; and were now arrived from Manilla, after a passage of ninety-six days; touching in their way hither at Dusky Bay in New Zealand, from which they had sailed about a fortnight.

On their coming up, they anchored just abreast of the two points which form Sydney Cove, declining saluting, as it was not in our power to return it. These ships were of three hundred and five tons burden each, and were built for the particular voyage on which they were sent. Great care was observable in their construction, both as to the strength of the vessels and the accommodation of the officers and the equipage. They were well manned, and had, beside the officers customary in king's ships, a botanist and limner on board each vessel.

N N

They

They had vifited all the Spanish poffeffions in South America and other parts of the world, afcertaining with precifion their boundaries .and fituations; gaining much information refpecting their cuftoms and manners, their importance with regard to the mother country, their various productions commercial, agricultural, botanical, and mineral. For all which purpofes the officers on board appeared to have been fe- lected with the happieft fuccefs. They moft forcibly reminded us of the unfortunate Count de la Peyroufe and his followers, of whom thefe gentlemen had only heard that they were no more; and for whofe deftiny they expreffed a feeling arifing from their having traverfed the ocean in the fame purfuit, and followed in the fame path. Equally fincere and polite as Count de la Peyroufe, the Spanish commodore paid a tribute to the abilities and memory of our circumnavigator Cook, in whofe fteps the Chevalier Malafpina, who was an Italian marquis and a knight of Malta, declared it was a pleafure to follow, as it left him nothing to attend to, but to remark the accuracy of his obferva- tions. They loft at the ifland of Luconia Don Antonio Pineda, a colonel of the Spanish guards, who was charged with that department of the expedition which refpected the natural hiftory of the places they vifited. They fpoke of him in high terms as a man of fcience and a gentleman, and favoured us with an engraving of the monument which they had caufed to be erected over his grave at the place where he died; and from which the following infcription was copied:

ANTONIO . PINEDA .
Tribuno . Militum .
Virtute . In . Patriam . Bello . Armifque . Infigni .
Naturæ . Demum . Indefeffo . Scrutatori .
Trienni . Arduo . Itinere . Orbis . Extrema . Adiit .
Telluris . Vifcera . Pelagi . Abyffos . Andiumque . Cacumina . Luftrans .
Vitæ . Simul . Et . Laborum . Gravium .
Diem . Supremum . Obiit . In . Luconia . Philippicarum .
VI Calendas . Julii . M.D.C.C.X.C.II.
Præmaturam . Optimi . Mortem .
Luget . Patria . Luget . Fauna . Lugent . Amici .
Qui . Hocce . Pofuere . Monumentum .

The

The monument was defigned by Don Fernando Drambila, the land-fcape-painter on board the Atrevida ; and the infcription did credit to the claffical knowledge of Señor Don Fadeo Hcencke, the botanift on board the Defcuvierta.

Having requefted permiffion to erect an obfervatory, they chofe the point of the cove on which a fmall brick hut had been built for Ben-nillong by Governor Phillip, making ufe of the hut to fecure their inftruments. They did not profefs to be in want of much affiftance ; but fuch as they did require was directed to be furnifhed them without any expence; it was indeed too inconfiderable to become an object of charge.

The arrival of thefe ftrangers, together with that of the fhip from Dengal, gave a pleafant diverfity to the dull routine that commonly prevailed in the town of Sydney; every one ftriving to make their abode among us as cheerful as poffible, and to convince them, that though fevered from the mother country, and refiding in woods and among favages, we had not forgotten the hofpitalities due to a ftranger.

The commiffion of offences was now fo frequent, that it had be-come neceffary to affemble the criminal court during this month ; and William Afhford, a lad who had been drummed out of the New South Wales corps, was tried for ftealing feveral articles of wearing apparel from fome of the convicts ; of which being convicted, he was fentenced to receive three hundred lafhes.

On the 21ft the Kitty returned from Norfolk Ifland, having on board Captain Paterfon and his company of the new corps, together with a number of free people and convicts ; amounting in all to one hundred and feventy-two perfons; Governor King having been de-fired to get rid of any fuch characters as might be dangerous or trou-blefome to him.

Mr. King wrote very favourably of the ftate of the fettlements under his command. The crops of wheat and maize had produced fo abun-dantly, as to infure him a fufficiency of that article for the next twelve months. The inhabitants were healthy; and fuch had been the effects of fome wholefome regulations, and the attention of the magiftrates to enforce them, that for the laft three months not any offence deferving of punifhment had been committed, nor a cob of corn purloined either of private or public property.

At the departure of the Kitty, he was bufied in erecting fome neceffary buildings, as barracks, a granary, florehoufes, &c. and had completed a very excellent houfe for his own ufe. Lime-ftone having been found in great abundance on Norfolk Ifland, enabled him to build with more extent and fecurity than had hitherto been done even in New South Wales. Several cafks of this ufeful article were now imported in the Kitty, with a quantity of plank.

Captain Johnfton's company in the new corps received fome addition by this fhip. Eight of the marine fettlers, whofe grounds, on extending the lines of their allotments, were found to interfect each other, and who had declined fuch accommodation as Governor King thought it proper to offer them, had refigned their farms, and preferred returning to their former profeffion.

Toward the latter end of the month information was received of fome nefarious practices which had been carrying on at the ftore at Parramatta; the fum of which was, that the two convicts who had been employed in iffuing the provifions under the ftorekeeper had been for fome time in the habit of ferving out on each iffuing-day an extra allowance of provifions to one, or occafionally to two meffes. The meffes confifted of fix people, and one of thefe fix (taking any mefs he chofe) ufed to be previoufly informed by one or other of the convicts who ferved the provifions, that an extra allowance for the whole mefs would be ferved to him, which he was to receive and convey away, taking care to return the allowance to them at night, then to be divided into three fhares. To accomplifh this fraud, an opportunity was to be taken of the ftorekeeper's abfence, which might happen during the courfe of a long ferving, and for which they took care to watch. On his return the mefs for which one allowance had juft been ferved was publicly called, and the whole ferved a fecond time. With this practice they had trufted nine or ten different people; and the wife of one man, who had affifted in the crime, in a fit of drunkennefs confeffed the whole.

On examination before the judge-advocate it appeared, in addition to the above circumftances, that this fcheme had been carried on for about

about two months paſt; but there was little doubt of its having exiſted much longer.

It was no difficult matter to diſcover the perſons who had aſſiſted in this practice; and on their being taken up ſeveral confeſſed the ſhare that they and others had had in it: upon which the lieutenant-governor ordered them all to be ſeverely puniſhed.

In the Kitty arrived one of the ſuperintendants who had at Norfolk Iſland been employed in manufacturing the flax plant; but which, for want of ſome neceſſary tools, he could not bring to much perfection. Theſe had been written for to England, and he came hither to be employed at theſe ſettlements till they ſhould arrive. He was now ſent up to Toongabbe, to ſuperintend the delivery of proviſions at that place.

Notwithſtanding the orders which had been given reſpecting ſpirits being in the poſſeſſion of the convicts, on a ſearch made in ſome ſuſpected houſes, fourteen or fifteen gallons were found in one night; and, being ſeized by the watchmen and the guard, were divided among them as a ſtimulus to future vigilance. The evil effect of this ſpirit was perceptible in the number of priſoners which were to be found every morning in the watch-houſe; for, when intoxicated, it could not be expected that people of this deſcription would be very careful to avoid breaking the peace.

CHAP. XXI.

THE SPANISH SHIPS SAIL.—THE CHESTERFIELD RETURNS FROM NORFOLK ISLAND.
—A CONTRACT ENTERED INTO FOR BRINGING CATTLE FROM INDIA TO
THIS COUNTRY.—PROVISIONS EMBARKED ON BOARD THE BENGAL SHIP FOR
NORFOLK ISLAND.—THE DÆDALUS ARRIVES.—CATTLE LOST.—DISCOVERIES
BY CAPTAIN VANCOUVER.—TWO NATIVES OF NEW ZEALAND BROUGHT IN.—
BENGAL SHIP SAILS.—PHÆNOMENON IN THE SKY.—THE HOURS OF LABOUR
AND RATION ALTERED.—LEAD STOLEN.—DETACHMENT AT PARRAMATTA
RELIEVED.—ACCIDENT AT THAT SETTLEMENT.—LANDS CLEARED BY OFFI-
CERS.—MUTINY ON BOARD THE KITTY.—THE KITTY SAILS FOR ENGLAND.—
HIS MAJESTY'S BIRTH-DAY.—STATE OF THE PROVISION STORE.—THE BRI-
TANNIA ARRIVES.—LOSS OF CATTLE.—GENERAL ACCOUNT OF CATTLE PUR-
CHASED, LOST IN THE PASSAGE, AND LANDED IN NEW SOUTH WALES.—
NATIVES.

April.] THE Spanish officers having nearly completed the astronomical observations which the commodore thought it necessary to make
in this port, that officer signified his intention of shortly putting to
sea on the further prosecution of the instructions and orders which he
had received from his court. Previous to their departure, however,
the lieutenant-governor, with the officers of the settlement and of the
corps, were entertained first on board the Descuvierta, and the next
day on board the Atrevida, the lieutenant-governor being each day
received with a salute of nine guns, with the Spanish flag hoisted on
the foretopmast-head, being the compliment that is paid in the Spanish
service to a lieutenant-general. The dinner was prepared and served
up after their own custom, and bore every appearance of having been
furnished from a plentiful market *. The healths of our respective
sovereigns, being united in one wish, were drank with every token of
approbation, under a discharge of cannon; and " Prosperity to the

* A small cow from Monterey was sacrificed on the occasion.

" British

" British colonies in New South Wales" concluded the ceremonials of each day.

The commodore presented the lieutenant-governor with two drawings of this settlement, and one of Parramatta, done in Indian ink, by F. Brambila; together with a copy of the astronomical observations which had been made at the observatory, and at Parramatta. From these it appeared that the longitude of the observatory which they had erected at the Point, deduced from forty-two sets of distances of the sun and moon, taken on the morning of the 2d of this month,

was - - - - - 151° 18′ 8′ E. from Greenwich ;
And the latitude, - - 33° 51′ 28′′ S.
The latitude of the governor's house
at Parramatta was - - 33° 48′ 0′′ S.

And the distance west from the observatory about nineteen miles.

The commodore left a packet with dispatches for the Spanish ambassador at the court of London, to be forwarded by the first ship which should depart hence direct for England; and on the 12th both ships sailed. Their future route was never exactly spoken of by them; but, from what the officers occasionally threw out, it appeared that they expected to be in Europe in about fourteen months from their departure. They spoke of visiting the Society and Friendly Islands, and of proceeding again to the coast of South America.

As it had been the general wish to render the residence of these strangers among us as pleasant as our situation would allow, we received with great satisfaction the expressions of regret which they testified at their departure, a regret that was at least equally felt on our part. Our society was very small; we could not therefore but sensibly feel the departure of these gentlemen, who united to much scientific knowledge those qualities of the heart which render men amiable in society; and the names of Malaspina, Bustamante, Tova, Espinosa, Concha, Cevallos, Murphy *, Robredo, Quintano, Viana, Novales, Pineda †, Bauza, Heencke ‡, Nee ‡, Ravenet §, and Brambila §, were not likely to be soon forgotten by the officers of this set-

* This gentleman was of Irish extraction.   † Brother to D. A. Pineda.
‡ The botanists.   § The limner, and landscape-painter.

dement.

tlement. During their stay here, the greatest harmony subsisted between the seamen of the two ships and our people, the latter in but
few instances exercising their nimble-fingered talents among them;
such, however, as did choose to hazard a display, and were detected,
were severely punished.

A few days before these ships left us, the Chesterfield returned
(after an absence of only thirty days) from Norfolk Island, where she
landed safely every thing she had on board for that settlement. Mr. Alt
anchored for some days in Cascade Bay, where Governor King had
constructed a wharf, and had hopes of making the landing more convenient than could ever be practicable at Sydney Bay. This was truly a
desideratum, as few ships had gone to this island without having in the
course of their stay either been blown off, or been in some danger on
the shore. It was understood that scarcely any thing less than a mi-
racle could have saved the Kitty from being wrecked on a rock just
off the reef.

The master of the Shah Hormuzear having laid before the lieutenant-governor some proposals for bringing cattle to this country, they
were taken into consideration; and as the introducing cattle into the
colony was a most desirable object, and Bengal had been pointed out
as the settlement from which they were to be procured, after some
days a contract was entered into between Mr. Bampton on his own
part, and the lieutenant-governor on behalf of the crown, wherein it
was covenanted, that Mr. Bampton should freight at some port in
India a ship with one hundred head of large draught cattle; one hundred and fifty tons of the best provision rice, and one hundred and
fifty tons of dholl, both articles to be equal in quality to samples then
produced and approved of; and one hundred tons of the best Irish
cured beef or pork; or, in lieu of the salt provisions, fifty tons of
rice. For the cattle, it was covenanted on the part of the crown that
Mr. Bampton should receive at the rate of thirty-five pounds sterling
per head for all that he should land in a merchantable condition in the
colony; for the rice he was to be paid twenty-six pounds sterling, and
for the dholl eighteen pounds sterling, for every merchantable ton
which should be landed; and, lastly, for the salt provisions he was to
receive four-pence halfpenny per pound for all that should be landed

14   in

in proper condition. In this contract there were several conditions and restrictions, and the master was bound in one thousand five hundred pounds penalty to fulfil them.

The lieutenant-governor, wishing to send a supply to Norfolk Island sufficient to place that settlement, as far as depended upon him, in a comfortable state in point of provisions, engaged the Shah Hormuzear to carry two hundred and twenty tons of provisions thither for the sum of 220l.; and the quantity now sent, added to what the Kitty and Chesterfield had already conveyed, insured to Governor King provisions for more than twelve months for all his people at the full ration. Mr. Bampton engaging the Chesterfield to carry some part of these provisions, both ships began taking them in, and by the 19th had quitted the cove, intending to sail the following morning; but the signal being made for a sail at daylight, they waited to see the event.

At the close of the evening of the 20th the Dædalus storeship anchored in the cove, from the north-west coast of America. The Dædalus left England with a cargo of provisions and stores, consisting chiefly of articles of traffic, for the use of the vessels under the command of Captain Vancouver, whom she joined at Nootka Sound on the north-west coast of America; and it was designed that she should, after delivering her cargo, be dispatched to this colony with such stock as she might be able to procure from the different islands whereat she might touch, and be afterwards employed as the service might require, should Captain Vancouver not make any application for her return; which was thought probable, as well as that he might require some assistance from the colony.

Captain Vancouver, after taking out as much of the cargo as could be received on board the vessels under his command, dispatched her according to his orders, although not so early as he could have wished, owing to particular circumstances; and he was now obliged to send with her a requisition for the remainder of the provisions and stores being returned to him, together with a certain quantity of provisions from the colony; the whole to be dispatched from hence so as to join him either at Nootka, or some of the Sandwich Islands, in the month of October next.

o e   The

The agent Lieutenant Richard Hergill, who left England in this ship, was unfortunately killed, together with a Mr. Gootch (an astronomer, on his way to join Captain Vancouver) and one seaman, at Wahoo, one of the Sandwich Islands, where they touched to procure refreshments. Captain Vancouver had replaced this officer, by Lieutenant James Hanson, of the Chatham armed-tender, who now arrived in the ship.

On board of the Dædalus were embarked at Monterrey, a Spanish settlement at a short distance from Nootka, six bulls, twelve cows, six rams, and eight ewes; and at Otaheite, Lieutenant Hanson took on board upwards of one hundred hogs, (most of them, unluckily, barrows,) of all which stock four sheep and about eighty hogs only survived the passage. The loss of the cattle was attributed to their having been caught wild from the woods, and put on board without ever having tasted dry food. The major part of the hogs, apparently of a fine breed, arrived in very poor condition.

Lieutenant Hanson, having touched at the northernmost island of New Zealand, brought away with him two natives of that country, having received directions to that effect for the purpose of instructing the settlers at Norfolk Island in the manufacture of the flax plant. They were both young men, and, as they arrived before the departure of the Shah Hormuzear, the lieutenant-governor determined to send them at once to Norfolk Island.

Captain Vancouver transmitted by Lieutenant Hanson a chart and drawings of a spacious harbour, which he discovered on the southwest coast of this country, and which he named King George the Third's Sound. Its situation was without the line prescribed as the boundary of the British possessions in this country, being in the latitude of 35° 05′ 30″ South, and longitude 118° 34′ 0″ E. He also sent an account of the discovery of a dangerous cluster of rocks, which he named the Snares, the largest of which was about a league in circuit, and lay in latitude 48° 03′ S. and longitude 166° 20′ East, bearing from the South-end of New Zealand S. 40 W. true, twenty leagues distant; and from the southernmost part of the Traps (rocks discovered by Captain Cook) S. 67½ W. true, twenty leagues distant. The largest of these rocks, which was the highest and the northeasternmost, ernmoft, might be feen in clear weather about eight or nine leagues: the whole clufter was compofed of feven barren rocks, extending in a direction about N. 70 E. and S. 70 W. true, occupying the fpace of about three leagues.

The Chatham, being feparated in a gale of wind from the Difco-very, fell in with an ifland, which was named " Chatham Ifland," and along the north-fide of which fhe failed for twelve leagues. Its in-habitants much refembled the natives of New Zealand, and it was fituated in latitude 43° 49' S. and longitude 183° 02' Eaft.

We learned from Lieutenant Hanfon, that the Matilda whaler, which failed hence in the latter end of the year 1791, on her fifhing voyage, was wrecked on a reef in 22° South latitude, and 138° 30' Weft longitude. The mafter and people reached Otaheite, from whence fome were taken by an American veffel, and fome by Captain Bligh of the Providence. Five failors only remained on the ifland, with one runaway convict from this place, when the Dædalus touched there in her route hither, and of that number one failor only could be prevailed on to quit it.

We had now the fatisfaction of learning that Captain Bligh had failed for Jamaica in July laft, with ten thoufand bread-fruit plants on board in fine order; having fo far accomplifhed the object of this his fecond miffion to that ifland.

The natives from New Zealand having been put on board the Shah Hormuzear at the laft moment of her ftay in port, Lieutenant Hanfon remaining with them until the fhip was without the Heads, fhe failed, together with the Chefterfield, on the 24th.

Mr. Bampton purpofed making his paffage to India through the ftraits at the fouth end of New Guinea, known by the name of Torres's Straits. Captain Hill, of the New South Wales corps, took his paffage to England by the way of India with Mr. Bampton.

But few convicts were allowed to quit the colony in thefe fhips; four men and one woman only, whofe terms of tranfportation were expired, being received on board.

Gray, who had abfconded from the hofpital in February laft, made his appearance about the latter end of this month at Toongabbe, where he was detected in ftealing Indian corn.

Richard Sutton was stabbed with a knife in the belly by one Abraham Gordon, at the house of a female convict, on some quarrel respecting the woman, and at a time when both were inflamed with liquor. In the struggle Sutton was also dangerously cut in the arm; and when the surgeon came to dress him, he found six inches of the omentum protruding at the wound in his belly. Gordon was taken into custody.

Some people were taken up at Parramatta on suspicion of having murdered one of the watchmen belonging to that settlement; the circumstances of which affair one of them had been overheard relating to a fellow-convict, while both were under confinement for some other offence. A watchman certainly had been missing for some time past; but after much inquiry and investigation nothing appeared that could furnish matter for a criminal prosecution against them.

A soldier, who had been sentenced by a court-martial to receive three hundred lashes, on being led out to receive his punishment, attempted to cut his throat, wounding himself under the ear with a knife. The punishment was put off until the evening, when he declared that he was the person who killed the watchman at Parramatta, which he effected by shooting him; and that he would lead any one to the place where the body lay. This, however, not preventing his receiving as much of his punishment as he could bear, he afterwards declared that he knew nothing of the murder, and had accused himself of perpetrating so horrid a crime solely in the hope of deferring his punishment.

The natives, who now and then shewed themselves about the distant settlements, toward the latter end of the month wounded a convict who was taking provisions from Parramatta to a settler at Prospect Hill. The wound was not dangerous; but it occasioned the loss of the provisions with which he was entrusted.

The rains of this month came too late to save the Indian corn of the season, which now wore a most unpromising appearance. A grain had been lately introduced into the settlement, and grown at Toongabbe, and other places, which promised to answer very well for stock. It was the caffre corn of Africa, and had every appearance of proving a useful grain.

An

An extraordinary appearance in the sky was observed by several people between five and six o'clock in the evening of Friday the 12th of this month. It was noticed in the north-west, and appeared as if a ray of forked lightning had been stationary in that quarter of the sky for about fifteen minutes, which was the time it was visible. It was not to be discerned, however, after the sun had quitted the horizon.

May.] The days being considerably shortened, and the weather having lately been bad, it became necessary to alter the hours of labour. On the first of May, therefore, the lieutenant-governor directed that the convicts employed in cultivation, those employed under the master bricklayer, and those who worked at the brick carts and timber carriages, should labour from seven in the morning until ten, rest from that time until three in the afternoon, and continue at their work till sunset. The carpenters, whose business mostly lay within doors, and who were therefore not exposed to the weather, were directed to work one hour more in the afternoon, beginning at one instead of two o'clock.

On the 4th the weekly ration was altered, the male convicts receiving (instead of seven) four pounds of flour, to which were added four pounds of wheat and four pounds of maize; the allowance of salt provisions continued the same; but, the oil being expended, six ounces of sugar were issued in lieu of that article. The wheat was that received from Bengal, and the maize was issued the first week shelled, but unground; on the second the people received it in the cob, getting six pounds in that state in lieu of four shelled. This was unquestionably a good ration, and when a sufficient number of mills were put up to grind the maize and the wheat, the people themselves allowed it to be so.

With a ration that they admitted to be a good one, with about six hours labour during five days of the week, and with the advantages of gardens and good huts, the situation of the convicts might at this period be deemed comfortable, and such as precluded all excuse for misconduct. Garden robberies were, notwithstanding, often committed at Sydney; and at the other settlements the maize which was still in the field suffered considerable depredation.

A distinction was made in the ration served to the civil and military, they receiving weekly six instead of eight pounds of flour, two pounds of wheat, and four pounds of maize per man.

About

About the middle of the month the weather was remarkably bad. In the forenoon of the 15th a report was spread, in the midst of a most violent squall of wind and rain, that a ship was coming in. The wind having blown from the southward for some days before favoured the story, and, every one who heard it believing it to be true, the town was soon in motion notwithstanding the storm; for, although it was not so rare as it had been to hear of a ship, yet there was always something cheering and grateful, and perhaps ever will be, in entertaining the idea that our society was perhaps about to be increased, and that we were on the point of receiving intelligence from our connections, or information of what was doing in that world from which we felt themselves almost severed. On this occasion, however, we were disappointed; for, on the return of a boat which had been sent to the South Head, we were informed that the signal had not been made, nor a ship seen to occasion it. But we had been well trained in New South Wales to meet and endure disappointment!

On the night of this day, during the very heavy rain which fell, some person or persons found means to take off, undiscovered by the centinel at the store on the east side, five hundred weight of sheet lead, which had been landed from the Dædalus, and rolled to the storehouse door, where, being an article not likely from its weight to become an easy object of depredation, it was supposed to be perfectly safe. A very diligent search was made, but without success; and it remained undiscovered until the 27th, when a seaman belonging to the Kitty transport, on the ebbing of a spring tide, perceived it lying on the shore at low-water mark, opposite to the spot where the Dædalus lay at anchor. From this circumstance suspicion fell upon the people belonging to that ship; but as any design they could have in stealing it was not very obvious, it was more probable that some of the convicts had dropped it there for the purpose of secreting it till a future day, when it would have been got up, and cast into shot for those who are allowed to kill game.

About the end of the month the detachment of the New South Wales corps on duty at Parramatta was relieved. The party that remained there was placed under the command of Lieutenant M'Arthur, the officer charged with the direction of the civil duties of that settlement.

ment. The relief took place by land, the party from Sydney march-
ing up in about seven hours, and that from Parramatta arriving at their
quarters in Sydney in something more than six. The computed distance
by land is between seventeen and eighteen miles.

On the 29th our colours were displayed at the fort, in grateful remembrance of the restoration of monarchy in England.

Information was the same day received from Parramatta, that on the
evening of Saturday the 24th a settler of the name of Lisk, having
been drinking at the house of Charles Williams with Rose Burk (a
woman with whom he cohabited) until they were very much intoxicated, as he was returning to his farm through the town of Parramatta,
a dispute arose between him and the woman, during which a gun that
he had went off, and the contents lodged in the woman's arm below the
elbow, shattering the bones in so dreadful a manner as to require immediate amputation; which Mr. Arndell, being fortunately at home, directly
performed. The unhappy woman acquitted her companion of any intention to do her so shocking an injury, and when the account reached
Sydney she was in a favourable way.

In this accident Williams, it is true, had no further share than what
he might claim from their having intoxicated themselves at his house;
but that, however, established him more firmly in the opinion of those
who could judge of his conduct as a public nuisance.

The principal labour in hand at Sydney at this time was what the
building of the barracks occasioned; and at the other settlements the
people were chiefly employed in getting into the ground the grain for
the ensuing season, and in preparing for sowing the maize. This
article of subsistence having in the late season proved very unprofitable, the average quantity being not more than six bushels per acre in
the whole, the lieutenant-governor determined to sow with wheat as
much of the public grounds as he could; and every settler who chose
to apply was permitted to draw as much wheat from the public granary as his ground required, proper care being taken to insure its being
applied solely to that use. At Toongabbe no addition had been made
to the public ground since Governor Phillip's departure; but by a survey made at the latter end of this month it appeared, that the officers
to whom lands had been granted, had cultivated and cleared two hundred

dred and thirty-three acres, and had cut down the timber from two hundred and nineteen more. All the settlers of a different description had added something to their grounds; and there were many who might be pronounced to be advancing fast toward the comfortable situation of independent farmers.

The quantity of land granted since the governor's departure amounted to one thousand five hundred and seventy-five acres, eight hundred and thirty of which lay between the towns of Sydney and of Parramatta, the lieutenant-governor wishing and purposing to form a chain of farms between these settlements. The advantages to be derived from this communication were, the opening of an extent of country in the neighbourhood of both townships, and the benefit that would ultimately accrue to the colony at large from the cultivation of a track of as good land as any that had been hitherto opened; by some indeed it was deemed superior to the land immediately about Parramatta or Toongabbe. In this chain, on the Parramatta side, were placed those settlers who came out in the Bellona; and although they had only taken possession of their farms about the middle of February, they had got some ground ready for wheat, and by their industry had approved themselves deserving of every encouragement.

June.] The Kitty transport, which, since her arrival from Norfolk Island on the 21st of April last, had been fitting for her return to England, at length hauled out of the cove on the 1st of this month, it being intended that she should sail on the following morning. Her departure, however, was delayed by the appearance of a mutiny among the sailors at the very moment of being ordered to get the anchor up and proceed to sea. The master, George Ramsay, had frequently complained of some of the sailors belonging to the ship for various offences, and several of them had been punished on shore; one in particular, Benjamin Williams, for resisting Mr. Ramsay's authority as master of this ship, had been punished with one hundred lashes. This man, and four or five of the other sailors, having procured half a gallon of liquor from a man who (his term of transportation having expired) was permitted to return to England, were found by the master drinking, and with a light burning in the forecastle, at the late and improper hour of twelve o'clock on the night preceding

14   their

their intended failing. On being ordered to put out the light, they refufed, Williams declaring with an oath, that if the mafter extinguifhed it, he would light it again. This, however, the mafter effected; but on his afterwards going forward for the purpofe of difcovering if they had procured another light, he was feized by Williams and the other failors, and thrown clear of the fhip into the water. Fortunately he could fwim, a circumftance unknown to thefe mifcreants, and he reached the fhip's fide, whence, the mate coming to his affiftance, he was, though with fome difficulty, being a very heavy man, got into the fhip. The mafter, notwithftanding the outrage which he had thus experienced at their hands, would have contented himfelf with making a depofition of the circumftance, and have put to fea the next morning; but when he ordered the topfails to be hoifted, and the fhip got under way, Williams ftood forward, and, for himfelf and the reft, declared with much infolence, that the anchor fhould not be moved until the proper number of hands belonging to the fhip were on board *. The anchor, however, was got up by the affiftance of the paffengers and fome people who had boats from the fettlement alongfide, and with the wind at weft fhe dropped gradually down the harbour. The lieutenant-governor, on being informed by fome officers who were prefent of the dangerous and alarming temper which the feamen manifefted on board, refolved, by taking a firm and very active part, to crufh the diforder at once. He accordingly went on board in perfon, with fome foldiers, and, ordering the fhip to be brought to an anchor, returned with Williams, and two others who were pointed out by the mafter as his confederates, not only in refufing the duty of the fhip, but in throwing him overboard during the preceding night. This refolute ftep was inftantly followed up by their being taken to the public parade, and there punifhed, Williams with one hundred and fifty, and his companions with one hundred lafhes each, by the drummers of the New South Wales corps. At the place and in the moment of punifhment Williams's courage forfook him, and the fpirit which he had difplayed on board the Kitty was all

---

* She was deficient three men and two boys. The latter had run away the night before.

evapo-

evaporated *. He would have faid or done any thing to have averted
the lafh.

The appearance of a mutiny is at all times and in every fituation to
be dreaded; but in this country nothing could be more alarming.
The lieutenant-governor faw the affair in that light; and with a cele-
rity and firmnefs adapted to the exigency of the cafe reftored tranquillity and fafety to all thofe who were concerned in the fate of the
Kitty. The day following feveral depofitions were taken by the
judge-advocate, for the purpofe of being tranfmitted to the navy-
board, and the three feamen who had been taken out of the Kitty
being replaced by two convicts and one feaman lately difcharged from
the Dædalus, fhe failed at day-light on the morning of the 4th inftant,
and by twelve o'clock at noon was not to be feen from the South-
head.

On board the Kitty were embarked Mr. Dennis Confiden, one of
the affiftant-furgeons of the fettlement, who had received permiffion
to return to England on account of his health, which had been formerly impaired in the Eaft Indies; Lieutenant Stephen Donovan, who
had been employed in fuperintending the landing of provifions and
ftores at Norfolk Ifland, and was now returning to England, having
been appointed a lieutenant in the navy; Mr. Richard Clarke, who
came out in the Bellona as a medical fuperintendant; Mr. Alexander
Purvis Cranfton, late furgeon of his Majefty's floop Difcovery, who
was returning to England, being from ill health no longer capable of
attending to the duties of his profeffion; Mr. Henry Phillips, late
carpenter of the fame veffel, who was fent hither to be forwarded to
England as a prifoner; two feamen and one marine, invalids from the
veffels under the command of Captain Vancouver; five men and one
woman †, who, their terms of tranfportation being expired, were permitted to return to their friends; the feaman who was left behind
from the Atrevida; alfo five men, who were permitted to enter on

* He pretty well knew what a flogging was; for he was recognifed by a foldier of the
New South Wales corps, who had feen him flogged from fhip to fhip at Spithead for a
fimilar offence.

† Dorothy Handland, who at the time of her departure was upwards of eighty years
of age, but who neverthelefs had not a doubt of weathering Cape Horn.

board

board the Kitty for the purpose of navigating her. For the officers
and invalids who were on board, provisions for six months were sent
from the colony; but the others provided for themselves.

The services of the Kitty were to be summed up in very few words.
Of ten artificers with which she sailed from England, she lost eight;
and of the cargo of stores and provisions which she brought out, a part
was damaged. In seventeen months that she had been in the service
of government, she had made a long and circuitous voyage from England, and had taken one freight of provisions, stores, and troops to
Norfolk Island from this place. For these services her owners were
to receive the sum of 3500 l.; and, allowing her to be seven months
on her passage to England, the total amount of her hire will be found
to be very little short of 5000 l.

His Majesty's birth-day passed with the usual marks of distinction.
The regiment fired three vollies on their own parade, and the convicts
were allowed the day to themselves. On this occasion also the lieutenant-governor caused twelve of the largest hogs which had been received by the Dædalus, to be killed and divided among the military,
superintendants, and sick at the hospital; sufficient being given to the
latter for two days.

Notwithstanding the purchases of provisions which had fortunately
been made from the Philadelphia brigantine before governor Phillip's
departure, and since that time from the Hope and from the Shah Hormuzear, the lieutenant-governor found it necessary on the 12th of the
month to give notice, " That unless supplies arrived before the 22d he
" should be under the disagreeable necessity of ordering the ration to
" be reduced on that day."

A view of the provisions remaining in store here and at Parramatta
on the 24th of last month, (the date of the return sent home by the
commissary in the Kitty,) will evince the necessity of such an alteration.

On the 24th of May there were in store

Of Flour - - - - -	137,944 lbs.
Wheat - - - - -	154,560
Paddy - - - - -	49,248

making a total of three hundred and forty-one thousand seven hundred
and fifty-two pounds of grain; which, at the established ration of
eight pounds per man per week, would last six weeks and three days.

Beef

Beef - - - - - - - 93,969 lbs.
Pork - - - - - - 125,178
which, at the ration of seven pounds of beef, or four pounds of pork, per man per week, would last, the beef five weeks, and the pork eleven weeks and a half.

There was also in store, though not at present issued, the Indian corn rendering it unnecessary, seventy-one thousand two hundred and eighty pounds of grain and pease; which, at the allowance of three pints per man per week, would last eight weeks and a half; and nineteen thousand eight hundred pounds of sugar; which, at six ounces per man per week, would last eighteen weeks and a half. This latter article had been issued since the beginning of the last month, when it was served as an equivalent for oil.

It must be remarked, that but for the purchases which had most fortunately been made of provisions, the colony must at this moment have been again groaning under the oppression of a very reduced ration.

From the Philadelphia were purchased Beef   109,817 lbs.
From the Hope - - - ditto   38,600
From the Shah Hormuzear - ditto   107,988
                                   ―――――――
            Total of Beef -   256,405
From the Hope were purchased Pork -   15,600
                                   ―――――――
        Whole quantity purchased -   272,005
of which, deducting the quantity remaining, we shall be found to have then consumed fifty-two thousand eight hundred and fifty-eight pounds, something more than equal to one-fifth part.

From the Hope were purchased   Flour   8,800 lbs.
From the Shah Hormuzear - ditto   36,539
                                   ―――――――
        Whole quantity purchased -   45,339
which deducted from the quantity remaining, we should then only have had in store - - - - -   92,605 lbs.
of the other articles of which the present ration was composed (the maize excepted) we should not have had any in the colony; for the wheat and the sugar were brought hither in the ship from Bengal.

A 2

As none of these incidental supplies could be known in England, it was fair to conclude, that our situation must have been adverted to, and that ships with provisions were now not very distant. Under this idea, although on the 22d no supplies had arrived, the lieutenant-governor did not make any alteration in the ration, determining to wait one week longer before he directed the necessary reduction. It was always a painful duty to abridge the food of the labouring man, and had been too often exercised here. The putting off, therefore, the evil day for another week in the hope of any decrease being rendered unnecessary by the arrival of supplies, met with general applause.

On the Monday following the signal was made for a sail, and about nine o'clock at night the Britannia was safe within the Heads, having to a day completed eight months since she sailed hence. The length of time she had been absent gave birth to some anxiety upon her account, and her arrival was welcomed with proportionate satisfaction.

Mr. Raven touched at Dusky Bay in New Zealand, where he left his second mate Mr. John Leith and some of his people, for the purpose of procuring seals (the principal object of his voyage from England); and of the timber which he found there he made a very favourable report, pronouncing it to be light, tough, and in every respect fit for masts or yards. From New Zealand the Britannia, after rounding Cape Horn in very favourable weather, proceeded to the island of Santa Catherina, on the Brasil coast, where the Portuguese have a settlement, and from whose governor Mr. Raven received much civility during the eighteen days that he remained there. Not being able to procure at this place any of the articles he was instructed to purchase, (one cow and one cow-calf excepted,) he stood over to the African continent, and arrived at the Cape of Good Hope on the 24th of March last. At this port he took on board thirty cows; three mares; twelve goats; a quantity of flour, sugar, tobacco, and spirits; and other articles, according to the orders of his employers. Mr. Raven afforded another instance of the great difficulty attending the transporting of cattle to this country; for, notwithstanding the extreme care and attention which were paid to them, twenty-nine of the cows and three goats unfortunately died. This he attributed solely, and no doubt

doubt justly, to their not being properly prepared for such a voyage, and previously fed for some weeks on dry food.

In her passage from the Cape of Good Hope to this port, the Britannia met with much bad weather, running for fourteen days under her bare poles. The prevailing winds were from S. W. to N. W. She came round Van Dieman's Land in a gale of wind without seeing it. To the southward of New Zealand Mr. Raven fell in with the rocks seen by Captain Vancouver, and named by him the Snares. In the latitude of them Mr. Raven differed from Captain Vancouver only four miles; their longitude he made exactly the same. Such similarity in the observations was rare and remarkable. He passed some islands of ice at three and five leagues distance, in latitudes 51° and 52° S. and longitudes 232° and 240° East.

At the Cape Mr. Raven found the Pitt, Captain Manning, from Calcutta, to whom he delivered his dispatches; and he received information from the captains of the Triton and Warley East Indiamen of the agitated state of Europe; of the naval and military preparations which were making in our own country; and of the spirit of loyalty and affection for our justly-revered sovereign which breathed throughout the nation, accompanied with firm and general determinations to maintain inviolate our happy constitution. These accounts, while they served to excite an ardent wish for the speedy arrival of a ship from England, seemed to throw the probability of one at a greater distance, particularly as Mr. Raven could not learn with any certainty of a ship being preparing for New South Wales.

Among other circumstances which he mentioned was one which deserved notice. The Royal Admiral East Indiaman, Captain Bond, was lying on the 19th of last December in the Tigris. She sailed hence on the 13th of November, and, admitting that she had only arrived on the day on which she was stated to a certainty to be at anchor in the river, she must have performed the voyage in thirty-seven days from this port. This ship, it may be remembered, made the passage from the Cape of Good Hope to this place in five weeks and three days; a run that had never before been made by any other ship coming to this country.

From the length of time which the Britannia had been absent, our observation was forcibly drawn to the distance whereat we were placed from

from any quarter which could furnish us with supplies; and a calculation of the length of time which had been taken by other ships to procure them confirmed the necessity that existed of using every exertion that might place the colony in a state of independence.

When the Sirius went to the Cape of Good Hope in 1788, she was absent seven months and six days.

The Supply, which was sent for provisions in 1789, returned herself in six months and two days; but the supplies which had been purchased for the colony were two months longer in reaching it.

The Atlantic sailed hence for Calcutta on the 26th of October 1791, touching at Norfolk Island, from which place she took her departure on the 13th of November; and, calculating her passage from that time, she will be found to have been seven months and one week in procuring the supplies for which she was sent out.

The Britannia too was eight months absent. From all this it was to be inferred, that there should not only be always provisions in the stores for twelve months beforehand; but that, to guard against accidents, whenever the provisions in the colony were reduced to that quantity and no more, then would be the time to dispatch a ship for supplies.

The difficulty of introducing cattle into the colony had been rendered evident by the miscarriage of the different attempts made by this and other ships. In this particular we had indeed been singularly unfortunate; for we had not only lost the greatest part of what had been purchased and embarked for the colony, as will appear by the following statement; but we had at the beginning, as will be remembered, lost the few that did survive the passage. Of these it never was known with any certainty what had been the fate. Some of the natives who resided among us did, in observing some that had been landed, declare that they had seen them destroyed by their own people; and even offered to lead any one to the place where some of their bones might be found; but, from the distance of the supposed spot, and our more important concerns, this had never been sought after. It was very probable that they had been so destroyed; if not, and that they had met with no other accident, their increase at this time must have been very considerable.

Account

Account of Black Cattle purchased for, lost in the passage to, and landed in New South Wales.

	Purchased			Lost in the Passage			Landed		
	Bulls	Cows	Calves	Bulls	Cows	Calves	Bulls	Cows	Calves
Embarked in 1787 on board the Sirius and one of the transports -	1	7	1	—	2	—	1	5	1
Embarked in 1789 on board the Guardian - - -	2	16	—	2	16	—	—	—	—
Embarked in 1791 on board the Gorgon, Admiral Barrington, and calved on the passage, - -	3	24	1	3	7	—	—	17	1
Embarked on board the Atlantic in 1792, at Calcutta, - -	2	2	1	—	1	1	2	1	—
Embarked on board the Pitt -	—	2	—	—	1	—	—	1	—
Embarked on board the Royal Admiral	—	1	—	—	—	—	—	1	—
Embarked on board the Shah Hormuzear in 1792, in India, -	1	24	2	1	23	—	—	1	2
Embarked on board the Dædalus -	6	12	—	6	12	—	—	—	—
Embarked on board the Britannia -	—	31	1	—	29	—	—	2	1

	Purchased	-	15 bulls, 119 cows, 6 calves;
Total	Lost in the passage		12 bulls, 91 cows, 1 calf;
	Landed	-	3 bulls, 28 cows, 5 calves.

Of the three bulls which were landed two only were living at this period, beside the bull calf produced on board the Gorgon. Of the twenty-eight cows only twenty, and of the five calves only two were living; but the cows which arrived in the Gorgon had produced three cow and two bull calves; and one small cow must be added to the number in the colony, which had been presented by the Spanish commodore to the lieutenant-governor.

Sheep, horses, and hogs were found, better than any other stock, to stand the rough weather which was in general met with between the Cape of Good Hope and this country.

The mortality which had happened among the stock on board the Britannia set a high price on those which survived. For the cows Mr. Raven bought at the Cape he gave twenty dollars each, and for each horse he gave thirty dollars. For the cow with her calf, which he purchased at Santa Catharina, he gave no more than sixteen Spanish dollars.

6   On

On Saturday the 29th, the lieutenant-governor determining to try the present ration yet another week, the usual allowance was issued, and on the next day the following general order appeared: " It being " unsafe to continue at the present ration, the commissary has received " instructions to reduce the weekly allowance, either one pound of " pork, or two pounds of beef, making a proportionate deduction " from the women and children. This alteration to take place on " Saturday the 6th of July."

The natives had lately become troublesome, particularly in lurking between the different settlements, and forcibly taking provisions and clothing from the convicts who were passing from one to another. One or two convicts having been wounded by them, some small armed parties were sent out to drive them away, and to throw a few shot among them, but with positive orders to be careful not to take a life.

Several of these people, however, continued to reside in the town, and to mix with the inhabitants in the most unreserved manner. It was no uncommon circumstance to see them coming into town with bundles of fire-wood which they had been hired to procure, or bringing water from the tanks; for which services they thought themselves well rewarded with any worn-out jacket or trowsers, or blankets, or a piece of bread. Of this latter article they were all exceedingly fond, and their constant prayer was for bread, importuning with as much earnestness and perseverance as if begging for bread had been their profession from their infancy; and their attachment to us must be considered as an indication of their not receiving any ill treatment from us.

CHAP. XXII.

THE DÆDALUS SAILS FOR NOOTKA.—A TEMPORARY CHURCH FOUNDED.—
CRIMINAL COURT.—THE COLONIAL VESSEL LAUNCHED.—A SCHEME TO
TAKE A LONG BOAT.—TWO SOLDIERS DESERT.—COUNTERFEIT DOLLARS IN
CIRCULATION.—A SOLDIER PUNISHED.—THE BODDINGTONS ARRIVES FROM
CORK.—GENERAL COURT MARTIAL HELD.—THE BRITANNIA HIRED AND
CHARTERED FOR BENGAL.—THE NEW CHURCH OPENED.—ACCIDENT.—PRO-
VISIONS IN STORE.—CORN PURCHASED FROM SETTLERS.—THE BRITANNIA
SAILS FOR BENGAL, AND THE FRANCIS SCHOONER FOR NEW ZEALAND.
—IRISH CONVICTS STEAL A BOAT.—THE SUGAR CANE ARRIVES.—INTENDED
MUTINY ON BOARD PREVENTED.—EXCURSION TO THE WESTWARD.—PUBLIC
WORKS.

July.] ON the first of this month the Dædalus sailed to convey to Captain Vancouver the provisions and stores which had been required by that officer. Lieutenant Hanson, the naval agent on board, received the most pointed orders for the ship to return to this port immediately after having executed the service on which she was then going. The Dædalus was considered as a colonial ship; and nothing but Captain Vancouver's express requisition to have the stores and provisions which were on board her (the stores being chiefly articles of traffic) sent back to him, to enable him to fulfil the instructions he had received, would have induced the lieutenant-governor, in the present state of the colony, to have parted with her, when it was not improbable that her services might be wanting to procure supplies, and at no very distant period, if ships did not arrive.

The Dædalus being, like other ships which had preceded her, short of hands, the master was permitted to recruit his numbers here, and took with him six convicts, who had served their several terms of transportation, and were of good character; and two seamen, who had been left behind from other ships. The extensive population of the islands at some of which the Dædalus might have occasion to touch rendered it absolutely necessary that she should be completely manned;

as we well knew the readineſs with which, at all times, their inhabitants availed themſelves of any inferiority or weakneſs which they
might diſcover among us.

On board of the Dædalus alſo was embarked a native of this country, who was ſent by the lieutenant-governor for the purpoſe of acquiring our language. Lieutenant Hanſon was directed by no means
to leave him at Nootka, but, if he ſurvived the voyage, to bring him
back ſafe to his friends and countrymen. His native names were
Gnung-a gnung-a, Mur-re-mur-gan; but he had for a long time entirely loſt them, even among his own people, who called him
" Collins," after the judge-advocate, whoſe name he had adopted on
the firſt day of his coming among us. He was a man of a more
gentle diſpoſition than moſt of his aſſociates; and, from the confidence
he placed in us, very readily undertook the voyage, although he left
behind him a young wife, (a ſiſter of Bennillong, who accompanied
Governor Phillip,) of whom he always appeared extremely fond.

On Saturday the 6th the intended change took place in the ration;
and it being a week on which pork was to be iſſued, three pounds of
that article were ſerved inſtead of four. The other articles remained
the ſame.

The clergyman, who ſuffered as much inconvenience as other people
from the want of a proper place for the performance of divine ſervice,
himſelf undertook to remove the evil, on finding that, from the preſſure
of other works, it was not eaſy to foreſee when a church would be
erected. He accordingly began one under his own inſpection, and
choſe the ſituation for it at the back of the huts on the eaſt ſide of the
cove. The front was ſeventy-three feet by fifteen; and at right angles with the centre projected another building forty feet by fifteen.
The edifice was conſtructed of ſtrong poſts, wattles, and plaſter, and
was to be thatched *. Much credit was due to the Rev. Mr. Johnſon
for his perſonal exertions on this occaſion.

Repreſentation having been made to the lieutenant-governor, that
ſeveral of the ſoldiers had been ſo thoughtleſs as to diſpoſe of the ſugar
and tobacco which had been ſerved out to them by their officers ſince

---

* The expence of building it was computed to be about forty pounds.

                                                    the

the arrival of the Britannia, almost as soon as they had received those articles, and that some artful people had availed themselves of their indiscretion, in many instances bartering a bottle of spirits (Cape brandy) for six times its value, he judged it necessary to give notice, that any convict detected in exchanging liquor with the soldiers for any article served out to them by their officers, would immediately be punished, and the articles purchased taken away: and further, (now become a most necessary restriction,) that any persons attempting to sell liquor without a licence might rely on its being seized, and the houses of the offending parties pulled down.

About the middle of the month all the wheat which was to be sown on the public account was got in at and near Toongabbe ; the quantity of ground was about three hundred and eighty acres. The wheat of last season being now nearly thrashed out, some judgment was formed of its produce, and it was found to have averaged between seventeen and eighteen bushels an acre. A large quantity of wheat was also sown this season by individuals, amounting to about one thousand three hundred and eighty-one bushels, every encouragement having been given to them to sow their grounds with that grain.

Several houses having been lately broken open, the criminal court of judicature was assembled on the 15th, when Samuel Wright, a convict who arrived in 1791, was tried for breaking into a hut in the day-time, and stealing several articles of wearing apparel ; of which offence being found guilty, he received sentence of death, and was to have been executed on the Monday following ; but the court having recommended him to mercy on account of his youth, being only sixteen years of age, the lieutenant-governor as readily forgave as the court had recommended him; but, that the prisoner might have all the benefit of so awful a situation, the change in his fate was not imparted to him until the very moment when he was about to ascend the ladder from which he was to be plunged into eternity. He had appeared since his conviction as if devoid of feeling ; but on receiving this information, he fell on his knees in an agony of joy and gratitude. The solemn scene appeared likewise to make a forcible impression on all his fellow prisoners, who were present.

The

The weather of this winter having been colder than any that we had before experienced, great exertions were made to clothe all the labouring convicts; and for that purpose the work of the taylors had for some time been confined to them. Every male convict received one cloth jacket, two canvas frocks, one pair of shoes, and one leathern cap. The females also had been clothed.

The vessel which had been received in frame by the Pitt was now completed, and, to avoid the labour which would have attended her being launched in the usual manner, Mr. Raven, the master of the Britannia, offered his own services and the assistance of his ship to lay her down upon her bilge, and put her into the water on rollers. This mode having been adopted, in the forenoon of Wednesday the 24th of this month she was safely let down upon the rollers, and by dusk, with the assistance of the Britannia, was hove down to low-water mark, whence, at a quarter before eight o'clock, she floated with the tide, and was hauled safely along-side the Britannia. The ceremony of christening her was performed at sun-rise the next morning, when she was named The Francis, in compliment to the lieutenant-governor's son, whose birth-day this was; and, Mr. Raven coinciding with the general opinion that she would be much safer if rigged as a schooner than as a sloop, for which she had been originally intended, the carpenters were directed to fit her accordingly; and that gentleman very obligingly supplied a spar, which he had procured for the Britannia at Dusky Bay, to make her a foremast.

The command of this little vessel, of whose utility great expectations were formed, was given by the lieutenant-governor to Mr. William House, late boatswain of the Discovery, who arrived here in the Dædalus for the purpose of proceeding to England as an invalid; but being strongly recommended by Captain Vancouver as an excellent seaman, with whom he was very unwilling to part, and signifying a wish to be employed in this country, the command of this vessel was given to him, with the same allowance that is made to a superintendant; on which list he was placed. The two boys who were left behind from the Kitty were also entered for her, and she was ordered to be fitted forthwith for sea. As it was well known that many people had their eyes upon this vessel as the means of their escaping from the

2   colony,

colony, it was intended, in addition to other precautions, that none but the most trusty people should ever be employed in her.

On the last day of the month a plan to take off one of the long-boats was revealed to the lieutenant-governor. The principal parties in it were soldiers; and their scheme was, to proceed to Java, with a chart of which they had by some means been furnished. If their plan had been put into execution, the evil would have carried with it its own punishment; for, had they survived the voyage, they would never have been countenanced by the Dutch, who were always very jealous of strangers coming among them, and had, no doubt, heard of the desertion of Bryant and his associates from this settlement. Two of the soldiers were immediately put into confinement; and in the night two others, one a corporal, went off into the woods, taking with them their arms, about one hundred rounds of powder and ball, which they collected from the different pouches in the barrack, their provisions and necessaries.

The principal works in hand by the people at Sydney were, erecting kitchens and storerooms for the officers' new barracks, bringing in timber for rollers for the sloop, and constructing huts at Petersham for convicts. At Toongabbe the Indian corn was not all gathered, and housing of that, and preparing the ground for the reception of the next season's crop, occupied the labouring convicts at that settlement.

Some counterfeit dollars were at this time in circulation; but the manufacturers of them were not discovered.

August.] The two soldiers who were put into confinement on suspicion of being parties in a plan to seize one of the long-boats, were tried by a regimental court-martial on the first day of this month, and one was acquitted; but Roberts, a drummer, who was proved to have attempted to persuade another drummer to be of the party, was sentenced to receive three hundred lashes, and in the evening did receive two hundred and twenty-five of them. While smarting under the severity with which his punishment was inflicted, he gave up the names of six or eight of his brother soldiers as concerned with him, among whom were the two who had absented themselves the preceding evening. These people, the day following their desertion, were met in the path to Parramatta, and told an absurd story of their

being

being sent to the Blue Mountains. They were next heard of at a settler's (John Nicholls) at Prospect Hill, whose house they entered forcibly, and, making him and a convict hutkeeper prisoners, passed the night there. At another settler's they took sixteen pounds of flour, which they sent by his wife to a woman well known to one of them, and had them baked into small loaves. They signified a determination not to be taken alive, and threatened to lie in wait for the game-killers, of whose ammunition they meant to make themselves masters. These declarations manifested the badness of their hearts, and the weakness of their cause; and the lieutenant-governor, on being made acquainted with them, sent out a small armed party to secure and bring them in, rightly judging that people who were so ready at expressing every where a resolution to part with their lives rather than be taken, would not give much trouble in securing them.

This desertion, and the disaffection of those who meant to take off a long-boat, was the more unaccountable, as the commanding officer had uniformly treated them with every indulgence, putting it entirely out of their power to complain on that head. Spirits and other comforts had been procured for them; he had distinguished them from the convicts in the ration of provisions; he had allowed them to build themselves comfortable huts, permitting them while so employed the use of the public boats; he had indulged them with women; and, in a word, had never refused any of them a request which did not militate against the rules of the service, or of the discipline which he had laid down for the New South Wales corps; at the same time, however, to prevent these indulgencies from falling into contempt, they were counterbalanced by a certainty of their being withdrawn when abused, and flagrant offenders were sure of meeting with punishment: yet there were many among them who were so ungrateful for the benefits which they received, and so unmindful of their own interest and accommodation, that they behaved ill whenever they had an opportunity.

The parties who had been sent after the runaways, by dividing themselves, fell in with them near Toongabbe on the 6th, and secured them without any opposition.

There were at this time in the New South Wales corps, distributed among the different companies, thirty recruits who had been selected

from

from among the convicts as people of good characters, and, having formerly been in the army, were permitted to enlist. These people had conducted themselves with remarkable propriety, one man only excepted, who had some time since been punished by the sentence of a court-martial, and who afterwards misbehaving was discharged from the corps. They were in general enlisted for life, a condition to which they subscribed on being attested; and such as had a long time to serve under their sentence, were emancipated on the above condition.

On the 7th the Boddingtons transport anchored in the cove from Ireland, having sailed from Cork on the 15th of February last, with one hundred and twenty-four male, and twenty female convicts of that kingdom on board, provisions calculated to serve them nine months * after their arrival, and a proportion of clothing for twelve months. As a guard, there was embarked a subaltern's party of the New South Wales corps; and this precaution was found to have been very necessary, the ignorance of the Irish convicts having displayed itself in an absurd scheme to take the ship; but which was happily frustrated by the vigilance and activity of the master † and the officers.

Mr. Richards jun., who had the contract for supplying the ships which sailed for this country in 1788 and the Lady Juliana transport, was employed again by government; a circumstance of general congratulation among the colonists on its being made known. On the present occasion he had contracted to furnish two ships to bring out three hundred male and female convicts from Ireland, with stores and provisions. The Boddingtons, being the first ready, sailed alone; the Sugar Cane (the second ship) was at Deptford ready to drop down to Gravesend when her intended companion was about leaving Ireland. Government were to pay four pounds four shillings per ton for such stores as should be put on board, and for the convicts at the rate of twenty-two pounds per head. This mode of payment was complained of in the contract made formerly with Messrs. Calvert and Co.; but in the present instance the evil attending that contract was avoided, by a part of the above sum (five pounds) being left to be paid by certificate

---

* Two hundred and twenty-eight barrels of flour; one hundred and eight tierces of pork, and fifty four tierces of beef; twenty-eight bales and thirteen cases of stores.

† Captain Robert Chalmers, on the captain's half pay of the marines.

for

for every convict which should be landed. No ship, however, could have brought out their convicts in higher order, nor could have given stronger proofs of attention to their health and accommodation, than did this vessel. Each had a bed to himself, and a new suit of clothes to land in. On the part of the crown also, to see justice done to the convicts, there was a surgeon of the navy on board, Mr. Kent, as a superintendent; and on the part of the contractor, a gentleman who had visited us before with Mr. Marshall, in the second voyage of the Scarborough to this country, Mr. A. Jac. Bier, a surgeon also. They had not any sick list, and had lost only one man on the passage.

Captain Chalmers informed us, that on his arrival at Rio de Janeiro, in which port he anchored on the 10th of last April, he heard that the Atlantic transport had sailed thence about three weeks, and had made her passage from this country round Cape Horn to Rio de Janeiro in fifty-eight days. He learned from the gentlemen about the palace, that his excellency Governor Phillip when he touched there appeared to be in perfect health. He had there too heard of the agitated state of Europe; and understanding that in all probability the Channel would be infested with French privateers, he purchased some guns, to strengthen the force which he had already on board the Atlantic.

Advices were received by this ship, that administration intended to make arrangements for our being supplied from Bengal with live cattle: and this became a favourite idea with every person in the colony; for the sheep, though small, were found to be very productive, breeding twice in the year, and generally bringing two lambs at a birth. The climate was also found to agree well with the cattle of the buffalo species which had been received.

The convicts received by the Boddingtons were disembarked a day or two after her arrival, and sent up to Toongabbe. On quitting the ship they with one voice bore testimony to the humane treatment they had received from Captain Chalmers, declaring that they had not any complaints to prefer, and cheering him when the boats which carried them put off from her side.

It being necessary to mark with some degree of severity the offence which had been committed by the two soldiers, a general court-mar-

tial

tial was assembled for their trial on the 12th. The lieutenant-governor, with much humanity, forebore to charge them with a capital offence ; bringing them to trial for absenting themselves from head-quarters without leave, instead of the more serious crime of desertion.

By the mutiny act, a general court-martial may, in Africa, consist of less than thirteen commissioned officers, but not less than five ; the like provision was also extended to New South Wales; and nine officers formed the court now assembled for the first time in this colony. Captain Collins officiated as deputy judge-advocate. The prisoners did not deny the crime they were charged with ; and the court, after reducing the corporal to the ranks, sentenced him to receive five hundred lashes, and the private soldier eight hundred. The sentence, being approved by the lieutenant-governor, was in part carried into execution on Saturday the 17th, the corporal receiving two hundred and seventy-five, and the soldier three hundred lashes.

The Britannia being now nearly ready for sea, having had some very necessary articles of repair done to her, and which the master declared had been as well executed by the artificers of the colony as if the ship had been in England, she was tendered to be employed for the service of the settlement wherever the lieutenant-governor might think it necessary to send her. In the charter-party of the Boddingtons, a clause was inserted, empowering the governor to send her to Norfolk Island, or elsewhere, should he have occasion, the crown paying the same hire as was paid for the Atlantic transport (fifteen shillings and sixpence per ton per month) during the time she should be so employed. The Britannia was tendered at one shilling per ton less, and had moreover the advantage of being a coppered ship.

It has been seen that the supply brought by the Boddingtons was very inconsiderable. No greater quantity was expected with any degree of certainty by the Sugar Cane. The salt provisions remaining in store (by a calculation made up to the 28th) were sufficient for only fourteen weeks at the full ration, including what had been received by the Boddingtons, and some surplus provisions which had been purchased of the agent to the contractor, and one hundred casks of pork, which had been omitted by an oversight in the last account taken in May a few days before the Kitty sailed. When it was considered

sidered

fidered that our fupplies would always be affected by commotions at
home, and that if a war fhould take place between England and any
other nation, which at the departure of the Boddingtons was hourly
expected, they might be retarded, or taken by the enemy, the lieutenant-governor determined, while he had in his own hands the means
of fupplying himfelf, to employ them; and on the 26th chartered the
Britannia for India. Our principal want was falt provifions; of flour
we well remembered that Bengal produced none, and a coming crop
was before us on our own grounds. The Britannia was therefore to
proceed to Bengal, to be freighted by the government of that prefi-
dency with falt provifions, Irifh beef or pork; and in the event of its
not being poffible to procure them, the fhip was to return loaded with
fugar, rice, and dholl, thefe being the articles which, next to falt provifions, were the moft wanted in the colony.

Mr. Raven, the mafter of the Britannia, having, as was before obferved, left a mate and fome of his people at Dufky Bay in New Zealand, the lieutenant-governor directed the Francis to be got ready
with all expedition, purpofing that fhe fhould accompany the Britannia as far on her way as that harbour, where fhe had permiffion
to touch; and Mr. Raven was directed to tranfmit by the mafter all
fuch information refpecting that extenfive bay, and the feal-fifhery in
its vicinity, as he fhould be of opinion might in anywife tend to the
prefent or future benefit of his Majefty's fervice as connected with
thefe fettlements.

The clergyman having completed the building which he began in
July laft, divine fervice was performed in it for the firft time on Sunday the 25th of this month; and for a temporary accommodation it
appeared likely to anfwer very well. Mr. Johnfon in his difcourfe,
which was intended to imprefs the minds of his audience with the
neceffity of holinefs in every place, lamented that the urgency of public works had prevented any undertaking of the kind before, and had
thus thrown it upon him; he declared that he had no other motive for
ftanding forward in the bufinefs, than that of eftablifhing a place fhel-
tered from bad weather, and from the fummer heats, where public
worfhip might be performed. He faid, that the uncertainty of a place
where they might attend had prevented many from coming; but he

now

now hoped the attendance would be full whenever he preached there.
The place was constructed to hold five hundred people.

It appeared by an estimate which Mr. Johnson afterwards gave in,
for the purpose of being reimbursed what it had cost him, that the expence of this building considerably exceeded his first calculation, the
whole amount of it being 67 l. 12 s. 11¼ d. ; of which Mr. Johnson
paid to the different artificers he had employed 59 l. 18 s. in dollars ;
twenty gallons and a half of spirits ; one hundred and sixteen pounds
of flour; fifty-two pounds of salt provisions; three pounds of tobacco;
and five ounces of tea. Spirits were at this time sold in the colony at
ten shillings per gallon; but Mr. Johnson observed in his estimate,
that he only charged that and other articles at the prices which they
had actually cost him. This account Mr. Johnson requested might be
transmitted to the secretary of state, and he accompanied it with a
letter stating his reasons for having undertaken the building.

The Boddingtons was cleared of her cargo, and discharged from
Government employ on the 26th. The cargo, when landed, was
found in most excellent condition, not a single article being damaged ;
far different from that received by the Bellona, where the ship was
overloaded. Had the Boddingtons been coppered, no ship could have
been better calculated for the transport of provisions to this country
from any part of the world.

A remarkable instance of fecundity in a female goat occurred at the
house of one of the superintendants at Sydney. She produced five
kids, three females and two males, all of which died, (a blow which
the animal received bringing them before their time,) excepting the
first which was kidded, a female. The same goat in March last
brought four kids, three males and one female, all of which lived.
She was a remarkably fine creature.

Much apprehension was now entertained for the wheat, which
began to look yellow and parched for want of rain. Toward the
latter end of the month, however, some rain fell during three days
and nights, which considerably refreshed it. But there being no fixed
period at which wet weather was to be expected in this country, it
might certainly be pronounced too dry for wheat.

An

An unpleasant accident occurred at the lieutenant-governor's farm. A convict of good character, who had the care of the sheep, was found dead in the woods. He had declined coming in to his breakfast, and was left eating some bread made of Indian corn and coarse-ground wheat. His body was opened, but no cause for his sudden dissolution could be assigned from its appearance.

At the Ponds, a district of settlers in the neighbourhood of Parramatta, John Richards, in possession of a grant of thirty acres of land, died of intoxication. This was the first death which had occurred among any of the people of that description.

By an account taken of the provisions remaining in store on the 28th of the month, it appeared that we had, (calculating each article at the established ration for two thousand eight hundred and forty-five persons, the numbers victualled at Sydney and Parramatta,)

			lbs.
Flour,	to last 4 weeks,	or	91,040
Beef,	3 ditto,	or	59,745
Pork,	11 ditto,	or	125,180
Wheat,	1 ditto,	or	22,760
Gram and Pease,	8 ditto,	or	68,280
Sugar,	3 ditto,	or	3,200
Paddy,			43,000

September.] Unproductive as the Indian corn proved which was sown last year on the public grounds, the settlers must have had a better crop; for, after reserving a sufficiency for seed for the ensuing season, and for their domestic purposes, a few had raised enough to enable them to sell twelve hundred bushels to Government, who, on receiving it into the public stores, paid five shillings per bushel to the bringer. Government, however, was not resorted to in the first instance by the settler, who preferred disposing of his corn where he could receive spirits in payment, (which he retailed for labour) to bringing it to the commissary for five shillings a bushel; but at this price, from whose hands soever it might come, it was received into the public stores.

The

The Britannia and Francis schooner sailed on Sunday the 8th for Dusky Bay. The Francis was manned with seamen and boys who had been left here from ships, and the master had for his assistant as mate Robert Watson, who formerly belonged to his Majesty's ship Sirius, and was afterwards a settler at Norfolk Island; but his allotment having been erroneously surveyed, he, being obliged to resign a part of it, gave up the whole, and gladly returned to his former way of life. One of the three seamen who had been taken out of the Kitty, and punished, was permitted to enter on board the schooner; another of them was taken by the captain of the Boddingtons; Williams, the principal, remained in the colony, not bearing that sort of character which would recommend him to any master of a ship.

Captain Nicholas Nepean, the senior captain in the New South Wales corps, having been for some time past in an ill state of health, obtained the lieutenant-governor's leave to return to England by the way of Bengal, and quitted the colony in the Britannia. Three men and one woman also received permission to leave the settlement.

It might have been supposed, that the fatal consequences of endeavouring to seek a place in the woods of this country where they might live without labour had been sufficiently felt by the convicts who arrived here in the Queen transport from Ireland, to deter others from rushing into the same error, as they would, doubtless, acquaint the new comers with the ill success which attended their schemes of that nature. Several of those, however, who came out in the Boddingtons went off into the woods soon after their landing; and a small party, composed of some desperate characters, about the same time stole a boat from Mr. Schaffer, the settler, with which, as they were not heard of for some days after, it was supposed they had either got out of the harbour, or were lying concealed until, being joined by those who had taken to the woods, they could procure a larger and a safer conveyance from the country.

A slight change took place in the ration this month; the sugar being expended, molasses was ordered to be served in lieu of that article, in the proportion of a pint of molasses to a pound of sugar.

On Sunday the 15th died James Nation, a soldier in the New South Wales corps, into which he had entered from the marine detachment.

He

He funk under an inflammatory complaint brought on by hard drinking. With this perfon Martha Todd cohabited at the time of her deceafe, which, as before related, was occafioned by the fame circumftance, and which, together with her death, Nation had been frequently heard to fay was the caufe of much unhappinefs to him.

On Tuefday the 17th the fignal was made at the South Head, and about fix o'clock in the evening the Sugar-Cane tranfport anchored in the cove from Cork, whence fhe failed the 13th of laft April, having on board one hundred and ten male and fifty female convicts, with a ferjeant's party of the New South Wales corps as a guard. Nothing had happened on board her until the 25th of May, when information was given to Mr. David Wake Bell, the agent on the part of Government, that a mutiny was intended by the convicts, and that they had proceeded fo far as to faw off fome of their irons. Infinuations were at the fame time thrown out, of the probability of their being joined by certain of the failors and of the guard. The agent, after making the neceffary inquiry, thought it indifpenfable to the fafety of the fhip to caufe an inftant example to be made, and ordered one of the convicts who was found out of irons to be executed that night. Others he punifhed the next morning; and by thefe meafures, as might well be expected, threw fuch a damp on the fpirits of the reft, that he heard no more during the voyage of attempts or intentions to take the fhip.

Since the arrival of the Boddingtons many circumftances refpecting the intended mutiny in that fhip had been difclofed by the convicts themfelves which were not before known. They did not hefitate to fay, that all the officers were to have been murdered, the firft * mate and the agent excepted, who were to be preferved alive for the purpofe of conducting the fhip to a port, when they likewife were to be put to death.

As intentions of this kind had been talked of in feveral fhips, the military guard fhould never have been lefs than an officer's command, and that guard (efpecially when embarked for the fecurity of a fhip

_____
* Mr. Duncan M'Ever. He belonged to the Atlantic, which fhip he quitted at Bengal.

full

full of wild lawlefs Irifh) ought never to have been compofed either of young foldiers, or of deferters from other corps.

This fhip had a quick paffage from Rio de Janeiro, arriving here in fixty-five days from that port. She brought the following quantity of provifions and ftores for the colony :

Beef,	- - -	46 tierces,	15,496, }	31,496 pounds ;
Shipped at Cork,	-	80 barrels,	16,000, }	
Pork,	- - -	92 tierces,	29,440, }	45,440 pounds ;
Shipped at Cork,	-	80 barrels,	16,000, }	
Flour,	- - -	192 barrels,	-	64,512 pounds ;
Lime-ftone, fhipped at Cork,	-	-	-	44 tons ;
Clothing and neceffaries,	-	-	-	17 bales and 5 cafes.

The convicts arrived in a very healthy ftate, nor was any one loft by ficknefs during the voyage.

Captain Paterfon, of the New South Wales corps, an account of whofe journies in Africa appeared in print fome years ago, conceiving that he might be able to penetrate as far as, or even beyond, the weftern mountains, (commonly known in the colony by the name of the Blue Mountains, from the appearance which land fo high and diftant generally wears,) fet off from the fettlement with a fmall party of gentlemen, (Captain Johnfton, Mr. Palmer, and Mr. Laing the affiftant-furgeon,) well provided with arms, and having provifions and neceffaries fufficient for a journey of fix weeks, to make the attempt. Boats were fent round to Broken Bay, whence they got into the Hawkefbury, and the fourth day reached as far as Richmond Hill. At this place, in the year 1789, the governor's progrefs up the river was obftructed by a fall of water, which his boats were too heavy to drag over. This difficulty Captain Paterfon overcame by quitting his large boats, and proceeding from Richmond Hill with two that were fmaller and lighter. He found that this part of the river carried him to the weftward, and into the chafm that divided the high land feen from Richmond Hill. Hither, however, he got with great difficulty and fome danger, meeting in the fpace of about ten miles with not lefs than five waterfalls, one of which was rather fteep, and was running at the rate of ten or twelve miles an hour. Above this part the water was about fifteen yards from fide to fide, and came down with
fome

some rapidity, a fall of rain having swollen the stream. Their navigation was here so intricate, lying between large pieces of rock that had been borne down by torrents, and some stumps of trees which they could not always see, that (after having loosened a plank in one boat, and driven the other upon a stump which forced its way through her bottom) they gave up any further progress, leaving the western mountains to be the object of discovery at some future day. It was supposed that they had proceeded ten miles farther up the river than had ever before been done, and named that part of it which until then had been unseen, " the Grose ;" and a high peak of land, which they had in view in the chasm, they called " Harrington Peak." .

Captain Paterson, as a botanist, was amply rewarded for his labour and disappointment by discovering several new plants. Of the soil in which they grew, he did not, however, speak very favourably.

He saw but few natives, and those who did visit them were almost unintelligible to the natives of this place who accompanied him. He entertained a notion that their legs and arms were longer than those of the inhabitants of the coast. As they live by climbing trees, if there really was any such difference, it might perhaps have been occasioned by the custom of hanging by their arms and resting on their feet at the utmost stretch of the body, which they practise from their infancy. —The party returned on the 22d, having been absent about ten days.

In their walk to Pitt Water, they met with the boat which had been stolen by some of the Irish convicts; and a few days after their return some of those who had run into the woods came into Parramatta, with an account of two of their party having been speared and killed by the natives. The men who were killed were of very bad character, and had been the principals in the intended mutiny on board the Boddingtons. Their destruction was confirmed by some of the natives who lived in the town.

The foundation of another barrack for officers was begun in this month. For the privates one only was yet erected ;. but this was not attended with any inconvenience, as all those who were not in quarters had built themselves comfortable huts between the town of Sydney and the brick-kilns. This indulgence might be attended with some convenience to the soldiers; but it had ever been considered, that soldiers

. B 3   could

could no where be so well regulated as when living in quarters, where, by frequent inspections and visitings, their characters would be known, and their conduct attended to. In a multiplicity of scattered huts, the eye of vigilance would with difficulty find its object, and the soldier in possession of a habitation of his own might, in a course of time, think of himself more as an independent citizen, than as a subordinate soldier.

On the 23d the first part of the cargo of the Sugar Cane was delivered, and in a very few days all that she had on board on account of government was received into the store, together with some surplus provisions of the contractor's. The convicts which she brought out were, very soon after her arrival, sent to the settlements up the harbour. At these places the labouring people were employed, some in getting the Indian corn for the ensuing season into such ground as was ready, and others in preparing the remainder. At the close of the month, through the favourable rains which had fallen, the wheat in general wore the most flattering appearance, giving every promise of a plenteous harvest. At Toongabbe the wheat appeared to bid defiance to any accident but fire, against which some precautions had however been judiciously and timely taken. From this place, and from the settlers, a quantity of corn sufficient to supply all our numbers for a twelvemonth was expected to be received into the public granaries, if those who looked so far forward, and took into their calculation much corn not yet in ear, were not too sanguine in their expectations.

CHAP. XXIII.

October.] THE Boddingtons and Sugar Cane being both bound for
the same port in India, (Bengal,) the masters agreed to proceed together;
and on the 13th, the Sugar Cane having set up her rigging, and hurried
through such refitting as was indispensably necessary, both ships left
the harbour with a fair wind, purposing to follow in the Atlantic's
track. The master of the Boddingtons was furnished by us with a
copy of a chart made on board the Pitt Indiaman, and brought hither
by the Britannia, of a passage or channel found by that ship in the land
named by Lieutenant Shortland New Georgia; which channel was
placed in the latitude of 8° 30' S. and in the longitude of 158° 30' E.
and named " Manning's Straits," from the commander of the Pitt.

The master of the Sugar Cane, had he been left to sail alone, determined to have tried the passage to India by the way of the South Cape
of this country, instead of proceeding to the northward, and seemed
not to have any doubt of meeting with favourable winds after rounding
the cape. By their proceeding together, however, it remained yet to be
determined, whether a passage to India round the South Cape of this
country was practicable, and whether it would be a safer and a shorter
route than one through Endeavour or Torres's Straits, the practicability
of which was likewise undetermined as to any knowledge which was
had of it in this colony.

Seven persons whose terms of transportation had expired, were permitted to quit the colony in these ships, and the master of the Sugar

Cane had shipped Benjamin Williams, the last of the Kitty's people who remained undisposed of. One free woman, the wife of a convict, took her passage in the Sugar Cane.

Notwithstanding the facility with which passages from this place were procured, (very little more being required by the masters than permission to receive them, and that the parties should find their own provisions,) it was found after the departure of these ships that some convicts had, by being secreted on board, made their escape from the colony; and two men, whose terms as convicts had expired, were brought up from the Sugar Cane the day she sailed, having got on board without permission; for which the lieutenant-governor directed them to be punished with fifty lashes each, and sent up to Toongabbe.

Early in the month an alteration took place in the weekly ration, the four pounds of wheat served to the convicts were discontinued, and a substitution of one pint of rice, and two pints of gram, (an East India grain resembling dholl,) took place. The serving of wheat was discontinued for the purpose of issuing it as flour; to accomplish which a mill had been constructed by a convict of the name of James Wilkinson, who came to this country in the Neptune. His abilities as a millwright had hitherto lain dormant, and perhaps would longer have continued so, had they not been called forth by a desire of placing himself in competition with Thorpe the millwright sent out by government.

His machine was a walking mill, the principal wheel of which was fifteen feet in diameter, and was worked by two men; while this wheel was performing one revolution, the mill-stones performed twenty. As it was in opposition to the public millwright that he undertook to construct this mill, he of course derived no assistance whatever from Thorpe's knowledge of the business, and had to contend not only with his opinion, but the opinion of such as he could prejudice against him. The heavy part of the work, cutting and bringing in the timber, and afterwards preparing it, was performed by his fellow-prisoners, who gave him their labour voluntarily. He was three months and five days from taking it in hand to his offering it for the first trial. On this trial it was found defective in some of the machinery, which was all constructed of the timber of the country, and not properly seasoned. Its effects in grinding were various; at first it

3   would

would grind no more than two bushels an hour; with some alteration, it ground more, and did for some time complete four bushels; it afterwards ground less, and at the end of the month produced not more than one bushel. Had the whole of the machinery been upon a larger scale, there was reason to suppose it would have answered every expectation of the most interested. The constructor, however, had a great deal of merit, and perceiving himself what the defects were in this, he undertook to make another upon a larger scale at Sydney, and on an improved plan. For this purpose, all the artificers and a gang of convicts were brought down from Parramatta, and were first employed in forming a timber-yard at Petersham, two hundred feet square.

At that place, a small district in the neighbourhood of Sydney so named by the lieutenant-governor, nine huts for labouring convicts were built, and sixty acres of government ground cleared of timber, twenty of which were sown with Indian corn. This was the only addition made to the public ground this season; and the sole difference that was observable in the progress of our cultivation consisted in sowing this year with wheat a large portion of that ground which last year grew Indian corn. The weather throughout the month continued extremely favourable for wheat.

The number of convicts which it was intended to receive for the present into the New South Wales corps being determined, a warrant of emancipation passed the seal of the territory, giving conditional freedom to three-and-twenty persons of that description, seven of whom were transported for life, and three had between six and nine years to serve, having been sent out for fourteen. The condition of the pardon was, their continuing to serve in the corps into which they had enlisted until they should be regularly discharged therefrom.

Several instances of irregularity and villainy among the convicts occurred during this month. From Parramatta, information was received, that in the night of the 15th four people broke into the house of John Randall, a settler, where with large bludgeons they had beaten and nearly murdered two men who lived with him. The hands and faces of these miscreants were blackened; and it was observed, that they did not speak during the time they were in the hut. It was supposed

posed that they were some of the new-comers, and meant to rob the house; and this they would have effected, but for the activity of the two men whom they attacked, and for the resistance which they met with from them. At this time seven of the male convicts lately arrived from Ireland, with one woman, had absconded into the woods. Some of these people were afterwards brought in to Parramatta, where they confessed that they had planned the robbing of the mill-house, the governor's, and other houses; and that they were to be visited from time to time in their places of concealment by others of their associates who were to reside in the town, and to supply them with provisions, and such occasional information as might appear to be necessary to their safety. They also acknowledged that the assault at Randall's hut was committed by them and their companions.

About the same time the house of Mr. Atkins at Parramatta was broken into, and a large quantity of provisions, and a cask of wine, removed from his store-room to the garden fence, where they left them on being discovered and pursued. They, however, got clear off, though without their booty.

At Sydney, in the night of the 26th, a box belonging to John Sparrow (a convict) was broke open, and three watches stolen out, one of which with the seals had cost thirty-two guineas, and belonged to an officer. This theft was committed at the hospital, where Sparrow was at the time a patient, although able to work occasionally at his business; and being a young man of abilities as a watchmaker, and of good character, was employed by most of the gentlemen of the settlement. Suspicion fell upon a notorious thief who was in the same ward, and who had some time before proposed to another man to take the box. On his examination he accused two others of the theft, but with such equivocation in his tale as clearly proved the falsehood of it. As there was no evidence against him, except the proposal just mentioned, he was discharged, and during the month nothing was heard of the watches. An old man belonging to the hospital was robbed at the same time of eight guineas and some dollars, which he had got together for the purpose of paying for his passage and provisions in any ship that would take him home.

During

During a storm of rain and thunder which happened in the after-noon of Saturday the 26th, two convict lads Dennis Reardon and William Meredith, who were employed in cutting wood just by the town when the rain commenced, ran to a tree for shelter, where they were found the next morning lying dead, together with a dog which followed them. There was no doubt that the shelter which they sought had proved their destruction, having been struck dead by light-ning, one or two flashes of which had been observed to be very vivid and near. One of them, when he received the stroke, had his hands in his bosom; the hands of the other were across his breast, and he seemed to have had something in them. The pupils of their eyes were considerably dilated, and the tongue of each, as well as that of the dog, was forced out between the teeth. Their faces were livid, and the same appearance was visible on several parts of their bodies. The tree at the foot of which they were found was barked at the top, and some of its branches torn off. In the evening they were decently buried in one grave, to which they were attended by many of their fellow-prisoners. Mr. Johnson, to a discourse which he afterwards preached on the subject, prefixed as a text these words from the first book of Samuel, chap. xx. verse 3. " There is but a step between me " and death."

This was the first accident of the kind that, to our knowledge, had occurred in the colony, though lightning more vivid and alarming had often been seen in storms of longer duration.

While every one was expecting our colonial vessel, the Francis, from New Zealand, the signal for a sail was made on the 29th ; and shortly after the Fairy, an American snow, anchored in the cove from Boston in New England, and last from the island of St. Paul, whence she had a passage of only four weeks. The master, Mr. Rogers, touched at False Bay; but from there not having been any recent arrivals from Europe, he procured no other intelligence at that port, than what we had already received. At the island of St. Paul he found five seamen who had been left there from a ship two years before, and who had procured several thousand seal-skins. They informed him, that Lord Macartney in his Majesty's ship the Lion, and the Hindostan East-Indiaman,

Indiaman, had touched there in their way to China, and Mr. Rogers expected to have heard that his lordship had visited this settlement.

The Fairy was to proceed from this place to the north-west coast of America, where the master hoped to arrive the first for the fur market. Thence he was to go to China with his skins, and from China back to St. Paul, where he had left a mate and two sailors. Their success was to regulate his future voyages.

Mr. Rogers expressed a surprise that we had not any small craft on the coast, as he had observed a plentiful harvest of seals as he came along. He came in here merely to refresh, not having any thing on board for sale, his cargo consisting wholly of articles of traffic for the north-west-coast of America.

Charles Williams, the settler so often mentioned in this narrative, wearied of being in a state of independence, sold his farm with the house, crop, and stock, for something less than one hundred pounds, to an officer of the New South Wales corps, lieutenant Cummings, to whose allotment of twenty-five acres Williams's ground was contiguous. James Ruse also, the owner of Experiment farm, anxious to return to England, and disappointed in his present crop, which he had sown too late, sold his estate with the house and some stock (four goats and three sheep) for forty pounds. Both these people had to seek employment until they could get away; and Williams was condemned to work as a hireling upon the ground of which he had been the master. But he was a stranger to the feelings which would have rendered this circumstance disagreeable to him.

The allotment of thirty acres, late in the possession of James Richards, a settler at the Ponds, deceased, was put into the occupation of a private soldier of the New South Wales corps; and a grant of thirty acres at the Eastern Farms was purchased for as many pounds by another soldier.

The greatest inconvenience attending this transfer of landed property was, the return of such a miscreant as Williams, and others of his description, to England, to be let loose again upon the public. The land itself came into the possession of people who were interested in making the most of it, and who would be more studious to raise plentiful crops for market.

                                                            Building

Building and covering the new barrack, and bringing in timber for the new mill-house, which was not to be built of brick, formed the principal labour of this month at Sydney. The shipwrights were employed in putting up the frame of a long-boat purchased of the master of the Britannia, and repairing the hoy, which had been lying for some months useless for want of repairs, having been much injured by the destructive worm that was found in the waters of this cove.

At the other settlements the convicts were employed in planting the Indian corn. About four hundred and twenty acres were planted with that article for this season's crop.

November.] In the night of Thursday the 7th of November, the Francis schooner anchored in the cove from Dusky Bay in New Zealand; her long absence from this place (nearly nine weeks) having been occasioned by meeting with contrary and heavy gales of wind. The alteration which had been made in this vessel by rigging her as a schooner instead of a sloop, for which she was built, was found to have materially affected her sailing; for a schooner she was too short, and, for want of proper sail, she did not work well. Four times she was blown off the coast of New Zealand, the Britannia having anchored in Dusky Bay sixteen days before the Francis.

Mr. Raven found in health and safety all the people whom he had left there. They had procured him only four thousand five hundred seal-skins, having been principally occupied in constructing a vessel to serve them in the event of any accident happening to the Britannia. This they had nearly completed when Mr. Raven arrived. She was calculated to measure about sixty-five tons, and was chiefly built of the spruce fir, which Mr. Raven stated to be the fittest wood he had observed there for ship-building, and which might be procured in any quantity or of any size. The carpenter of the Britannia, an ingenious man, and master of his profession, compared it to English oak for durability and strength.

The natives had never molested the Britannia's people: indeed they seemed rather to abhor them; for if, by chance, in their excursions (which were but very few,) they visited and left any thing in a hut, they were sure, on their next visit, to find the hut pulled down, and their present remaining where it had been left. Some few articles

T T   which

which Mr. Raven had himself placed in a hut, when he touched there to establish his little fishery, were found three months after by his people in the same spot.

Their weather had been very bad; severe gales of wind from the north-west and heavy rains often impeding their fishery and other labour. A shock of an earthquake too had been felt. They had an abundance of fresh provisions, ducks, wood-hens, and several other fowl; and they caught large quantities of fish. The soil, to a great depth, appeared to be composed of decayed vegetable substances.

From Mr. Raven, who had waited some days for the appearance of the Francis, the master received such assistance as he stood in need of; and on the 20th of October she sailed from Dusky Bay, in company with the Britannia, with whom she parted immediately, leaving her to pursue her voyage to Bengal.

Nothing appeared by this information from Dusky Bay, that held out encouragement to us to make any use of that part of New Zealand. So little was said of the soil, or face of the country, that no judgment could be formed of any advantages which might be expected from attempting to cultivate it; a seal fishery there was not an object with us at present, and, beside, it did not seem to promise much. The time, however, that the schooner was absent was not wholly misapplied; as we had the satisfaction of learning the event of a rather uncommon speculation, that of leaving twelve people for ten months on so populous an island, the inhabitants whereof were known to be savages, fierce and warlike. We certainly may suppose that these people were unacquainted with the circumstance of there being any strangers near them; and that consequently they had not had any communication with the few miserable beings who were occasionally seen in the coves of Dusky Bay.

A few days after the arrival of the Francis, Mr. Rogers sailed for China, taking with him two women and three men who had received permission to quit the colony. On board of the Fairy was found a convict, John Crow, who for some offence had been confined in the military guardhouse at Parramatta, whence he found means to make his escape, and reached Sydney in time to swim on board the American. On being brought on shore he received a slight punishment,

6   and

and was confined in the black hole at the guardhouse at Sydney, out of which he escaped a night or two after, by untiling a part of the roof. After this he was not heard of, till the watch apprehended him at Parramatta, where he had broken into two houses, which he had plundered, and was caught with the property upon him.

The frequency of enormous offences had rendered it necessary to inflict a punishment that should be more likely to check the commission of crimes than mere flagellation at the back of the guardhouse, or being sent to Toongabbe. Crow, therefore, was lodged in the custody of the civil power, and ordered for trial by the court of criminal judicature.

During the time the Fairy lay at anchor in this cove, a serjeant and three privates of the New South Wales corps were sent and remained on board, for the purpose of preventing all improper visitations from the shore, and inspecting whatever might be either received into or sent from the ship in a suspicious manner: a regulation from which the master professed to have found essential service, as he thereby kept his decks free from idle or bad people, and his seamen went on unmolested with the duty of the vessel.

On Saturday the 23d, the flour and rice in store being nearly expended, the ration was altered to the following proportions of those articles, viz.:

To the officers, civil and military, soldiers, overseers, and the settlers from free people, were served,

Of biscuit or flour, - - - - - -	2 pounds ;
Wheat, - - - - - -	2 pounds ;
Indian corn, - - - - - -	5 pounds ;
Pease, - - - - - -	3 pints.

To the male convicts were served, women and children receiving in the proportions always observed,

(Of biscuit or flour, none,—and for the first time since the establishment of the colony,)

Wheat, - - - - - -	3 pounds ;
Indian corn, - - - - - -	5 pounds ;
Paddy, - - - - - -	2 pints ;
Gram, - - - - - -	2 ditto.

T T 2   This

This was univerfally felt as the worft ration that had ever been ferved from his Majefty's ftores; and by the labouring convict particularly fo, as no one article of grain was fo prepared for him as to be immediately made ufe of. The quantity that was now to be ground, and the numbers who brought grain to the mill, kept it employed all the night as well as the day; and as, from the fcarcity of mills, every man was compelled to wait for his turn, the day had broke, and the drum beat for labour, before many who.went into the mill houfe at night had been able to get their corn ground. The confequence was, that many, not being able to wait, confumed their allowance unprepared. By the next Saturday, a quantity of wheat fufficient for one ferving having been paffed through the large mill at Parramatta, the convicts received their ration of that article ground coarfe.

The lumber yard near Sydney being completed, the convict millwright Wilkinfon was preparing his new mill with as much expedition as he could ufe; and John Baughan, an ingenious man, formerly a convict, had undertaken to build another mill upon a conftruction fomewhat different from that of Wilkinfon's, in which he was affifted by fome artificers of the regiment. Both thefe mills were to be erected on the open fpot of ground formerly ufed as a parade by the marine battalion.

Short as was the quantity of flour in ftore, we did not, however, defpair of being able to iffue fome meal of this feafon's growth before it could be entirely expended. About the middle of the month, the wheat that was fown in April laft, about ninety acres, being perfectly ripe, the harveft commenced, and from that quantity of ground it was calculated that upwards of twenty-two bufhels an acre would be received. Moft of the fettlers had alfo begun to reap; and they, as well as others who had grown that grain, were informed, that " Wheat " properly dried and cleaned would be received at Sydney by the " commiffary at ten fhillings the bufhel; but that none could be " purchafed from any other perfons than thofe who had grown it " on their own farms; neither could any be taken into the ftores at " Parramatta."

The precaution of receiving wheat only from thofe perfons who had raifed it on their own farms was intended to prevent the petty and

rafcally

raſcally traffic which would otherwiſe have been carried on between free people off the ſtores and perſons who might employ them to ſell the fruits of their depredations on the public and other grounds.

December.] Early in this month a criminal court was aſſembled, at which Charles Williams, a boy of fourteen years of age, and John Bevan, a notorious offender, though alſo very young, were tried for breaking into a houſe at Toongabbe; but, for want of evidence, were acquitted. John Crow was alſo tried for the burglary in the hut at Parramatta, out of which he had ſtolen a quantity of wearing apparel and proviſions; and, being clearly convicted, he received ſentence of death.

An idea very generally prevailed among the ignorant part of the convicts, that the lieutenant-governor was not authoriſed to cauſe a ſentence of death to be carried into execution, a notion that was in their minds confirmed by the mercy which he had extended to Samuel Wright, who was pardoned by him in July. It became, therefore, abſolutely neceſſary, for their own ſakes, to let them ſee that he was not only poſſeſſed of the power, but that he would alſo exerciſe it. On this account the priſoner, after petitioning more than once for a reſpite, which he received, was executed on Tueſday the 10th, eight days after his trial. There did not exiſt in the colony at this time a fitter object for example than John Crow. Unfortunately, the poor wretch to his laſt moment cheriſhed the idea that he ſhould not ſuffer; and conſequently could have been but ill prepared for the change he was about to experience. He had endeavoured to effect his eſcape by jumping down a privy a few hours before his execution; and it was afterwards found, that he had with much ingenuity removed ſome bricks in the wall of the hole in which he was confined, whence, had he obtained the reſpite of another day, he would eaſily have eſcaped.

Independent of the conſideration that this man had long been a proper object of ſevere puniſhment, to have pardoned him (even on any condition) would only have tended to ſtrengthen the ſuppoſition that the lieutenant-governor had not the power of life and death; and many daring burglaries and other enormities would have followed. Crow pretended that he was in the ſecret reſpecting the watches which were ſtolen from the hoſpital in October laſt; but all that he knew
amounted

amounted to nothing that could lead to a discovery either of them or of the thief. He did not appear to be at all commiserated or regretted by any of his fellow prisoners; a certain proof of the absence of every good quality in his character.

In the night of the 6th, during a violent storm of rain and thunder, a long-boat, which had arrived in the evening from Parramatta with grain for the next day's serving, and was then lying at the wharf on the west side under the care of a centinel, filled with the quantity of water which ran from the wharf, and sunk. By this accident two hundred and eighty bushels of Indian corn in cob, and a few bushels of wheaten meal, were totally lost. The natives who could dive availed themselves of the circumstance, and recovered a great quantity of the corn, of which they were very fond. The boats were not injured.

Sudden storms of this kind were frequent; and gusts of wind have been so sudden and violent, that ships, loosely moored, have driven at their anchors in the cove.

On Saturday the 7th a change took place in the ration; this was, the discontinuing of the three pints of pease which were served to the civil and military, and the three pints of gram which were served to the convicts, and giving them instead an equal quantity of wheat.

Notwithstanding every supply of flour which had been purchased, or received into the store from England, it was at length entirely exhausted; the civil and military receiving the last on Monday the 9th. This total deprivation of so valuable, so essential an article in the food of man happened, fortunately, at a season when its place could in some measure be supplied immediately, the harvest having been all safely got in at Toongabbe by the beginning of this month. About the middle of it, eight hundred bushels were threshed out, and on Monday the 16th the civil and military received each seven pounds of wheat coarsely ground at the mill at Parramatta. This mill, from the brittleness of the timber with which it was constructed, was found to be unequal to the consumption of the settlements. The cogs frequently broke, and hence it was not of any very great utility. To remedy this inconvenience, a convict blacksmith undertook to produce one iron hand-mill each week, for which he was to be paid at the rate of two guineas;

guineas; and by his means several mills were distributed in the settlements.

The salt meat being the next article which threatened a speedy expenditure, on Saturday the 28th one pound was taken from the weekly allowance of beef; and but a small quantity of Indian corn remaining in store, the male convicts received eight pounds of new wheat, whole; and only three pounds of Indian corn, or paddy, were served.

On Christmas day, the Reverend Mr. Johnson preached to between thirty and forty persons only, though on a provision day some four or five hundred heads were seen waiting round the storehouse doors. The evening produced a watchhouse full of prisoners; several were afterwards punished, among whom were some servants for stealing liquor from an officer.

The passion for liquor was so predominant among the people, that it operated like a mania, there being nothing which they would not risk to obtain it: and while spirits were to be had, those who did any extra labour refused to be paid in money, or any other article than spirits, which were now, from their scarcity, sold at six shillings per bottle. Webb, the settler near Parramatta, having procured a small still from England, found it more advantageous to draw an ardent diabolical spirit from his wheat, than to send it to the store and receive ten shillings per bushel from the commissary. From one bushel of wheat he obtained nearly five quarts of spirit, which he sold or paid in exchange for labour at five and six shillings per quart.

M'Donald, a settler at the Field of Mars, made a different and a better use of the produce of his farm. Having a mill, he ground and dressed his wheat, and sold it to a baker at Sydney at four-pence per pound, procuring forty-four pounds of good flour from a bushel of wheat, which was taken at fifty-nine pounds. This person also killed a wether sheep (the produce of what had been given to him by Governor Phillip) at Christmas, and sold it at two shillings per pound, each quarter weighing about fifteen pounds.

The town of Sydney had this year increased considerably; not fewer than one hundred and sixty huts, beside five barracks, having been added since the departure of Governor Phillip. Some of these huts were large, and to each of them upwards of fourteen hundred bricks
were

were allowed for a chimney and floor. These huts extended nearly to the brickfields, whence others were building to meet them, and thus to unite that diſtrict with the town.

About the latter end of the month a large party of the natives attacked ſome ſettlers who were returning from Parramatta to Toongabbe, and took from them all the proviſions which they had juſt received from the ſtore. By flying immediately into the woods, they eluded all purſuit and ſearch. They were of the Hunter's or Woodman's tribe, people who ſeldom came among us, and who conſequently were little known.

The natives who lived about Sydney appeared to place the utmoſt confidence in us, chooſing a clear ſpot between the town and the brickfield for the performance of any of their rites and ceremonies; and for three evenings the town had been amuſed with one of their ſpectacles, which might properly have been denominated a tragedy, for it was attended with a great effuſion of blood. It appeared from the beſt account we could procure, that one or more murders having been committed in the night, the aſſaſſins, who were immediately known, were compelled, according to the cuſtom of the country, to meet the relations of the deceaſed, who were to avenge their deaths by throwing ſpears, and drawing blood for blood. One native of the tribe of Cammerray, a very fine fellow named Carradah *, who had ſtabbed another in the night, but not mortally, was obliged to ſtand for two evenings expoſed to the ſpears not only of the man whom he had wounded, but of ſeveral other natives. He was ſuffered indeed to cover himſelf with a bark ſhield, and behaved with the greateſt courage and reſolution. Whether his principal adverſary (the wounded man) found that he poſſeſſed too much defenſive ſkill to admit of his wounding him, or whether it was a neceſſary part of his puniſhment, was not known with any certainty; but on the ſecond day that Carradah had been oppoſed to him and his party, after having received ſeveral of their ſpears on his ſhield, without ſuſtaining any injury, he ſuffered the other to pin his left arm (below the elbow) to

---

* So he was called among his own people before he knew us; but having exchanged names with Mr. Ball (who commanded the Supply,) he went afterwards by that name, which they had corrupted into Midjer Bool.

his

his side, without making any resistance; prevented, perhaps, by the uplifted spears of the other natives, who could easily have destroyed him, by throwing at him in different directions. Carradah stood, for some time after this, defending himself, although wounded in the arm which held the shield, until his adversaries had not a whole spear left, and had retired to collect the fragments and piece them together. On his sitting down his left hand appeared to be very much convulsed, and Mr. White was of opinion that the spear had pierced one of the nerves. The business was resumed when they had repaired their weapons, and the fray appeared to be general, men, women, and children mingling in it, giving and receiving many severe wounds, before night put an end to their warfare.

What rendered this sort of contest as unaccountable as it was extraordinary was, that friendship and alliance were known to subsist between several that were opposed to each other, who fought with all the ardour of the bitterest enemies, and who, though wounded, pronounced the party by whom they had been hurt to be good and brave, and their friends.

Possessing by nature a good habit of body, the combatants very soon recovered of their wounds; and it was understood, that Carradah, or rather Midjer Bool, had not entirely expiated his offence, having yet another trial to undergo from some natives who had been prevented by absence from joining in the ceremonies of that evening.

About this time several houses were attempted to be broken into; many thefts were committed; and the general behaviour of the convicts was far from that *propriety* which ought to have marked them. The offences were various, and several punishments were of necessity inflicted. The Irish who came out in the last ships were, however, beginning to shew symptoms of better dispositions than they landed with, and appeared only to dislike hard labour.

Among the conveniencies that were now enjoyed in the colony must be mentioned the introduction of passage-boats, which, for the benefit of settlers and others, were allowed to go between Sydney and Parramatta. They were the property of persons who had served their respective terms of transportation; and from each passenger one shilling was required for his passage; luggage was paid for at the rate of one shilling per cwt.; and the entire boat could be hired by one person for six shillings. This was a great accommodation to the description of people whom it was calculated to serve, and the proprietors of the boats found it very profitable to themselves.

The boat-builders and shipwrights found occupation enough for their leisure hours, in building boats for those who could afford to pay them for their labour. Five and six gallons of spirits was the price, and five or six days would complete a boat fit to go up the harbour; but many of them were very badly put together, and threatened destruction to whoever might unfortunately be caught in them with a fail up in blowing weather.

On the 24th ten grants of land passed the seal of the territory, and received the lieutenant-governor's signature. Five allotments of twenty-five acres each, and one of thirty, were given to six non-commissioned officers of the New South Wales corps, who had chosen an eligible situation nearly midway between Sydney and Parramatta; and who, in conjunction with four other settlers, occupied a district to be distinguished in future by the name of *Concord*. These allotments extended inland from the water's side, within two miles of the district named Liberty Plains.

The settlers at this latter place appeared to have very unproductive crops, having sown their wheat late. They were, indeed, of opinion, that they had made a hasty and bad choice of situation; but this was nothing more than the language of disappointment, as little judgment could be formed of what any soil in this country would produce until it had been properly worked, dressed, cleansed, and purged of that four quality that was naturally inherent in it, which it derived from the droppings of wet from the leaves of gum and other trees, and which were known to be of an acrid destructive nature.

Another barrack for officers was got up this month at Sydney; but, for want of tiles, was only partly covered in. The millwrights Wilkinson and Baughan had got up the frames and roofs of their respective mill-houses, and, while waiting for their being tiled, were proceeding with preparing the wood-work of their mills.

The great want of tiles that was occasionally felt, proceeded from there being only one person in the place who was capable of moulding tiles,

14

tiles, and he could never burn more than thirty thousand tiles in six weeks, being obliged to burn a large quantity of bricks in the same kilns. It required near sixty-nine thousand bricks to complete the building of one barrack, and twenty-one thousand tiles to cover it in. The number of tiles rendered useless by carriage, and destroyed in the kilns, was estimated at about three thousand in each kiln, and fifteen thousand were generally burnt off at a time.

To furnish bricks for these barracks, and other buildings, three gangs were constantly at work, finding employment for three overseers and about eighty convicts.

To convey these materials from the brickfield to the barrack-ground, a distance of about three-quarters of a mile, three brick-carts were employed, each drawn by twelve men, under the direction of one overseer. Seven hundred tiles, or three hundred and fifty bricks, were brought by each cart, and every cart in the day brought either five loads of bricks, or four of tiles. To bring in the timber necessary for these and other buildings, four timber-carriages were employed, each being drawn by twenty-four men. In addition to these, to each carriage were annexed two fallers, and one overseer, making a total of two hundred and twenty-eight men, who must be employed in any such heavy labour as the building of a barrack or a storehouse, exclusive of the sawyers, carpenters, smiths, painters, glaziers, and stone-masons, without whose labour they could not be completed.

The expence of victualling and clothing these people (both their provisions and the materials for making their clothes being augmented above their prime cost, by freight and by the cost of what might be damaged and useless) must be supposed to be considerable; and must be taken into account, together with the cost of tools and of such materials as were not to be procured in the country, when calculating the expences of the public works erected in this colony.

There died between the 1st of January and 31st of December, both inclusive, two settlers, seven soldiers, seventy-eight male convicts, twenty-six female convicts, and twenty-nine children. One male convict was executed; six male convicts were lost in the woods; one male convict was found dead in the woods; one male convict was killed by the fall of a tree, and two male convicts were killed by

lightning;

lightning; making a decrease by death and accidents of one hundred and fifty-three persons. To this decrease may be added, four male convicts, who found means to escape from the colony on board of some of the ships which had been here.

The following were the prices of grain, live and dead stock, grocery, spirits, &c. as they were sold or valued at Sydney and Parramatta at the close of the year 1793:

At SYDNEY.

Grain.

Wheat per bushel, for cash, 10s.
Ditto, in payment for labour, 14s.
Maize per bushel, for cash, 7s.
Ditto, in payment for labour, 12s. 6d.
Caffre corn 5s.
English flour per lb. 6d.
Flour of this country, for cash, 3d.
Ditto, for labour, 4d.

Vegetables.

Potatoes per cwt. 10s.
Ditto per lb. 1½d.

Live and dead stock.

Ewes (Cape) from 6l. to 8l. 8s.
Wethers (Cape) from 4l. to 5l. 10s.
She goats, full grown, 8l. 8s.
Ditto, half grown, 4l. 4s.
Male goat, full grown, 2l.
Breeding sows from 3l. to 6l.
Sucking pigs 6s.
A full grown hog from 3l. to 3l. 10s.
Turkeys per couple, nearly full grown, 2l. 2s.
Ducks per couple, nearly ditto, 10s.
Laying hens, each 5s.
A full grown cock 4s.
Half grown fowls 2s.
Chickens, six weeks old, per couple 2s.
Fresh pork per lb. 9d.
Mutton per lb. from 2s. to 2s. 6d.
Kangooroo per lb. 4d.
Salt pork per lb. 9d.
Salt beef per lb. 6d.

At PARRAMATTA.

Grain.

Wheat per bushel, for cash, 10s.
Ditto, in payment for labour, 14s.
Maize per bushel, for cash, 7s. 6d.
Ditto, in payment for labour, 10s.
Caffre corn, none.
English flour per lb. 6d.
Flour of this country, for cash, 4d.
Ditto, for labour, 6d.

Vegetables.

Potatoes per lb. 3d.
Greens per hundred 6s.

Live and dead stock.

Ewes from 4l. to 10l.
Wethers from 2l. 10s to 4l.
She goats from 4l. to 10l. 10s.
A young male goat 3l.
Breeding sows from 3l. to 7l.
Sucking pigs from 4s. to 7s. 6d.
Turkeys per couple, nearly full grown, 2l. 1s.
Ducks per couple, full grown, 1l. 1s.
Laying hens, each from 4l. to 7s. 6d.
A full grown cock 5s.
Half grown fowls 3s.
Chickens, six weeks old, per couple 2s.
Fresh pork per lb. 9d.
Mutton per lb. from 2s. to 2s. 6d.
Kangooroo per lb. 4d.
Salt pork per lb. 9d.
Salt beef per lb. 5d.

A2

At SYDNEY.

Groceries.

Tea (green) from 12s. to 16s.
Tea (black) from 10s. to 12s.
Loaf sugar per lb. 2s. 6d.
Fine moist sugar per lb. 2s.
Coarse moist sugar per lb. 1s. 6d.
Butter from 2s. per lb. to 2s 6d.
Cheese from 2s. per lb. to 2s. 6d.
Soap per lb. from 2s. to 3s.
Tobacco per lb. from 1s. to 1s. 6d.
Lamp oil, made from shark's liver, per gall. 4s.

Wine,—Spirits,—Porter.

Jamaica rum per gallon from 1l. to 1l. 8s.
Rum (American) from 16s. per gall. to 1l.
Coniac brandy per gallon from 1l. to 1l. 4s.
Cape brandy per gallon from 16s. to 1l.
Cherry brandy per dozen 3l. 12s.
Wine (Cape Madeira) per gallon 12s.
Porter per gallon from 4s. to 6s.

At PARRAMATTA.

Groceries.

Tea (green) from 16s. to 1l. 1s.
Black tea from 10s. to 16s.
Moist sugar (coarse) 2s.
Butter per lb. 2s. 6d.
Cheese per lb. 2s. 6d.
Soap per lb. 3s.
Tobacco per lb. 2s.
Lamp oil, made from shark's liver, per gall. 4s.

Wine,—Spirits,—Porter.

Neat spirits per gallon from 1l. 10s. to 2l.
Wine of the most inferior quality per gall. 16s.

The high prices of wine, spirits, and porter, proceeded not only from their scarcity, but from the great avidity with which they were procured by the generality of the people in these settlements, with whom money was of so little value, that the purchaser had been often known (instead of asking) to name himself a price for the article he wanted, fixing it at as high again would otherwise have been required of him.

The live stock in the country belonging to individuals was confined to three or four persons, who kept up the price in order to create an interest in the preservation of it. An English cow, in calf by the bull which was brought here in the Gorgon, was sold by one officer to another for eighty pounds; and the calf, which proved a male, was sold for fifteen pounds. A mare, brought in the Britannia from the Cape, was valued at forty pounds, and, although aged and defective, was sold twice in the course of a few days for that sum. It must however be remarked, that in these sales stock itself was generally the currency of the country, one kind of animals being commonly exchanged for another.

Labour

Labour was also proportionably high. For sawing one hundred feet of timber, in their own time, for individuals, a pair of sawyers demanded seven shillings; a carpenter for his day's work charged three shillings; and for splitting paling for fences, and bringing it in from the woods, they charged from one shilling and six-pence to two shillings and six-pence per hundred. An officer who had an allotment of one hundred acres of land near the town of Sydney having occasion for a hundred thousand bricks to build a dwelling-house, contracted with a brick-maker and his gang, and for that number of bricks paid him the sum of forty-two pounds ten shillings. In the fields, for cutting down the timber of an acre of ground, burning it off, and afterwards hoeing it for corn, the price was four pounds. Five-and-twenty shillings were demanded and paid for hoeing an acre of ground already cleared.

For all this labour, where money was paid, it was taken at its reputed value; but where articles were given in lieu of labour, they were charged according to the prices stated.

The masters of merchantmen, who generally made it their business immediately on their arrival to learn the prices of commodities in the colony, finding them so extravagantly high as before related, thought it not their concern to reduce them to anything like a fair equitable value; but, by asking themselves what must be considered a high price, after every proper allowance for risk, insurance, and loss, kept up the extravagant nominal value which every thing bore in the colony.

CHAP. XXIV.

A MURDER COMMITTED NEAR PARRAMATTA.—THE FRANCIS SAILS FOR
NORFOLK ISLAND.—PROVISIONS.—STORM OF WIND AT PARRAMATTA.—
CROPS.—A SETTLEMENT FIXED AT THE HAWKESBURY.—NATIVES.—
A BURGLARY COMMITTED.—SAMUEL BURT EMANCIPATED.—DEATH OF
WILLIAM CROZIER COOK.—THE WATCHES RECOVERED.—THE FRANCIS
RETURNS FROM NORFOLK ISLAND.—INFORMATION.—THE NEW ZEALAND
NATIVES SENT TO THEIR OWN COUNTRY.—DISTURBANCE AT NORFOLK
ISLAND.—COURT OF INQUIRY AT SYDNEY.—THE FRANCIS RETURNS TO
NORFOLK ISLAND.—NATIVES TROUBLESOME.—STATE OF PROVISIONS.

January 1794.] THE report that was spread in April last, of a murder having been committed on a watchman belonging to the township of Parramatta, never having been confirmed, either by finding the body among the stalks of Indian corn as was expected, or by any one subsequent circumstance, it was hoped that the story had been fabricated, and that murder was a crime which for many years to come would not stain the annals of the colony. In proportion, indeed, as our numbers increased, and the inhabitants began to possess those comforts or necessaries which might prove temptations to the idle and the vicious, that high and horrid offence might, in common with others of the same tendency, be expected to exist; but at this moment all thought their persons secure, though their property was frequently invaded. On the 5th of this month, however, John Lewis, an elderly convict, employed to go out with the cattle at Parramatta, was most barbarously murdered. The cattle, having lost their conductor, remained that night in the woods; and when they were found, the absence of Lewis excited an apprehension that some accident had happened to him. His body was not discovered however until the Wednesday following, when, by the snorting and great uneasiness of the cattle which had been driven out for the purpose, it was perceived lying in a hollow or ravine, into which it had been thrown by those who had butchered him, covered with logs, boughs, and

and grafs. Some native dogs, led by the fcent of human blood, had found it, and by gnawing off both the hands, and the entire flesh from one arm, had added confiderably to the horrid fpectacle which the body exhibited on being freed from the load of rubbifh which had been heaped upon it.

This unfortunate man had imprudently boafted of being worth much money, and that he always carried it with him fewed up in fome part of his clothes, to guard againft lofing it while abfent from his hut. If this was true, what he carried with him certainly proved his deftruction; if not, the cataftrophe muft be attributed to his indifcreet declarations. By the various wounds which he had received, it appeared that he muft have well defended himfelf, and could not have parted with his life until overpowered by numbers; for, though advanced in years, he was a ftout, mufcular man; and it was from this circumftance concluded, that more than one perfon was concerned in the murder of him. To difcover, if poffible, the perpetrators of this atrocious offence, one or two men of bad characters were taken up and examined, as well as all the people employed about the flockyard: but nothing came out that tended to fix it upon any one of them; and, defirable as it was that they fhould be brought to that punifhment which fooner or later awaited them, it was feared that until fome riot or difagreement among themfelves fhould occur, no clue would be furnifhed that would lead to their detection. The body was therefore brought in from the fpot where it had been concealed, about four miles from Parramatta, and buried at that place, after having been very carefully examined by the affiftant-furgeon Mr. Arndell.

In tracing the motives that could lead to this murder, the pernicious vice of *gaming* prefented itfelf as the firft and grand caufe. To fuch excefs was this purfuit carried among the convicts, that fome had been known, after lofing provifions, money, and all their fpare clothing, to have ftaked and loft the very clothes on their wretched backs, ftanding in the midft of their affociates as naked, and as indifferent about it, as the unconfcious natives of the country. Money was, however, the principal object with thefe people; for with money they could purchafe fpirits, or whatever elfe their paffions made them covet, and the colony could furnifh. They have been feen playing at their favourite

games

games cribbage and all-fours, for six, eight, and ten dollars each game; and those who were not expert at these, instead of pence, tossed up for dollars. Their meetings were scenes of quarrelling, swearing, and every profaneness that might be expected from the dissolute manners of the people who composed them; and to this improper practice must undoubtedly be attributed most of the vices that existed in the colony, pilferings, garden-robberies, burglaries, profanation of the Sabbath, and murder.

On the 5th the Francis sailed for Norfolk Island. The last accounts from thence were dated in March 1793; and as we were uncertain that the supplies which had been sent in the April following by Mr. Bampton had been safely landed, we became extremely anxious to learn the exact state of the settlement there. This information was all the advantage that was expected to be derived from the voyage; for, whatever Mr. King's wants might be, the stores at Sydney were incapable of alleviating them. Little apprehension was however entertained of his being in any need of supplies, as, at the date of his last letter, he reckoned that his crops of wheat and maize would produce more grain than would be sufficient for twelve months consumption.

At this time, an account of the salt provisions remaining in store at Sydney and Parramatta being taken, it appeared, that there were sufficient for only ten weeks at the ration then issued, viz. three pounds per man per week. In this situation, every addition that could be made to the ration was eagerly sought after. Wheat was paid to the industrious in exchange for labour; and those who were allowed to subsist independent of the public stores availed themselves of that indulgence to its fullest extent. It might therefore have been expected, that every advantage was taken of such a situation, and that no opportunity would be lost from which any profit could be derived. As an instance of this, one Lane, a person who had been a convict, and who was allowed to support himself how he could, was detected in buying a kangooroo of a man employed by an officer to shoot for him. The game-killer, with the assistance of six or seven greyhounds, had killed three kangooroos, two of which he brought in; the third he sold or lent to Lane, but said he had cut it up for his dogs.

As most of the officers in the colony were allowed people to shoot for them, it became necessary to make some example of the man who bought, rather than of him who sold; for it was a maxim pretty generally adopted, that the receiver was more culpable than the thief. The lieutenant-governor, therefore, ordered Lane to be punished with one hundred lashes, placed upon the commissary's books for provisions, and sent up to labour at Toongabbe.

About the middle of the month one small cow and a Bengal steer, both private property, were killed, and issued to the non-commissioned officers and privates of two companies of the New South Wales corps. This was but the third time that fresh beef had been tasted by the colonists of this country; once, it may be remembered, in the year 1788, and a second time when the lieutenant-governor and the officers of the settlement were entertained by the Spanish captains. At that time however, had we not been informed that we were eating beef, we should never have discovered it by the flavour; and it certainly happened to more than one Englishman that day, to eat his favourite viand without recognising the taste *.

The beef that was killed at this time was deemed worth eighteen-pence per pound, and at that price was sold to the soldiers. The two animals together weighed three hundred and seventy-two pounds.

About this time accounts were received from Parramatta of an uncommon storm of wind, accompanied with rain, having occurred there. In its violence it bordered on a hurricane, running in a vein, and in a direction from east to west. The west end of the governor's hut was injured, the paling round some farms which lay in its passage were levelled, and a great deal of Indian corn was much damaged. It was not however felt at Sydney, nor, fortunately, at Toongabbe; and was but of short duration; but the rain was represented as having been very heavy. The climate was well known to be subject to sudden gusts of wind and changes of weather; but nothing of this violence had been before experienced within our knowledge.

It was found that the settlers, notwithstanding the plentiful crops which in general they might be said to have gathered, gave no assist-

* We understood that the Spanish mode of roasting beef, or mutton, was, first to boil and then to brown the joins before the fire.

ance

ance to government by sending any into store. Some small quantity (about one hundred and sixty bushels) indeed had been received; but nothing equal either to the wants or expectations of government. They appeared to be most sedulously endeavouring to get rid of their grain in any way they could; some by brewing and distilling it; some by baking it into bread, and indulging their own propensities in eating; others by paying debts contracted by gaming. Even the farms themselves were pledged and lost in this way; those very farms which undoubtedly were capable of furnishing them with an honest comfortable maintenance for life.

No regular account had been obtained of what these farms had produced; but it was pretty well ascertained, that their crops had yielded at the least nearly seven thousand bushels of wheat. Of the different districts, that of Prospect Hill proved to be the most productive; some grounds there returned thirty bushels of wheat for one. Next to the district of Prospect Hill, the Northern Boundary farms were the best; but many of the settlers at the other districts ascribed their miscarriage more to the late periods at which their grounds were sown, than to any poverty in the soil; and seemed to have no doubt, if they could procure seed-wheat in proper time, (that is, to be in the ground in April,) and the season were favourable, of being repaid the expences which they had been at, and of being enabled to supply themselves and families with grain sufficient for their sustenance without any aid from the public stores.

The ground in cultivation on account of government, which had been sown with wheat, (three hundred and sixty acres,) was found to have produced about the same quantity as that raised by the settlers. Through the want of flour, the consumption of this article was however very great; and toward the latter end of the month half of the whole produce of the last season (reserving twelve hundred bushels for seed) had been issued. This afforded but a gloomy prospect; for it was much feared, that unless supplies arrived in time, the Indian corn would not be ripe soon enough to save the seed-wheat.

On the 25th, the grain from Bengal being expended, and no more Indian corn of last year's growth remaining that could be served, the public were informed, that from that time no other grain than wheat

could

could be issued; and accordingly on that day the male convicts received for their week's subsistence three pounds of pork and eight pounds of wheat. One pound of wheat more than was issued to the convicts was received on the Monday following by the civil and military.

In this unprovided state of the settlement, the return of Mr. Bampton with his promised cargo of cattle, salt provisions, rice, and dholl, began to be daily and anxiously expected. The completion of the Britannia's voyage was also looked forward to as a desirable event, though to be expected at a somewhat later period; and every shower of rain, as it tended to the benefit of the Indian corn then growing, was received as a sort of presage that at least the seed wheat, the hopes of next season, would be safe. Some very welcome rain had fallen during this month, which considerably revived the Indian corn that was first sown, and improved the appearance of that which had been sown later.

Another division of settlers was this month added to the list of those already established. Williams and Ruse, having got rid of the money which they had respectively received for their farms, were permitted, with some others, to open ground on the banks of the Hawkesbury, at the distance of about twenty-four miles from Parramatta. They chose for themselves allotments of ground conveniently situated for fresh water, and not much burdened with timber, beginning with much spirit, and forming to themselves very sanguine hopes of success. At the end of the month they had been so active as to have cleared several acres, and were in some forwardness with a few huts. The natives had not given them any interruption.

These people, however, though they had not been heard of where it might have been expected they would have proved troublesome, had not been so quiet in the neighbourhood of Parramatta. Between that settlement and Prospect Hill some settlers had been attacked by a party of armed natives and stripped of all their provisions. Reports of this nature had been frequently brought in, and many, perhaps, might have been fabricated to answer a purpose; but there was not a doubt that these people were very desirous of possessing our clothing and provisions; and it was noticed, that as the corn ripened, they constantly

stantly drew together round the settlers farms and round the public grounds, for the purpose of committing depredations.

Several gardens were robbed and some houses broken into during this 'month, the certain effect of a reduced ration. One burglary which was committed was of some magnitude, and deserving of mention. A serjeant of the New South Wales corps having been on guard, on his return to his hut in the morning, had the mortification of finding he had been robbed during his absence of a large quantity of wearing apparel, and twenty-seven pounds in guineas and dollars; in fact the thief had stripped him of all his moveable property, except only a spare suit of regimentals. The hut stood the first of a new row just without the town, and ought not to have been left without some person to take care of it. The spoil, no doubt, soon passed from one hand to another in the practice of that vice which, as already mentioned, too generally prevailed among the lower class of the people in the colony.

At Parramatta some people were taken up and punished, on being detected in issuing to themselves from the stores, where they were employed, a greater proportion of provisions than the ration. This offence had often been committed; and though it was always punished with severity, yet while convicts were employed, it was likely, notwithstanding the utmost vigilance, to continue. Vigilance seemed only to incite to deeper contrivances; and perhaps, though discoveries of this practice had often occurred, yet too many had been guilty of it with impunity, and, being alarmed, had withdrawn in time from the danger.

But very few appeared deserving of confidence; for, sooner or later, wherever it had been placed, either temptation was too strong, or opportunity proved too favourable; and many who had been deemed honest enough to be trusted ended their services by being detected in a breach of that duty which they owed to the public as a return for the faith which had been reposed in them.

This perhaps was owing to the uncertainty of reward for any services that they might render while in the class of convicts. As an exception to this rule, however, must be mentioned those people to whom unconditional emancipation had been held out at the expiration of a

7

certain

certain period, if then confidered as deferving of his Majefty's mercy as at the time of making the promife. In the hope of this reward they continued to conduct themfelves without incurring the flighteft cenfure; and one of them, Samuel Burt, was deemed, through a confcientious and rigid difcharge of his duty, to have merited the pardon he looked up to. Accordingly, on the laft day of the month he was declared abfolutely free. In the inftrument of his emancipation it was ftated, " that the remainder of his term of tranfportation was remitted " in confideration of his good conduct in difcovering and thereby pre-" venting the intended mutiny on board the Scarborough in her voyage " to this country in the year 1790, and his faithful fervices in the " public ftores under the commiffary fince his arrival." Independent of his integrity as a ftorekeeper, he was certainly deferving of fome diftinguifhing mark of favour for having been the means of faving the tranfport in which he came out at the rifk of his own life.

At the end of this month nearly four hundred acres were got ready for wheat at Sydney, and every exertion was making to increafe that quantity.

A large number of flops having been prepared, a frock, fhirt, and trowfers, were ferved out to each male convict at Sydney and the interior fettlements. Shoes were become an article of exceeding fcarcity; and the country had hitherto afforded nothing that could be fubftituted for them. A convict who underftood the bufinefs of a tanner had fhewn that the fkin of the kangooroo might be tanned; but the animal was not found in fufficient abundance to anfwer this purpofe for any number of people; and the fkin itfelf was not of a fubftance to be applied to the foling of fhoes.

Among the number of deaths this month was that of William Crozier Cook, who expired in confequence of eating two pounds of unground wheat, which was forced, by his immediately drinking a quantity of water, into the inteflines, whence it could not pafs; and though the moft active medicines were adminiftered a mortification took place in the lower part of his inteflines, which put an end to his life. Cook had, for a length of time after his arrival in this country, been a worthlefs vagabond; but had latterly appeared fenfible how much more to his advantage a different character would prove, and

had

had gained the good word and opinion of the overseers and superintendants under whom he laboured.

February.] On the 4th of this month the watches which had remained so long undiscovered were brought down from Parramatta by
Lieutenant M'Arthur. By a chain of circumstances it appeared that
they had been stolen by John Bevan, who at the time had broken out
of the prison hut at Toongabbe, and coming immediately down to
Sydney, in conjunction with Sutton, (the man who was tried for
stealing Mr. Raven's watch in October 1792,) committed the theft,
returning with the spoil to his hut at Toongabbe before he had been
missed from it by any of the watchmen. He afterwards played at
cards with another convict, and exchanged the watches for a nankeen
waistcoat and trowsers. From this man they got into the possession of
two or three other people, and were at last, by great accident, found
to be in the possession of one Batty, an overseer, in the thatch of
whose hut they, together with ten dollars, were found safe and unin-
jured. The dollars were supposed to be part of the money stolen at
the same time from Walsh at the hospital *, with whom Bevan, some
time before, had made acquaintance, winning from him not only a
hundred weight of flour, which he had almost starved himself to lay
by, but deluding him also out of the secret of his money, with every
particular that was necessary to his design of stealing it.

This was the information given against Bevan by the people through
whose hands the watches had passed; but as it was entirely unsupported by any corroborating circumstance, he was discharged without
punishment; but Batty and another man, Luke Normington, of whose
guilt there was not a doubt, received each a severe corporal punishment by order of the lieutenant-governor. In all the examinations
which took place, nothing appeared that affected Sutton, farther than
the unsupported assertions of one or two other convicts; but if Bevan
was assisted by any one, Sutton, from his general character, having
already dealt in the article of watches, was very probably his friend
on the occasion.

The constancy of this wretched young man (Bevan) was astonish-
ing. He most steadily denied knowing any thing of the transaction,

* This wretched old man did not long survive the loss of his money.

treating

treating with equal indifference both promises of rewards and threats of punishment. Crow, who was executed in December last, declared a short time before he suffered, that he had been shewn the watches by Bevan in the corn ground between Parramatta and Toongabbe; but as they had never been found in his possession, he resolved on obstinately persisting in the declaration that, however guilty of others, he was at least innocent of this offence; and he thus escaped this time from justice, to be led, perhaps at no very distant period, if not sufficiently warned, with surer step to the gallows that he had so often merited, and in the high road to which he seemed daily to be walking.

On the 12th the Francis returned from Norfolk Island, having been absent five weeks and three days.

The information received from that settlement was, that the Shah Hormuzear and Chesterfield arrived there from this place, on the 2d day of May last, when, every article of stores and provisions which had been put on board of them being safely landed, both ships sailed for India on the 27th day of the same month; Captain Bampton purposing to attempt making the passage between New Holland and New Guinea, that was expected to be found to the northward of Endeavor Straits.

While these ships were off Lord Howe Island, they experienced a heavy gale of wind, in which the Shah Hormuzear lost her topmasts, and the Chesterfield was in much danger from a leak which she sprung. Captain Bampton having, in some bad weather off Norfolk Island, lost his long-boat, he, with the assistance given him by Lieutenant-governor King, built, in ten days, a very fine one of two-and-thirty feet keel, with which he sailed, and without which it would not have been quite safe for him to have proceeded on a voyage where much of the navigation lay among islands and shoals, and where part of it had certainly been unexplored.

Mr. King had the satisfaction of stating, that his crops had been abundant, plenty reigning among all descriptions of people in the island. His wheat was cut, the first of it on the 25th of November last, and the harvest was well got in by Christmas-day. About two thousand bushels were the calculated produce of this crop, which would have been greater had it not, during its growth, been hurt by the

wind

want of rain. Of the maize, the firſt crop (having always two) was gathering while the ſchooner was there, and, notwithſtanding the drought, turned out well; from one acre and a quarter of ground, one hundred and ſix buſhels had been gathered; but it was pretty generally eſtabliſhed on the iſland, that thirty-ſix buſhels of maize might be taken as the average produce of an acre of ground.

The ſuperior fertility of the ſoil at Norfolk Iſland to that of New South Wales had never been doubted. The following account of laſt year's crop was tranſmitted by Lieutenant-governor King :

From November 1792 to November 1793 the crop of maize
    amounted to   -   -   -   -   3247 buſhels;
Wheat, -   -   -   -   -   -   1302 ditto ;
Calavances, -   -   -   -   -   50 ditto.
Purchaſed in the above time from ſettlers and others, at five
    ſhillings per buſhel,   -   3600 buſhels.
Reſerved by them for ſeed,   3000 ditto of maize ;
                        300 ditto of wheat ;
                        300 ditto of calavances; and
                        50 tons of potatoes :

Which, together with three hundred and five buſhels of maize brought from thence with the detachment of the New South Wales corps at the relief in March 1793, made a total of
                  10,152 buſhels of maize,
                  1602 ditto of wheat,
                  350 ditto of calavances,
                  50 tons of potatoes,
raiſed on Norfolk Iſland in one twelvemonth, on about two hundred and fifty-ſix acres of ground.

Of this crop, and of what had been purchaſed, there remained in the public ſtores, when the ſchooner left the iſland, forty-three weeks maize and wheat; in addition to which Lieutenant-governor King ſuppoſed he ſhould have of this ſeaſon's growth, after reſerving five hundred buſhels of wheat for ſeed, ſufficient of that article for the conſumption of ſix hundred and ninety-nine perſons *, the whole number

---

* The whole number in the ſettlement amounted to one thouſand and eight perſons.

of people victualled there from the stores for fourteen weeks and a half, at the rate of ten pounds per man per week; and fifty-eight weeks maize at twelve pounds per man per week. He had besides, at the established ration, twelve weeks beef, twenty-nine weeks pork, five weeks molasses, and thirty weeks oil and sugar. The whole forming an abundance that seemed to place the evil hour of want and distress at too great a distance to excite much alarm or apprehension of its occurring there.

The settlement had been so healthy, that no loss by death had happened since we last heard from them; and when the schooner sailed very few people were sick. There had died, between the 10th of November 1791 (the date of Lieutenant-governor King's return to the command at Norfolk Island) and the 27th of January 1794, only one soldier, forty male convicts, three female convicts, and nineteen children, making a total of sixty-three persons, in two years and sixty-eight days; and ninety-five * children had been born. Every description of stock, except some Cape sheep which did not breed, was equally healthy as the inhabitants, and were increasing fast.

On the 22d of October the Doddingtons and Sugar-Cane touched at that island, for the purpose of landing John Cole, a convict who had secreted himself on board the former of these ships. Many articles of comfort were sold among the settlers and others from the Sugar-Cane.

On the 2d of the succeeding month Mr. Raven called there in the Britannia, in his way to Bengal, to procure a supply of fresh provisions and vegetables for his people.

The two natives of New Zealand, who had been sent to Mr. King in April last by the Shah Hormuzear, having completed the purpose for which they had been sent thither, by giving such instruction in the process of preparing the flax plant, that even with very bad materials a few hands could manufacture thirty yards of good canvas in

* By the commissary's books there were, on the 20th of February 1794, two hundred and fifty-four children in the three-settlements here. On the 30th of January, by Lieutenant-governor King's return, there were one hundred and forty-eight children at Norfolk; making a total of four hundred and two children here and at Norfolk Island.

a week;

a week; and having manifested much anxiety, on the appearance of
any ship, to return to their friends and native country, though treated
with every attention and kindness that could dispel their fears and con-
ciliate their good opinion; Mr. King thought this a favourable opportunity of gratifying their wishes; and that he might himself be a
witness of their not experiencing on the voyage any interruption to
the good treatment they had met with from every one while under his
care, he determined to accompany them himself. He accordingly,
giving Mr. Raven the necessary order, embarked on board of the Britannia, with a guard from the New South Wales corps, and sailed for
New Zealand on the 9th. Their passage thither was short; for on the
fourth day, having rounded the North Cape, the two natives were
landed among some of their friends and acquaintance, though not
exactly at the district whereat their families and kindred resided (the
Bay of Islands); and Mr. King returned to Norfolk Island on the 18th,
having been ten days on board the Britannia. Captain Nepean, who
was proceeding in that ship to Europe by the way of India, remained
on shore in the government of Norfolk Island during Mr. King's absence; but, on his return, reimbarked in the Britannia; and on the
20th of the same month she sailed on the further prosecution of her
voyage.

It was not imagined that this delay in the Britannia's voyage would
be of any consequence, as Mr. Raven purposed making what is called
the Eastern Passage; that is, between the south end of Mindanao and
Borneo; and it was known that the eastern monsoon did not set well
in, nor was attended with good weather in those seas before December
or January.

Mr. King found himself compelled to send by the Francis ten soldiers
of the detachment of the New South Wales corps on duty there, under
a charge of mutinous behaviour. A jealousy which had grown up
between the soldiers and the free men, settlers and others, occasioned
by some acts of violence and improper behaviour on either side, broke
out in the evening of the 18th of last month, at a place in which the
lieutenant-governor had permitted plays to be represented by the convicts, as an innocent recreation after labour. Mr. King, who was
present, having thought it necessary to order one of the soldiers into

con-

confinement when the play was ended, the detachment repaired to
their own commanding-officer, and demanded the release of their
comrade. On his declaring his inability to comply with such request,
they signified a resolution to release him themselves; upon which the
officer remonstrated with them, and they dispersed. It did not appear
that they made any attempts to release the prisoner; but on the following morning, when the lieutenant-governor was made acquainted
with the above circumstances, he convened all the officers in the settlement, and laid before them what he had heard, together with an
account of a determination among the soldiers, to release from the
halberts any of their comrades who should be ordered punishment for
any offence or injury done to a settler; all of which he had caused
to be authenticated upon oath. The result of this meeting was, that
the detachment should be disarmed, and that the settlers late of the
marines, and Sirius's ship's company, should be embodied and armed
as a militia. This resolution was accordingly put in execution on the
21st, by sending the detachment from their quarters unarmed, upon
different duties; while the new-raised militia took possession of their
arms. On their return, twenty were selected as mutineers to be sent
to this place, the remainder returning to their duty immediately; (but
of that number ten were, after a few days confinement, pardoned and
liberated;) and two days after Mr. King had restored good order in
the settlement the Francis appeared. By her he sent the ten prisoners
under a guard of an officer and as many soldiers as the vessel could
conveniently receive.

A court of inquiry, composed of the officers of the regiment present
at Sydney, was assembled immediately after the arrival of the Francis,
to inquire into the complaint which had accompanied the soldiers from
Norfolk Island; when, after five days deliberation, and examination
of papers, witnesses, &c. they reported, that the conduct of the soldiers, in disobeying the orders of their officers, was reprehensible; but,
on considering the provocations which had given birth to that disobedience, they recommended them to their commanding officer's
clemency.

On the 27th the schooner sailed a second time for Norfolk Island,
for the purpose of conveying two officers of the New South Wales

corps,

corps, and some non-commissioned officers and privates, in lieu of those who had been sent hither, and without whom the detachment on duty there would have been too much weakened.

The natives were again troublesome this month. Two several accounts were sent down from Parramatta, of their having attacked, robbed, and beaten some of the settlers' wives who were repassing between their farms and Parramatta; and great quantities of corn continued to be stolen by them. One of these women (married to Trace, a settler at the foot of Prospect Hill) was so severely wounded by a party who robbed and stripped her of some of her wearing apparel, that she lay for a long time dangerously ill at the hospital. It was said, that the people who committed this and other acts of violence and cruelty were occasional visitors with others at Sydney. Could their persons have been properly identified, the lieutenant-governor would have taken serious notice of the offenders.

Notwithstanding the woods were infested by these people, numbers of the male convicts, idle, and dreading labour as a greater evil than the risk of being murdered, absented from the new settlements, and, after wandering about for a few days, got at length to Sydney almost naked, and so nearly starved, that in most cases humanity interfered between them and the punishment which they merited. They in general pleaded the insufficiency of the present ration to support a labouring man; but it was well known that the labour required was infinitely short of what might have been justly exacted from them, even had the ration been much less. They mostly wrought by tasks, which were so proportioned to their situation, that after the hour of ten in the forenoon their time was left at their own disposal; and many found employment from settlers and other individuals who had the means of paying them for their labour. At this period, it was true, the labouring convict was menaced with the probability of suffering greater want than had ever been before experienced in the settlement. On Saturday the 22d (the last provision-day in this month) there remained in store a quantity of salt meat only sufficient for the inhabitants until the middle of the second week in the next month, at which time there would not be an ounce of provisions left, if some supplies did not arrive before that period. But even this situation, bad

a a

as it certainly was, was still alleviated by the assistance that the officers, settlers, and others were able to afford to those whom they either retained in their service or occasionally hired for labour as they wanted them. Some who were off the store, and who well remembered their own distresses in the years 1789 and 1791, declared, that with a little industry, and being allowed the indulgence of going out in a boat, they could, even at this time, earn a better subsistence than if they were employed by Government, and fed from a full store. Nothing was lost; even the shark was found to be a certain supply; the oil which was procured from the liver was sold at one shilling the quart, and but very few houses in the colony were fortunate enough to enjoy the pleasant light of a candle.

The seed-wheat as yet escaped, and might remain untouched for another fortnight. The Indian corn was ripening; and it was hoped, that by making some little deduction from the wheat, it would be ready in time to save all the seed that had been reserved for the next season. To lose the seed-wheat would be to repel every advance which had been made toward supporting ourselves, and to crush every hope of independence. All that had been done in cultivation, every acre which was preparing for the ensuing crop, would long have remained a memorial of our distress; and where existed the mind that could have returned to the labour of the field with that cheerful spirit or energy that would have been necessary to ensure future success?

The watch at Parramatta, under the direction of Barrington the constable, ever on the look-out for the murderers of Lewis, detected a man of bad character in offering a dollar in payment for some article that he had purchased, and which dollar appeared to have been buried in the ground. He had been taken up before, and on searching him at that time was not in possession of any money. As nothing more, however, than this circumstance was adduced against him, he was discharged, it being admitted that he might have earned something since that time by his labour.

The foundation of a second barrack for soldiers at Sydney was begun in the latter part of this month; and Baughan's mill-house was covered in with tiles.

Mutton

Mutton was this month fold for one shilling and nine-pence per pound. The Bengal sheep, by crossing the breed with the Cape ram, were found to improve considerably in appearance and size.

CHAP. XXV.

ALARMING STATE OF THE PROVISIONS.—THE WILLIAM ARRIVES WITH SUPPLIES FROM ENGLAND, AND THE ARTHUR FROM BENGAL.—THE AMOR PATRIÆ NATURAL TO MAN IN ALL PARTS OF THE EARTH.—INFORMATION.—MR. BAMPTON.—CAPTAIN BLIGH.—ADMIRAL BARRINGTON TRANSPORT LOST.—FULL RATION ISSUED.—INGRATITUDE AND JUST PUNISHMENT OF THE SETTLERS.—BUFFIN'S CORN-MILL SET TO WORK.—GAMING.—HONESTY OF A NATIVE.—THE DÆDALUS ARRIVES FROM AMERICA.—INFORMATION.—FEMALE INCONSTANCY, AND ITS CONSEQUENCES.—THE ARTHUR SAILS.—THE FRANCIS RETURNS FROM NORFOLK ISLAND.—A BOAT STOLEN.—NATIVES KILLED.—A NEW MILL.—DISORDER IN THE EYES PREVALENT.

March.] TO fave as much of the feed-wheat as possible, a deduction of two pounds was made in the allowance of that article which was served to the convicts on Saturday the first of the month. The provision-store was never in so reduced a state as at this time; one serving of salt-meat alone remained, and that was to be the food of only half a week. After that period, the prospect, unless we were speedily relieved, was miserable; mere bread and water appeared to be the portion of by far the greater part of the inhabitants of these settlements, of that part too whose bodily labour must be called forth to restore plenty, and attain such a state of independence on the parent country as would render delay or accident in the transport of supplies a matter of much less moment to the colony than it had ever hitherto been considered.

As at this time the stock of swine in the possession of individuals was rather considerable, some saving of the salt provisions, it was thought, might be made, by purchasing a quantity sufficient to issue

to

to the military at the rate of four pounds and a half to each man for the week, in lieu of the three pounds of salt meat. A quantity was therefore purchased by the commissary and issued in the above proportion, the soldiers receiving the fresh instead of the salt provisions (to which latter they must have given the preference, being able to make them go the farthest) with that cheerfulness which at all times marked their conduct when compliance with any wish of their commanding-officer was the question.

Both public and private stock appeared to be threatened with destruction. The sheep and goats in the colony were not numbered far within one thousand. The cows had increased that species of stock by thirteen calves, which were produced in the last year. The exact number of hogs was not, nor could it well be ascertained; it must, however, have been considerable, as every industrious convict had been able to keep one or more breeding sows. All this wore, indeed, the appearance of a resource; yet what would it all have been (admitting that an equal partition had been made) when distributed among upwards of three thousand people? But an equal partition of private stock, as most of this was such, could not have been expected. The officers holding this stock in their own hands would certainly take care to keep it there, and from it would naturally supply their own people. How far, in an hour of such distress, the convicts would have sat quietly down on their return from labouring in the field to their scanty portion of bread and water, and looked patiently on while others were keeping want and hunger at a distance by the daily enjoyment of a comfortable meal of fresh viands? was a question with many who thought of their situation.

Happily, however, for all descriptions of people, they were not this time to be put to the trial.

On Saturday the 8th, at that critical moment when the doors of the provision-store had closed, and the convicts had received their last allowance of the salt provisions which remained, the signal for a sail was made at the South-head. We expected a ship from India in pursuance of the contract entered into with Mr. Bampton, who had been absent from us nearly eleven months. We also looked daily for the return of the Dædalus. We hoped for a ship from England.

But

But whence the ship came for which the signal had been made was to remain for some time unknown. One boat alone, with an officer, went down; (in compliance with an order which had some days before been given to that purpose;) and on its return at night we were told that a ship with English colours flying had stood into the harbour as far as Middle-head; but meeting with a heavy squall of wind at south, in which she split her fore-top-sail, was compelled again to put to sea. It was conjectured that she was a stranger; for if any person on board her had had any knowledge of the harbour, she might have been run with much ease from the Middle-head into safety in Spring-cove. The officer who went down (Captain Johnston) unfortunately could not board her, such a sea ran within the Heads; and the wind blew with so much violence as to render any attempt to get near her extremely dangerous.

At night the wind increased with much rain, and morning was anxiously looked for, to tell us where and who the stranger was. Nothing more however was known of her during that day (Sunday), the same causes as those of the preceding day operating against our receiving any other information, than that she was to be seen from the flag-staff, whence in the evening word was brought up over land, that another vessel, a brig, was in sight.

Anxiety and curiosity, now strained to the utmost, were obliged to wait the passing of another night; but about three o'clock on Monday the 10th, the wind and weather having both changed, to our great satisfaction we saw the ship William, Mr. William Folger of London master, anchor safely in the cove. With her also came up the Arthur, a small brig of about ninety-five tons, from Bengal.

The William, we found, had sailed from the river Thames on the first of July last, whence she proceeded to Cork, where she took on board a cargo of beef and pork for this colony*; but had not an ounce of flour. She left Ireland on the 20th of September, having

* She had likewise on board a machine for dressing flour; a small quantity of iron; two pairs of millstones, and some tools for the smiths; all which were received in the river.

z z   waited

waited some weeks for a convoy, (the war with France in which England was engaged having rendered the protection of some of his Majesty's ships necessary,) and made her passage to this country by the route of Rio de Janeiro. She arrived at that port on the 22d day of November; left it the third of the following month; and made Van Dieman's Land on the second of this month. Mr. Folger reported, that his weather from the American coast to this port had been in general good.

We learned that Governor Phillip reached England in the Atlantic on the 21st of May last. That ship (which it may be remembered sailed from this place on the 11th of December 1792) passed Cape Horn on the 17th of the following January; anchored at Rio de Janeiro on the 7th of February; and sailed thence on the 4th of March; arriving in the channel without any interruption, save what was given by a French privateer which chased her when within eight-and-forty hours sail of the land. The natives Benillon and Yem-mer-ra-wan-nie were well, but not sufficiently divested of the genuine, natural love for liberty and their native country, to prefer London with its pleasures and its abundance to the woods of New South Wales. They requested that their wives might be taught to expect their return in the course of this year. Had it been possible to eradicate in any breast that love for the place of our birth, or where we have lived and grown from infancy to manhood, which is implanted in us by the kind hand of Nature, it surely would have been effected on two natives of New Holland, whose country did not possess a single charm in the eye even of a savage inhabitant of New Zealand *. But we now found that in every breast that sentiment is the same; and that a love for our native country is not the result of her being the seat of arts and arms; the residence of worth, beauty, truth, justice; of all the virtues that adorn and dignify human nature; and of all the pleasures and enjoyments that render life valuable; but that it can be

---

* The New Zealanders who were brought hither in the Dædalus in April last expressed both here and at Norfolk Island the utmost abhorrence of this country and its inhabitants.

excited

excited even in a land where wretchedness, want, and ignorance have laid their iron hands on the inhabitants, and marked with misery all their days and nights.

In the William arrived an assistant-chaplain, the Rev. Mr. Marsden, to divide the religious duties of the colony with Mr. Johnson.

Had it been known on the evening of the 8th, when the report was received that the ship had been blown out to sea, that she contained so valuable a cargo as four months beef and pork (eleven hundred and seventy-three barrels of the former, and nine hundred and seven of the latter) at the full ration, how would our anxiety have been increased upon her account, particularly as it still lived in our remembrance, that the Justinian with a similar cargo, after making the North-head of this harbour, was blown off to the Northward, was three weeks before she regained the port, and was once within that time nearly lost in a heavy gale of wind! Had the William been blown off the coast for three weeks, how deeply would distress have been felt in these settlements!

The brig from Bengal had on board a small quantity of beef and pork; some sugar, Bengal rum, and coarse callicoes.

To the great surprise and regret of every one, it was heard from Mr. Barber the master, that at the time of his departure from Calcutta, no accounts had been received of the arrival of Mr. Bampton in any port in India.

' As well at his departure from Norfolk Island, as when he quitted this place, he had expressed his resolution of attempting a passage between this country and New Guinea, in the hope of being, if successful, the first to establish a fact that would be attended with singular advantages to his Majesty's settlements in this part of the world.

Captain Bligh, of the happy conclusion of whose second voyage for the bread fruit we now heard by the William, was particularly instructed to survey the straits which separate New Holland from New Guinea. By the accounts of his voyage which reached us, we found that the two ships Providence and Assistance were twenty days from their entrance into the strait to their finding themselves again in an open sea. The navigation through this passage was described as the

Z Z 2　　　　　　　　　　　most

moft dangerous ever performed by any navigator, abounding in every
direction with iflands, breakers, and fhoals, through which they purfued their courfe with the utmoft difficulty. In one day, on anchoring to avoid danger, the Providence broke two of her anchors; and as
the eaftern monfoon was blowing, (the month of September 1792,)
and the paffage which they were exploring was extremely narrow, it
became impoffible to beat back. From fome of the iflands, eight canoes formed the daring attempt of attacking the armed tender, and
with their arrows killed one and wounded two of the feamen. Some
of thefe canoes were fixty or feventy feet long, and in one of them
twenty-two perfons were counted.

This account excited many apprehenfions for Mr. Bampton's fafety.
On taking his leave of Lieutenant-governor King, he affured him that
he hoped to fee Norfolk Ifland again in November, expecting to be
here early in the month of October. It was known that he had on
board fome articles of merchandize which he meant to difpofe of at
Batavia; but by accounts received at Calcutta from that place a very
fhort time before the Arthur failed, he had not touched at that port.
It was therefore more than probable, that both the Shah Hormuzear
and Chefterfield had been wrecked on fome of the fhoals with which
the ftrait abounded, and that their officers and people, taking to their
long-boats, had fallen facrifices to the natives who had attacked the
Affiftance, by whofe guns many had been wounded in their attempt
to carry that veffel.

To the difappointment which the colony fuftained from the failure
of the contract already mentioned for cattle and provifions which were
to have been brought hither by Mr. Bampton, was added the regret
which every thinking being among us felt on contemplating the calamitous moments that had, in all probability, brought deftruction on fo
many of our fellow-creatures.

Mr. Barber alfo informed us, that Captain Patrickfon, who was here
in the Philadelphia brig in October 1792, had purchafed or hired a
large fhip, on board of which he had actually put a quantity of provifions and other articles, with which he defigned to return to this
country; but under fome apprehenfion that his cargo might poffibly
not

not be purchased, he gave up the intention, and when the Arthur
failed was left proceeding to Europe under Imperial colours.

The Government of Bengal too had advertised for terms to freight
a vessel for this country with cattle and provisions; but were diverted
from the design by the equipment of the armaments which it was necessary to enter into at that time.

Thus had the infant colony of New South Wales still been doomed
to be the sport of contingency, the jarring interests of men co-operating
with the dangers of the sea to throw obstacles in the way of that long-
desired independence which would free the mother country from a
heavy expence, and would deliver the colonists from the constant apprehension under which they laboured, of being one day left to seek
their subsistence among the woods of the country, or along the shores
of its coast *.

The report of the probable loss of the Admiral Barrington transport,
which was received here in February 1793, was now confirmed. It
appeared, that after sailing from Batavia she reached so near her port
as to be in sight of the shipping at Bombay, but was driven off the
coast by a gale of wind, in which she was forced on shore on one of
the Malouine Islands, where she was wrecked, and her crew (the
master, chief mate, and surgeon excepted) were murdered by the
natives. These people saved themselves by swimming to an East-India
country ship which was riding at anchor near the island.

The sight of two vessels at anchor in the cove laden with provisions
gave at this time greater satisfaction than had been known on any
other arrival; for never before had the colony verged so near to the
point of being without a pound of salt provisions. On Monday the
10th, (the issuing-day to the civil and military,) when all were served
their provisions, there remained only eighteen hundred and three
pounds of salt meat in store; and even this quantity had been saved by

* It had been proposed, on the account reaching Bengal of the loss of his Majesty's
ship Guardian, to raise by subscription a sum sufficient to purchase and freight a ship
with provisions to this country; but, from some accident or other, this benevolent purpose was never put in execution.

issuing

issuing fresh pork to the non-commissioned officers and men of the regiment on the two last serving-days *.

In consequence of these fortunate arrivals, the full ration of salt meat was ordered to be issued; and as soon as part of the cargo was got on shore from the storeship, the deficiency on the last serving days was completed to the full allowance. The last of the wheat was served on the 17th, (a proper quantity being reserved for seed,) and on the next provision-day ten pounds of Indian corn were substituted instead of the allowance of wheat. Nothing but dire necessity could have induced the gathering and issuing this article in its present unripened state, the whole of it being soft, full of juice, and wholly unfit to grind. Had the settlers, with only a common share of honesty, returned the wheat which they had received from Government to sow their grounds the last season, the reproach which they drew upon themselves, by not stepping forward at this moment to assist Government, would not have been incurred; but though, to an individual, they all knew the anxiety which every one felt for the preservation of the seed-wheat, yet when applied to, and told (in addition to the sum of ten shillings per bushel) that any quantity which they might choose to put into the store should be brought from their farms without any expence of carriage to them, they all, or nearly all, pleaded an insufficiency to crop their ground for the ensuing season; a plea that was well known to be made without a shadow of truth. In consequence of this refusal, (for their excuses amounted to as much,) the lieutenant-governor directed all those settlers †, whose limited time ‡ for being victualled from the public stores had expired, to be struck off the provision list, and left to provide for themselves, a very just punishment for their ingratitude; for some had been fed and supplied from the colonial stores for more than twelve months beyond the time prescribed for them when they were settled. This indulgence had been

---

* Saved on the 3d and 10th of March by issuing fresh pork to the non-commissioned officers and privates of the New South Wales corps, their wives and children,   1803 lbs.
There were issued to the above people,   -   -   -   -   fresh pork,   5094' lbs.
The hogs that were purchased on this occasion from individuals cost government the sum of 254 l. 19 s. 6 d.

† Sixty-three in number.   ‡ Eighteen months.

continued

continued to them from quarter to quarter on account of bad crops, unfavourable seasons, and the reduced ration, with which all of them, more or less, had had to struggle; and every accommodation had constantly been afforded them which was consistent with the situation of the colony. It was, however, now seen, that they were not the description of settlers from whom, whatever indulgences they might receive, Government had any assistance to expect; their principal object was their own immediate interest; and to serve that, they would forget every claim which the public had upon them.

The small cargo of salt provisions brought by the brig from Bengal was purchased on account of Government for 307¹. 16s.; the beef at five-pence and the pork at eight-pence per pound; the remainder of her cargo was purchased by the officers of the civil and military departments. The cargo of the William, which arrived in very good order, was all landed, and the ship cleared and discharged from Government employ on the 28th.

The Rev. Mr. Marsden entered on the duties of his function the first Sunday after his arrival, preaching to the military in a barrack prepared for the occasion in the forenoon, and to the convicts at the church erected by Mr. Johnson in the afternoon.

On the day when the William anchored in the cove Bussin's new mill was completed and set to work; and Wilkinson's was in some forwardness. At first it went rather heavily; but in a few days, with nine men's labour, it ground sixty-three pounds of wheat in seventeen minutes. It must be observed, that not any mill was yet erected in the colony whereat corn was ground for the public, the military as well as the convicts grinding their own grain themselves. Whenever wind or water-mills should be erected, this labour would be saved, and the allowance of wheat or Indian corn be issued ground and dressed.

The late distress of the colony was not found to have made any amendment in the morals of the convicts. Gaming still prevailed among them in its fullest extent; and a theft which was committed at one of these meetings shewed how far it was carried. Among those who made a daily practice of gaming was one who, in his situation as an overseer, had given such offence to some of his fellow-prisoners, that

that a plan was formed to plunder him the first time that he should
have a sum worthy of their attention.   He was accordingly surrounded
when engaged at play, by a party who, watching their opportunity,
rushed upon him when he had won a stake of five-and-twenty dollars,
and, in the confusion that ensued, secured the whole.   He was, however, fortunate enough to seize one of them, with ten of the dollars in
his hand, but was not able to recover any more.   The man whom he
secured proved to be Samuel Wright, who in the month of July last
had been reprieved at the foot of the gallows; so soon had he forgotten the terror of that moment.   On this circumstance being reported
to the lieutenant-governor, Wright received an immediate corporal
punishment.

M'Koy, the overseer, confessed that gaming had been for many
years his profession and subsistence, though born of honest and reputa-
ble parents; and he acknowledged, that but for his pursuit of that
vice he should never have visited this country in the situation of a
convict.

A better principle shewed itself shortly after in Ca-ru-ey, a native
youth, who, from long residence among us, had contracted some of
our distinctions between good and ill.   Being fishing one morning in
his canoe near the lieutenant-governor's farm, he perceived some convicts gathering and secreting the Indian corn which grew there; and,
knowing that acts of that nature were always punished, he instantly
came to the settlement, and gave an account of what he had seen, in
time to secure the offenders on the spot, with the corn in their possession.

As he made no secret of what he had done, it was apprehended that
some revenge might, if they were punished, be levelled at him on a
future opportunity, they were therefore pardoned; but Ca-ru-ey was
nevertheless applauded and recompensed for his attention and honesty.

Among other articles of information received by the William, we
were assured, that it had been industriously circulated in England, that
there was not in this country either grass for graminivorous animals,
or vegetables for the use of man.   This report was, however, rather
forcibly contradicted by the abundant increase of all descriptions of
live stock at this time in the colony, and by the plenty which was to

3   be

be found in every garden, whether cultivated by the officer or by the
convict. A striking instance of this plenty occurred at Parramatta a
few days before the arrival of the storeship, when six tons and two
hundred weight of potatoes were gathered as the produce of only
three quarters of an acre of ground. From the then reduced state of
the stores, they were sold for fifty pounds.

Mutton was sold in this month for one shilling and nine-pence per
pound.

April.] In the forenoon of Thursday the 3d of April, the signal
was made at the South-head for a sail, and about four o'clock the
Dædalus storeship anchored in the cove from the north-west coast of
America; but last from Owhyhee, one of the Sandwich Islands, from
which place she sailed on the 8th day of February last.

Lieutenant Hanson, on his arrival at Nootka Sound the 8th of last
October, found only a letter from Captain Vancouver, directing him
to follow the Discovery to another port; between which and Nootka
he fortunately met with her and the Chatham, and was afterwards
obliged to proceed with them to the Sandwich Islands, before Captain
Vancouver could take out of the Dædalus the stores which were consigned to his charge. The harbour of Nootka was still in the hands
of the Spaniards, and some jealousy on their part prevented the
delivery of the stores from the vessel in any of the Spanish ports on
the coast.

Mr. Hanson was informed, that three natives of Whahoo (the
island whereat his predecessor in the Dædalus, Lieutenant Hergest,
with the astronomer, Mr. Gooch, and the seaman were killed,) had
been delivered up by the chief of the island to Captain Vancouver,
for the purpose of being offered as an expiatory sacrifice for those
murders; and that they were accordingly, after remaining some short
time on board the Discovery, taken one by one into a canoe, and put
to death alongside that ship by one of their chiefs. A pistol was the
instrument made use of on this occasion, which certainly was as extraordinary as unexpected.

The great accommodation which those islands proved to ships trading on the north-west coast of America rendered it absolutely necessary, that the inhabitants should be made to understand that we never

3 A   would

would nor could pafs unnoticed an act of fuch atrocity. With this view Captain Vancouver had demanded of the chief of Whahoo the murderers of Mr. Hergeft and his unfortunate companions. It was not fuppofed that the people facrificed were the actual perpetrators of thefe murders; but that an equal number of the natives had been given up as an atonement for the Europeans we had loft.

The native of this country who accompanied Lieutenant Hanfon we had the fatisfaction of feeing return fafe in the Dædalus. He had conducted himfelf with the greateft propriety during the voyage, readily complying with whatever was required of him, and not incurring, in any one inftance, the diflike or ill-will of any perfon on board the fhip. Wherever he went he readily adopted the manners of thofe about him; and when at Owhyhee, having difcovered that favours from the females were to be procured at the eafy exchange of a looking-glafs, a nail, or a knife, he was not backward in prefenting his little offering, and was as well received as any of the white people in the fhip. It was noticed too that he always difplayed fome tafte in felecting the object of his attentions. The king of Owhyhee earneftly wifhed to detain him on the ifland, making fplendid offers to Mr. Hanfon, of canoes, warlike inftruments, and other curiofities, to purchafe him; but if Mr. Hanfon had been willing to have left him, Collins would not have confented, being very anxious to return to New South Wales.

He did not appear to have acquired much of our language during his excurfion; but feemed to comprehend a great deal more than he could find words to exprefs. .

On his arrival at Sydney he found his wife, whom he had left in a ftate of pregnancy, in the poffeffion of another native, a very fine young fellow, who fince his coming among us had gone by the name of Wyatt. The circumftance of his return, and the novelty of his appearance, being habited like one of us, and very clean, drew many of his countrymen about him; and among others his rival, and his wife. Wyatt and Collins eyed each other with indignant fullennefs, while the poor wife (who had recently been delivered of a female child, which fhortly after died) appeared terrified, and as if not knowing which to cling to as her protector, but expecting that fhe fhould
be

be the sufferer, whether ascertained to belong to her former or her present husband. A few days, however, determined the point: her travelled husband shivered a spear with Wyatt, who was wounded in the contest, and the wife became the prize of the victor, who, after thus ascertaining his right by arms, seemed indifferent about the reward, and was soon after seen traversing the country in search of another wife.

Three young gentlemen of the Discovery and Chatham's quarter-decks arrived here in the Dædalus, to procure passages from hence to England. Among them was the Honourable Thomas Pitt, who on his arrival here first learnt the death of his father, the late Lord Camelford.

Captain Vancouver not having room for all the provisions which were sent him from the public stores of this settlement, the greatest part of them were returned.

While the Dædalus was in the morning standing in for the harbour, the Arthur went out, bound to that part of the world from which she was just arrived, the north-west coast of America. Four convicts whose terms of transportation had expired were permitted to quit the colony in her. She also took away the carpenter of the Fairy, American brig, who had been left on shore dangerously ill when Mr. Rogers sailed, but who had perfectly recovered through the great attention and medical assistance which he received at the hospital.

The day following the arrival of the Dædalus, the Francis schooner returned from Norfolk Island, having been absent five weeks and one day. In her arrived the Rev. Mr. Bayne, the chaplain of the New South Wales corps, and Mr. Grimes, the deputy-surveyor of lands, with some few other passengers.

Lieutenant-governor King's second crop of Indian corn had been so productive, that he was enabled to make an offer of sending five thousand bushels of that article to this colony, if required.

The peace and good order which universally prevailed at Norfolk Island having rendered unnecessary the keeping together the settlers as a militia, they had some time before the arrival of the Francis returned to their several avocations on their respective farms.

3 A 2   Notwith-

Notwithstanding the ill success which had hitherto attended the
endeavours of the Irish convicts stationed at Toongabbe and Parramatta to find a way from this country to China, a few of them were
again hardy enough to attempt effecting their escape, and getting
thither in a small boat, which they took from a settler, and with
which they got out of the harbour in the night of the 12th of this
month. They had furnished themselves with some provisions; but
the wretchedness of their boat must have ensured to them the same
end which certainly befel Tarwood and his companions, particularly
as it blew a gale of wind the day succeeding their departure. It was
at first imagined that they would be heard of at the Hawkesbury; but
no accounts having been received of them at the end of the month,
there could be little doubt of their having perished.

From the settlement on the banks of that river the best reports continued to be received from time to time: every where the settlers
found a rich black mould of several feet depth, and one man had in
three months planted and dug a crop of potatoes. The natives, however, had given them such interruption, as induced a necessity for
firing upon them, by which, it was said, one man was killed.

At Toongabbe, where the Indian corn was growing, their visits
and their depredations were so frequent and extensive, that the watchmen stationed for the protection of the corn-grounds were obliged to
fire on them, and one party, considerable in number, after having
been driven off, returning directly to the plunder, was pursued by the
watchmen for several miles, when a contest ensued, in which the natives were worsted, and three were left dead on the spot. The watchmen had so often come in with accounts of this nature, that, apprehensive lest the present transaction should not be credited, they
brought in with them, as a testimonial not to be doubted, the head
of one of those whom they had slain. With this witness to support
them, they told many wonderful circumstances of the pursuit and subsequent fight, which they stated to have taken place at least fourteen
miles from the settlement, and to have been very desperately and obstinately sustained on the part of the natives. It was remarked, however, that not one of the watchmen had received the slightest injury,
                                        a cir-

a circumstance that threw a shade over their story, which, but for the production of the head, would have been altogether disbelieved.

Whatever might have been the truth, it is certain that a party of natives appeared the following day about the corn grounds, but conducted themselves with a great deal of caution, stationing one of their party upon the stump of a tree which commanded an extensive view of the cultivated grounds, and retreating the instant they perceived themselves to be observed.

From the quantities of husks and leaves of corn which were found scattered about the dwelling places of these people, their depredations this season must have been very extensive.

At Sydney a large party of natives assembled for the purpose of burning the body of Carradah, the native mentioned in the transactions of the month of December last, by the name of Midjer Bool. He had been put to death while asleep in the night by some people who were inimical to his tribe; and the natives who witnessed the performance of the last rite assured us, that when the murderers should be discovered several severe contests would ensue. It was at this time that the rencounter between Collins and Wyatt took place; and some other points of honour which remained unsettled were then determined, not without much violence and bloodshed, though no one was killed.

Cropping the ground with wheat formed the general and most material labour of this month. On the public account nearly four hundred acres were sown with that essential grain. At this time wheat bore the price of twenty shillings a bushel.

The crops of Indian corn in general turned out very productive. An officer who held an allotment of an hundred acres near Parramatta, from each acre of nineteen, on a light sandy soil, gathered fifty bushels of shelled corn; and a patch of Caffre corn, growing in the like soil, produced the same quantity per acre. This grain had been introduced into our settlement from the Cape of Good Hope by Captain Paterson, and was found to answer well for fattening of stock. No one having attempted to separate the farinaceous part of the grain from the husk, which was of an astringent quality, no judgment had been formed of its utility as a flour; but some who had ground it and mixed the whole together

together into a paste pronounced it to be equal to any preparation of oatmeal.

Wilkinson's grinding machine was set in motion this month. It was a walking mill, upon a larger construction than that at Parramatta. The diameter of the wheel in which the men walked was twenty-two feet, and it required six people to work it. Those who had been in both mills (this and Buffin's, which was worked by capstan-bars and nine men,) gave the preference to the latter; and in a few days it was found to merit it; for, from the variety and number of the wheels in Wilkinson's machinery, something was constantly wrong about it. Finding, after a fair trial, that it was imperfect, it was taken to pieces; and Buffin was employed to replace it by another mill upon the same principle as that which he had himself constructed; and Wilkinson returned to Parramatta.

An inflammation of the eyes appeared to be a disorder generally prevalent among all descriptions of people at this time. It raged at first among children; but when got into a house, hardly any person in it escaped the complaint. It was accounted for by the variable and unsettled weather which we had during this month.

CHAP. XXVI.

May.] EARLY in this month the William sailed on her fishing voyage to the coast of Peru. Mr. Folger, her master, purposed trying what success might be met with on this coast for a few weeks, it being the wish of his owners in consequence of the reports brought home by fome of the whaling fhips which were here in 1792. If he fhould be at all fortunate, he intended to return to this port with the account; it being the anxious wifh of every officer in the colony to hear of any thing that was likely to make a return to the mother country for the immenfe fums which muft annually have been expended on this fettlement.

Some difpatches and returns being fent by this fhip, it appeared, that here and at Norfolk Ifland were exifting, at the latter end of laft month, four thoufand four hundred and fourteen perfons of all defcriptions, men, women, and children. Eftimating the daily expence of thefe at two fhillings a head, (a fair calculation, when every article of provifions, clothing, ftores, freight of fhips, allowance for civil and military eftablifhments, damaged cargoes, &c. &c. was confidered,) it will be found to amount annually to the fum of one hundred and fixty-one thoufand one hundred and eleven pounds; an expence that called loudly for every exertion toward eafing the mother country of fuch a burden, by doing away our dependence on her for many of the above articles, or by affording a return that would be equal to fome part of this expence.

Separated as we were from Europe, conftantly liable to accidents interrupting our fupplies, which it might not always be poffible to guard againft or forefee, how cheering, how grateful was it to every thinking mind among us, to obferve the rapid ftrides we were making toward that defirable independence! The progrefs made in the cultivation of the country infured the confequent increafe of live ftock; and it muft be remembered, that the colony had been fupplied with no other grain than that raifed within itfelf fince the 16th day of laft December.

The permiffion given to officers to hold lands had operated powerfully in favour of the colony. They were liberal in their employment of people to cultivate thofe lands; and fuch had been their exertions, that it appeared by a furvey taken in the laft month by Mr. Alt, that nine hundred and eighty-two acres had been cleared by them fince that permiffion had been received. Mr. Alt reported, that there had been cleared, fince Governor Phillip's departure in December 1792, two thoufand nine hundred and fixty-two acres and one quarter; which,

added

added to seventeen hundred and three acres and a half that were cleared at that time, made a total of four thousand six hundred and sixty-five acres and three quarters of cleared ground in this territory. It must be farther remarked in favour of the gentlemen holding ground, that in the short period of fifteen months *, the officers, civil and military, had cleared more than half the whole quantity of ground that had been cleared by government and the settlers, from the establishment of the colony to the date of the governor's departure. The works of government, however vigilantly attended to, always proceeded slowly, and never with that spirit and energy that are created by interest.

The people who were to labour for the public had in general been but scantily fed, and this operated against any great exertions. The settlers were not fed any better; and though they had an interest in working with spirit, yet they always looked to be supplied from the public stores beyond the time allowed them; and were consequently careless, indolent, and poor: while the officer, from the hour he received his grant, applied himself with activity to derive a benefit from it; and it was not too much to say, that the independence of the colony was more likely to be attained through their exertions, than by any other means. To encourage them, therefore, was absolutely necessary to accelerate and promote the prosperity of the colony.

One woman and six men, whose terms of transportation had expired, were permitted to quit the colony in the William.

Some natives, who had observed the increasing number of the settlers on the banks of the Hawkesbury, and had learned that we were solicitous to discover other fresh-water rivers, for the purpose of forming settlements, assured us, that at no very great distance from Botany Bay, there was a river of fresh water which ran into the sea. As very little of the coast to the Southward was known, it was determined to send a small party in that direction, with provisions for a few days, it not being improbable that, in exploring the country, a river might be found which had hitherto escaped the observation of ships running along the coast.

* The officers did not begin to open ground until February 1793.

Two

Two people of fufficient judgment and difcretion for the purpofe being found among the military, they fet off from the fouth fhore of Botany Bay on the 14th, well armed, and furnifhed with provifions for a week. They were accompanied by a young man, a native, as a guide, who profeffed a knowledge of the country, and named the place where the frefh water would be found to run. Great expectations were formed of this excurfion, from the confidence with which the native repeatedly afferted the exiftence of a frefh-water river; on the 20th, however, the party returned, with an account, that the native had foon walked beyond his own knowledge of the country, and trufted to them to bring him fafe back; that having penetrated about twenty miles to the fouthward of Botany Bay, they came to a large inlet of the fea, which formed a fmall harbour; the head of this they rounded, without difcovering any river of frefh water near it. The country they defcribed as high and rocky in the neighbourhood of the harbour, which, on afterwards looking into the chart, was fuppofed to be fomewhere about Red Point. The native returned with the foldiers as chearfully and as well pleafed as if he had led them to the banks of the firft river in the world.

An excurfion of another nature was at this time framing among fome difcontented Irifh convicts, and was on the point of being carried into execution when difcovered. Among thofe who came out in the laft fhips from Ireland was a convict who had been an attorney in that kingdom, and who was weak enough to form the hazardous fcheme with feveral others of feizing a long-boat, in which they were to endeavour to reach Batavia. A quantity of provifions, water-cafks, fails, and other neceffary articles, were provided, and were found, at the time of making the difcovery, in the houfe of the principal. Thefe people had much greater reafon to rejoice at, than to regret, the difcovery of their plot; for the wind, on the day fucceeding the night in which they were to have gone off, blew a heavy gale; and, as there were no profeffed feamen in the party, it was more than probable that the boat would have been loft. The greateft evil that attended thefe defertions was the lofs of the boats which were taken off; for the colony could not fuftain much injury by the abfence of a few wretches

3 B   who

who were too idle to labour, and who muſt be conſtantly whiſpering their own diſcontents among the other convicts.

On the 24th of this month we had the ſatisfaction of ſeeing the Indiſpenſable, a ſtoreſhip, anchor in the cove from England, with a cargo conſiſting principally of proviſions for the colony. We under-ſtood that ſhe was the firſt of ſix or ſeven ſhips which were all to bring out ſtores and proviſions, and which, if no accident happened in the paſſage, might be expected to arrive in the courſe of two months. The ſupply of clothing and proviſions intended to be conveyed by them, together with what had been received by the William, was calculated for the conſumption of a twelvemonth. The quantity which now arrived in the Indiſpenſable formed a ſupply of flour for twelve weeks, beef for four ditto, pork for four ditto, and of peaſe for fourteen ditto. She ſailed from Spithead the 26th of laſt December, touched at Teneriffe and at the Cape of Good Hope, from which place ſhe ſailed on the 30th of March laſt, and made the South Cape of this country the 17th of this month. Between the Cape of Good Hope and this port, the maſter ſtated that he found the weather in general very rough, and the prevailing winds to have blown from W. N. W. to S. W.

At the Cape of Good Hope Mr. Wilkinſon met with the Cheſter-field, which ſailed hence in April 1793 with the Shah Hormuzear; and one of her people, who had been formerly a convict in this country, wiſhing to return to it, we now collected from him ſome information reſpecting Mr. Bampton's voyage. He told us, that the two ſhips were ſix months in their paſſage hence to Timor, owing to the diffi-culty which they met with in the navigation of the ſtraits between New Holland and New Guinea. On one of the iſlands in theſe ſtraits they loſt a boat, which had been ſent on ſhore to trade with the na-tives. In this boat went, never to return, (according to this perſon's account,) Captain Hill; Mr. Carter, a friend of Mr. Bampton's; —— Shaw, the firſt mate of the Cheſterfield; —— Aſcott, who had been a convict here, and who had diſtinguiſhed himſelf at the time the Sirius was loſt; and two or three black people belonging to the Shah Hormuzear. It was conjectured that they were, immediately

after

after landing, murdered by the natives, as the people of a boat that was sent some hours after to look for them found only the clothes which they had on when they left the ship, and a lantern and tinder-box which they had taken with them; the clothes were torn into rags. At a fire they found three hands; but they were so black and disfigured by being burnt, that the people could not ascertain whether they had belonged to black or white men. If the account of this man might be credited, the end of these unfortunate gentlemen and their companions must have been truly horrid and deplorable; it was how-ever certain that the ships sailed from the island without them, and their fate was left in uncertainty, though every possible effort to dis-cover them was made by Mr. Bampton.

At Timor Mr. Bampton took in a very valuable freight of sandal wood, with which he proceeded to Batavia; and when the Chester-field parted company, he hoped soon to return to this country.

In consequence of the supplies received by the Indispensable, the full ration of flour was directed to be issued, and the commissary was ordered not to receive for the present any more Indian corn that might be brought to the public stores for sale. The following weekly ration was established until further orders, and commenced on the 27th:

Flour eight pounds; beef seven pounds, or pork four pounds; Indian corn three pints, in lieu of pease.

The whole quantity of Indian corn purchased by the commissary on account of Government from settlers and others amounted to six thousand one hundred and sixty-three bushels and a quarter, which, taken at five shillings per bushel, came to the sum of 1540 l. 16 s. 3 d.

Toward the latter end of this month, Wilkinson, the millwright, was drowned in a pond in the neighbourhood of the Hawkesbury River. He had been there on a Sunday with some of the settlers to shoot ducks, and getting entangled with the weeds in the pond was drowned, though a good swimmer; thus untimely perishing before he could reap any reward from his industry and abilities.

Several people still continued to complain of sore eyes, but the dis-order was disappearing fast.

June.] The signal for a sail was made in the morning of the first of June, and was conjectured to be for one of the ships expected to arrive from England; but in a few hours word was brought that the

Britannia was safe within the harbour. This arrival gave general satisfaction, as many doubts about her return had been created by some accounts which the master of the Indispensable had heard at the Cape of Good Hope, of the Bay of Bengal being full of French privateers.

On Mr. Raven's arrival at the settlement, we learned that he had been forced to go to Batavia instead of Bengal, having been attacked in the Straits of Malacca by a fleet of piratical Proas, which engaged him for six hours, and from whom he might have found some difficulty to escape, had he not fortunately killed the captain of the one which was nearest to the Britannia when in the act of making preparations for boarding him. At Batavia he was informed that his passage to Bengal was very precarious, from the number of French privateers which infested the bay, as well as the west coast of Sumatra, several vessels having arrived at Batavia which had been chased by them. Mr. Raven, therefore, determined to load the Britannia at Batavia, and, after some necessary arrangements with the governor-general and council, purchased the following cargo at the annexed prices for the settlements in New South Wales: viz.

		Rix-dollars.	Stivers.
250 Casks of beef - 111,264½ lbs. at 9 stivers *		20,862	2
250 Casks of pork - 83,865½ lbs. at ditto -		15,724	37
500 Pecols † of sugar, at 7 rix-dollars 27 stivers per Pecol.		3781	12
35 Coyangs ‡ of rice, at 55 rix-dollars per Coyang		1925	0
To these must be added for extra boat-hire. Hire of twenty black people for twenty days, and commission on the purchase at 2½ per cent. - - -		1493	0
Rix-dollars -		42,786	3
The bills drawn on the treasury for this cargo bearing a premium of 16 per cent, there was deducted from the whole - - - -		6040	0
Which reduced the total amount to rix-dollars -		37,746	3

* Forty-eight stivers the rix-dollar.
† Pecol, one hundred and thirty-three pounds English.
‡ Coyang, three thousand three hundred and seventy-five pounds Dutch.

Or

		£	s.	d.
Or in sterling money of Great Britain	-	7549	4	3
To which the hire * of the ship being added,	-	2210	7	7

The whole of the expence amounted to   -   £. 9759 11 10

Captain Nepean, who left this place as a passenger in the Britannia, and took with him some dispatches for government, and the private letters of the officers, left Batavia on the 17th of February last in the Prince William Henry, a fast sailing schooner, bound direct for England.

The Britannia arrived at Batavia on the 11th of February, and sailed for this country on the 10th of April following. While she lay at Batavia, the season was extremely unhealthy, and some of her people fell victims to the well-known insalubrity of the climate.

At Batavia Mr. Raven learned that the Shah Hormuzear sailed from thence for Bombay three months before he arrived there; and the report we had heard of the disaster which befel the boat and people from that ship, in the passage through the Straits between this country and New Guinea, was confirmed at Batavia. As, however, Mr. Bampton had not since been heard of, it was more than probable he had fallen a prize to some of the privateers which were to be met with in those seas.

His Majesty's birth-day did not pass without that distinction which we all, as Englishmen devoted to our sovereign, had infinite pleasure in shewing it.

On the 8th the Speedy, a storeship commanded by Mr. Melville, who was here in 1791 in the Britannia whaler, anchored in the cove from England, with a cargo of stores and provisions for the colony, and clothing for the New South Wales corps. Mr. Melville sailed a few hours before the Indispensable, and touched at Rio de Janeiro, whence he had a long passage of several weeks. He made the south cape of this country the 2d Instant; and arrived here in a leaky and weak condition.

Good fortune befriended us in the passage of this ship; for she ran safely through every part where there could be danger, without a

* She was chartered at fourteen shillings and sixpence per ton per month, and to be paid for two hundred and ninety-six tons, her registered measurement.

gun

gun on board to defend her from an enemy if she should have met with any.

On the 14th, a few hours after the signal was made at the South-head, arrived in the harbour the Halcyon, a ship from Rhode Island, commanded by Mr. Benjamin Page, who was here in the ship Hope at the close of the year 1792, and who had ventured here again with a cargo of provisions and spirits * on speculation.

Mr. Page made his passage from Rhode Island in one hundred and fifteen days, and without touching at any port. His run from the south cape of New Holland was only five days. The ship he built himself at Providence, after his return from China in the Hope. That ship was only two months in her voyage from hence to Canton, and Mr. Page did not see any land until he made the Island of Tinian. This place he now represented as well calculated to furnish a freight of cattle for this colony.

Of the convicts that Mr. Page was permitted to ship at this port in his last voyage, William Murphy behaved so extremely ill, having more than once endeavoured to excite the crew to mutiny, that at St. Helena he delivered him to the captain of his Majesty's ship Powerful, whom he found there. This proved in the event a circum-stance of great good fortune to Murphy, for, being directly rated on that ship's books (his abilities as a sail-maker entitling him to that situ-ation), and a French East Indiaman being captured by the Powerful a very few hours after, he became entitled to a seaman's share of the produce of her cargo, which was a very valuable one.

Bateman he carried on with him to Rhode Island, where he mar-ried, but had more than once exhibited symptoms of returning to habits which he had not forgotten, and which would soon bring him to disgrace in his new situation. Shepherd he had put on board a ship bound to Ostend, and spoke well of his conduct.

Captain Page at first thought he had come to a bad market with his provisions; for the day was arrived when we found ourselves enabled to say that we were not in want of any casual supplies; but by the end of the month he declared he had not made a bad voyage; his

* Eight hundred barrels of beef and pork, American cured. About five thousand gallons of spirits; a small quantity of tobacco, tea, snakeroot, &c.

spirits

spirits and provisions were nearly all purchased by individuals; and what he at first thought an unprofitable circumstance to him (the sight of four ships at anchor in the cove) proved favourable, for the most of his provisions were disposed of among the shipping. The whole of the spirits were purchased by the officers of the settlement and of the garrison at the rate of six shillings per gallon; and afforded, together with what had been received from Batavia by the Britannia, a large and comfortable supply of that article for a considerable time.

It might be safely pronounced, that the colony never wore so favourable an appearance as at this period: our public stores filled with wholesome provisions; five ships on the seas with additional supplies; and wheat enough in the ground to promise the realizing of many a golden dream; a rapidly increasing stock; a country gradually opening, and improving every where upon us as it opened; with a spirit universally prevalent of cultivating it.

The ships which had lately arrived from England were fraught with the dismal and ill-founded accounts, which through some evil design continued to be insidiously propagated, of the wretched unprofitable soil of New South Wales. It was hoped, however, that when the present appearance and state of the colony should reach England, every attempt to mislead the public would cease; and such encouragement be held out as would induce individuals to settle in the country.

In the Halcyon arrived an American gentleman (Mr. W. Megee) in the character of supercargo. This person, on seeing the Toongabbe hills covered with a most promising crop of wheat, declared that he had never seen better in America, even at Rhode Island, the garden of America; and on being shewn some Indian corn of last year's growth, gave it as his opinion, that we wanted nothing but large herds of grazing cattle, to be a thriving, prosperous, and great colony, possessing within itself all the essential articles of life.

We ourselves had long been impressed with an idea of the advantage that grazing cattle would give to the country; every possible care was taken of the little that was in it, and all means used to promote its increase. One step toward this was the keeping up the price; an article, by which the proprietor was always certain of making a great profit, was as certain to be taken the greatest care of; every individual
possessing

poſſeſſing ſtock found it his intereſt to preſerve it in the higheſt order, that it might be deemed equal to the general high value which ſtock bore.

By an account which was taken at the end of this month of the live ſtock in the colony, the following numbers appeared to be in the poſſeſſion of government and of individuals: viz.

	Horſes.		Aſſes.		Oxen.		Sheep.		Goats.		
	Mares.	Stallions.	Male.	Female.	Bulls.	Cows.	Ewes.	Rams & Wethers.	Female.	Male.	Total.
Government ſtock - -	6	6	—	—	14	18	59	49	10	3	165
Private ditto - - - -	5	3	2	1	1	7	257	161	342	167	946
Total	11	9	2	1	15	25	316	210	352	170	1111

In this account the hogs (from their being ſo diſpoſed as not eaſily to be aſcertained) were not included; but they were ſuppoſed to amount to ſeveral hundreds.

As a reſerve in time of great diſtreſs, when alone it could be made uſe of, this ſtock was, when compared with our numbers, no very great dependance; but it was every thing as a ſtock to breed from, and well deſerving of attention to cheriſh it and promote its increaſe.

On the laſt day of the month the Francis ſchooner ſailed for Nor-folk Iſland, whither ſhe was ſent merely to appriſe Mr. King that the Dædalus would be diſpatched to him immediately after the return of the ſchooner, with ſuch ſtores and proviſions as he ſhould require.

During this month the houſe of the Rev. Mr. Johnſon was broken into at night, and robbed of ſugar, coffee, arrack, Ruſſia ſheeting, and other articles to a large amount. There was little doubt but that ſome of his own people had either committed the burglary, or had given information to others how and when it might be committed, as the part of the houſe broken into was that which Mr. Johnſon had applied to a ſtore-room. Several people were taken up, and ſome of the articles found concealed in the woods; but thoſe who ſtole them had addreſs enough to avoid diſcovery.

3   Very

Very shortly after this a most daring burglary was committed in a house in the old marine quarters occupied by Mr. Kent, who arrived here in the Boddingtons from Ireland in August last, as agent of convicts on the part of Government. He had secured the door with a padlock, and after sun-set had gone up to one of the officers' barracks, where he was spending the evening, when, before nine o'clock, word was brought him that his house had been broken into. On going down, he found that the staple, which was a very strong one, had been forced out, and a large chest that would require four men to convey it out of the door had been taken off. It contained a great quantity of wearing apparel, money, bills, and letters; but, though the theft could not have been long committed, all the search that twenty or thirty people made for some hours that night was ineffectual, no trace being seen of it, and nothing found but a large caulking-iron, with which it was supposed the staple was wrenched off. The chest was found the next morning behind a barrack, (which had lately been fitted up as a place of divine worship for the accommodation of the chaplain of the New South Wales corps,) and some of the wearing apparel was brought in from the woods; but Mr. Kent's loss was very little diminished by this recovery.

In addition to these burglaries a highway robbery was committed on the supercargo of the American, who was attacked in the dusk of the evening, close by one of the barracks, by two men, who, in the moment of striking him, seized hold of his watch, and with a violent jerk wrenched off the seals, the watch falling on the ground. The place was, however, too public to risk staying to look for it; and the owner was fortunate enough to find it himself; but the seals, which were of gold, were carried off.

All these offences against peace and good order were to be attributed to the horrid vice of gaming, which was still pursued in this place, and which, from the management and address of those who practised it, could not be prevented. The persons of the peace-officers were well known to them; and, that they might never be detected in the fact, one of the party, commonly the greatest loser, was always stationed on the look-out to alarm in time.

During

During this month the millwright Buffin completed the mill which he was constructing in the room of Wilkinson's; and, on its being worked, it was found to answer still better than the first which he made. The body of Wilkinson, after being dragged for several days in vain, was found at last floating on the surface of the pond where he lost his life, and being brought into Parramatta was there decently interred.

Of the few who died in this month was one, a male convict, of the name of Peter Gillies, who came out to this country in the Neptune transport in the year 1791. His death took place on the morning of the arrival of the Speedy from England, by which ship a letter was received addressed to him, admonishing him of the uncertainty of life, recommending him early to begin to think of the end of it, and acquainting him of the death of his wife, a child, and two other near relations. He had ceased to breathe before this unwelcome intelligence reached the hospital.

July.] The signal for a sail was made at the South-head between seven and eight o'clock in the morning of the 5th of July; and soon after the Hope, an American ship from Rhode Island, anchored in the cove, having on board a cargo of salted provisions and spirits on speculation. This ship was here before with Captain Page, the commander of the Halcyon, and now came in the same employ, the house of Brown and Francis at Providence. Brown was the uncle of Page, between whom there being some misunderstanding, Page built and freighted the Halcyon after the departure of the Hope, whose master being ordered to touch at the Falkland's Islands, Page determined to precede him in his arrival at this country, and have the first of the market, in which he succeeded.

This proved a great disappointment to the master of the Hope, who indeed sold his spirits at three shillings and sixpence per gallon; but his salted provisions no one would purchase.

The Hope was seven days in her passage from the South Cape to this port; and the master said, that off Cape St. George he met with a current which carried him during the space of three days a degree to the southward each day.

On

On the 8th the Indispensable and Halcyon sailed on their respective voyages, the former for Bengal, and the latter for Canton. The Indispensable was a large stout ship, provided with a letter of marque, well manned and armed; and had been captured from the French at the beginning of the present war. The master was permitted to receive on board several persons from the colony, on his representing that he was short of hands to navigate his ship; and two convicts found means to make their escape from the settlement. A third was discovered concealed on board for the same purpose, and being brought on shore, it appeared that the coxswain of the lieutenant-governor's boat had assisted him in his attempt; for which he was punished and turned out of the boat, such a breach of trust deserving and requiring to be particularly noticed.

By the Halcyon were sent some dispatches to be forwarded by the way of China to his Majesty's secretary of state for the home department. The day following the departure of these two ships, the Fancy snow arrived from Bombay, having on board a small quantity of rice and dholl *, intended as part of the contract entered into by Captain Bampton, who, we now learned, had arrived safe at Bombay, after a long passage from this place of between six and seven months. This vessel was commanded by Mr. Thomas Edgar Dell, formerly chief mate of Mr. Bampton's ship the Shah Hormuzear, from whom the following information was received.

The ships Shah Hormuzear and Chesterfield sailed, as before related, from Norfolk Island on the 27th of May 1793. On the 2d of the following month a reef was seen in latitude 19° 28' S. and longitude 158° 32' 15" East. On the 1st of July, being then in latitude 9° 39' 30" S. and longitude 142° 59' 15" East of Greenwich, they fell in with an island which obtained the name of Tate's Island, and at which they had the misfortune to stave a boat as beforementioned. The circumstances of the murder of Captain Hill, Mr. Carter, Shaw the first mate of the Chesterfield, and the boat's crew, were related by Mr. Dell. It appeared from his account, that they had landed to search for fresh

---

* Thirty-eight tons of rice, and thirty-eight tons of dholl. Captain Bampton also sent twenty-four bags of seed-wheat.

water, and purposed remaining one night on the island to barter with
the natives, and procure emu feathers from them. The day after they
were put on shore the weather changed, coming on to blow hard; the
ship was driven to leeward of the bay in which they landed; and it was
not until the third day that it was possible to send a boat after them. Mr.
Dell himself was employed on this occasion, and returned with the melancholy account of his being unable to discover their lost companions.
An armed force was then sent on shore, but succeeded only in burning
the huts and inclosures of the natives. At a fire they found some incontestable proofs that their friends could not be living; of three human
hands which they took up, one, by some particular marks, was positively thought by Mr. Dell to have belonged to Mr. Carter; their
great coats were also found with the buttons cut off; a tinder-box, a
lantern, a tomahawk, and other articles from the boat, were also found;
but though they rowed entirely round the island, looking into every cove
or creek, the boat could not be seen. Mr. Dell was, if possible, to procure
two prisoners; but he could not succeed. In the intercourse, however,
which he had with them, they gave him to understand by signs, that they
had killed all who were in the boat, except two: at least, so Mr. Dell
thought; but if it was so, nothing could be hoped from the exception,
nor could any other conclusion be formed, than that they were reserved
perhaps for more deliberate torture and a more horrid end.

This island was described as abounding with the red sweet potatoe,
sugar-cane, plantains, bamboo, cocoa trees, and mangroves. The natives appeared stout, and were in height from five feet eight to six feet
two inches; their colour dark, and their language harsh and disagreeable. The weapons which were seen were spears, lances made of
a hard black wood, and clubs about four feet in length. They lived
in huts resembling a hay-cock, with a pole driven through the middle,
formed of long grass and the leaves of the cocoa-tree. These huts
might contain six or eight persons each, and were inclosed with a fence
of bamboo. In a corner of some of the huts which they entered, they
perceived a wooden image, intended to resemble a man; in others the
figure of a bird, very rudely carved, daubed with red, and curiously
decorated with the feathers of the emu. Over these images were suspended from the roof several strings of human hands, each string

4   having

having five or six hands on it. In some they found small piles of human sculls; and in one, in which there was a much larger pile of sculls than in any other that they had visited, they observed some gum burning before a wooden image.

This island was supposed to be about eight miles in length, five in breadth, and fifteen in circumference; a coral reef seemed to guard it from all approach, except on the north-west part which formed a bay, where the ship anchored in thirteen fathoms water. Fresh water was seen only in one place.

Mr. Bampton did not arrive at Timor until the 11th of September, having been detained in the straits by a most difficult and dangerous navigation. By this passage he had an opportunity of discovering that the straits which were named after Torres, and supposed to have been passed first by him in the year 1606, and afterwards by Green in 1722, could never have existed; for Mr. Bampton now observed, that New Guinea extended ninety miles to the southward of this supposed track.

Of the two convicts taken from hence by the Shah Hormuzear, John Ascot was killed by the natives with Captain Hill, and Catharine Pryor, Ascot's wife, died two days before the ship got to Batavia, of a spotted fever, the effect of frequent inebriety while at Timor. Ascot was the young man whose activity prevented the Sirius, with the stores and provisions on board, from being burnt the night after she was wrecked off Norfolk Island, and thereby saved that settlement from feeling absolute want at that time.

Captain Dell was full three months in his passage from Bombay; during the latter part of which time the people on board suffered great distress from a shortness of water and fuel. Out of seventy-five persons, mostly Lascars, with whom he sailed, nine died, and a fever existed among those who remained on his arrival.

The people who had broken into Mr. Kent's house were so daring as to send to that gentleman a letter in miserable verse, containing some invectives against one Devan, a prisoner in confinement for a burglary, and a woman who they supposed had given information of the people that broke into the clergyman's store-room, which affair they took upon themselves.

themfelves. The letter was accompanied by a pocket-book belonging to Mr. Kent, and fome of his papers; but none of the bills which
were in it when it was ftolen were returned.

The infolence of this proceeding, and the frequency of thofe nocturnal vifits, furprifed and put all perfons on their guard; but that the
enemy was within our own doors there was no doubt. An honeft
fervant was in this country an invaluable treafure; we were compelled
to take them as chance fhould direct from among the common herd;
and if any one was found who had fome remains of principle in him,
he was fure to be foon corrupted by the vice which every where fur-
rounded him.

It became neceffary at length for the criminal juftice of the feulement
to interfere, and three convicts were tried for burglaries. John Beran,
though tried on two charges, was acquitted from a want of evidence;
the others, John Flemming and Archibald M'Donald, were convicted.
The latter of thefe two had broken into a foldier's hut the night before
the court fat, and at a time when it was publicly known in the fettlement that it was to fit for the trial of fuch offenders as might be
brought before it. The ftate of the colony called loudly for their
punifhment, and they were both executed the third day after their
conviction. It was afterwards faid, that M'Donald was one of the
party who broke into the clergyman's houfe.

Soon after thefe executions, Cæfar *, ftill incorrigible, took up
again his former practice of fubfifting in the woods by plundering the
farms and huts at the outfkirts of the towns. He was foon taken; but
on his being punifhed, and that with fome feverity, he declared with
exultation and contempt, that " all that would not make him better."

The Hope failed this month for Canton, the mafter being fuffered
to take with him one man, John Pardo Watts, who had ferved his
time of tranfportation.

The Britannia was alfo hired in this month by fome of the officers
of the civil and military departments, to procure them cattle and other
articles at the Cape of Good Hope.

* See page 70, et feq.

During

During this month a building, confisting of four cells for prisoners, was added to the guard-house on the eaft side of the cove. This had long been greatly wanted; and, the whole being now inclofed with a ftrong high paling, fome advantage was expected to be derived from confinement adopted only as a punifhment.

CHAP. XXVII.

THE SPEEDY SAILS AND RETURNS.—EXCURSION TO THE WESTERN MOUNT-AINS.—THE FRANCIS RETURNS FROM NORFOLK ISLAND.—CORN BILLS NOT PAID.—THE BRITANNIA SAILS FOR THE CAPE, AND THE SPEEDY ON HER FISHING VOYAGE.—NOTIFICATION RESPECTING THE CORN BILLS.—THE RESOLUTION AND SALAMANDER ARRIVE FROM ENGLAND.—IRISH PRISON-ERS TROUBLESOME.—GALES OF WIND.—NATIVES.—DÆDALUS SAILS FOR NORFOLK ISLAND.—EMANCIPATIONS.—THE FANCY SAILS.—A DEATH.—BEVAN EXECUTED.—A SETTLER MURDERED AT PARRAMATTA.—THE MERCURY ARRIVES.—SPANISH SHIPS.—EMANCIPATION.—SETTLERS AND NATIVES.—CIVIL COURT.—THE SURPRIZE ARRIVES.—DEATHS.—RESOLU-TION AND SALAMANDER SAIL.—TRANSACTIONS.—THE DÆDALUS RETURNS FROM NORFOLK ISLAND.—THE MERCURY SAILS FOR AMERICA.—THE LIEU-TENANT-GOVERNOR LEAVES THE SETTLEMENT.—THE DÆDALUS SAILS FOR ENGLAND, AND THE SURPRIZE FOR BENGAL.—THE EXPERIMENT ARRIVES.—CAPTAIN PATERSON ASSUMES THE GOVERNMENT PRO TEMPORE.—RA-TION.—DEATHS IN 1794.

Auguft.] MR. Melville failed on his intended fifhing voyage on the fecond of this month. He talked of returning in about fourteen days, during which time he meant to vifit Jervis and Bateman Bays to the fouthward, as well as to try once more what fortune might attend him as a whaler upon the coaft. He returned, however, on the 8th, without having feen a fifh, or vifited either of the bays, having experienced a conftant and heavy gale of wind at E. S. E. fince he left the port, which forced him to fail under a reefed forefail during the whole of its continuance.

In

In the evening of the day on which he failed hence, the people at the South-head made the signal for a fail; but it was imagined, that as they had loft fight of the Speedy in the morning, they had perhaps feen her again in the evening on another tack, as the wind had fhifted. But when this was mentioned to Mr. Melville at his return, he faid that it was not poffible for the Speedy to have been feen in the evening of the day fhe failed, as fhe ftood right off the land; and he added, that he himfelf, in the clofe of the evening, imagined he faw a fail off Botany Bay. No fhip, however, making her appearance during the month, it was generally fuppofed that the people at the Look-out muft have been miftaken.

A paffage over the inland mountains which form the weftern bound-ary of the county of Cumberland being deemed practicable, Henry Hacking, a feaman, (formerly quarter-mafter in the Sirius, but left here from the Royal Admiral,) fet off on the 20th of the month, with a companion or two, determined to try it. On the 27th they re-turned with an account of their having penetrated twenty miles further inland than any other European. Hacking reported, that on reaching the mountains, his further route lay over eighteen or nineteen ridges of high rocks; and that when he halted, determined to return, he ftill had in view before him the fame wild and inacceffible kind of country. The fummits of thefe rocks were of iron-ftone, large fragments of which had covered the intermediate valleys, in which water of a reddifh tinge was obferved to ftagnate in many fpots. The foil midway up the afcent appeared good, and afforded fhelter and food for feveral red kangooroos. The ground every where bore figns of being fre-quently vifited by high winds; for on the fides expofed to the fouth and fouth-eaft it was ftrewed with the trunks of large trees. They faw but one native in this defolate region, and he fled from their ap-proach, preferring the enjoyments of his rocks and woods, with li-berty, to any intercourfe with them. Thefe hills appearing to extend very far to the northward and fouthward, an impaffable barrier feemed fixed to the weftward; and little hope was left of our extending cul-tivation beyond the limits of the county of Cumberland.

On the following day the Francis fchooner returned from Nor-folk Ifland, having been abfent about eight weeks and three days. Her

Her paſſage thither was made in ten days, and her return in thirty-eight days, having met with very bad weather.

From Mr. King we learned that his harveſt had been prodigiouſly productive. He had purchaſed from the firſt crops which the ſettlers brought to market upwards of eleven thouſand buſhels of maize; and bills for the amount were drawn by him in favour of the reſpective ſettlers; but, requiring the ſanction of the lieutenant-governor, they were now ſent to Port Jackſon. Mr. King had been partly induced to make this proviſional kind of purchaſe, under an idea that the corn would be acceptable at Port Jackſon, and alſo in compliance with the conditions on which the ſettlers had received their reſpective allotments under the regulations of Governor Phillip; that is to ſay, that their overplus grain and ſtock ſhould be purchaſed from them at a fair market price. Being, however, well ſtocked with that article already, the lieutenant-governor did not think himſelf juſtifiable in putting the crown to ſo great an expence, (nearly three thouſand pounds ſterling,) and declined accepting the bills.

Had we been in want of maize, Mr. King could have ſupplied us with twenty thouſand buſhels of it, much of which muſt now inevitably periſh, unleſs the ſettlers would, agreeably to a notification which the governor intended to ſend them by the firſt opportunity, receive their corn again from the public ſtores.

Mr. King had the ſatisfaction to write that every thing went on well in his little iſland, excepting that ſome diſcontent appeared among the marine ſettlers, and ſome others, on account of his not purchaſing their ſecond crops of corn. As ſome proof of the exiſtence of this diſſatisfaction, one marine ſettler and three others arrived in the ſchooner, who had given up their farms and entered into the New South Wales corps; and it was reported that moſt of the marine ſettlers intended to follow their example.

This circumſtance naturally gave riſe to an inquiry, what would be the conſequence if ever Government ſhould, from farming on their own account, raiſe a quantity of wheat and maize ſufficient for the conſumption of thoſe in the different ſettlements who were victualled by the crown. If ſuch a ſyſtem ſhould be adopted, the ſettler would be deprived of a market for his overplus grain, would find himſelf cut

3 D   off

off from the means of purchasing any of those comforts which his family must inevitably require, and would certainly quit a country that merely held out to him a daily subsistence; as he would look, if he was ordinarily wise, for something beyond that. It might be said, that the settler would raise stock for the public; but government would do the same, and so prevent him from every chance of providing for a family beyond the present day.

As it was desirable that those settlers who had become such from convicts should remain in this country, the only inducement they could have would be that of raising to themselves a comfortable independence for the winter of their own lives and the summer of their progeny. Government must therefore, to encourage the settler, let him be the farmer, and be itself the purchaser. The Government can always fix its own price; and the settler will be satisfied if he can procure himself the comforts he finds requisite, and lay by a portion of his emoluments for that day when he can no longer till the field with the labour of his own hands. With this encouragement and prospect, New South Wales would hold out a most promising field for the industrious; and might even do more: it might prove a valuable resource and acceptable asylum for many broken and reduced families, who, for want of it, become through misfortunes chargeable to their respective parishes.

Notwithstanding the weather was unfavourable during the whole of this month, the wheat every where looked well, particularly at the settlement near the Hawkesbury; the distance to which place had lately been ascertained by an officer who walked thither from Sydney in two minutes less than eight hours. He computed the distance to be two-and-thirty miles.

The weather during the whole of this month was very unpleasant and turbulent. Much rain, and the wind strong at south, marked by far the greatest part of it. On the 25th, the hot land-wind visited us for the first time this season, blowing until evening with much violence, when it was succeeded (as usually happened after so hot a day) by the wind at south.

September.] On the 1st of September the Britannia sailed for the Cape of Good Hope, on a second voyage of speculation for some of
the

the civil and military officers of the settlement. In her went, with dispatches, Mr. David Wake Bell, and Mr. Richard Kent (gentlemen who arrived here in the Boddingtons and Sugar Cane transports, charged with the superintendance and medical care of the convicts from Ireland). The Speedy also sailed on her fishing voyage, the master intending not to consume any longer time in an unsuccessful trial of this coast. Several persons were permitted to take their passage in these ships; among others, Richard Blount, for whom a free pardon had some time since been received from the secretary of state's office.

Soon after the departure of these ships, the lieutenant-governor, having previously transmitted with his other dispatches an account of the transaction to the secretary of state, thought it necessary to issue a public order, calculated to impress on the minds of those settlers and others at Norfolk Island who might think themselves aggrieved by his late determination of not ordering payment to be made for the corn purchased of them by Lieutenant-governor King, a conviction that although he should on all occasions be ready to adopt any plan which the lieutenant-governor might devise for the accommodation or advantage of the inhabitants at Norfolk Island, yet in this business he made objections, because he did not consider himself authorised to ratify the agreement.

He proposed to those who held the bills to take back their corn ; or, if they preferred leaving it in the public stores until such time as an answer could be received from the secretary of state, he assured them that they might depend on the earliest communication of whatever might be his decision; and that if such decision should be to refuse the payment of the bills, he promised that grain should be returned equal in quantity and quality to what had been received from them *.

How far the settlers (who in return for the produce of their grounds looked for something more immediately beneficial to them and their families, than the waiting eighteen months or two years for a refusal,

---

* Governor Hunter on his arrival ordered the bills to be paid, which was afterwards confirmed by the secretary of state.

instead

inftead of payment of thefe bills) would be fatisfied with this order, was very queftionable. It has been feen already, that they were dif-fatisfied at the produce of their fecond crops not being purchafed; what then muft be their ideas on finding even the firft received indeed, but not accounted for; purchafed, but not paid for? It was fair to conclude, that on thus finding themfelves without a market for their overplus grain, they would certainly give up the cultivation of their farms and quit the ifland. Should this happen, Lieutenant-governor King would have to lament the neceffity of a meafure having been adopted which in effect promifed to depopulate his government.

On the 10th and 11th of this month we had two very welcome arrivals from England, the Refolution and Salamander ftorefhips. They were both freighted with ftores and provifions for the colony; but immediately on their anchoring we were given to underftand, that from meeting with uncommon bad weather between the Cape of Good Hope and Van Dieman's Land, the mafters apprehended that their cargoes had fuftained much damage.

The Refolution failed in company with the Salamander (from whom fhe parted in a heavy gale of wind about the longitude of the iflands Amfterdam and St. Paul's) on the 20th of March laft; anchored on the 16th of April at the Ifle of May, whence fhe failed on the 20th; croffed the equator on the 3d of May; anchored on the 25th of the fame month in the harbour of Rio de Janeiro; left it on the 10th of June, and, after a very boifterous paffage, made the fouthern extremity of New Holland on the 30th of Auguft, having been ninety-three days in her paffage from the Brazils, during which time fhe endured feveral hard gales of wind, three of which the mafter, Mr. Matthew Lock, reported to have been as fevere as any man on board his fhip had ever witneffed. He ftated, in the proteft which he entered before the judge-advocate, that his fhip was very much ftrained, the main piece of the rudder fprung, and moft of the fails and rigging worn out. The Salamander appeared to have met with weather equally bad; but fhe was at one time in greater hazard, having broached-to in a tremendous gale of wind; during which time, according to the tale of the fuperftitious feamen, and which they took

care

care to infert in their protest, blue lights were seen dancing on each maft-head and yard in the fhip.

By thefe fhips we learned that the Surprife transport, with male and female convicts for this country, was left by them lying at. Spithead ready for fea, and that they might be fhortly expected. The Kitty, which failed from this place in June 1793, had arrived fafely at Cork on the 5th of February laft, not lofing any of her paffengers or people in fo long a voyage and in fuch a feafon.

His Majefty's appointment of John Hunter Efq. to be our governor, in the room of Captain Phillip who had refigned his office, we found had been officially notified in the London Gazette of the 5th of February laft. Mr. Phillip's fervices, we underftood, were remunerated by a penfion of five hundred pounds per annum.

The Irifh prifoners were now again beginning to be troublefome; and fome of them being miffing from labour, it was directly rumoured that a plan was in agitation to feize the boat named the Cumberland, which had recently failed with provifions for the fettlers at the Hawkefbury. By feveral it was faid, that fhe had actually been attacked without the Heads, and carried. Notice was therefore immediately fent over-land to the river, to put the people in the boat on their guard, and to return fhould fhe reach that fettlement fafely: an armed long-boat was alfo fent to protect her paffage round. After a few days fufpence we found, that while providing againft any accident happening to the Cumberland, fome of the Irifh prifoners at Parramatta had ftolen from the wharf at that place a fix-oar'd boat belonging to Lieutenant M'Arthur, with which they got without the harbour undifcovered. She was found however, fome days after, at Botany Bay. The people who were in her made fome threats of refiftance, but at length took to the woods, leaving the boat with nearly every thing that they had provided for their voyage. From the woods they vifited the farms about Sydney for plunder, or rather for fuftenance; but one of them being fired at and wounded, the reft thought it their wifeft way to give themfelves up. They made no hefitation in avowing that they never meant to return; but at the fame time owned that they fuppofed they had reached Broken Bay inftead of Botany Bay, ignorant whether it lay to the northward or

3   fouthward

southward of this harbour. The man who had been wounded died at the hospital the next day; and his companions appeared but very ill able to provide for themselves, even by those means which had occasioned our being troubled with them in this country.

On the 17th, we were visited by a violent gale of wind at south-west, which blew so strong, that the Resolution was at one time nearly on shore. At Parramatta, during the gale, a public granary, in which were upwards of two thousand four hundred bushels of shelled maize or Indian corn, caught fire, through the carelessness of some servants who were boiling food for stock close to the building (which was a thatched one), and all the corn, together with a number of fine hogs the property of an individual, were destroyed.

Some severe contests among the natives took place during this month in and about the town of Sydney. In fact, we still knew very little of the manners and customs of these people, notwithstanding the advantage we possessed in the constant residence of many of them among us, and the desire that they shewed of cultivating our friendship. At the Hawkesbury they were not so friendly; a settler there and his servant were nearly murdered in their hut by some natives from the woods, who stole upon them with such secrecy, as to wound and overpower them before they could procure assistance. The servant was so much hurt by them with spears and clubs, as to be in danger of losing his life. A few days after this circumstance, a body of natives having attacked the settlers, and carried off their clothes, provisions, and whatever else they could lay their hands on, the sufferers collected what arms they could, and following them, seven or eight of the plunderers were killed on the spot.

This mode of treating them had become absolutely necessary, from the frequency and evil effects of their visits; but whatever the settlers at the river suffered was entirely brought on them by their own misconduct: there was not a doubt but many natives had been wantonly fired upon; and when their children, after the flight of the parents, have fallen into the settlers hands, they have been detained at their huts, notwithstanding the earnest entreaties of the parents for their return.

On the 26th, the Dædalus sailed for Norfolk Island, having on board a quantity of the stores and provisions lately received from England,

England, and a detachment of officers and men of the New South Wales corps to relieve those on duty there.

Two female natives, wishing to withdraw from the cruelty which they, with others of their sex, experienced from their countrymen, were allowed to embark in the Dædalus, and were consigned to the care of the lieutenant-governor. One of them was sister to Bennillong; the other was connected with the young man his companion. Perhaps they wished to wait in peace and retirement the arrival of those who were bound to protect them.

At the latter end of the month some warrants of emancipation passed the seal of the territory, and received the lieutenant-governor's signature. The objects of this indulgence were, Robert Sidaway, who received an unconditional pardon in consideration of his diligence, unremitting good conduct, and strict integrity in his employment for several years as the public baker of the settlement; and William Leach, who was permitted to quit this country, but not to return to England during the unexpired term of his sentence of transportation, which was for seven years. Eight convicts were pardoned on condition of their serving in the New South Wales corps until regularly discharged therefrom. James Larra, James Ruffler, and Richard Partridge (convicts for life), received a conditional pardon, or (as was the term among themselves on this occasion) were made free on the ground, to enable them to become settlers; as were also William Joyce and Benjamin Carver for the same purpose. Joyce had been transported for fourteen years, and Carver for life. Freedom on the ground was also given to William Waring, a convict for life.

It was pleasing to see so many people withdrawing from the society of vice and wretchedness, and forming such a character for themselves as to be thought deserving of emancipation.

On the 29th, the Fancy snow left this port. Mr. Dell, the commander, purposed running to Norfolk Island, but affected a secrecy with respect to his subsequent destination. It was generally surmised, however, that he was bound to some island whereat timber fit for naval purposes was to be procured; and at which whatever ship Mr. Hampton should bring with him might touch and load with a cargo for India. The snow was armed, was about one hundred and seventy

tons

tons burden, had a large and expensive complement of officers and
men, a guard of sepoys, and a commission from the Bombay marine*. New Zealand was by us supposed to be the place; as force, or
at least the appearance of it, was there absolutely requisite.

The wife of Griffin the drummer, whose hoarded guineas were
supposed to have been stolen by Charles, or (as he was more commonly named) Pat Gray, killed herself with drinking, expiring in a
fit of intoxication while the husband was employed in the lower part
of the harbour in fishing for his family. She left him four children
to provide for.

October.] This month opened with an indispensable act of justice:
John Bevan, a wretched convict, whose name has been frequently
mentioned in this narrative, broke into the house of William Fielder
at Sydney, and being caught in the fact, it was substantiated against
him beyond the chance of escape; he was of course fully convicted,
and received sentence of death. The trial was on the 1st, and at nine
in the morning of the 6th he was executed. At the tree he confessed
nothing, but seemed terrified when he found himself so near the ignominious death that he had so long merited. On being taken to hear
divine service the Sunday preceding his execution, he seemed not to
be in the smallest degree affected by the clergyman's discourse, which
was composed for the occasion; but was visibly touched at the singing
of the psalm intitled the " Lamentation of a Sinner."

On the evening preceding the day of his execution, information
was received from Parramatta, that Simon Burn, a settler, had been
stabbed to the heart about eight o'clock in the evening before, of
which wound he died in an hour. The man who perpetrated this
atrocious act was a convict named Hill, a butcher by trade. It appeared on the trial, which lasted five hours, that Hill had borne the
deceased much animosity for some time, and, having been all the day
(which, to aggravate the offence, happened to be Sunday) in company
drinking with him, took occasion to quarrel with a woman with whom
he cohabited, and following her into an empty house, whither she had

* Mr. Dell had likewise on board a much greater number of cross-cut saws than were
necessary to procure wood for the mere use of the vessel.

run to avoid a beating, the deceased, unhappily for him, interfered, and was by Hill stabbed to the heart; living, as has been said, about an hour, but having just strength enough to declare in the presence of several witnesses, that the butcher had killed him. The prisoner attempted to set up an alibi for his defence; but the fact of killing was incontrovertibly fixed upon him, as well as the malice which urged his hand to take away the life of his fellow-creature, and to send him, with the sin upon his head of having profaned the Lord's day by rioting and drunkenness, unprepared before his Maker.

This poor man was buried by his widow (an Irish woman) in a corner of his own farm, attended by several settlers of that and the neighbouring districts, who celebrated the funeral rites in a manner and with orgies suitable to the disposition and habits of the deceased, his widow, and themselves.

Hill was executed on the 16th, and his body dissected according to his sentence.

On the 17th the Mercury, an American brig, commanded by Mr. William Barnet, anchored in the cove from Falkland's Islands. He had nothing on board for sale, but brought us the very welcome information of his having seen the officers of the Spanish ship Descuvierta at that place. Being in want of biscuit, he made application to the commodore Malaspina for a supply, proffering to settle the payment in any manner that he should choose to adopt; but the commodore, after sending him a greater quantity than he had required, assured him that he was sufficiently satisfied in having assisted a ship whose people, whether English or American, spoke the language of those gentlemen from whom himself and the officers of the ships under his command had received, while in New South Wales, such attention and hospitality. Mr. Barnet understood the Atrevida was in the neighbourhood, and that no loss or accident had happened in either ship since their departure from Port Jackson. The Mercury was bound to the north-west coast of America, and her master purposed quitting this port as soon as his people, who were all afflicted with that dreadful sea distemper the scurvy, should be sufficiently recovered.

The period of probation which had been allotted by the late governor to the services of William Stephenson (one of the people serving

3 E   in

in the stores) expiring this month, his pardon was delivered to him
accordingly. No one among the prisoners could be found more deserving of this clemency; his conduct had been uniformly that of a
good man, and he had shewn that he was trust-worthy by never having
forfeited the good opinion of the commissary under whom he was
placed in the provision-store.

From the Hawkesbury were received accounts which corroborated
the opinion that the settlers there merited the attacks which were from
time to time made upon them by the natives. It was now said, that
some of them had seized a native boy, and, after tying him hand and
foot, had dragged him several times through a fire, or over a place
covered with hot ashes, until his back was dreadfully scorched, and in
that state threw him into the river, where they shot at and killed him.
Such a report could not be heard without being followed by the closest
examination, when it appeared that a boy had actually been shot when
in the water, from a conviction of his having been detached as a spy
upon the settlers from a large body of natives, and that he was returning to them with an account of their weakness, there being only one
musquet to be found among several farms. No person appearing to
contradict this account, it was admitted as a truth; but many still considered it as a tale invented to cover the true circumstance, that a boy
had been cruelly and wantonly murdered by them.

The presence of some person with authority was become absolutely
necessary among those settlers, who, finding themselves freed from
bondage, instantly conceived that they were above all restrictions;
and, being without any internal regulations, irregularities of the worst
kind might be expected to happen.

On the morning of the 25th a civil court was assembled, for the purpose of investigating an action brought by one Joyce (a convict lately
emancipated) against Thomas Daveny, a free man and superintendant
of convicts at Toongabbe, for an assault; when the defendant, avail-
ing himself of a mistake in his christian name, pleaded the misnomer.
His plea being admitted, the business was for that time got over, and
before another court could be assembled he had entered into a compro-
mise with the plaintiff, and nothing more was heard of it.

In

In the evening of the same day the Surprise transport arrived from England, whence she sailed on the 2d of last May, having on board sixty female and twenty-three male convicts, some stores and provisions, and three settlers for this colony.

Among the prisoners were, Messrs. Muir, Palmer, Skirving, and Margarot, four gentlemen lately convicted in Scotland of the crime of sedition, considered as a public offence, and transported for the same to this country.

We found also on board the Surprise a Mr. James Thompson, late surgeon of the Atlantic transport, but who now came in quality of assistant-surgeon to the settlement; and William Baker, formerly here a serjeant in the marine detachment, but now appointed a superintendant of convicts.

A guard of an ensign and twenty-one privates of the New South Wales corps were on board the transport. Six of these people were deserters from other regiments brought from the Savoy; one of them, Joseph Draper, we understood had been tried for mutiny (of an aggravated kind) at Quebec.

This mode of recruiting the regiment must have proved as disgusting to the officers as it was detrimental to the interests of the settlement. If the corps was raised for the purpose of protecting the civil establishment, and of bringing a counterpoise to the vices and crimes which might naturally be expected to exist among the convicts, it ought to have been carefully formed from the best characters; instead of which we now found a mutineer, (a wretch who could deliberate with others, and consent himself to be the chosen instrument of the destruction of his sovereign's son,) sent among us, to remain for life, perhaps, as a check upon sedition, now added to the catalogue of our other imported vices.

This ship touched only at Rio de Janeiro, between which port and the south-west cape of this country the winds which they met with very much favoured, in the idea of Mr. Campbell the master, the opinion of a passage being readily made to the Cape of Good Hope, or to India, round by Van Dieman's Land.

Among other articles of information now received, we learned that Governor Hunter, with the Reliance and Supply, two ships intended to be employed in procuring cattle for the colony, might be expected to arrive in about three months. The governor was to bring out with him a patent for establishing a court of criminal judicature at Norfolk Island.

The two natives in England were said to be in health, and anxious for the governor's departure, as they were to accompany him. They had made but little improvement in our language.

The Surprise anchoring in the cove after dark, she saluted at sunrise the following morning with fifteen guns.

A theft was committed in the course of the month in one of the out-houses belonging to Government-House, used as a regimental storeroom; the articles stolen were fifteen shirts and seventeen pair of shoes. In searching among the rocks and bushes for this property, three white and two check shirts, one pair of trowsers, and one pair of stockings, were found; but so damaged by the weather as to be entirely useless. These must have been planted (to use the thief's phrase) a considerable time; for every mark or trace which could lead to a discovery of the owner was entirely effaced.

The storeships being cleared of their cargoes, a survey was made upon such part of them as was damaged, which was found to be very considerable. A serving of slops was immediately issued to the male and female convicts; the men receiving each one jacket, one waistcoat, one shirt, one hat, and one pair of breeches; the women one petticoat, one shift, one pair of stockings, one cap, one neck-handkerchief, one hat, and one jacket made of raven duck. A distinction was made in the articles of the slops served to watchmen and overseers, each receiving one coat instead of a jacket, one pair of duck trowsers instead of a pair of breeches, and one pair of shoes.

On the 21st died an industrious good young man, Joseph Webb, a settler at the district named Liberty Plains. He had been working in his ground, and suddenly fell down in an apoplectic fit. We have seen that another settler was murdered, and two male convicts were executed. Burn had been an unfortunate man; he had lost one of his eyes, when, as a convict, he was employed in splitting paling for government; his farm had never succeeded; himself and his wife were too fond of spiritous liquors to be very industrious; and he was at last

2   forced

forced out of the world in a state and in a manner shocking to human nature.

November.] Since our establishment in this harbour but few accidents had happened to boats. On the 1st of this month, however, the long-boat of the Surprise, though steered by one of the people belonging to the settlement, was overset on her passage from the cove to Parramatta, in a squall of wind she met with off Goat Island, with a number of convicts and stores on board. Fortunately, no other loss followed than that occasioned by the drowning of one very fine female goat, the property of Baker the superintendant.

On the following day died Mr. Thomas Freeman, the deputy-commissary of stores and provisions employed at Parramatta. He was in his fifty-third year, and in this country ended a life the greater part of which had been actively and usefully employed in the king's service. His remains were interred in the burial-ground at Parramatta, and were attended by the gentlemen of the civil department residing in that township.

On the morning of the 9th the ships Resolution and Salamander left the cove, purposing to sail on their fishing voyage; soon after which, it being discovered that three convicts, Mary Morgan and John Randall and his wife, were missing, a boat was sent down the harbour to search the Resolution, on board of which ship it was said they were concealed. No person being found, the boat returned for further orders, leaving a serjeant and four men on board; but before she could return, Mr. Locke the master, after forcing the party out of his ship, got under way and stood out to sea. Mr. Irish, the master of the Salamander, did not accompany him; but came up to the town, to testify to the lieutenant-governor his uneasiness at its being supposed that he could be capable of taking any person improperly from the colony.

On the day following it appeared that several persons were missing, and two convicts in the night swam off to the Salamander, one of whom was supposed to have been drowned, but was afterwards found concealed in her hold and sent on shore. The Resolution during this time was seen hovering about the coast, either waiting for her companion,

panion, or to pick up a boat with the runaways. On the 13th, the Salamander got under way, with a southerly wind; but it falling calm when the ship was between the Heads, she drifted, and was set with the ebb tide so near the north head of the harbour as to be obliged to anchor suddenly in eighteen fathoms water. When anchored they got a kedge-anchor out, and began to heave; but the surf on the head and the swell from the sea were so great, occasioned by the late southerly winds, that in heaving the cable parted. Fortunately the stream-hawser hung her; and a breeze from the northward springing up, she was brought into the harbour with the loss of an anchor. This loss being repaired by her getting another from the Surprise, she was enabled to sail finally on the 15th.

The impropriety of the conduct of the Resolution's master was so glaring, that the lieutenant-governor caused some depositions to be taken respecting it, which he purposed transmitting to the navy-board. This man had been permitted to ship as many persons from the settlement as he stated to be necessary to complete his ship's company; notwithstanding which, there was not any doubt of his having received on board, without any permission, to the number of twelve or thirteen convicts whose terms of transportation had not been served. No difficulty had ever been found by any master of a ship, who would make the proper application, in obtaining any number of hands that he might be in want of; but to take clandestinely from the settlement the useful servants of the public was ungrateful and unpardonable. It was to be hoped that government, if the facts could be substantiated against him, would make this person a severe example to other masters of ships coming to this port.

On the 23d, after an absence of eight weeks and two days, the Dædalus returned from Norfolk Island. Ten days of this time were passed in going thither, and sixteen in returning; the intermediate time was consumed in landing one, and receiving on board the other detachment, with their baggage.

Several persons, whose sentences of transportation had expired, and who preferred residing in New South Wales, together with ten of the marine settlers, who had given up their grounds in consequence of the
late

late difappointment which they experienced in refpect of their corn
bills, and had entered into the New South Wales corps, arrived in
this fhip.

We underftood that Phillip Ifland had been found to anfwer extremely well for the purpofe of breeding flock. Some hogs which
were allowed to be placed there in Auguft 1793, the property of an
individual, had increafed fo prodigioufly, as to render the raifing
hogs there on account of government an object with the lieutenant-
governor.

The Dædalus immediately began preparations for her departure for
England ; and Lieutenant-governor Grofe fignified his intention of
quitting the fettlement by that opportunity.

The lieutenant-governor having fet apart for each of the gentlemen
who came from Scotland in the Surprife a brick hut, in a row on the
eaft fide of the cove, they took poffeffion of their new habitations,
and foon declared that they found fufficient reafon for thinking their
fituations " on the bleak and defolate fhores of New Holland" not
quite fo terrible as in England they had been taught to expect.

The Surprife was difcharged this month from government employ,
and Mr. Campbell began to prepare for making his paffage to Bengal
(whither he was bound) by the fouth cape of this country. Of the
female prifoners who came out in this fhip one was buried on the 21ft ;
fhe had lain in of a dead child, and died fhortly after of a milk
fever. Her hufband, a free man, came out with her to fettle in the
country.

Reaping our wheat-harveft commenced this month.

December.] The people of the Mercury being perfectly recovered
from the diforder which afflicted them when they arrived, that veffel
failed on the 7th of December for the north-weft coaft of America.
The mafter had permiffion to fhip five perfons belonging to the colony,
and on the day of his failing feveral others were miffing from the labouring gangs, and were fuppofed to have made their efcape in her ;
but on the following morning they were all at their refpective labours,
not having been able to get on board.

                                                          Some

Some of the seamen belonging to this vessel, preferring the pleasures they met with in the society of the females and the free circulation of spirituous liquors which they found on shore, to accompanying Mr. Barnet to the north-west coast of America, had left his vessel some days previous to her sailing. Application being made to the lieutenant-governor, several orders were given out calculated to induce them to return to their duty, informing them, that if they remained behind they would be certainly sent to hard labour, and the persons who had harboured them severely punished. But our settlements had now become so extensive, that orders did not so readily find their way to the settlers, as runaways and vagrants, who never failed of finding employment among them, particularly among those at the river.

On the 8th a farm of five-and-twenty acres of ground in the district of Concord was sold by public auction for thirteen pounds. Four acres were planted with Indian corn, and half an acre with potatoes; there was beside a tolerable hut on the premises. This farm was the property of Samuel Crane, a soldier, who, too industriously for himself, working on it on the Sunday preceding his death, received a hurt from a tree which fell upon him, and proved fatal.

Every preparation for accommodating the lieutenant-governor and his family being completed on board the Dædalus, he embarked in the evening of the 15th. Previous to his departure, such convicts as were at that time confined in the cells, or who were under orders for punishment, were released; several grants of lands were signed, conveying chiefly small allotments of five-and-twenty acres each to such soldiers of the regiment as were desirous of, and made application for that favour; and some leases of town lots were given.

With the lieutenant-governor went Mr. White, the principal surgeon of the colony; Mr. Bain, the chaplain, in whose absence the Rev. Mr. Marsden was to do his duty; Mr. Laing, assistant-surgeon of the settlement, and mate of the New South Wales corps; three soldiers; two women, and nine men. The master of the transport had permission to ship twelve men and two women, whose sentences of transportation had expired.

The

The . North View of . Sydney . Cove, taken from the end of . Pitt. Row .

The Surprise sailed on the 17th. Mr. Campbell, being in want of hands, was allowed to receive on board sixteen men. He had shipped a greater number; but some, regardless of their own situation, and of the effect such an act might have on others, had been detected in the act of robbing the ship, and were turned on shore.

Mr. Campbell at his departure expressed his determination of trying his passage to Bengal by the south cape of this country. The route of the Dædalus was round the southern extremity of New Zealand.

The lieutenant-governor took with him all the documents which were necessary to lay before government to explain the state of the different settlements under his command; such as the commissary's accounts, returns of stock, remains of provisions, &c. &c.; vouchers, in fact, of that true spirit of liberality which had marked the whole of his administration of the public affairs of this settlement.

Our society was much weakened by this departure of our friends; they carried with them, however, letters to our connexions, and our earnest wishes for their speedy, pleasant, and safe passage to England.

The number of small boats at this time in the settlement was considerable, although wretchedly put together. Two of them were stolen during the month by several Irish prisoners, accompanied by some who came out in the Surprise. In it they went down to the South-head, whence they took what arms they could find, and made off to sea. In a very few days they were all brought in from the adjacent bays, and punished for their rashness and folly. No example seemed to deter these people from thinking it practicable to escape from the colony; the ill success and punishment which had befallen others affected not them, till woeful experience made it their own; and then they only regretted their ill fortune, never attributing the failure to their own ignorance and temerity.

In the morning of Wednesday the 24th the signal was made at the South-head for a vessel (which they had seen the day before). She came in about three o'clock, and proved to be the Experiment, a snow from Bengal, laden with spirits, sugar, piece-goods, and a few casks of provisions; the speculation being suggested by Mr. Beyer, the agent for the Sugar Cane and Boddingtons. Those ships had arrived safely at Bengal, and had sailed thence for England.

The

The Experiment had had a paffage of three months from Calcutta, one month of which fhe had paffed fince fhe faw the fouthern extremity of this country.

We learned from Mr. F. M'Clellan, the mafter, that a large fhip named the Neptune had been freighted with cattle, &c. in purfuance of the contract entered into with Mr. Bampton, and had failed from Bombay in July laft, but was unfortunately loft in the river by failing againft the monfoon. When Mr. Bampton might be expected was uncertain.

The direction of the colony during the abfence of the governor and lieutenant-governor devolving upon the officer higheft in rank then on fervice in the colony, Captain William Paterfon, of the New South Wales corps, on Chriftmas-day took the oaths prefcribed by his Majefty's letters patent for the perfon who fhould fo take upon him the government of the fettlement. This officer, expecting every day the arrival of Governor Hunter, made no alteration in the mode of carrying on the different duties of the fettlement now entrufted to his care and guidance.

At the latter end of the month a general mufter was ordered of all the male convicts, together with the perfons who had ferved their feveral terms of tranfportation, as well thofe refiding at Sydney and Parramatta, as thofe on the banks of the river Hawkefbury. The following ration was alfo ordered, the maize being nearly expended: videlicet,

To Civil, Military, Free People, and Free Settlers.	To Male Convicts.
8 lbs. of flour. 7 lbs. of beef, or	4 lbs. of flour. 7 lbs. of beef, or
4 lbs. of pork. 3 pints of peafe.	4 lbs. of pork. 3 pints of peafe.
6 oz. of fugar.	6 ozs. of fugar, and 3 pints of rice.

Women and children were to receive the ufual proportion, and a certain quantity of flops was directed to be iffued to the male and female convicts who came out in the Surprife tranfport, they being very much in want of clothing.

A jail gang was alfo ordered to be eftablifhed at Toongabbe, for the employment and punifhment of all bad and fufpicious characters.

Wheat was this month directed to be purchafed from the fettlers at ten fhillings per bufhel. Much of that grain was found to have been
blighted

blighted this feafon. The ground about Toongabbe was pronounced
to be worn out, the produce of the laft harveft not averaging more
than fix or feven bufhels an acre, though at firft it was computed at
feventeen. The Northern farms had alfo failed through a blight.

Our lofs by death in the year 1794 was, two fetlers ; four foldiers ;
one foldier's wife; thirty-two male convicts ; ten female convicts ; and
ten children ; making a total of fifty-nine perfons.

CHAP. XXVIII.

GANGS SENT TO TILL THE PUBLIC GROUNDS.—THE FRANCIS SAILS.—REGU-
LATIONS FOR THE HAWKESBURY.—NATIVES.—WORKS.—WEATHER.—
DEATHS.—PRODUCE AT THE RIVER.—TRANSACTIONS THERE.—NATIVES.
—THE FRANCIS RETURNS FROM PORT STEPHENS.—TRANSACTIONS.—
THE BRITANNIA ARRIVES FROM THE CAPE.—THE FANCY FROM NEW
ZEALAND.—INFORMATION.—THE EXPERIMENT SAILS FOR INDIA.—A
NATIVE KILLED.—WEATHER.—WHEAT.—CRIMINAL COURT.—RATION
REDUCED.—THE BRITANNIA HIRED TO PROCURE PROVISIONS.—NATIVES
AT THE HAWKESBURY.—THE ENDEAVOUR ARRIVES WITH CATTLE FROM
BOMBAY.—DEATHS.—RETURNS OF GROUND SOWN WITH WHEAT.—THE
BRITANNIA SAILS FOR INDIA—THE FANCY FOR NORFOLK ISLAND.—CON-
VICTS.—CASUALTIES.

January 1795.] FROM the great numbers of labouring convicts
who were employed in the town of Sydney, and at the grounds about
Peterfham ; of others employed with officers and fetlers ; of thofe
who, their terms of tranfportation having expired, were allowed to
provide for themfelves ; and of others who had been permitted to
leave the colony, public field-labour was entirely at a ftand. The
prefent commanding officer wifhing to cultivate the grounds belonging
to government, collecting as many labourers as could be got together,
fent a large gang, formed of bricklayers, brickmakers, timber-carriage
men, &c. &c. to Parramatta and Toongabbe, there to prepare the
ground for wheat for the enfuing feafon. At the mufter which had

3 F 2   been

been lately taken fifty people were found without any employment, whose services still belonged to the public; most of these were laid hold of, and sent to hard labour; and it appeared at the same time that some few were at large in the woods, runaways, and vagabonds. These people began labouring in the grounds immediately after New Year's day, which as usual was observed as a holiday.

On the 22d, the convict women who had children attended at the store, when they received for each child three yards of flannel, one shirt, and two pounds of soap.

On the day following, the colonial schooner sailed for the river, having on board a mill, provisions, &c. for the settlers there. A military guard was also ordered, the commanding officer of which was to introduce some regulations among the settlers, and to prevent, by the effect of his presence and authority, the commission of those enormities which disgraced that settlement. For the reception of such quantity of the Indian corn and wheat grown there this season as might be purchased by government, a store-house was to be erected under the inspection of the commissary; and Baker, the superintendant who arrived in the Surprise, was sent out to take the charge of it when finished. The master of the schooner was ordered, after discharging his cargo, to receive on board Mr. Charles Grimes, the deputy surveyor-general, and proceed with him to Port Stephens, for the purpose of examining that harbour.

About the middle of the month a convict, on entering the door of his hut, was bit in the foot by a black snake; the effect was, an immediate swelling of the foot, leg, and thigh, and a large tumour in the groin. Mr. Thompson, the assistant-surgeon, was fortunately able to reduce all these swellings by frequently bathing the parts in oil, and saved the man's life without having recourse to amputation. While we lived in a wood, and might naturally have expected to have been troubled with them, snakes and other reptiles were by no means so often seen, as since, by clearing and opening the country about us, the natives had not had opportunities of setting the woods so frequently on fire. But now they were often met in the different paths about the settlements, basking at mid-day in the sunshine, and particularly after a shower of rain.

We

We heard and faw much of the natives about this time. At the Hawkefbury a man had been wounded by fome of the Wood tribe. Two women (natives) were murdered not far from the town of Sydney during the night, and another victim, a female of Pe-mul-wy's party, (the man who killed M'Intyre,) having been fecured by the males of a tribe inimical to Pe-mul-wy, dragged her into the woods, where they fatigued themfelves with exercifing acts of cruelty and luft upon her.

The principal labour performed In January was preparing the ground for wheat. The Indian corn looked every where remarkably well, it was now ripening, and the fettlers on the banks of the Hawkefbury fuppofed that at leaft thirty thoufand bufhels of that grain would be raifed among them.

Several native boys, from eight to fourteen years of age, were at this time living among the fettlers in the different diftricts. They were found capable of being made extremely ufeful; they went cheerfully into the fields to labour, and the elder ones with eafe hoed in a few hours a greater quantity of ground than that generally affigned to a convict for a day's work. Some of thefe were allowed a ration of provifions from the public ftores.

In confequence of the heavy rains, the river at the Hawkefbury rofe many feet higher than it had been known to rife in other rains, by which feveral fettlers were fufferers. At Toongabbe the wheat belonging to government was confiderably injured. At Parramatta the damage was extenfive; the bridge over the creek, which had been very well conftructed, was entirely fwept away; and the boats with their moorings carried down the river. At Sydney fome chimnies in the new barracks fell in.

Mr. Jones, the quarter-mafter ferjeant of the New South Wales corps, a perfon of much refpectability, and whofe general demeanor indicated an education far beyond what is met with in the fphere of life in which he moved, died this month.

A convict lad, in the fervice of Mr. William Smith the ftore-keeper, died on the 26th, having fwallowed arfenic. It was remarkable in his untimely end, that he himfelf placed the poifon with a view of deftroying

ing the rats with which the house was infested, and was particularly
cautioned against it. How he came, after that, to take it himself, was
not to be accounted for.

BAKER's FARM,
High land on the banks of the — River

February.] Early in February, the storehouse at the Hawkesbury
being completed, the provisions which had been sent round in the
schooner were landed and put under the care of Baker. Some officers
who had made an excursion to that settlement, with a view of selecting
eligible spots for farms, on their return spoke highly of the corn which
they saw growing there, and of the picturesque appearance of many
of the settlers' farms. The settlers told them, that in general their
grounds which had been in wheat had produced from thirty to
thirty-six bushels an acre; that they found one bushel (or on some
spots five pecks) of seed sufficient to sow an acre; and that, if sown
as early as the month of April or May, they imagined the ground
would

would produce a fecond crop, and the feafon be not too far advanced
to ripen it. Their kitchen gardens were plentifully flocked with vegetables. The mafter of the fchooner complained that the navigation
of the river was likely to be hurt. The fettlers having fallen many
trees into the water, he was apprehenfive they would drift afhore on
fome of the points of the river where, in procefs of time, fand, &c.
might lodge againft them, and form dangerous obftructions in the
way of craft which might be hereafter ufed on the river. No doubt
remained of the ill and impolitic conduct of fome of the fettlers toward
the natives. In revenge for fome cruelties which they had experienced,
they threatened to put to death three of the fetlers, Michael Doyle,
Robert Forrefter, and ——— Nixon; and had actually attacked and
cruelly wounded two other fettlers, George Shadrach and John Akers,
whofe farms and perfons they miftook for thofe of Doyle and Forrefter. Thefe particulars were procured through the means of one
Wilfon, a wild idle young man, who, his term of tranfportation being
expired, preferred living among the natives in the vicinity of the
river, to earning the wages of honeft induftry by working for fettlers.
He had formed an intermediate language between his own and theirs,
with which he made fhift to comprehend fomething of what they
wifhed him to communicate; for they did not conceal the fenfe they
entertained of the injuries which had been done them. The tribe
with whom Wilfon affociated had given him a name, Buo-bo-é, but
none of them had taken his in exchange. As the gratifying an idle
wandering difpofition was the fole object with Wilfon in herding with
thefe people, no good confequence was likely to enfue from it; and
it was by no means improbable, that at fome future time, if difgufted
with the white people, he would join the blacks, and affift them in
committing depredations, or make ufe of their affiftance to punifh or
revenge his own injuries. Mr. Grimes purpofed taking him with
him in the fchooner to Port Stephens.

There were at this time feveral convicts in the woods fubfifting by
theft; and it being faid that three had been met with arms, it became
neceffary to fecure them as foon as poffible. Watchmen and other
people immediately went out, and in the afternoon of the 14th a
wretched fellow of the name of Suffini was killed by one of them.
This circumftance drove the reft to a greater diftance from Sydney,
                                                            and

and they were reported, some days afterwards, to have been met on their route to the river. Suffini would not have been shot at, had he not refused to surrender when called to by the watchman while in the act of plundering a garden.

About the latter end of the month the natives adjusted some affairs of honour in a convenient spot near the brick-fields. The people who live about the south shore of Botany Bay brought with them a stranger of an extraordinary appearance and character; even his name had something extraordinary in the sound—Gòme-boak. He had been several days on his journey from the place where he lived, which was far to the southward. In height he was not more than five feet two or three inches; but he was by far the most muscular, square, and well-formed native we had ever seen. He fought well; his spears were remarkably long, and he defended himself with a shield that covered his whole body. We had the satisfaction of seeing him engaged with some of our Sydney friends, and of observing that neither their persons nor reputations suffered any thing in the contest. When the fight was over, on our praising to them the martial talents of this stranger, the strength and muscle of his arm, and the excellence of his sight, they admitted the praise to be just (because when opposed to them he had not gained the slightest advantage); but, unwilling that we should think too highly of him, they assured us, with horror in their countenances, that Gòme-boak was a cannibal *.

March.] On the 1st of March the Francis returned from Port Stephens. Mr. Grimes reported, that he went into two fresh-water branches, up which he rowed, until, at no very great distance from the entrance, he found them terminate in a swamp. He described the land on each side to be low and sandy, and had seen nothing while in this harbour which in his opinion could render a second visit necessary. The natives were so very unfriendly, that he made but few observations on them. He thought they were a taller and a stouter race of people than those about this settlement, and their language was entirely different. Their huts and canoes were something larger than those which we had seen here; their weapons were the same. They wel-

* Gòme-boak, we learned, was afterwards killed among his own people in some affair to the southward.

comed

comed him on fhore with a dance, joined hand in hand, round a tree, to exprefs perhaps their unanimity ; but one of them afterwards, drawing Mr. Grimes into the wood, poifed a fpear, and was on the point of throwing it, when he was prevented by young Wilfon, who, having followed Mr. Grimes with a double-barrelled gun, levelled at the native, and fired it. He was fuppofed to be wounded, for he fell ; but rifing again, he attempted a fecond time to throw the fpear, and was again prevented by Wilfon. The effect of this fecond fhot was fuppofed to be conclufive, as he was not feen to rife any more. Mr. Grimes got back to his boat without any other interruption.

Mr. Houfe in his way thither ran clofe along the fhore, and faw not any fhelter for a fhip or veffel from Broken Bay to Port Stephens. The fchooner was only fourteen hours on her return.

About this time, the fpirit of inquiry being on foot, Mr. Cummings, an officer of the corps, made an excurfion to the fouthward of Botany Bay, and brought back with him fome of the head bones of a marine animal, which, on infpection, Captain Paterfon, the only naturalift in the country, pronounced to have belonged to the animal defcribed by M. de Buffon, and named by him the Manatee. On this excurfion Mr. Cummings received fome information which led him to believe that the cattle that had been loft foon after our arrival were in exiftence. The natives who converfed with him were fo particular in their account of having feen a large animal with horns, that he fhortly after, taking fome of them with him as guides, fet off to feek them, but returned without fuccefs, not having met with any trace that could lead him to fuppofe they might ever be found.

On the 4th the Britannia returned from the Cape of Good Hope, having been abfent fix months and three days. Mr. Raven brought alive to his employers, one ftallion, twenty-nine mares, three fillies, and twelve fheep. He failed from the Cape with forty mares on board ; but thofe that died were the worft, and had not been kept up long enough on dry food before they were embarked.

It was evident, on vifiting the fhip, that every attention had been paid to their accommodation ; but horfes were generally fuppofed

3 O   better

better calculated than other cattle to endure the weather usually met with between the Cape and this country *.

We had the gratification of hearing that our fleet under Earl Howe had been victorious in a gallant and severe action with the enemy.

On the 15th, when anxiously expecting an arrival from England, we saw Mr. Dell come to anchor in the cove from Norfolk Island.

Though this arrival proved a disappointment to most of us, yet the information we received by it was rather interesting. We now learned, that Mr. Dell had been at New Zealand, where he passed three months in the river named by Captain Cook the Thames, employed in cutting spars, for the purpose (as was conjectured here at the time of his departure) of freighting such ship as might arrive from India on Mr. Dampton's account. In the course of that time they cut down upwards of two hundred very fine trees, from sixty to one hundred and forty feet in length, fit for any use that the East-India Company's ships might require. The longest of these trees measured three feet and a half in the butt, and differed from the Norfolk Island pines in having the turpentine in the centre of the tree instead of between the bark and the wood. From the natives they received very little interruption, being only upon one occasion obliged to fire on them. Like other uncivilised people, these islanders saw no crime in theft, and stole some axes from the people employed on shore, gratifying thereby their predilection for iron, which, strange as it may sound to us, they would have preferred to gold. Unfortunately, iron was too precious even here to part with, unless for an equivalent; and it became necessary to convince them of it. Two men and one woman were killed, the seamen who fired on them declaring (in their usual enlarged style of relation) that they had driven off and pursued upwards of three thousand of these cannibals. They readily parted with any quantity of their flax, bartering it for iron. As the valuable qualities of this flax were well known, it was not uninteresting to us to learn, that so small a vessel as the Fancy had lain at an anchor for three months in the midst of numerous and warlike tribes of savages, without any attempt on their

* It may be remembered, that in a former voyage to the Cape on a similar errand, she lost twenty-nine cows.

S,   part

part to become the maſters; and that an intercourſe might ſafely and advantageouſly be opened between them and the coloniſts of New South Wales, whenever proper materials and perſons ſhould be ſent out to manufacture the flax, if the governor of that country ſhould ever think it an object worthy of his attention.

From New Zealand the Fancy proceeded to Norfolk Iſland, and now came hither in the hope of meeting with, or hearing of Mr. Bampton.

From that ſettlement we gained the following information:

The Salamander touched there, and the Reſolution appeared off the Iſland, but had no communication with the ſhore.

A heavy gale of wind, accompanied with a ſlight ſhock of the earth, had done conſiderable damage, waſhing away a very uſeful wharf and crane at Caſcade, but which the governor meant immediately to replace.

The produce of the wheat this ſeaſon on government's account amounted to three thouſand buſhels, and that of ſettlers to fifteen hundred. The Indian corn promiſed a very plentiful crop; but the ſettlers were much diſcouraged by their bills of the laſt year remaining ſtill unpaid. Much of that corn was obliged to be ſurveyed, and two thouſand buſhels had been condemned.

Swine were increaſing ſo rapidly on Phillip Iſland, now ſtocked by government, that Mr. King thought he ſhould be able for ſome time to iſſue freſh pork during four days in the week. The flour was expended; of ſalt meat there was a ſufficiency in ſtore for eight months. The whole number of perſons on the iſland amounted to nine hundred and forty-five.

A convict well known in this ſettlement, Benjamin Ingraham, being detected in the act of houſebreaking, put an end to his own exiſtence by hanging himſelf, thus terminating by his own hand a life of wretchedneſs and villany.

On the 17th St. Patrick found many votaries in the ſettlement. Some Cape brandy lately imported in the Britannia appeared to have arrived very ſeaſonably; and libations to the ſaint were ſo plentifully poured, that at night the cells were full of priſoners.

Settlers, and other perſons who had Indian corn to diſpoſe of, were this month informed, that they would receive five ſhillings per buſhel for all they might bring to the public ſtores. They were likewiſe told,

that

that a preference would be given to those who had difpofed of their wheat to government.

On the 23d the Experiment failed for India. Mr. M'Clellan had been with his veffel to the Hawkefbury, where he had taken in fixty large logs of the tree which we had named the cedar. He had alfo purchafed fome of the mahogany of this country. Whether cedar and mahogany were or were not to be readily procured at Bengal, ought to have been well known to this gentleman before he put himfelf to the trouble, delay, and expence of procuring fuch a quantity*; but it was here generally looked upon as a fpeculation that would not produce him much profit.

On the day of his failing, fufpecting (as was reported) fome defign to feize his veffel, he fent on fhore three people whom he had fhipped here. They rendezvoufed at a hut in the town occupied by one John Chapman Morris; and, on fearching it, in the bed of one of them were found a dozen of new Indian fhirts marked D. W.; twenty-two new pulicate handkerchiefs; and three pieces of ftriped gingham. On the poffeffor being queftioned, he faid, that they were fold to him while he was at Norfolk Ifland by the fteward of Captain Manning's fhip, the Pitt. As this was a very improbable ftory, the houfe they were in was ordered by the commanding officer to be pulled down. The property, having been difclaimed by Mr. M'Clennan, was lodged with the provoft-marfhal; and the parties given to underftand, that a reference would be made to Norfolk Ifland by the firft opportunity.

On the 26th, fome of our people witneffed an extraordinary tranf-action which took place among the natives at the brick-fields. A young man of the name of Bing-yi-wan-ne, well known in the fettlement, being detected in the crifis of an amour with Maw-ber-ry, the companion of another native, Ye-ra-ni-be Go-ru-ey, the latter fell upon him with a club, and being a powerful man, and of fuperior ftrength, abfolutely beat him to death. Bing-yi-wan-ne had fome friends, who on the following day called Ye-ra-ni-be to an account for the murder; when, the affair being conducted with more regard to honour than juftice, he came off with only a fpear-wound in his thigh.

* He was to allow one hundred pounds for as many trees; but we underftood that it was to be in the way of barter with articles, fugar, fpirits, &c.

The

The farmers began gathering their Indian corn about the latter end of this month. The weather during the former and latter part of it was wet. About the time of the equinox, the tides in the cove were observed to be very high.

On the 28th Thomas Webb, a settler, who had removed from his farm at Liberty Plains to another on the banks of the Hawkesbury, was dangerously wounded there, while working on his grounds by some of the wood natives, who had previously plundered his hut. About the same time a party of these people threw a spear at some soldiers who were going up the river in a small boat. All these unpleasant circumstances were to be attributed to the ill treatment the natives had received from the settlers.

At Prospect Hill a woman was bitten by a snake; but by the timely application of some volatile salts by Mr. Irving, her life was saved.

A WESTERN VIEW OF TOONGABBE

Published May 20th 1798 by Cadell & Davies Strand

April]

April.] It was determined to let the Toongabbe Hills remain fallow for a season, they being reported to be worn out. Other ground, which had been prepared, was now sown; a spot called the Ninety Acres, and the hills between Parramatta and Toongabbe.

On the 15th, a criminal court was assembled for the trial of John Anderson and Joseph Marshall, settlers; and John Hyams, Joseph Dunstill, Richard Watson, and Morgan Bryan, convicts; for a rape committed on the body of one Mary Hartley, at the Hawkesbury, The court was obliged to acquit the prisoners, owing to glaring contradiction in the witnesses, no two of them, though several were examined, agreeing in the same point. But as such a crime could not be passed with impunity, they were recommitted, and on the 22d tried for an assault, of which being very clearly convicted, the two settlers and Morgan Bryan were sentenced to receive each five hundred lashes, and the others three hundred each; of which sentence they received one half, and were forgiven the remainder. This was a most infamous transaction; and, though the sufferer was of bad character, would have well warranted the infliction of capital punishment on one of the offenders, if the witnesses had not prevaricated in their testimony. They appeared to have cast off all the feelings of civilized humanity, adopting as closely as they could follow them the manners of the savage inhabitants of the country. One prisoner, John Rayner, was also tried for a burglary, and being convicted received sentence of death.

On the 29th, a liberal allowance of slops was issued to the male and female convicts in the different settlements, among which were some soap to the men, and some thread, tape, and soap to the women.

A shed for the purpose of receiving their Indian corn was this month begun by the settlers at the river, they and their servants bringing in the materials, and government supplying the carpenters, tools, nails, &c.

The farmers now every where began putting their wheat into the ground, except at the river, where they had scarcely made any preparations, consuming their time and substance in drinking and rioting; and trusting to the extreme fertility of the soil, which they declared would produce an ample crop at any time without much labour. So

silly

filly and thoughtlefs were thefe people, who were thus unworthily placed on the banks of a river which, from its fertility and the effect of its inundations, might not improperly be termed the *Nile* of New South Wales.

May.] From the reduced ftate of the falted provifions, it became neceffary (fuch had often been the preamble of an order) to diminifh the ration of that article iffued weekly to each perfon, and half the beef and half the pork was flopped at once. In fome meafure to make this great deduction lighter, three pints of peafe were added. This circumftance induced the commanding officer, on the day this alteration took place, to hire the Britannia to proceed to India for a cargo of falted provifions. Supplies might arrive before fhe could return; but the war increafed the chances againft us. He therefore took her up at fifteen fhillings and fixpence per ton per month; and, in order to fave as much falt meat as was poffible, he directed the commiffary to purchafe fuch frefh pork as the fettlers and others might bring in good condition to the ftore, iffuing two pounds of frefh, in lieu of one of falt meat. During the time this order continued, a barrow was killed and part fent to the ftore, which weighed five hundred pounds, and a fow which weighed three hundred and thirty-fix pounds. They had both been fed a confiderable time * on Indian corn, and, according to the rate they fold at (the pork one fhilling per pound, and the corn five fhillings per bufhel) could neither of them have repaid the expence of their feed.

On the 21ft the colonial fchooner returned from the Hawkefbury, bringing upwards of eleven hundred bufhels of remarkably fine Indian corn from the ftore there. The mafter again reported his apprehenfions, that the navigation of the river would be obftructed by the fettlers, who continued the practice of falling and rolling trees into the ftream. He found five feet lefs water at the ftore-wharf than when he was there in February laft, owing to the dry weather which had for fome time paft prevailed.

At that fettlement an open war feemed about this time to have commenced between the natives and the fettlers; and word was received

* The barrow two years and a half, and the fow about two years.

over—

over-land, that two people were killed by them; one a settler of the name of Wilson, and the other a freeman, one William Thorp, who had been left behind from the Britannia, and had hired himself to this Wilson as a labourer. The natives appeared in large bodies, men, women, and children, provided with blankets and nets to carry off the corn, of which they appeared as fond as the natives who lived among us, and seemed determined to take it whenever and wherever they could meet with opportunities. In their attacks they conducted themselves with much art; but where that failed they had recourse to force, and on the least appearance of resistance made use of their spears or clubs. To check at once, if possible, these dangerous depredators, Captain Paterson directed a party of the corps to be sent from Parramatta, with instructions to destroy as many as they could meet with of the wood tribe (Bè-dia-gal); and, in the hope of striking terror, to erect gibbets in different places, whereon the bodies of all they might kill were to be hung. It was reported, that several of these people were killed in consequence of this order; but none of their bodies being found, (perhaps if any were killed they were carried off by their companions,) the number could not be ascertained. Some prisoners however were taken, and sent to Sydney; one man, (apparently a cripple,) five women, and some children. One of the women, with a child at her breast, had been shot through the shoulder, and the same shot had wounded the babe. They were immediately placed in a hut near our hospital, and every care taken of them that humanity suggested. The man was said, instead of being a cripple, to have been very active about the farms, and instrumental in some of the murders which had been committed. In a short time he found means to escape, and by swimming reached the north shore in safety; whence, no doubt, he got back to his friends. Captain Paterson hoped, by detaining the prisoners and treating them well, that some good effect might result; but finding, after some time, that coercion, not attention, was more likely to answer his ends, he sent the women back. While they were with us, the wounded child died, and one of the women was delivered of a boy, which died immediately. On our withdrawing the party, the natives attacked a farm nearly opposite Richmond Hill, belonging to one William Rowe, and put him and a very fine child to death;

the

the wife, after receiving several wounds, crawled down the bank, and concealed herself among some reeds half immersed in the river, where she remained a confiderable time without affiftance: being at length found, this poor creature, after having seen her hufband and her child flaughtered before her eyes, was brought into the hofpital at Parramatta, where she recovered, though flowly, of her wounds. In confequence of this horrid circumftance, another party of the corps was fent out; and while they were there the natives kept at a diftance. This duty now became permanent; and the foldiers were diftributed among the fettlers for their protection; a protection, however, that many of them did not merit.

Pemulwy, or fome of his party, were not idle about Sydney; they even ventured to appear within half a mile of the brickfield huts, and wound a convict who was going to a neighbouring farm on bufinefs. As one of our moft frequent walks from the town was in that direction, this circumftance was rather unpleafant; but the natives were not feen there again.

On Sunday the 31ft, about one o'clock, the fignal was made at the South-head for a fail; and about five there anchored in the cove the Endeavour, a fhip of eight hundred tons from Bombay, under the command of Mr. Bampton, having on board one hundred and thirty-two head of cattle, a quantity of rice, and the other articles of the contract engaged by Lieutenant-governor Grofe, except the falt provifions. She had been eleven weeks from Bombay.

The cattle arrived, in general, in good condition; and Mr. Bampton had been very fuccefsful in his care of them. He embarked one hundred and thirty at Bombay, out of which he loft but one cow, and that died the morning before his arrival.

On vifiting the fhip, the fight was truly gratifying; the cattle were ranged on each fide of the gun-deck, fore and aft, and not confined in feparate ftalls; but fo conveniently ftowed, that they were a fupport to each other. They were well provided with mats, and were conftantly cleaned; and when the fhip tacked, the cattle which were to leeward were regularly laid with their heads to windward, by people (twenty in number) particularly appointed to look after them, independent of any duty in the fhip. The grain which was their food

was,

was, together with their water, regularly given to them, and the deck they flood on was well aired, by scuttles in the sides, and by wind sails *. Of this number of cattle forty were for draught, sixty for breeding, and the remainder calves; but some of them so large, as to be valued and taken at fifteen guineas per head.

On their landing, we were concerned to find that many of the draught cattle were very aged; they were, it was true, in health; but younger animals undoubtedly ought to have been procured; for of little use could toothless, old, and blind beasts be to us.

At the settlement at the Hawkesbury, a woman who had been drinking was found dead in her husband's arms. Webb the settler, who was wounded in March last, died; and one settler (Rowe) and his child were killed in this month.

June.] On the 4th of this month, being the anniversary of his Majesty's birth, the commissary issued to each of the non-commissioned officers and privates of the New South Wales corps, one pound of fresh pork and half a pint of spirits; and to all other people victualled from the store one gill each. At noon the regiment fired three vollies; and at one o'clock the Britannia and Fancy twenty-one guns each in honour of the day.

Preparatory to the departure of the Britannia, some returns were procured, which were necessary to be transmitted with the dispatches then making up. Among others it appeared, that the following quantity of ground had been this season sown with wheat: viz.

	Acres
On account of government at and about Parramatta	340
Individuals at and about ditto -	1214
Individuals at the River † - -	548½
Individuals at and about Sydney -	618½
Total -	2711½

* These circumstances are mentioned so particularly, in the hope that they may prove useful hints to any persons intending, or who may be in future employed, to convey cattle from India, or any other part of the world, to New South Wales.

† This was the account given by the settlers; but their conduct gave little room to believe they had been so industrious: they certainly ought to have had a greater quantity.

6   On

On the 18th the Britannia failed for India. As the ftate of the fettlement at the time of her departure required every exertion to be made in procuring an immediate fupply of provifions, Mr. Raven was directed to repair to Batavia, to procure there if poffible a cargo of European falted meat. The neceffity of his immediate return was fo urgent, that if he found on his arrival that only half a cargo could be got, he was to fill up the remainder of the flowage with rice and fugar, and make the beft of his way back. If falted provifions were not to be got at Batavia, he was to proceed to Calcutta. Should circumftances run fo much againft us, as to caufe his failure at both thefe ports, Mr. Raven was at liberty to return by the way of the Cape of Good Hope, as provifions were at any rate to be procured, if poffible.

On the 21ft, the Fancy failed for Norfolk Ifland, taking a cargo of rice and dholl for the ufe of that fettlement; the Rev. Mr. Marfden alfo embarked in her to marry and baptife fuch as flood in need of thofe rites.

On the 29th the colonial fchooner brought another cargo of Indian corn (one thoufand one hundred and twelve bufhels) from the Hawkefbury. For want of ftorehoufe room, great quantities were left lying before the door, expofed to, and fuffering much by the weather. As it had not been meafured or received by the ftore-keeper, the lofs fell upon the owners.

. The cattle lately arrived feemed to fuffer by their change of climate; one cow and feveral calves died; perhaps as much from mifmanagement, as by the weather; for, with very few exceptions, it was impoffible to felect from among the prifoners, or thofe who had been fuch, any who would feel an honeft intereft in executing the fervice in which they were employed. They would pilfer half the grain entrufted to their care for the cattle; they would lead them into the woods for pafturage, and there leave them until obliged to conduct them in; they would neither clean them nor themfelves. Indolent, and by long habit worthlefs, no dependance could be placed on them. In every inftance they endeavoured to circumvent; and whenever their exertions were called for, they firft looked about them to difcover how thofe exertions might be turned to their own advantage.

Could

Could it then be wondered at, if little had been done since our eftablifhment? and muft it not rather excite admiration to fee how much had been done? Whatever was to be feen was the effect of the moft unremitting, and perhaps degrading vigilance on the part of thofe in whom the executive power had been from time to time vefted, and of the intereft that many individuals had felt in raifing this country from its original infignificance to fome degree of confequence.

Among the cafualties of the month muft be noticed the death of a man unfortunately drowned in attempting to fave the life of a woman who was overfet with himfelf in a paffage-boat, coming from Parramatta. He had juft got her into fafety when fhe pulled him under water, and he perifhed. It is extremely hazardous, and requires very great caution in thofe who meddle with perfons that are drowning.

On the 27th, two foldiers, going with their arms to Parramatta, ftopped on the road to fire at a mark. One of them, inconfiderately, placing himfelf behind the tree which was the mark, and prefenting himfelf in the unfortunate moment of his companion's firing, received the ball in his thigh near the groin. He was brought to Sydney as foon as it was poffible, when Mr. Harris the furgeon of the regiment amputated the limb. The wound was fo near the groin, however, that the tourniquet was fixed with much difficulty and hazard *.

There was at this time under the care of the furgeon Jofeph Harton, a fettler at the Eaftern Farms, an elderly man, who had been dangeroufly ftabbed in the belly by his wife, a young woman, (named before their marriage Rofamond Sparrow,) in a fit of jealoufy and paffion. On his recovery, he earneftly requefted that no punifhment might be inflicted on her, but that fhe might be put away from him.

* The patient's name was Nicholas Downie. He recovered, after feveral weeks care and attention on the part of Mr. Harris; but his comrade fuffered much anxiety during the cure.

CHAP. XXIX.

July.] THE salted provisions being all expended, except a few
casks which were reserved for the non-commissioned officers and private soldiers of the corps, on Saturday the 11th of the month the convicts received the following ration :

Indian corn,	- - - -	12 pounds (unground) ;
Rice,	- - - -	5 ditto ;
Dholl,	- - - -	3 pints ;
Sugar,	- - - -	1½ pound ;

being the first time, since the establishment of the colony, that they
had gone from the store without receiving either salted or fresh provisions. On the Monday following the military received,

Salt pork,	- - - -	2 pounds ;
Indian corn,	- - - -	12 ditto (unground) ;
Pease,	- - - -	3 pints ;
Rice,	- - - -	3 ditto ;
Sugar,	- - - -	6 ounces.

This

This being the state of the stores, supplies were ardently to be desired. It was truly unfortunate, that Mr. Bampton had not been able to procure any salted provisions at Bombay, but in lieu thereof had brought us a quantity of rice. We now began to grow grain sufficient for our consumption from crop to crop, and grain that was at all times preferred to the imports from India. Dholl and rice were never well received by the prisoners as an equivalent for flour, particularly when pease formed a part of the ration; and it was to be lamented that a necessity ever existed, of forcing upon them such trash as they had from time to time been obliged to digest.

The effects of this ration soon appeared; several attacks were made on individuals; the house occupied by Mr. Muir was broken into, and all or nearly all that gentleman's property stolen: some of his wearing apparel was laid in his way the next day; but he still remained a considerable sufferer by the visit. Some private stock yards were attacked; but finding them too vigilantly watched, a fellow played off a trick that he thought would go down with the hungry; he stole a very fine greyhound, and, instead of secretly employing him in procuring occasionally a fresh meal, he actually killed the dog, and sold it to different people in the town for kangooroo at nine-pence per pound. Being detected in this villainous traffic, he was severely punished.

A criminal court was assembled on the 20th for the trial of Mary Pawson, a settler's wife at the river, for the crime of arson. On the trial there was strong evidence of malice in the prisoner against the wife of the owner of the house; but not any that led directly to convict her of having set the house on fire. She was therefore acquitted; but the adjoining settlers disliking such a character in their neighbourhood, the husband, who had nothing against him but this wife, sold a very good farm which he possessed on a creek of the river, and withdrew to another situation, remote and less advantageous. At the same time a notorious offender, James Darry, was tried for attempting to break into a settler's house at the Ponds with an intent to steal, the proof of which was too clear to admit of his escape. He was sentenced to suffer one thousand lashes, and on the Saturday following received two hundred and seventy of them.

On

On the same day a civil court was held for the purpose of granting probate of the will of Thomas Daveney, late a superintendant of convicts, who died on the 3d of the month. The cause of his death was extraordinary. He had been appointed a superintendant of the convicts employed in agriculture at Toongabbe by the late Governor Phillip, who, considering him trust-worthy, placed great confidence in him. Some time after Governor Phillip's departure, his conduct was represented to the lieutenant-governor in such a light, that he dismissed him from his situation, and he retired to a farm which he had at Toongabbe. He had been always addicted to the use of spirituous liquors; but he now applied himself more closely to them, to drown the recollection of his disgrace. In this vice he continued until the 3d of May last, on which day he came to Sydney in a state of insanity. He went to the house of a friend in the town, determined, as it seemed, to destroy himself; for he there drank, unknown to the people of the house, as fast as he could swallow, nearly half a gallon of Cape brandy. He fell directly upon the floor of the room he was in (which happened to be of brick); where the people, thinking nothing worse than intoxication ailed him, suffered him to lie for ten or twelve hours; in consequence he was seized with a violent inflammation which broke out on the arm, and that part of the body which lay next the ground; to this, after suppuration had taken place, and several operations had been performed to extract the pus, a mortification succeeded, and at last carried him off on the 3d of July. A few hours before his death he requested to see the judge-advocate, to whom he declared, that it had been told him that he had been suspected of having improperly and tyrannically abused the confidence which he had enjoyed under Governor Phillip; but that he could safely declare, as he was shortly to appear before the last tribunal, that nothing lay on his conscience which could make his last moments in this life painful. At his own request he was interred in the burying ground at Parramatta. He had been advancing his means pretty rapidly; for, after his decease, his flock of goats, consisting of eighty-six males and females, sold by public auction for three hundred and fifty-seven pounds fifteen shillings. He left a widow (formerly Catharine Hounson,) who had for several years been deranged in her intellects.

In

In addition to the superintendant, there died in this month a woman, Jane Forbes, the wife of ——— Butler, a settler at Prospect Hill, who fell into the fire while preparing their breakfast, and received such injury that she shortly after expired.

August.] From the scantiness of salted provisions, the article salt was become as scarce. There came out in the Surprise, as a settler, a person of the name of Boston. Among other useful knowledge * which we were given to understand he possessed, he at this time offered his skill in making salt from sea-water. As it was much wanted, his offers were accepted, and, an eligible spot at Bennillong's Point (as the east point of the cove had long been named) being chosen, he began his operations, for which he had seven men allowed him, whose labour, however, only produced three or four bushels of salt in more than as many weeks.

His Royal Highness the Prince of Wales's birth-day was duly noticed. At one o'clock the Endeavour fired twenty-one guns.

Wilson (Bun-bo-è), immediately after his return from Port Stephens with the deputy-surveyor, went off to the natives at the river. Another vagabond, who like himself had been a convict, one Knight, thinking there must be some sweets in the life which Wilson led, determined to share them with him, and went off to the woods. About the middle of this month they both came into the town, accompanied by some of their companions. On the day following it appeared that their visit was for the purpose of forcing a wife from among the women of this district; for in the midst of a considerable uproar, which was heard near the bridge, Wilson and Knight were discovered, each dragging a girl by the arm (whose age could not have been beyond nine or ten years) assisted by their new associates. The two white men being soon secured, and the children taken care of, the mob dispersed. Wilson and Knight were taken to the cells and punished, and it was intended to employ them both in hard labour; but they found means to escape, and soon mixed again with companions whom they preferred to our overseers.

* Having been sent out by government to supply us with salted fish, he had some time before offered to procure and salt fish for the settlement; but he required boats and men, and more assistance than it was possible to supply. He proposed to try Broken Bay.

About

About this time the natives were, during two days, engaged in very severe contests. Much blood was shed, and many wounds inflicted; but no one was killed. It appeared to afford much diversion; for they were constantly well attended by all descriptions of people, notwithstanding the risk they ran of being wounded by a random spear.

On the 26th the settlement was gratified by the arrival of his Majesty's ship Providence, of twenty-eight guns, commanded by Captain Broughton, from England. She sailed thence on the 25th of February last, in company with his Majesty's ships Reliance and Supply, which ships she left at Rio de Janeiro some time in May last. We had the satisfaction of learning that Governor Hunter was on board the Reliance, and might be daily expected.

The Providence met with very bad weather on her passage from the Brazil coast, and was driven past this harbour as far to the northward as Port Stephens, in which she anchored. There, to the great surprise of Captain Broughton, he found and received on board four white people, (if four miserable, naked, dirty, and smoak-dried men could be called white,) runaways from this settlement. By referring to the transactions of the month of September 1790, it will be found that five convicts, John Tarwood, George Lee, George Connoway, John Watson, and Joseph Sutton, escaped from the settlement at Parramatta, and, providing themselves with a wretched weak boat, which they stole from the people at the South Head, disappeared, and were supposed to have met a death which, one might have imagined, they went without the Heads to seek. Four of these people (Joseph Sutton having died) were now met with in this harbour by the officers of the Providence, and brought back to the colony. They told a melancholy tale of their sufferings in the boat; and for many days after their arrival passed their time in detailing to the crowds both of black and white people which attended them their adventures in Port Stephens, the first harbour they made. Having lived like the savages among whom they dwelt, their change of food soon disagreed with them, and they were all taken ill, appearing to be principally affected with abdominal swellings. They spoke in high terms of the pacific disposition and gentle manners of the natives. They were at some distance inland when Mr. Grimes

3 I   was

was in Port Stephens; but heard soon after of the schooner's visit, and
well knew, and often afterwards saw, the man who had been fired at,
but not killed at that time as was supposed, by Wilson. Each of them
had had names given him, and given with several ceremonies.
Wives also were allotted them, and one or two had children. They
were never required to go out on any occasion of hostility, and were
in general supplied by the natives with fish or other food, being considered by them (for so their situation only could be construed) as
unfortunate strangers thrown upon their shore from the mouth of the
yawning deep, and entitled to their protection. They told us a ridiculous story, that the natives appeared to worship them, often assuring
them, when they began to understand each other, that they were undoubtedly the ancestors of some of them who had fallen in battle, and
had returned from the sea to visit them again ; and one native appeared
firmly to believe that his father was come back in the person of either
Lee or Connoway, and took him to the spot where his body had
been burnt. On being told that immense numbers of people existed
far beyond their little knowledge, they instantly pronounced them to
be the spirits of their countrymen, which, after death, had migrated
into other regions.

It appeared from these four men, that the language to the northward differed wholly from any that we knew. Among the natives
who lived with us, there were none who understood all that they said,
and of those who occasionally came in, one only could converse with
them. He was a very fine lad, of the name of Wur-gan. His mother
had been born and bred beyond the mountains, but one luckless day,
paying a visit with some of her tribe to the banks of the Dee-rab-bun,
(for so the Hawkesbury was named,) she was forcibly prevented returning, and, being obliged to submit to the embraces of an amorous
and powerful Be-dia-gal, the fruit of her visit was this boy. Speaking
herself more dialects than one, she taught her son all she knew, and he,
being of quick parts, and a roving disposition, caught all the different
dialects from Botany Bay to Port Stephens.

We understood that Lieutenant-governor Grose in the Dædalus
had reached Rio de Janeiro in eleven weeks from his sailing hence,
and that all on board were in health.

Public labour was scarcely any where performed in this month, owing to the extreme badness of the weather which prevailed. The rain and wind were so violent for some days after the arrival of the Providence, that neither that ship nor the Endeavour had much communication with the shore. Accounts were received from the Hawkesbury, that several farms on the creeks were under water; and the person who brought the account was nearly drowned in his way over a plain named the Race-Ground. Paling could no where stand the force of the storm. Several chimnies and much plaster fell, and every house was wet. At Parramatta much damage was done; and at Toongabbe (a circumstance most acutely felt) a very large barn and threshing-floor were destroyed. The schooner had been loading with corn at the river, and, though she left the store on the 11th, did not reach Sydney until the 20th, having met with much bad weather. During the storm, the column at the South Head fell in. This, however, could be more readily repaired than the barn and the threshing-floor at Toongabbe, which were serious losses, and had cost government a much larger sum than the beacon.

Several of the cattle lately arrived perished in this bad weather.

To eke out the salt meat that was reserved for the military, two Cape cows, which would not breed, were killed and served out to them during this month.

September.] After an absence of eleven weeks, the Fancy arrived on the 3d from Norfolk Island. Her passage thither was made in six days; but on her return she ran within one hundred and thirty miles of this port in three or four days; yet afterwards met with contrary and heavy gales of wind which kept her out a month. On the 28th of last month she was off the south head of Broken Bay in a heavy gale of wind, and was, by being close in with the land in thick weather, in extreme danger. Of a large quantity of stock (the property of Mr. Balmain, who left Norfolk Island to take upon him the charge of the general hospital here), but a very small quantity remained alive after the gale.

The most favourable accounts were received from that settlement. Plenty reigned throughout. Every barn was full. Four thousand pounds of fresh pork having been cured, the lieutenant-governor had

forty

forty tons of falt provifions to fpare, which he offered to this colony.
The wharf and crane at Cafcade were rather improved than fimply
repaired, and an overfhot water-mill had been erected at the trifling
expence of three ewe fheep to the conftructor, which ground and
dreffed eighteen bufhels of flour in a day.

' William Hogg, a prifoner well known and approved at this place
for his abilities as a filverfmith, and an actor in the walk of low comedy, put an end to his exiftence in a very deliberate manner a few
days before the Fancy failed. Spirits being in circulation after her
arrival, he went to the " Grog-fhop" as long as he had money; but,
finding that he had no credit, he could no longer endure the lofs of
character which he thought attached to it; and though he did not
" make his quietus with a bare bodkin," yet he found a convenient
rope that put him out of the world.

The 7th of September was marked by the arrival of the governor
in chief of thefe fettlements. The fignal was made for two fail between
eight and nine o'clock in the morning. The wind being from the
northward, they did not reach the anchorage until late; his Majefty's
fhip the Supply, commanded by Lieutenant William Kent, getting in
about fun-fet; and the Reliance, with the governor on board, about
eight at night. Their paffage from Rio de Janeiro was long (fourteen
weeks) and very rough, until the fhips came off Van Dieman's Land.
Of our late bad weather they had felt nothing.

Situated as the colony was in point of provifions, we learned with
infinite concern, that a ftorefhip which had once been under Governor
Hunter's orders, had, from being overloaded, been unavoidably left
behind, and had yet to run the chance of being taken by the enemies'
cruizers; and that by the two fhips now arrived we had only gained
a few barrels of provifions falted at Rio de Janeiro; a town clock;
the principal parts of a large wind-mill; two officers of the New South
Wales corps; Mr. S. Leeds an affiftant-furgeon, and Mr. D. Payne
a mafter boat-builder.

His excellency did not take upon him the exercife of his authority
until the 11th, on which day his Majefty's commiffion was publicly
read by the judge-advocate, all defcriptions of perfons being prefent.
His excellency, in a very pertinent fpeech, declared the expectations

he

he had from every one's conduct, touching with much delicacy on that of the persons lately sent here for a certain offence, (some of whom were present, but who unfortunately kept at too great a distance to hear him,) and strongly urging the necessity of a general unanimity in support of his Majesty's government. He was afterwards sworn in by the judge-advocate at his office *. An address, signed by the civil and military officers on occasion of his return among them as governor, was presented to his excellency a few days after his public appearance in that important capacity.

That he might as speedily as possible be acquainted with the state of the colony, he ordered a general muster to be taken by the commissary, appointing different days at Sydney, Parramatta, and the Hawkesbury, in order that correct accounts might be obtained of the number and distribution of every person (the military excepted) in those districts; and he purposed in person to inspect the state of the different farms. He recommended it to all persons who had lands in cultivation to plant with Indian corn as much of them as might not at that time be under any other grain; urging them, as it was the proper season, not to let it pass by, it being an essential article in the nourishment of live stock, the increase of which was of such importance to the settlement, that he could not but advise the utmost care and œconomy in the use of what might then and in future be in the possession of settlers and other persons.

Mr. Bampton having given his ship such repairs as he was able in this port, the Endeavour and Fancy sailed for India on the 18th. He purposed touching at New Zealand and at Norfolk Island. We found after their departure, that, notwithstanding so many as fifty persons whose transportation had expired had been permitted to leave the colony in the Endeavour, nearly as many more had found means to secrete themselves on board her. As she was to touch at Norfolk Island, hopes were entertained of getting the runaways back again, as

* Before Captain Paterson gave up his command, all the prisoners in confinement were pardoned and liberated. Rayner, under sentence of death, was pardoned by the governor some time after. In consequence of this act of grace, several runaways gave themselves up.

the

the loss even of one man's labour was at this time an object of consequence.

As many labouring people as could be got together were employed during the month in receiving such articles as had been brought in the king's ships for the colony.

The weather during the month was very variable; and three women and two men died. Of these one was much regretted, as his loss would be severely felt; this was Mr. J. Irving, who, dying before the governor arrived, knew not that he had been appointed an assistant to the surgeons with a salary of fifty pounds per annum.

October.] The police and civil duties of the town and district of Sydney were now regulated by civil magistrates. At Parramatta, Lieutenant M'Arthur continued to carry on the duties to which he had been appointed by Lieutenant-governor Grose, the public service at that place requiring the inspection and superintendance of an officer.

On Sunday the 4th of this month the Young William, the storeship whose unavoidable delay in her sailing we had regretted on the arrival of the governor without her, anchored safe in the cove from England, after a short passage of four months and nine days, with a cargo of provisions only. She sailed from Spithead in company with the Sovereign, another storeship, on the 25th of May, taking her route by the way of Rio de Janeiro, where she anchored on the 12th of July, leaving it on the 21st of the same month; and meeting with very bad weather nearly the whole of the voyage, she shipped great quantities of water; and, being very deeply laden, the vessel was considerably strained.

By letters received from this ship we learned, that some promotions had taken place in the New South Wales corps. Captain Nicholas Nepean had obtained the commission of second major; Lieutenant John M'Arthur had succeeded to his company; Lieutenant John Townson had got the company late belonging to Captain Hill; and Ensigns Clephan and Piper were made lieutenants, all without purchase. Messrs. Kent and Bell, the naval agents, who left this country in the Britannia in September 1794, arrived safely in England in March last.

In

In confequence of this arrival the governor had it in his power to iſſue a better, though not ſo ample a ration of proviſions as he could have defired. The ſupply had not been ſufficient to allow him to order more than four pounds ten ounces and two thirds of an ounce of beef, or two pounds ten ounces and two thirds of an ounce of pork, and four pounds of flour, to the convicts. The ſame quantity of ſalt meat was ordered for the military; but they received two pounds of flour more than the priſoners. The other parts of the weekly ration remained nearly the ſame as before, except the article of ſugar, the convicts receiving ſix ounces inſtead of one pound and a half of that article.

The report of the general muſter which was ordered in the laſt month having been laid before the governor, he thought proper to make ſome regulations in the aſſiſtance afforded by government to ſettlers and others holding grants of land. To the officers who occupied grounds was continued the number of men allowed them by Lieutenant-governor Groſe; viz. ten for agriculture, and three for domeſtic purpoſes. Notwithſtanding this far exceeded the number which had at home been thought neceſſary, the governor did not conceive this to be the moment for reducing it, much as he wanted men. A wheat harveſt was approaching; ground was planting with Indian corn; not a man was unemployed; but he ſaw and explained that a reduction muſt take place; that government could not be ſuppoſed much longer to feed, maintain, and clothe the hands that wrought the ground, and at the ſame time pay for the produce of their labour, particularly when every public work was likely to ſtand ſtill for want of labourers. He was ſenſible that the aſſiſtance which had been given had not been thrown away, and that the ſmall number allowed by government could never have produced ſuch rapid approaches toward that Independence which he thought, from what he had already ſeen of the cultivation of the country, was now much nearer than at his leaving it in 1791 he could have conceived to be poſſible. To the ſettlers * who arrived in the Surpriſe he allowed five male convicts; to the ſuperintendants, conſtables, and ſtore-keepers, four; to ſettlers from

* Meſſrs. Boſton, Pearce, and Ellis.

free

free people *, two; to settlers from prisoners, one; and to serjeants of the New South Wales corps, one.

As much inconvenience also was felt, and the end for which government gave up the services of these convicts to individuals liable to be defeated by their not residing at their respective farms, the settlers were directed as much as possible to prevent their servants from having any intercourse, particularly during the night, with the towns in their neighbourhood; as most of the robberies which were committed were not unjustly laid to their account.

It appeared likewise by this muster, that one hundred and seventy-nine people subsisted themselves independent of the public stores, and resided in this town. To many of these, as well as to the servants of settlers, were to be attributed the offences that were daily heard of; they were the greatest nuisances we had to complain of; and there was not a doubt that they were concerned about this time in rolling two casks of meat from a pile at the store in a very hard storm of wind and rain. Enough to fill a cask was found concealed in different holes the following morning.

An indulgence had been allowed to some of the military and others, which was now found to have produced an evil. Having been permitted to build themselves huts on each side of and near the stream of water which supplied the town of Sydney, they had, for the convenience of procuring water, opened the paling, and made paths from each hut; by which, in rainy weather, a great quantity of filth ran into the stream, polluting the water of which every one drank. It therefore became an object of police; and the governor prohibited removing the paling, or keeping hogs in the neighbourhood of the stream, under penalty to the offender that his house should be pulled down.

On the 13th, the Providence sailed for Nootka Sound. She was followed by the Supply, which sailed on the 16th for Norfolk Island, having on board three officers of the New South Wales corps, and a detachment of the regiment to relieve those now on duty there. On

* Such as the marine settlers, those at Liberty Plains, and others who never had been prisoners.

the

the 29th the Young William, having been expeditiously cleared of her cargo, failed for Canton.

Clearing the store-ship, which was completed on the 19th, and stowing in the public store the provisions she brought out, was the principal labour of the month. Every effort was made to collect together a sufficient number of working people to get in the ensuing harvest; and the muster and regulation respecting the servants fortunately produced some. The bricklayer and his gang were employed in repairing the column at the South-head; to do which, for want of bricks at the kiln, the little hut built formerly for Bennillong, being altogether forsaken by the natives, and tumbling down, the bricks of it were removed to the South-head. A person having undertaken to collect shells and burn them into lime, a quantity of that article was sent down; and the column, being finished with a thick coat of plaster, and whitened, was not only better guarded against the weather, but became a more conspicuous object at sea than it ever had been before.

November.] On the 5th of November, the Sovereign store-ship arrived from England; her cargo a welcome one, being provisions. Like the Young William, she touched at Rio de Janeiro, and like her also had met with very bad weather after she had left that port until her arrival; from making the south cape of this country to her anchoring she had a passage of three weeks. In this ship arrived Mr. Thomas Hibbins, the deputy judge-advocate for Norfolk Island; but unfortunately without the patent under the great seal for holding the court. One settler also arrived, a Mr. Kennedy and his family (a sister and three nieces); and Mr. Joseph Gerald, a prisoner, whose present situation afforded another melancholy proof of how little profit and honor were the endowments of nature and education to him who perverted them. In this gentleman we saw, that not even elegant manners, (evidently caught from good company,) great abilities, and a happy mode of placing them in the best point of view, the gifts of nature matured by education, could (because he misapplied them) save him from landing an exile, to call him by no worse a name, on a barbarous shore, where the few who were civilized must pity, while

3 K   they

they admired him. He arrived in a very weak and impaired state of health. We learned that two other ships with convicts, the Marquis Cornwallis and the Maria, might be expected to arrive in the course of this summer.

On the 7th, a criminal court was assembled, when the following persons were tried; viz. Samuel Chinnery (a black) servant to Mr. Arndell *, the assistant surgeon, for robbing that gentleman; but he was acquitted: —— Smith and Abraham Whitehouse, for breaking into the dwelling-house of Willam Potter, a settler at Prospect Hill, and after cruelly treating the only person in the house, William Thorn, (a servant,) stripping it of all the moveables they could find, and killing and taking away some valuable stock; these were found guilty, and' condemned to die: and two settlers, and six convicts, for an assault on one Marianne Wilkinson, (attended with like circumstances of infamy as that on Mary Hartley in April last,) of which three were found guilty, and sentenced, —— Merchant, alias Jones, the principal, to receive one thousand lashes; the others, Ladley and Everitt, eight hundred each.

These unmanly attacks of several men on a single woman had frequently happened, and had happened to some females who, through shame, concealed the circumstance. To such a height indeed was this dissolute and abandoned practice carried, that it had obtained a cant name; and the poor unfortunate objects of this brutality were distinguished by a title expressive of the insults they had received.

On the 16th the two prisoners Smith and Whitehouse were led out to execution. Smith suffered, after warning the crowd which attended him to guard against breaking the Sabbath. Whitehouse, being evidently the tool of Smith, and a much younger man, was pardoned by the governor. His excellency, after the execution, expressed in public orders, his " hope that neither the example he had that day found " himself compelled to make of one offender, nor the lenity which " he had shewn to another, would be without their effect: it would " always be more grateful to him to spare than to punish; but he felt

* This gentleman had, on the arrival of Mr. Leeds, been permitted to retire from the civil duties of the colony with a salary of fifty pounds per annum.

" it

" it neceffary on that occafion to declare, that if neither the juflice
" which had been done, nor the mercy which had been fhewn, tended
" to decreafe the perpetration of offences, it was his determination in
" future to put in execution whatever fentence fhould be pronounced
" on offenders by the court of criminal judicature."

A fmall printing-prefs, which had been brought into the fettlement
by Mr. Phillip, and had remained from that time unemployed, was
now found very ufeful; a very decent young man, one George
Hughes, of fome abilities in the printing line, having been found
equal to conducting the whole bufinefs of the prefs. All orders were
now printed, and a number thrown off fufficient to enfure a more
general publication of them than had hitherto been accomplifhed.

Some time after the arrival of the Sovereign the full allowance of
falt meat was iffued, and the hours of public labour regulated, more
to the advantage of government than had for a confiderable time,
owing to the fhortnefs of the ration, been the cafe. Inftead of completing in a few hours the whole labour which was required of a man
for the day, the convicts were now to work the whole day, with the
intermiffion of two hours and a half of reft. Many advantages were
gained by this regulation; among which not the leaft was, the diminution of idle time which the prifoners before had, and which, empha-
tically terming *their own time*, they applied as they chofe, fome in-
duftrioufly, but by far the greater part in improper purfuits, as gaming,
drinking, and ftealing.

The full ration of flour was iffued to the military, on account of the
" hard duty which had lately fallen upon the regiment;" but they
were informed, that the quantity of flour in the public ftore would
not admit of their receiving fuch allowance for any length of time.
Four pounds were iffued to the prifoners, and fome other grain given
to them to make up the difference.

On the 20th his Majefty's fhip Supply returned from Norfolk Ifland,
having been abfent four weeks and four days. She had a long paffage
back of feventeen days. When Mr. Kent left the ifland, the lieutenant-governor was dangeroufly ill with the gout in his ftomach. We
underftood that cultivation was nearly at a ftand there. The grounds
were fo over-run with two great enemies to agriculture, rats, and a

J K 2   pernicious

pernicious weed called cow-itch *, that the settlers despaired of ever being able to get rid of either.

A circumstance happened this month not less extraordinary and unexpected than the discovery of the four convicts at Port Stephens.

The contests which had lately taken place very frequently in this town, and the neighbourhood of it, among the natives, had been attended by many of those people who inhabited the woods, and came from a great distance inland. Some of the prisoners gathering from time to time rumours and imperfect accounts of the existence of the cattle lost in 1788, two of them, who were employed by some officers in shooting, resolved on ascertaining the truth of these reports, and trying by different excursions to discover the place of their retreat. On their return from the first outset they made, which was subsequent to the governor's arrival, they reported, that they had seen them. Being, however, at that moment too much engaged in perfecting the civil regulations he had in view for the settlement, the governor could not himself go to that part of the country where they were said to have been found; but he detached Henry Hacking, a man on whom he could depend. His report was so satisfactory, that on the 18th the governor set off from Parramatta, attended by a small party, when after travelling two days, in a direction S. S. W. from the settlement at Prospect Hill, he crossed the river named by Mr. Phillip the Nepean; and, to his great surprise and satisfaction, fell in with a very fine herd of cattle, upwards of forty in number, grazing in a pleasant and apparently fertile pasturage. The day being far advanced when he saw them, he rested for the night in their neighbourhood, hoping in the morning to be gratified with a sight of the whole herd. A doubt had been started of their being cattle produced from what we had brought into the country from the Cape; and it was suggested that they might be of longer standing. The governor thought this a circumstance worth determining, and directed the attendants who were with him (Hacking and the two men who had first found them) to endeavour in the morning to get near enough to kill a calf. This they were not able to effect; for, while lying in wait for the whole herd to pass

* The Prurima, a species of the Dolichos.

(which

(which now confifted of upwards of fixty young and old,) they were furioufly fet upon by a bull, which brought up the rear, and which in their own defence they were compelled to kill. This however an-fwered the purpofe better perhaps than a calf might have done; for he had all the marks of the Cape cattle when full grown, fuch as wide-fpreading horns, a moderate rifing or hump between his fhoulders, and a fhort thin tail. Being at this time feven or eight-and-thirty miles from Parramatta, a very fmall quantity of the meat only could be fent in; the remainder was left to the crows and dogs of the woods, much to the regret of the governor and his party *, who confidered that the prifoners, particularly the fick at the hofpital, had not lately received any meat either falt or frefh.

The country where they were found grazing was remarkably plea-fant to the eye; every where the foot trod on thick and luxuriant grafs; the trees were thinly fcattered, and free from underwood, except in particular fpots; feveral beautiful flats prefented large ponds, covered with ducks and the black fwan, the margins of which were fringed with fhrubs of the moft delightful tints; and the ground rofe from thefe levels into hills of eafy afcent.

The queftion how thefe cattle came hither appeared eafy of folution. The few that were loft in 1788, two bulls and five cows, travelled without interruption in a weftern direction until they came to the banks of the Nepean. Arrived there, and finding the croffing as eafy as when the governor forded it, they came at once into a well-watered country, and amply ftored with grafs. From this place why fhould they move? They found themfelves in poffeffion of a country equal to their fupport, and in which they remained undifturbed. We had not yet travelled quite fo far weftward; and but few natives were to be found thereabouts; they were likely therefore to remain for years un-molefted, and fecurely to propagate their fpecies.

It was a pleafing circumftance to have in the woods of New Holland a thriving herd of wild cattle. Many propofals were made to bring them into the fettlement; but in the day of want, if thefe fhould be facrificed, in what better condition would the colony be for having

* Captain Waterhoufe and Mr. Bafs (furgeons) of the Reliance, and the writer of this Narrative.

poffeffed

possessed *a herd of cattle in the woods?*—a herd which, if suffered to remain undisturbed for some years, would, like the cattle of South America, always prove a market sufficient for the inhabitants of the country; and, perhaps, not only for their own consumption, but for exportation. The governor saw it in this light, and determined to guard, as much as was in his power, against any attempts to destroy them.

On his return he found some very fine ground at the back of Prospect Hill. The weather during this excursion was so intensely hot, that one day as the party passed through a part of the country which was on fire, a terrier dog died by the way.

Discharging the store-ship, some part of the cargo of which appeared to be injured by the weather she had met with, formed the principal labour of the month. On account of the small number of working men which could be got together, the governor required two able men to be sent in for this purpose from each farm having ten, to be returned as soon as the provisions were stowed in the public store.

It having been the practice for some time past to shoot such hogs (pursuant to an order which their destructive qualities had rendered necessary in the lieutenant-governor's time) as were found trespassing in gardens or cultivated grounds, and the loss of the animals being greatly felt by the owners, as well as detrimental to the increase of that kind of stock, the governor directed, that instead of firing at them when found trespassing, they should be taken to the provost-marshal, by whom (if the damage done, which was to be ascertained before a magistrate, was not paid for within twenty-four hours) they were to be delivered to the commissary as public property, and the damages paid as far as the value of the animal would admit.

A combination appearing among the labouring people to raise the price of reaping for a day, the governor, being as desirous to encourage industry as to check every attempt at imposition, thought it necessary, on comparing our's with the price usually paid in England, to direct that ten shillings, and no more, should be demanded of, or given by any settler, under pain of losing the assistance of government, for reaping an acre of wheat. It was much feared that this order would be but little attended to; and that some means would be devised on both sides to evade the letter of it.

We heard nothing of the natives at the river; all was quiet there. About this settlement their attention had been for some time engroffed by Ben-nil-long, who arrived with the governor. On his firft appearance, he conducted himfelf with a polished familiarity toward his fifters and other relations; but to his acquaintance he was diftant, and quite the man of confequence. He declared, in a tone and with an air that feemed to expect compliance, that he fhould no longer fuffer them to fight and cut each other's throats, as they had done; that he fhould introduce peace among them, and make them love each other. He expreffed his wifh that when they vifited him at Government-houfe they would contrive to be fomewhat more cleanly in their perfons, and lefs coarfe in their manners; and he feemed abfolutely offended at fome little indelicacies which he obferved in his fifter Car-rang-ar-rang, who came in fuch hafte from Botany Bay, with a little nephew on her back, to vifit him, that fhe left all her habiliments behind her.

Ben-nil-

Ben-nil-long had certainly not been an inattentive obferver of the manners of the people among whom he had lived; he conducted himfelf with the greateft propriety at table, particularly in the obfervance of thofe attentions which are chiefly requifite in the prefence of women. His drefs appeared to be an object of no fmall concern with him; and every one who knew him before he left the country, and who faw him now, pronounced without hefitation that Ben-nil-long had not any defire to renounce the habits and comforts of the civilized life which he appeared fo readily and fo fuccefsfully to adopt.

His inquiries were directed, immediately on his arrival, after his wife Go-roo-bar-roo-bool-lo; and her he found with Caruey. On producing a very fafhionable rofe-coloured petticoat and jacket made of a coarfe ftuff, accompanied with a gypfy bonnet of the fame colour, fhe deferted her lover, and followed her former hufband. In a few days however, to the furprife of every one, we faw the lady walking unincumbered with clothing of any kind, and Ben-nil-long was miffing. Caruey was fought for, and we heard that he had been feverely beaten by Ben-nil-long at Rofe Bay, who retained fo much of our cuftoms, that he made ufe of his fifts inftead of the weapons of his country, to the great annoyance of Caruey, who would have preferred meeting his rival fairly in the field armed with the fpear and the club. Caruey being much the younger man, the lady, every inch a woman, followed her inclination, and Ben-nil-long was compelled to yield her without any further oppofition. He feemed to have been fatisfied with the beating he had given Caruey, and hinted, that refting for the prefent without a wife, he fhould look about him, and at fome future period make a better choice.

His abfences from the governor's houfe now became frequent, and little attended to. When he went out he ufually left his clothes behind, refuming them carefully on his return before he made his vifit to the governor.

During this month one man and a woman, attempting to crofs one of the creeks at the Hawkefbury by a tree which had been thrown over,

over, fell in, and were drowned; and one man had died there of the
bite of a fnake. Three male convicts * died at Sydney.

December.] The court of civil judicature had hitherto been but
rarely affembled. The few debts which had been contracted were not
of fufficient moment, and had feldom remained long enough in doubt,
to require an action to recover them. But now the poffibility having
been difcovered of acquiring in this country a property worth pre-
ferving, it was probable, when the talents and difpofition of the men
of landed property (the fettlers) in New South Wales were confidered,
that many difputes would occur among them which the civil court
alone could decide.

A court of civil judicature was affembled this month. Some debts
were fworn to, and writs granted. An action for an affault was alfo
tried. About the latter end of the month of October, a large fow,
the property of Mr. J. Bofton, having trefpaffed with two or three
other hogs on a clofe belonging to an officer of the New South Wales
corps, was fhot by a foldier of the regiment (the officer's fervant).
The owner, Mr. Bofton, repairing immediately to the fpot, on feeing
the fow, then near farrowing, lying dead on the ground, made ufe of
fome intemperate expreffions; which being uttered in the hearing of
two of the officers and fome other foldiers of the corps, the officers
were faid by Mr. Bofton to have encouraged and urged the foldiers to
beat him. Mr. Bofton had been ftruck, and, as it appeared on the
trial, with a mufket, which at the time was loaded. Mr. Bofton laid
his damage at five hundred pounds. The court however, after feveral
days very attentive examination of the bufinefs, gave him a verdict
againft two of the defendants, with twenty fhillings damages from
each. One of thefe defendants, a foldier, was advifed to appeal from
the decifion of the court to the governor, who, after hearing the appeal, confirmed the verdict of the civil court.

On the 6th the Francis fchooner failed for Norfolk Ifland. The governor, being anxious to learn the fituation of the lieutenant-governor,
fent her merely with a letter, that if unhappily any accident fhould

* One of them, William Lawler, from the extraordinary deformity of his left leg,
had been offered 100l. for it in England.

3 L.   have

have happened to him, a proper perfon might be fent in the Reliance to command the fettlement, until a fucceffor could arrive from England. Having nothing to deliver or receive that could detain him, the mafter determined to try in what time his veffel could run thither and back again.

The harveft was begun in this month. The Cape wheat (a bearded grain differing much from the Englifh) was found univerfally to have failed. An officer who had fown feven acres with this feed at a farm in the diftrict of Peterfham Hill, on cutting it down, found it was not worth the reaping. This was owing to a blight; but every where the Cape wheat was pronounced not worth the labour of fowing.

A quantity of ufeful timber having been for fome time paft indifcriminately cut down upon the banks of the River Hawkefbury, and the creeks running from it, which had been wafted or applied to purpofes for which timber of lefs value might have anfwered, the governor, among other colonial regulations, thought it neceffary to direct, that no timber whatever fhould be cut down on any ground which was not marked out on either the banks or creeks of that river: and, in order to preferve as much as poffible fuch timber as might be of ufe either for building or for naval purpofes, he ordered the king's mark to be immediately put on all fuch timber, after which any perfons offending againft the order were to be profecuted. This order extended only to *grounds not granted to individuals*, there being a claufe in all grants from the crown, exprefsly referving, under pain of forfeiture, for the ufe thereof, " fuch timber as might be growing or to " grow hereafter upon the land fo granted, which fhould be deemed " fit for naval purpofes."

It was feared, that the certainty of the exiftence of our cattle to the fouthward being incontrovertibly eftablifhed, fome of our vagabonds might be tempted to find them out, and fatisfy their hunger on them from time to time, as they might find opportunity. We were therefore not furprifed to hear that two of them had been killed. A very ftrict inquiry into the report, however, convinced us that it had been raifed only for the purpofe of trying how fuch a circumftance would be regarded. The governor thought it neceffary therefore to ftate in public orders, that " Having heard it reported, that fome perfon or
" perfons,

" perfons, who had been permitted to carry arms for the protection
" of themfelves and property, had lately employed that indulgence in
" an attempt to deftroy the cattle belonging to government, which
" were at large in the woods; and as the prefervation of that ftock
" was of the utmoft importance to the colony at large, he declared,
" that if it fhould be difcovered that any perfon whatever fhould ufe
" any meafure to deftroy or otherwife annoy them, they would be
" profecuted with the utmoft feverity of the law."   A reward was alfo
held out to any perfon giving information, and the order was made
as public as poffible that no one might plead ignorance of it.

The harveft having commenced, the governor on the 22d fignified
to the fettlers, that " although it had hitherto been the intention and
" the practice of government to give them every poffible encourage-
" ment, as well as others who had employed themfelves in growing
" corn, by taking off their hands all their furplus grain at fuch prices
" as had from time to time been thought fair and reafonable, it was
" not, however, to be expected, as the colony advanced in the means
" of fupplying itfelf with bread, that fuch heavy expences could be
" continued.   He therefore recommended to them to confider what
" reduction in the price of wheat and Indian corn they could at pre-
" fent fubmit to, as their offers in that refpect would determine him
" how far it might be neceffary in future to cultivate on the part of
" government, inftead of taking or purchafing a quantity from indi-
" viduals at fo great a price."

This propofal, he thought, could not be confidered otherwife than
as fair and reafonable, when they recollected that the means by which
individuals had fo far improved their farms had arifen from the very
liberal manner in which government had given up the labour of fo
great a number of its own fervants, to affift the induftry of others.   If
this reprefentation fhould not have the effect which he hoped and expected, by a reduction of the prefent high price of grain, he thought
it his duty to propofe, that thofe who were affifted with fervants from
government, fhould at leaft undertake to furnifh thofe fervants with
bread.

To thofe who had farms on the banks of the Hawkefbury he thought
it neceffary to obferve, that, there not being any granaries in that dif-

trict

trict belonging to government, the expence of conveying their grain from thence to this part of the settlement rendered it absolutely necessary that they should lower their prices; otherwise they must be at that expence themselves, and bring their surplus corn to market either at Sydney or Parramatta, where government had stores wherein to deposit it, and where only the commissary could be permitted to receive it.

A report from the river was current about this time, that the natives had assembled in a large body, and attacked a few settlers who had chosen farms low down the river, and without the reach of protection from the other settlers, stripping them of every article they could find in their huts. An armed party was directly sent out, who, coming up with them, killed four men and one woman, badly wounded a child, and took four men prisoners. It might have been supposed that these punishments, following the enormities so immediately, would have taught the natives to keep at a greater distance; but nothing seemed to deter them from prosecuting the revenge they had vowed against the settlers for the injuries they had received at their hands.

A savage of a darker hue, and full as far removed from civilisation, black Cæsar, once more fled from honest labour to the woods, there to subsist by robbing the settlers. It was however reported, that he had done one meritorious action, killing Pe-mul-wy, who had just before wounded Collins (the native) so dangerously, that his recovery was a matter of very great doubt with the surgeons at our hospital, whose assistance Collins had requested as soon as he was brought into town by his friends. A barbed spear had been driven into his loins close by the vertebræ of the back, and was so completely fixed, that all the efforts of the surgeons to remove it with their instruments were ineffectual. Finding, after a day or two, that it could not be displaced by art, Collins left the hospital determined to trust to nature[*]. He was much esteemed by every white man who knew him, as well on

_____

[*] And he did not trust in vain. We saw him from time to time for several weeks walking about with the spear unmoved, even after suppuration had taken place; but at last heard that his wife, or one of his male friends, had fixed their teeth in the wood and drawn it out: after which he recovered, and was able again to go into the field. His wife War-re-weer shewed by an uncommon attention her great attachment to him.

14   ACCOUNT

account of his perfonal bravery, of which we had witneffed many diftinguifhing proofs, as on account of a gentlenefs of manners which
ftrongly marked his difpofition, and fhaded off the harfher lines that
his uncivilifed life now and then forced into the fore-ground.

On the 27th the Sovereign failed for Bengal; and on the laft day
of the year the fignal for a fail was made at the South-head, too late
in the day for it to be known what or whence the veffel was.

The harveft formed the principal labour this month both public and
private. At Sydney, another attempt being made to fteal a cafk of
pork from the pile of provifions which ftood before the ftore-houfe,
the whole was removed into one of the old marine barracks. The
full ration of falt provifions being iffued to every one, it was difficult
to conceive what could be the inducement to thefe frequent and wanton attacks on the provifions, whenever neceffity compelled the commiffary to truft a quantity without the ftore. Perhaps, however, it
was to gratify that ftrong propenfity to thieving, which could not
fuffer an opportunity of exercifing their talents to pafs, or to furnifh
them with means of indulging in the baneful vice of gaming.

At the Hawkefbury, in the beginning of the month, an extraordinary meteorological phænomenon occurred. Four farms on the
creek named Rufe's Creek were totally cut up by a fall, not of hail or
of fnow, but of large flakes of ice. It was ftated by the officer who
had the command of the military there, Lieutenant Abbott, that the
fhower paffed in a direction N. W. taking fuch farms as fell within its
courfe. The effect was extraordinary; the wheat then ftanding was
beaten down, the ears cut off, and the grain perfectly threfhed out.
Of the Indian corn the large thick ftalks were broken, and the cobs
found lying at the roots. A man who was too far diftant from a
houfe to enter it in time was glad to take fhelter in the hollow of a
tree. The fides of the trees which were oppofed to its fury appeared
as if large fhot had been difcharged againft them, and the ground was
covered with fmall twigs from the branches. On that part of the
race-ground which it croffed, the ftronger fhrubs were all found cut to
pieces, while the weaker, by yielding to the ftorm, were only beaten
down. The two fucceeding days were remarkably mild; notwithftanding which the ice remained on the ground nearly as large as
when it fell. Some flakes of it were brought to Lieutenant Abbott

on the fecond day, which meafured from fix to eight inches long, and at that time were two fingers at the leaft in thickneſs.

On this officer's reprefenting to the governor the diftrefs which the fetlers had fuffered whofe farms had lain in the courfe of the ſhower, fuch relief was given them as their fituations required. Nothing of this kind had been felt either at Parramatta or at Sydney.

There died this month Mr. Barrow, a midfhipman belonging to his Majefty's ſhip Supply. His death, which was rather fudden, was occafioned by an obftruction in the bowels, brought on by bathing when very much heated and full. He had attended divine fervice on the Sunday preceding his death, and heard Mr. Johnfon preach on the uncertainty of human life, little thinking how foon he was himfelf to prove the verity of the principal point of his difcourfe—" that death " ftole upon us like a thief in the night."

Two male convicts died at Sydney. One of them, John Durham, had been for upwards of two years a venereal patient in the hofpital; and died at laft a wretched but exemplary fpectacle to all who beheld him, or who knew his fufferings. There died, during the year 1795, one affiftant to the furgeons; one ferjeant of the New South Wales corps; two fetlers; thirteen male convicts; feven female convicts and one child; and one male convict was executed. Making a total of twenty-fix perfons who loft their lives during the year.

CHAP. XXX.

THE ARTHUR ARRIVES FROM INDIA—FRANCIS FROM NORFOLK ISLAND.—
A PLAY-HOUSE OPENED. —HER MAJESTY'S BIRTH-DAY KEPT.—STILLS DE-
STROYED. —CERES STORE-SHIP ARRIVES—AND EXPERIMENT FROM INDIA
—SHIP OTTER FROM AMERICA.—NATIVES.—HARVEST GOT IN.—DEATHS
—A HUT DEMOLISHED BY THE MILITARY.—A TRANSPORT ARRIVES WITH
PRISONERS FROM IRELAND.—A CRIMINAL COURT HELD.—CÆSAR SHOT.
—GENERAL COURT MARTIAL.—OTTER TAKES AWAY MR. MUIR.—
ABIGAIL FROM AMERICA ARRIVES.—A FORGERY COMMITTED.—WORKS.—
THE RELIANCE.—PARTICULARS RESPECTING MR. BAMPTON, AND OF THE
FATE OF CAPTAIN HILL AND MR. CARTER.—A SCHOONER ARRIVES FROM
DUSKEY-BAY.—CROPS BAD.—ROBBERIES COMMITTED.—SUPPLY FOR NOR-
FOLK ISLAND. —NATIVES.—BENNILLONG.—CORNWALLIS SAILS.—GERALD
AND SKIRVING DIE.

January 1796.] ON the first of this month, the Arthur brig anchored
in the cove from Calcutta. Mr. Barber, who was here in 1794 in the
same vessel, had been induced by the success he then met with to pay
us a second visit, with a cargo similar as to the nature of the articles,
but of much larger value than that which he then sold. He had been
thirteen weeks on his passage, and had heard nothing of the Britannia.

It appeared from the information he brought us, that the Cape of
Good Hope might at that time be in the possession of the English.
Trincomale had surrendered to our arms; but of Batavia he could
only say, that a strong party in the French interest existed there.

The Surprise, Captain Campbell, had arrived at Bengal after a long
passage of eight months from this port.

In the evening of the following day the colonial vessel returned
from Norfolk Island, having been absent just four weeks. Lieutenant-
governor King continued extremely ill.

In consequence of the order issued last month respecting a reduction
in the price of wheat, the settlers, having consulted among themselves,
deputed

deputed a certain number from the different districts to state to the governor the hardships they should be subjected to by a reduction in the price of grain, at least for that season. He therefore consented to purchase their present crops of wheat at ten shillings per bushel; but at the same time assured them, that a reduction would be made in the ensuing season, unless some unforeseen and unavoidable circumstances should occur to render it unnecessary.

The officers who held ground offered to give up two of the number of men the governor had allowed them, and to take two others off the provision-store, which proposal was directed to be carried into execution.

Some of the more decent class of prisoners, male and female, having some time since obtained permission to prepare a play-house* at Sydney, it was opened on Saturday the 16th, under the management of John Sparrow, with the play of The Revenge and the entertainment of The Hotel. They had fitted up the house with more theatrical propriety than could have been expected, and their performance was far above contempt. Their motto was modest and well chosen— " We cannot command success, but will endeavour to deserve it." Of their dresses the greater part was made by themselves; but we understood that some veteran articles from the York theatre were among the best that made their appearance.

At the licensing of this exhibition they were informed, that the slightest impropriety would be noticed, and a repetition punished by the banishment of their company to the other settlements; there was, however, more danger of improprieties being committed by some of the audience than by the players themselves. A seat in their gallery, which was by far the largest place in the house, as likely to be the most resorted to, was to be procured for one shilling. In the payment of this price for admission, one evil was observable, which in fact could not well be prevented; in lieu of a shilling, as much flour, or

* The building cost upwards of one hundred pounds. The names of the principal performers were, H. Green, Sparrow, (the manager,) William Fowkes, G. H. Hughes, William Chapman, and Mrs. Davis. Of the men, Green best deserved to be called an actor.

21

as much meat or spirits, as the manager would take for that sum, was often paid at the gallery door. It was feared that this, like gambling, would furnish another inducement to rob; and some of the worst of the convicts, ever on the watch for opportunities, looked on the play-house as a certain harvest for them, not by picking the pockets of the audience of their purses or their watches, but by breaking into their houses while the whole family might be enjoying themselves in the gallery. This actually happened on the second night of their playing.

The 18th was observed as the day on which her Majesty's birth is celebrated in England *. The troops fired three vollies at noon, and at one o'clock the king's ships fired twenty-one guns each, in honour of the day.

Among other objects of civil regulation which required the go-vernor's attention was one to remedy an evil of great magnitude. Some individuals formed the strange design of making application to the governor for his licence to erect stills in different parts of the set-tlement. On inquiry it appeared, that for a considerable time past they had been in the practice of making and vending a spirit, the quality of which was of so destructive a nature, that the health of the settlement in general was much endangered.

A practice so iniquitous and ruinous, being not only a direct dis-obedience of his Majesty's commands, but destructive of the welfare of the colony in general, the governor in the most positive manner forbade all persons on any pretence whatsoever to distil spirituous liquors of any kind or quality, on pain of such steps being taken for their punishment as would effectually prevent a repetition of so dan-gerous an offence. The constables of the different districts, as well as all other persons whose duty it was to preserve order, were strictly enjoined to be extremely vigilant in discovering and giving informa-tion where and in whose possession any article or machine for the pur-pose of distilling spirits might then be, or should hereafter be erected in opposition to this notification of the governor's resolution. Inform-

* The anniversary of her Majesty's birth might with greater propriety be kept in the colonies, particularly in New South Wales, on the 19th of May, the day on which it happened, than at any other time; the same reasons for observing it at a time distant from the king's not existing there. This is attended to in India.

ation

ation on this subject was to be given to the nearest magistrate, who was to send the earliest notice in his power to the judge-advocate at Sydney.

In pursuance of these directions several stills were found and destroyed, to the great regret of the owners, who from a bushel of wheat (worth at the public store ten shillings) distilled a gallon of a new and poisonous spirit, which they retailed directly from the still at five shillings per quart bottle, and sometimes more. This was not merely paid away for labour, as was pretended, but sold for the purposes of intoxication to whoever would bring ready money.

Little or no attention having been paid to the order issued in October last respecting removing the paling about the stream, the governor found it necessary to repeat it, and to declare in public orders, " to every description of persons, that when an order was given by " him, it was given to be obeyed." This had become absolutely necessary, as there were some who, in open defiance of his directions, not only still opened the paling, but took with dirty vessels the water which they wanted above the tanks, thereby disturbing and polluting the whole stream below.

Several attempts had been made by the commissary to ascertain the number of arms in the possession of individuals; it being feared, that, instead of their being properly distributed among the settlers for their protection, many were to be found in the hands of persons who used them in shooting, or in committing depredations. It was once more attempted to discover their number, by directing all persons (the military excepted) who were in possession of arms to bring them to the commissary's office, where, after registering them, they were to receive certificates signed by him, of their being permitted to carry such arms.

Some few settlers, who valued their arms as necessary to their defence against the natives and against thieves, hastened to the office for their certificate; but of between two and three hundred stands of arms which belonged to the crown not fifty were accounted for.

The many robberies which were almost daily and nightly committed rendered it expedient that some steps should be taken to put a stop to an evil so destructive of the happiness and comfort of the industrious duftrious inhabitants. Cæfar was ftill in the woods, with feveral other vagabonds, all of whom were reported, by people who faw them from time to time, to be armed; and as he had fent us word, that he neither would come in, nor fuffer himfelf to be taken alive, it became neceffary to fecure him. Notice was therefore given, that whoever fhould fecure and bring him in with his arms fhould receive as a reward five gallons of fpirits. The fettlers, and thofe people who were occafionally fupplied with ammunition by the officers, were informed, that if they fhould be hereafter difcovered to have fo abufed the confidence placed in them, as to fupply thofe common plunderers with any part of this ammunition, they would be deemed accomplices in the robberies committed by them, and fteps would be taken to bring them to punifhment as acceffaries.

To relieve the mind from the contemplation of circumftances fo irkfome to humanity, on the 23d the Ceres ftore-fhip arrived from England. It was impoffible that a fhip could ever reach this diftant part of his Majefty's dominions, from England, or from any other part of the world, without bringing a change to our ideas, and a variety to our amufements. The introduction of a ftranger among us had ever been an object of fome moment; for every civility was confidered to be due to him who had left the civilized world to vifit us. The perfonal intereft he might have in the vifit we for a while forgot; and from our folicitude to hear news he was invited to our houfes and treated at our tables. If he afterwards found himfelf neglected, it was not to be wondered at; his intelligence was exhaufted, and he had funk into the mere tradefman.

This fhip, whofe mafter's name was Hedley, had on board ftores and provifions for the fettlement. She failed from England on the 5th of Auguft laft; took the route of moft other fhips which had preceded her, anchoring at Rio de Janeiro on the 18th of October, whence fhe failed on the 22d of the fame month, and made Van Dieman's Land on the 9th inftant, her paffage occupying fomething more than five months.

We found that a fhip (the Marquis Cornwallis) had failed for Cork to take in her convicts three weeks before the Ceres left England; and

3 M 2   that

that it was reported at Rio de Janeiro, that the Cape of Good Hope was in our poffeffion.

The Ceres, touching at the ifland of Amfterdam in her way hither, took off four men, two French and two Englifh, who had lived there three years, having been left from a brig, (the Emilia,) which was taken on to China by the Lion man of war. One of the Frenchmen, M. Perron, apparently deferved a better kind of fociety than his companions fupplied. He had kept an accurate and neatly-written journal of his proceedings, with fome well-drawn views of the fpot to which he was fo long confined. It appeared that they had, in the hope of their own or fome other veffel arriving to take them off, collected and cured feveral thoufands of feal-fkins, which, however, they were compelled to abandon. M. Perron had fubfifted for the laft eighteen months on the flefh of feals.

On the day following this arrival the fignal was again made; and before noon the fnow Experiment, commanded by Mr. Edward M'Clellan, who was here in the fame veffel in the year before laft, from Bengal, and the fhip Otter, Mr. Ebenezer Dorr mafter, from Bofton in North America, anchored in the cove.

Mr. M'Clellan had on board a large inveftment of India goods, muflins, calicoes, chintzes, foap, fugar, fpirits, and a variety of fmall articles, apparently the fweepings of a Bengal bazar; the fale of which inveftment he expected would produce ten or twelve thoufand pounds.

The American, either finding the market overftocked, or having had fome other motive for touching here, declared he had nothing for fale; but that he could, as a favour, fpare two hogfheads of Jamaica rum, three pipes of Madeira, fixty-eight quarter cafks of Lifbon wine, four chefts and a half of Bohea tea, and two hogfheads of melaffes. He had touched at the late refidence of M. Perron, the ifland of Amfterdam, and brought off as many of the feal-fkins (his veffel being bound to China after vifiting the north-weft coaft of America) as he could take on board. He had been five months and three days from Bofton, touching no where but at the above-mentioned ifland.

We had the fatisfaction of hearing, through Mr. M'Clellan, from the mafter of the Britannia. He had, according to his inftructions, proceeded

proceeded to Batavia, where judging from his own obfervation, and by what he heard, that it was unfafe to make any ftay, he after four or five days left the port, and by that means fortunately efcaped being detained, which, from information that he afterwards received at Bengal, he found would have happened to him. He was to leave Calcutta about the end of December.

The report of the Cape of Good Hope being in our poffeffion had reached that place before the Experiment failed. On this fubject we were rather anxious, as the armed fhips which had lately arrived, the Reliance and Supply, were intended to proceed to that port as foon as the feafon would admit, for cattle for the colony.

Ben-nil-long's influence over his countrymen not extending to the natives at the river, we this month again heard of their violence. They attacked a man who had been allowed to ply with a paffage-boat between the port of Sydney and the river, and wounded him, (it was feared mortally,) as he was going with his companion to the fettlement ; and they were beginning again to annoy the fettlers there.

Notwithftanding the reward that had been offered for apprehending black Cæfar, he remained at large, and fcarcely a morning arrived without a complaint being made to the magiftrates of a lofs of property fuppofed to have been occafioned by this man. In fact, every theft that was committed was afcribed to him ; a cafk of pork was ftolen from the mill-houfe, the upper part of which was acceffible, and, the centinels who had the charge of that building being tried and acquitted, the theft was fixed upon Cæfar, or fome of the vagabonds who were in the woods, the number of whom at this time amounted to fix or eight.

The harveft was all well got in during this month. At Sydney, the labouring hands were employed in unloading the ftore-fhip ; for which purpofe three men from each farm having ten were ordered in to public work.

On the 21ft of this month his Majefty's fhip the Reliance failed for Norfolk Ifland. In her went Mr. Hibbins, the judge-advocate of that fettlement who arrived from England in the Sovereign ; and a captain of the New South Wales corps, to take the command of the troops there.

On

On the 7th the surgeon's mate of the Supply died of a dysenteric complaint. He had attended Mr. Barrow to his grave, who died in December last. On the evening of the 23d a soldier of the name of Eades, having gone over to the north shore to collect thatch to cover a hut which he had built for the comfort of his family, fell from a rock and was drowned. He left a widow and five small children, mostly females, to lament his loss. He was a quiet man and a good soldier.

February.] The players, with a politic generosity, on the 4th of this month performed the play of The Fair Penitent with a farce, for the benefit of the widow Eades and her family. The house was full, and it was said that she got upwards of twelve pounds by the night.

A circumstance of a disagreeable nature occurred in the beginning of this month. John Baughan *, the master carpenter at this place, being at work in the shed allotted for the carpenters in one of the mill-houses, overheard himself grossly abused by the centinel who was planted there, and who for that purpose had quitted his post, and placed himself within hearing of Baughan. This centinel had formerly been a convict, and, while working as such under Baughan in the line of his business, thought himself in some circumstance or other ill-treated by him, for which he " owed him a grudge," and took this way to satisfy his resentment. Baughan, a man of a sullen and vindictive disposition, perceiving that the centinel was without his arms, took them, unobserved by him, from the post where he had left them, and delivered them to the serjeant of the guard.

The centinel being confined, the company to which he belonged, indignant at the injury done to their comrade, and too much irritated either to act with prudence, or to consider the conduct they determined to pursue, repaired the following morning to Baughan's house, (a neat little cottage which he had built below the hospital,) where in a few minutes they almost totally demolished his house, out-houses, and furniture, and Baughan himself suffered much personal outrage.

* John Baughan, alias Buffin, alias Bingham. He had served the term of his transportation, and had for a considerable time been employed in the direction of the carpenters and sawyers at this place.

5   They

They were so sudden in the execution of this business, that the mischief was done before any steps could be taken either by the civil or military power to prevent it.

Baughan, after some days had elapsed, swearing positively to the persons of four of the principals in this transaction, a warrant was made out to apprehend them; but before it could be executed, the soldiers expressing themselves convinced of the great impropriety of their conduct, and offering to indemnify the sufferer for the damage they had done him, (who also personally petitioned the governor in their behalf,) the warrant was withdrawn.

It was observed, that the most active of the soldiers in this affair had formerly been convicts, who, not having changed their principles with their condition, thus became the means of disgracing their fellow-soldiers. The corps certainly was not much improved by the introduction of people of this description among them. It might well have been supposed, that being taken as good characters from the class of prisoners, they would have felt themselves above mixing with any of them afterwards; but it happened otherwise; they had nothing in them of that pride which is termed *l'esprit du corps*; but at times mixed with the convicts familiarly as former companions; yet when they chose to quarrel with, or complain of them, they meanly asserted their superiority as soldiers.

This intercourse had been strongly prohibited by their officers; but living (as once before mentioned) in huts by themselves, it was carried on without their knowledge. Most of them were now, however, ordered into the barracks; but to give this regulation the full effect, a high brick wall, or an inclosure of strong paling, round the barracks, was requisite; the latter of these securities would have been put up some time before, had there not been a want of the labouring hands necessary to prepare and collect the materials.

On the 11th of this month the ship Marquis Cornwallis anchored in the cove from Ireland, with two hundred and thirty-three male and female convicts of that country. We understood from her commander, Mr. Michael Hogan, that a conspiracy had been formed to take the ship from him; but, the circumstances of it being happily disclosed in time, he was enabled to prevent it, and having sufficient evidence of
the

the exiftence of the confpiracy, he caufed the principal part of thofe concerned to be feverely punifhed, firft taking the opinions of all the free people who were on board. A military guard, confifting of two fubalterns and a proportionate number of privates of the New South Wales corps, (principally drafts from other regiments,) was embarked in this fhip. The prifoners were in general healthy; but fome of thofe who had been punifhed were not quite recovered, and on landing were fent to the hofpital. It appeared that the men were for the moft part of the defcription of people termed Defenders, defperate, and ripe for any fcheme from which danger and deftruction were likely to enfue. The women were of the fame complexion; and their ingenuity and cruelty were difplayed in the part they were to take in the purpofed infurrection, which was the preparing of pulverifed glafs to mix with the flour of which the feamen were to make their puddings. What an importation!

A few months provifions for thefe people, and the remainder* of the mooring chains intended for his Majefty's fhips the Reliance and the Supply, together with a patent under the great feal for affembling criminal courts at Norfolk Ifland, arrived in this fhip. She failed from Cork on the 9th of Auguft laft, and touched at the ifland of St. Helena and the Cape of Good Hope, which latter place, we had the fatisfaction of hearing, had furrendered to his Majefty's arms, and was in our poffeffion. General Craig, the commander in chief on fhore, and Commodore Blankett, each fent an official communication of this important circumftance to Governor Hunter, and ftated their defire to affift in any circumftance that might be of fervice to the fettlement, when the feafon fhould offer for fending the fhips under his orders to the Cape for fupplies.

With infinite regret we heard of the death of Colonel Gordon, whofe attentions to this fettlement, when opportunities prefented themfelves, can never be forgotten. He was a favoured fon of fcience, and liberally extended the advantages which that fcience gave him wherever he thought they could promote the welfare of his fellow-creatures.

* Some part had arrived in the Reliance and Supply.

On Monday the 15th a criminal court was held for the trial of two prisoners, William Britton a soldier, and John Reid a convict, for a burglary in the house of the Rev. Mr. Johnson, committed in the night of Sunday the 7th of this month. The evidence, though strong, was not sufficient to convict them, and they were acquitted. While this court was sitting, however, information was received, that black Cæsar had that morning been shot by one Wimbow. This man and another, allured by the reward, had been for some days in quest of him. Finding his haunt, they concealed themselves all night at the edge of a brush which they perceived him enter at dusk. In the morning he came out, when, looking round him and seeing his danger, he presented his musquet; but before he could pull the trigger Wimbow fired and shot him. He was taken to the hut of Rose, a settler at Liberty Plains, where he died in a few hours. Thus ended a man, who certainly, during his life, could never have been estimated at more than one remove above the brute, and who had given more trouble than any other convict in the settlement.

On the morning of the 18th the Otter sailed for the north-west coast of America. In her went Mr. Thomas Muir (one of the persons sent out in the Surprise for sedition) and several other convicts whose sentences of transportation were not expired. Mr. Muir conceived that in withdrawing (though clandestinely) from this country, he was only asserting his freedom; and meant, if he should arrive in safety, to enjoy what he deemed himself to have regained of it in America, until the time should come when he might return to his own country with credit and comfort. He purposed practising at the American bar as an advocate; a point of information which he left behind him in a letter. In this country he chiefly passed his time in literary ease and retirement, living out of the town at a little spot of ground which he had purchased for the purpose of seclusion.

A few days after the departure of this ship, the Abigail, another American, arrived. As several prisoners had found a conveyance from this place in the Otter, the governor directed the Abigail to be anchored in Neutral Bay (a bay on the north shore, a little below Rock Island), where he imagined the communication would not be so easy as the ships of that nation had found it in Sydney Cove. Her master, Christopher Thornton, gave out that he was bound to Manilla and Canton, having on board a cargo for those places. For part of that cargo, however, he met with purchasers at this place, notwithstanding the glut of articles which the late frequent arrivals must have thrown in. He expected to have found here a snow, named the Susan, which he knew had sailed from Rhode Island with a cargo expressly laid in for this market. He came direct from that port without touching any where.

The frequent attacks and depredations to which the settlers situated on the banks of the Hawkesbury, and other places, were exposed from the natives, called upon them, for the protection of their families, and the preservation of their crops, mutually to afford each other their assistance upon every occasion of alarm, by assembling without delay whenever any numerous bodies of natives were reported to be lurking about their grounds; but they seldom or never shewed the smallest disposition to assist each other. Indolent and improvident even for their own safety and interest, they in general neglected the means by which either could be secured. This disposition being soon manifested to the governor, he thought it necessary to issue a public order, stating his expectations and directions, that all the people residing in the different districts of the settlements, whether the alarm was on their own farm, or on the farm of any other person, should upon such occasions immediately render to each other such assistance as each man if attacked would himself wish to receive; and he assured them, that if it should be hereafter proved, that any settlers or other persons withdrew or kept back their assistance from those who might be threatened, or who might be in danger of being attacked, they would be proceeded against as persons disobeying the rules and orders of the settlement. Such as had fire-arms were also positively enjoined not wantonly to fire at, or take the lives of any of the natives, as such an act would be considered a deliberate murder, and subject the offender to such punishment as (if proved) the law might direct to be inflicted. It had been intimated to the governor, that two white men (Wilson and Knight) had been frequently seen with the natives in their excursions, and

were

were supposed to direct and assist in those acts of hostility by which the settlers had lately suffered. He therefore recommended to every one who knew or had heard of these people, and particularly to the settlers who were so much annoyed by them, to use every means in their power to secure them, that they might be so disposed of as to prevent their being dangerous or troublesome in future. The settlers were at the same time strictly prohibited from giving any encouragement to the natives to lurk about their farms; as there could not be a doubt, that if they had never met with the shelter which some had afforded them, they would not at this time have furnished so much cause of complaint.

Those natives who lived with the settlers had tasted the sweets of a different mode of living, and, willing that their friends and companions should partake, either stole from those with whom they were living, or communicated from time to time such favourable opportunities as offered of stealing from other settlers what they themselves were pleased with.

At this time several persons who had served their term of transportation were applying for permission to provide for themselves. Of this description were Wilson and Knight; but they preferred a vagrant life with the natives; and the consideration that if taken they would be dealt with in a manner that would prevent their getting among them again, now led them on to every kind of mischief. They demonstrated to the natives of how little use a musquet was when once discharged, and this effectually removed that terror of our fire-arms with which it had been our constant endeavour to inspire them.

Several articles having been brought for sale in the Marquis Cornwallis, a shop was opened on shore. As money, or orders on or by any of the responsible officers * of the colony, were taken at this shop for goods, an opportunity was afforded to some knowing ones among the prisoners to play off, not only base money, as counterfeit Spanish dollars and rupees, but forged notes or orders. One forged note for ten pound ten shillings, bearing the commissary's name, was passed at

---

* Such as the commissary, paymaster of the corps, and officers who paid companies.

the

the shop, but fortunately discovered before the recollection of the persons who offered it was effaced, though not in time to recover the property. The whole party was apprehended, and committed for trial.

Discharging the storeships formed the principal labour of this month; which being completed, the assistants required from the farms to unload them were returned.

The bricklayers' gang were employed in erecting a small hut for the accommodation of an officer within the paling of the guardhouse at Sydney, the main guard being now commanded by a subaltern officer.

Mr. Henry Brewer, the provost-marshal of the territory, worn out with age and infirmities, being incapable of the duties of his office, which now required a very active and a much younger man to execute, and at this time very much indisposed, the governor appointed to that situation Mr. Thomas Smyth, then acting as a storekeeper at this place, until Mr. Brewer should be able to return to the duties of it.

During one or two hot days in this month the shrubs and brushwood about the west point of the cove caught fire, and burnt within a few yards of the magazine. On its being extinguished, the powder was removed for a few days on board the Supply, until some security against any future accident of that kind could be thrown up round the building.

March.] Late in the evening of the 5th of March his Majesty's ship the Reliance returned from Norfolk Island. In her came Mr. D'Arcy Wentworth. This person arrived at New South Wales in the Neptune transport, and went immediately to Norfolk Island, where he was employed, first as a superintendant of convicts, and afterwards as an assistant to the surgeon at the hospital there, having been bred to that profession.

By letters received from Mr. Bampton, who sailed from this place in the Endeavour in the month of September last, we now heard, that on his reaching Dusky Bay in New Zealand his ship unfortunately proved so leaky, that with the advice and consent of his officers
and

and people she was run on shore and scuttled. By good fortune the vessel which had been built by the carpenter of the Britannia (when left there with Mr. John Leith the mate, and others, in that ship's first voyage hence to the Cape of Good Hope) being found in the same state as she had been left by them, they completed and launched her, according to a previous agreement between the two commanders. It may be remembered, that in addition to the large number of persons which Mr. Bampton had permission to ship at this port, nearly as many more found means to secrete themselves on board his ship and the Fancy. For these, as well as his officers and ship's company, he had now to provide a passage from the truly desolate shores of New Zealand. He accordingly, after fitting as a schooner the vessel which he had launched, and naming her the Providence, sailed with her and the Fancy for Norfolk Island, having on board as many of the officers and people who reached Dusky Bay with him as they could contain, leaving the remainder to proceed in a vessel which one Hatherleigh (formerly a carpenter's mate of the Sirius, who happened to be with him) undertook to construct out of the Endeavour's long-boat. The Fancy and Providence arrived safe at Norfolk Island, whence they sailed for China on the 31st day of January last.

This unlucky termination of the voyage of the Endeavour brought to our recollection the difficulties and dangers which Mr. Bampton met with in the Shah Hormuzear, when, on his return to India from this country, he attempted to ascertain a passage for future navigators between New Holland and New Guinea.

In the course of this narrative, the different reports received respecting the fate of the boat which landed on Tate Island have been stated. In a Calcutta newspaper, brought here by Mr. M'Clellan in the Experiment, we now found a printed account of the whole of that transaction, which filled up that chasm in the story which the parties themselves alone could supply.

By referring to the account given in the month of July 1794, as communicated by Mr. Dell, it will appear, that the ship, having been driven to leeward of the island after the boat left her, was three days before she could work up to it. When Mr. Dell went on shore to

S　　　　　　　　　　　　　　　　　　　　　　search

search for Captain Hill and his companions, he could only, at his return, produce, what he thought incontestable proofs of their having been murdered; such as their great-coats, a lanthorn, tomahawk, &c. and three hands, one of which, from a certain mark, was supposed to have belonged to Mr. Carter. Of the boat, after the most diligent search round the island, he could find no trace. By the account now published, and which bore every mark of authenticity, it appeared, that when the boat, in which these unfortunate gentlemen were, had reached the island (on the 3d of July 1793), the natives received them very kindly, and conducted them to a convenient place for landing. After distributing some presents among them, with which they appeared very much satisfied, it was proposed that Mr. Carter, Shaw (the mate of the Chesterfield), and Ascott, should proceed to the top of a high point of land which they had noticed, and that Captain Hill should stay by the boat, with her crew, consisting of four seamen belonging to the Chesterfield.

The island party, taking the precaution to arm, and provide themselves with a necessary quantity of ammunition, set off. Nothing unfriendly occurred during their walk, though several little circumstances happened, which induced Ascott to suspect that the natives had some design on them; an idea, however, which was scouted by his companions.

On their return from the hill, hostile designs became apparent, and the natives seemed to be deterred from murdering them merely by the activity of Ascott, who, by presenting his musket occasionally, kept them off; but, notwithstanding his activity and vigilance, the natives at length made their attack. They began by attempting to take Ascott's musket from him, finding he was the most likely to annoy them; directly after which, Mr. Carter, who was the foremost of the party, was heard to exclaim, " My God, my God, they " have murdered me." Ascott, who still retained his musket, immediately fired, on which the natives left them and fled into the bushes. Ascott now had time to look about him, and saw what he justly deemed a horrid spectacle, Mr. Carter lying bleeding on the ground, and Mr. Shaw with a large wound in his throat under the left

left jaw. They were both however able to rise, and proceed down the hill to the boat. On their arrival at the beach they called to their companions to fire; but, to their extreme horror, they perceived Captain Hill and one of the seamen lying dead on the sand, cut and mangled in a most barbarous manner. Two others of the seamen they saw floating on the water, with their throats cut from ear to ear. The fourth sailor they found dead in the boat, mangled in the same shocking manner. With much difficulty these unhappy people got into their boat, and, cutting her grapnel, pulled off from this treacherous shore. While this was performing, they clearly saw the natives, whom in their account they term voracious cannibals, dragging the bodies of Captain Hill and the seamen from the beach toward some large fires, which they supposed were prepared for the occasion, yelling and howling at the same time most dismally.

These wretched survivors of their companions having seen, from the top of the hill whither their ill-fated curiosity had led them, a large sand-bank not far from the island, determined to run under the lee of it, as they very reasonably hoped that boats would the next morning be sent after them from the ship. They experienced very little rest or ease that night, and when daylight appeared found they had drifted nearly out of sight of the island, and to leeward of the sand-bank.

Deeming it in vain to attempt reaching the bank, after examining what was left in the boat, (a few of the trifles which they had put into her to buy the friendship of the natives, and Ascon's great-coat, but neither a compass nor a morsel of provisions,) they determined, by the advice of Shaw, who of these three miserable people was the only one that understood any thing of navigation, to run direct for Timor, for which place the wind was then happily fair. To the westward, therefore, they directed their course, trusting (as the printed account stated) to that Providence which had delivered them from the cannibals at Tate Island [*].

* The narrative of this most horrible affair, as printed at Calcutta, was reprinted entire in the European Magazine for May and June 1797.

Without

Without provisions, destitute of water, and almost without bodily strength, it cannot be doubted that their sufferings were very great before they reached a place of safety and relief. They left the island on the 3d of July, the day on which their companions were butchered. On the 7th, having the preceding day passed a sand-bank covered with birds, they providentially, in the morning, found two small birds in the boat, one of which they immediately divided into three parts, and were considerably relieved by eating it. On the 8th they found themselves with land on both sides. Through these straits they passed, and continued their course to the westward. All that could be done with their wounds was to keep them clean by opening them occasionally, and washing them with salt water. On the 11th they saw land, and pushed their boat into a bay, all agreeing that they had better trust to the chance of being well received on shore, than to that of perishing in the course of a day or two more at sea. Here they procured some water and a roasted yam from the natives, who also gave them to understand that Timor was to the southward of them. Not thinking themselves quite so safe here as they would be at Coupang, they again embarked. They soon after found a proa in chace of them, which they eluded by standing with their boat over a reef that the proa would not encounter. On the morning of the 14th they saw a point of land a-head, which, with the wind as it then was, they could not weather. They therefore ran into a small bay, where the natives received them, calling out " Bligh! Bligh!" Here they landed, were hospitably received, and providentially saved from the horror of perishing by famine.

This place was called by the natives Sarrett, and was distinct from Timor Land, which was the first place they refreshed at. They were also informed, that there was another small island to the northward, called by them Fardatte, but which in some charts was named Ta-na-bor. They also understood that a proa came yearly from Banda to trade at Tanabor, and that her arrival was expected in the course of seven or eight months.

They

They were much gratified with this information, and soon found that they had fallen into the hands of a hospitable and humane race of people.

On the 25th of July Mr. Carter's wound was entirely healed, after having had thirteen pieces of the fractured skull taken out. But this gentleman was fated not long to survive his sufferings. He remained in perfect health until the 17th of November, when he caught a fever, of which he died on the 10th of December, much regretted by his two friends (for adversity makes friends of those who perhaps, in other situations, would never have shaken hands).

The two survivors waited in anxious expectation for the arrival of the annual trading proa from Banda. To their great joy she came on the 12th of March 1794.

For Banda they sailed on the 10th of April, and arrived there on the 1st of May following, where they were received with the greatest hospitality by the governor, who supplied them with every thing necessary for people in their situation, and provided them with a passage on board an Indiaman bound to Batavia, where they arrived on the 10th of the following October; adding another to the many instances of escape from the perils which attend on those whose hard fate have driven them to navigate the ocean in an open boat.

Hard indeed was the fate of Captain Hill and Mr. Carter. They were gentlemen of liberal education, qualified to adorn the circles of life in which their rank in society placed them. How lamentable thus to perish, the one by the hands and rude weapons of barbarous savages, cut off in the prime of life and most perfect enjoyment of his faculties, lost for ever to a mother and sister whom he tenderly loved, his body mangled, roasted, and devoured by cannibals; the other, after escaping from those cannibals, to perish * in a country where all were strangers to him, except his two companions in misery Shaw and Ascott, to give up all his future prospects in life, never

* It is evident, if this account be true, that Mr. Dell must have been mistaken in his opinion of having carried on board the Shah Hormuzear a band which, from a certain mark on it, he knew to have belonged to Mr. Carter.

more to meet the cheering eye of friendfhip or of love, and without
having had the melancholy fatisfaction of recounting his perils, his
efcape, and fufferings, to thofe who would fympathife with him in the
tale of his forrows.

On the 17th the veffel built by the fhipwright Hatherleigh at Dufky
Bay arrived, with fome of the people left behind by Mr. Bampton.
They were fo diftreffed for provifions, that the perfon who had the
direction of the veffel could not bring away the whole; and it was
fingularly fortunate that he arrived as he did, for with all the œconomy that could be ufed, his fmall ftock of provifions was confumed
to the laft mouthful the day before he made the land.

This veffel, which the officer who commanded her (Waine, one of
the mates of the Endeavour) not unappropriately named the Affiftance, was built entirely of the timber of Dufky Bay, but appeared
to be miferably conftructed. She was of near fixty tons burden, and
was now to be fold * for the benefit of Mr. Bampton.

The fituation of the people ftill remaining at Dufky Bay was not,
we underftood, the moft enviable; their dependence for provifions
being chiefly on the feals and birds which they might kill. They had
all belonged to this colony, and one or two happened to be perfons of
good character.

On the 10th the American failed for the north-weft coaft of America. In her went Mr. James Fitzpatrick Knarefbro', a gentleman
whofe hard lot it was to be doomed to banifhment for life from his
native country, Ireland, and the enjoyment of a comfortable fortune
which he there poffeffed. He arrived here in the Sugar Cane tranfport, in the year 1793, and had lived conftantly at Parramatta with
the moft rigid œconomy and fevere felf-denial even of the common
comforts of life.

It was feen with concern that the crops of this feafon proved in
general bad, the wheat being almoft every where mixed with a weed
named by the farmers Drake. Every care was taken to prevent this
circumftance from happening in the enfuing feafon, by cleaning with

* Notwithftanding all her imperfections, fhe was valued at and fold for two hundred
and fifty pounds.

the greatest nicety not only such wheat as was intended for seed, but such as was received into the public store from settlers. It was occasioned by the ground being overwrought, from a greediness to make it produce golden harvests every season, without allowing it time to recruit itself from crop to crop, or being able to afford it manure. Had this not happened, the crops would most likely have been immense.

At the Hawkesbury, where alone any promise of agricultural advantages was to be found, the settlers were immersed in intoxication. Riot and madness marked their conduct; and this was to be attributed to the spirits that, in defiance of every precaution, found their way thither.

Early in the month a store-room belonging to Captain Paterson was broken into, and articles to a large amount stolen thereout. A centinel was stationed in the front of the house; notwithstanding which, the thieves had time to remove, through a small hole that they made in a brick wall, all the property they stole.

In the course of the month Captain Townson, another officer of the corps, was also robbed. He had that morning received in trust sixty pounds in dollars; these, together with his watch, were stolen from him in the following night. His servants were suspected, as were also Captain Paterson's; but nothing could be fixed upon them that bore the semblance of proof.

Robberies were more frequent now than they had been for some time past, scarcely a night passing without at least an attempt being made. On the 17th, the festival of St. Patrick, the night-watch were assaulted by two fellows, Matthew Farrel and Richard Sutton, (better known by the title of the Newgate Bully,) while the latter was pursued by them from a house which he was endeavouring to break into, to the house of Farrel, who tried to secrete him, and afford him protection.

A woman was stopped in the street at night, and a piece of callico forcibly taken from her. A convict being taken up as the man who had robbed her, she at first was positive to his person, but when brought before a magistrate, on recollecting that his life might be in danger, she was ready to swear that, it being very dark at the time, it

was

was not poffible fhe fhould know his features. Thus difficult was it too often found to bring thefe people to juftice.

On the 24th his Majefty's fhip Supply failed for Norfolk Ifland. The patent for holding criminal courts there, which was brought hither by the Cornwallis, was fent by this conveyance, together with R. Sutton (the Newgate Bully) and fome other very bad charaders, who, it was not unlikely, would foon entitle themfelves to the benefit of the patent which accompanied them.

Hogs again became fuch a public nuifance, by running loofe in the town without rings or yokes, that another order refpeding them was given out, direding the owners either to fhut them up, or appoint them to be watched when at large.

Reports were again received this month of frefh outrages committed by the natives at the river. The fchooner which had been fent round with provifions faw fome of thefe people off a high point of land named Portland Head, who menaced them with their fpears, and carried in their appearance every mark of hoftility. The governor being at this time on an excurfion to that fettlement (by water), one of his party landed on the fhore oppofite Portland Head, and faw at a fhort diftance a large body of natives, who he underflood had affembled for the purpofe of burning the corpfe of a man who had been killed in fome conteft among themfelves.

About this time Bennillong, who occafionally fhook off the habits of civilized life, and went for a few days into the woods with his fifters and other friends, fent in word that he had had a conteft with his bofom friend Cole-be, in which he had been fo much the fufferer, that until his wounds were healed he could not with any pleafure to himfelf appear at the governor's table. This notification was accompanied with a requeft, that his clothes, which he had left behind him when he went away, might be fent him, together with fome victuals, of which he was much in want.

On his coming among us again, he appeared with a wound on his mouth, which had divided the upper lip and broke two of the teeth of that jaw. His features, never very pleafing, now feemed out of all proportion, and his pronunciation was much altered. Finding himfelf badly received among the females, (although improved by his
                                                                        travels

travels in the little attentions that are supposed to have their weight
with the sex,) and not being able to endure a life of celibacy, which
had been his condition from the day of his departure from this country
until nearly the present hour, he made an attack upon his friend's
favourite, Boo-ree-a, in which he was not only unsuccessful, but was
punished for his breach of friendship, as above related, by Cole-be,
who sarcastically asked him, " if he meant that kind of conduct to be
" a specimen of English manners ?"

The Ceres, having been discharged from government employ, sailed
in the beginning of the month for Canton. Being well manned, the
master was not in want of any hands from this place ; but eight convicts found means to secrete themselves on board a day or two before
she sailed. They were however, by the great vigilance of Mr. Hedley, discovered in time to be sent back to their labour. Among them
we were not surprised to find two or three of the last importation from
Ireland.

We lost four persons by death during this month. On the 6th died
of a severe dysentery, Richard Hudson, the serjeant-major of the New
South Wales corps. At three in the morning of the 16th Mr. Joseph
Gerald breathed his last. A consumption which accompanied him
from England, and which all his wishes and efforts to shake off could
not overcome, at length brought him to that period when, perhaps,
his strong enlightened mind must have perceived how full of vanity
and vexation of spirit were the busiest concerns of this world; and
into what a narrow limit was now to be thrust that frame which but
of late trod firmly in the walk of life, elate and glowing with youth-
ful hope, glorying in being a martyr to the cause which he termed
that of Freedom, and considering as an honour that exile which
brought him to an untimely grave *. He was followed in three days
after by another victim to mistaken opinions, Mr. William Skirving.
A dysentery was the apparent cause of his death, but his heart was
broken. In the hope of receiving remittances from England, which
might enable him to proceed with spirit and success in farming, of

* He was buried in the garden of a little spot of ground which he had purchased at
Farm Cove. Mr. F. Palmer, we understood, had written his epitaph at large.

7   which,

which he appeared to have a thorough knowledge, he had purchased from different persons, who had ground to sell, about one hundred acres of land adjacent to the town of Sydney. He soon found that a farm near the sea-coast was of no great value. His attention and his efforts to cultivate the ground were of no avail. Remittances he received none; he contracted some little debts, and found himself neglected by that party for whom he had sacrificed the dearest connexions in life, a wife and family; and finally yielded to the pressure of this accumulated weight. Among us, he was a pious, honest, worthy character. In this settlement his political principles never manifested themselves; but all his solicitude seemed to be, to evince himself the friend of human nature. *Requiescat in pace!*

CHAP. XXXI.

SLOPS SERVED.—ORDERS.—LICENCES GRANTED.—THE SUPPLY RETURNS FROM NORFOLK ISLAND—THE SUSAN FROM NORTH AMERICA—AND THE INDISPENSABLE FROM ENGLAND.—A CRIMINAL AND CIVIL COURT HELD.—SICK.—THEFTS COMMITTED.—THE BRITANNIA ARRIVES FROM BENGAL.—MR. RAVEN'S OPINION AS TO THE TIME OF MAKING A PASSAGE TO INDIA.—A CIVIL COURT.—THE CORNWALLIS AND EXPERIMENT SAIL FOR INDIA.—CAUTION TO MASTERS OF SHIPS.—A WIND-MILL BEGUN.—THEFTS COMMITTED.—STATE OF THE SETTLERS.—THE GOVERNOR GOES TO MOUNT HUNTER.—REGULATIONS.—PUBLIC WORKS.—DEATHS.

April] IN the beginning of this month a very liberal allowance of slops was served to the prisoners male and female. As it had been too much the practice for these people to sell the clothing they received from government as soon as it was issued to them, the governor on this occasion gave it out in public orders, that whenever it should be proved that any person had either sold or otherwise made away with any of the articles then issued, the buyer and seller or receiver thereof would both subject themselves to corporal or other punishment. Orders, however, had never yet been known to have much weight with these people.

Thefts

Thefts were ftill nightly committed. At the Hawkefbury the corn ftore was broken into, and a quantity of wheat and other articles ftolen; and two people were apprehended for robbing the deputy-furveyor's fowl-houfe. All thefe depredations were chiefly committed by thofe public nuifances the people off the ftores.

Toward preventing the indiferiminate fale of fpirits which at this time prevailed in all the fettlements, the governor thought that granting licences to a few perfons of good character might have a good effect. Ten perfons were felected by the magiftrates, and to them licences for twelve months, under the hands of three magiftrates, were granted. The principals were bound in the ufual penalties of twenty pounds each, and obliged to find two fureties in ten pounds: and as from the very frequent ftate of intoxication in which great numbers of the lower order of people had for fome time paft been feen, there was much reafon to fufpect that a greater quantity of fpirituous liquors had been landed from the different fhips which had entered this port than permits had been obtained for, it became highly neceffary to put a ftop, as early as poffible, to a practice which was pregnant with all kinds of mifchief. The governor judged it neceffary, the more effectually to fupprefs the dangerous practice of retailing fpirits in this indiferiminate way, not only to grant licences under the reftrictions abovementioned, but to defire the aid of all officers, civil and military, and in a more particular manner of all magiftrates, conftables, &c. as they regarded the good of his Majefty's fervice, the peace, tranquillity, and good order of the colony, to ufe their utmoft exertions for putting an end to a fpecies of traffic, from which the deftruction of health and the ruin of all induftry were to be expected; and urged them to endeavour to difcover who thofe people were, that, felf-licenced only, had prefumed to open public-houfes for this abominable purpofe.

He alfo informed thofe who might, after knowing his intentions, be daring enough to continue to act in oppofition to them, that the houfe of every offender fhould be pulled down as a public nuifance, and fuch other fteps be taken for his further punifhment as might be deemed neceffary.

In

In the evening of the 18th his Majesty's ship Supply returned from Norfolk Island, having been absent only three weeks and four days, the quickest passage that had yet been made to and from that island. At night word was sent up from the Look-out, that another vessel was off, and on the following evening the snow Susan arrived from Rhode Island, having been at sea two hundred and thirty-one days, not touching any where on her passage.

The Americans were observed to make these kind of voyages from motives of frugality, sailing direct for this port; but they were at the same time observed to bring in their people extremely healthy. On our enquiring what methods they took so to secure the health of their seamen, they told us, that in general they found exercise the best preventive against the scurvy, and considered idleness as the surest means of introducing it. In addition to exercise, however, they made frequent use of acids in the diet of their seamen, and of fumigations from tobacco in their between-decks. Certain it was that none of our ships, which touched in their way out at other ports, arrived so generally healthy.

A Mr. Trotter was the master of this vessel. He was an Irishman by birth, but had for some time been a citizen of the United States. Strong currents and foul winds had been his enemies in the late voyage. His cargo consisted of spirits, broad-cloth, and a variety of useful and desirable articles, adapted to the necessities of this country.

On the last day of this month the Indispensable transport arrived from England, with one hundred and thirty-one female convicts, and a small quantity of provisions on board for their consumption.

Mr. Wilkinson, who commanded this ship, we found, to our great regret, had not touched at the Cape of Good Hope; he had stopped only at the port of Rio de Janeiro. This was unfortunate, as it was intended that the king's ships should sail early in the ensuing month of September for that part of the world. That the war still raged in Europe we heard with concern, feeling as every humane mind must do for the sufferings of its fellow-creatures; but it was in the highest degree gratifying to us to know that our situation was not wholly forgotten at home, proof enough of which we experienced in the late frequent arrivals of ships from England.

At

At a criminal court which was held in this month four prisoners were tried for forging, and uttering with a forged indorsement, the note which had been passed at Mr. Hogan's store in February last, when James M'Carthy was convicted of the same, and received sentence of death; the others who were tried with him were acquitted. This trial had been delayed for some time, M'Carthy having found means to break out of the cells, and remain for some weeks sheltered at the Hawkesbury, the refuge of all the Sydney rogues when in danger of being apprehended.

Three prisoners were tried for stealing some articles out of the store at the river, one of whom was found guilty, viz. James Ashford, a young lad who had been formerly drummed out of the New South Wales corps. He was sentenced to seven years labour at Norfolk Island. One soldier was accused by an old man, a settler at the river, of an unnatural crime, but acquitted.

Two people off the store were found guilty of stealing some geese, the property of Mr. Charles Grimes, the deputy-surveyor, and sentenced to receive corporal punishment. Another of the same class was found guilty of cutting and wounding a servant of the commissary, who had prevented his committing a theft, and was sentenced to receive eight hundred lashes; and one man, George Hyson, for an attempt to commit the abominable crime of bestiality, was sentenced to stand three times in the pillory, an hour each time.

How unpleasing were the reflections that arose from this catalogue of criminals and their offences! No punishment however exemplary, no reward however great, could operate on the minds of these unthinking people. Equally indifferent to the pain which the former might occasion, and the gratification that the other might afford, they blindly pursued the dictates of their vicious inclinations, to whatever they prompted; and when stopped by the arm of justice, which sometimes reached them, they endured the consequences with an hardened obstinacy and indifference that effectually checked the sensations of pity which are naturally excited by the view of human sufferings.

A civil court also was assembled this month, by which some writs and some probates of wills were granted.

At the Hawkesbury, where the settlers were consuming their subsistance in drunkenness, a very excellent barrack was erecting for the use of the commandant, on a spot which had been selected sufficiently high to preclude any danger of the building being affected by a flood.

In this and the preceding month many people, adults as well as children, were again afflicted with inflammations in the eyes. Having been visited by this disorder in the month of April 1794, about which time we had the same variable weather as was now experienced, we attributed its appearance among us at this time to the same cause. The medical gentlemen could not account for it on any other principle. One man, Serjeant-major Jones of the New South Wales corps, died.

May.] Sixty of the women received by the Indispensable were sent up to Parramatta, there to be employed in such labour as was suited to their sex and strength. The remainder were landed at this place.

On the 4th the governor notified in public orders his appointment of Mr. D'Arcy Wentworth to the situation of assistant-surgeon to the settlement, in the room of Mr. Samuel Leeds, (the gentleman who came out with Governor Hunter,) he being permitted to return to England for the recovery of his health.

Daily experience proved, that those people whose sentences of transportation had expired were greater evils than the convicts themselves. It was at this time impossible to spare the labour of a single man from the public work. Of course, no man was allowed to remove himself from that situation without permission. But, notwithstanding this had been declared in public orders, many were known to withdraw themselves from labour and the provision-store on the day of their servitude ceasing. On their being apprehended, punished for a breach of the order, and ordered again to labour, they seized the first opportunity of running away, taking either to the woods to subsist by depredations, or to the shelter which the Hawkesbury settlers afforded to every vagabond that asked it.

By thefe people we were well convinced every theft was committed. Their information was good; they never attempted a houfe that was not an object of plunder; and wherever there was any property they were fure to pay a vifit. The late robberies at the clergyman's and at Captain Townfon's were among the moft ftriking inftances.

It was on thefe occafions generally conjectured, that the domeftics of the houfe muft aid and affift in the theft; for the perpetrator of it always feemed to know where to lay his hand on the article for which he thus rifked his neck; and we never found them make an attempt on the houfe of a poor individual.

On Wednefday the 11th, to the great fatisfaction of the fettlement at large, the Britannia ftorefhip arrived fafe from Calcutta and Madras, entering this port for the fifth time with a valuable cargo on board.

She was now freighted with falted provifions, and a fmall quantity of rice on account of government, procured by order of the prefidencies of Calcutta and Madras. On private account, the different officers of the civil and military departments received the various commiffions which they had been allowed to put into the fhip; and one young mare, five cows, and one cow-calf, of the Bengal breed, were brought for fale.

On board of this fhip arrived two officers of the Bengal army, Lieutenant Campbell and Mr. Phillips, a furgeon of the military eftablifhment, for the purpofe of raifing two hundred recruits from among thofe people who had ferved their refpective terms of tranfportation. They were to be regularly enlifted and attefted, and were to receive bounty-money; and a provifional engagement was made with Mr. Raven, to convey them to India, if no other fervice fhould offer for his fhip.

On the firft view of this fcheme it appeared very plaufible, and we imagined that the execution of it would be attended with much good to the fettlement, by ridding it of many of thofe wretches whom we had too much reafon to deem our greateft nuifances: but when we found that the recruiting officer was inftructed to be nice as to the characters of thofe he fhould enlift, and to entertain none that were of known bad morals, we perceived that the fettlement would derive

lefs

lefs benefit from it than was at firft expected. There was alfo fome
reafon to fuppofe, that feveral fettlers would abandon their farms, and,
leaving their families a burden to the ftore, embrace the change which
was offered them by enlifting as Eaft-India foldiers. It was far better
for us, if any were capable of bearing arms and becoming foldiers,
to arm them in defence of their own lives and poffeffions, and, by
embodying them from time to time as a militia, fave to the public the
expence of a regiment or corps raifed for the mere purpofe of protecting the public ftores and the civil eftablifhment of the colony.

Recruiting, therefore, in this colony for the Bengal army, being a
meafure that required fome confideration, and which the governor
thought fhould firft have obtained the fanction of adminiftration, he
determined to wait the refult of a communication on the fubject with
the fecretary of ftate, before he gave it his countenance. At the fame
time he meant to recommend it in a certain degree, as it was evident
that many good recruits might be taken, without any injury to the
interefts of the fettlement, from that clafs of our people who, being
no longer prifoners, declined labouring for government, and, without any vifible means of fubfifting, lived where and how they chofe.

The Britannia, in her paffage to Batavia, anchored in Gower's
Harbour, New Ireland, (on the 16th of July,) where fhe completed
her wood and water, and failed on the 23d. On the 2d of September
following fhe arrived at Batavia; and it appearing to Mr. Raven (as
before obferved) but too probable that he fhould be detained by the
government if he ventured to wait even for their determination refpecting fupplying the provifions, he failed on the 7th for Bengal,
arriving in the Ganges on the 12th of October. Not being able to
procure at Calcutta the full quantity of provifions that his fhip could
contain, he failed for Madras on the 1ft of February, where he anchored on the 15th. There he completed his cargo, and failed, with
five homeward-bound Indiamen, on the 27th of the fame month.
His paffage to this country was long and tedious, owing to the prevalence of light and contrary winds; but we were all well pleafed to be
in poffeffion of the comforts he brought us from that part of the world,
and to congratulate him on his perfonal efcape from the fickly and

now

now inimical port of Batavia, as well as from the cruisers of the enemy, with which he had reason to suppose he might fall in on the Indian coast.

On his return from this his second voyage to India, Mr. Raven gave it as his opinion, " that the passage to be pursued from New South Wales to India depended wholly upon the season in which the ship might leave Port Jackson. From the month of November to April, or rather from October to the beginning of March, which ought to be the latest period that any ship should attempt a northern passage, he recommended making Norfolk Island; and thence, passing between the Loyalty Islands * and New Caledonia, to keep as nearly as circumstances would allow in the longitude of 165° East; until the ship should reach the latitude of 8° South; and then shape a course to cross the equator in 160° East; after which the master should steer to the N. W. by N. or N. N. W. until in the latitude of 5° 20' or 5° 30' North; in which latitude Mr. Raven would run down his longitude, and pass the south end of Mindanao, and between that island and Bascelan; and thence through the straits of Banguey into the China Sea. In running this passage, it would be necessary to pay attention to Mr. Dalrymple's charts of those islands, &c. which Mr. Raven found very accurate.

" If leaving Port Jackson any time between the beginning of March and the 1st of September, Mr. Raven would prefer passing through a strait in the longitude of 156° 10' E. or thereabout; and from the latitude of 7° 06' E. to 6° 42' S. which divides some part of the islands of the New Georgia of Captain Shortland; thence through St. George's Channel to the northward of New Guinea, through

---

* The Loyalty Islands are situated between New Caledonia and the New Hebrides, and extend from about 21° 30' to 20° 50' S. and from the longitude of 168° to 167° E. Mr. Raven supposed them to be a large group of islands, which, being pressed for time, he could not stop to survey. All that he had opportunity to determine was, the longitude and latitude of some of the head-lands. Many fires were seen on them in the night; the whole appeared to be full of wood, and in some places in high cultivation. These islands, certainly a discovery belonging to Mr. Raven, may be thought worthy of being explored at some future day, and become an object of consequence to the settlement in New South Wales.

Dampier's

Dampier's Strait, down Pitt's Passage, to the southward of Boutton, and through the Straits of Salayer, into the Banda or Amboyna Sea. This passage the Britannia performed in sixty-five days from Port Jackson to Batavia ; which, had it not been for calms she met with off the coast of New Guinea, would in all probability have been performed in six weeks, or thereabout."

Mr. Raven furnished these observations in the hope that they might benefit the settlement, by proving useful to the commanders of any ships which the governor might have occasion to send into those seas on the service of the colony.

The governor, convinced that an example was necessary to check the present practice of villainy, had ordered James M'Carthy, the prisoner under sentence of death for forgery, to be executed on Saturday the 14th of this present month ; but yielded to the request of Mr. Johnson (the clergyman who attended the prisoner) to spare his life, it appearing evidently on the trial, that, guilty though he certainly was, he had in the present instance been rather the victim of the vice of others, than of his own.   He was accordingly pardoned, on condition of his serving for seven years at hard labour at Norfolk Island.

About this time the Marquis Cornwallis and Experiment sailed for India.   Previous to their departure, Mr. Hogan, the commander of the former, had requested an examination might be taken as to the circumstances of his conduct toward the convicts and others on board his ship during their passage from Ireland to this country.   The examination upon oath was made by the judge-advocate, assisted by two other magistrates, to whom it appeared, that Mr. Hogan, but for the fortunate and timely discovery of it, would with his ship have fallen a sacrifice to as daring and alarming a conspiracy as, perhaps, ever had been entered into by a set of desperate wretches on board of any ship ; and that nothing was left for him, to save himself from the danger of a similar circumstance occurring during the voyage, but to inflict immediate punishment on the persons who were concerned in it.

A civil court was assembled nearly about the same time, to try an assault, the action for which was brought by Mr. Matthew Austin (a gentleman who came out in the Marquis Cornwallis, as a superintending

ing

ing furgeon of the convicts in that fhip, on the part of government) againft Mr. Michael Hogan the commander, Mr. John Hogan the furgeon, and Henry Hacking the pilot. The circumftances of the affault being proved, the court adjudged Mr. M. Hogan to pay damages to the amount of fifty pounds; the others were acquitted.

On Mr. M'Clellan's arrival from Bengal, he reminded us, that fome property had been found concealed in the bed of one of our people, which property had been fhewn to him at the time, under a fuppofition that it might have been ftolen from his fhip. On his return to India, he found that a fmall bale, containing the very articles which had been fhewn him here, had been put on board him at Bengal, to be delivered as a prefent to a gentleman at Batavia, the initials of whofe name were marked on the bale. On his ftating thefe circumftances to the judge-advocate, that part of the property which had been found, and placed in the cuftody of the provoft-marfhal, was given up to Mr. M'Clellan. Rogers, who had been either the principal or the receiver, perhaps forefeeing that the offence might fooner or later be brought home to him, had taken himfelf off in the Endeavour, and was one of thofe perfons who had been unavoidably left behind at Dufky Bay by Mr. Waine when he quitted that place in the Affiftance.

From the addrefs with which this bufinefs muft have been managed, mafters of fhips might fee the neceffity that exifted for their keeping a vigilant eye over the people whom they admitted on their decks, and be perfectly affured, that many vifited them for the exprefs purpofe of difcovering what vigilance was obferved by the mafter, his mates, and people. Many inftances of this kind had occurred, although it might have been readily fuppofed, that a ftranger would have been on his guard, and never have loft the idea of the defcription of people by whom he was likely to be vifited. A large quantity of tobacco had been ftolen out of the Bellona ftorefhip fhortly after fhe arrived here; half a cafk of gunpowder had been ftolen out of the Britannia, at the very time that the mafter was entertaining fome of the gentlemen of the fettlement in the cabin; Mr. Page, the mafter of the American fhip Hope, was robbed of feveral articles, and the buckles out of his fhoes, which ftood in the cabin wherein he lay afleep; and this theft

of

of the bale from on board the Experiment was an additional instance of the management and ability displayed by our people in conducting an affair of that kind.

From this recapitulation of some of the offences which had been committed on board of ships while riding in this cove, (to which many others might have been added,) let the masters of those which may hereafter be sent out, and who may have perused this account, be cautious who they receive on board during the day, let their pretext of business, or coming from an officer, be what it may; never should they be suffered to mix with their seamen, nor to see where the stores of the ship are placed; nor should a boat be ever permitted to come alongside during the night, except with or for an officer, which might sometimes unavoidably happen; and in that case the people should not be allowed to come into the ship. The masters of ships were long since forbidden to receive any convict on board without a pass signed by the judge-advocate, who, from his official situation, was the best qualified to know the character of those who might apply; but the decks of ships were often filled with convicts, who went off with merely the sanction of the masters they lived with, although known perhaps at the time to be as suspicious characters as any in the settlement.

Among the Irish prisoners who arrived in the Marquis Cornwallis was one who professed to understand the business of a millwright, and who undertook with very little assistance to construct a mill at this place. He appeared rough and uncouth in his manners; but our want of a mill was so great, that it was determined to try what his abilities were, and place some hired artificers under his direction. A spot was chosen on the summit of the ground which forms the western side of the cove, and, saw-pits being dug for him, he began the work.

With a mill once erected competent to the grinding of all our wheat, a reduction in the ration of flour would not be felt. So sensible of this advantage had the governor been, that he brought out with him the most material parts of a windmill, with a model, by which any millwright he might find here would be enabled to set up the different parts; and Thorp the millwright was employed in collecting

3   lecting

lecting and preparing the timber necessary for putting up this mill at Parramatta.

The weather was very variable during the month. The cattle brought by Mr. Raven, though in Smithfield they would not all together have been worth fifty pounds, were sold by auction at enormous prices. The mares went at one hundred pounds, one of the cows at eighty-four pounds, and the others at prices something inferior.

June.] His Majesty's birth-day was observed by the settlement with that attention which, as English subjects, we were proud to pay to it. The Susan (with American colours flying), though provided with only six or eight guns, contrived to fire at one o'clock with the king's ships, a well-timed salute of twenty-one guns in honour of the day.

On this occasion the governor pardoned all culprits, except James M'Carthy, who was under orders for Norfolk Island. It might be looked upon as a sort of encouragement to the commission of crimes, thus by a periodical pardon to render punishment less certain. If men were led to suppose, that on the king's birth-day all culprits would be pardoned, they would be emboldened to offend, at least for a month or two previous to that time; but the governor did not mean to extend this act of mercy beyond the present occasion, being the first birth-day of his sovereign that had occurred since his arrival.

Several daring thefts were committed early in this month. William Waring, a prisoner who had been allowed to cultivate a farm of thirty acres on the banks of the Hawkesbury, having occasion to move a cask of salted provisions, which he had purchased from the master of a ship riding in this cove, entrusted it to the care of two people his servants, to convey it from his farm to that of a neighbouring settler. The temptation was too great to be resisted, and the cask was stolen out of the boat, while the servants landed for the night at some farm by the way. They pretended to have no concern in it; but as that was too improbable to be believed, they were ordered to make restitution by their labour.

About the same time the brick-hut occupied by Thomas Clark, a superintendant of convicts, was broken into; and, notwithstanding the door of the room in which he slept with his wife was open, they plundered the house of several articles to a great amount.

Some runaways from the jail-gang at this place were suspected; and our watch, being dispatched immediately on receipt of this in-

formation,

formation, were very near falling in with the thieves; but these latter deserted them in time to make their escape. Information being afterwards received, that two runaway vagabonds were concealed at a house near the brick-fields, some of the watch repaired to the spot, and found two notorious offenders, James M'Manus and George Collins. These two people had repeatedly broken out of the jail-hut, and one of them, M'Manus, had some time since been fired at and wounded in an attempt to commit a burglary. On the present occasion, he had sufficient address to effect his escape from the watch; the other was secured and brought in. The hut in which they were found was pulled down the following morning, to deter others (if possible) from harbouring thieves and vagabonds.

The settlers in the different districts, and particularly those at the Hawkesbury, had long been supposed to be considerably in debt; and it was suspected, that their crops for two or more seasons to come were pledged to pay these debts. As this was an evil of great magnitude, the governor set on foot such an inquiry as he thought would ascertain or contradict the report. By this inquiry, it appeared, that the settlers at the districts of Prospect Hill, the Ponds, the Field of Mars, the Eastern Farms, and Mulgrave Place on the banks of the river Hawkesbury, stood indebted in the sum of 5098 l. The inquiry was farther directed as well to the appearance of the farms, and the general character of the settlers, as to their debts. Many were reported to be industrious and thriving; but a great number were stated to be idle, vicious, given to drinking, gaming, and other such disorders as lead to poverty and ruin. One man, a settler at the Eastern Farms, Edward Elliot, had received a ewe sheep from the late Governor Phillip before his departure in the year 1792. He had resisted many temptations to sell it, and at the time this inquiry took place was found possessing a flock of two-and-twenty sheep, males and females. He had been fortunate in not meeting with any loss, but had not added to his flock by any purchase. This was a proof that industry did not go without its reward in this country. Other instances were found to corroborate this observation.

At the settlement of the Hawkesbury one man had been drowned, and another killed by the natives.

The

The gentlemen who conducted the inquiry found most of the settlers there oftener employed in carousing in the fronts of their houses, than in labouring themselves, or superintending the labour of their servants in their grounds. There was at this time a considerable quantity of spirits in the colony from the Susan, the Britannia, and Indispensable, and no doubt much of it had found its way to the settlers; but that they could be so lost to their own true interest, could be only accounted for by recollecting their former habits of life, in which the frequent use of intoxicating liquors formed a part of their education.

With a view to check the drunkenness that prevailed in the different districts, the governor had directed licences for retailing spirituous liquors to be given to certain deserving characters in each; but it was not found to answer the effect he expected. Instead of the settlers being disposed to industry, they still indulged themselves in inebriety and idleness, and robberies now appeared to be committed more frequently than formerly. He therefore judged it necessary to direct, that none of those persons who had obtained licences should presume to carry on a traffic with settlers or others who might have grain to dispose of, by paying for such grain in spirits. He assured them, that should any persons be thereafter discovered to have carried on so destructive a trade, their licences would immediately be recalled, and such steps taken for their further punishment as they might be thought to deserve. He also desired it might be understood, that trading with spirits to the extent which he found practised was strictly forbidden to others, as well as to those who had licensed public houses.

The practice of purchasing the crops of the settlers for spirits had too long prevailed in the settlement; and the governor thought it absolutely necessary, by all the means in his power, to put an end to it; for it was not possible that a farmer who should be idle enough to throw away the labour of twelve months, for the gratification of a few gallons of poisonous spirits, could expect to thrive, or enjoy those comforts which were only to be procured by sobriety and industry. From such characters he determined to withdraw the assistance of government, since when left to themselves they would have less time to waste in drunkenness and riot.

3 Q 2

In

In the night of the 19th of this month some thieves broke into the house of William Miller, (a young man who, on account of his good behaviour, had been allowed to exercise the trade of a baker,) and stole articles to the amount of fifty-six pounds, mostly property not belonging to himself. Suspicion falling upon some people off the store, they were apprehended; but in the morning the greater part of what had been stolen was found placed in a garden where it could be easily discovered, and restored to the owner.

On the day following, the governor, with a small party, undertook a second excursion to the retreat of the cattle. A few days previous to the governor's departure, Mr. Bass, the surgeon of the Reliance, and two companions, set off in an attempt to round the mountains to the westward; but having soon attained the summit of the highest, they saw at the distance of forty or fifty miles another range of mountains, extending to the northward and southward. Mr. Bass reported, that he passed over some very fine land, and he brought in some specimens of a light wood which he met with.

The governor was not long absent. He saw the cattle ranging as before, although not exactly in the same spot, in the finest country yet discovered in New South Wales, and ascended a hill which from every point of view had appeared the highest in our neighbourhood. He fixed, by means of an artificial horizon, its latitude to be 34° 09' S. nine miles to the southward of Botany Bay. The height of this hill, which obtained the name of Mount Hunter, was supposed to be near a mile from the base; and the view from the summit was commanding, and full of grand objects, wood, water, plains, and mountains. Every where on that side of the Nepean, the soil was found to be good, and the ground eligible for cultivation. The sides of Mount Hunter, though very steep, were clothed with timber to the summit, and the ground filled with the Orchis root.

The knowledge derived from this excursion was, that the cattle had not been disturbed, and that they had increased; ninety-four were at this time counted.

About the same time the people of a fishing-boat returned from a bay near Port Stephens, into which they had been driven by bad weather, and brought in with them several large pieces of coal, which they said they found at some little distance from the beach, lying in con-

confiderable quantity on the furface of the ground. Thefe people having conducted themfelves improperly while on fhore, two of them were feverely wounded by the natives, one of whom died foon after he reached the hofpital.

The Francis fchooner failed on the 21ft with difpatches for Norfolk Ifland; the king's fhips, the Reliance and Supply, began the neceffary preparations for their intended voyage to the Cape of Good Hope, and the firft day of September was fixed for their departure.

Toward the latter end of the month two men from each officer were ordered to join the public gangs, it being found wholly impracticable to erect without more affiftance any of the buildings which had now become indifpenfably neceffary. Storehoufes were much wanted; the barracks were yet unfinifhed; houfes were to be built for the affiftant-furgeons, thofe which had been erected foon after our arrival being now no longer tenable. A church too, of more fubftantial materials than lath and plaifter, was wanted here and at Parramatta; as well as court-houfes, or places where the courts of civil and criminal judicature might be held, and where the magiftrates might meet to do the public bufinefs.

At Sydney, the bricklayers' gang was employed during this month in erecting a temporary court-houfe of lath and plaifter; as it was uncertain when one to be built of bricks could be begun; and great inconvenience was felt by the judge-advocate and other magiftrates in being obliged to tranfact bufinefs at their own houfes.

We had at laft the fatisfaction of feeing ufefully employed fome of the cattle brought hither in the Endeavour. A careful perfon being found to conduct them, the timber-carriage was now, inftead of men, drawn by fix or eight ftout oxen; and all the timber which was wanted for building, or other purpofes, was brought to the pits by them, both here and at Parramatta. This was fome faving of men, but eight people were ftill employed with each carriage.

The carpenters continued erecting the temporary fhed for provifions; the town gang was employed delivering the florefhips; and at Toongabbe fome women were employed in making hay, intended to be put on board the king's fhips for the cattle to be purchafed at the Cape for the colony.

One man, Matthew Farrel, died in this month. He had been hurt in an affray with fome watchmen in the night of the 17th of March laft.

CHAP. XXXII.

TWO MEN KILLED; CONSEQUENT REGULATIONS.—THE BRITANNIA HIRED
TO PROCEED TO ENGLAND.—REPORT OF THE NATIVES.—THE FRANCIS
ARRIVES FROM NORFOLK ISLAND.—PUBLIC WORKS.—DEATHS.—A CRIMI-
NAL COURT ASSEMBLED.—A SETTLER EXECUTED FOR MURDER.—THE
SUSAN SAILS.—A CIVIL COURT HELD.—AN AMERICAN SHIP ARRIVES FROM
BOSTON.—A LONG-BOAT LOST.—DEATHS.—WEATHER.—A TEMPORARY
CHURCH OPENED AT PARRAMATTA.—APPOINTMENTS.—THE SUPPLY SAILS
FOR NORFOLK ISLAND AND THE CAPE.—ACCOUNT OF STOCK.—LAND IN
CULTIVATION, AND NUMBERS IN THE COLONY.—A MURDER COMMITTED.
—BRITANNIA SAILS FOR ENGLAND.—GENERAL OBSERVATIONS.

July.] AMONG the many evils that were daily seen flowing from
that state of dissipation which had found its way into the different settlements, we had to regret that two men lost their lives by the hand of
violence. On Tuesday the 4th of this month, John Smith, a seaman
belonging to the Indispensable, was shot at Sydney in the house of
Mr. Daniel Payne, the master boat-builder, by a convict-servant of
his; and on the same day, at the Hawkesbury, David Lane was shot
by his master, John Fenlow, a settler at that place. The latter of
these unfortunate men lived but a few hours; Smith the seaman was
taken to the hospital, where he languished until the 9th, and then
died. Fenlow and the convict were taken into custody, and would
have been immediately brought to trial; but, through the carelessness
of one of the watchmen, Fenlow found means, though incumbered
with heavy irons, to escape from the cells, and was not retaken until
the latter end of the month, when some natives discovered him lurking
near his own grounds at the river, and, giving information, he was
easily apprehended and secured.

These transactions were productive of some internal regulations
which had long been wanting. Several settlers, with whose conduct
the governor had had but too much cause to be displeased, were at
length deprived of all assistance from government, and left to the exercise of their own abilities, pursuant to a notice which they received

to that effect in the last month. Several other settlers also, who had
been victualled from the public stores long beyond the period allowed
them by the crown, were struck off from the victualling books. All
persons off the stores, who of course did not labour for government,
were ordered forthwith to appear at Sydney, in order to their being
mustered and examined relative to their respective terms of transportation; when certificates were to be given to such as were regularly
discharged from the commissary's books, and the settlers were directed
not to employ any but such as could produce this certificate. Frequent
visits were directed to be made by the magistrates, for the purpose of
settling such differences as might arise among the settlers and other
persons; and the governor signified his determination of inspecting
their conduct himself from time to time, and of punishing such as were
proved to afford shelter or employment to the thieves and vagabonds
who ran to the river and other districts from this town and Parramatta.

These regulations being made known as publicly and generally as
was possible, in order that none might plead ignorance, the town of
Sydney was shortly after filled with people from the different settlements, who came to the judge-advocate for certificates of their having
served their respective sentences. Among these were many who had
run away from public labour before their time had expired; some
who had escaped from confinement with crimes yet unpunished hanging over their heads; and some who, being for life, appeared by
names different from those by which they were commonly known in
the settlement. By the activity of the watchmen, and a minute investigation of the necessary books and papers, they were in general
detected in the imposition, and were immediately sent to hard labour
in the town and jail gangs.

To the latter of these gangs additions were every day making;
scarcely a day or a night passed but some enormity was committed or
attempted either on the property or persons of individuals. Two notorious characters, Luke Normington and Richard Elliott, were detected on the night of the 13th in a very suspicious situation in the
commissary's stock-yard, which was well filled at the time with sheep
and other stock. These were sent to the jail-gang, in company with
one

one Sharpless, a convict, who, after marrying a woman that was a perfect antidote to desire, pretended to be jealous, and gave her such a dreadful beating, that her life was for some time in danger.

Stock of all denominations was at this time fast increasing in the different districts. An officer of the New South Wales corps, having obtained the governor's sanction for his quitting the colony in one of the ships now preparing for the Cape of Good Hope, sold to government a flock of goats, consisting of about one hundred animals, for 490 l. 10 s. This was a valuable acquisition, and promises of stock to several deserving settlers were now performed.

The Britannia, being now cleared of the cargo she brought from Bengal on government account, was fitting again for sea, when Mr. Raven, the master, proffered her to the governor for the purpose of going direct to England, if his excellency should have any occasion to employ her in such a voyage. There were at this time several soldiers in the New South Wales corps wholly unfit for service; the governor had for some time intended to send home Mr. Clark, a superintendant of convicts, whose engagement with the crown had expired; and James Thorp, a person who had been sent out with a salary of 105 l. per annum as a master millwright, but who was at this time unemployed in the settlement. To ease government at once of these expences, the governor thought it adviseable to charter the Britannia, for the purpose of taking home such invalids and passengers as might be ordered, at the rate of fifteen shillings per ton per month; the charter to be in force on the first day of the ensuing month.

The public stores were opened during this month at Parramatta and the river for receiving Indian corn; which was taken in at five shillings per bushel for this season; but it was generally supposed, that there would not be occasion to give that price for it again.

Fresh pork was at this time purchased by the commissary at one shilling per pound, and issued as a ration, in the proportion of two pounds of fresh for one of salt meat.

It having been represented to the governor, that several people in the town of Sydney employed themselves in building boats for sale, and without obtaining any permission, a liberty which had crept into the settlement in opposition to all former orders and regulations on

that

that head; and as it was well known that, notwithstanding the great convenience which must attend the having boats for various uses in this extensive harbour, many abuses were carried on through their means; it was ordered, that no boat whatever, of any size or description, should be built until application had been made to the governor, and permission in writing obtained, either signed by the governor for the time being, or by some person properly authorised by him. It was also ordered, that all boats at that time in the possession of individuals should be forthwith taken to the master boat-builder, where a number was to be cut on the stern, and a register of such number was to be kept by the provost-marshal. All boats found without a number were to be liable to seizure.

The natives appeared less troublesome lately than they had been for some time past. The people of a fishing-boat, which had been cast on shore in some bad weather near Port Stephens, met with some of these people, who without much entreaty, or any hope of reward, readily put them into a path from thence to Broken Bay, and conducted them the greatest part of the way. During their little journey, these friendly people made them understand, that they had seen a white woman among some natives to the northward. On their reporting this at Sydney, this unfortunate female was conjectured to be Mary Morgan, a prisoner, who it was now said had failed in her attempt to get on board the Resolution store-ship, which sailed from hence in 1794. There was indeed a woman, one Ann Smith, who ran away a few days after our sitting down in this place, and whose fate was not exactly ascertained; if she could have survived the hardships and wretchedness of such a life as must have been hers during so many years residence among the natives of New Holland, how much information must it have been in her power to afford! But humanity shuddered at the idea of purchasing it at so dear a price.

Toward the latter end of the month, there not remaining any more flour in the store than what was necessarily reserved for the use of his Majesty's ships Reliance and Supply to carry them to the Cape of Good Hope, nine pounds of wheat were added to the allowance of that article (three pounds) served to the civil, military, and free people.

A court

A court of civil judicature was held on the 27th and 28th, when several debts were sworn to, and writs taken out.

In the night of the 29th, the Francis schooner returned from Norfolk Island, having been absent five weeks and three days. From her we learned, that the criminal court of judicature had been assembled, and one man, a convict, had suffered death, being convicted of a most daring burglary, which he and two others his accomplices effected with some circumstances of cruelty. The accomplices were sentenced to hard labour on Phillip Island for a certain term of years.

It was observed that the gangs at this place employed in different public works were seldom to be seen in the afternoon. On inquiry, it appeared that, notwithstanding the orders which had been given for the regulation of the public labour, the superintendants had taken it upon themselves to task the working people in such manner as they thought proper, and upon no other authority than their own will. By this abuse the work of government was almost wholly neglected, and the time of the labourers applied to the use of private individuals.

To remedy this evil, the governor repeated the order in which the hours of public labour were pointed out, and informed the superintendants and overseers, that if they should be known to take the liberty of applying to any other use or purpose the time designed to be employed for the public, they would be instantly dismissed from their employments, as persons who could not be depended upon; and they might rest assured, that any one, who had been proved unworthy the trust he had placed in him, would never be restored to a situation of which he was so little tenacious.

During this month died Mr. Henry Brewer, the provost-marshal of the territory, at the age of fifty-seven years. He came out with Governor Phillip as his clerk, and on our landing was appointed to act as provost-marshal in the room of the person appointed by the crown, Mr. Alexander, who never came out. Mr. Brewer afterwards received his Majesty's commission appointing him to the vacancy. There also died Andrew Fishburn, a private in the New South Wales corps, but formerly belonging to the marine detachment serving in this country, who had been very useful as a carpenter in the settlement;

ment; a foldier, who came out in the Cornwallis; one male convict, who died fuddenly; one unfortunate man, John Williams, who was crufhed to death by the wheel of a timber-carriage going over his head; and the fettler's fervant who was killed at the Hawkefbury; befide the feaman belonging to the Indifpenfable who was fhot.

Auguft.] A court of criminal judicature was affembled early in the month for the trial of feveral offenders who were at that time in confinement under different charges.

Four prifoners were. tried for a burglary in the houfe of William Miller, but acquitted through a defect in evidence. David Lloyd was tried for the wilful murder of John Smith, the feaman belonging to the fhip Indifpenfable. It appeared, that the feaman had repaired in a ftate of intoxication to the houfe of Mr. Payne, for the exprefs purpofe of taking from a female convict (then living as a fervant at Mr. Payne's, and with whom he, the feaman, had cohabited during the paffage) fome clothes which he had given her. A riot, the natural confequence of fuch a proceeding, enfued; and the prifoner endeavoured to make it appear that he had been compelled in his own defence to fire the piftol which caufed the death of the feaman. The court admitted that the prifoner had not any of that malice in his heart againft the deceafed which is neceffary to conftitute the crime of murder, and therefore acquitted him of that charge; but found him guilty of manflaughter, and fentenced him to receive fix hundred lafhes. John Fenlow was tried for the wilful murder of his fervant, David Lane. This charge was fully made out, and the prifoner received fentence to die. Matthew Farrel, who (with Richard Sutton, the Newgate Bully) affaulted the watch on the night of the 17th of March laft, having in the courfe of that conteft received a wound on the temple which proved incurable, and occafioned his death fome time after, the watchmen were now brought forward to account for the death of the deceafed. This they did very fatisfactorily, and were difcharged. Four vagabonds, who had repeatedly broken out of prifon, and run away from the jail-gang, were tried as incorrigible rogues, and being found guilty, were fentenced to three years hard labour at Norfolk Ifland; and one man was tried for a rape, but acquitted. Fenlow, being tried on the Saturday, was executed on the

3 R 2   following

following Monday. His body being delivered to the surgeons for dissection pursuant to his sentence, a stone was found in his gall bladder, of the size of a lark's egg. This unhappy man was remarkable for an extreme irascibility of temper: might it not have been occasioned by the torment that such a substance must produce in so irritable a situation? He however, the night before his execution, confessed that the murder which he committed was premeditated. Notwithstanding which, he had, the day before he was tried, prepared an opening through the brick wall of his cell, purposing, if it had not been discovered in time, to have availed himself of it to escape after his trial. It could scarcely be supposed, that among the description of people of which the lower class was formed in this place, any would have been found sufficiently curious to have attended the surgeons on such an occasion; but they had no sooner signified that the body was ready for inspection, than the hospital was filled with people, men, women, and children, to the number of several hundreds; none of whom appeared moved with pity for his fate, or in the least degree admonished by the sad spectacle before their eyes.

On Monday the 8th the snow Susan sailed on her voyage to Canton. Two women, Sarah Nitchell and Elizabeth Robinson, and a few men, were allowed to quit the colony in this vessel.

His Royal Highness the Prince of Wales's birth-day was duly distinguished by us on the 12th of this month. Such days had never been neglected by the colonists of New South Wales.

A civil court was again held on the day following, when several persons who had been arrested by writs issued from the last court were brought up; many of whom, being settlers, gave assignments on their coming crops of wheat for the different sums in which they were indebted. Several other debts were sworn to, and writs issued. Had those defendants who were thus suffered to give assignments on their crops then in the ground been thrown into prison at the suit of the different plaintiffs, their ruin would have been certain, and the debt would have remained unsatisfied. This method was tried, as being something more beneficial to both parties; but they were in general of such a thoughtless worthless description, that even this indulgence might induce them to be, if possible, more worthless and thoughtless than

                                                                        before,

before, as, to use their own expression, they had now " to work for " a dead horse."

On the 23d (the signal for a sail having been made at the South-head, the day before), there anchored in the stream, just without the two points of Sydney Cove, the ship Grand Turk, from Boston, after a passage of five months from that port. She had been twenty-three days from Van Dieman's Land, meeting with a current, during several days, that set her each day twenty-one miles either to the S. E. or N. E. We found on board as supercargo, Mr. M'Gee, who was here before in the Halcyon with Mr. Benjamin Page. He brought news from Europe as late as January last, by which we learned that the war still raged. Mr. M'Gee had on board for sale, spirits, tobacco, wine, soap, iron, linseed-oil, broad-cloth, &c. &c. for this market, Manilla, and Canton. The tobacco (eighteen hogsheads) were immediately bought for one shilling and three half-pence per pound, and government pur-chased some of his spirits at seven shillings per gallon.

During this month a long-boat belonging to his Majesty's ship Re-liance, which had been sent to Botany Bay in July to procure fish, was given up for lost, with five or six seamen. They were known to have quitted Botany Bay, and, not having been heard of for some weeks, were conjectured to have taken the boat away to the north-ward, where, being without compass or provisions, (except the few fish they had caught,) it was more than probable they had perished.

The jail-gang at this time, notwithstanding the examples which had been made, consisted of upwards of five-and-twenty persons ; and many of the female prisoners were found to be every whit as in-famous as the men.

One settler was executed this month, and one soldier lost his life by a tree falling on him at the Hawkesbury.

The first and middle parts of the month were wet. The branch of the harbour named Duck River was so swollen as to overflow its banks, which were very steep.

September.] A temporary church, formed out of the materials of two old huts, was opened at Parramatta by the Rev. Mr. Marsden on the first Sunday in this month. Decent places of worship were now

to

to be feen at the two principal fettlements. At the time when we were vifited by the Spanifh fhips Mr. Johnfon preached wherever he could find a fhady fpot. The prieft belonging to the commodore's fhip, obferving that we had not any church built, lifted up his eyes with aftonifhment, and declared, that had the place been fettled by his nation, a houfe for God would have been erected before any houfe for man.

The fhips being now on the point of failing, the Britannia for England, and the Reliance and Supply for the Cape of Good Hope, the following appointments were notified in the public orders: viz. Captain George Johnfton, of the New South Wales corps, was appointed aid-de-camp to the governor. The Rev. Mr. Johnfon and William Balmain Efq. were nominated the acting magiftrates in the diftrict of the town of Sydney. Mr. James Williamfon (a gentleman who came from England with the governor) was to do the duty of commiffary in the abfence of Mr. Palmer, who was returning to England on leave. Mr. Thomas Smyth was appointed provoft-marfhal, in the room of Mr. Henry Brewer, by warrant bearing date the day after his deceafe. Mr. Thomas Moore, carpenter of the fhip Britannia, was appointed mafter boat-builder in the room of Mr. Daniel Payne. William Stephenfon was placed under the commiffary as a ftore-keeper, in the room of Mr. Thomas Smyth ; and George Barrington, whofe conduct, ftill uniform and upright, recommended him to the notice of the governor, was, after receiving an abfolute pardon under the feal of the territory, appointed a fuperintendant of convicts, with a falary of fifty pounds per annum, in the room of Mr. Thomas Clark, returning to England *.

On the 20th, his Majefty's fhip Supply failed for Norfolk Ifland and the Cape of Good Hope, having on board part of the military relief intended for that fettlement, and part of a thoufand bufhels of wheat which had been written for from thence.

On the following day the fhips Indifpenfable and Grand Turk failed for Canton. The American had not fucceeded in his fpeculation fo

* Mr. Richard Atkins had fome time before been nominated by the fecretary of ftate to do the duty of judge-advocate, whenever Captain Collins fhould return to England.

wdl

well as he had expected; the market was over-stocked with goods, and by the governor's regulations he was compelled to take away, with many other articles, his ground-tier full of spirits, which he hoped to have fold here.

The invalids and passengers who were returning to England in the Britannia being embarked, that ship, the Reliance, and the Francis schooner, hauled out of the cove preparatory to their departure.

As a proof that stock was not falling in its value, Mr. Palmer, the commissary, sold two Cape cows and one steer for 189l. sterling. The stock in the colony at this time was of considerable extent and value, as will appear by the following account of it, which was taken for the purpose of being transmitted to government:

Account of live stock in the possession of government and the civil and military officers of the settlement, on the 1st of September 1796.

To whom belonging.	Mares and Stock.	Cows and Cow-Calves.	Ox's and Bull-Calves.	Oxen.	Sheep.	Goats.	Hogs.
To government, - -	14	67	37	46	191	111	59
Officers civil and military,	43	34	37	6	1310	1176	889
Total of government and officers,	57	101	74	52	1501	1287	948
To settlers, - - -	-	-	-	-	30	140	921
General total,	57	101	74	52	1531	1427	1869

The wild cattle to the westward of the river Nepean were not included in this account.

All kinds of poultry were numerous.

The

The following account of the land in cultivation was taken at the same time :

To whom belonging.	Land in Cultivation. Acres.	Observations.
To government, - -	1700	By our weakness in public labourers, and wanting many necessary buildings, the land cleared by government was unemployed this year.
Officers civil and military, -	1172	About four fifths of which were at this time sown with wheat.
Total of government and officers,	2872	
To settlers, - - -	2547	Of which much timber was cut down but not burnt off.
General total,	5419	

It was satisfactory to those gentlemen who were now about to quit the colony to reflect that they left it not only with a prospect of plenty before it, but with stores and granaries abundantly filled at the time. Of these, the judge-advocate and the commissary, who had been in the settlement from its establishment, had witnessed periods of distress and difficulty; but they had the gratification of seeing them fairly surmounted, and the probability of their ever recurring thrown to a very great distance. In the houses of individuals were to be found most of the comforts, and not a few of the luxuries of life. For these the island was indebted to the communications it had had with India, and other parts of the world; and the former years of famine, toil, and difficulty, were now exchanged for years of plenty, ease, and pleasure.

The

The following state of the settlement was made up to the 31st of last month:

Salt provisions and grain in store.

Quality.					To last at the established ration.	
					Weeks.	Days.
Beef,	-	-	-	-	31	1
Pork,	-	-	-	-	44	6
Total of salt meat,	-	-	-	76	0
Pease,	-	-	-	-	22	
Wheat,	-	-	-	-	29	1
Maize,	-	-	-	-	41	4
Sugar,	-	-	-	-	4	

To consume this quantity of food, there were victualled at Sydney	-	-	-	2219 persons;
At Parramatta,	-	-	-	965
At the Hawkesbury,	-	-	-	454
Making a total of	-	-	-	3638

There were 321 people off the public stores, which, added to the 3638 who were victualled, gave a general total of 3959 persons in the different settlements, of all descriptions and ages; not including those at Norfolk Island, in which settlement were

889 persons;

to which add   -   3959 persons in New South Wales;

there will be found 4848 persons under the British government in New South Wales and its dependencies.

A few days previous to the sailing of the ships, information was received of a most inhuman murder having been perpetrated on the body of —— Williams, a settler's wife, at the district of the Ponds. A female neighbour of their's was accused by an accomplice of having committed this diabolical act, for the purpose of enriching herself with the property which she knew this unfortunate woman had in the house. She was immediately apprehended, and search made for the

3 s   property

property which had been taken away. Some of this was found, and there was little doubt but the avenging arm of justice would soon fall upon the head of the murderer.

On the 29th his Majesty's ship Reliance, the Britannia hired transport, and the Francis schooner, sailed from Port Jackson. They were all to touch at Norfolk Island, whence the ships were to proceed to the Cape of Good Hope, and the schooner was to return to New South Wales. The Britannia's call at Norfolk Island was for the purpose of taking on board Lieutenant-governor King, who, from a long state of ill health, had found himself compelled to apply to Governor Hunter for leave to return to England, to which the governor had consented.

On board of the Reliance were the commissary, the remainder of the military relief, and such part of the thousand bushels of wheat as the Supply did not receive. In the transport were Captain Paterson; Lieutenants Abbott and Clephan; one serjeant and seventeen privates (invalids) of the New South Wales corps, with their wives and children; the judge-advocate of the settlement, who was charged with dispatches from the governor; Mr. Leeds, an assistant-surgeon; Thomas Clark, late a superintendant of convicts; James Thorp, the master millwright; and several other persons, male and female, who had been allowed a passage to England by the governor.

The following were the prices of various articles, as they were sold at Sydney about the time the ships sailed, viz.

Stock.

Cows 80 l.
Horses 90 l.
Sheep 7 l. 10 s.
Goats 4 l.
Turkeys 1 l. 1 s.
Geese 1 l. 1 s.
Fowls, full grown, 5 s.
Ducks 5 s.

Provisions.

Fresh pork per lb. 1 s. 3 d.
Mutton 2 s.

Provisions.

Goat per lb. 1 s. 6 d.
Kangooroo 6 d.
Fish 2½ d.
Eggs per dozen 2 s.
Salted pork per lb. 1 s.
Salted beef, ditto, 6 d.
Potatoes per cwt. 12 s.
Ditto per lb. 3 d.
Flour, ditto, 7½ d.
Wheat-meal, sifted, 4½ d.
Ditto, unsifted, 3½ d.
Wheat per bushel 12 s.

Provisions.

Provisions.

Barley, per bushel, 10 s.
Pease, ditto, 7 s.
Maize, ditto, 5 s.
Ditto ground, ditto, 8 s.
Cheese per lb. 3 s.
Butter, ditto, 3 s.
White-wine vinegar per gallon 6 s.

Groceries.

Hyson tea per lb. 1 l. 4 s.
Coffee, ditto, 2 s.
Sugar (soft), ditto, 1 s.
Soap, ditto, 2 s.
Virginia leaf-tobacco, ditto, 5 s.
Brasil roll, ditto, 7 s.
Black pepper, ditto, 4 s.
Ginger, ditto, 3 s.
Pipes per gross 1 l. 10 s.

Wine and Spirits.

Red port per bottle 5 s.

Wine and Spirits.

Madeira, per bottle, 4 s.
Cape wine, ditto, 3 s.
Rum, ditto, 5 s.
Gin, ditto, 6 s.
Porter, ditto, 3 s.
Beer made at Sydney 5 s. 6 d.

India Goods.

Long cloth per yard from 3 s. to 6 s.
Callicoes, ditto, from 1 s. 6 d. to 2 s. 6 d.
Muslins, ditto, from 7 s. to 12 s.
Nankeen per piece 10 s.
Coarse printed callicoes, ditto, 1 l. 5 s.
Silk handkerchiefs, ditto, 12 s.

English Goods.

Black hats from 15 s. to 3 l.
Shoes per pair from 9 s. to 13 s.
Cotton Stockings from 6 s. to 12 s.
Writing paper per quire 6 s.

The beer mentioned in the preceding account as being made at Sydney was brewed from Indian corn, properly malted, and bittered with the leaves and stalks of the love-apple, (Lycopersicum, a species of Solanum,) or, as it was more commonly called in the settlement, the Cape gooseberry. Mr. Boston found this succeed so well, that he erected at some expence a building proper for the business, and was, when the ships sailed, engaged in brewing beer from the abovementioned materials, and in making soap.

At this time the following prices were demanded and paid for labour and work done at Sydney and the different settlements, viz.

	£.	s.	d.
A carpenter for a day's work, - -	0	5	0
A labourer for a day's work, - -	0	3	0
For clearing an acre of ground, - -	3	0	0
For breaking up an acre of ground, - -	1	0	0

3 S 2

For

	£.	s.	d.
For threshing a bushel of wheat, - -	0	1	6
For reaping an acre of wheat, - -	0	10	0
For felling an acre of timber, - -	0	17	0

The price of ground was from 12 s. to 1 l. an acre.

	£.	s.	d.
For making a pair of men's shoes, - -	0	3	6
For making a pair of women's shoes, -	0	3	0
For making a coat, - - -	0	6	0
For making a gown, - - -	0	5	0

For washing, three-pence for each article was paid; and the person who washed found soap, &c. If a woman was hired, she had one shilling and six-pence for the day, and her meals.

It must here be remarked, that the mechanic and the labourer were generally contented to be paid the above prices in such articles as they or their families stood in need of, the values of which had not as yet been regulated by any other authority, or guided by any other rule, than the will of the purchaser.

The want at this time of several public buildings in the settlement has already been mentioned. To this want must be added, as absolutely necessary to the well-being and comfort of the settlers and the prosperity of the colony in general, that of a public store, to be opened on a plan, though not exactly the same, yet as liberal as that of the Island of St. Helena, where the East-India Company issue to their own servants European and Indian goods, at ten per cent. advance on the prime cost. Considering our immense distance from England, a greater advance would be necessary; and the settlers and others would be well satisfied, and think it equally liberal, to pay fifty per cent. on the prime cost of all goods brought from England; for at present they pay never less than one hundred, and frequently one thousand per cent. on what they have occasion to purchase. It may be supposed that government would not choose to open an account, and be concerned in the retail of goods; but any individual would find it to his interest to do this, particularly if assisted by government in the freight; and the inhabitants would gladly prefer the manufactures of their own country to the sweepings of the Indian bazars.

The

The great want of men in the colony muſt be ſupplied as ſoon as a peace ſhall take place; but the want of reſpectable ſettlers may, perhaps, be longer felt; by theſe are meant men of property, with whom the gentlemen of the colony could aſſociate, and who ſhould be thoroughly experienced in the buſineſs of agriculture. Should ſuch men ever arrive, the adminiſtration of juſtice might aſſume a leſs military appearance, and the trial by jury, ever dear and moſt congenial to Engliſhmen, be ſeen in New South Wales.

That we had not a thorough knowledge of the coaſt from Van Dieman's Land as far as Botany Bay, though to be regretted, was not to be wondered at. As a ſurvey of the coaſt cannot very conveniently be made by any of the ſhips belonging to the ſettlement, it muſt be the buſineſs of government to provide proper veſſels and perſons for this ſervice; and it is to be hoped that we ſhall not be much longer without a knowledge of the various ports, harbours, and rivers, and of the ſoil and productions of the country to the ſouthward of the principal ſettlement.

The ACCOUNT of the ENGLISH COLONY of NEW SOUTH WALES muſt here be cloſed for a time, the writer being embarked in the Britannia on his return to England. On reviewing the pages he has written, the queſtion involuntarily ariſes in his mind, In what other colony under the Britiſh government has a narrator of its annals had ſuch circumſtances to record? No other colony was ever eſtabliſhed under ſuch circumſtances. He has, it is true, occaſionally had the gratification of recording the return of principle in ſome, whoſe want of that ingredient, ſo neceſſary to ſociety, had ſent them thither; but it has oftener been his taſk to ſhow the predilection for immorality, perſeverance in diſſipation, and inveterate propenſity to vice, which prevailed in many others. The difficulty under ſuch diſadvantages of eſtabliſhing the bleſſings of a regular and civil government muſt have occurred to every well-informed mind that has reflected on our ſituation. The duties of a governor, of a

judge-

judge-advocate, and of other magistrates and civil officers, could not be compared with those in other countries. From the disposition to crimes and the incorrigible characters of the major part of the colonists, an odium was, from the first, illiberally thrown upon the settlement; and the word " Botany Bay" became a term of reproach that was indiscriminately cast on every one who resided in New South Wales. But let the reproach light on those who have used it as such. These pages were written to demonstrate, that the bread of government has not been eaten in idleness by its different officers; and that if the honour of having deserved well of one's country be attainable by sacrificing good name, domestic comforts, and dearest connections in her service, the officers of this settlement have justly merited that distinction.

CONCLUSION:

COMPRISING

Particulars of the BRITANNIA's VOYAGE to ENGLAND; with Remarks on the STATE of NORFOLK ISLAND, and some Account of NEW ZEALAND.

THE Britannia sailed from Port Jackson, in company with his Majesty's ship Reliance and the Francis colonial schooner, on the 29th of September.

On the 4th of October, we had Ball Pyramid off Lord Howe's Island distant about five leagues, and were from that day until the 15th, owing to light and contrary winds, before we reached Norfolk Island; where we found his Majesty's ship Supply, which had been there several days. On the following morning we had communication with the shore.

The interval between the 16th and 23d was occupied in receiving on board the Britannia Lieutenant-governor King and his family, who were returning to England. On the 25th the colonial schooner, which had attended for that purpose, received Captain King's letters to Governor Hunter, and the three ships made sail from the island.

During the time we were there, the weather fortunately proved extremely favourable for communicating with the shore, and large quantities of stock and grain were received on board, in addition to what we brought from Port Jackson, and sufficient for a much longer passage than we had any reason to expect in the run to the Cape of Good Hope.

With

With the following Particulars of the State of NORFOLK ISLAND to the time when the ships left it, the Writer has been favoured by LIEUTENANT-GOVERNOR KING.

Court of Judicature.

A court of criminal judicature existed there similar to that in New South Wales, differing only in being composed of five instead of seven members. No civil court, however, had been established.

Number of Inhabitants.

The civil department consisted of a lieutenant-governor, a deputy judge-advocate, a deputy provost-marshal, and deputy commissary; a surgeon, a store-keeper, and four subordinate officers.

The military consisted of a company of the New South Wales corps.

The settlers were, four seamen who belonged to his Majesty's ship Sirius; fifteen marines who were discharged at the relief of that detachment; fifty-two settlers from among those whose respective terms of transportation had expired; three officers, and others who held ground by grant or lease, or had purchased allotments from settlers; fourteen from those whose terms of transportation were unexpired, but who held allotments exceeding five acres. The whole number (exclusive of the officers), with their families, was about two hundred and forty.

One hundred and forty-nine men, and sixty-three women, whose terms of sentence had expired, supported themselves by hiring ground from settlers, working for individuals, or at their different callings, (some few were employed as overseers,) and labouring for the public; for which they were clothed and fed from the stores, and received such other encouragement as their behaviour merited. The number of this class, with their women and children, was about one hundred and thirty.

Male

Male Convicts.

The numbers of these who remained under the sentence of the law were as follow:

For life - - - - -	36
From 10 to 5 years - - -	10
5 to 3 - - - -	4
3 to 1 - - - -	26
1 year to 6 months - -	60
Total -	**136**

of which number fifty-seven were assigned to settlers and others, on condition of being maintained by them; the rest were occupied as hereafter stated; from which it will be obvious, that no progress in cultivation for the crown could be made, as not more than thirty men were employed in cultivating ground for the public advantage, and even these were much interrupted by incidental work, and by attending the artificers in carrying on the different buildings which were indispensable.

State of Cultivation.

The island contains about eleven thousand acres of ground. In the level parts where the earth cannot be washed away by the heavy rains, the soil varies from a rich brown mould to a light red earth, without any intermixture of sand. These are again varied by some extensive pieces of light black mould and fine gravel, which are found to produce the best wheat. The rains which fall during the winter months wash the mould from the sides of the steep hills into the bottoms, leaving a grey marly substance, which will not admit of cultivation in that state. This, however, is the case only among the very steep hills that are cleared of timber, and have been four or five years in cultivation. Those of an easy ascent preserve their depth of soil, and many of them have borne six successive crops of wheat. From the quantity of soil thus washed away from the sides of the steep hills into the bottom, (some of which were only a water-way between the hills,) there

3 T were

were level fpots of ground covered to a great depth with the richeft mould. Of the eleven thoufand acres of ground in this ifland, there are not two hundred that might not be cultivated to the greateft advantage, if cleared of timber, and allowed a fufficiency of labourers, of cattle, and of ploughs.

Appropriation of the Land.

The ground cleared of timber for the public ufe, and that marked out for the fettlers lots, comprifed one half of the ifland, and was diftributed in the following manner:

	Number of Acres.	Acres cleared of Timber.
Ground allotted to fettlers on grant or leafe -	3,239	920
Ground allotted to officers by grant, leafe, or permiffion - - - -	132	132
Ground allotted to individuals of different defcriptions - - - -	100	100
Ground referved for government, and contiguous to the above allotments - -	1,400	——
Ground cleared of timber, and occupied for the public benefit - - -	376	376
Total quantity of ground occupied as above	5,247	1,528
Suppofed contents of the ifland, about	11,000	
Suppofed quantity of ground unoccupied, about	5,753	
Suppofed quantity of ground not cleared of timber - - - -	9,472	

Moft of the ground cleared of timber was under cultivation in 1793 and 1794, and produced above thirty-four thoufand bufhels of grain; but, from the fudden and effectual check given to private induftry during the year 1794, and the great proportion of the labourers working for their own fupport and other ways difpofed of, not more than a third of the government-ground, and a fifth of the ground belonging to individuals, was in any ftate of cultivation during the laft year. That portion of the ground thus neglected became over-run with rank and ftrong weeds, which formed a great cover to the numerous

merous rats; beside that the injury done to the soil by the growth of these weeds was very much to be deplored. The humane attention, however, shewn to the wants of the industrious individual by Governor Hunter, in directing the maize bills to be paid, it was hoped would not only relieve many deserving people, but also revive that industrious disposition which the settlers had in general manifested.

The small number of convicts at public work, and the labour necessary for preparing the ground to receive wheat, did not admit of more than one hundred acres of wheat, and eighteen of maize being sown last year for the crown; the produce of which had been abundant; but the quantity was much reduced by the weeds that grew with it, and from an attack by lightning when in blossom.

Cultivation was confined to maize, wheat, potatoes, and other garden-vegetables. The heat of the climate, occasional droughts, and blighting winds, rendered wheat an uncertain crop; nor could it be averaged at more than eighteen bushels an acre, though some had yielded twenty-five.

Owing to the quick and constant growth of rank weeds few individuals could sow more wheat than was necessary to mix with their maize, which hitherto had rarely exceeded five acres each family. Some few indeed among the settlers, who were remarkably industrious, or who had greater advantages than others, had generally from five to eleven acres in wheat; but the number of these was very small.

The harvests of maize were constant, certain, and plentiful; and two crops were generally procured in twelve months. The produce of one crop might be averaged at forty-five bushels per acre, and many had yielded from seventy to eighty.

By the statement before given it appears, that there were five thousand two hundred and forty-seven acres occupied; of which only one thousand five hundred and twenty-eight were cleared of timber: that there also remained five thousand seven hundred and fifty-three neither occupied nor cleared, making in the whole nine thousand four hundred and seventy-two acres not cleared of timber. If six thousand of the nine thousand four hundred and seventy-two acres not cleared could be put under cultivation in addition to the one thousand five

3 T 2   hundred

hundred and twenty-eight already cleared of timber, its produce at one crop only, and allowing no more than thirty bushels of maize to the acre, would be two hundred and twenty-five thousand eight hundred and forty bushels of grain; and even this might be doubled, if, as before said, there were labourers to procure a second crop.

The remaining three thousand four hundred and seventy-two acres might be reserved for fuel, building-timber, and other purposes.

From these data some calculation may be made of the number of people that the island might be made to maintain.

The following is a statement of the stock belonging to government and individuals on the 18th October 1796:

To whom belonging.	Cattle.		Horses.		Asses.		Sheep.	Goats.	Swine.	Poultry.
	Male.	Female.	Male.	Female.	Male.	Female.	Male and Female.	Male and Female.	Male and Female.	
Government - -	3	3	—	—	2	4	22	55	710	A very great abundance.
Individuals - -	—	—	1	2	—	—	148	328	4125	
Total -	3	3	1	2	2	4	170	383	4835	

Exclusive of the above stock, five hundred and ninety-two thousand four hundred and eighty pounds of swine's flesh and mutton had been expended on the island and exported from it; all which were produced from the following quantity received from November 1791 to October 1796.

	Cattle.		Horses.		Asses.		Sheep.		Goats.		Swine.	
	Male.	Female.	Male.	Female.	Male.	Female.	Male.	Female.	Male.	Female.	Male.	Female.
Total received -	1	2	1	1	1	3	2	21	2	11	4	157

When the settlers were informed that payment for the maize lodged in the stores in January 1794 could not be made until orders were received from England, and that no more grain could be received, but that the purchase of fresh pork would be continued, the course of their industry

industry became changed, though raising grain still continued necessary for rearing their stock.

On most part of the nine thousand four hundred and seventy-two acres not cleared of timber the trees and underwood were covered with succulent herbage, which, with the fern and other soft roots, afford the best food for swine. Several individuals had taken advantage of this convenience, by inclosing from ten to one hundred acres of the uncleared parts, into which they turned their swine, whereof many had from twenty to one hundred and fifty, that required nothing more than a sufficiency of maize to accustom them to their owner's call.

Another resource of animal food was on Phillip Island, which abounded with the best feed for swine. On it were at least three hundred and seventeen swine belonging to government, which were unconfined, and required no other attendance than the being called together occasionally by a man who resided there with his family. But those which were first sent, and their progeny, were so wild, that it was not thought an easy matter to take them. Several large hogs and boars had been brought from thence which had weighed, when fattened, from one hundred and eighty to three hundred and six pounds.

Salting pork in the cool months had been successfully tried; but it would not answer in the summer. It was intended that the swine belonging to government which could be killed during the winter should be salted down, as a sufficiency of salt was making to answer that purpose.

From these resources it might fairly be presumed, that if no unforeseen mortality should attack the stock, the settlers and other individuals would be able to continue supplying the stores with half the ration of animal food, and that government in the course of twelve months might furnish the other half. And farther, that if the industry of the settlers and other individuals were encouraged by their overplus grain and animal food being purchased at a fair price, the produce of the grounds cleared would be more than sufficient for the maintenance of the present inhabitants, three hundred and thirty-seven of whom supported themselves without any expence to the crown: and this might be further secured, if cattle and sheep could be sent there, as the

former

former were much wanted for labour, and the latter for a change of
food; for it is certain that sheep breed there as well as in any part of
the world, and have not as yet been subject to the distempers common
to that kind of stock. The Bengal ewes yean twice in the thirteen
months, and have commonly two, often three, and sometimes four
lambs at a yeaning; and these have increased so much, by being
crossed with the Cape ram, that a lamb six weeks old is now as large
as one of the old ewes.

The goats too are extremely prolific, and generally breed thrice in
the year, having commonly from two to four kids at a time.

Any number of sheep and goats, and a large quantity of cattle
might be bred here, as the cleared ground affords the best of pasture
for those species of stock. But it will be a long time before the present stock will be of much use, unless more are sent thither.

The want of artificers of all descriptions, and the scarcity of labourers at public work, much retarded the construction of a number
of necessary buildings. The island possessed the best of stone, lime,
and timber; but, unfortunately, there never had been but one mason
(a marine settler) on the island.

At Cascade Bay a great advantage had been obtained in the construction of a very strong wharf, one hundred and twenty-six feet
long, which connects the shore with the landing rock. At the end
of it is a swinging crane and capstern, by which boats are loaded and
unloaded with the heaviest articles; and in bad weather are hoisted up
with perfect safety.

Near this wharf, a large storehouse, and barracks for the guard, are
built. One of the great advantages attending this work is, that no
risk need be run by ships keeping in Sydney Bay, as the landing is
generally good at Cascade Bay, when it becomes in the least degree
hazardous at the former place. And here it may be noticed, that no
casualty by boats had happened since the lieutenant-governor's arrival
in 1791.

The utility of a well-constructed water-mill is sufficiently obvious.
From an addition of three feet to the height of the dam, it ground
twenty bushels of wheat daily; which had removed the great inconvenience of every man being obliged to grind his own ration before

it could be dreffed. The abundance of mill-ftones, and the quantity of wood fit for millwrights' work, with the convenient fituation of the different ftreams, will admit of any number of water-mills being erected.

Two well-finished wind-mills had alfo been erected by fettlers, which anfwered extremely well.

Not more than ten fettlers had been able to erect dwellings better than log-huts, which are neither warm nor durable. Better, indeed, could hardly be expected, when it was confidered how much their labour and attention muft have been employed in raifing food for their families, and in procuring fuch articles of accommodation as they needed. Many, however, of this as well as of other defcriptions were building comfortable framed and weather-boarded habitations at their own expence.

Of fchools there were two, viz. one for young children, who were inftructed by a woman of good character; and the other kept by a man, who taught reading, writing, and arithmetic, for which he was well qualified, and was very attentive. A third inftitution on a permanent footing was added, for the reception of fuch orphan female children as had loft or been deferted by their parents. Moft of thefe were of fuch an age as to require a ftrict hand and careful eye over them. Unfortunately they, as well as the other children, were deftitute of every article of clothing, except fuch as the ftore afforded, which was by no means calculated for children in that warm climate. By the application of fines impofed for breaches of the peace, &c. and a fub-fcription raifed among the officers, the orphan children had for fome time paft been clothed, and about twenty-eight pounds remained to be applied in the fame manner.

Hours of Labour.

To explain this article, it will be neceſſary to ſtate the different deſcriptions that compoſe the inhabitants; to do which in a perſpicuous form the following claſſification has been adopted:

Claſs.	Deſcription.	Number.	By whom ſupported.
1ſt,	Civil and military, - - -	83	government.
2d,	Settlers, by grant or leaſe, and freemen who are under-tenants to the ſettler, -	104	labour.
	Freemen who are hired by the year, &c. or who hire themſelves out daily, - -	138	ditto.
	Convicts who are taken off the ſtores by officers, &c.	5	ditto.
3d,	Ditto aſſigned to officers, &c. - -	67	government.
4th,	Ditto employed as overſeers, artificers, watchmen, &c. for the public benefit, many of whom are invalids,	106	ditto.
	Ditto cultivating ground for the public uſe, and other incidental work, - - -	30	ditto.
	Total males,	**533**	
5th,	Women belonging to civil and military, and at public labour, - - - -	40	ditto.
	Ditto, who belong to the ſecond claſs of men, -	155	labour.
6th,	Children belonging to the firſt and fourth claſſes,	116	government.
	Ditto to the ſecond and third claſſes, - -	73	labour.
	Total females and children,	**354**	

From the foregoing ſtatement it appears, that not more than one hundred and thirty-ſix men, compoſing the fourth claſs, are employed in carrying on public work, of which number only twenty-eight can be employed (when other works of public neceſſity do not intervene) in raiſing grain, &c. without expence to the crown, for the firſt, third, fourth, and a part of the fifth and ſixth claſſes; making together four hundred and forty-two perſons.

Thoſe of the fourth claſs who labour as carpenters, ſawyers, blackſmiths, &c. work from daylight till eight o'clock; from nine till noon; and from two in the afternoon till ſun-ſet; and as long as they
do

do their work properly, they have Fridays and Saturdays to themselves, which they employ in working at their grounds, or in building, &c. for settlers and others who can employ them. As those works are in fact of a private nature, although in the end they become more or less of public utility, the artificers are indulged with the use of government-tools and such materials as can be spared.

Those employed in cultivation, and other incidental labour, for the public benefit, work at all seasons from daylight until one o'clock, which is found much more advisable than dispersing them at the hours for meals, and collecting them again to resume their labour. As very few of this description have any persons to dress their meal, or grind their maize, they have by this management a great part of the day at their own disposal; and from the 21st of September to the 21st of February no public work is done on Saturdays. Those of this description who are industrious employ a great part of their leisure time in cultivating pieces of ground for their own use, or labouring for others.

The second and a part of the fifth and sixth classes, making together three hundred and thirty-one persons, support themselves by the produce of their labour without expence to the crown; as the clothing with which they and the settlers are occasionally furnished from the stores is paid for in grain or stock.

Ordinary Price of Labour.

To a convict taken off the stores by an officer or settler, from 5 l. to 6 l. per annum.

To a freeman hired by the year, victualled and clothed, from 10 l. to 12 l. per annum.

A day's work for a labourer, with victuals, is 3 s.; without, 5 s.

Cutting down and burning off an acre of wood, 2 l.

Ditto - ditto - an acre of weeds, 1 l. 10 s.

Threshing one bushel of wheat, 10 lbs.; equal to 1 s. 8 d.

Other works are in proportion. The mode of payment for labour is various, and depends entirely on the employer's circumstances; but it is in general made by what arises from the grain or fresh pork put

3 U   into

into the stores by settlers, &c.; sometimes (but very rarely) in cash; and often by equal labour, or by produce, which is rated as underneath.

And, in order to prevent disputes respecting the payment, these agreements, as well as all others, are entered in a book kept by a person for that purpose, and properly witnessed.

Average prices of provisions raised on the island, either for sale, for barter, or in payment for labour.

PLENTIFUL ARTICLES.

Fresh pork 6 d. per lb.
Pickled ditto 8 d.
Wheat from 7 s. 6 d. to 10 s. per bushel.
Maize from 1 s. 6 d. to 5 s.
Potatoes from 1 s. to 3 s. 6 d. per cwt.
Full-grown fowls from 6 d. to 1 s. each.
Ditto ducks 10 d. to 1 s. 3 d. each.
Ditto turkeys 7 s. 6 d. each.

SCARCE ARTICLES.

Geese 10 s. each.
Female goats 8 l. each.
Goats' flesh or mutton to government 9 d. per lb.
Ditto to individuals 1 s. 6 d. ditto.

N. B. When the latter is taken into the stores for the sick, it is issued as five pounds of mutton for seven pounds of salt beef stopped in the stores; by which method government does not pay more than six-pence per pound as for fresh pork.

Account of grain raised by those employed in cultivating ground for the public use; and that raised by officers, settlers, and others, on Norfolk Island, from the 6th of March 1788 (when it was first settled) to October 1796.

Year.	By whom raised.	Quantity of maize and wheat in bushels.	Bushels of maize and wheat purchased from individuals for the public use.
From March 1788 to May 1789, -	government,	46	
	individuals,	10	
May 1789 to May 1790, -	government,	450	
	individuals,	50	
The lieutenant-governor was absent this year.			
From May 1791 to May 1792, -	government,	1681	
	individuals,	391	40
May 1792 to May 1793, -	government,	4549	
	individuals,	6900	3610½
May 1793 to May 1794, -	government,	6000	
	individuals,	28,676	11,688
May 1794 to May 1795, -	government,	3300	
	individuals,	14,000	none.
May 1795 to May 1796, -	government,	1803	
	individuals,	11,500	389

Account of births and deaths from November 12th, 1791, to September 31st, 1796.

Births.				Deaths.				
Civil.	Military.	Convicts.	Total.	Civil.	Military.	Convicts.	Children.	Total.
10	3	178	191	1	4	94	38	137

From

From 1 month to 2 years 36 have died.			Teething,	-	-	23 have died.
2 years	to 18	2	Dysentery,	-	-	45
18	to 30	36	Cholera morbus 1, obstipation 1,	-	-	2
30	to 45	30	Fevers 7, consumptions 8,			15
45	to 65	31	Debility,	-	-	22
	Total	137	Lues venerea,	-	-	5
			Dropsy 3, putrid sore throat 1,			4
			Convulsions and epilepsy,			4
			Surfeit 1, scalded 1, abscess and canker 2,	-		5
			Eruptions, scald head, and mortifications,	-		3
			Iliac passion,	-	-	1
			Shot 1, casualties 2, executed 1, suicide 2,	-		6
			Ophthalmia,	-	-	2
					Total	137

State of the Flax Manufactory.

Not more than nine men and nine women can be employed in preparing and manufacturing the flax, which barely keeps them in practice. There is only one loom on the island, and the slay or reed is designed for coarse canvas; nor do they possess a single tool required by flax-dressers or weavers, beyond the poor substitutes which they are obliged to fabricate themselves. If there were introduced proper slays or reeds, brushes, and other articles indispensably necessary for flax-dressing and weaving, with more people to work the flax and a greater number of weavers, this island would soon require very little assistance in clothing the convicts; but, for the want of these necessary articles, the only cloth that can be made is a canvas something finer than No. 7, which is thought to be equally strong and durable as that made from European flax.

This useful plant needs no cultivation. An experiment has been made to cultivate it, and answered extremely well; but the produce

14

was

was not so much superior to that growing in a natural state as to make it advisable to bestow any pains on its culture.

Before the arrival of the two New Zealanders in May 1793, no effectual progress had been made in its manufacture; nor was it without much intreaty that our visitors were induced to furnish the information we required. And indeed, as this work is principally performed by the women in New Zealand, our friends were by no means competent to give us the fullest instructions. Sufficient, however, was obtained from them to improve upon. Since that time those women that could be spared from other work, not exceeding from six to twelve, had been employed in preparing the flax; and a flax-dresser, weaver, and three other assistants, in manufacturing it into canvas, rope, &c.

When the leaves are gathered, the hard stalk running through the centre is taken out with the thumb-nail; and the real edges of the leaf are also stripped off. The two parts are then separated in the middle, making four slips of about three-quarters of an inch wide, and the length of from eighteen inches to three or four feet. These slips are cut across the centre with a muscle-shell, but not so deep as to separate the fibres, which is the flax. The slips thus prepared are held in the left hand, with the thumb resting on the upper part of the slip just above the cut. The muscle-shell held in the right hand is placed on the upper part just below the cut, with the thumb resting on the upper part. The shell is drawn to the end of the slip, which separates the vegetable covering from the flaxen filaments. The slip is then trimmed, and the same operation is performed on the remaining part, which leaves the flax entire. If it be designed for fishing-lines, or other coarse work, nothing more is done to it; but if intended for cloth, it is twisted and beaten for a considerable time in a clear stream of water; and when dried, twisted into such threads as the work requires. It has been before observed, that the New Zealand instructors were not very conversant in the mode of preparing the flax; but on what was learnt from them it was our business to improve. Instead of working it as soon as gathered, our people found it work better for being placed in a heap in a close room for five days or a week, after which

which it became fofter and pleafanter to work. They alfo found it
eafier, and more expeditious, to fcrape the vegetable covering from
the fibres, which is done with three ftrokes of a knife. It is then
twifted, and put into a tub of water, where it remains until the day's
work is finifhed. The day following it is wafhed and beaten in a
running ftream. When fufficiently beaten it is dried, and needs no
other preparation, until it is hackled and fpun into yarn for weaving.

The numbers employed at this work were as follow :

Invalids gathering the flax	- -	3 men;
Preparing it - -	- -	7 women;
Beating and wafhing it	- -	3 who are invalids;
Flax-dreffer - -	- -	1
Spinners - -	- -	2 women;
Weaver and affiftant	- -	2 men;

Total   -   18;

by whofe weekly labour fixteen yards of canvas of the fize of
No. 7 was made. It is to be remarked, that the women, and moft of
the men, could be employed at no other work; and that the labour of
manuring and cultivating the ground; the lofs of other crops; the
many proceffes ufed in manufacturing the European hemp, and the
accidents to which it is liable during its growth, are all, by ufing this
flax, avoided, as it needs no cultivation, and grows in fufficient abundance on all the cliffs of the ifland (where nothing elfe will grow) to
give conftant employment to five hundred people. Indeed, fhould it
be thought an object, any quantity of canvas, rope, or linen, might be
made there, provided there were men and women, weavers, flax-
dreffers, fpinners, and rope-makers, with the neceffary tools; but
deftitute as our people were of thefe aids, all that could be done was
to keep in employ the few that could be fpared from other effential
work. If a machine could be conftructed to feparate the vegetable
covering from the flaxen filaments, any quantity of this ufeful article
might be prepared with great expedition.

The

The New Zealanders mentioned in the preceding account of the Flax Manufactory at Norfolk Island, remained, as has been already shewn, six months at that settlement. As they resided at the Lieutenant-governor's, and under his constant observation, some information respecting NEW ZEALAND, and its inhabitants, was procured, which was obligingly communicated by GOVERNOR KING, in substance as follows :

Hoo-doo Co-co-ty To-wa-ma-how-ey is about twenty-four years of age; five feet eight inches high; of an athletic make; his features like those of an European, and very interesting. He is of the district of Teer-a-witte, which, by the chart of Too-gee the other New Zealander, is a district of the same name, but does not lie so far to the southward as the part of Ea-hei-no-mawe, called Teer-a-witte by Captain Cook; for we are certain that Too-gee's residence is about the Bay of Islands; and they both agree that the distance between their dwellings is only two days journey by land, and one day by water [*]. That part called by Captain Cook Teer-a-witte is at a very considerable distance from the Bay of Islands.

Hoo-doo is nearly related to Po-vo-reek, who is the principal chief of Teer-a-witte. He had two wives and one child, about whose safety he seemed very apprehensive; and almost every evening at the close of the day, he, as well as Too-gee, lamented their separation in a sort of half-crying and half-singing, expressive of grief, and which was at times very affecting.

Too-gee Te-ter-re-nu-e Warri-pe-do is of the same age as Hoo-doo; but about three inches shorter; he is stout and well made, and like Hoo-doo of an olive complexion, with strong black hair. Both are tattowed on the hips. Too-gee's features are rather handsome and

[*] Since the return of the Fancy from New Zealand, it appears that Too-gee's residence is at Doubtless Bay, in which place the Fancy anchored, and Too-gee with his wife went on board; but he said that he would not return to Norfolk Island until Lieutenant-governor King came to fetch him. Two lads, at Too-gee's recommendation, were going thither; but as they became sea-sick were set on shore again. Hoo-doo's residence must be between the Bay of Islands and Doubtless Bay, according to the information given by Too-gee to the master of the Fancy.

interesting;

interefting; his nofe is aquiline, and he has good teeth. He is a native of the diftrict of Ho-do-doe, (which is in Doubtlefs Bay,) of
which diftrict Too-gee's father is the Etang-a-roñh, or chief prieft;
and to that office the fon fucceeds on his father's death. Befide his
father, who is a very old man, he has left a wife and child; about all
of whom he is very anxious and uneafy, as well as about the chief,
(Moo-de-wy,) whom he reprefents as a very worthy character. Too-gee
has a decided preference to Hoo-doo both in difpofition and manners;
although the latter is not wanting in a certain degree of good-nature,
but he can at times be very much of the favage. Hoo-doo, like a true
patriot, thinks there is no country, people, nor cuftoms, equal to his
own; on which account he is much lefs curious as to what he fees
about him than his companion Too-gee, who has the happy art of
infinuating himfelf into every perfon's efteem. Except at times, when
he is lamenting the abfence of his family and friends, he is cheerful,
often facetious, and very intelligent. And were it not for the different
difpofition of Hoo-doo, the moft favourable opinion might be formed
of the New Zealanders in general. It is not, however, meant to be faid,
that if Too-gee were not prefent, an indifferent opinion would have been
formed of Hoo-doo; on the contrary, the manners and difpofition of
the latter are far more pleafing than could have been expected to be
found in a native of that country.

At the time they were taken from New Zealand, Too-gee was on a
vifit to Hoo-doo; and the mode of their capture was thus related by
them [*]: The Dædalus appeared in fight of Hoo-doo's habitation in
the afternoon, and was feen the next morning, but at a great diftance
from the main land. Although the was near two iflands which are
inhabited, and which Too-gee in his chart calls Ko-mootu-Kowa, and
Opan-a-ké, curiofity, and the hopes of getting fome iron, induced Povoreek the chief, Too-gee, and Hoo-doo, with his brother, one of his
wives, and the prieft, to launch their canoes. They went firft to the
largeft of the two iflands, where they were joined by Tee-ah-wor-rack,
the chief of the ifland, by Komootookowa, who is Hoo-doo's father-
in-law, and by the fon of that chief who governs the fmaller ifland,

[*] This account has fince been corroberated by Lieutenant Hanfon.

called

called Opan-a-ké. They were some time about the ship before the canoe in which were Too-gee and Hoo-doo ventured alongside, when a number of iron tools and other articles were given into the canoe. The agent, Lieutenant Hanson, (of whose kindness they speak in the highest terms,) invited and pressed them to go on board, with which Too-gee and Hoo-doo were anxious to comply immediately, but were prevented by the persuasion of their countrymen. At length they went on board, and, according to their own expression, they were blinded by the curious things they saw. Lieutenant Hanson prevailed on them to go below, where they ate some meat. At this time the ship made sail. One of them saw the canoes astern; and when they perceived that the ship was leaving them, they both became frantic with grief, and broke the cabin windows with an intention of leaping overboard, but were prevented. While those in the canoes remained within hearing, they advised Povoreek to make the best of his way home, for fear that he also should be taken.

For some time after their arrival at Norfolk Island they were very sullen, and as anxiously avoided giving any information respecting the flax, as our people were desirous of obtaining it. The apprehension of being obliged to work at it was afterwards found to have been a principal reason for their not complying so readily as was expected. By kind treatment, however, and indulgence in their own inclinations, they soon began to be more sociable. They were then given to understand the situation and short distance of New Zealand from Norfolk Island, and were assured that as soon as they had taught our women "emou-ka ea-ra-ka-ke," (i. e.) to work the flax, they should be sent home again. On this promise they readily consented to give all the information they possessed, and which turned out to be very little. This operation was found to be among them the peculiar province of the women; and as Hoo-doo was a warrior, and Too-gee a priest, they gave the governor to understand that dressing of flax never made any part of their studies.

When they began to understand each other, Too-gee was not only very inquisitive respecting England, &c. (the situation of which, as well as that of New Zealand, Norfolk Island, and Port Jackson, he well knew how to find by means of a coloured general chart); but

3 X   was

was also very communicative respecting his own country. Perceiving he was not thoroughly understood, he delineated a sketch of New Zealand with chalk on the floor of a room set apart for that purpose. From a comparison which Governor King made with Captain Cook's plan of those islands, a sufficient similitude to the form of the northern island was discoverable to render this attempt an object of curiosity; and Too-gee was persuaded to describe his delineation on paper. This being done with a pencil, corrections and additions were occasionally made by him, in the course of different conversations; and the names of districts and other remarks were written from his information during the six months he remained there. According to Too-gee's chart and information, Ea-hei-no-maue, the place of his residence, and the northern island of New Zealand, is divided into eight districts governed by their respective chiefs, and others who are subordinate to them. The largest of those districts is T'Souduckey, the inhabitants of which are in a constant state of warfare with the other tribes, in which they are sometimes joined by the people of Moo-doo When-u-a, Tettua Whoo-doo, and Wangaroa; but these tribes are oftener united with those of Choke-han-ga, Teer-a-witte, and Ho-do-doc against T'Souduckey (the bounds of which district Governor King inclines to think is from about Captain Cook's Mount Egmont, to Cape Runaway). They are not, however, without long intervals of peace, at which times they visit, and carry on a traffic for flax and the green talc-stone, of which latter they make axes and ornaments. Too-gee obstinately denied that the whole of the New Zealanders were canibals*; it was not without much difficulty that he could be persuaded to enter on the subject, or to pay the least attention to it; and whenever an inquiry was made, he expressed the greatest horror at the idea. A few weeks after, he was brought to own, that all the inhabitants of Poo-nam-moo (i. e. the southern island) and those of T'Souduckey ate the enemies whom they took in battle, which Hoo-doo corroborated, for his father was killed and eaten by the T'Souduckey people. " Notwithstanding the general probity of

---

* During the Fancy's stay in the river Thames, they had many and almost daily proofs of Too-gee's want of veracity on this head.

                                                                    " our

" our visitors, particularly Too-gee, (says Captain King,) I am inclined
" to think that horrible banquet is general through both islands."

Too-gee described a large fresh-water river on the west side of
Ea-hei-no-maue; but he said it was a bar river, and not navigable
for larger vessels than the war canoes. The river, and the district
around it, is called Cho-ke-han-ga. The chief, whose name is
To-ko-ha, lives about half-way up on the north side of the river.
The country he stated to be covered with pine-trees of an immense
size. Captain King says, that he made Too-gee observe, that Captain
Cook did not in his voyage notice any river on the west side, although
he coasted along very near the shore. On this Too-gee asked with much
earnestness, if Captain Cook had seen an island covered with birds.
Gannet Island being pointed out, he immediately fixed on Albatross
Point as the situation of the river, which Captain Cook's account
seems to favour, who says, ' On the north side of this point (Albatross)
' the shore forms a bay, in which there appears to be anchorage and
' shelter for shipping.' Governor King on this subject remarks as follows : " The probable situation of this river (if there be one) being
" thus far ascertained, leads me to suppose, that the district of
" T'Souduckey extends from Cape Runaway on the east side, to Cape
" Egmont on the west, and is bounded by Cook's Strait on the south
" side, which is nearly one half of the northern island. Of the river
" Thames I could not obtain any satisfactory account ; but I have
" great reason to suppose, that the river he has marked in the district
" of Wonga-ro-ah is the Thames. Too-gee's residence appears to be
" on the north side of the Bay of Islands, in the district called by him
" Ho-do-do, which he says contains about a thousand fighting men,
" and is subject to the following chiefs ; i. e. Te-wy-te-wye, Wy-
" to-ah, Moo-de-wye, Wa-way, To-mo-co-mo-co, Pock-a-roo, and
" Tee-koo-ra, the latter of whom is the principal chief's son. The
" subordinate distinctions of persons at New Zealand are as follow :
" [We are told, that the inferior classes are perfectly subordinate to
" their superiors ; and such I suppose to be the case by the great de-
" ference always paid by Too-gee to Hoo-doo.]

" Etang-a-téda Eti-ket-ti-ca, a principal chief, or man in very great
" authority. His superior consequence is signified by a repetition
" of the word eti-ket-ti-ca. This title appears hereditary.

" Etanga-

" Etanga-roah, or E-ta-hon-ga, a prieſt, whoſe authority in many
" caſes is equal, and in ſome ſuperior to the etiketica.

" Etanga-teda Epo-di, a ſubordinate chief or gentleman.

" Ta-ha-ne Emo-ki, a labouring man.

Reſpecting the cuſtoms and manners of theſe people, the governor
favoured the writer with the following particulars:

" The New Zealanders inter their dead; they alſo believe that the
" third day after the interment the heart ſeparates itſelf from the corpſe;
" and that this ſeparation is announced by a gentle breeze of wind,
" which gives warning of its approach to an inferior Ea-tooa (or di-
" nity) that hovers over the grave, and who carries it to the clouds.
" In his chart Too-gee has marked an imaginary road which goes
" the lengthways of Ea-hei-no-maue, viz. from Cook's Strait to the
" North Cape, which Too-gee calls Terry-inga. While the ſoul is
" received by the good Ea-tooa, an evil ſpirit is alſo in readineſs to
" carry the impure part of the corpſe to the above road, along which
" it is carried to Terry-inga, whence it is precipitated into the ſea.

" Suicide is very common among the New Zealanders, and this
" they often commit by hanging themſelves on the ſlighteſt occaſions;
" thus a woman who has been beaten by her huſband will perhaps
" hang herſelf immediately. In this mode of putting an end to their
" exiſtence, both our viſitors ſeemed to be perfect adepts, having often
" threatened to hang themſelves, and ſometimes made very ſerious
" promiſes of putting it into execution if they were not ſent to their
" own country. As theſe threats, however, were uſed in their
" gloomy moments, they were ſoon laughed out of them.

" It could not be diſcovered that they have any other diviſion of
" time than the revolution of the moon, until the number amounted
" to one hundred, which they term " Ta-iee E-tow," i. e. one Etow
" or hundred moons; and it is thus they count their age, and calcu-
" late all other events.

" Hoo-doo and Too-gee both agreed that a great quantity of ma-
" nufactured flax might be obtained for trifles *, ſuch as axes, chiſſels,

* This circumſtance all the people belonging to the Fancy fully confirmed; for
during the three months that veſſel lay in the Thames, they replaced all their running-
rigging by ropes made of the flax-plant.

" &c.;

" &c. ; and faid, that in moft places the flax grows naturally in great
" quantities ; in other parts it is cultivated by feparating the roots,
" and planting them out, three in one hole, at the diftance of a foot
" from each other. They give a decided preference to the flax-plant
" that grows here, both for quantity and fize.

" It may be expected (fays Governor King) that after a fix
" months acquaintance between us and the two New Zealanders,
" we fhould not be ignorant of each other's language. Myfelf and
" fome of the officers (who were fo kind as to communicate the ob-
" fervations they obtained from our vifitors) could make our ideas
" known, and tolerably well underftood by them. They too, by
" intermixing what Englifh words they knew with what we knew of
" their language, could make themfelves fufficiently underftood by us.
" During the time they were with us I did not poffefs any account
" of Captain Cook's voyages ; but fince their departure, I find from
" his firft voyage, that it has great fimilitude to the general language
" fpoken in thofe feas. The vocabulary which I have appended to
" thefe memoranda was collected by myfelf and the furgeon, and is, I
" believe, very correct, particularly the numerals. Much other infor-
" mation was given us by our two friends ; but as it may be liable to
" great errors, I forbear repeating it."

It has been already faid *, that Governor King went himself to New
Zealand to return Hoo-doo and Too-gee to their country and friends.
The following are the governor's remarks on his voyage thither :

" Having rounded the north cape of New Zealand on the 12th of
" November 1793, the fourth day after leaving Norfolk, we faw a
" number of houfes and a fmall hippah on an ifland which lies off
" the north cape, and called by Too-gee, Moo-de Moo-too. Soon
" after we opened a very confiderable hippah or fortified place,
" fituated on a high round hill, juft within the cape, whence fix
" large canoes were feen coming toward the fhip. As foon as they
" came within hail, Too-gee was known by thofe in the canoes,
" which were foon increafed to feven, with upwards of twenty men
" in each. They came alongfide without any intreaty, and thofe

° Page 347.

" who

" who came on board were much rejoiced to meet with Too-gee,
" whose first and earnest inquiries were after his family and chief.
" On those heads he received the most satisfactory intelligence from
" a woman, who, as he informed us, was a near relation of his
" mother. His father and chief were still inconsolable for his loss;
" the latter (whom Too-gee always mentioned in the most respectful
" manner) had been about a fortnight past on a visit to the chief of
" the hippah above mentioned, where he remained four days; and
" Te-wy-te-wye, the principal chief of Too-gee's district, was daily
" expected. With this information he was much pleased. It was
" remarked, that although there were upward of a hundred New
" Zealanders on board and alongside, yet Too-gee confined his caresses
" and conversation to his mother's relation, and one or two chiefs,
" who were distinguished by the marks (a-mo-ko) on their faces, and
" by the respectful behaviour which was shewn them by the emokis
" (i. e. the working men) who paddled the canoes, and who at times
" were beaten most unmercifully by the chiefs. To those who by
" Too-gee's account were epodis (subaltern chiefs), and well known
" to him, I gave some chissels, hand-axes, and other articles equally
" acceptable. A traffic soon commenced. Pieces of old iron hoop
" were given in exchange for abundance of manufactured flax, cloth,
" patoo-patoos, spears, tale ornaments, paddles, fish-hooks, and lines.
" At seven in the evening they left us, and we made sail with a light
" breeze at west, intending to run for the Bay of Islands, (which we
" understood was Too-gee's residence,) and from which we were
" twenty-four leagues distant. At nine o'clock a canoe with four men
" came alongside, and jumped on board without any fear. The master
" of the Britannia being desirous to obtain their canoe, the bargain
" was soon concluded, (with Too-gee's assistance,) much to the satis-
" faction of the proprietors, who did not discover the least reluctance
" at sleeping on board, and being carried to a distance from their
" homes. Our new guests very satisfactorily corroborated all the cir-
" cumstances that Too-gee had heard before. After supper Too-gee
" and Hoo-doo asked the strangers for the news of their country since
" they had been taken away. This was complied with by the four
" strangers, who began a song, in which each of them took a part,

2   " sometimes

" fometimes ufing fierce and favage geftures, and at other times fink-
" ing their voices, according to the different paffages or events that
" they were relating. Hoo-doo, who was paying great attention to
" the fubject of their fong, fuddenly burft into tears, occafioned by an
" account which they were giving of the T'Souduckey tribe having
" made an irruption on Teer-a-witte, (Hoo-doo's diftrict,) and killed
" the chief's fon with thirty warriors. He was too much affected to
" hear more; but retired into a corner of the cabin, where he gave
" vent to his grief, which was only interrupted by his threats of
" revenge.

" Owing to calm weather, little progrefs was made during the
" night. At daylight on the 13th, a number of canoes were feen
" coming from the hippah; in the largeft of which was thirty-fix
" men and a chief, who was ftanding up making fignals with great
" earneftnefs. On his coming alongfide, Too-gee recognifed the chief
" to be Ko-to-ko-ke, who is the etiketica, or principal chief of the
" hippah whence the boats had-come the preceding evening. The
" old chief, who appeared to be about feventy years of age, had not
" a vifible feature, the whole of his face being tattowed with fpiral
" lines. At his coming on board he embraced Too-gee with great
" affection; Too-gee then introduced me to him; and after the
" ceremony of " ehong-i," (i. e. joining nofes,) he took off his
" ah-a-how, or mantle, and put it on my fhoulders. In return
" I gave him a mantle made of green baize, and decorated with
" broad arrows. Soon after feven, other canoes, with upwards of
" twenty men and women in each, came alongfide. At Too-gee's
" defire the poop was " eta-bon," i. e. all accefs to it by any others
" than the old chief forbidden. Not long before Ko-to-ko-ke came
" on board, I afked Too-gee and Hoo-doo if they would return to
" Norfolk Ifland or land at Moo-dee When-u-a in cafe the calm con-
" tinued, or the wind came from the fouthward, of which there was
" fome appearance. Too-gee was much averfe to either. His reafon
" for not returning to Norfolk was the natural wifh to fee his family
" and chief; nor did he like the idea of being landed at Moo-dee
" When-u-a, as, notwithftanding what he had heard refpecting the
" good underftanding there was between his diftrict and that of
                                                    " Moo-dee

" Moo-dee When-u-a, the information might turn out to be not strictly
" true. Nothing more was said about it ; and it was my intention to
" land them nearer to their homes, if it could be done in the course
" of the day, although it was then a perfect calm. Soon after the
" chief came on board they told me with tears of joy that they
" wished to go with Ko-to-ko-ke, who had fully confirmed all they
" had heard before, and had promised to take them the next morning
" to Too-gee's residence, where they would arrive by night. To
" wait the event of the calm, or the wind coming from the north-
" ward, might have detained the ship some days longer. Could I
" have reached in four days from leaving Norfolk the place where
" Too-gee lived, I certainly should have landed him there; but that
" not being the case, (as this was the fifth day,) I did not consider
" myself justifiable in detaining the ship longer than was absolutely
" necessary to land them in a place of safety, and from which they
" might get to their homes.

" Notwithstanding the information Too-gee had received, and the
" confidence he placed in the chief, I felt much anxiety about our
" two friends, and expressed to Too-gee my apprehensions that what
" he had heard might be an invention of Ko-to-ko-ke's and his people
" to get them and their effects into their power. I added, that as the
" ship could not be detained longer, I would rather take them back
" than leave them in the hands of suspicious people. To this Too-gee
" replied with an honest confidence, that " etiketica no eteka,"
" i. e. a chief never deceives. I then took the chief into the
" cabin, and explained to him, assisted by Too-gee, (who was present
" with Hoo-doo,) how much I was interested in their getting to
" Ho-do-do; and added, that in two or three moons I should return
" to Ho-do-do, and if I found Too-gee and Hoo-doo were safe ar-
" rived with their effects, I would then return to Moo-dee When-u-a,
" and make him some very considerable presents, in addition to those
" which I should now give him and his people for their trouble in
" conducting our two friends to their residence. I had so much
" reason to be convinced of the old man's sincerity, that I considered
" it injurious to threaten him with punishment for failing in his en-
" gagement. The only answer Ko-to-ko-ke made was, by putting
                                                                " both

" both his hands to the fides of my head (making me perform the
" fame ceremony,) and joining our nofes ; in which pofition we re-
" mained three minutes, the old chief muttering what I did not
" underftand. After this he went through the fame ceremony with
" our two friends, which ended with a dance, when the two latter
" joined nofes with me, and faid that Ko-to-ko-ke was now become
" their father, and would in perfon conduct them to Ho-do-doe *.
" While I was preparing what I meant to give them, Too-gee (who
" I am now convinced was a prieft) had made a circle of the New
" Zealanders round him, in the centre of which was the old chief,
" and recounted what he had feen during his abfence. At many
" paffages they gave a fhout of admiration. On his telling them, that
" it was only three days fail from Norfolk to Moo-doo When-u-a,
" whether his veracity was doubted, or that he was not contented
" with the affertion alone, I cannot tell, but with much prefence of
" mind he ran upon the poop, and brought a cabbage, which he in-
" formed them was cut five days ago in my garden. This convincing
" proof produc:d a general fhout of furprife.
" Every thing being now arranged, and ready for their departure,
" our two friends requefted that Ko-to-ko-ke might fee the foldiers
" exercife and fire. To this I could have no objection, as the requeft
" came from them ; but I took that opportunity of explaining to the
" chief, (with Too-gee's help,) that he might fee, by our treatment of
" him and his two countrymen, that it was our wifh and intention to
" be good neighbours and friends with all Ea-hei-no-mau-e; that thefe
" weapons were never ufed but when we were injured, which I hoped
" would never happen ; and that no other confideration than the
" fatisfying of his curiofity could induce me to fhew what thofe in-
" ftruments were intended for.
" About one hundred and fifty of the New Zealanders were feated
" on the larboard fide of the deck, and the detachment paraded on
" the oppofite fide. After going through the manual, and firing
" three vollies, two great guns were fired, one loaded with a fingle
" ball, and the other with grape-fhot, which furprifed them greatly,

* Which was very faithfully performed.

3 Y

" as

" as I made the chief obferve the diftance at which the fhot fell from
" the fhip. The wind had now the appearance of coming from the
" fouthward; and as that wind throws a great furf on the fhore, they
" were anxious to get away. Too-gee and Hoo-doo took an affec-
" tionate leave of every perfon on board, and made me remember my
" promife of vifiting them again, when they would return to Norfolk
" Ifland with their families. The venerable chief, after having taken
" great pains to pronounce my name, and made me well acquainted
" with his, got into his canoe and left us. On putting off from the
" fhip, they were faluted with three cheers, which they returned as
" well as they could, by Too-gee's directions. It was now feven in
" the morning of the 13th: at nine a breeze came from the north,
" with which we ftood to the eaftward. After a paffage of five days
" from New Zealand, (having had light winds,) and ten days abfence
" from Norfolk Ifland, I landed at three o'clock in the afternoon of
" the 18th.

" The little intercourfe that I had with the New Zealanders (as I
" was only eighteen hours off that ifland, twelve of which were in
" the night) does not enable me to fay much refpecting them, or to
" form any decifive opinion of them, as much of their friendly be-
" haviour in this flight interview might be owing to our connexion
" with Too-gee and Hoo-doo, and their being with us. Thefe two
" worthy favages (if the term may be allowed) will, I am confident,
" ever retain the moft grateful remembrance of the kindneffes they
" received on Norfolk Ifland; and if the greater part of their country-
" men have but a fmall portion of the amiable difpofition of Too-gee
" and Hoo-doo, they certainly are a people between whom and the
" Englifh colonifts a good underftanding may with common prudence
" and precaution be cultivated. I regret very much that the fervice
" on which the Britannia was ordered did not permit me to detain
" her longer; as in a few days, with the help of our two friends,
" much ufeful information might have been obtained refpecting the
" quantity of manufactured flax that might be procured, which I
" think would be of high importance if better known. The great
" quantity that was procured in exchange for fmall pieces of iron hoop

8   " is

" is a proof, that an abundance of this valuable article is manufac-
" tured among them.

" The articles that I gave Too-gee and Hoo-doo confifted of hand-
" axes; a fmall affortment of carpenters' tools, fix fpades, fome hoes,
" with a few knives, fciffors, and razors; two bufhels of maize, one
" of wheat, two of peafe, and a quantity of garden feeds; ten young
" fows, and two boars, which Too-gee and the chief faithfully pro-
" mifed fhould be preferved for breeding, a promife which I am in-
" clined to think they will ftrictly obferve *."

---

* The firft place the Fancy made at New Zealand was Doubtlefs Bay, which the
mafter defcribes as a very dangerous place for a veffel to go into, and ftill worfe to lie at,
as it is open to the eafterly winds. On their coming to an anchor, which was not till
late in the evening (in December 1795), feveral canoes came round the veffel, but did
not venture alongfide until Too-gee was inquired for, when the New Zealanders exclaimed " My-ty Governor King! My-ty Too-gee! My-ty Hoo-doo!" Some went on
board, and others put in to fhore, returning foon after with Too-gee and his wife. He
had not forgotten his Englifh, at leaft the more common expreffions. He informed Captain Dell, that he had one pig remaining alive, and fome peafe growing; but what became of the reft of his ftock he did not fay. As Doubtlefs Bay was found a bad place to
remain in, the Fancy endeavoured to get out, but was obliged to return, when the two
lads who wifhed to fee Norfolk Ifland, being fea-fick, left her.

A Short

A Short VOCABULARY of the NEW ZEALAND LANGUAGE.

New Zealand.	English.
E-ba-ha,	Fire.
E-when-ua,	Earth, or ground.
E-wy,	Water,
E-mu-da,	Flame of the fire.
E-dou-ma-te,	Summer.
E-ho-ho-tou-ké,	Winter.
E-ma-ran-gi,	North.
E-sow-how-oo-doo,	South.
E-ton-ga,	East.
E-te-hu,	West.
E-te-te-do,	To see.
E-don-go,	To hear.
E-do-mi-do-mi,	To feel.
E-hon-gi,	To smell.
E-mei-te,	To taste.
He-te-te-how, or Ye-te-de-how,	New moon.
E-po-po-e-e-nue,	Full moon.
E-de-de-ke,	{ Last quarter of the moon.
E-ma-ra-ma,	The moon.
E-da,	Sun.
E-pu-ta,	Sun-rise.
E-a-wa-tere,	Noon.
E-a-hi-au, or E-po,	Sun-set.
E-wha-tú,	Star.
Ye-rew-a-new-a,	Rainbow.
E-Ma-tan-gee,	Wind.
E-bu-a,	Rain.
E-ue-da,	Lightning.
E-wet-e-te-da,	Thunder.

New Zealand.	English.
Em-ma-ha-né,	Hot.
Ma-ka-ree-deé,	Cold.
E-ko-how,	Fog.
E-po-ka-ka,	Dew.
E-paw-ha,	Smoke.
E-mo-an-na,	{ Salt water, or the sea.
E-a-o,	The day.
E-po,	The night.
E-co-pee-ce.	To freeze, or ice.
E-wha-tu,	Snow.
In-an-hai,	Yesterday.
N'A-goo-nai,	To-day.
A-po-po,	To-morrow.
A-ta-by-da,	{ Day after to-morrow.
A-wa-ka,	Day following.
A-wa-ka-ett ue,	Four days hence.
E-hon-gi,	{ The ceremony of joining nose as a falute.
Yen-gang,	The head.
Hé-ho-do-ho-do,	{ The hair of the head.
Eta-din-ga,	The ear.
Etould-Eta-din-ga,	Deaf.
E-da-hú,	The Forehead.
Ca-no-wei, or F-ca-no-che,	The eye.
E-pu-di E'Ca-no-wei,	Blind.
Pa-pa-reen-gi,	The cheek.
	Fe-Eea-ho,

New Zealand.	English.
Ec-Eee-fhu,	The nose.
E-cou-wye,	The beard.
E-ka-ke,	The neck.
Po-co-fee-fee, or Edinga-ringa,	The arm.
E-dai-ee,	The breast.
He-ooo, lengthened out,	The nipple.
E-pee-too,	The navel.
Eu-wa,	The thigh.
E-tu-di-po-na, or E-wa-wye,	The leg.
E-mata-ka-ra,	The fingers.
E-coro-E-te,	Finger-nails.
He-l-a-dar-re,	The fkin.
Ing-oo-too,	The lips.
E-wa-ha,	The mouth.
In-ni-fhow,	The teeth.
Ecoro-coro,	The throat.
E-pa-ro,	The hand.
E-co-pu,	The belly.
E-to-to,	Blood.
E-tu-di-po-na,	Knees.
E-da-pa-ra-pa,	The feet.
E-too-o-ra,	The back.
E-cu-mo,	The backfide.
E-kau-wai,	The chin.
E-ki,	The mouth.
E-u-de,	The penis.
E-ai,	The vulva.
E-tek-ké,	To copulate.
E-ma-mi,	To go to make water.
E-tu-tai,	To go to ftool.
Pa-ke-da,	Bald-headed.
E-fha-pu,	Pregnant.
E-ko-ki,	A cripple.
E-ka-ta,	To laugh.
E-tan-gé,	To cry.
E-too-ha,	To fpit.
E-co-we-ra,	To breathe.
E-ma-my,	To groan.
E-fha, founded expreffive of the action,	To figh.

New Zealand.	English.
Te-zee-ou-wa, founded expreffive of	Sneezing *.
E-co-fhew,	To hiccough.
E-mo-a,	To fleep.
E-ta-ko-te,	To lie down to fleep.
E-a-ra,	To rife from fleep.
E-kow-hae-ra,	To yawn.
E-to-u,	To break wind.
E-ku-pa,	To belch.
E-du-a-ke,	To puke.
E-da-hee,	Fat.
Eet, pronounced as Eat,	Lean.
E-o-ra,	In health.
E-mat-tee, means alfo death	Sick.
E-pi,	Handfome, alfo clean.
E-ko-no,	Ugly, alfo dirty.
E-ni-a-ymi,	Pain in general.
In-ni-fhou, E-to-on-ga	Tooth-ach.
E-hu-de,	Head-ach.
E-de-ka-ra-ka,	An itching.
E-huf-fé,	Love.
He-de-de,	Hatred, or being diffatisfied.
He-ma-ta-kú,	Fear.
E-ka-tou,	Joy.
E-ko-ko-pe,	Shame.
E-kow-wa,	Loathing.
E-wa-ra-wa-ra,	An error or miftake.

* A compliment is paid (by the New Zealanders when one of the company fneezes, by repeating the following lines:

" Tee-zee, Tee-zee, Pa-woy, Pa-woy, wa- " cou-te-ma-hé co-to-ko-cee," drawn out very long.

" Tu-tu-ra a-té na tan-gu-ta kiti-ga,

" Tu-tu-ra ma-liié na-ta-na-ta kit-can

" Tee-zee, Tee-zee, &c." as in the firft line.

All which means wifhes for health from night to morning, and that no hours may be broken by the fhock of fneezing.

E-ko-cut,

New Zealand.	English.	New Zealand.	English.
E-ko-cut,	A cut.	E-moo-roo,	To clean.
E-mo-to,	A blow.	Eo-roo-ee,	To wash.
E-hou-dang-e,	To faint.	E-yhang-a,	{ To build a house or boat.
He-kye,	To eat.		
E-e-nue,	To drink.	E-ka-wa,	Ill-tasted, bitter.
E-matti-he-a-kye,	Hungry.	He-i-de-mal!	Come here!
Ka-ke,	Satisfied.	Sey-ede, or Ei-ra,	To go.
E-i-ra,	To walk.	E-ko-re-roo,	To converse.
E-o-niu,	To run.		
E-da-re,	To jump.	Pat-too pat-too,	{ To beat, also the name of a principal weapon.
E-ka-ou,	To swim.		
E-su-ti-ke,	To meet any one.	E-te-ka,	To tell a lie.
Ke-o-ro-mi,	To make haste.	E-po-no,	To tell truth.
E-no-ho,	To sit down.	E-wa-ka,	A canoe.
E-tu,	Standing up.	E-fhoo,	{ To paddle a canoe.
E-mo-ki,	To work.		
Ka-ko-p-i,	To shut a door.	E-i-ka,	A fish.
Eu-wa-ke,	To open.	E-a-ho,	To catch a fish.
E-de-ding-ee,	To sell.	E-wa-du,	{ A fish-hook made of wood.
E-o-mi,	To give or reach.		
Wha-ka-de-de,	I'll give you.	E-ma-ka,	A fishing-line.
Z'Shocke-e-mai,	Ditto.	E-nue,	Big, large.
E-wa-k-a-tu,	To plant.	E-mo-ro-ce-te,	Small.
E-o-boo-tee,	To pluck up.	My-ty,	Good.
E-da-fe,	To tie or bind.	Mack-row-a,	Bad.
E-wa-wai-te,	Untie.	Ki-e-dow,	Fit to eat.
E-ma-ca,	To throw away.	E-whan-na,	To kick.
E-te-te-do,	To look or observe.	E-ha-ka,	To dance.
E-ko-re,	{ To break any thing, as a plate.	E-wy-ette,	To sing.
		E-wa-du,	To dream.
E-whau-te,	{ To break any thing, as a stick.	E-ta po-ke,	To drown.
		E-ka-ya,	To steal.
E-hi-yi,	To tear, as paper.	E-ta-ro-na,	{ To hang one's self.
Car-co-rei,	{ To pull down or destroy, as a building, ship, &c.	E-ee-ta,	I understand.
		Na?	Do you mean this?
		Ha ya-ha,	What is this?
E-ko-cout,	To cut.	Ko-ai,	Who is this?
Iog-ha-roo,	To see or look for.	An-ga,	There.
E-hu-na,	To hide.	Pah-hee,	{ A ship, or very large canoe.
Ea-ke-tere,	To find.	E-whar-re,	A house.
E-ke-no,	{ To stain or dirty any thing.	E-ta-o,	A spear.
		E-da-kow,	{ A tree, or piece of wood.

E-ma-ra,

New Zealand.	English.	New Zealand.	English.
E-ma-ra,	A sharp stone with which they cut their hair.	E-po-to,	Short.
		E-wā-nui,	Wide.
		E-wa-eté,	Narrow.
Paf-aa-te-ra,	A stone.	E-tl-mā-hā,	Heavy.
E-ko-ha-tuo,	A rock.	E-mā-mā,	Light.
E-bo-ne,	Sand-beach.	E-de-ding-é,	Full.
E-a-wha,	A harbour.	E-ma-dia-gé,	Empty.
E-pa-pā,	A beard.	E-ma-row,	Hard.
E-to-ki,	An axe.	E-kī-rā-de,	A dog.
E-whow,	A chissel, nail, or iron.	E-kere,	A rat.
		E-mānu,	A bird.
E-va-te-to-ka,	A door.	E-wy-you,	Milk.
E-pu-ki,	A hill.	E-whairo,	Red.
E-pa-poo,	Shells.	E-ema,	White.
E-wak-e-te-ca,	Ear-rings.	E-man-goe,	All dark colours.
E-u-pu,	The flax plant when growing.	Kā-de-dā,	Green.
		Ka-nap-pa,	Blue.
E-mu-ka,	The flax when dressed.	Ta-āh-ne a founded long,	A man.
E-mu-ka Yera-ka-kee	The operation of drawing the flax from the plant.	Wha-hei-né,	A woman.
		E-co-ro-wa-ké,	An old man.
		E-du-a-hei-né,	An old woman.
		E-Ta-ma-ree-keé,	A young man.
Eka-ka-how,	Cloth wove from the flax.	E-Ta-mā-hei-né,	A young woman.
		Ta-ma-i-eté,	A male child.
		E-co-téro,	An infant.
A-mo-ko,	The marks on their face and different parts of their bodies.	Ma-tu-a-Tā-a-ne,	Father.
		Ma-tu-a-wa-hei-ne,	Mother.
		Tu-a-hei-né,	Sister.
To-ko-hai-ya?	How many?	Tu-a-Can-na Tei-né	Elder brother. Younger brother.
E-mā-hā,	A great many, speaking of things.	E-mi-yan-ga,	Twins.
		Pah-pah,	Children call their father.
Ka-tā-puk-e-mai,	A great many, speaking of people.	Hah-ty-yee,	Children call their mother.
Yen-gé-engé, and founded hard,	Tired.	E forem to be used as the article, pronounced as in the English.	
E-o-ho-ro-hā,	A whale.	A is always founded long, as in the French.	
E-he-nue,	Whale oil, or any other fat.		
E-mata-to-too-roo,	Thick.	Numerals.	
E-da-edó-hi,	Thin.	Ta-hie,	One.
E-do-āw,	High, or tall, and long.	Du-o,	Two.
		Too-roo,	Three.
		Whā,	Four.
			Dee-ma-h,

New Zealand.	English.	New Zealand.	English.
Dee-mah,	Five.	Ca-te-cow, Ca, F.-wha,	Ninety.
O-no,	Six.	Kah-row,	A hundred.
Whee-too,	Seven.	Carow, Ca, Ta-hie,	One hundred.
Wha-roo,	Eight.		
F.-whā,	Nine.	Carow, Ca, Du-o, and so on to	Two hundred. Nine hundred.
Ng-a-hu-du,	Ten.		
Ca-te-cow signifies One Ten.		Kom-ma-roo,	A thousand,
Ma-ta-hie,	Eleven.	Com-mā-no, Ca, Tahie,	One thousand.
Ma-duo,	Twelve, and so on, the numeral being preceded by Ma, until nineteen (Ma-Ew-ha) then Twenty is		
		Com-mā-no, Ca-du-o, and so on to	Two thousand, Nine thousand.
Ca-te-cow, Ca, du-o,	Twenty.	Cā-tee-nee,	Ten thousand, which appears to be the extent of their numerals.
Ca-te-cow, Ca, Too-roo,	Thirty.		
Ca-te-cow, Ca, Wha,	Forty,		
and so on to Ninety.			

[Thus far Lieutenant-governor King.]

From the 25th of October, the day on which the ships made sail from Norfolk Island, till the 31st of the same month, nothing material occurred. On that day Mr. Raven stated to Captain Waterhouse, the commander of the Reliance, the necessity there was for the Britannia's making the best of her way to England; and as he thought she sailed rather better than that ship, he requested permission to part company, which Captain Waterhouse not objecting to, we separated and made sail from them.

On the 5th of November we passed an island named by Lieutenant Watts (who first saw it in the Lady Penrhyn transport) Macauley Island.

Sunday the 6th was passed in examining an island, which Mr. Raven was decidedly of opinion had never been seen before. It was situated in the latitude of 29° 15′ S. and longitude of 181° 56′ E. We found the land high, and it appeared to be well covered with wood. On the south-west side of it is a bay in which, from the colour of the water,

water, Mr. Raven thought there was good anchorage; but at this time there was too much furf breaking on the beach to render it prudent to fend a boat in. The afpect on this fide of the ifland was romantic and inviting; but on the other fide the fhore was bold, and in many parts rugged and bare. The whole appeared to confift, like Norfolk Ifland, of hills and dales. We conjectured that there was frefh water in the bay on the fouth-weft fide. The knowledge of the exiftence of this ifland can be of no other importance, than to caufe navigators failing in that route to keep a good look-out, particularly in the night-time, as many ftraggling rocks lie off the north fide.

From the circumftance of its being feen on a Sunday it obtained the name of Sunday Ifland.

Leaving this, we proceeded toward Cape Horn; but it was not till the 16th of December that we faw the fouthern part of the vaft continent of America. Mr. Raven intended to have made the Jafons, and touched at Falkland's Iflands in the hope of procuring fome information refpecting the Cape of Good Hope; but, after paffing Cape Horn, and finding the wind hang to the northward, he altered his courfe for the Ifland of St. Helena, or the Cape of Good Hope, as circumftances might direct.

On the 21ft, in latitude 51° 56' S. and longitude 306° 25' E. to our great furprife, we fell in with and joined our companions the Reliance and Supply. We found that, by keeping nearer to the north end of New Zealand than we had done, they had met with more favourable winds. We now proceeded together toward the Cape of Good Hope.

On the 23d, being about the latitude of 50° S. we fell in with feveral iflands of ice; which, however, we cleared without any accident, and ftood more to the northward. Mr. Raven was of opinion, that ice would always be found in or about thofe latitudes, and recommended that all fhips, after paffing Cape Horn, fhould keep more to the northward than we did.

On the 9th of January we croffed the three hundred and fixtieth degree of eaft longitude. Our weather now was much too moderate; for it was not till the 15th of January that we faw the coaft of Africa. Some neceffary precautions were taken by the king's fhip on coming

3 z   in

in with it; and, finding every thing as we wished, on the next day we completed our long voyage of sixteen weeks from Port Jackson by anchoring safely in Table Bay.

Here, almost the whole of our ship's company having been pressed, or voluntarily entered into the king's service, and with difficulty getting some necessary repairs done to the ship, we were compelled most reluctantly to remain for eight weeks. The place was very unhealthy, and lodging and every article of comfort extravagantly high.

A few days before we sailed, the ship Ganges, commanded by Mr. Patrickson, arrived with convicts from Cork. She sailed from Ireland with another ship, the Britannia, having on board a similar cargo; but the master, intending to touch at Rio de Janeiro, had parted company with the Ganges off Palma. We learned by the Ganges, that two storeships, the Sylph and Prince of Wales, had sailed in June last for New South Wales. Much as Governor Hunter wanted labourers, the provisions would be more welcome to him than the Irish convicts, who had hitherto always created more trouble than any other.

Before we sailed we had the satisfaction of seeing seventy head of very fine young Cape cattle purchased by Mr. Palmer, the commissary for the colony, to be sent thither in the Reliance and Supply; the latter of which ships sailed with her proportion a few days before we left Table Bay. These ships would return well stored with useful articles for the settlement, and comforts for every officer in it.

We left the Cape on the 16th of March, and arrived at the pleasant island of St. Helena on the 26th of the same month. Here we remained till the 17th of April, having waited some time for a convoy, and sailed at last without any, in company with the ship Brothers, a South-Sea whaler, who was returning loaded.

During our stay at St. Helena we made several excursions into the interior part of the island. A visit from the French was daily expected; but we saw with pleasure preparations made for their reception that caused every one to treat the probability of their coming as an event more to be wished for than dreaded. From the hospitality of Governor Brooke and his family, and the pleasant society of this

6   place,

place, we felt a regret at leaving the island, which nothing but the prospect of soon reaching our own happy shores alleviated.

Every one now was anxious for the succesful termination of the passage before us. On the 27th of April we crossed the equator in the longitude of 19° 02′ W. On the 4th of May we spoke the ship Elizabeth, (an American,) Isaac Stone master. They had only been twenty-eight days from Dover, and gave us the first intelligence we received of the victory obtained by our fleet under Earl St. Vincent over that of the Spaniards.

On the 7th of June we spoke a schooner under American colours, the Federal George of Duxbury from Bourdeaux, bound to Boston. The master informed us, that the channel was full of the enemy's cruisers, who were looking out for our West-India fleet, then expected home. Though we felt persuaded that our cruisers would counteract their designs, Mr. Raven determined, from this information, and from the wind having long hung to the eastward, to stand to the northward. From this time to the 18th our weather was very unfavourable, and our wind mostly contrary. On the 18th we saw the rock laid down in the charts by the name of Isle Rokal, being then in the latitude of 57° 51′ N. and longitude 13° 56′ W. The rock then bore N. 23° E. distant eight miles and a half. Our foul wind continued many days; but on the 23d we found ourselves off Innishone on the north part of Ireland. Here a man came off, who, to our inquiries respecting the progress of the war, answered, that he knew nothing about war, except that the strongest party always got the better of the weakest, thus uttering a truth in the midst of the profoundest ignorance. We now determined to steer for Liverpool, at which port, after much anxiety, we arrived in safety on the 27th.

On the 29th the judge-advocate delivered at the Duke of Portland's office the dispatches with which he was charged.

He now learned, that previous to his arrival in London there had sailed for New South Wales, exclusive of the ships Sylph and Prince of Wales, Ganges and Britannia, the Lady Shore transport, having on board two male and sixty-six female convicts. On the 6th of last November the Barwell sailed, having on board Mr. Dore, the present judge-advocate of that territory, and two hundred and ninety-eight

male

male convicts. The Britannia, a ship belonging to the house of Enderby and Co. sailed on the 17th of last February with ninety-six female convicts on board. This ship went out with orders to try the whale-fishery on the coast of New South Wales for one season. If this should succeed, the settlement and the public at large will owe much to the spirited exertions of the house of Enderby to promote a beneficial commerce from that country.

The king's ships on that station being ill calculated for the services expected from them, having on board expensive complements of men and officers, and consequently but little room for cattle; and being beside so defective and impaired by time as to be unsafe to navigate much longer; two others have been provided, newer and more capable of rendering service to the colony. One of them, the Buffalo, commanded by Mr. William Raven, late master of the Britannia, is on the point of sailing, and is to take cattle to New South Wales from the Cape of Good Hope. The other is named the Porpoise, and has the same service to perform. A ship, called the Minerva, is also proceeding to Cork to take in a number of Irish convicts.

Letters have been received from New South Wales, dated about six weeks after the author sailed from that colony. Governor Hunter had received by the Sylph and Prince of Wales storeships two thousand six hundred and fifty casks of salted provisions. Several persons had been tried by the court of criminal judicature for robbing the public stores, and had been found guilty. One man had been executed for murder, and his body hung in chains on Rock Island, a small spot at the mouth of Sydney Cove, and by which every boat and ship coming into the cove must necessarily pass. The governor was on the point of visiting Portland Head, some high land on the banks of the Hawkesbury, where he purposed establishing a settlement.

Had that river and its fertile banks been discovered before the establishment at Sydney Cove had proceeded too far to remove it, how eligible a place would it have been for the principal settlement! A navigable river possesses many advantages that are unknown in other
situations.

fituations. Much benefit, however, was to be derived from this even as an inferior fettlement. Its extreme fertility would always infure a certain fupply of grain; and the fettlers on its banks muſt produce a quantity equal to the confumption of the civil and military, and of their own families; and thus, while rendering a fervice to the ſtate, they might in time become opulent farmers. Yet our pity is excited, when it is confidered, that they are of fo unworthy a defcription as has clearly been made appear in the preceding narrative. That a river juſtly termed the Nile of New South Wales ſhould fall into fuch hands is to be lamented. In procefs of time, however, their productive farms will have yielded them all that they afpire to, and may then fall into the poffeffion of perfons who will look beyond the mere gratification of the moment, and caufe the fettlements in New South Wales to ſtand as high in the public eſtimation as any colonies in his Majeſty's dominions.

SAUNDERSON'S FARM.

looking down the River

Publiſhed May 20ᵗʰ 1798 by Cadell & Davies Strand

A P P E N D I X.

GENERAL REMARKS.

THE reader of the preceding narrative will have feen, that after many untoward occurrences, and a confiderable lapfe of time, that friendly intercourfe with the natives which had been fo earneftly defired was at length eftablifhed; and having never been materially interrupted, thefe remote iflanders have been fhewn living in confiderable numbers among us without fear or reftraint; acquiring our language; readily falling in with our manners and cuftoms; enjoying the comforts of our clothing, and relifhing the variety of our food. We faw them die in our houfes, and the places of the deceafed inftantly filled by others, who obferved nothing in the fate of their predeceffors to deter them from living with us, and placing that entire confidence in us which it was our intereft and our pleafure to cultivate. They have been always allowed fo far to be their own mafters, that we never, or but rarely, interrupted them in any of their defigns, judging that by fuffering them to live with us as they were accuftomed to do before we came among them, we fhould fooner attain a knowledge of their manners and cuftoms, than by waiting till we had acquired a competent fkill in their language to converfe with them. On this principle, when they affembled to dance or to fight before our houfes, we never difperfed, but freely attended their meetings. To them this attention of ours appeared to be agreeable and ufeful; for thofe who happened to be wounded in their contefts inftantly looked out for one of our furgeons, and difplayed entire confidence in his fkill, and great bravery in the firmnefs with which they bore the knife and the probe.

By

By flow degrees we began mutually to be pleafed with, and to underftand each other. Language, indeed, is out of the queftion; for at the time of writing this, (September 1796,) nothing but a barbarous mixture of Englifh with the Port Jackfon dialect is fpoken by either party; and it muft be added, that even in this the natives have the advantage, comprehending, with much greater aptnefs than we can pretend to, every thing they hear us fay. From a pretty clofe obferv-ation, however, affifted by the ufe of the barbarous dialect juft men-tioned, the following particulars refpecting the natives of New South Wales have been collected.

No. I.

GOVERNMENT AND RELIGION.

Government.

WE found the natives about Botany Bay, Port Jackfon, and Broken Bay, living in that ftate of nature which muft have been common to all men previous to their uniting in fociety, and acknowledging but one authority. Thefe people are diftributed into families, the head or fenior of which exacts compliance from the reft. In our early inter-courfe with them (and indeed at a much later period, on our meeting with families to whom we were unknown) we were always accofted by the perfon who appeared to be the eldeft of the party, while the women, youths, and children, were kept at a diftance. The word which in their language fignifies father was applied to their old men; and when, after fome time, and by clofe obfervation, they perceived the authority with which Governor Phillip commanded, and the obe-dience which he exacted, they beftowed on him the diftinguifhing appellation of (Be-anna) or Father. This title being conferred folely on him (although they perceived the authority of mafters over their fervants) places the true fenfe of the word beyond a doubt, and proves, that

that to those among them who enjoyed that diflinction belonged the authority of a chief.

When any of these came into the town, we have been immediately informed of their arrival, and they have been pointed out to our notice in a whifper, and with an eagernefs of manner which, while it drew our attention, imprefled us with an idea that we were looking at perfons to whom fome confequence was attached even among the favages of New Holland. Another acceptation of the word Be-anna, however, foon became evident; for we obferved it to be frequently applied by children to men who we knew had not any children of their own. On inquiry we were informed, that in cafe a father fhould die, the neareft of kin, or fome deputed friend, would take the care of his children; and for this reafon thofe children ftyled them Be-anna, though in the lifetime of their natural parent. This Ben-nil-long (the native who was fome time in England) confirmed to us at the death of his firft wife, by configning the care of his infant daughter Dil-boong (who at the time of her mother's deceafe was at the breaft) to his friend Governor Phillip, telling him that he was to become the Be-anna or Father of his little girl. Here, if the reader paufes for a moment to confider the difference between the general conduct of our baptifmal fponfors (to whofe duties this cuftom bears much refemblance) and the humane practice of thefe uncivilifed people, will not the comparifon fuffufe his cheek with fomething like fhame, at feeing the enlightened Chriftian fo diftanced in the race of humanity by the untutored favage, who has hitherto been the object of his pity and contempt? But forry am I to recollect, and as a faithful narrator to be impelled to relate, one particular in their cuftoms that is wholly irreconcilable with the humane duties which they have prefcribed to themfelves in the above Inftance; duties which relate only to thofe children who, in the event of lofing the mother, could live without her immediate aid. · A far different lot is referved for fuch as are at that time at the breaft, or in a ftate of abfolute helpleffnefs, as will be feen hereafter.

We have mentioned their being divided into families. Each family has a particular place of refidence, from which is derived its diftinguifhing name. This is formed by adding the monofyllable Gal to the name of the place: thus the fouthern fhore of Botany Bay is called

4 A   Gwea,

Gwea, and the people who inhabit it stile themselves Gweagal. Those who live on the north shore of Port Jackson are called Cam-mer-ray-gal, that part of the harbour being distinguished from others by the name of Cam-mer-ray. Of this last family or tribe we have heard Ben-nil-long and other natives speak (before we knew them ourselves) as of a very powerful people, who could oblige them to attend where-ever and whenever they directed. We afterwards found them to be by far the most numerous tribe of any within our knowledge. It so happened, that they were also the most robust and muscular, and that among them were several of the people styled Car-rah-dy and Car-rah-di-gang, of which extraordinary personages we shall have to speak particularly, under the article *Superstition*.

To the tribe of Cam-mer-ray also belonged the exclusive and extra-ordinary privilege of exacting a tooth from the natives of other tribes inhabiting the sea-coast, or of all such as were within their authority. The exercise of this privilege places these people in a particular point of view; and there is no doubt of their decided superiority over all the tribes with whom we were acquainted. Many contests or decisions of honour (for such there are among them) have been delayed until the arrival of these people; and when they came, it was impossible not to observe the superiority and influence which their numbers and their muscular appearance gave them over the other tribes.

These are all the traces that could ever be discovered among them of government or subordination; and we may imagine the deference which is paid to the tribe of Cam-mer-ray to be derived wholly from their superiority of numbers; but this superiority they may have maintained for a length of time before we knew them; and indeed the privilege of demanding a tooth from the young men of other families must have been of long standing, and coëval with the obedience which was paid to them: hence their superiority partakes something of the nature of a constituted authority; an authority which has the sanction of custom to plead for its continuance.

Religion.

Religion.

IT has been asserted by an eminent divine *, that no country has yet been discovered where some trace of religion was not to be found. From every observation and inquiry I could make among these people, from the first to the last of my acquaintance with them, I can safely pronounce them an exception to this opinion. I am certain that they do not worship either sun, moon, or star; that, however necessary fire may be to them, it is not an object of adoration; neither have they respect for any particular beast, bird, or fish. I never could discover any object, either substantial or imaginary, that impelled them to the commission of good actions, or deterred them from the perpetration of what we deem crimes. There indeed existed among them some idea of a future state, but not connected in anywise with religion; for it had no influence whatever on their lives and actions. On their being often questioned as to what became of them after their decease, some answered that they went either on or beyond the great water; but by far the greater number signified, that they went to the clouds. Conversing with Ben-nil-long after his return from England, where he had obtained much knowledge of our customs and manners, I wished to learn what were his ideas of the place from which his countrymen came, and led him to the subject by observing, that all the white men here came from England. I then asked him where the black men (or Eora) came from? He hesitated.—Did they come from any island? His answer was, that he knew of none: they came from the clouds (alluding perhaps to the aborigines of the country); and when they died, they returned to the clouds (Boo-row-e). He wished to make me understand that they ascended in the shape of little children, first hovering in the tops and in the branches of trees; and mentioned something about their eating, in that state, their favourite food, little fishes.

If this idea of the immortality of the soul should excite a smile, is is more extraordinary than the belief which obtains among some of us,

* Blair's Sermons, vol. i. Sermon 5.

4 A 2   that

that at the last day the various disjointed bones of men shall find out each its proper owner, and be re-united?—The savage here treads close upon the footsteps of the Christian.

The natives who inhabit the harbour to the northward, called by us Port Stephens, believed that five white men who were cast away among them (as has been before shewn) had formerly been their countrymen, and took one of them to the grave where, he told him, the body he at that time occupied had been interred. If this account, given us by men who may well be supposed to deal in the marvellous, can be depended upon, how much more ignorant are the natives of Port Stephens, who live only thirty leagues to the northward of us, than the natives of and about Port Jackson!

The young people who resided in our houses were very desirous of going to church on Sundays, but knew not for what purpose we attended. I have often seen them take a book, and with much success imitate the clergyman in his manner, (for better and readier mimics can no where be found,) laughing and enjoying the applause which they received.

I remember to have seen in a news-paper or pamphlet an account of a native throwing himself in the way of a man who was about to shoot a crow; and the person who wrote the account drew an inference, that the bird was an object of worship: but I can with confidence affirm, that so far from dreading to see a crow killed, they are very fond of eating it, and take the following particular method to ensnare that bird: a native will stretch himself on a rock as if asleep in the sun, holding a piece of fish in his open hand; the bird, be it hawk or crow, seeing the prey, and not observing any motion in the native, pounces on the fish, and, in the instant of seizing it, is caught by the native, who soon throws him on the fire and makes a meal of him.

That they have ideas of a distinction between *good* and *bad* is evident from their having terms in their language significant of these qualities. Thus, the sting-ray was (wee-re) bad; it was a fish of which they never ate. The pat-ta-go-rang or kangooroo was (bood-yer-re) good, and they ate it whenever they were fortunate enough to kill one of these animals.

To

To exalt thefe people at all above the brute creation, it is neceffary to fhew that they had the gift of reafon, and that they knew the diftinction between *right* and *wrong*, as well as between what food was good and what was bad. Of thefe latter qualities their fenfes informed them; but the knowledge of right and wrong could only proceed from reafon. It is true, they had no diftinction in terms for thefe qualities—wee-re and bood-yer-re alike implying what was good and bad, and right and wrong. Inftances however were not wanting of their ufing them to defcribe the fenfations of the mind as well as of the fenfes; thus their enemies were wee-re; their friends bood-yer-re. On our fpeaking of cannibalifm, they expreffed great horror at the mention, and faid it was wee-re. On feeing any of our people punifhed or reproved for ill-treating them, they expreffed their approbation, and faid it was bood-yer-re, it was right. Midnight murders, though frequently practifed among them whenever paffion or revenge were uppermoft, they reprobated; but applauded acts of kindnefs and generofity, for of both thefe they were capable. A man who would not ftand to have a fpear thrown at him, but ran away, was a coward, jee-run, and wee-re. But their knowledge of the difference between right and wrong certainly never extended beyond their exiftence in this world; not leading them to believe that the practice of either had any relation to their future ftate; this was manifeft from their idea of quitting this world, or rather of entering the next, in the form of little children, under which form they would re-appear in this.

No. II.

STATURE AND APPEARANCE.

WE obferved but few men or women among them who could be faid to be tall, and ftill fewer who were well made. I once faw a dwarf, a female, who, when fhe ftood upright, meafured about four feet two inches. None of her limbs were difproportioned, nor were the features

of

of her face unpleasant; she had a child at her back, and we were told came from the south shore of Botany Bay. I thought the other natives seemed to make her an object of their merriment. In general, indeed almost universally, the limbs of these people were small; of most of them the arms, legs, and thighs were thin. This, no doubt, is owing to the poorness of their living, which is chiefly on fish; otherwise the fineness of the climate, co-operating with the exercise which they take, might have rendered them more muscular. Those who live on the sea-coast depend entirely on fish for their sustenance; while the few who dwell in the woods subsist on such animals as they can catch. The very great labour necessary for taking these animals, and the scantiness of the supply, keep the wood natives in as poor a condition as their brethren on the coast. It has been remarked, that the natives who have been met with in the woods had longer arms and legs than those who lived about us. This might proceed from their being compelled to climb the trees after honey and the small animals which resort to them, such as the flying squirrel and opossum, which they effect by cutting with their stone hatchets notches in the bark of the tree of a sufficient depth and size to receive the ball of the great toe. The first notch being cut, the toe is placed in it; and while the left arm embraces the tree, a second is cut at a convenient distance to receive the other foot. By this method they ascend very quick, always cutting with the right hand and clinging with the left, resting the whole weight of the body on the ball of either foot.

In an excursion to the westward with a party, we passed a tree (of the kind named by us the white gum, the bark of which is soft) that we judged to be about one hundred and thirty feet in height, and which had been notched by the natives at least eighty feet, before they attained the first branch where it was likely they could meet with any reward for so much toil.

The features of many of these people were far from unpleasing, particularly of the women: in general, the black bushy beards of the men, and the bone or reed which they thrust through the cartilage of the nose, tended to give them a disgusting appearance; but in the women, that feminine delicacy which is to be found among white people

7

ple was to be traced even upon their fable cheeks; and though entire
ftrangers to the comforts and conveniencies of clothing, yet they
fought with a native modefty to conceal by attitude what the want of
covering would otherwife have revealed. They have often brought
to my recollection,

" The bending ftatue which enchants the world,"

though it muft be owned that the refemblance confifted folely in the
pofition.

Both women and men ufe the difgufting practice of rubbing fifh-oil
into their fkins; but they are compelled to this as a guard againft the
effects of the air and of mufquitoes, and flies; fome of which are
large, and bite or fting with much feverity. But the oil, together
with the perfpiration from their bodies, produces, in hot weather, a
moft horrible ftench. I have feen fome with the entrails of fifh frying
in the burning fun upon their heads, until the oil ran down over their
foreheads. A remarkable inftance once came under my obfervation of
the early ufe which they make of this curious unguent. Happening to
be at Camp Cove at a time when thefe people were much preffed with
hunger, we found in a miferable hut a poor wretched half-ftarved native and two children. The man was nearly reduced to a fkeleton,
but the children were in better condition. We gave them fome falted
beef and pork, and fome bread, but this they would not touch. The
eldeft of the children was a female; and a piece of fat meat being
given to her, fhe, inftead of eating it inftantly as we expected, fqueezed
it between her fingers until fhe had nearly preffed all the fat to a liquid;
with this fhe oiled over her face two or three times, and then gave it to
the other, a boy about two years of age, to do the like. Our wonder
was naturally excited at feeing fuch knowledge in children fo young.
To their hair, by means of the yellow gum, they faften the front teeth
of the kangooroo, and the jaw-bones of large fifh, human teeth, pieces
of wood, feathers of birds, the tail of the dog, and certain bones taken
out of the head of a fifh, not unlike human teeth. The natives who
inhabit the fouth fhore of Botany Bay divide the hair into fmall par-
cels, each of which they mat together with gum, and form them
into

into lengths like the thrums of a mop. On particular occasions they ornament themselves with red and white clay, using the former when preparing to fight, the latter for the more peaceful amusement of dancing. The fashion of these ornaments was left to each person's taste; and some, when decorated in their best manner, looked perfectly horrible. Nothing could appear more terrible than a black and dismal face, with a large white circle drawn round each eye. In general waved lines were marked down each arm, thigh, and leg; and in some the cheeks were daubed; and lines drawn over each rib, presented to the beholder a truly spectre-like figure. Previous either to a dance or a combat, we always found them busily employed in this necessary preliminary; and it must be observed, that when other liquid could not be readily procured, they moistened the clay with their own saliva. Both sexes are ornamented with scars upon the breast, arms, and back, which are cut with broken pieces of the shell they use at the end of the throwing stick. By keeping open these incisions, the flesh grows up between the sides of the wound, and after a time, skinning over, forms a large wale or seam. I have seen instances where these scars have been cut to resemble the feet of animals; and such boys as underwent the operation while they lived with us, appeared to be proud of the ornament, and to despise the pain which they must have endured. The operation is performed when they are young, and until they advance in years the scars look large and full; but on some of their old men I have been scarcely able to discern them. As a principal ornament, the men, on particular occasions, thrust a bone or reed through the *septum nasi*, the hole through which is bored when they are young. Some boys who went away from us for a few days, returned dignified with this strange ornament, having, in the mean time, had the operation performed upon them; they appeared to be from twelve to fifteen years of age. The bone that they wear is the small bone in the leg of the kangooroo, one end of which is sharpened to a point. I have seen several women who had their noses perforated in this extraordinary manner.

The women are, besides, early subjected to an uncommon mutilation of the two first joints of the little finger of the left hand. The operation is performed when they are very young, and is done

with

with a hair, or some other slight ligature. This being tied round at the joint, the flesh soon swells, and in a few days, the circulation being destroyed, the finger mortifies and drops off. I never saw but one instance where the finger was taken off from the right hand, and that was occasioned by the mistake of the mother. Before we knew them, we took it to be their marriage ceremony; but on seeing their mutilated children we were convinced of our mistake; and at last learned, that these joints of the little finger were supposed to be in the way when they wound their fishing lines over the hand. On our expressing a disgust of the appearance, they always applauded it, and said it was very good. They name it Mal-gun; and among the many women whom I saw, but very few had this finger perfect. On my pointing these out to those who were so distinguished, they appeared to look at and speak of them with some degree of contempt.

The men too were not without their mutilation. Most of those who lived on the sea-coast we found to want the right front tooth; some, whom we met in the interior part of the country, had not been subjected to the authority of the tribe of Cam-mer-ray-gal; but a particular account of the ceremonies used on this occasion will be given under the article *Customs and Manners.*

I noticed but few deformities of person among them; once or twice I have seen on the sand the print of inverted feet. Round shoulders or hump-backed people I never saw. Some who were lame, and assisted themselves with sticks, have been met with; but their lameness might proceed from spear wounds, or by accident from fire; for never were women so inattentive to their young as these. We often heard of children being injured by fire, while the mother lay fast asleep beside them, these people being extremely difficult to awaken when once asleep. A very fine little girl, belonging to a man well known and much beloved among us, of the name of Cole-be, had two of its toes burnt off, and the sinews of the leg contracted in one night, by rolling into a fire out of its mother's arms, while they both lay asleep.

Their sight is peculiarly fine, indeed their existence very often depends upon the accuracy of it; for a short-sighted man (a misfortune unknown to them, and not yet introduced by fashion, nor relieved by the use of a glass) would never be able to defend himself from their

4 B   spears,

spears, which are thrown with amazing force and velocity. I have noticed two or three men with specks on one eye, and once at Broken Bay saw in a canoe an old man who was perfectly blind. He was accompanied by a youth who paddled his canoe, and who, to my great surprise, sat behind him in it. This may, however, be in conformity to the idea of respect which is always paid to old age.

The colour of these people is not uniform. We have seen some who, even when cleansed from the smoke and filth which were always to be found on their persons, were nearly as black as the African negro; while others have exhibited only a copper or Malay colour. The natural covering of their heads is not wool as in most other black people, but hair; this particular may be remembered in the two natives who were in this country, Ben-nil-long and Yem-mer-ra-wan-nie. The former, on his return, by having some attention paid to his dress while in London, was found to have very long black hair. Black indeed was the general colour of the hair, though I have seen some of a reddish cast; but being unaccompanied by any perceptible difference of complexion, it was perhaps more the effect of some outward cause than its natural appearance.

Their noses are flat, nostrils wide, eyes much sunk in the head, and covered with thick eyebrows; in addition to which, they wear tied round the head, a net the breadth of the forehead, made of the fur of the opossum, which, when wishing to see very clearly, I have observed them draw over the eyebrows, thereby contracting the light. Their lips are thick, and the mouth extravagantly wide; but when opened discovering two rows of white, even, and sound teeth. Many had very prominent jaws; and there was one man who, but for the gift of speech, might very well have passed for an orang-outang. He was remarkably hairy; his arms appeared of an uncommon length; in his gait he was not perfectly upright; and in his whole manner seemed to have more of the brute and less of the human species about him than any of his countrymen. Those who have been in that country will, from this outline of him, recollect old We-rahng.

No. III.

HABITATIONS.

THEIR habitations are as rude as imagination can conceive. The hut of the woodman is made of the bark of a single tree, bent in the middle, and placed on its two ends on the ground, affording shelter to only one miserable tenant. These they never carry about with them; for where we found the hut, we constantly found the tree from which it had been taken withered and dead. On the sea-coast the huts were larger, formed of pieces of bark from several trees put together in the form of an oven with an entrance, and large enough to hold six or eight people. Their fire was always at the mouth of the hut, rather within than without; and the interior was in general the nastiest smoke-dried place that could be conceived. Their unserviceable canoes were commonly broken up and applied to this use. Beside these bark huts, they made use of excavations in the rock; and as the situations of these were various, they could always choose them out of the reach of wind and rain. At the mouths of these excavations we noticed a luxuriancy of soil; and on turning up the ground, found it rich with shells and other manure. These proved a valuable resource to us, and many loads of shells were burnt into lime, while the other parts were wheeled into our gardens.

When in the woods I seldom met with a hut, but at the mouth of it was found an ant's nest, the dwelling of a tribe of insects about an inch in length, armed with a pair of forceps and a sting, which they applied, as many found to their cost, with a severity equal to a wound made by a knife. We conjectured, that these vermin had been drawn together by the bones and fragments of a venison feast, which had been left by the hunter.

In their huts and in their caves they lie down indiscriminately mixed, men, women, and children together; and appear to possess under them much the same enjoyment as may be supposed to be found by the brute beast in his den, shelter from the weather, and, if not disturbed by external enemies, the comfort of sleep.

4 B 2   The

The extreme foundnefs with which they fleep invites jealoufy, or revenge for other wrongs, to arm the hand of the affaffin. Several inftances of this kind occurred during our acquaintance with them, one
of which was too remaikable to pafs unnoticed: Yel-lo-way, a native,
who feemed endowed with more urbanity than the reft of our friends,
having poffeffed himfelf (though not, as I could learn, by unfair means)
of Noo-roo-ing the wife of Wat-te-wal, another native well known
among us, was one night murdered in his fleep by this man, who could
not brook the decided preference given by Noo-roo-ing to his rival. This
murder he feveral months after repaid in his own perfon, his life being
taken by Cole-be, one of Yel-lo-way's friends, who ftole upon him in the
night, and put him to death while afleep. It was remarkable, that Cole-be
found an infant lying in his arms, whom he firft removed, before he
drove the fatal fpear into the father; he afterwards brought the child
with him into the town. Yel-lo-way was fo much efteemed among
us, that no one was forry he had been fo revenged.

Being themfelves fenfible of the danger they ran in the night, they
eagerly befought us to give them puppies of our fpaniel and terrier
breeds; which we did; and not a family was without one or more of
thefe little watch-dogs, which they confidered as invaluable guardians
during the night; and were pleafed when they found them readily devour the only regular food they had to give them, fifh.

No. IV.

MODE OF LIVING.

THE natives on the fea-coaft are thofe with whom we happened to
be the moft acquainted. Fifh is their chief fupport. Men, women,
and children are employed in procuring them; but the means ufed are
different according to the fex; the males always killing them with the
fiz-gig, while the females ufe the hook and line. The fiz-gig is made of
the wattle; has a joint in it, faftened by gum; is from fifteen to
twenty feet in length, and armed with four barbed prongs; the barb
being

being a piece of bone secured by gum. To each of these prongs they gave a particular name; but I never could discover any sensible reason for the distinction.

The lines used by the women are made by themselves of the bark of a small tree which they find in the neighbourhood. Their hooks are made of the mother-of-pearl oyster, which they rub on a stone until it assumes the shape they want. It must be remarked, that these hooks are not barbed; they neverthelefs catch fish with them with great facility.

While fishing, the women generally sing; and I have often seen them in their canoes chewing muscles or cockles, or boiled fish, which they spit into the water as a bait. In these canoes, they always carry a small fire laid upon sea-weed or sand; wherewith, when desirous of eating, they find a ready material for dressing their meal. This fire accounted for an appearance which we noticed in many of the women about the small of the back. We at first thought it must have been the effect of stripes; but the situation of them was questionable, and led us to make inquiry, when we found it to be the effect of the fires in the canoes.

In addition to fish, they indulge themselves with a delicacy which I have seen them eager to procure. In the body of the dwarf gum tree are several large worms and grubs, which they speedily divest of antennæ, legs, &c. and, to our wonder and difgust, devour. A servant of mine, an European, has often joined them in eating this luxury; and has assured me, that it was sweeter than any marrow he had ever tasted; and the natives themselves appeared to find a peculiar relish in it.

The woods, exclusive of the animals which they occasionally find in their neighbourhood, afford them but little sustenance; a few berries, the yam and fern-root, the flowers of the different banksia, and at times some honey, make up the whole vegetable catalogue.

The natives who live in the woods and on the margins of rivers are compelled to seek a different subsistence, and are driven to a harder exercise of their abilities to procure it. This is evinced in the hazard and toil with which they ascend the tallest trees after the opossum and flying squirrel. At the foot of Richmond Hill, I once found several places constructed expressly for the purpose of ensnaring animals or birds. These were wide enough at the entrance to admit a person

without

without much difficulty; but tapering away gradually from the entrance to the end, and terminating in a small wickered grate. It was
between forty and fifty feet in length; on each side the earth was
thrown up; and the whole was conftructed of weeds, rufhes, and
brambles; but fo well fecured, that an animal once within it could not
poffibly liberate itfelf. We fuppofed that the prey, be it beaft or bird,
was hunted and driven into this toil; and concluded, from finding one
of them deftroyed by fire, that they force it to the grated end, where it
is foon killed by their fpears. In one I faw a common rat, and in another the feathers of a quail.

By the fides of lagoons I have met with holes which, on examining,
were found excavated for fome fpace, and their mouths fo covered
over with grafs, that a bird or breaft ftepping on it would inevitably
fall in, and from its depth be unable to efcape.

In an excurfion to the Hawkefbury, we fell in with a native and his
child on the banks of one of the creeks of that noble river. We had
Cole-be with us, who endeavoured, but in vain, to bring him to a conference; he launched his canoe, and got away as expeditioufly as he
could, leaving behind him a fpecimen of his food and the delicacy of his
ftomach; a piece of water-foken wood (part of the branch of a tree)
full of holes, the lodgment of a large worm, named by them eah-bro,
and which they extract and eat; but nothing could be more offenfive
than the fmell of both the worm and its habitation. There is a tribe of
natives dwelling inland, who, from the circumftance of their eating
thefe loathfome worms, are named Cah-bro-gal.

They refort at a certain feafon of the year (the month of April) to
the lagoons, where they fubfift on eels which they procure by laying
hollow pieces of timber into the water, into which the eels creep, and
are eafily taken.

Thefe wood natives alfo make a pafte formed of the fern-root and the
large and fmall ant bruifed together; in the feafon they alfo add the
eggs of this infect.

No. V.

COURTSHIP AND MARRIAGE.

HOW will the refined ear of gallantry be wounded at reading an account of the courtſhip of theſe people! I have ſaid that there was a delicacy viſible in the manners of the females. Is it not ſhocking then to think that the prelude to love in this country ſhould be violence? yet ſuch it is, and of the moſt brutal nature: theſe unfortunate victims of luſt and cruelty (I can call them by no better name) are, I believe, always ſelected from the women of a tribe different from that of the males, (for they ought not to be dignified with the title of men,) and with whom they are at enmity. Secreſy is neceſſarily obſerved, and the poor wretch is ſtolen upon in the abſence of her protectors; being firſt ſtupified with blows, inflicted with clubs or wooden ſwords, on the head, back, and ſhoulders, every one of which is followed by a ſtream of blood, ſhe is dragged through the woods by one arm, with a perſeverance and violence that one might ſuppoſe would diſplace it from its ſocket; the lover, or rather the raviſher, is regardleſs of the ſtones or broken pieces of trees which may lie in his route, being anxious only to convey his prize in ſafety to his own party, where a ſcene enſues too ſhocking to relate. This outrage is not reſented by the relations of the female, who only retaliate by a ſimilar outrage when they find it in their power. This is ſo conſtantly the practice among them, that even the children make it a game or exerciſe; and I have often, on hearing the cries of the girls with whom they were playing, ran out of my houſe, thinking ſome murder was committed, but have found the whole party laughing at my miſtake.

The women thus raviſhed become their wives, are incorporated into the tribe to which the huſband belongs, and but ſeldom quit him for another.

Many of the men with whom we were acquainted did not confine themſelves to one woman. Ben-nil-long, previous to his viſit to England, was poſſeſſed of two wives, (if wives they may be called,) both

14   living

living with him and attending on him wherever he went. One named Ba-rang-a-roo, who was of the tribe of Cam-mer-ray, (Ben-nil-long himself was a Wahn-gal,) lived with him at the time he was seized and brought a captive to the settlement with Cole-be; and before her death he had brought off from Botany Bay, by the violence before described, Go-roo-bar-roo-bool-lo, the daughter of an old man named Met-ty, a native of that district; and she continued with him until his departure for England. We were told, on the banks of the Hawkesbury, that all the men there, and inland, had two wives. Cole-be, Ben-nil-long's friend, had two female companions; and we found, indeed, more instances of plurality of wives than of monogamy. I do not recollect ever noticing children by both; and observed, that in general, as might be expected, the two women were always jealous of and quarrelling with each other. I have heard them say, that the first wife claimed a priority of attachment and exclusive right to the conjugal embrace; while the second or latter choice was compelled to be the slave and drudge of both.

Chastity was a virtue in which they certainly did not pride themselves; at least, we knew women who, for a loaf of bread, a blanket, or a shirt, gave up any claim to it, when either was offered by a white man; and many white men were found who held out the temptation. Several girls, who were protected in the settlement, had not any objection to passing the night on board of ships, though some had learned shame enough (for shame was not naturally inherent in them) to conceal, on their landing, the spoils they had procured during their stay. They had also discovered that we thought it shameful to be seen naked; and I have observed many of them extremely reserved and delicate in this respect when before us; but when in the presence of only their own people, perfectly indifferent about their appearance.

No. VI.

CUSTOMS AND MANNERS.

DURING the time of parturition thefe people fuffer none but femalea to be prefent. War-re-weer, Bennillong's fifter, being taken in labour in the town, an opportunity offered of obferving them in that critical juncture, of which fome of our women, who were favourites with the girl, were defired to avail themfelves; and from them we learned, that during her labour one female, Boo-roong, was employed in pouring cold water from time to time on the abdomen, while another, tying one end of a fmall line round War-re-weer's neck, with the other end rubbed her own lips until they bled. She derived no actual affiftance from thofe who were about her, the child coming into the world by the fole efforts of nature; neither did any one receive it from her; but, having let it drop, one of our women divided the umbilical cord; after which, fhe retired to a fmall hole which had been prepared for her, over which fhe fat until the after-birth took place. The perfon who cut the navel-ftring wafhed the child, which fhe readily permitted, though Boo-roong and the other natives objected to it. She appeared much exhaufted, and, being faint, fell acrofs a fire that was in the place, but without receiving any injury.

I faw Bennillong's wife a few hours after fhe had been delivered of a child. To my great furprife fhe was walking about alone, and picking up fticks to mend her fire. The infant, whofe fkin appeared to have a reddifh caft, was lying in a piece of foft bark on the ground, the umbilical cord depending about three inches from the navel. I remained with her for fome time, during which fhe was endeavouring to get it off; to effect which fhe made ufe of the fmall bone of the leg of the kangooroo, round the point of which Bennillong had rolled fome punk, fo that it looked not unlike the button of a foil. She held it every now and then to the fire, then applied and preffed it to the navel until it cooled. This was perfevered in, till the mother

4 c   thought

thought the cord sufficiently deadened, and then with a shell she separated it [*].

The infant thus produced is by the mother carried about for some days on a piece of soft bark; and, as soon as it acquires strength enough, is removed to her shoulders, where it sits with its little legs across her neck; and, taught by necessity, soon catches hold of her hair to preserve itself from falling.

The reddish cast of the skin soon gives place to the natural hue, a change that is much assisted by the smoke and dirt in which, from the moment of their existence, these children are nurtured. The parents begin early to decorate them after 'the custom of the country. As soon as the hair of the head can be taken hold of, fish-bones and the teeth of animals are fastened to it with gum. White clay ornaments their little limbs; and the females suffer the extraordinary amputation which they term mal-gun before they have quitted their seat on their mother's shoulders.

In about a month or six weeks the child receives its name. This is generally taken from some of the objects constantly before their eyes, such as a bird, a beast, or a fish, and is given without any ceremony. Thus Bennillong's child Dilboong was so named after a small bird, which we often heard in low wet grounds and in copses. An elderly woman who occasionally visited us was named Mau-ber-ry, the term by which they distinguish the gurnet from other fish. Bennillong told me, his name was that of a large fish, but one that I never saw taken. Bal-loo-der-ry signified the fish named by us the leathern-jacket; and there were two girls in the town named Pat-ye-go-rang, a corruption of Pat-ta-go-rang, the name of the large grey kangooroo. Other instances might be adduced; but these are sufficient to show the prevalence of the custom.

At an early age the females wear round the waist a small line made of the twisted hair of the opossum, from the centre of which depend a few small uneven lines from two to five inches long, made of the same materials. This they term bar-rin, and wear it until they are grown into women and are attached to men.

[*] I here find in my papers a note, that for some offence Bennillong had severely beaten this woman in the morning, a short time before she was delivered.

The

The union of the fexes takes place at an earlier period than is ufual in colder regions. We have known feveral inflances of very young girls having been much and fhamefully abufed by the males.

From their earlieft infancy the boys are accuftomed to throwing the fpear, and to the habit of defending themfelves from it. They begin by throwing reeds at each other, and are foon very expert. They alfo, from the time when they can run, until prompted by man-hood to realize their fports, amufe themfelves with ftealing the females, and treat them at this time very little worfe than they do then.

Among their juvenile exercifes I obferved that of throwing up a ball, and paffing it from one to another. They alfo provide themfelves with fmall fticks, and range themfelves in a row, when the one at the upper end rolls a ball or any other round fubftance along the front of his com-panions, every one of whom endeavours to ftrike it as it paffes. This is a favourite exercife with them, and of courfe they excel at it.

Between the ages of eight and fixteen, the males and females undergo the operation which they term Gnah-noong, viz. that of hav-ing the *feptum nafi* bored, to receive a bone or reed, which among them is deemed a great ornament, though I have feen many whofe articu-lation was thereby rendered very imperfect. Between the fame years alfo the males receive the qualifications which are given to them by lofing one of the front teeth. This ceremony occurred twice during my refidence in New South Wales; and in the fecond operation I was fortunate enough to attend them during the whole of the time, at-tended by a perfon well qualified to make drawings of every particular circumftance that occurred. A remarkable coincidence of time was noticed as to the feafon in which it took place. It was firft performed in the beginning of the month of February 1791; and exactly at the fame period in the year 1795 the fecond operation occurred. As they have not any idea of numbers beyond three, and of courfe have no regular computation of time, this can only be afcribed to chance, par-ticularly as the feafon could not have much fhare in their choice, February being one of the hot months.

On the 25th of January 1795 we found that the natives were affem-bling in numbers for the purpofe of performing this ceremony. Seve-ral youths well known among us, never having fubmitted to the

4 C 2   operation,

operation, were now to be made men. Pe-mul-wy, a wood native,
and many strangers, came in ; but the principals in the operation not
being arrived from Cam-mer-ray, the intermediate nights were to be
passed in dancing. Among them we observed one man painted white
to the middle, his beard and eye-brows excepted, and all together a
frightful object. Others were distinguished by large white circles round
the eyes, which rendered them as terrific as can well be imagined. It
was not until the 2d of February that the party was complete. In the
evening of that day the people from Cam-mer-ray arrived, among
whom were those who were to perform the operation, all of whom
appeared to have been impatiently expected by the other natives. They
were painted after the manner of the country, were mostly provided
with shields, and all armed with clubs, spears, and throwing sticks.
The place selected for this extraordinary exhibition was at the head of
Farm Cove, where a space had been for some days prepared by clearing
it of grass, stumps, &c. ; it was of an oval figure, the dimensions of it
27 feet by 18, and was named Yoo-lahng.

When we arrived at the spot, we found the party from the north
shore armed, and standing at one end of it ; at the other we saw a
party consisting of the boys who were to be given up for the purpose of
losing each a tooth, and their several friends who accompanied them.

They then began the ceremony. The armed party advanced from
their end of the Yoo-lahng with a song or rather a shout peculiar to
this occasion, clattering their shields and spears, and raising a dust with
their feet that nearly obscured the objects around them. On reaching
the farther end of the Yoo-lahng, where the children were placed, one
of the party stepped from the crowd, and seizing his victim returned
with him to his party, who received him with a shout louder than usual,
placing him in the midst, where he seemed defended by a grove of
spears from any attempts that his friends might make to rescue him.
In this manner the whole were taken out, to the number of fifteen ;
among them appeared Ca-ru-ey, a youth of about sixteen or seventeen
years of age, and a young man, a stranger to us, of about three and
twenty.

The number being collected that were to undergo the operation,
they were seated at the upper end of the Yoo-lahng, each holding
down

down the head ; his hands clasped, and his legs crossed under him. In this position, aukward and painful as it must have been, we understood they were to remain all night; and, in short, that until the ceremony was concluded, they were neither to look up nor take any refreshment whatsoever.

The carrahdis now began some of their mystical rites. One of them suddenly fell upon the ground, and throwing himself into a variety of attitudes, accompanied with every gesticulation that could be extorted by pain, appeared to be at length delivered of a bone, which was to be used in the ensuing ceremony. He was during this apparently painful process encircled by a crowd of natives, who danced around him, singing vociferously, while one or more beat him on the back until the bone was produced, and he was thereby freed from his pain.

He had no sooner risen from the ground exhausted, drooping, and bathed in sweat, than another threw himself down with similar gesticulations, who went through the same ceremonies, and ended also with the production of a bone, with which he had taken care to provide himself, and to conceal it in a girdle which he wore.

We were told, that by these mummeries (for they were in fact nothing else) the boys were assured that the ensuing operation would be attended with scarcely any pain, and that the more these carrahdis suffered, the less would be felt by them.

It being now perfectly dark, we quitted the place, with an invitation to return early in the morning, and a promise of much entertainment from the ensuing ceremony. We left the boys sitting silent, and in the position before described, in which we were told they were to remain until morning.

On repairing to the place soon after day-light, we found the natives sleeping in small detached parties ; and it was not until the sun had shown himself that any of them began to stir. We observed that the people from the north shore slept by themselves, and the boys, though we heard they were not to be moved, were lying also by themselves at some little distance from the Yoo-lahng. Towards this, soon after sun-rise, the carrahdis and their party advanced in quick movement, one after the other, shouting as they entered, and running twice or thrice round it. The boys were then brought to the Yoo-lahng, hanging
                                                            their

their heads and clafping their hands.   On their being feated in this
manner, the ceremonies began, the principal performers in which appeared to be about twenty in number, and all of the tribe of Cam-
mer-ray.

The exhibitions now. performed were numerous and various; but
all of. them in their tendency pointed toward the boys, and had fome
allufion to the principal act of the day, which was to be the concluding
fcene of it.   The ceremony will be found pretty accurately reprefented
in the annexed ENGRAVINGS.

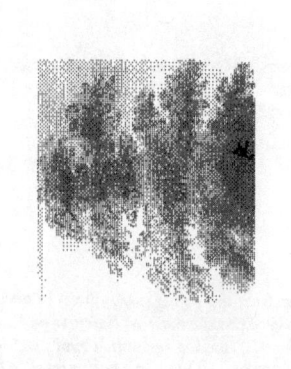

No. 1.—Reprefents the young men, fifteen in number, feated at the head of the Yoo-lahng, while thofe who were to be the operators paraded feveral times round it, running upon their hands and feet, and imitating the dogs of the country. Their drefs was adapted to this purpofe; the wooden fword, ftuck in the hinder part of the girdle which they wore round the waift, did not, when they were crawling on all fours, look much unlike the tail of a dog curled over his back. Every time they paffed the place where the boys were feated, they threw up the fand and duft on them with their hands and their feet. During this ceremony the boys fat perfectly ftill and filent, never once moving themfelves from the pofition in which they were placed, nor feeming in the leaft to notice the ridiculous appearance of the carrahdis and their affociates.

We underftood that by this ceremony power over the dog was given to them, and that it endowed them with whatever good or beneficial qualities that animal might poffefs.

The dogs of this country are of the jackal fpecies; they never bark; are of two colours, the one red with fome white about it; the other quite black. They have an invincible predilection for poultry, which the fevereft beatings could never reprefs. Some of them are very handfome.

Hunting Irish Surlieny. 2.

No. 2.—Reprefents the young men feated as before. The firft figure
in the plate is a ftout robuft native, carrying on his fhoulders a pat-ta-
go-rang or kangooroo made of grafs ; the fecond is carrying a load of
brufh-wood. The other figures, feated about, are finging, and beating
time to the fteps of the two loaded men, who appeared as if they were
almoft unable to move under the weight of the burthen which they
carried on their fhoulders. Halting every now and then, and limping,
they at laft depofited their load at the feet of the young men, and retired
from the Yoo-lahng as if they were excelfively fatigued by what they
had done. It muft be noticed, that the man who carried the brufh-
wood had thruft one or two flowering fhrubs through the *feptum nafi.*
He exhibited an extraordinary appearance in this fcene.

By this offering of the dead kangooroo was meant the power that
was now given them of killing that animal ; the brufh-wood might reprefent its haunt.

4 D

No. 3.—The boys were left feated at the Yoo-lahng for about half an hour; during which the actors went down into a valley near the place, where they fitted themfelves with long tails made of grafs, which they faftened to the hinder part of their girdles, inftead of the fword, which was laid afide during the fcene. Being equipped, they put themfelves in motion as a herd of kangooroos, now jumping along, then lying down and fcratching themfelves, as thofe animals do when bafking in the fun. One man beat time to them with a club on a fhield, while two others armed, attended them all the way, pretending to fteal upon them unobferved and fpear them.

This was emblematical of one of their future exercifes, the hunting of the kangooroo.

The fcene was altogether whimfical and curious; the valley where they equipped themfelves was very romantic, and the occafion extraordinary and perfectly novel.

No. 4.—On the arrival of this curious party at the Yoo-lahng, it passed by the boys as the herd of Kangooroo, and then quickly divesting themselves of their artificial tails, each man caught up a boy, and, placing him on his shoulders, carried him off in triumph toward the last scene of this extraordinary exhibition.

It must be remarked, that the friends and relations of the young people by no means interfered, nor attempted to molest these north shore natives in the execution of their business.

No. 5.—After walking a short distance, the boys were let down from the shoulders of the men, and placed in a cluster, standing with their heads inclined on their breasts, and their hands clasped together. Some of the party disappeared for above ten minutes to arrange the figure of the next scene. I was not admitted to witness this business, about which they appeared to observe a greater degree of mystery and preparation than I had noticed in either of the preceding ceremonies. We were at length desired to come forward, when we found the figures as placed in the plate No. 5.

The group on the left are the boys and those who attended them; fronting them were seen two men, one seated on the stump of a tree bearing another man on his shoulders, both with their arms extended: behind these were seen a number of bodies lying with their faces toward the ground, as close to each other as they could lie, and at the foot of another stump of a tree, on which were placed two other figures in the same position as the preceding.

As the boys and their attendants approached the first of these figures, the men who formed it began to move themselves from side to side, lolling out their tongues, and staring as wide and horribly with their eyes as they could open them. After this mummery had continued some minutes, the men separated for them to pass, and the boys were now led over the bodies lying on the ground. These immediately began to move, writhing as if in agony, and uttering a mournful dismal sound, like very distant thunder. Having passed over these bodies, the boys were placed before the second figures, who went through the same series of grimaces as those who were seated on the former stump; after which the whole moved forward.

A particular name, boo-roo-moo-roong, was given to this scene; but of its import I could learn very little. I made much inquiry; but could never obtain any other answer, than that it was very good; that the boys would now become brave men; that they would see well, and fight well.   4

Hamburg Fischbrücking 6.

No. 6.—At a little diftance from the preceding fcene the whole party halted; the boys were feated by each other, while oppofite to them were drawn up in a half circle the other party, now armed with the fpear and the fhield. In the centre of this party, with his face toward them, ftood Boo-der-ro, the native who had throughout taken the principal part in the bufinefs. He held his fhield in one hand, and a club in the other, with which he gave them, as it were, the time for their exercife. Striking the fhield with the club, at every third ftroke the whole party poifed and prefented their fpears at him, pointing them inwards, and touching the centre of his fhield.

This concluded the ceremonies previous to the operation; and it appeared fignificant of an exercife which was to form the principal bufinefs of their lives, the ufe of the fpear.

No. 7.—They now commenced their preparations for striking out the tooth. The first subject they took out was a boy of about ten years of age: he was seated on the shoulders of another native who sat on the grass, as appears in this Plate.

The bone was now produced which had been pretended to be taken from the stomach of the native the preceding evening; this, being made very sharp and fine at one end, was used for lancing the gum, and but for some such precaution it would have been impossible to have got out the tooth without breaking the jaw-bone. A throwing-stick was now to be cut about eight or ten inches from the end; and to effect this, much ceremony was used. The stick was laid upon a tree, and three attempts to hit it were made before it was struck. The wood being very hard, and the instrument a bad tomahawk, it took several blows to divide it; but three feints were constantly made before each stroke. When the gum was properly prepared, the operation began: the smallest end of the stick was applied as high up on the tooth as the gum would admit of, while the operator stood ready with a large stone apparently to drive the tooth down the throat of his patient. Here their attention to the number three was again manifest; no stroke was actually made until the operator had thrice attempted to hit the throwing-stick. They were full ten minutes about this first operation, the tooth being, unfortunately for the boy, fixed very firm in the gum. It was at last forced out, and the sufferer was taken away to a little distance, where the gum was closed by his friends, who now equipped him in the style he was to appear in for some days. A girdle was tied round his waist, in which was stuck a wooden sword; a ligature was put round his head, in which were stuck slips of the grass-gum tree, which, being white, had a curious and not unpleasing effect. The left hand was to be placed over the mouth, which was to be kept shut; he was on no account to speak; and for that day he was not to eat.

In like manner were all the others treated, except one, a pretty boy about eight or nine years of age, who, after suffering his gum to be lanced, could not endure the pain of more than one blow with the stone, and breaking from them made his escape.

4 E 2   During

During the whole of the operation the assistants made the most hideous noise in the ears of the patients *, sufficient to distract their attention, and to drown any cries they could possibly have uttered ; but they made it a point of honour to bear the pain without a murmur.

Some other peculiarities, however, were observed. The blood that issued from the lacerated gum was not wiped away, but suffered to run down the breast, and fall upon the head of the man on whose shoulders the patient sat, and whose name was added to his. I saw them several days afterwards, with the blood dried upon the breast. They were also termed Ke-bar-ra, a name which has reference in its construction to the singular instrument used on this occasion, Ke-bah in their language signifying a rock or stone. I heard them several months after address each other by this significant name.

* Crying e-wah e-wah, gä-ga gä-ga, repeatedly.

Halting for midday.

No. 8.—This Plate reprefents the young men arranged and fitting upon the trunk of a tree, as they appeared in the evening after the operation was over. The man is Cole-be, who is applying a broiled fifh to his relation Nan-bar-ray's gum, which had fuffered from the ftroke more than any of the others.

Suddenly, on a fignal being given, they all ftarted up, and rufhed into the town, driving before them men, women, and children, who were glad to get out of their way. They were now received into the clafs of men; were privileged to wield the fpear and the club, and to oppofe their perfons in combat. They might now alfo feize fuch females as they chofe for wives.

All this, however, muft be underftood to import, that by having fubmitted to the operation, having endured the pain of it without a murmur, and having loft a front tooth, they received a qualification which they were to exercife whenever their years and their ftrength fhould be equal to it.

Ben-nil-long's fifter, and Da-ring-ha, Cole-be's wife, hearing me exprefs a great defire to be poffeffed of fome of thefe teeth, procured three of them for me, one of which was that of Nan-bar-ray, Cole-be's relation.

I found that they had faftened them to pieces of fmall line, and were wearing them round their necks. They were given to me with much fecrecy and great dread of being obferved, and with an injunction that I fhould never let it be known that they had made me fuch a prefent, as the Cam-mer-ray tribe, to whom they were to be given, would not fail to punifh them for it; and they added that they fhould tell them the teeth were loft. Nan-bar-ray's tooth Da-ring-ha wifhed me to give to Mr. White, the principal furgeon of the fettlement, with whom the boy had lived from his being brought into it, in the year 1789, to Mr. White's departure; thus with gratitude remembering, after the lapfe of fome years, the attention which that gentleman had fhewn to her relative.

Having remained with them while the operation was performed on three or four of the boys, I went into the town, and returned after fun-fet, when I found the whole equipped and feated on the trunk of the tree, as defcribed in the Plate. It was then that I received the three

three teeth, and was conjured by the women to leave the place, as they did not know what might ensue. In fact, I observed the natives arming themselves; much confusion and hurry was visible among them; the savage appeared to be predominating; perhaps the blood they had drawn, and which was still wet on the heads and breasts of many of them, began to make them fierce; and, when I was on the point of retiring, the signal was given, which animated the boys to the first exercise.of the spirit which the business of the day had infused into them, (for I have no doubt that their young bosoms were warmed by the different ceremonies which they had witnessed, of which they had indeed been something more than mere spectators, and which they knew had been exhibited wholly on their account,) and they rushed into the town in the manner before described, every where as they passed along setting the grass on fire.

On shewing the teeth to our medical gentleman there, and to others since my return to England, they all declared that they could not have been better extracted, had the proper instrument been used, instead of the stone and piece of wood.

On a view of all these circumstances, I certainly should not consider this ceremony in any other light than as a tribute, were I not obliged to hesitate, by observing that all the people of Cam-mer-ray, which were those who exacted the tooth, were themselves proofs that they had submitted to the operation. I never saw one among them who had not lost the front tooth. I well recollect Ben-nil-long, in the early period of our acquaintance with him and his language, telling us, as we then thought, that a man of the name of Cam-mer-ra-gal wore all the teeth about his neck. But we afterwards found that this term was only the distinguishing title of the tribe which performed the ceremonies incident to the operation. Ben-nil-long at other times told us, that his own tooth was bour-bil-liey pe-mul, buried in the earth, and that others were thrown into the sea. It is certain, however, that my female friends, who gave me the teeth, were very anxious that the gift should not come to the knowledge of the men of Cam-mer-ray, and repeatedly said that they were intended for them.

In alluding to this ceremony, whether by pointing to the vacancy occasioned by the lost tooth, or by adverting to any of the curious
scenes

scenes exhibited on the occasion, the words Yoo-lahng erah-ba-diahng
were always used ; but to denote the loss of any other tooth the word
bool-bag-ga was applied. The term Yoo-lahng erah-ba-diahng must
therefore be considered as applying solely to this extraordinary occasion ; it appears to be compounded of the name given to the spot
where the principal scenes take place, and of the most material qualification that is derived from the whole ceremony, that of throwing
the spear. I conceive this to be the import of the word erah-ba- ·
diahng, erah being a part of the verb to throw, erah, throw you,
erailley, throwing.

Being thus entered on " the valued file," they quickly assume the
consequence due to the distinction, and as soon as possible bring their
faculties into action. The procuring of food really seems to be but a
secondary business with them ; the management of the spear and the
shield, dexterity in throwing the various clubs they have in use among
them, agility in either attacking or defending, and a display of the
constancy with which they endure pain, appearing to rank first among
their concerns in life. The females too are accustomed to bear on
their heads the traces of the superiority of the males, with which they
dignify them almost as soon as they find strength in the arm to imprint the mark. We have seen some of these unfortunate beings with
more scars upon their shorn heads, cut in every direction, than could
be well distinguished or counted. The condition of these women is
so wretched, that I have often, on seeing a female child borne on its
mother's shoulders, anticipated the miseries to which it was born, and
thought it would be a mercy to destroy it. Notwithstanding, however, that they are the mere slaves of the men, I have generally
found, in tracing the causes of their quarrels, that the women were at
the head of them, though in some cases remotely. They mingled in
all the contests of the men ; and one of these, that was in the beginning attended with some ceremony, was opened by a woman:

                                                                We

We had been told for some days of their making great preparations for a fight, and gladly heard that they had chosen a clear spot near the town for the purpose. The contending parties consisted of most of our Sydney acquaintance, and some natives from the south shore of Botany Bay, among whom was Còme-boak, already mentioned in page 408. We repaired to the spot an hour before sun-set, and found them seated opposite each other on a level piece of ground between two hills. As a prelude to the business, we observed our friends, after having waited some time, stand up, and each man stooping down, take water in the hollow of his hand, (the place just before them being wet,) which he drank. An elderly woman with a cloak on her shoulders, (made of opossum skins very neatly sewn together,) and provided with a club, then advanced from the opposite side, and, uttering much abusive language at the time, ran up to Cole-be, who was on the right, and gave him what I should have considered a severe blow on the head, which with seeming contempt he held out to her for the purpose. She went through the same ceremony with the rest, who made no resistance, until she came up to Ye-ra-ni-be, a very fine boy, who stood on the left. He, not admiring the blows that his companions received, which were followed by blood, struggled with her, and had he not been very active, I believe she would have stabbed him with his own spear, which she wrested from him. The men now advanced, and gave us many opportunities of witnessing the strength and dexterity with which they threw their spears, and the quickness of sight which was requisite to guard against them. The contest lasted until dark, when throwing the spear could no longer be accounted fair, and they beat each other with clubs, until they left off by mutual consent. In this part of the contest many severe wounds were given, and much blood was drawn from the heads of each party; but nothing material happened while they had light enough to guard against the spear.

In the exercise of this weapon they are very expert. I have seen them strike with certainty at the distance of seventy measured yards. They are thrown with great force, and where they are barbed are very formidable instruments. The wo-mer-ra, or throwing-stick, is always made use of on such occasions. This is a stick about three feet long,

with

with a hook at one end (and a shell at the other, secured by gum), to receive which there is a small hole at the head of the spear. Both are held in the right hand, the fingers of which are placed, two above the throwing-stick, and two between it and the spear, at about the distance of two feet from the hook. After poising it for some time, and measuring with the eye the distance from the object to be thrown at, the spear is discharged, the throwing-stick remaining in the hand. Of these instruments there are two kinds; the one, named Wo-mer-ra, is armed with the shell of a clamm, which they term Kah-dien, and which they use for the same purposes that we employ a knife. The other, which they name Wig-goon, has a hook, but no shell, and is rounded at the end. With this they dig the fern-root and yam out of the earth, and it is formed of heavy wood, while the wo-mer-ra is only part of a wattle split. They have several varieties of spears, every difference in them being distinguished by a name. Some are only pointed; others have one or more barbs, either shaped from the solid piece of wood of which the spear is made, or fastened on with gum; and some are armed with pieces of broken oyster-shell for four or five inches from the point, and secured by gum. All these barbed spears are dangerous, from the difficulty of extracting them. Of shields they have but two sorts. One, named E-lee-mong, is cut from the bark of the gum tree, and is not so capable of resisting the spear as the Ar-ra-gong, which is formed of solid wood, and hardened by fire. This shield is not so much in use as the e-lee-mong, as I imagine from its greater weight, and perhaps also from the superior difficulty they meet with in procuring it. Of clubs they use several sorts, some of which are of very large dimensions. They have one, the head of which is flat, with a sharp point in the centre. The flat part is painted with red and white stripes from the centre, and does not look unlike what they term it, Gnal-lung-ul-la, the name given by them to a mushroom. They have yet another instrument, which they call Ta-war-rang. It is about three feet long, is narrow, but has three sides, in one of which is the handle, hollowed by fire. The other sides are rudely carved with curved and waved lines, and it is made use of in dancing, being struck upon for this purpose with a club. An instrument very common among them must not be omitted in this account

4 F   of

of their weapons of hostility, for such, I fear, some of our miserable straggling convicts have found it to their cost, though it generally is applied to more peaceful purposes. This is the Mo-go*, or stone-hatchet. The stone is found in the shallows at the upper part of the Hawkesbury, and a handle being fixed round the head of it with gum, the under part is brought by friction to an edge fine enough to divide the bark of such trees as they take their canoes or hunters huts from, and even the shields which are cut from the body of the tree itself. There is no doubt of their readily applying this as a weapon, when no other offers to their necessities.

It must be observed, that the principal tribes have their peculiar weapons. Most of us had made collections of their spears, throwing-sticks, &c. as opportunities occurred; and on shewing them to our Sydney friends, they have told us that such a one was used by the people who live to the southward of Botany Bay; that another belonged to the tribe of Cam-mer-ray. The spear of the wood tribes, Be-dia-gal, Tu-ga-gal, and Boo-roo-bir-rong-gal, were known from being armed with bits of stone, instead of broken oyster-shells. The lines worn round the waist by the men belonged to a peculiar tribe, and came into the hands of others either by gift or plunder. The nets used by the people of the coast for carrying their fish, lines, &c. differed in the mesh from those used by the wood natives; and they extend this peculiarity even to their dances, their songs, and their dialect.

Among other customs which these people invariably practise, is one that is highly deserving of notice, as it carries with it some idea of retributive justice.

The shedding of blood is always followed by punishment, the party offending being compelled to expose his person to the spears of all who choose to throw at him; for in these punishments the ties of consanguinity or friendship are of no avail. On the death of a person, whether male or female, old or young, the friends of the deceased must be punished, as if the death were occasioned by their neglect. This is sometimes carried farther than there seems occasion for, or than can be reconcilable with humanity.

* A representation of this and other instruments is given in the Vignette in page 439.

After

After the murder of Yel-lo-way by Wat-te-wal, his widow Noo-roo-ing being obliged, according to the cuftom of her country, to avenge her hufband's death on fome of the relations of the murderer, meeting with a little girl named Go-nang-goo-lie, who was fomeway related to Wat-te-wal, walked with her and two other girls to a retired place, where with a club and a pointed ftone they beat her fo cruelly, that fhe was brought into the town almoft dead. In the head were fix or feven deep incifions, and one ear was divided to the bone, which, from the nature of the inftrument with which they beat her, was much injured. This poor child was in a very dangerous way, and died in a few days afterwards. The natives to whom this circumftance was mentioned expreffed little or no concern at it, but feemed to think it right, neceffary, and inevitable ; and we underftood that whenever wo-men have occafion for this fanguinary revenge, they never exercife it but on their own fex, not daring to ftrike a male. Noo-roo-ing, per-ceiving that her treatment of Go-nang-goo-lie did not meet our appro-bation, denied having beaten her, and faid it was the other girls ; but fuch men as we converfed with on the fubject affured us it was Noo-roo-ing, and added, that fhe had done no more than what cuftom obliged her to. The little victim of her revenge was, from her quiet tractable manners, much beloved in the town ; and what is a fingular trait of the inhumanity of this proceeding, fhe had every day fince Yel-lo-way's death requefted that Noo-roo-ing might be fed at the officer's hut, where fhe herfelf refided. Savage indeed muft be the cuftom and the feelings which could arm the hand againft this child's life ! Her death was not avenged, perhaps becaufe they confidered it as an expiatory facrifice.

Wat-te-wal, who committed the crime for which this little girl fuffered fo cruelly, efcaped unhurt from the fpears of Ben-nil-long, Cole-be, and feveral other natives, and was afterwards received by them as ufual, and actually lived with this very woman for fome time, till he was killed in the night by Cole-be, as before related.

This Wat-te-wal was in great union with Ben-nil-long, who twice denied his having committed offences which he knew would forfeit our favour. In this laft inftance Ben-nil-long betrayed more duplicity than we had given him credit for. On afking him with fome earneftnefs if Wat-te-wal had killed Yel-lo-way, he affured us with much confidence

that

that it was not Wat-te-wal who had killed him, but We-re-mur-rah. Little did we suspect that our friend had availed himself of a circumstance which he knew we were unacquainted with, that Wat-te-wal had more than one name. By giving us the second, he saved his friend, and knew that he could at all times boldly maintain that he had not concealed his name from us, We-re-mur-rah being as much his name as Wat-te-wal, though we had never known him by it. On apprising him some time afterwards, that we had discovered his artifice, and that it was a meanness we did not expect from him, he only laughed and went away.

The violent death of Yel-lo-way we have seen followed by a cruel proceeding, which terminated in the death of the murderer's relation, Go-nang-goo-lie. I shall now shew what followed where the person died a natural death.

Bone-da, a very fine youth, who lived at my house for several months, died of a cold, which, settling in his face, terminated in a mortification of his upper and lower jaws, and carried him off. We were told that some blood must be spilt on this occasion; but six weeks elapsed before we heard of any thing having happened in consequence of his decease. About that time having passed, however, we heard that a large party of natives belonging to different tribes, being assembled at Pan-ner-rong *, (or, as it is named with us, Rose Bay,) the spot which they had often chosen for shedding blood, after dancing and feasting over-night, early in the morning, Mo-roo-ber-ra, the brother, and Cole-be, another relation of Bone-da, seized upon a lad named Tar-ra-bil-long, and with a club each gave him a wound in his head, which laid the skull bare. Da-ring-ha, the sister of Bone-da, had her share in the bloody rite, and pushed at the unoffending boy with a doo-ull or short spear. He was brought into the town and placed at the hospital, and, though the surgeon pronounced from the nature of his wounds that his recovery was rather doubtful, he was seen walking about the day following. On being spoke to about the business, he said he did not weep or cry out like a boy, but like a man cried Ki-yah when they struck him; that the persons who treated him in this unfriendly manner were no longer his enemies, but would eat or drink or sit with him as friends.

* Pan-ner-rong in the language of the country signifies Blood.

Three

Three or four days after this, Go-roo-bine, a grey-headed man, apparently upwards of sixty years of age, who was related to Bone-da, came in with a severe wound on the back part of his head, given him on account of the boy's decease; neither youth nor old age appearing to be exempted from those sanguinary customs.

When Ba-rang-a-roo, Ben-nil-long's wife, died, several spears were thrown by the men at each other, by which many were wounded; and Ben-nil-long had a severe contest with Wil-le-mer-ring, whom he wounded in the thigh. He had sent for him as a car-rah-dy to attend her when she was ill; but he either could not or would not obey the summons. Ben-nil-long had chosen the time for celebrating these funeral games in honour of his deceased wife when a whale feast had assembled a large number of natives together, among whom were several people from the northward, who spoke a dialect very different to that with which we were acquainted.

Some officers happening once to be present in the lower part of the harbour when a child died, perceived the men immediately retire, and throw their spears at one another with much apparent anger, while the females began their usual lamentations.

When Dil-boong, Ben-nil-long's infant child, died, several spears were thrown, and Ben-nil-long, at the decease of her mother, said repeatedly, that he should not be satisfied until he had sacrificed some one to her *manes*.

Ye-ra-ni-be Go-ru-ey having beaten a young woman, the wife of another man, and she having some time after exchanged a perilous and troublesome life for the repose and quiet of the grave, a contest ensued some days after, on account of her decease, between Ben-nil-long and Go-ru-ey, and between the husband and Go-ru-ey, by both of whom he was wounded. Ben-nil-long drove a spear into his knee, and the husband another into his left buttock. This wound he must have received by failing to catch the spear on his shield, and turning his body to let it pass beside him; other spears were thrown, but he alone appeared to be the victim of the day. Signifying a wish to have his wounds dressed by the surgeon, he was in the evening actually brought up to the hospital by the very man who had wounded him.

The bay named Pan-ner-rong was the scene of this extraordinary transaction.

4 F   Not

Not a long time before I left the country, I witnessed another contest among them, which was attended with some degree of ceremony. The circumstance was this. A native of the Botany Bay district, named Collindiun, having taken off by force Go-roo-boo-roo-bal-lo, the former wife of Ben-nil-long, but now the wife of Car-ru-ey, and carried her up the harbour, Car-ru-ey with his relation Cole-be, in revenge, stole upon this Collindiun one night while he lay asleep, and each fixed a spear in him. The wounds, though deep and severe, yet did not prove mortal, and on his recovery he demanded satisfaction. He came accompanied by a large party of natives from the south shore of Botany Bay, and rather reluctantly, for he had wished the business to be decided there, rather than among Car-ru-ey's friends, as many of his associates in arms were entire strangers to us. Thirsting after revenge, however, he was prevailed with to meet him on his own ground, and the Yoo-lahng formerly used for a different purpose was the place of rendezvous.

At night they all danced, that is to say, both parties, but not mixed together; one side waiting until the other had concluded their dance. In the manner of dancing, of announcing themselves as ready to begin, and also in their song, there was an evident difference.

Our friends appeared to have some apprehension of the event not proving favourable to them; for perceiving an officer there with a gun, Car-ru-ey strenuously urged him, if any thing should happen to him, to shoot the Botany Bay black fellows. The women, to induce us to comply with his request, told us that some of the opposite party had said they would kill Car-ru-ey. Some other guns making their appearance, the strangers were alarmed and uneasy, until assured that they were intended merely for our own security.

The time for this business was just after ten in the forenoon. We found Car-ru-ey and Cole-be seated at one end of the Yoo-lahng, each armed with a spear and throwing-stick, and provided with a shield. Here they were obliged to sit until some one of their opponents got up; they also then arose and put themselves en garde. Some of the spears which were thrown at them they picked up and threw back; and others they returned with extraordinary violence.

The

The affair was over before two o'clock ; and, what was remarkable, we did not hear of any person being wounded. We understood, however, that this circumstance was to produce another meeting.

In this as in all the contests I ever witnessed among them, the point of honour was rigidly observed. But spears were not the only instruments of warfare on these occasions. They had also to combat with words, in which the women sometimes bore a part. During this latter engagement I have seen them, when any very offensive word met their ears, suddenly place themselves in the attitude of throwing the spear, and at times let it drop on the ground without discharging; and others threw it with all their strength; but always scrupulously observing the situation of the person opposed, and never throwing at him until he covered himself with his shield. The most unaccountable trait in this business was, the party thrown at providing his enemy with weapons; for they have been repeatedly seen, when a spear has flown harmless beyond them, to pick it up and fling it carelessly back to their adversary. This might proceed from contempt, or from there being a scarcity of spears; and I have thought that when, instead of flinging it carelessly back, they have thrown it with much violence, it was because it had been thrown at them with a greater visible degree of malevolence than the others.

This rigid attention to the point of honour, when fairly opposed to each other, is difficult to reconcile with their treacherous and midnight murders.

Their mode of retaliating an insult or injury was extraordinary. Children, if when at play they received a blow or a push, resented it by a blow or a push of equal force to that which they felt. This retaliating spirit appeared also among the men, of a remarkable instance of which several of us were witnesses. A native of the name of Bur-ro-wan-nie had some time before been beaten by two natives of the tribe of Gwe-a, at the head of Botany Bay. One of these being fixed on, he was in return to be beaten by Bur-ro-wan-nie. For this purpose a large party attended over-night at the head of the stream near the settlement to dance; at which exercise they continued from nine till past twelve o'clock. The man who was to be beaten danced with the rest until they ceased, and then laid himself down among them

them to sleep. Early in the morning, while he was yet on the ground, and apparently asleep at the foot of a tree, Cole-be and Bur-ro-wan-nie, armed each with a spear and a club, rushed upon him from among some trees. Cole-be made a push at him with his spear, but did not touch him, while the other, Bur-ro-wan-nie, struck him with his club two severe blows on the hinder part of the head. The noise they made, if he was asleep, awaked him; and when he was struck, he was on his legs. He was perfectly unarmed, and hung his head in silence while Cole-be and his companion talked to him. No more blows were given, and Ben-nil-long, who was present, wiped the blood from the wounds with some grass. As a proof that Bur-ro-wan-nie was satisfied with the redress he had taken, we saw him afterwards walking in the town with the object of his resentment, who, on being asked, said Bur-ro-ween-nie was good; and during the whole of the day, wheresoever he was seen, there also was this poor wretch with his breast and back covered with dried blood; for, according to the constant practice of his countrymen, he had not washed it off. In the evening I saw him with a ligature fastened very tight round his head, which certainly required something to alleviate the pain it must have endured.

In some of these contests they have been seen on the field of battle attended by a person who appeared to be the friend of both parties. In a single combat which Mo-roo-ber-ra had with Ben-nil-long, they were attended by Cole-be, who took a position on one side about half-way between them, armed with a spear and throwing-stick, but unprovided with a shield. This I saw he frequently shook, and talked a great deal, but never threw it. While in this situation he was styled Cä-bah-my.

I had long wished to be a witness of a family party, in which I hoped and expected to see them divested of that restraint which perhaps they might put on in our houses. I was one day gratified in this wish when I little expected it. Having strolled down to the Point named Too-bow-gu-liè, I saw the sister and the young wife of Ben-nil-long coming round the Point in the new canoe which the husband had cut in his last excursion to Parramatta. They had been out to procure fish, and were keeping time with their paddles, responsive to the

the words of a song, in which they joined with much good humour and harmony. They were almoſt immediately joined by Ben-nil-long, who had his ſiſter's child on his ſhoulders. The canoe was hauled on ſhore, and what fiſh they had caught the women brought up. I obſerved that the women ſeated themſelves at ſome little diſtance from Ben-nil-long, and then the groupe was thus diſpoſed of:—The huſband was ſeated on a rock, preparing to dreſs and eat the fiſh he had juſt received. On the ſame rock lay his pretty ſiſter War-re-weer aſleep in the ſun, with a newborn infant in her arms; and at ſome little diſtance were ſeated, rather below him, his other ſiſter and his wife, the wife opening and eating ſome rock-oyſters, and the ſiſter ſuckling her child, Kah-dier-rang, whom ſhe had taken from Ben-nil-long. I cannot omit mentioning the unaffected ſimplicity of the wife: immediately on her ſtepping out of her canoe, ſhe gave way to the preſſure of a certain neceſſity, without betraying any of that reſerve which would have led another at leaſt behind the adjoining buſh. She bluſhed not, for the cheek of Go-roo-bar-roo-bool-lo was the cheek of rude nature, and not made for bluſhes. I remained with them till the whole party fell aſleep.

They have great difficulty in procuring fire, and are therefore ſeldom ſeen without it. Ben-nil-long, or ſome other native, once ſhewed me the proceſs of procuring it. It is attended with infinite labour, and is performed by fixing the pointed end of a cylindrical piece of wood into a hollow made in a plane: the operator twirling the round piece ſwiftly between both his hands, ſliding them up and down until fatigued, at which time he is relieved by another of his companions, who are all ſeated for this purpoſe in a circle, and each one takes his turn until fire is procured.

Moſt of their inſtruments are ornamented with rude carved-work, effected with a piece of broken ſhell, and on the rocks I have ſeen various figures of fiſh, clubs, ſwords, animals, and even branches of trees, not contemptibly repreſented.

No. VII.

SUPERSTITION.

LIKE all other children of ignorance, these people are the slaves of superstition.

I think I may term the car-rah-dy their high priest of superstition. The share they had in the tooth-drawing scenes was not the only instance, that induced me to suppose this. When Cole-be accompanied Governor Phillip to the banks of the Hawkesbury, he met with a car-rah-dy, Yel-lo-mun-dy, who, with much gesticulation and mummery, pretended to extract the barbs of two spears from his side, which never had been left there, or, if they had, required rather the aid of the knife than the incantations of Yel-lo-mun-dy to extract them; but his patient was satisfied with the car-rah-dy's efforts to serve him, and thought himself perfectly relieved.

During the time that Boo-roong lived at the clergyman's house she paid occasional visits to the lower part of the harbour. From one of these she returned extremely ill. On questioning her as to the cause, for none was apparent, she told us that the women of Cam-mer-ray had made water in a path which they knew she was to cross, and it had made her ill. These women were inimical to her, as she belonged to the Botany Bay district. On her intimating to them that she found herself ill, they told her triumphantly what they had done. Not recovering, though bled in the arm by Mr. White, she underwent an extraordinary and superstitious operation, where the operator suffers more than the patient. She was seated on the ground, with one of the lines worn by the men passed round her head once, taking care to fix the knot in the centre of her forehead; the remainder of the line was taken by another girl, who sat at a small distance from her, and with the end of it fretted her lips until they bled very copiously; Boo-roong imagining all the time that the blood came from her head, and passed along the line until it ran into the girl's mouth, whence it was spit into a small vessel which she had beside her, half filled with water, and into which she

occasion-occafionally dipped the end of the line. This operation they term be-an-ny, and is the peculiar province of the women.

Another curious inftance of their fuperftition occurred among fome of our people belonging to a boat that was lying wind-bound in the lower part of the harbour. They had procured fome fhell-fifh, and during the night were preparing to roaft them, when they were obferved by one of the natives, who fhook his head and exclaimed, that the wind for which they were waiting would not rife if they roafted the fifh. His argument not preventing the failors from enjoying their treat, and the wind actually proving foul, they, in their turn, gave an inftance of fu-perftition by abufing the native, and attributing to him the foul wind which detained them. On queftioning Ye-ra-ni-be refpecting this cir-cumftance, he affured me that the natives never broil fifh by night.

In a reach of the Hawkefbury, about midway up fome high land, ftands a rock which in its form is not unlike a centry-box. Refpecting this rock, they have a fuperftitious tradition, that while fome natives were one day feafting under it, fome of the company whiftling, it hap-pened to fall from a great height, and crufhed the whole party under its weight. For this reafon they make it an invariable rule never to whiftle under a rock.

Among their other fuperftitions was one which might be naturally expected from their ignorance, a belief in fpirits.

Of this belief we had at different times feveral accounts. Ben-nil-long, during his firft acquaintance with us, defcribed an apparition as advancing to a perfon with an uncommon noife, and feizing hold of him by the throat. It came flowly along with its body bent, and the hands held together in a line with the face, moving on till it feized the party it meant to vifit. We were told by him and others, and that after we underftood each other, that by fleeping at the grave of a deceafed perfon, they would, from what happened to them there, be freed from all future apprehenfions refpecting apparitions; for during that awful fleep the fpirit of the deceafed would vifit them, feize them by the throat, and, opening them, take out their bowels, which they would replace and clofe up the wound. We underftood that very few chofe to en-counter the darknefs of the night, the folemnity of the grave, and the vifitation of the fpirit of the deceafed; but that fuch as were fo hardy

became

became immediately car-rah-dys, and that all those who exercised that profession had gone through this ceremony.

It is very certain, that even in the day-time they were strangely unwilling to pass a grave; but I believe that their tale of being seized by the throat by a ghost was nothing more than their having felt the effects of what we term the night-mare during an uneasy sleep.

To the shooting of a star they attach a degree of importance; and I once, on an occasion of this kind, saw the girl Boo-roong greatly agitated, and prophesying much evil to befal all the white men and their habitations.

Of thunder and lightning they are also much afraid; but have an idea, that by chanting some particular words, and breathing hard, they can dispel it. Instances of this have been seen.

No. VIII.

DISEASES.

THEIR living chiefly on fish (I speak of those whom we found on the sea-coast) produces a disorder which greatly resembles the itch; they term it Djee-ball djee-ball; and at one time, about the year 1791, there was not one of the natives, man, woman, nor child, that came near us, but was covered with it. It raged violently among them, and some became very loathsome objects.

The venereal disease also had got among them; but I fear our people have to answer for that; for though I believe none of our women had connection with them, yet there is no doubt but that several of the black women had not scrupled to connect themselves with the white men. Of the certainty of this an extraordinary instance occurred. A native woman had a child by one of our people. On its coming into the world she perceived a difference in its colour; for which not knowing how to account, she endeavoured to supply by art what she found deficient in nature, and actually held the poor babe, repeatedly, over the

smoke

fmoke of her fire, and rubbed its little body with afhes and dirt, to reftore it tot he hue with which her other children had been born. Her hufband appeared as fond of it as if it had borne the undoubted fign of being his own, at leaft fo far as complexion could afcertain to whom it belonged. Whether the mother had made ufe of any addrefs on the occafion, I never learned.

It was by no means afcertained whether the lues venerea had been among them before they knew us, or whether our people had to anfwer for having introduced that devouring plague. Thus far is certain, however, that they gave it a name, Goo-bah-roong; a circumftance that feems rather to imply a pre-knowledge of its dreadful effects.

In the year 1789 they were vifited by a diforder which raged among them with all the appearance and virulence of the fmall-pox. The number that it fwept off, by their own accounts, was incredible. At that time a native was living with us; and on our taking him down to the harbour to look for his former companions, thofe who witnefled his expreffion and agony can never forget either. He looked anxioufly around him in the different coves we vifited; not a veftige on the fand was to be found of human foot; the excavations in the rocks were filled with the putrid bodies of thofe who had fallen victims to the diforder; not a living perfon was any where to be met with. It feemed as if, flying from the contagion, they had left the dead to bury the dead. He lifted up his hands and eyes in filent agony for fome time; at laft he exclaimed, " All dead! all dead!" and then hung his head in mournful filence, which he preferved during the remainder of our excurfion. Some days after he learned that the few of his companions who furvived had fled up the harbour to avoid the peftilence that fo dreadfully raged. His fate has been already mentioned. He fell a victim to his own humanity when Boo-roong, Nan-bar-ray, and others were brought into the town covered with the eruptions of the diforder. On vifiting Broken Bay, we found that it had not confined its effects to Port Jackfon, for in many places our path was covered with fkeletons, and the fame fpectacles were to be met with in the hollows of moft of the rocks of that harbour.

Notwithftanding the town of Sydney was at this time filled with children, many of whom vifited the natives that were ill of this diforder,

not

not one of them caught it, though a North-American Indian, a sailor belonging to Captain Ball's vessel, the Supply, sickened of it and died.

To this disorder they also gave a name, Gal-gal-la; and that it was the small-pox there was scarcely a doubt; for the person seized with it was affected exactly as Europeans are who have that disorder; and on many that had recovered from it we saw the traces, in some the ravages of it on the face.

As a proof of the numbers of those miserable people who were carried off by this disorder, Ben-nil-long told us, that his friend Cole-be's tribe being reduced by its effects to three persons, Cole-be, the boy Nan-bar-ray, and some one else, they found themselves compelled to unite with some other tribe, not only for their personal protection, but to prevent the extinction of their tribe. Whether this incorporation ever took place I cannot say; I only know that the natives themselves, when distinguishing between this man and another of the same name at Botany Bay, always styled him Cad-i Cole-be; Cad-i being the name of his district; and Cole-be, when he came into the field some time after, appeared to be attended by several very fine boys who kept close by his side, and were of his party.

Whenever they feel a pain, they fasten a tight ligature round the part, thereby stopping the circulation, and easing the part immediately affected. I have before mentioned the quickness with which they recovered from wounds; but I have even known them get the better in a short time of a fractured skull. That their skulls should be fractured will be no wonder, when it is recollected that the club seems to be applied alone to the head. The women who are struck with this weapon always fall to the ground; but this seldom happens to the men, though the blows are generally more severe.

No. IX.

PROPERTY.

THEIR spears and shields, their clubs and lines, &c. are their own property; they are manufactured by themselves, and are the whole of
their

their perfonal eflate. But, ftrange as it may appear, they have alfo
their real eflates.' Ben-nil-long, both before he went to England and
fince his return, often affured me, that the ifland Me-mel (called by us
Goat Ifland) clofe by Sydney Cove was his own property; that it was
his father's, and that he fhould give it to By-gone, his particular friend
and companion. To this little fpot he appeared much attached; and
we have often feen him and his wife Ba-rang-a-roo feafting and enjoying themfelves on it. He told us of other people who poffeffed this
kind of hereditary property, which they retained undifturbed.

No. X.

DISPOSITIONS.

FROM the different circumftances that have been related of thefe
people in the foregoing account, a general idea of their character and
difpofition may be gathered. They are revengeful, jealous, courageous,
and cunning. I have never confidered their ftealing on each other in
the night for the purpofes of murder as a want of bravery, but have
looked on it rather as the effect of the diabolical fpirit of revenge,
which thus fought to make furer of its object than it could have done
if only oppofed man to man in the field. Their conduct when thus
oppofed, the conftancy with which they endured pain, and the alacrity
with which they accepted a fummons to the fight, are furely proofs of
their not wanting courage. They difclaim all idea of any fuperiority
that is not perfonal; and I remember when Ben-nil-long had a fhield,
made of tin and covered with leather, prefented to him by Governor
Phillip, he took it with him down the harbour, whence he returned
without it, telling us that he had loft it; but in fact it had been taken
from him by the people of the north fhore diftrict and deftroyed; it
being deemed unfair to cover himfelf with fuch a guard.

They might have been honeft before we came among them, not
having much to covet from one another; but from us they often ftole
fuch things as we would not give them. While they pilfered what

9　　　　　　　　　　　　　　could

could gratify their appetites, it was not to be wondered at; but I have seen them steal articles of which they could not possibly know the use. Mr. White once being in the midst of a crowd of natives in the lower part of the harbour, one of them saw a small case of instruments in his pocket, which, watching an opportunity, he slyly stole, and ran away with; but, being observed, he was pursued and made to restore his prize. We were very little acquainted with them at this time, and therefore the native could not have known the contents of the case. Could he have been watched to his retreat, I have no doubt but he would have been seen to lay the case on his head, as an ornament, the place to which at first every thing we gave them was usually consigned.

That they are not strangers to the occasional practice of falsehood, is apparent from the words truth and falsehood being found in their language; but, independent of this, we had many proofs of their being adepts in the arts of evasion and lying; and I have seen them, when we have expressed doubts of some of their tales, assure us with much earnestness of the truth of their assertions; and when speaking to us of other natives they have as anxiously wished us to believe that they had told us lies.

Their talent for mimicry is very great. It was a favourite diversion with the children to imitate the peculiarities in any one's gait, and they would go through it with the happiest success.

They are susceptible of friendship, and capable of feeling sorrow; but this latter sensation they are not in the habit of encouraging long. When Ba-loo-der-ry, a very fine lad who died among us, was buried, I saw the tears streaming silently down the sable cheek of his father Maugo-ran; but in a little time they were dried, and the old man's countenance indicated nothing but the lapse of many years which had passed over his head.

With attention and kind treatment, they certainly might be made a very serviceable people. I have seen them employed in a boat as usefully as any white person; and the settlers have found some among them, who would go out with their flock, and carefully bring home the right numbers, though they have not any knowledge of numeration beyond three or four.

Their

Their acquaintance with aſtronomy is limited to the names of the ſun and moon, ſome few ſtars, the Magellanic clouds, and the milky way. Of the circular form of the earth they have not the ſmalleſt idea, but imagine that the ſun returns over their heads during the night to the quarter whence he begins his courſe in the morning.

As they never make proviſion for the morrow, except at a whale-feaſt, they always eat as long as they have any thing left to eat, and when ſatisfied, ſtretch themſelves out in the ſun to ſleep, where they remain until hunger or ſome other cauſe calls them again into action. I have at times obſerved a great degree of indolence in their diſpoſitions, which I have frequently ſeen the men indulge at the expence of the weaker veſſel the women, who have been forced to ſit in their canoe, expoſed to the ſervour of the mid-day ſun, hour after hour, chaunting their little ſong, and inviting the fiſh beneath them to take their bait; for without a ſufficient quantity to make a meal for their tyrants, who were lying aſleep at their eaſe, they would meet but a rude reception on their landing.

No. XI.

FUNERAL CEREMONIES.

THE firſt peculiarity noticeable in their funeral ceremonies is the diſpoſal of their dead: their young people they conſign to the grave; thoſe who have paſſed the middle age are burnt. Ben-nil-long burnt the body of his firſt wife Ba-rang-a-roo, who, I ſuppoſe, was at the time of her deceaſe turned of fifty. I have attended them on both occaſions. The interment of Ba-loo-der-ry was accompanied with many curious ceremonies. From being one day in apparent perfect health, he was brought in the next extremely ill, and attended by Ben-nil-long, whom we found ſinging over him, and making uſe of thoſe means which ignorance and ſuperſtition pointed out to him to recover his health. Ba-loo-der-ry lay extended on the ground, appearing to

4 H

be

be in much pain. Ben-nil-long applied his mouth to those parts of his patient's body which he thought were affected, breathing strongly on them, and singing: at times he waved over him some boughs dipped in water, holding one in each hand, and seemed to treat him with much attention and friendship. On the following morning he was visited by a car-rah-dy, who came express from the north shore. This man threw himself into various distortions, applied his mouth to different parts of his patient's body, and at length, after appearing to labour much, and to be in great pain, spit out a piece of a bone about an inch and a half long (which he had previously procured). Here the farce ended, and Ba-loo-der-ry's friends took the car-rah-dy with them and entertained him with such fare as they had to give him. He was at this time at our hospital; during the night his fever increased, and his friends, thinking he would be better with them, put him into a canoe, intending to take him to the north shore; but he died as they were carrying him over. This was immediately notified to us by a violent clamour among the women and children; and Ben-nil-long soon after coming into the town, it was agreed upon between him and the governor that the body should be buried in the governor's garden.

In the afternoon it was brought over in a canoe, and deposited in a hut at the bottom of the garden, several natives attending, and the women and children lamenting and howling most dismally. The body was wrapped up in the jacket which he usually wore, and some pieces of blanketing tied round it with bines. The men were all armed, and, without any provocation, two of them had a contest with clubs; at the same time a few blows passed between some of the women. Boo-roong had her head cut by Go-roo-ber-ra, the mother of the deceased. Spears were also thrown, but evidently as part of a ceremony, and not with an intention of doing injury to any one. At the request of Ben-nil-long, a blanket was laid over the corpse, and Cole-be his friend sat by the body all night, nor could he be prevailed on to quit it.

They remained rather silent till about one in the morning, when the women began to cry, and continued for some time. At daylight Ben-nil-long brought his canoe to the place, and cutting it to a proper
length,

length, the body was placed in it, with a spear, a fiz-gig, a throwing-
stick, and a line which Ba-loo-der-ry had worn round his waist.
Some time was taken up in adjusting all this business, during which
the men were silent, but the women, boys, and children uttered the
most dismal lamentations. The father stood alone and unemployed, a
silent observer of all that was doing about his deceased son, and a perfect picture of deep and unaffected sorrow. Every thing being ready,
the men and boys all assisted in lifting the canoe with the body from
the ground, and placing it on the heads of two natives, Collins and
Yow-war-re. Some of the assistants had tufts of grass in their hands,
which they waved backwards and forwards under the canoe, while it
was lifting from the ground, as if they were exorcising some evil
spirit. As soon as it was fixed on the heads of the bearers, they set
off, preceded by Ben-nil-long and another man, Wat-te-wal, both
walking with a quick step towards the point of the cove where Ben-
nil-long's hut stood. Mau-go-ran, the father, attended them armed
with his spear and throwing-stick, while Ben-nil-long and Wat-te-wal
had nothing in their hands but tufts of grass, which as they went they
waved about, sometimes turning and facing the corpse, at others
waving their tufts of grass among the bushes. When they fronted
the corpse, the head of which was carried foremost, the bearers made
a motion with their heads from side to side, as if endeavouring to
avoid the people who fronted them. After proceeding thus to some
little distance, Wat-te-wal turned aside from the path, and went up
to a bush, into which he seemed to look very narrowly, as if searching for something that he could not find, and waving about the tufts
of grass which he had in either hand. After this fruitless search, they
all turned back, and went on in a somewhat quicker pace than before.
On their drawing near the spot where the women and children were
sitting with the other men, the father threw two spears towards, but
(evidently intentionally) short of them. Here Ben-nil-long took his
infant child, Dil-boong, in his arms, and held it up to the corpse, the
bearers endeavouring to avoid it as before described. Bè-dia Bè-dia,
the reputed brother of the deceased, a very fine boy of about five
years of age, was then called for, but came forward very reluctantly,

and

and was prefented in the fame manner as the other child. After this they proceeded to the grave which had been prepared in the governor's garden. Twice they changed the bearer who walked the foremoft, but his friend Collins carried him the whole of the way. At the grave fome delay took place, for unfortunately it was found not to be long enough; but after fome time, it being completed according to their wifhes, Yel-lo-way levelled the bottom with his hands and feet, and then ftrewed fome grafs in it, after which he ftretched himfelf at his length in it, firft on his back, and then on his right fide. Ben-nil-long had earneftly requefted that fome drums might be ordered to attend, which was granted, and two or three marches were beat while the grave was preparing; Ben-nil-long highly approving, and pointing at the time firft to the deceafed and then to the fkies, as if there was fome connexion between them at that moment. When the grave was ready, the men to the number of five or fix got in with the body, but being ftill fomewhat too fhort, the ends of the canoe were cut, in doing which the bines were loofened and the corpfe expofed to view. It appeared to be in a very putrid ftate. Every thing was however adjufted, and the grave was filled in by the natives and fome of our people.

On laying the body in the grave, great care was taken fo to place it, that the fun might look at it as he paffed, Ben-nil-long and Cole-be taking their obfervations for that purpofe, and cutting down every fhrub that could at all obftruct the view. He was placed on his right fide with his head to the N. W.

The native Yow-war-re appeared to have much to do in this ceremony. When the grave was covered in, and laid up round, he collected feveral branches of fhrubs, and placed them in a half circle on the fouth fide of the grave, extending them from the foot to the head of it. He alfo laid grafs and boughs on the top of it, and crowned the whole with a large log of wood. This log appeared to be placed there for fome particular purpofe; for having fixed it he ftrewed fome grafs over it, and then laid himfelf on it at his length for fome minutes, with his face towards the fky. Every rite being performed, the party retired, fome of the men firft fpeaking in a menacing tone to the women, and telling Boo-roong not to eat any fifh nor meat that day. We underftood that at
night

night two of the men were to fleep at the grave, but I have reafon to think that they did not. Cole-be and Wat-te-wal were painted red and white over the breaft and fhoulders, and on this occafion were dif-tinguifhed by the title of Moo-by ; and we learned from them that while fo diftinguifhed they were to be very fparing in their meals.

They enjoined us on no account to mention the name of the deceafed, a cuftom they rigidly attended to themfelves whenever any one died ; and in purfuance of this cuftom, Nan-bar-ray, one of whofe names was Ba-loo-der-ry, had actually relinquifhed that, and obtained another name.

The ceremony of fleeping at the grave of the deceafed, we knew, was obferved by Ben-nil-long after the death of his little child Dil-boong, he and two or three other natives pafling the night in the governor's garden, not very far from the fpot where it was buried.

Such were the ceremonies attendant on the interment of Ba-loo-der-ry. When Ba-rang a-roo Da-ring-ha, Ben-nil-long's wife, died, he determined at once to burn her, and requefted Governor Phillip, Mr. White, and myfelf, to attend him. He was accompanied by his own fifter Car-rang-ar-rang, Collins, Ca-ru-ey, Yem-mer-ra-wan-nie, and one or two other women.

Collins prepared the fpot whereon the pile was to be conftructed, by excavating the ground with a ftick, to the depth of three or four inches, and on this part fo turned up were firft placed fmall fticks and light brufh-wood ; larger pieces were then laid on each fide of thefe ; and fo on till the pile might be about three feet in height, the ends and fides of which were thus formed of large dry wood, while the middle of it confifted of fmall twigs and branches, broken for the pur-pofe and thrown together. When wood enough had been procured, fome grafs was fpread over the pile, and the corpfe, covered with an old blanket, was borne to it by the men, and placed on it with the head to the northward. A bafket with the fifhing apparatus and other fmall furniture of the deceafed was placed by her fide ; and, Ben-nil-long having laid fome large logs of wood over the body, the pile was lighted by one of the party. Being conftructed of dry wood, it was quickly all in a flame, and Ben-nil-long himfelf pointed out to us a black fmoke,

which

which proceeded from the centre of the pile where the body lay,
and signified that the fire had reached it.

We left the spot long before the last billet was consumed, and Ben-
nil-long appeared during the day more cheerful than we had expected,
and spoke about finding a nurse from among the white women to suckle
his child.

The following day he invited us to see him rake the ashes of his
wife together, and we accompanied him to the spot, unattended by
any of his own people. He preceded us in a sort of solemn silence,
speaking to no one until he had paid Ba-rang-a-roo the last duties of a
husband. In his hand he had the spear with which he meant to punish
the car-rah-dy Wil-le-me-ring for non-attendance on his wife when she
was ill, with the end of which he raked the calcined bones and ashes
together in a heap. Then, laying the spear upon the ground, he
formed with a piece of bark a tumulus that would have done credit to a
well-practised grave-digger, carefully laying the earth round, smooth-
ing every little unevenness, and paying a scrupulous attention to the
exact proportion of its form. On each side the tumulus he placed a log
of wood, and on the top of it deposited the piece of bark with which
he had so carefully effected its construction. When all was done he
asked us " if it was good," and appeared pleased when we assured him
that it was.

His deportment on this occasion was solemn and manly ; an expressive silence marked his conduct throughout the scene ; in fact we attended him as silently, and with close observation. He did not suffer
any thing to divert him from the business he had in hand, nor did he
seem to be in the least desirous to have it quickly dispatched, but paid
this last rite with an attention that did honour to his feelings as a man,
as it seemed the result of an heartfelt affection for the object of it, of
whose person nothing now remained but a piece or two of calcined bone.
When his melancholy work was ended, he stood for a few minutes
with his hands folded over his bosom, and his eye fixed upon his
labours in the attitude of a man in profound thought. Perhaps in that
small interval of time many ideas presented themselves to his imagination. His hands had just completed the last service he could render to

a woman

a woman who, no doubt, had been useful to him; one to whom he was certainly attached, (of many instances of which we had at different times been witnesses,) and one who had left him a living pledge of some moments at least of endearment. Perhaps under the heap which his hands had raised, and on which his eyes were fixed, his imagination traced the form of her whom he might formerly have fought for, and whom he now was never to behold again. Perhaps when turning from the grave of his deceased companion, he directed all his thoughts to the preservation of the little one she had left him; and when he quitted the spot his anxiety might be directed to the child, in the idea that he might one day see his Ba-rang-a-roo revive in his little motherless Dil-boong.

Cole-be's wife, who bore the same names as the deceased, lost them both on this occasion, and was called by every one Bo-rahng-al-le-on. This peculiarity was also observed by them with respect to a little girl of ours, of whom Ba-rang-a-roo was so fond as to call her always by her own name. On her decease she too was styled Bo-rahng-al-le-on.

Cole-be's wife, the namesake of the Ba-rang-a-roo I have just mentioned, did not survive her many months. She died of a consumption, brought on by suckling a little girl who was at her breast when she died. This circumstance led to the knowledge of a curious but horrid custom which obtains among these people. The mother died in the town, and when she was taken to the grave her corpse was carried to the door of every hut and house she had been accustomed to enter during the latter days of her illness, the bearers presenting her with the same ceremonies as were used at the funeral of Ba-loo-der-ry, when the little girl Dil-boong and the boy Bè-dia Bè-dia were placed before his corpse.

When the body was placed in the grave, the bye-standers were amazed to see the father himself place the living child in it with the mother. Having laid the child down, he threw upon it a large stone, and the grave was instantly filled in by the other natives. The whole business was so momentary, that our people had not time or presence of mind sufficient to prevent it; and on speaking about it to Cole-bé, he, so far from thinking it inhuman, justified the extraordinary act by assuring us that as no woman could be found to nurse the child, it must die a much worse death than that to which he had put it. As a similar

circum-

circumſtance occurred a ſhort time after, we have every reaſon to ſuppoſe the cuſtom always prevails among them; and this may in ſome
degree account for the thinneſs of population which has been obſerved
among the natives of the country[*].

I have ſaid that theſe women were nameſakes. Ben-nil-long's wife
was called Ba-rang-a-roo Daring-ha; Cole-be's, Daring-ha Ba-rang-
a-roo. A peculiarity in their language occurs to me in this place. The
males of the ſame name call each other Da-me-li, the women call each
other Da-me-li-ghen.

I have mentioned their taking particular names on certain occaſions.
The mutual friend who attends them to the field is ſtyled Ca-bah-my;
the perſons who at their funerals are painted red and white, are named
Moo-by; the nameſake of a deceaſed perſon, if a male, is ſtyled Bo-
rahng; if a woman, Bo-rahng-al-le-on. When Nor-roo-ing came into
the town to acquaint us with the death of Yel-lo-way, ſhe was perfectly
a diſmal ſorrowing figure. She had covered herſelf entirely with aſhes,
was named while ſhe continued ſo Go-lahng, and refuſed all kinds of
ſuſtenance.

The annexed PLATE repreſents the burning of the corpſe of a native
who was killed by a limb of a tree falling on him. He was brought to
the ſpot with all the preceding ceremonies. His head was laid to the
northward, and in his hands were depoſited his ſpear and his throwing-
ſtick. His aſhes were afterwards raked together, and a tumulus erected
over them, ſimilar to that which Ben-nil-long had raiſed over his wife.

No. XII.

LANGUAGE.

IN giving an account of an unwritten language many difficulties
occur. For things cognizable by the external ſenſes, names may be
eaſily procured; but not ſo for thoſe which depend on action, or addreſs

[*] Cole-be's child was about four or five months old, and ſeemed to have partaken of
in mother's illneſs. I think it could not have lived.

them-

themfelves only to the mind: for inflance, a fpear was an objeó both
vifible and tangible, and a name for it was eafily obtained; but the ufe
of it went through a number of variations and inflexions, which it was
extremely difficult to afcertain; indeed I never could, with any degree
of certainty, fix the infinitive mood of any one of their verbs. The following fketch is therefore very limited, though, as far as it does proceed,
the reader may be affured of its accuracy.

Their language is extremely grateful to the ear, being in many inflances
expreffive and fonorous. It certainly has no analogy with any other
known language, (at leaft fo far as my knowledge of any other language
extends,) one or two inflances excepted, which will be noticed in the fpecimen. The dialeó fpoken by the natives at Sydney not only differs entirely from that left us by Captain Cook of the people with whom he
had intercourfe to the northward, (about Endeavour river,) but alfo from
that fpoken by thofe natives who lived at Port Stephens, and to the
fouthward of Botany-Bay, (about Adventure Bay,) as well as on the
banks of the Hawkefbury. We often heard, that people from the
northward had been met with, who could not be exaófly underftood by
our friends; but this is not fo wonderful as that people living at the
diftance of only fifty or fixty miles fhould call the fun and moon by
different names; fuch, however, was the faéf. In an excurfion to the
banks of the Hawkefbury, accompanied by two Sydney natives, we
firft difcovered this difference; but our companions converfed with the
river natives without any apparent difficulty, each underftanding or
comprehending the other.

We have often remarked a fenfible difference on hearing the fame
word founded by two people; and, in faóf, they have been obferved
fometimes to differ from themfelves, fubftituting often the letter. b for
p, and g for c, and vice verfa. In their alphabet they have neither s nor
v; and fome of their letters would require a new charaóter to afcertain
them precifely.

What follows is offered only as a fpecimen, not as a perfeóf vocabulary of their language.

4 I   Names

Names chiefly of Objects of Sense.

New South Wales.	English.
Co-ing,	The sun.
Yen-na-dah,	The moon.
Bir-rong,	A star.
Mo-loo-ino-long,	The Pleiades.
War-re-wull,	The Milky Way.
Ca-ra-go-ra,	A cloud.
Boo-do-en-ong, *general name*	
Cal-gal-le-on, *the greater,*	The Magellanic clouds.
Gnar-rang-al-le-on, *the lesser,*	
Tu-ru-gā,	A star falling.
Co-ing bi-bo-bā,	Sun-rising.
Boot-ra,	The sky.
Co-ing bur-re-goo-lab,	Sun-setting.
Gnoo-wing,	Night.
Can-mar-roo,	Day.
Tar-re-ber-re,	
Gwe-yong,	Fire.
Cad-jet,	Smoke.
Gil-le,	A spark.
Per-mul,	Earth.
Ta-go-rā,	Cold.
Yoo-roo-gā,	Heat.
Men-nie-mo-long,	Dew.
Pan-nā, and Wāl-lan,	Rain.
Bā-do,	Water.
Chi-a-ra,	Name.
Car-rig-er-rang,	The sea.
Go-nie,	A boat.
Now-ey,	A canoe.
Beng-al-le,	A basket.
Car-rah-jun,	A fishing-line.
Gnam-mul,	A sinker *.
Bur-rā,	A book.

New South Wales.	English.
Ke-bā,	A stone or rock.
Bwo-mar,	A grave.
Bow-wan,	A shadow.
Ma-hn,	A ghost.
Wir-roong,	Scars on the back.
Cong-ar-ray,	Do. on the breast.
Jee-run,	A coward.
Can-ning,	A cave.
Me-diong,	A sore †.
Ya-goo-na,	To-day.
Bo-rā-ne,	Yesterday.
Par-ry-boo-go,	To-morrow.
Mul-lm-ow-ool,	In the morning.
Jen-ni-be,	Laughter.
Boo-roo-wāng,	An island ‡.
Gno-rāng,	A place.
E-rāng,	A valley.
Boo-do,	A torch made of reeds.
Mi-yal §,	A stranger.
Ar-rung-a,	A calm.
Moo-roo-bin,	Woman's milk.
Ew-ing,	Truth.
Ca-bahn,	An egg.
Yab-bun,	Instrumental music.
Yoo-long, or Yoo-lahng,	Cleared ground for public ceremonies.

Adjectives.

Bood-jer-re,	Good.
Wee-re,	Bad.
Mur-ray,	Great.
Gnar-rang,	Small.
Coo-rar-re,	Long.

* A small stone to suk the line.
† On noticing a hole in any part of our dress they term it Me-diong.
‡ This word they applied to our ships.
§ This word has reference to sight ; Mi, the eye.

Too-

New South Wales.	English.	New South Wales.	English.
Too-mur-ro,	Short.	No-gro, or No-gur-ro,	} Nose.
Go-jy, Go-jay-by,	} Rotten.	Kar-gä,	Mouth.
Bin-nicc,	Pregnant.	Wil-ling,	Lips.
Par-rat-ber-rl,	Empty.	Da-ra,	Teeth.
Bo-ruck,	Full.	Tal-lang,	Tongue.
Pe-mul-gine,	Dirty.	Wäl-lo,	Chin.
Bar-gat,	{ Afraid. { Frightened.	Go-ray,	Ear.
Ba-diel,	Ill.	Cad-le-ar, Cad-le-ang,	} Neck.
Moo-la,	Sick.	Nä-bung,	Breast or Nipple.
Boo-row-a,	Above or upward.	Yar-rin,	Beard*.
Cad-i,	Below or under.	De-war-ra,	Hair †.
Bar-bug-gä,	Left.	Bar-rong,	Belly.
War-räng-i,	Right.	Go-rook,	Knee.
Doo-room-i,	Left.	Dar-ra,	Leg.
Goo-lar-ra,	Angry.	Ma-no-e,	Foot.
Yu-ro-ra,	Passionate.	Tam-mir-ra,	Hand.
Wo-gul, and Wo-cul,	} One.	Ber-ril-le,	Fingers.
Yoo-blow-re, and Boo-la,	} Two.	Car-rung-un,	Nail.
Brew-y,	Three.	Bib-be,	Ribs.
Mur-ray-too-lo,	A great many.	Ba-rongle,	Vein.
Gnal-le-a,	Both.	Pä-dl-el,	Flesh or lean.
Moo-jel,	Red.	Bog-gay, or Pog-gay,	} Fat.
Ta-bo-a,	White.	Tar-rang,	Arm.
Gni-na,	Black.	O-nur,	Elbow.
Bool-gi-ga,	Green.	Wy-o-man-no,	Thumb.
Moo-ton-ore,	Lame.	Dar-ra-gal-lie,	Fore-finger.
Yu-roo, and Yu-roo-gur-ra,	} Hungry.	Ba-roo-gal-lie,	Middle or ring'd.
Mo-rem-me,	Yes.	Wel-leng-al-lie,	Little finger.
Beall,	No.		
Mar-rey,	Wet.		

Parts of the Human Body.

Ca-ber-ra,	Head.		
Gnul-lo,	Forehead.		
Mi,	Eye.		
Yin-ner-ry,	Eye-brow.		

Consanguinity.

Eo-rä,	{ The name com- mon for the natives.

* This they often singe, and describe it as a painful operation.
† This is commonly full of vermin, which I have seen them eat, and change from one soil to another.

New South Wales.	English.	New South Wales.	English.
Mul-lā,	A man.	Cam-mar-rade, and Cā-mong-al-lay,	Terms of affection used by girls.
Din,	A woman.		
Din-al-le-ong, Gin-al-le-ong,	Women*.		
Be-an-na; (this they shorten to Be-an and Be-a, and when in pain, they exclaim Be-a-ri,	A father.		
		Spears and other Instruments.	
Wy-an-na, and Wy-ang,	Mother.	Goong-un,	A spear with four barbs cut in the wood, which they do not throw, but strike with hand to hand.
Go-mang,	Grandfather.		
Ba-bun-na,	Brother.		
Ma-oun-na,	Sister.	Noo-ro Cā-my,	A spear with one barb, fastened on.
Go-roong,	A child.		
We-row-ey,	A female child.		
Wong-er-ra,	A male ditto.		
Nā-bung-ay wui-dal-liea †,	Infant at the breast.	Cā-my,	A spear with two barbs.— This word is used for spear in general.
	Child eight months old.		
Boro-goo-roo,			
Guy-a-nay-yong,	An old man.		
Mau-gohn,	A wife.	Bil-larr,	A spear with one barb, cut from the wood.
Mau-gohn-nal-ly,	A temporary ditto.		
Go-rah-gal-long,	A handsome man.		
Go-rah-gal-long-al-le-ong,	A handsome woman.	Wal-lang-al-le-ong,	A spear armed with pieces of shell.
Mā-lin, Nurkine, Mud-gin, Gnar-ra-mal-ta,	A relation ‡.	Can-na-diul,	A spear armed with stones.
		Ghe-rub-bine,	A spear without a barb.
Cow-ul,	Male of animals.	Doo-ull,	A short spear.
We-ring,	Female of ditto.	Ne-roo-gal Cā-my,	Holes made by a shield.
Dn-roon,	A son.		
Do-roon-e-nāng,	A daughter.	E-lee-mong,	A shield made of bark.
Go-mul,	A term of friendship.	Ar-rā-gong,	A shield cut out from the solid wood.
		Moo-ting, Cal-larr,	Fragigt.
		Car-rab-ba,	Prong of the moo-ting.

* One of the few instances I could ever discover of a plural or dual number.
† Compounded of Nā-bung its breast, and Wui-dal-liea relating to drinking.
‡ To these I never could affix precise meanings.

Dam-

New South Wales.	English.
Dam-moo-ne, }	Prong of the callarr.
Woo-dah,	
Can-na-ral-ling,	
Doo-win-aul, }	Names of clubs.
Can-ni-cull,	
Car-ru-wāng,	
Wo-mur-rāng.	
Goal-lung-ul-la, }	
Tar-ril-ber-re,	
Mo-go,	Stone hatchet.
We-bat,	Handle of ditto.
Wo-mcr-ra,	Throwing-stick.

Pronouns, Adverbs, and Mode of Address.

Gni-a,	I, or myself.
Gnæ-ne,	You.
Gnee-ne-de,	Yours.
Dīn-nai,	Mine.
Dar-ring-al,	His.
Gnā-ni,	Whose.
Wau,	Where.
De,	There.
Diam,	Here.
Diam o waw?	Where are you?
Diam o diam o,	Here I am.
Gnahn Chiara, gnahn? }	What is your name?
Bir-rong,	Appertaining.

Winds.

Bow-wān,	North.
Bol-gay-al-lang,	South.
Boo-roo-wee,	East.
Bain-mar-ray,	West.
Doo-loo-gal,	North-west.
Yare-bā-lahng,	South-west.
Go-nie-mah,	North-east.
Gwār-ra,	A high wind.

Inflexions of the Verbs.

New South Wales.	English.
Gnia-na,	Sighing.
Bwo-me,	Breathing.
Dere-rign-ang,	Sneezing.
Car-re-nar-re-bil-le,	Coughing.
Yen-no-rā,	Walking.
Yen-mow,	I will walk or go.
Yenn,	Go or walk.
Yen-mā-nia,	We will walk or go.
Yen-wor-ro,	He is gone.
Yen-nim-me,	You are going.
Yen-nool, Yen-noong, Yen-nore-yen, }	Relating to walking.
Yen-nang-allea,	Let us both walk.
Al-loey,	Stay.
Wo-roo-wo-roo, War-re-war-re, }	Go away.
Pat-ta-diow,	I have eaten.
Pat-tā-die-mi,	You have eaten.
Pat-ty,	He has eaten.
Pat-ta-bow,	I will eat.
Pat-tā-baw-me,	{ You will eat, or will you eat?
Pat-tā-ne,	They eat.
Wul-da-diow,	I have drank.
Wul-da-die-mi,	You have drank.
Nwya je-uning-a,	Give me.
Py-yay,	Killed.
Jung-ara py-yay,	Killed by dogs.
Par-rat-ben-ni-diow, }	I have emptied.
Py-ya-bow,	I will strike or beat.
Py-yee,	He did beat.
E-ra-bow,	I will throw.
E-ra,	Throw you.
E-rail-leiz,	Throwing.
Mahn-me-diow,	I have taken it.
Mahu-iow,	{ Shall I, or I shall take.
Goo-rā,	Sunk.
Ton-ga-bil-lie,	Did cry.
Wau-me,	Scolding or abusing.

Wau-me-

New South Wales.	English.	New South Wales.	English.
Wau-me-bow,	I will scold or abuse.	Bo-gay,	Diving.
Wau-me-diow,	{ I have scolded or abused.	Ta-yo-ra, Me-diang-a,	{ Severely cold. Medianga is compounded of Mediong, a sore.
Wau-me-diang-ha,	{ They have scolded or abused.		
Nang-er-ra,	} He sleeps.	Mul-lā-ra,	{ Married. Compounded of Mulla a man.
Nang-a,			
Nang-a-bow,	I will sleep.		
Nang-a-diow,	I have slept.		
Nang-a-diem-me,	Tou have slept.		
Nang-a-bau-me?	Will you sleep?		
Gn-ro-da,	He snores.		**Beasts.**
Gnā-nā le-cnā,	She or he breathes.		
Al-lo-wan,	He lives or remains.	Jung-o,	Common name.
Al-lo-wah,	Stay here, or sit down.	Pat-a-go-rāng,	{ A large grey kangaroo-roo.
Wal-loo-me-yen-wal-loo?	} Where are you going?	Bag-gar-ray,	Small red ditto.
War-re-me-war-re?	Where have you been?	Wal-li-bah,	Black ditto.
Gnā- diow,	Tou have seen.	Tein-go,	} Dog.
Gnā-diem-me,	I have seen.	Din-go,	
Gnā-bōw,	I will see.	Wor-re-gal,	
Gnā,	See.	Boo-roo-min,	{ Grey vulpine opossum.
Era-mad-jow-in-nia,	Forced from him.	Go-ra-go-ro,	Red ditto.
Car-rah-mā,	Stealing.	Wob-bin,	Flying squirrel.
Wor-ga-wee-na,	{ He whistles, or whistling.	Ga-ni-mong,	Kang-oo-roo rat.
Goo-lar-ra py-yel-la,	} Snarling with anger.	Wee-ree-a-min, Wee-ree-am-by,	} Large fox rat.
Man-nie mong-alla,	Surprised.	Bo-gul,	Rat or mouse.
Yare-bā,	Tired.	Me-rea-gine,	Spotted rat.
Pe-to-e,	Sought for.		
Man-nie mal-lee,	He was startled.		**Birds.**
Nwya-bow-in-nia,	I will give you.		
Wan-ye-wan-yi,	He lies.	Ma-ray-ong,	Emu.
Ma-row-e,	He creeps.	Go-ree-ail,	A parrot.
Bāng-a-ja-bun,	He did paddle.	Mul-go,	A black swan.
Noy-go,	Howling as a dog.	Car-rāng-a bo mur-ray,	} A pelican. When they see this bird over their heads, they sing the following words:
Toll,	Biting.		
Co-e, Cow-e, Cwoi, Cow-ana,	} Come here.		
Wad-be,	Swimming.		

Goo-roo-me ta-twī-mitwī na-twī.—Goo-roo me ta-twī na-twī, m-twī, tar-ra wow, tar-ra wow*.

* On seeing a shoal of porpoises, they sing while the fish is above water, No-tā-le-bre lā-lā, No-tā-le-bre lā-lā, until it goes down, when they sing the words No-ter, No-ter, until it rises again.

Yoo-.

New South Wales.	English.
Yoo-rong-i,	A wild duck.
Goad-gäng,	A wild pigeon.
Wir-gan,	Bird named by us the Friar.
Go-gan-ne-gine,	Bird named by us the Laughing Jack-Ass.
Po-book,	Musquito hawk.
Wau-gan,	Crow.
Jam-mul jam-mul,	Common hawk.
Gare-a-way,	White cockatoo.
Cä-rite,	Black ditto.
Ur-win-ner-ri-wing,	Curlew.

Insects, Reptiles.

New South Wales.	English.
Mar-rae-gong,	A spider.
Mi-a-nong,	A fly.
Go-nis-go-nia,	A beetle.
Gil-be-nong,	A grashopper.
Bur-roo-die-ra,	A butterfly.
Go-na-long,	Caterpillar.
Can-nar-ray,	Centipede.
Cahn,	Snake.
Po-boo-nång	A black ant.

Peculiarities of Language.

To the men when fishing they apply the word Mah-ni; to the women, Mähn.

They make some distinction in another instance when speaking of crying, they say the men Tong-i, the women Tong-e.

The following difference of dialect was observed between the natives at the Hawkesbury and at Sydney.

Coast.	Inland.	English.
Ca-ber-ra,	Co-co,	Head.
De-war-ra,	Ke-war-ra,	Hair.
Gnul-lo,	Nar-ran,	Forehead.
Mi,	Ma,	Eye.
Go-ray,	Ben-ne,	Ear.
Cad-lian,	Gang-a,	Neck.
Ba-rong,	Ben-de,	Belly.
Moo-nur-ro,	Boom-boong,	Navel.
Boong,	Bay-ley,	Buttocks.
Yen-na-dah,	Dil-luck,	Moon.
Co-ing,	Con-do-in,	Sun.
Go-rä,	Go-ri-ba,	Hail.
Go-gen-ne-gine,	Go-con-de,	Laughing Jack-ass.

World

Words of a Song.

Mäng-en-ny-wau-yen-go-nah, bar-ri-boo-lah, bar-re-mah. This they begin at the top of their voices, and continue as long as they can in one breath, sinking to the lowest note, and then rising again to the highest. The words are the names of deceased persons.

E-i-ah wan-ge-wah, ehian-go, wan-de-go. The words of another song, sung in the same manner as the preceding, and of the same meaning.

I met with only two or three words which bore a resemblance to any other language.

The middle head of Port Jackson is named Cä-ba Cä-ba—in Portuguese Cäba signifies a head. Cam-ma-räde, a term of affection used among girls, has a strong resemblance to the French word Cammerade; and may not some similitude be traced between the word E-lee-mong, a shield, and the word Telamon, the name given to the greater Ajax, on account of his being lord of the seven-fold shield? How these words came into their language must be a mystery till we have a more intimate knowledge of it than I can pretend to.

—————

I could have enlarged very much the foregoing account of the natives of New South Wales; but, both in describing their customs and in detailing their language, I have chosen to mention only those facts about which, after much attention and inquiry, I could satisfy my own mind. That they are ignorant savages cannot be disputed; but I hope they do not in the foregoing pages appear to be wholly incapable of becoming one day civilized and useful members of society.

POST-

POSTSCRIPT.

SINCE the preceding account was printed, letters have been received from New South Wales of as late date as the 20th of August 1797. By these it appears, that his Majesty's ship Reliance, in her passage from the Cape of Good Hope to Port Jackson, met with uncommon bad weather, which kept her out eleven weeks and one day. About the latitude of 41° S. and 77° E. longitude, the sea suddenly became violently agitated, and at last broke on board the ship, staving a boat which was over the stern, and doing considerable damage to the ship. Captain Waterhouse, however, landed safely thirty-nine head of black cattle, three mares, and near sixty sheep.

Information was also received through the same channel, that a ship called the Sydney-Cove had been fitted out for Port Jackson from Bengal; but springing a leak at sea, she was run ashore on the southernmost part of the coast of New Holland: seventeen of the crew attempted to get to Port Jackson in their long-boat, but were driven on shore, and lost their boat. They then attempted to reach it by land, in which hazardous undertaking only three of them succeeded, the others either dying on the route or being killed by the natives. They were eighty days in performing this journey, and reported that in their way they had found great quantities of coal. This was afterwards confirmed by the surgeon of the Reliance, who went down to the wreck, and brought specimens of it back with him, having found immense strata of this useful article. Some part of the cargo was got on shore and housed where the ship was stranded.

When these letters left the colony, it continued in as flourishing a state as when the Britannia sailed. May it continue to prosper!

THE END.

LIST OF ENGRAVINGS.

www.ingramcontent.com/pod-product-compliance
Lightning Source LLC
Chambersburg PA
CBHW021927110726
47901CB00003B/744